I0677882

Flight of the Lost
by
Ashley Causey

ISBN: 978-0-9897089-4-4
Text 2017 © Ashley Causey
Map 2013, 2016 © Ashley Causey
Cover 2016 © Ashley Causey
Edited by Ashley Causey

WRITTEN BY ASHLEY CAUSEY

Immortal Flight

Flight of the Broken
Flight of the Lost
Flight of a Hero (in progress)

Immortal Spirit (planned)

Spirit Destroyer
Spirit Healer
Spirit Protector

Map featuring the Lands of the Shadowborn and neighboring territories as visited during the events of **Flight of the Lost**

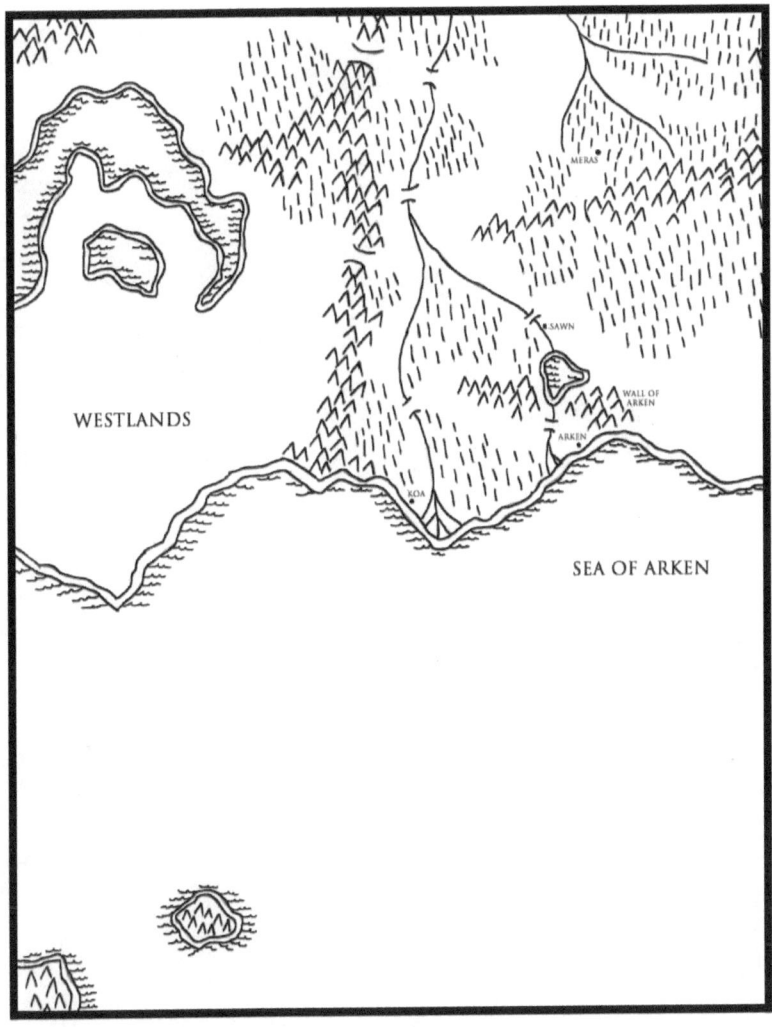

Map featuring the Lands of the Mortal people and neighboring territories as visited during the events of **Flight of the Lost**

DEDICATION

This book is for the readers, writers, and book lovers of the world.

FOREWORD

So I have reached the second book in this grand writing adventure of mine. Flight of the Lost joins Flight of the Broken and the to be written Flight of a Hero to become the Immortal Flight trilogy. I already know that the story won't end there for there are endless possibilities to explore. Does that mean more novels or short stories? Of course!

Flight of the Lost is more than just the continuation of the story. It is the continuation of a dream to tell a story that I would enjoy reading. It is my voice, thoughts, feelings, and experiences on paper.

Well? What can you expect from the second book of a trilogy? Changes, both physical and mental, are coming for the characters. In a way, this book is much darker and as such, the positive moments shine more brightly. You will also get to visit more places on the map and meet more characters of different races, powers, and backgrounds. Legends will come to life like never before and not always in the way expected by the characters involved. More secrets and background stories that I did not reveal in Flight of the Broken will be unveiled. Of course, I will leave some things for Flight of a Hero and other future works.

I recommend reading Flight of the Broken before you read Flight of the Lost. It will help you get a better understanding of the characters, world, and plot. Immerse yourself in a fantasy world with Gryphons, Dragons, Spirits, and sword wielding mystical warriors. Let yourself be taken by the fear and the courage of a world desperate to stop the march of Kaiser Adonis. Happy reading and enjoy Flight of the Lost!

Ashley Causey

SUMMARY FOR FLIGHT OF THE BROKEN

In a land where Gryphons soar and Spirits walk, Kaiser Adonis is the name of unspoken fear that grips the hearts of all. With a tongue as sharp as a sword and a soul as black as night, he has the power to bring forth the darkest of nightmares. His reach stretches across a thousand years, orchestrating his rise to greatness with rivers of blood.

The world is quickly spiraling towards an echo of the tumultuous past, noble war heroes long gone. Cries for help go unheard. Danger lurks around every corner as Kaiser tightens his hold over the crumbling Shadowborn throne. No one is safe.

All that stands in Kaiser's way are two sons of the ancient Silvanus bloodline: the royal heir Onyx Silvanus and the bastard rebel Ryder Coba. They are the last hope to rescue their ancestral throne and bring courage back to a world preparing for war.

TABLE OF CONTENTS

FEAR NOT THE NIGHT

The screams. The shattering of something deeper than flesh and bone. The overwhelming darkness of a reality that he could no longer escape from. Nightmares so terrible that they threatened to destroy him. Onyx woke, the sheets tangled around his body like chains. His pillow had been mashed into an unrecognizable mess beneath his head. He took several deep breaths in an attempt to calm his fear and anxiety. His breath was ragged and his throat was raw from yet another consecutive night of crying and screaming until there was nothing left within him. All Onyx could think about was when would it end?

Onyx wished that he had a window in his room so that he could look at the stars. He sat up and ran his fingers through his hair, his bangs slick against his forehead. His right leg twitched with a dull pain. He looked down and rubbed his calf, feeling the tender scars beneath the fabric of his pants. He had once been proud of the scars for they told the story of how he fought a Demon and won. Now, they only served as a painful reminder of his father's sad fate. He gripped his calf and bowed his head, slamming his eyes shut.

His father was dead and though people tried to convince him otherwise, he had been the one to end his life. It was his sword that plunged through his father's chest, stabbing him in the heart. The blood had been so red. He bit his tongue to avoid screaming again. A copper taste inundated his mouth. He swallowed a mouthful, forcing it down.

It was still the middle of the night but Onyx found that he could no longer sleep. Nor did he have the will to revisit the endless cycle of nightmares. He got out of bed and stepped over to the wash basin, not expecting the water to be warm. He grumbled when he discovered that the basin was bone dry. A part of him longed for the comforts of his former home where chamber servants made sure his bed was always made and his washing water warm. Even after two months with the rebels, Onyx had still not gotten used to the spartan living. And yet, he knew there was no going back to that life. He leaned over the basin, fighting back tears of anger and sorrow. When would the torrent of emotion end?

Onyx slid down to the floor and leaned his head back against the wall. He stared at the ceiling, willing stars to appear so he could have something besides stone to look at. He thought about going to sit beside the pond outside. It would provide him a semblance of peace and a chance to calm his mind. But he did not want the attention of anyone. He did not want to appear like a blubbering child. He was a man now albeit a young one. He did not have centuries or even decades of experience to give him strength. He had no close friends or family left that he could talk to. Maybe Ryder but even then, they were not close. Plus, his cousin was too busy organizing the rebel offensive to even properly train him. As if Onyx really wanted to learn battle tactics or whatever else Ryder could think of.

But the reality was that they were at war with Kaiser Adonis, a powerful and enigmatic psychopath. At least, that was what Ryder had said at the only war council Onyx had attended. He had figured that Ryder invited him out of sympathy or as an example of someone else who had personally suffered under Kaiser's influence. During that single meeting, Zoras stared hard at Ryder, suspicious of the details of his many childhood stories regarding Kaiser and his conduct. Ryder's stories only horrified Onyx and after that, he refused to attend. Since then, he had been plagued by the horrible nightmares of his father's death.

Onyx got up from the floor and stood in front of the lone mirror in his room. The small mirror sat behind the wash basin and had a crack across the top right hand corner. In it, Onyx could see his tired, haggard appearance. His midnight black hair was messy and hanging to his shoulders. His gray eyes were lusterless and dark. He was at least remotely pleased to see the growth of facial hair and he imagined that it made him look older. A mottled purple and yellow bruise still lingered on his jaw. He studied his frame, pleased at the muscle filling in at his shoulders. But his cousin was still bigger and stronger than him in both appearance and skill. Ryder looked like a noble leader and commander. Onyx felt and looked like neither.

His thoughts strayed to the endless stream of comparisons. Onyx was the true born Prince and heir but he felt that he had none of the skills necessary to assume the role. Ryder was everything he was not. He was everything his father Aku never was. Onyx gritted his teeth and threw his fist forward. His right hand connected with the mirror, breaking the glass. He immediately seethed with pain as he held his bleeding right hand with his left. What a stupid decision to punch the mirror or as Onyx figured, to punch his reflection. The action did nothing but rip open his knuckles. He tried to flex his hand, wiggling his fingers. The self-inflicted injury stung.

Onyx ripped a strip of fabric from his linen shirt and crudely wrapped it around his injured hand. Blood seeped through the thin bandage within seconds. He had to wonder if there were slivers of glass embedded in his knuckles. He knew that such a wound could fester if not properly cleaned and bandaged. Gathering his resolve, Onyx exited his room.

The stone tunnel that served as a hallway was empty though he could hear the distant sound of metal scrapping upon metal coming from another room. Someone was repairing and cleaning their armor. The torches snapped and flickered in irregular intervals on the wall. Onyx paused for a moment, trying to remember which direction the healer's quarters were in. He walked towards the left, thinking he had decided upon the right path before stopping. Which way was it again, he asked himself. He bit his lip in frustration.

The rebel base was unusually quiet to him for it being a time of war. Onyx expected a watchman to be pacing the halls especially since so much emphasis was placed on the protection of him and Ryder. They were the last two descendants of Shadow Night after all. As such, they were targets for Kaiser and his army of followers. Onyx was certain that the rebellion would have happened even if he and Ryder were dead for he believed that Kaiser was not going to stop his assault. Kaiser had declared many times over that it was his intent to destroy the Silvanus bloodline. But would it stop there? One secret that Onyx knew was that though Ryder was a Silvanus like himself, Ryder also was Kaiser's lone descendent. Onyx had nothing like that for protection though he wondered how long Ryder's Adonis blood would protect him.

Remembering where the healer's quarters were, Onyx turned around and headed towards the right, passing his bedroom door. As he strode down the hallway, he tried to flex his injured hand. It stung at each attempt. Part of him fought the desire to shout out for aid. It was a hammered in habit from his childhood

as a royal. Why was he resisting? He could issue an order and due
to his position, that order would be followed. But Onyx did not feel
like a true Prince anymore. He felt weak and insignificant. He was
only a name without a story. In reality, he was nothing but his
royal name. Kaiser had shaken the very fabric of his identity,
taking away those that cared about him. He was alone.

The door to the healer's quarters was open when Onyx
arrived. The smell of dried herbs and plants seeped out into the
hallway. He paused by the open door when he heard the soft
clinking of a stone mortar and pestle being used. He listened to the
scrapping and mushing of some unknown salve being prepared.
He kept himself as still and quiet as possible when he heard a voice
singing in a low tone.

Fear not the night
The moon will show you the way
Follow the silver light
And return to me one day

Come back to me
My lost and wandering soul
Come back to me
Come back to me

A whistle continued the tune before drifting off into a
whisper of breath. Onyx thought he heard a sniffle of sadness. He
then heard the singer mumbling about something. Perhaps an
argument? He strained to listen, trying to discern the exact nature
of the singer's private conversation. His hand throbbed and he was
reminded of why he was here in the first place.

Onyx slowly opened the door more, the iron hinges creaking
loudly. Sitting at the square table was Haven, her long raven hair
cascading over her shoulders in waves. Her shirt sleeves were
rolled back to her elbows. Her leather pants and boots were
covered in patches of dirt and plant debris. He could see why
Ryder was so attracted to Haven. She was a beautiful woman with
luxurious hair and a slender frame.

"Stare at me long enough and Ryder might appear to box
your ears," Haven scoffed as she paused to inspect her salve. She
bent forward to sniff it and nodded.

Onyx gulped. "Sorry. I did not mean to intrude."

Haven sat up from her work to look at Onyx. She gestured
with her eyes towards his bandaged hand. "Would you like me to
take care of that for you?"

Onyx held his injured hand in embarrassment. "It's stupid

really," he mumbled.

Haven pulled out a wooden stool from under the table and patted the seat, indicating for Onyx to sit down. "I've punched enough mirrors in my life to know," she stated once he sat down.

He watched Haven as she went about the room, picking up various instruments, bandages, and medicines. She came back to the table, spreading out the items. After preparing a bowl of hot water, she finally sat down. Onyx winced as Haven grabbed his injured right hand and proceeded to unwrap it.

"Well, it doesn't look like you severed any ligaments. That's good," Haven commented once the bandage was cleared away. "What were you doing punching mirrors?"

Onyx was reluctant to answer and he did not know why. He watched as Haven took a pair of tweezers, removing slivers of glass from his knuckles. He grimaced when she plucked a rather large piece of glass from near his thumb. He wiggled his thumb in relief. Haven tapped the back of his hand to get him to stop. When Onyx made eye contact with her, she waved the tweezers before plunging in to remove a thin sliver from the same spot.

"There. All gone," Haven declared as she set the tweezers aside. She then dunked a small cloth in the bowl, soaking it.

"Thank you," Onyx said softly as Haven cleaned his hand.

"It's nice to treat a non-Demon wound for once. I am honestly surprised how Ryder manages to function after his recent set of injuries. He pretends like they don't bother him but I know they do. The blood soaked stinking bandages are starting to pile up," Haven said, at first sounding pleasant but ending with an annoyed tone. "Stupid, inconsiderate jack ass," she added, throwing the cloth into the bowl with a splash.

"I'm sorry?" Onyx asked in confusion.

Haven continued to grumble in an unintelligible stream of words. She completely ignored Onyx's grimace of pain when she rubbed a white salve over his knuckles. With deft movements, Haven wrapped Onyx's hand with a set of clean bandages.

Onyx expected the bandages to feel clunky on his hand but was surprised by how easily he could move his fingers. He massaged the palm of his hand while Haven cleaned up the mess.

"There is nothing that you need to be sorry for," Haven said as she bottled up the salve she had made earlier. "Just your cousin," she added as she tightened the cork.

"What did he do?" Onyx asked.

Haven set the newly bottled salve on a shelf with other concoctions. She turned around to face him. "He left eight days ago on some sort of personal mission that he would not tell anyone about. Not even me. Last time he did that, he did not come home for one hundred years. There are many reasons why that pisses me off but mostly, he left you in your time of mourning."

Onyx slumped down on the stool and looked away. He closed his eyes in a desperate attempt to hold back tears. The myriad of smells became muddled and he felt like he was slipping down a dark tunnel. His chest tightened. He felt himself getting hot before quickly becoming cold again. His senses jolted him back to reality when he felt Haven's small hand on his shoulder.

"I cannot pretend to understand what you are going through but I know that you are hurting. If you need anything, just ask," Haven said softly as she sat down.

"What was Ryder like when his father died? I mean, when he was executed?" Onyx blurted out. He instantly regretted the personal question.

Haven let out a deep breath. "That I do not know. Some would say he felt nothing for Akakios. Others would say he blamed himself for his father's death. He took the death of his mother very hard though. He became very angry and lashed out. He often locked himself away or went off into the wilds alone."

Onyx looked away and shrugged. He wanted to find a way to cope with how he lost his father. Not only that but the shattering of what he perceived as reality. His life was not the idyllic fairytale of a Prince living in a castle full of servants. He had once thought that he was going to be a great warrior and leader worthy of praise. Memories he had once passed off as nothing to be concerned about flashed in his mind. Now that he had a moment to reflect, he asked himself how he could not have seen his happiness fading away into the terror he felt now. He was a part of a war long in the making and he was not sure that he was ready. He felt alone and afraid. Everyone he had loved was gone. How could he mourn any of them when he was so afraid of Kaiser?

"Are you afraid of Kaiser?" Onyx asked Haven in an honest tone.

"I have been afraid of him since the beginning. Many people from Umbra are. No one is sure just what he is capable of or what it is that he wants. But my parents always told me: Fear not this night for the day will come when all will be right again," Haven explained. She then smiled softly. "It may be dark now but you are not alone in this. It will be hard but Kaiser will be defeated."

The conversation was interrupted when a stout Shadowborn man that Onyx knew was from Zoras' office slid to a stop by the door. "Ryder is back," he stated quickly before bolting down the hallway.

Haven stood up and clenched her fists. "Good because I need to punch him."

Onyx followed Haven, trying to keep up with her determined pace. He stumbled when he tripped on the door threshold. He caught himself but had fallen several paces behind Haven. He ran to catch up. It became clear to him that Haven and Ryder must have had a massive argument that she believed warranted a physical strike. She had mentioned that she was angry at Ryder for leaving but Onyx did not think much of it. War time was busy for all. He did wonder how someone as small as Haven could cause someone as big as Ryder any real damage.

The hallway outside of Zoras' office was a hotbed of activity. People jostled to get inside or listen by the door. Two steel armored guards blocked the way with their pole arms, snapping at anyone that got too close. Haven boldly approached the guards and set her hands on her hips, tapping her foot. Onyx came up behind her.

"You dare block my way?" Haven growled. She made eye contact with both guards until they shuttered. The hallway quieted when the guards stepped back in submission. "Thank you."

Onyx stood slack jawed as Haven waltzed past the two guards, her shoulders thrown back and head held up high. It took him several seconds to realize that he should follow her. The guards had no hesitation in letting him pass for he was still seen as a royal Prince. Onyx had to wonder how the guards would react to Ryder, a royal bastard with a powerful reputation. Certainly they had heard how Ryder won the Arena in Crossroads, beating the more experienced Eru the Airborn. In a sense, Ryder had earned his name. Onyx had nothing like that to his. Not only was Ryder a better version of him, he was a greater version of his father. His heart shuddered as he thought about how his father met his end. He stepped into the office just as Haven launched a verbal tirade at Ryder.

"What do you mean you went to Cross? Cross?! Of all places why would you risk yourself by going there? And why did you not tell anyone?" Haven shouted, getting in Ryder's face. She poked his chest hard. "Why did you not trust me enough to tell me what you were planning on doing?"

Ryder looked completely dumbfounded by Haven's reaction. He cleared his throat. "This was a personal mission..."

Everyone gasped when Haven punched him hard on the jaw with an audible crunch. "Personal mission?!"

Onyx watched as Haven reared back for another strike. She threw her fist forward but Ryder deftly caught it. They struggled for a moment until Haven relented. She stepped back and crossed her arms, frowning. Onyx waited for her to respond but she only snorted loudly.

"This was not a mission for myself but I had to do it all the same," Ryder said. He reached over towards the table and picked up a long item wrapped in cloth. He turned his gaze towards Onyx and presented the item towards him. He gestured with his eyes for Onyx to approach.

It made Onyx nervous to suddenly be the center of attention. He gulped before he took a few tentative steps. "What is it?"

Ryder unwrapped the item to reveal the royal Silvanus Moon Blade. Its crescent moon cross guard was chipped and the jewel was cracked. The leather on the hilt was frayed. The steel blade was gleaming in stark contrast to the poor condition of the rest of the sword.

"Last time I saw that sword was in Kaiser's hand," Zoras said, reflexively scratching his chest. He edged in closer. "That Dragon forged steel is something impressive."

The tall, brawny Zoras was mesmerized by the shining blade even though his last memory of it was unpleasant. He hesitated to touch it. Onyx was even more transfixed by the sword, seeing a deeper meaning in Ryder presenting to him instead of keeping it. He wondered why Ryder would risk himself by going to Cross just to get an item that could easily be replaced. A sword was just a sword but a life was beyond valuable. Especially his.

"This sword has history and many famous hands have touched it. It has killed and it has named leaders for many years. But in the end, it is just a piece of steel. It is those that have wielded it that made it great. Onyx, I have had a lifetime of experiences to make me who I am today," Ryder stated as he handed Onyx the sword. "It felt only right that this familial blade represent the knowledge I wish to pass to you as a teacher."

Onyx graciously took the sword, remembering how he had asked Ryder to train him. Now, his cousin was making it official before witnesses. "Thank you."

Ryder nodded before he made eye contact with both Haven and Zoras. His expression was hard and serious. "Kaiser was not in Cross. He is on the move. To where? I do not know."

"Then we must be ready for our night is long and we have much to fear before the day breaks," Zoras said with a bow of the head.

*****

Onyx let out a sigh of exhaustion as he and Ryder entered his sleeping quarters. He slumped down on to the edge of his mattress, gripping the edges. He looked up when he heard the door shut. Ryder leaned back against the door frame, wiggling his jaw. Onyx watched as Ryder rubbed the left side of his face where Haven had struck him once again before leaving Zoras' office. He had even heard her growl under her breath that she was not happy. The dark tone of her voice unnerved him and he wondered what Ryder had done to make her so angry. It was more than just him leaving without telling anyone. It had to be much deeper than that.

"Why was Haven so mad?" Onyx asked tentatively when Ryder paused to check and see if there was any blood on his lip.

Ryder manipulated his jaw, wincing. "She hates it when I leave. Damn, she's got a good right hook."

"You taught her," Onyx said, remembering that Ryder had trained Haven.

"Maybe too well. If Kaiser had to face her in a fight, I am sure that she would win," Ryder stated with an exacerbated laugh. "She has a kind of ferocity in her that is almost Dragon like."

Onyx had to wonder what his cousin saw in himself. He could barely think that within his own being that he was comparable to a Dragon. Maybe a water logged puppy in his current state. Onyx dropped his shoulders and leaned back against the wall. He side glanced at the broken mirror by the empty wash basin. Yes, he felt broken and incomplete. He looked up to see Ryder watching him from his standing position by the closed door.

"I had to end my father's life. How can I ever be as fierce as a Dragon or expect to survive a fight with Kaiser if I cannot accept that I killed my father," Onyx blurted before bursting into tears.

Ryder sat down beside Onyx and wrapped his arm around Onyx's shoulder. Onyx continued to sob, his face buried against Ryder's chest.

> *Fear not the night*
> *For all is not lost*
> *Fight with all your might*
> *No matter the cost*

*****

THE WINGS OF DEATH

He adjusted the helmet strap to rest more comfortably under his chin. The leather piece had already rubbed him hard enough to create a sore along the right side of his jaw. He resisted the urge to scratch it. It could not be a good sign to start his shift like this. There was a nervous energy in the air. In fact, there had been since he had woken up that morning. The city had been unusually quiet. Well at least it was to him. The sea gulls that crowded the docks, crying out for handouts from the fishermen, did not seem as loud as he remembered. His grandmother had told him before he left for his watchman duties that it was a bad sign for the docks to be quiet. She kept going on about how it was the calm before the storm or at least a pirate attack. His grandfather had tried to quiet her to no avail. Finally he just had to leave to get away from the resulting argument.

Anxiety followed the young Shadowborn all the way to his post on the city wall. Even his watch captain had noticed. The older man was his usual self; harsh and unforgiving. Actually, the watchman thought that his captain was more on edge. The captain snapped at everyone for the smallest imperfection or deviation from the rules. Wrinkled tunic? Verbal lashing about proper uniforms. His captain's angry voice reverberated in his head. He did not think that his tunic, complete with royal sigil emblazoned on his front, was all that wrinkled. He resisted the urge to pull at the hem in an attempt to neaten his attire.

The watchman paused in his scheduled walk around the

southwestern wall, perplexed at what he saw. He approached the stone railing and rubbed his eyes. On the fields and roadway before the city of Eclipse was a fog so thick that he could no longer see the distant road sign that pointed the way to Cross. The watchman strained his far reaching sight to the limit but still he could see nothing. It was if the rolling sea mists had settled over the land. He sniffed the air but could not detect any hint of salt or moisture, the usual smells he associated with the ocean side city.

"Weird," the watchman muttered to himself. He started to walk away but stopped before he reached three feet from the railing. He turned back towards the mysterious fog.

He knew that fog was fog, especially when it had been raining day and night for the last eight days. The ground was saturated and the air was humid. He was also familiar with the mist that rose daily from the Mirror Sea. This was something completely different.

The mysterious fog crept along slowly as if it had a life of its own. Tentative silver tendrils reached out before the cloud like mass would roll forward to follow. The watchman was both fascinated and confused by what he saw. He approached the railing.

"Hey, Captain. Do you see this?" the watchman shouted to a waiting Shadowborn man in light steel armor.

The captain of the watch glanced towards the fog with little interest. He repeated the watchman's sensory investigation, ending with a deep sniff of the air. He turned briefly to the small watch tower, eyes darting towards a wind chime hanging from the door frame. It was not moving.

"The fog is moving as if the wind is blowing but there is no wind," the captain stated as he approached the watchman. He looked back towards the inner city before turning his gaze back towards the fog. "None of the flags or banners are moving either."

"You know, my gran told me..." the watchman started to say.

"Enough about your gran and her superstitions!" the captain snapped. The watchman shrunk back. "Some Waterborn pirate probably conjured up this mess just to scare us before an attack. Go make yourself useful and find someone to go to the docks to warn them."

Before the watchman could turn around and leave, a black mass came out of the silver wall. It was a few seconds before the shadowy mass completely separated from the reaching tendrils. It was a cloaked rider on the back of a massive warhorse.

"May the Spirits protect me and all my kin," the watchman frantically cried while crossing his heart with a ward. He clasped his hands together in prayer. He squeaked when the captain knocked him across the back of the head.

Both turned to watch the rider's approach. The warhorse was a magnificent white beast with a glimmering hide and thick muscled legs. Its riding gear was leather straps with glided silver fastenings. To the captain and the watchman, it was the most beautiful creature they had ever seen. The rider was another story entirely. There were no fancy designs or jeweled adornments on the voluminous cloak. They could not even tell if the rider was a man or a woman. What was obvious was that the rider moved with confidence, no hint of the confusion that came with riding through a fog.

The rider finally came to a stop, the horse snorting in protest at the tug of the reins. By now, other watchmen on the wall had noticed the stranger before the gates. The captain ordered everyone to stand down and the wall fell silent. Without the sound of the wind chime or snap of a flag in the breeze, the silence was eerie and deafening.

"Who comes to Eclipse masked and through the fog?" the captain called out.

The rider turned around and looked back at the silver fog bank, the hood of the sable cloak dropping. A steel helm shaped like the head of an eagle was revealed.

"It's an Adonis helm, Captain," the nervous watchman pointed out.

"Worn by only one, if even, in these days for he has not ridden to our fair city since the days of my youth," the captain gritted his teeth. What he did not tell his companion was that the sight of the helm was not good.

"It would seem that your young companion has quite the eye for the armor of my family. He should be rewarded for recognizing this dusty old thing." The rider removed the helm and revealed himself to be Kaiser Adonis. Kaiser examined the helm in his hands, twisting and turning it around in careful study. He scratched at a nick on the brow. "A little scuffed but it suits me as it suited my father."

"Should we open the gates? It is the Lord's Chancellor after all," the watchman asked sheepishly.

The captain hesitated and his reaction was not lost on the young watchman. What the captain could not tell or would not tell was that he had received a secret order from Zoras Rokar, the ex Saber Commander and leader of the rebellion, not to let Kaiser into Eclipse for any reason. The order had been transmitted by secret channels through word of mouth and had reached Eclipse's own rebel captain. The message in the order had quickly been dispersed among the loyal and faithful, the secret fighters in the city. The watch captain wanted to shout out the rebel order but he had to consider what it would cost him and those he cared about. Ultimately, he was afraid. And there was still the strange fog before the city to figure out.

"Your arrival is most unexpected. We have not received word of your visit and we are grossly unprepared," the captain deftly said.

Kaiser scoffed as he set his helm over the pommel of the saddle. "But I though Master Rokar sent word to your superior. Perhaps I was mistaken. My question to you is why are the gates of your fair city closed? Certainly the stormy weather has not spooked you." He chuckled softly.

"Sir, what is the Lord's Chancellor talking about?" the young watchman asked. He was utterly confused by the conversation. "And if the Lord's Chancellor has business in the city, is it against the Shadowlord's law to forbid him entrance?"

"Be silent!" the captain shouted.

Kaiser then laughed out loud at the exchange. It took him a minute to calm down. "I do not need your permission or authorization to enter. Your bumbling subordinate is however correct. I am on the Shadowlord's business and I am here on his command to address a few problems within Eclipse," he declared.

The captain shuddered when Kaiser set his eyes upon him. He swallowed hard. A cold sweat broke out on his brow. It was if Kaiser was looking deep into his soul, picking apart every piece of his innermost being. The eighty foot stone wall offered him no protection. Why did they have the gates closed? Why should he listen to an ambiguous message from a man he had never met? At least, Kaiser had made a point of presenting himself in person. Zoras rarely travelled west of Cross. And what was that damn fog! His mind screamed with confusion.

"Perhaps you can assist me," Kaiser directed towards the watchman at the captain's side. He smirked as the Shadowborn shuddered. "I am looking for a Shadowborn man who has threatened the stability of our good Lord's throne and I believe that he has sought the safety of a woman known as the Silver Dancer. Has you or your captain heard of such a thing?"

"We have heard nothing of a sort," the captain said quickly after slapping a hand over the watchman's mouth.

"Then why are you acting so strangely?" Kaiser inquired in an innocent voice.

The other Shadowborn on the watch had to agree. Their captain was acting in an odd and confused manner though he still retained some of his snarkiness. They began to suspect that their captain was hiding something. Perhaps a piece of information that could threaten the Shadowlord. That angered them and they started to curse and accuse the captain of treachery. They ripped off their city badges and threw them to the ground, stomping on them. Kaiser shushed them and they immediately stopped.

"It would seem that you are harboring some dark secret from your fellow watchmen. That kind of secrecy, especially when the throne is involved, is the sign of a rebel and traitor. As Lord's Chancellor, I must deal with it as His Majesty commands," Kaiser stated. He raised his right hand and snapped his fingers.

The strange fog disappeared in an instant, revealing a massive army in full war regalia. Shouts and jeers rang out from the armored crowd. They were separated from Kaiser by a distance of one hundred feet and they blanketed the fields to the horizon. Kaiser's well known masked servant was mounted on a black warhorse with an even more shocking companion at his side: Loran Win.

"It's the Mirror Sea Pirate!" several of the watchmen shouted with fear.

One thin Shadowborn on the wall turned to rush down the stairs, intent on alerting the city guard. Kaiser smirked and snapped his fingers again. Instantly, the Shadowborn burst into white hot flames. He shrieked and howled before tumbling over the wall in his desperate attempt to put out the fire. His body hit the ground with a loud thump, the still burning flames now spreading to the grass.

Kaiser looked at his hand as if he was confused. He shook it lightly and stretched out his fingers. He looked back up and grinned. "My apologies. Hair trigger. I can never tell when that will happen." He tapped the side of his head as if he had forgotten.

The captain could not believe what he had just witnessed. If Kaiser was capable of setting someone on fire without touching them, there was no possible way that he could stop him from blasting through the gates and entering the city. No! He had to stop him. He had to stay strong. He clenched his fists, cutting into his palms with his fingernails.

"I see that polite conversation will get us nowhere. No matter. I have been charged to purge Eclipse of its rebellious thoughts and ways," Kaiser stated as he set the helm back on his head. He sat up straight in the saddle.

The captain forced himself to look straight at Kaiser. His heart was pounding in his chest. His knees shook and he felt like throwing up. All around him, the air chilled him to the bone. His fellow watchmen were not as calm, frozen with fear. They were too afraid to move or speak for none of them wanted to be set on fire like their comrade.

Kaiser raised his right hand as his horse stamped beneath him. The army behind him roared with eager anticipation but held, waiting for his command.

"The Silver Dancer left the city four days ago!" the captain shouted without understanding why. He did not know her or her name. He only felt a sense that he must protect her.

Kaiser frowned and slowly put his arm back down. The army cursed and shouted behind him but Loran and the masked servant kept the massive force in check. The pair rode back and forth, shouting orders to remain still.

"Is that so? Trouble is that you are just lying to save your own skin. You care nothing for those around you. What kind of soul would want to follow such a selfish man?" Kaiser declared with a smirk. "I would relieve you of your command but it would be pointless. You will not survive to see the next dawn." He paused as he raised his right hand again to the cheers of the assembled army. "None of you will. This city will burn."

Until this point, it seemed as if Kaiser was solely focused on attacking the watch captain. Now it was clear to everyone on the wall. Kaiser was going to attack, raze Eclipse to the ground, and leave no one alive. Already, the carrion birds assembled in the sky, crying out in anticipation of blood. They soared above Eclipse, flapping their black wings. They were waiting.

THE FALL OF ECLIPSE

"RACHE!"

The flame haired Demon smirked as he dismounted from his war horse, tossing the reins towards Loran. Loran sneered as he fought to collect the leather straps before they could fall out of reach. Rache twisted around on his feet and shrugged as if to say he was sorry for the inconvenience. He laughed before turning back around, letting his cloth hood and mask fall to rest around his neck. He continued to snicker as he sauntered over to Kaiser's side, bowing his head once to acknowledge him. Kaiser growled before he smacked Rache across the back of the head.

"Leave your pissing contest with Loran upon these fields. Your target is beyond these gates," Kaiser snapped from the back of his war horse. The beast snorted and stepped back until Kaiser drew the reins taut.

Rache walked up to the gates, tapping the thick iron and wood with his knuckle. "It will take more than fire to get into Eclipse. This city knows how to handle raiders both from sea and land."

"But not you and certainly not me. Tear down these gates," Kaiser ordered.

"You want to show the world just how powerful you are. Why don't you do it?" Rache asked as he ran his hand over a rusted piece of iron. He scratched at the orange red build up, flicking the debris from his fingertips. He snorted.

"Fine. If you won't do it, hold my horse here," Kaiser

growled as he swung his leg over and dropped down to the dirt road. He stomped over to the gates and pushed Rache out of the way. "Let the city know that no matter what that idiot Zoras says, I will enter Eclipse."

Rache walked back towards Kaiser's horse and slapped its hip. The horse reared and kicked at the Demon but he only laughed as it took off towards the waiting army. He turned around and put his arms out to the side.

"Dear people of Eclipse. You deny the Lord's Chancellor entry? Well prepare yourselves for absolute annihilation. I would have been lenient and left a survivor. He plans on killing every last one of you!" Rache declared with a booming voice.

Kaiser pulled off his gloves and threw them to the ground. He then pressed his bare hands on the heavy gates, stretching his fingers out. Listening for the protective Spirit energy shield, Kaiser waited. It was common practice to use Spirit energy to reinforce the walls and gates of a major city. Kaiser had used this same idea to raise his Shadow Mirror at the borders though his purpose was entirely different. His ancestor Adonis Anu had helped to create the protective shields using a kind of mirror controlled by the life of the sitting Shadowlord. As his descendant, Kaiser knew how to dismantle the power. His hands locked on to the gates.

"What is he doing?" Loran asked Rache once the Demon came back to the front of the army.

Rache laughed. "Using a power more ancient than even your ancestors were capable of understanding," he replied as he crossed his arms.

The ground began to shake, slow at first and then more violently. Only Rache understood what was happening and found himself amused by Loran's fearful reaction. Yes, this was ancient power more fearsome and strong than anything the Spiritborn could come up with. Even Vorin the Dragonlord would be hard pressed to challenge it and win. The most that Vorin could do was activate the deep defensive power. Only Kaiser was capable of breaking through it.

Ripples of silver energy pulsated out from where Kaiser was touching the gates. The stone, wood, and metal loosened from their fittings with each pass. The furious movement of energy intensified quickly before suddenly withdrawing back to where Kaiser was touching the gates. He pulled his hands away and stepped back. It was completely silent for several long seconds. Kaiser then snorted and kicked the gates hard. With that one strike, the gates came crumbling down in a cloud of rubble and dust. He snorted before he turned around to face his army. He lifted his left hand into the air and snapped his fingers.

With the signal, Loran gave the shout to charge forward. Like a violent wave breaking on jagged rocks, the steel clad soldiers parted around Kaiser who stood with hands out to his side. He kept his back to the city walls, smirking. Soldiers shouted and jeered long after they passed him and poured into Eclipse.

Rache came to Kaiser's side, the only one not to charge into the city. Kaiser snatched him by his tunic collar and dragged the Demon close to his face. "Find her. If she has gone, find who helped her escape and bring them to me. Alive."

"Who?" Rache stupidly asked.

Kaiser shifted his grip from Rache's collar to his chin. His fingers dug into Rache's face. "You know who," he snarled in a low and terrible voice. "I would go myself but I have other priorities that require my focus. Secrets that need to be uncovered." Rache started to protest but Kaiser quickly shushed him. "Just do as you are told."

*****

The first wave of Kaiser's army spread quickly through the streets, cutting down any bystanders. Those that were caught in the streets and managed to run never got far before they ran into another battalion of soldiers. Blood curdling screams filled the air that was becoming thick with the odor of acrid smoke. Shops and houses closest to the city walls were burning, the fire spreading across the rooftops. Stalls were kicked down and ripped apart, spilling an assortment of goods. The first wave had struck Eclipse before any defense could be mounted to seal the broken gates.

Loran led the charge, shouting orders to the officers underneath his command. He was pleased when none of them hesitated, marching off with their assembly of foot soldiers. His experience as the Mirror Sea Pirate had given him a fearsome reputation. Several of the officers had even said how they respected him more as a Commander than his hapless cousin. At any other time, he would have lashed out in response, forbidding the mention of Morin's name in his presence. The thirst for battle kept him distracted enough from responding.

"Let us fight, my brothers! Let us take the city in our true Lord's name! For Kaiser!" Loran paused to shout. He pumped his sword hand in the air, the steel blade glinting in the fire light. At least thirty soldiers responded with a declaration for their leader.

"Eclipse has no hope when Lord Kaiser takes to the field!" a burly youth shouted as he bounded past.

"Eclipse will always have hope so long as a Silvanus lives!" The confident shout halted the boisterous attitude of the attacking soldiers. Loran growled as he looked down the main street towards a large battalion of city guards. At the head of the group was a shiny steel armored officer. The man was tall with broad shoulders and long black hair that spilled out from under his wolf head helmet.

"Your name is of no consequence to Lord Kaiser as is your defense which is useless against him," Loran shouted as a contingent of warriors pressed up behind him.

"He may think to take this city and burn it to the ground but all is does is reveal his true intentions against His Majesty and that of his righteous kin. I do not care if my name means nothing but you will learn to fear my Spirit!" the officer replied boldly. He pointed his sword at Loran. "You are nothing but a salted old Pirate and we of Eclipse know how to deal with your ilk."

Loran scoffed. "Is that so? Then let us duel or whatever you land lovers call it. Our men can watch us and judge the victor. Pick your champion."

The officer appeared pleased as he whispered to the guards under his command. "I will fight for the honor of the Shadowlord and the Immortal Truth. Tell your men to stand down as I will mine. Let us have a proper duel."

Loran waved his hand up in the air but suddenly the motion was halted. He ripped his hand back down, rubbing his wrist and preparing to curse who ever dared to touch him. He immediately held his tongue when Kaiser stepped forward a few paces before stopping.

"My Lord?" Loran squeaked in surprise.

Kaiser chuckled as his eyes focused in on the officer. "You were one of those who fought against the authority of Morin Win. Rightly so as he was a worthless and complete idiot. But he did serve his purpose. Everyone does in the grand scheme of things."

"Then your purpose is to cause discord, destruction, and death to those who believe in the Immortal Truth. I refuse to delude myself to your supposed grand vision of a better world and it angers me that there are Shadowborn who have chosen to gather under your banner," the officer exclaimed with a bold voice. He brandished his sword and threw back his shoulders.

"It is not about what is right or wrong. It is about cleansing." Kaiser took a deep breath and let it out slowly. "The world is so infected by the virus that is the Immortal Truth that it has become blind to what was and what could be. Is it really a better place? Are the Spirits really something to be loved or feared as entities of a hidden plane of existence? I am doing something our ancestors did not do. I am giving you a choice to experience the world as it should be."

The officer shook his head to avoid being taken by Kaiser's venomous speech. He knew the old tales about the Dark Days and they never ceased to frighten him. "But..."

"Oh no. There will be no such negotiations as a duel or questions against the real truth. By your words, you have refused to see reality. I made myself clear before the gates that are now in pieces: this city will burn and everyone will die. There will be no survivors or prisoners of war. Commander Win, do as you are ordered and burn this salted shit hole to the ground. I will deal with the pathetically brave," Kaiser stated as he slowly pulled out his sword. He looked at it, acting as if he was confused. He shrugged before throwing it to the ground. The steel blade clattered at his feet. "I do not need a weapon in my hand to destroy those that seek to oppose me. It is just a worthless piece of metal."

In that single act, the once confident officer shivered with fear. One thing he knew was that Kaiser was no fool. He glanced from the sword to the smirking Loran. "Run!" he ordered with a shriek.

Kaiser watched with evil delight as the Eclipse guards struggled to keep up with their commanding officer. He picked up his sword, using his cloak to clean the blade before resheathing it at his left hip.

"How did you do that?" Loran asked with surprise.

Kaiser turned around and patted Loran's shoulder. "Easy. People do not know whether to believe the stories my enemies tell them as myth or truth. People know you as the Mirror Sea Pirate. They have seen your once mighty ships attack and raid. You are fearsome plain as day. Me? I am as dark as the night. My true skill unknown and unseen. But surely someone as old as myself in this day and age has found a way to conquer what tries to destroy him and has been made greater because of it. It is the unknown that frightens them and the idea of the truth that makes their blood run cold." He came in closer. "Rumor is often more powerful in swaying the masses than truth."

*****

Eclipse had defended itself against countless pirate raids but the attack by Kaiser's army was something it had never seen. Even the Dominion War against the Demons during the days of Shadow Night Silvanus could not compare. For never before had the gates been broken and the city invaded by its own countrymen. Kaiser's army was thousands strong and frighteningly loyal to his command. Skirmishes erupted all over the city between the invaders and the guards. Soon, Eclipse's own standing army joined the fray while its fire brigade battled against the fast spreading inferno of flames consuming everything in its path. The two greatest powers, Kaiser and Rache, were rarely spotted in the city and when they were, the fear and desperation increased tenfold. Rache's reputation was obvious. He was a known Demon and famous killing machine. Kaiser was more mysterious and dangerous. Tales of his actions outside the wall had spread faster than the fire and had increased the panic.

Kaiser's army penetrated deep into the main residential area much to the horror of the city defenders. People were ripped from their homes only to be slaughtered on the streets. Those that refused to die were murdered in their homes and left to be burned by the flames. The scent of blood became thick as the streets ran red. Shrieks of desperation and begging for salvation were quickly silenced by the pass of many steel blades. Soon, the idea of defense was abandoned for retreat to the docks where merchant ships waited to take survivors.

Those desperate to live rushed to the docks, flanked by Eclipse's guards to protect the retreat. Some were cut down by the pursuing army, their bodies trampled to pulp beneath the army's feet. The mixed throng of attackers and city people exchanged blows only when someone was unfortunate enough to fall behind. When the streets opened for the docks, there was a collective sigh of relief. The feeling barely lasted for between the retreat and the salvation of the ships was Kaiser. He stood with his sword pointed to the ground, palms resting on the pommel.

"I never said any of you could run," Kaiser snarled. He stabbed the sword into the stone ground, shattering the steel from the force. He threw his arms out to the side, palms down. "I can set a man on fire with a snap of my fingers. I can destroy ancient gates with a single kick. That is only the beginning."

With sharp, precise movements, Kaiser swung his arms and twisted his waist. At his command, the sea water shot up into the air, forming a swirling torrent. A twitch of his finger sent a shockwave to wrap around the column. He brought his hands together and then quickly threw them apart, transforming the column into a wall that spread across the docks. Ships were thrown back and consumed by the thunderous waves, removing all hope.

"Where are your precious rebels now!" Kaiser roared with evil delight. "Run! Run now to the Spirit World!"

Kaiser leaned back at his waist before throwing his body forward. The force pulled the thunderous wave up over the docks and it crashed around him. The mass of water rushed towards both the survivors and his soldiers as if it was his own summoned army from the Mirror Sea. Shouts could be heard coming from the rushing water. Everyone in its path scrambled to get out of the way. People from Eclipse were swallowed, ripped from their feet to disappear from sight. Kaiser's own soldiers fared little better. Their armor weighed them down and few escaped the wrath of the attack.

When the water cleared and left the rubble and bodies soaking wet, Kaiser smiled and rubbed his palms together. He glanced down at the broken sword.

"My Lord, you could have killed us. We who are most loyal to you," one of his soldiers pointed out before coughing up a fountain of salt water.

"Oops," Kaiser simply replied.

*****

The salty smell of blood was intoxicating and distracting. Rache clenched his jaw in resistance. He had to stay focused on his mission to find who many called the Silver Dancer. He knew better as did Kaiser. She was no great leader or secret rebel warrior. To many who did know her identity, she was a gifted dancer that had captivated Kaiser many centuries ago or so it seemed. Rache only knew of three people alive who were privy to the truth: himself, Kaiser, and Ryder Coba.

In truth, the Silver Dancer was the code name given to Myra by Kaiser himself and was subsequently adopted by the senior members of the rebellion. All they knew was that she was a part of Kaiser's past. She had been a frequent visitor to Cross, invited to dance with her troupe from Eclipse for the royal court. Her moves were graceful and dazzling to all who had seen her troupe's show. Rache did not see the appeal in her beauty then. He often wondered why Kaiser took her to his bed.

No! He had to focus on the hunt! Not upon the past! Rache shook his head gripping the roofing shingles before he could slide off. His mind refused to settle and thus his senses were disrupted. His hand cracked the roof under his grip as he fought the errant thoughts. He roared in defiance as the flames rose up behind him. His shadow reared up like a great beast, a dark glimpse of his true nature in the fire. Rache leapt off the roof top, soaring high into the air. He landed hard on the stone street in a cloud of dust and ash.

Rache ignored the chaos raging around him as he stalked the streets. He quickly slayed anyone that dared to get in his way, paying no mind to if they were of Kaiser's army or from Eclipse. It actually pleased him when a soldier of the army fell victim to his deadly power. Though he was loyal to Kaiser, he was not wholly so. He was sure that Kaiser already knew of his rebellious thoughts but kept him around for his strength and ferocity. He smirked as he dispatched the latest victim, not even bothering to taste the blood. He stepped over the body and sniffed the air with a renewed sense of focus. Few could compete with his ability to find people by their auras and especially by the smell of their blood.

For what seemed like hours, Rache searched the city high and low. At first, he commended the Silver Dancer for hiding well but now he was becoming annoyed. The split blood was not so thick that he could not find her. She simply was not in Eclipse. This surprised him as he knew that Myra was deathly afraid of Kaiser. She was so afraid that she had not left Eclipse since Kaiser threatened her with instant death if she disobeyed him. Only one person could have given her the courage to leave. Rache growled in fury, angry at himself for not arriving at the conclusion sooner. Kaiser was not going to be happy.

*****

ENTER THE SILVER DANCER

"What if he finds out? What if he comes after us?"

Not for the first time, Ryder took the panicked woman in his arms in an effort to calm her down. She continued to mutter and shiver with a deep sense of fear. It was if all warmth had left her body. Ryder held the woman close to his chest, the top of her head barely reaching his chin. Her faded black hair was streaked with gray and was tied together in a messy bun. It was still as soft as Ryder remembered from his childhood. She was now so small and frail, her being diminished from too many years living in constant fear. She clung to Ryder, desperate to find strength through his own physical being.

"I will protect you, Nana," Ryder said softly. "I promised you that I would when I came to fetch you from Eclipse. Already you are breaking free when you agreed to come with me. He is losing his hold on you."

Ryder knew that Kaiser was going to come after her after the events in Cross and he had been desperate to get away and rescue her. To him and Kaiser, his grandmother represented a link into their shared past. Likely, Kaiser saw her as a weakness but Ryder saw her as a strength. The woman known as Myra was more than a court dancer and Kaiser's former lover. Unknown except to a rare few, Myra was the mother of Kaiser's daughter and thus his grandmother. But he knew that her relationship with Kaiser was not one of love. Behind closed doors, her relationship with Kaiser was one of abuse and terror. He had frightened her so badly that she had not set foot outside of Eclipse since the death of Ryder's mother and their daughter. Myra had been devastated by the loss of Aylin while Kaiser could have cared less. It took a great deal on Ryder's part to convince her to leave Eclipse.

Myra wiped her eyes as she pulled away from Ryder, sniffling loudly. "I'm sorry. It's just I have been afraid for so long that my next breath will be my last. When you disappeared, I could hardly even think. What was my grandson's fate?"

"It appears I will be answering for that decision for a very long time," Ryder said, taking his gaze away from her. He let out a deep breath.

Myra stepped forward and put a hand on Ryder's shoulder. "You are here now. That is all that matters."

"Try telling Haven. Sometimes I think that she has forgiven me and other times, she curses my name," Ryder laughed half-heartedly.

"So you are still seeing the woman from Umbra. The sword smith's daughter? Now that is a person with a great Spirit. No wonder you find her attractive though I am sure her form pleases you as well," Myra teased, managing to smile.

Ryder's face flushed red. He stammered to find something to say.

"You are a mighty and powerful Spirit yourself. So much so that even the Lord of the Fireborn thought you worthy to wed his daughter. A Princess for the Prince in blood but not in name," Myra stated rather proudly.

"Nana, I am no Prince," Ryder quickly said.

Myra chuckled. "You can keep telling yourself that all you like. You are still the son of a former Shadowlord and your father's heir. In a strange and twisted way, you are Kaiser's heir too. Which legacy will you choose to follow?"

"First, I think we need to get to the base before he picks up your trail. You know he can and will wipe us both off the face of the planet with his mind alone," Ryder said as he stepped back from Myra. He turned around in a circle, examining the cave and feeling the stone.

Myra had been fearful that the cave was not enough to hide her from Kaiser's wrath. But as she watched Ryder systematically apply Spirit energy to the stone, she knew that if anyone could protect her, it was her grandson. Physically, Ryder was bigger than Kaiser and would likely be able to crush him. Ryder was four inches taller and had a bulky muscular frame to match. She continued to watch him. As he worked, the small opening of the cave began to shimmer. With each tap of his finger, the shimmering energy grew brighter. Ryder stood back up and waved his right hand in a small circle. The bright energy disappeared in an instant and a cool breeze wafted in from outside. Ryder turned back around and knocked his head on the ceiling.

"Oww!" Ryder grumbled as he rubbed his forehead.

Myra chuckled though she shivered from the cold. She rubbed her arms, trying to feel some semblance of warmth. Her eyes darted towards the cave opening. Stepping outside was daunting. A breath caught in her throat and her heart fluttered in her chest. She shuddered when Ryder dropped his heavy cloak around her shoulders. The cloak was lined with soft fur though it was ratty from the road.

"Won't you be cold?" Myra asked as she pulled the cloak around her tightly.

Ryder shrugged. "It's summer. Besides, I learned a few tricks from the Fireborn on how to stay warm." He pulled back his tunic collar to reveal a twisted set of runes on the top of his chest. "Can you Shadow Slide at all?"

Myra looked down as she felt an instant chill in her heart that went deeper than eyes could see. She did not want to admit that she had lost touch of her own Spirit energy many years ago. "Fear is a powerful weapon that cannot easily be broken, Peredur."

"Then I will break him for what he has done to you. Even if I have to rip his f…"

"RYDER!" Myra shrieked in shock. She grabbed his chin and made him look her in the eyes. "Don't you dare curse like that in front of me even if it is about him. Now I do not want to hear you talk like that again. Got it?" Ryder nodded. "That's a good man."

Nothing like his grandmother scolding him for a foul mouth could make Ryder feel quite as young. Even if he was two hundred and fifty years old. He did not even dare to move until Myra's hand dropped from his face. He rubbed his chin as a reflex, feeling the stubble beneath his fingertips.

"The night is still young. Can we go now before this boldness gets the best of me and lets the fear back in?" Myra asked, raising an eyebrow.

Ryder nodded. Myra then stepped next to him, her side pressing against his. He put his arm around her and closed his eyes. It took a sliver of thought to center himself and find the pulse of energy within his being. Every errant thought that threatened to break him of his focus were brushed away like leaves in the wind. He took in one breath and let it out slowly. In an instant, the energy enveloped them both, enhanced by the dark night. He was grateful that the small cave was not far from the base for the short distance lessened the chance that Kaiser would be able to detect them.

Zoras, Haven, Onyx, and the others at the rebel base fully believed that he spent the entire eight days in Cross, retrieving the old royal sword. In actuality, he spent most of his time in Eclipse. That part of his absence had to be absolutely secret until he brought Myra back to the base alive and in one piece. Haven was the most angry at him and he doubted that the truth would have lessened her rage. She seemed more emotional as of late. He felt Myra nudge him, reminding him to stay focused on his Shadow Slide.

He bypassed the scouts that Zoras had ordered to inspect the terrain surrounding the mountain base with expert ease. One scout looked in his direction as he passed, nodding. Good. At least one of them was alert. Ryder slowed his Slide and with a spin, jumped out of it into view. The dozen Shadowborn in the yard fell back in some form of disarray and shock by his sudden appearance. More so, they were surprised and curious about the older woman clinging to his side. Ryder kept his arm tight around his grandmother, the look on his face forbidding comments as he walked in the stone dwellings.

The first room was sparsely decorated and immediately led into a long hallway that ended with a split in two directions. Ryder took the left hand direction without hesitation. The new hallway was lit by lanterns, flames bounded in an iron cage. As Ryder expected, the door to Zoras' study was wide open and the usual crowd was bent over a map. Also as usual, they were arguing over plans for the next rebel mission.

""We need to have more information about Kaiser's movements before we can do anything. For years, he stuck close to Cross and the throne. But if Ryder is correct, he has abandoned his base for who knows where," Zoras argued as he slapped his hand over the aged ink marking for Cross.

Ryder cleared his throat loudly. Everyone's heads shot up in his direction. Of the four assembled at the table, Haven and Zoras were the most surprised to see Myra. Donovan appeared clueless as to her identity. True to his Saber training, Hayden hid all reaction.

"Silver Dancer?" Zoras asked, familiar with Myra's code name.

Before Ryder could speak, Haven launched into him with a tirade of words. "Why in the world didn't you tell me that you were going to fetch your grandmother from Eclipse?!"

The room immediately silenced as Haven stared hard into Ryder's eyes. "In truth, I knew that Kaiser leaving Cross meant he was making a bee line for Eclipse. I had to get her out of there before he could kill her." He stopped speaking when he felt Myra squeeze his forearm.

"Perhaps this is a matter best left for morning when we are all rested and had a chance to calm ourselves," Myra said, looking fiercely at Haven. The younger Shadowborn woman snorted and looked away, crossing her arms tightly. "If anything, I am not as young as I used to be and I am in need of rest. Lady Ombre, would you kindly show me a place where the women of this base get to sleep?"

"I share his room and bed," Haven said, gesturing towards Ryder. She glared at him. Her tone was matter of fact and harsh.

"I will make sure proper quarters are found for you, close to your grandson if you like," Zoras suggested in hopes of diffusing the situation. He lifted his hand from the map. Ryder shook his head, anticipating the question before Zoras could even ask it. "Yes, we all could use a little rest. Captain Hayden. You have the night command. Donovan will switch off with you at dawn."

Hayden glanced in Ryder's direction, seeming to guess at what was being left unsaid. Donovan still appeared clueless. The Saber captain bowed his head towards Ryder as he passed, pulling Donovan with him and closing the door behind them both.

Myra visibly relaxed though Ryder remained tense. "Master Rokar, it would be best not to speak too openly of mine and my grandson's relationship. Those of the older generation know of my history with Kaiser and may let spread certain truths that we both wish to remain quiet."

"Hayden and Donovan will keep their peace out of loyalty to Ryder and his Silvanus blood. I cannot guarantee what others will say and eventually the matter will have to be addressed. At some point, the Shadowborn will have to know that we are led by Kaiser's own blood. As desperate as we are to destroy him, there will be those who want to destroy all trace of him," Zoras explained as he leaned over the map.

Haven stepped in between Zoras' gaze and Ryder. "We are supposed to be in this together and yet you could not tell me that you were rescuing your grandmother. I would have gladly gone with you to help."

"This was something I had to do on my own. To show Kaiser that I am not afraid of him despite the fact that I am terrified of his retribution. The loss of the sword was a trifle. The loss of," Ryder said as he glanced towards Myra. "Is even greater. It proves that fear can be broken and his hold over the world is not as strong as he thinks it is. He will be more angry and vengeful because of it."

After a long silence, Haven's shoulders dropped and she

relented. Myra welcomed her embrace. When the two women parted, Myra grabbed Haven's left hand and turned it over.

"Peredur, you still haven't wedded the girl? How long do you think she will be willing to wait," Myra admonished. Ryder turned beet red and Haven chuckled.

"He has made his intentions to me known though he claims he must wait for the war to end," Haven stated with a grin.

"Do not wait for a war to end for it may never. Besides, a wedding might perk this dreary bunch up," Myra suggested. She too started giggling at Ryder's expense

Ryder ran a hand over his face, sweat beading on his brow. "Try getting her into a dress first. Then we will talk."

Haven wiggled her left hand towards Ryder as if to invite him putting a ring on her finger. "Lady Myra, perhaps you can tell me a few secrets on how to handle your grandson better. Of everyone here, you know him best."

The two women giggled as they exited the room, old times and feelings returning to them. Ryder hung his head in embarrassment.

"Your grandmother is right. A wedding would be something worthwhile to celebrate," Zoras said as he sat in an ebony wood chair. The chair creaked loudly.

"And put an even bigger target on Haven's back? I cannot risk it. Kaiser had all this time to kill her and chose not to much as he did with my grandmother. He does not make such decisions lightly," Ryder stated, letting out a deep breath.

"Marrying Haven might make her feel a little more secure in this world. That she has a future to dream of when the war brings down her Spirits," Zoras suggested with a shrug.

Ryder looked back at Zoras. "And what do you dream of?"

"That my son's sacrifice was not in vain. That he died for a cause and a hope that he believed in with all his heart.

*****

INTO THE STORM

He had been pushed to the limits of his physical being and his mind was beginning to fray. His muscles burned with every frantic wing beat as he fought against the cold and blistering wind. Ice hardened over his eyes and he blinked to clear his vision. Blinding snow pelted him from every direction as he struggled to stay in the air. But flying through a blizzard was the last of Gyr's worries. He was being hunted by a force desperate to kill him.

Gyr threw his tattered wings forward as he pressed his limbs against his body. His thick muscular tail whipped to the right but before he could shift his body weight, a feather tearing gust slammed into his back and forced him down. He dropped several hundred feet in the span of a second. But the experienced Gryphon barrel rolled to the right to avoid losing the lift of the air. He flared out his wide wings and pumped four times to regain altitude.

He was a Gryphon born on the high mountains of the north by the waters of the Dragon's Neck. Flying through snow and ice was a skill he had mastered by the time he was a young adult. His ease at flying through storms was praised by all who lived in the mountains. But Gyr was a descendent of the famous Mistress Gia and not only did he inherit her pure white looks, he inherited her masterful flight skills. He knew how to fly through blizzards but escaping a hunter was another story.

The hunter to his knowledge was a malevolent Spirit hell bent on killing him and thus preventing him from reaching Bane.

Gyr at first thought that the hunter was an average Shadowborn for he never saw him. But the chill in his heart said otherwise for this murderous creature's pursuit had him on constant edge. Gyr did not know what the hunter looked like or what he was truly capable of. All he knew was that he was afraid. Afraid of dying. Afraid of failing Proto Avis and the Northern Alliance.

Gyr strengthened his will before plunging into a headwind. He threw his shoulders forward like a battering ram and used his wings like blades to cut through the air. He pumped all four limbs to give him more forward thrust. It was a battle that lasted for an agonizing half hour before the headwind receded. Gyr managed to have a moment of pride and relief before he spotted a pelting sheet of ice ahead of him. Determination to beat the blizzard swelled within him and he quickly tilted his head and chest up before tucking his wings and limbs in. His weight dropped him into a power dive.

The change from snow to ice was a sign to Gyr that he had left the high mountain peaks and entered the foothills. He knew that the wind gusts would be slow and not as sharp. But here he had to be more careful for now he had to maneuver around the tops of pine trees. The sweet but earthy smell of pine sap was a welcome change from the cold, bland high air. Gyr could hear better at the lower altitude and he felt more at ease and able to conquer the storm. He took a deep breath.

There it was! The dark and ominous chill entered Gyr's heart again and he was aware of the hunter's presence. Now he could hear footsteps on the edge of his hearing. It was a quick pounding sound that was muffled by the wind. Another even more frightening sound reached him. The stretch of a bowstring. Gyr rolled to his right to avoid the first arrow and he decided to move higher. He pumped his wings as hard as he could but the ice had frozen on the trailing edge of his wings. He would have to dislodge the ice first before he could climb any higher. And the quickest way was to fly through a net of tree branches.

The Gryphon powered through an icy wind gust, keeping aware of the hunter's movements. The trees were already thinning as a white grassland opened up before him. But as he suspected, a lone pine tree stood tall at the mouth of the valley end and he flew straight towards it. His chest swelled as he bent his wings above his shoulders. He closed his eyes tightly, not seeing a black shadow climb up the tree.

*****

The hunter saw his target and grinned. He had planned it perfectly by driving the snow white Gryphon through the Sol Mountains, a range notorious for its blustery weather. This particular Gryphon had lasted longer than the last one who was a pathetically thin creature. He reached the high branch and quickly armed his bow with a poisoned arrow. Demon's blood dripped from its tip. The hunter took aim and smirked.

*****

At the last minute, Gyr saw the hunter and tried to slow his speed. He jerked his wings back and flailed his limbs in a panic. The hunter's arrow buried itself in his exposed chest and Gyr immediately lost his balance. He crashed through the tree branches, tearing up his wings and shearing the muscle away from his right thigh. He collided with another pine, cracking the trunk into splinters. His body spun before hitting the ground, sliding thirty feet before crashing into a snow drift. Gyr's senses were swimming in a haze as he tried to push himself up. He did not know if he had broken bones but his wings were ripped to shreds. His chest burned as if his feathers had been set on fire. And the pain continued to radiate in throbbing waves.

On the edge of the crash site, the hunter landed like a dark and dangerous shadow. The unearthly black mist that shielded him dissipated with a gust of wind. He held a crudely shaped ebony bow in his right hand and a rusty iron arrow in his left. Frost black leather adorned his thin body with a white fur lined hood draw up over his head. His steps were slow and deliberate as he approached Gyr.

Gyr's hackles rose up in aggressive fury as he shifted his broken body into attack position. If he was going to die, he would go down fighting. A wave of pain made him wince and he struggled to keep his will from sinking. He wanted to scream curses in the sharp Gryphon whistles for Gyr felt he could not spend the effort to shout in the common tongue. And nothing felt better than cursing in his mother tongue where so many words were considered taboo and dirty. He had once gotten in trouble when he had insulted his prim and proper aunt's gray speckled wings. As punishment for his foul words, he was forced to clean the family fire pit and thus dirty his feathers. It was not one of his finer moments but as Gyr faced down the hunter, he prepared the worst of all Gryphon curses.

"And thus falls another Gryphon in the snow filled Sol

Mountains though I must commend you for your tenacious strength," the hunter mused as he set the arrow against the bow.

The hunter's breath stank of old blood and rotten flesh. It reminded Gyr of a Demon and he shuddered. In response, he shrieked and hissed his well thought out curse, bristling his feathers in a threat display. He whipped his leonine tail back and forth. As he took a deep breath to repeat his curse, his lungs burned like a raging fire. He winced and squeezed his eyes shut. When he opened them again, his vision was tinged with a red color.

The hunter chuckled as he pulled back on the bowstring and raised his weapon. "Demon's blood is such a fantastic poison. It burns as it courses through the body, destroying organs and melting your bones. But once it reaches the brain." He put the arrow point between Gyr's eyes. "Death."

Gyr gritted the edges of his charcoal colored beak as the hunter stepped backwards and took aim. It was an execution shot. He hardened his heart against the sense of failure and against his fear of death. Gyr began to will his Spirit into his core as his grandfather had taught him. It was an old Gryphon technique that when one died away from home, their Spirit could be sent to their loved ones with a message. The technique required a great deal of focus and Gyr needed to make sure that Proto Avis would learn of his fate.

Suddenly, the hunter appeared to be on edge as Gyr saw his red eyes dart about and his grip on the arrow slackened. The hunter looked around the area until his gaze settled back on Gyr. But no, he was looking beyond Gyr into the grasslands and he raised his weapon up in a tight stance. Something or someone was approaching as Gyr now heard distant footsteps in the snow. It seemed as if the longer he focused on the sound, everything else quieted down around him. Even the screaming wind submitted.

"Reveal yourself!" the hunter shouted.

No one called back in answer. Gyr pushed through his pain to look over his shoulder to see just what was coming towards them. At first, all he saw was a hazy shadow of a man whose outline was obscured by weather and distance. But then he saw the shadowy newcomer reach up to his shoulder and pull a long shining object free. He slowly brought it to his side and twisted it enough for Gyr to see that it was a sword. The blade shimmered as the icy rain pelted it.

In a burst of wind, Gyr was blown back to the ground, his wings pinned. He heard the twang of the hunter's bow and the furious growl of a his Demon voice. A rush of air pelted him as the once distant shadow man leaped over him with his sword raised. Gyr fought his failing vision to see the shadow man hit the ground with his right foot before jumping again. The Gryphon watched as the hunter struggled to arm his bow, spilling several arrows on the ground as he backpedaled. His efforts were in vain as the shadow man swung his sword to slice off the hunter's forearms. The hunter cried out in pure agony, tears of blood streaming down his face. His screams were then quickly ended with another cut of the sword.

The shadow man landed with his back to Gyr, sword held out to his right side. He looked back over his shoulder with a pair of sky blue eyes and Gyr knew exactly who had saved him. Hidden beneath the gray fur lined cloak was Bane. It had to be him. It just had to be for no one could frighten a Demon like the Daylord. Gyr had found him! Gyr smiled as the sight of Bane filled him with a sense of relief as he finally passed out from the Demon's poisonous blood.

FEVERISH DREAMS

Heat. Intense, burning heat. Gyr could not understand where the sensation was coming from for it seemed to attack him from all directions. Every sense was filled with it. The hiss and sizzle filled his ears. His eyes were blinded by the light. All he could smell was ash and the sickening odor of burnt feathers. His mouth was completely dry as his tongue stuck to the inside of his beak. Worst of all, he felt his body being consumed by the raging inferno. He had no sense of where he was or who he was anymore. All he knew was heat and pain.

Suddenly, a dark shadow swelled up before him and Gyr saw that he was back on the snowy field. The snow had long since turned to water which now was steaming amidst the flames. The shadow twisted and transformed into the hunter. Now, Gyr was starting to remember. The hunter had shot him, the crude arrow buried deep in his chest. Surely, the dangerous weapon had pierced his heart, its Demon poison consuming his body. Gyr tried to breathe but his chest burned hotter than the white hot flames surrounding him. The dark shadow cackled as it revealed its eerie glowing eyes.

The memory was coming back to Gyr. This moment had already happened. He was certainly dead and reliving the moment as he traveled to the Spirit World. But why would the Spirit World show him this? He was a good soul or at least he believed himself to be. He was a Gryphon after all. No Gryphon was evil.

The fires framed the dark shadow like the wings of a

creature. A creature from the depths of the Spirit World where no good souls walked. No! Gyr refused to be consumed by the darkness before him. He screeched or at least he thought he did. He screeched again, pushing all of his energy into a Spirit rending curse. Nothing. Nothing was swaying this dark and terrible force from coming for him. Gyr knew he had to prepare for his ultimate end.

The hunter was more than some errant Shadowborn or lifeless shade of darkness. He was a force beyond Gyr's reckoning, full of the desire to kill. Gyr snarled, his eyes blazing. This Gryphon was going to go down fighting, no matter what injuries he had or the poison in his veins. His determination filled him with new strength. But it wasn't enough. The hunter lurched forward, ready to deliver the final blow. But then, the hunter hesitated and looked off into the distance. Another man who was cloaked in shadow was approaching.

Those eyes! That piercing gaze! The image filled Gyr's senses with greater force than the fire or the darkness of the hunter. He thought that he knew those eyes though he could not possibly know where from. But in his heart, Gyr knew those eyes. The legends spoke true of the Daylord's ice blue gaze, a cold and mysterious look. The power from them overwhelmed the hunter and the fire like a fierce wind. All of the bright flames disappeared beneath a blizzard.

In the midst of the snow and ice dancing around him, Gyr saw a door in the distance. It appeared to be made of white stone and wood, etched with designs too detailed and intricate to make out. It was absolutely beautiful and it invited him to open it. Unlike the hunter and the eyes of the Daylord, he hesitated with how to respond. Was he afraid? Was he joyous? Was he not ready to open the door and go inside? The poison burned so badly that part of him desired to reach out for the door. No! Gyr knew that he was stronger than this and that his mission was not complete. As those thoughts consumed his mind, the door seemed to grow more distant and faded.

Still, Gyr could not shake the feeling that something was lurking in the shadows. He did not think that this presence was evil but it was still foreign to him. In his state, he screeched and began to lash out. He flailed and flapped his wings violently.

"Whoa! Hold on!" a voice cried out in a clear tone.

Gyr paused. That voice came from everywhere and yet it came from nowhere. Did the blizzard call out to him? No, that could not be it but he knew that he heard a voice. He chawed and whistled sharply in his native tongue, issuing a warning.

"I don't speak bird lion or whatever this language is but if you don't calm down, you will tear open your wounds."

There it was again! The clear voice. Gyr knew he had heard it before yet the tone was different. It was almost Spiritborn and yet it wasn't. He could hear rough yet refined tones of a young Shadowborn though they were muddled beneath a simple inflection. As Gyr fought to decipher the voice and the visions before him, he began to hear new sounds. A fire spat and crackled from somewhere close by. The sound of a raging blizzard was distant and muffled behind something. A flap of animal skin perhaps?

Gyr was slow to open his eyes for part of him feared that this was all an illusion. To open one's eyes was to open the mind and to let mental focus drift away into nothingness. Gyr had been taught early on how to reclaim that focus but something was keeping him from it. The world around him was fuzzy. A bright light flickered a few feet before him. His vision cleared some more and he could see the form of a man standing a distance away. Again, his vision sharpened. It quickly became apparent that Gyr was inside of a cave of brown stone and gray moss. His head swam from the sensory overload.

"Please, be still," the voice urged. It was coming from the man in the cave.

Heeding the man's words, Gyr closed his eyes again and took a painful deep breath. He let it out slowly before opening his eyes again. He discovered that he was lying on a pile of thick animal skins, his wounds dressed, and a blanket laid over him. He could smell salve of some kind. Even more appealing, he could smell rabbit meat. Gyr refocused on the man.

The strange man was young and certainly not the Daylord. His hair was as dark as night, loosely tied back in a ponytail. His face spoke of his youth but Gyr could tell by looking into his gray eyes that he was older than he appeared. The man was tall and well-muscled. He wore a pair of wool pants, leather boots, and a wool long sleeve shirt. His clothes were travel worn and dark, the true colors hidden beneath a splattering of mud, snow, and blood. The man's expression was worried but curious.

"Have you never seen a Gryphon before?" Gyr asked, starting to be annoyed by the man's lack of knowledge for his race's name. Bird lion? How insulting!

The man shrugged. "Only from a distance. This is my first time meeting one. You really are a Gryphon? I thought they were just fairytales. Well people act like they are fairytales south of Garhune. I mean a bird and a beast combined into one creature? It is odd."

Gyr scoffed. How could this man not know what a Gryphon

was and that they were very real? His description of one was insulting. Gyr decided to let the slight slide for the time being. "You must know for you dressed my wounds and bandaged them well."

"That was not me. Whoever it was led me here," the man stated.

"The Daylord? You saw the Daylord? Is he still here?" Gyr frantically asked. "I need to find him. Can you lead me to him?"

The man let out a deep breath. "The Daylord hasn't been seen in years beyond count. Certainly not in my lifetime."

Gyr felt deflated by the comment but his heart screamed at him to push harder. "Then how did you find me?"

"I'm not really sure how to explain it. I felt a call to come to you and render you aid. I could not ignore it," the man said curiously. He tilted his head to the side and let out a deep breath. "It was odd."

Gyr knew exactly what had happened. "Spirit Call. Whoever sent the message compelled you to come to this spot." He slowly shifted his weight as his right thigh had fallen asleep from the pressure of his body leaning on it. "And very few have a power great enough to compel others not known to them to follow an order."

"Everyone knows of the Daylord here. He is a legend to us, a king from a distant land and a warrior of great power. I don't know who you think you saw but it was not him," the man said apologetically. He sat down on the other side of the fire, tending to the two skinned rabbits cooking over the coals.

Maybe he did imagine that Bane had saved him but Gyr simply refused to believe that. It was Bane he saw. He was sure of it. His would be killer had been frozen with fear when Bane appeared. No one else could have done that to another person. Gyr closed his eyes and shook his head in an attempt to settle his mind. His mind refused to accept that his savior was anyone but the Daylord. It would be pointless trying to convince the dumb man of anything else. Where was his hope? Where was his belief that great heroes still roamed the land even if they were unseen?

"Well I refuse to believe that. If you will not lead me to him, then I will find him myself. I will fly this land shore to shore until I find my king," Gyr confidently stated. He started to stand up and immediately fell back down. He seethed and stiffened.

"Look. I'm no expert but I don't think you can fly in your condition. Either way," the man said before gesturing back towards the cave opening. "This blizzard isn't going anywhere anytime soon."

Gyr looked past the man. Every time the animal skin

flapped in the wind, he could see the heavy snowfall. His shoulders drooped and he bowed his head in defeat. He then looked up. "Where in the Southlands am I?"

"Eastern branch of the Sol Mountains. I believe that your city of Crossroads is northwest of here by many leagues," the man said as he poked at the fire with a stick. He was silent for a long time.

"Who are you?" Gyr asked, cocking his head.

The man paused. "Charon of Garhune. You?"

Gyr bowed his head as his culture dictated when introducing oneself. "My name is Gyr," he first said in his native tongue before repeating it in the common tongue. "I am charged with great purpose and thus have flown into the Southlands in order to find my king and bring him home."

Charon pulled the two rabbits off of the fire and passed one to Gyr. "I'm charged by whoever pays me to hunt, chase, fight, scout, and lead. A jack of all trades."

"I must be forward but you have to be of Spiritborn blood to have heard a Spirit Call. Is that true?" Gyr asked in between bites of meat.

"My father was Shadowborn according to my mother. Never knew the guy though so I can't tell you more," Charon replied with a shrug. "She was Mortal like most Southlanders."

Gyr immediately caught on and did not need to ask Charon about the fate of his mother. If she was indeed Mortal, it was clear that she was deceased. It made Gyr wonder just how old Charon was. Instead of pressing for more answers, Gyr tore into the rabbit and ate. It was nice to have something warm in his stomach. In between bites, Gyr looked up at Charon who had turned his attention to the blizzard raging outside. He snapped up the last piece of meat, savoring the taste

"Hopefully by morning, the blizzard will have stopped. I need to report back to Meras as soon as possible," Charon commented with a deep sigh.

"Why don't you just Shadow Slide? That should get you there quickly and safely," Gyr suggested.

Charon turned to look at him. "Shadow Slide? What is that?"

Gyr was flabbergasted that a Shadowborn, even one that was half-blooded, did not know what Shadow Slide was. It confused him and he jerked his head back. His chest burned with pain in response to the quick motion. "It is one of the most basic Shadowborn Spirit energy techniques. All Shadowborn know it before they can even perform it with any skill."

"Spirit energy? The only thing my mother said about that

was to never use it. She told me that it was dangerous and evil," Charon stated. He shrugged his shoulders.

"Yes, it can be dangerous and used for evil but it is also good and can be used in helpful ways. As a Gryphon, I cannot use it as the Spiritborn can but I can sense it," Gyr proudly said. He pushed out a puff of breath through his nostrils. "I suspect that the relationship between your mother and father was not a loving one."

"She rarely spoke of my father and when she did, it was never positive," Charon replied with a nod. "What about you?"

Gyr resisted the urge to puff out his chest in pride due to his injury. "My egg mother and egg father are noble Gryphons serving in the court of Lord Stellaris, my Lord of War. It is through my mother that I have my superior weather flight skills."

Charon chuckled. "Do you have any siblings?"

The get to know you conversation continued long into the night. Gyr found that despite initial impressions, he really liked Charon and his rough but genuine nature. He wanted to talk more but his wounds were getting the best of him. His eyes began to droop, his lids heavy with exhaustion. He was surprised that he had lasted even this long. As Gyr fell asleep, Charon tossed a blanket over the Gryphon and returned to tending the fire.

*****

IN THE RUINS

The air was thick with the smell of ash and salt. On every street were the ruins of burnt down buildings, debris strewn about in haphazard piles. Smoke blanketed the sky with clouds of gray and black. If one was not careful, stone and wood from crumbling walls would fall and hit them on the head. Kaiser walked through the mess, stepping over bodies and splashing his boots in puddles of congealed blood. The hem of his cloak dragged behind him, accumulating a layer of filth on the bottom edge.

Chaos amused him as he strode through the ruined streets of Eclipse. Soldiers terrorized survivors, chasing them with blood soaked swords in hand. Kaiser paused long enough to listen to the screams begging for mercy. The screams escalated in volume and desperation when a soldier cut down a survivor. Kaiser smirked before continuing on, leaving the massacre behind. He pushed all thoughts into his singular mission: find the vaults of Eclipse. Not the vaults where treasures were kept. He was looking for a place more secret and precious: the Silvanus family library. Sure, the destruction of Eclipse could be considered overkill. While he thought about it, he realized that he had forgotten to order his army to leave the citadel untouched. Perhaps it was foolish to forget that. He shrugged his shoulders as the thought crossed his mind.

Kaiser had done his research in his bid to find out the fate of Sage Silvanus. Sage was the one son of Shadow Night that had eluded him. Ensuring himself that Sage was dead, whether by his hand or some other end, was top priority. To him, Sage was outside of his control and he hated not having some semblance of an upper hand. He could not be harmed by Vorin's Dragonfire. Oren and the Earthborn were too afraid to move or say anything against him. The Waterborn were too withdrawn and unwilling to participate in the goings on of the world. The same could be said of Evander and the Lightborn. Kaiser did not think much of the Fireborn being a credible threat. Gryphons were just stupid beasts that were far too easy to kill. Aves, Bane, his grandson, and Sage were the last threats to his power that he could think of.

He paused to consider each of the four and to clean off the thick coat of blood on the soles of his boots. He stepped into the skeleton of a burnt down house and dragged his feet across a large piece of blackened stone. On their own, Aves was the eldest and strongest. Combined, Bane and his grandson could prove a credible threat but each had their own share of problems. Kaiser scoffed as he thought about the masterful manipulation he had achieved to drive Bane away. He was also responsible for training and shaping his grandson's power. But Sage was an unknown. He swiped his right foot one more time before stepping back out on to the street.

Kaiser had to admit to himself that he was proud of his followers. They were very thorough in their work. Everywhere he looked, glass windows had been shattered, homes gutted, and copious amounts of blood had been spilt. He had long though that many of the willing soldiers were idiots that had hooked on to his rhetoric of power and greater opportunity than their lives had held. It had been easy to convince so many of false truths, whether lies the world had told them or lies he was currently telling them. Of course not every one of his followers had come willingly. That required a little push. Kaiser smirked as he thought about how he twisted their minds into believing what he wanted them to believe. He wiggled and turned his fingers in response.

Up ahead loomed what remained of the stone citadel that sat in the center of Eclipse. The stone had been blackened by fire and several holes had been blasted in the walls. The wood and iron doors hung haphazardly from their bearings. Kaiser was thankful that the courtyard before the doors was abandoned. The only person that was present was the mangled body of a guard. Kaiser chuckled as he passed the body and approached the doors. The doors were twenty feet tall and usually required a whole team of guards pulling on the iron rings to open and close them. Kaiser ran his hand over the edge of the door to his left. It leaned against his touch. With a pop of his shoulder, Kaiser shoved it out of the way and it crashed to the ground.

The entryway was dark with a beam of sunlight streaming through the broken ceiling by the stairs to the second floor. Leaves and ash drifted through the hole in the ceiling like snow falling to the ground. The beam of sunlight hit the floor in between the second floor stairs. Behind the beam was a large burnt banner of the Silvanus royal crest. To any other person, the scene would have been eerie and frightening. There were few things that Kaiser feared and none he would admit to another. He appreciated scenes like the one before him. He sniffed the air. A sense of age and history filled his eleven hundred year old soul with the deep breath he took.

His steps echoed as he crossed the dark entryway. Each thud of his foot was loud and only emphasized the emptiness of the place. Kaiser turned his head about, pushing the vast reaching strength of his mind outwards in every direction. His senses twisted and turned around corners, blasting through physical barriers. The upper floors of the citadel were quickly eliminated as a possible location for the vaults. Kaiser drew his mental strength back and focused them more on the floors below him. He paused when he hit a source of resistant Spirit energy. Smart, he thought. Whoever set the entrance to the vaults used Spirit energy to lock it. Too bad they did not consider someone stronger than themselves coming along to open the door.

Kaiser followed the path of his senses, descending many stairs until he could go no further. Or so the builders of the citadel would have thought for the average person. He snickered at the thought that these master builders probably believed that no one could outsmart their designs. The room he ended up in had no other openings save the archway he had just come through. There were no windows and no sources of light as the torches had long been snuffed out. Kaiser raised his left hand and flicked his wrist with a snap of the fingers. The torches immediately lit at his command. He studied the shadows with a careful eye. Most would only see the shadows for what they are: an absence of light. Kaiser was not like most people. Age was partly to thank for he had his lifetime of experience and training. He could read the darkest of shadows, using them like another set of eyes. He took in a deep breath and slowly let it out, centering his focus.

Under his feet was a sealed chamber, one with no door. Kaiser laughed out loud. The builders were smart enough to ensure that only a Shadowborn could access the vaults via the innate technique Shadow Slide. Even then, it had to be a Shadowborn strong enough to pass through the stone and throw himself at the Spirit energy seal. Kaiser closed his eyes and immediately went into Shadow Slide. A few seconds passed as he slowly made his way downward through the stone floor. He hit the first barrier, slowing his descent. Kaiser amplified his Spirit energy into a battering ram and easily broke through the barrier. The path took him through five more barriers, requiring more strength and power to pass through. Each of the barriers represented the Spiritborn nations and required Kaiser to tap into his Anu blood to pass them. Going through the final barrier, Kaiser pulled himself out of Shadow Slide and slowly descended to the floor.

It moderately surprised him to find that the vaults contained a library. He had expected to find weapons or ancient treasure inside. The rows of books and old tomes appealed to his inner scholar. He was more passionate about books than he ever was about instruments of war. Kaiser gritted his teeth as he thought about all of the times his father pushed him to his physical limit and how his mother did nothing to stop her husband. He broke so many bones. His body bled until there was nothing left in him. At the time, he found quiet and solace in books. He had vowed as a small child to make his mind just as powerful as his physical body. He read constantly, often staying up far into the night. He explored the reaches of his Spirit energy at every moment. Now all of that training would pay off.

Kaiser took a moment to appreciate the books and scrolls that surrounded him. He slowly walked, dragging his fingers over the bindings as he passed. The air was stale and dust laid heavy on every surface. He wondered when the last person visited the vaults. Surely, they had to be of Anu blood or perhaps knew a secret code or had a key to get in. If anything, this vault had to hold the most ancient secrets of the Shadowborn. Kaiser hoped it would lead him to Sage Silvanus, the elusive last son of Shadow Night.

Eclipse had been the first capital of the Shadowborn in the earliest days of Terra. Shadow Night had been born here by the shores of the Mirror Sea, not in Cross as many had been led to believe. His wife and three sons had been born in the city of Cross and thus cemented the eventual capital as the home of the Silvanus family. Much of Shadow Night's history prior to his rise as Lord of the Shadowborn was muddled and lost to time. Kaiser could not even think of anyone alive that knew the old leader's past, not even Vorin the Dragonlord. His own ancestor Adonis Anu was long since dead and likely the last person to know the first Shadowlord's true past.

Kaiser paused when a silver covered book caught his eye. It stood out brightly among the dark leather tomes that dominated the library. He felt the ridges on the spine before pulling the book free. A hush of breath whispered out of the silence. Kaiser thought he heard the tones of his ancestor's voice, reminiscent of his father's own voice. For a moment, he thought it odd. Was a Spirit of one of his Adonis relatives in the room with him? Were they trying to lead him to the truth or were they trying to warn him of it? If anything, the whispers indicated that he had found the right book.

On the front of the book was the Adonis family crest and Adonis Anu's signature in gold trim. He brushed his fingers over a strip of dust, revealing the title.

"Last Will and Truths of Adonis Anu," Kaiser read to himself.

The whispers brushed past his ears again as he moved to open the book. He paused to snarl before forcing the old book to open. The first page was blank. Not unusual, Kaiser thought, for the page was there to protect the ink inscription on the following page from bleeding through. He turned the page. Blank again! Kaiser kept turning pages, finding them completely void of any writing or pictures. In a fury, he started ripping the paper sheets out before throwing the entire book into the air and blasting it with fire. The burning book fell to the floor, crumbling quickly into a pile of ash. He stomped on the ash angrily.

It had been too easy for him to find and enter the vaults. Surely his ancestor, who he now believed was the last to enter them, knew that a child of his bloodline would return here. It was of course impossible for Adonis Anu to know the intentions of his descendants. But why go through the trouble of creating such a place or leaving it for someone else to find. Kaiser growled and clenched his fists tightly.

"Is it your voice? Your Spirit?" he shouted to the emptiness. "Is it truly your last will to protect a secret kept here?" Kaiser threw out his arms, inviting whatever energy or Spirit was present to challenge him.

As Kaiser had been taught, Spirits could do incredible things in the world of the living. Omu the great wolf of the Shadowborn could lead the dead to the Spirit World. According to the Waterborn, a sea serpent guarded the Mirror Sea from the Darklands. Even the Airborn believed that an eagle Spirit blessed the first Gryphons, giving them their majestic bodies. All foolish drivel, Kaiser thought. The true power of the Spirits lay in their world where anything was possible. It was because of this that the Covenant of Spirits was written. At that moment, the world was separated into two separate domains: that of the living and that of Spirits and the dead. Dragons knew this story best for it had been a truly fearsome beast of their race that aided in separating the worlds. Such great and terrible power being suppressed was a pity to Kaiser.

The thoughts made him consider why finding Sage was so important to him. Sage was not that much older than he was and was not known to have been a warrior. No one even knew if the last of Shadow Night's sons was alive. If he was, what use could he be to a world that was different from the days of his youth? If he was indeed alive, Kaiser wanted to crush his throat and rip out his heart. In his current anger, he wanted to wipe away Sage's existence. Kaiser paused long enough to collect his thoughts and rein in his emotions. He let out a deep breath. Kaiser knew that he had to focus or he would achieve nothing in the vaults.

Sage would know his father's past. That was the answer. Kaiser smirked at the thought. Uncovering the past of Shadow Night would unlock the secrets behind the Silvanus royal power. A power denied to him by sheer legacy. He was a descendant of Begin Anu, the powerful Farlander killed by Rache, and if history had taught him, the Farlanders were greater in power than any Spiritborn. With his death, why did Adonis Anu come second to Shadow Night? It could not have been on his choices. Kaiser refused to believe that. But what if Sage was dead? How could that help him uncovered the necessary secrets? Kaiser knew that he had to risk his belief that Sage was still alive, hidden from the world by a power he could not overcome on his own. The power of an Anu had to be holding him prisoner somewhere.

The Anus had not been prolific in producing descendants due to their Farlander blood. Kaiser and his grandson were the last of that bloodline. Kaiser thought it extremely fortunate that Ryder was also a direct descendant of Shadow Night. Perhaps he could be of more use if his heart wasn't aligned with that of his parents. Both Akakios and Kaiser's daughter, Aylin, were free minded and believed in greater things such as the noble Spirits. But Kaiser had broken Akakios and killed Aylin. He would break Ryder before the end.

The whispers had fallen silent as if they were glad that the silver book proved useless. Maybe they could sense his dark heart or what he truly was. Kaiser did not want to think on that for long as he decided to renew his search. This time, he chose to be respectful of the books, reminding himself of his inner bibliophile. As he searched, he came to realize that the silver book he had torn apart was the only one in a sea of black. At first, he found that insignificant. Why should the color of a book's binding matter? But Kaiser started to think that it was indeed significant and that he would find no written directions to Sage's location. A silver book in a sea of black. A silver book in a sea of black. Kaiser kept repeating the observation to himself, forcing his mind to focus on it.

He paused as the realization came to him.
"Silver."

*****

MYRA SPEAKS

"How did you get out of Eclipse?" Onyx asked as he sat across the table from Myra. Haven sat to her right side, picking at her food. She giggled as she flicked a large piece of biscuit at Ryder.

"It's not like Kaiser put my grandmother in a prison with chains and guards. It was actually quite easy. Escaping unnoticed was the trickiest part," Ryder grumbled as he batted Haven's repeated attempts to flick food at his face.

Myra chuckled softly at the pair before returning her attention to Onyx. "My residence was on the eastern side of Eclipse at the furthest point from the shipyard. The house was actually my childhood home. I knew the neighborhood well. Every house, wall, loose gate, and sewer pipe. Haven, you better tell my grandson to make sure he scrubs himself well. I swear I can still smell the sewer stench."

"I have bathed since then," Ryder pointed out.

"You escaped Eclipse through the sewer pipes? Why not just Shadow Slide?" Onyx asked.

"I may not have been in chains and locked inside a cell but Kaiser has other means of detecting my movements. According to Ryder, there were several Spirit energy wards that surrounded my home. Wards that only activated if I or someone else used Spirit energy to leave. Ask Ryder about the finer points of such things. It is a bit beyond my understanding," Myra explained. She pushed back a lock of hair from her face. Her expression changed from jovial to subdued.

"Kaiser is a very smart man and one must admire his intelligence despite his evil nature. But even a smart man can make mistakes," Myra stated as she wiggled a finger. "Fear is a powerful prison or so Kaiser thought. He believed it strong enough to prevent me from leaving Eclipse. I doubt he figured on our grandson breaking the chains and setting me free."

She glanced over at Ryder who stood in the doorway, arms crossed and leaning against the frame. A fine layer of biscuit crumbs covered his right shoulder. She smiled but Ryder only let out a huff of breath. He turned away. He had to be embarrassed by an earlier story she had told about his childhood. The thought made her smile.

"Oh come on, Ryder. You've got to be able to laugh at yourself. I find it adorable that you cried over thinking you had lost a favorite stuffed toy," Haven teased and snickered. "Did you ever find it?"

"No," Ryder grumbled, gripping his biceps tightly.

"Well maybe for your birthday, I can get you another one," Haven said before she burst out laughing. She giggled louder when Ryder shot her a venomous glare.

Onyx smiled, amused at seeing his usually serious cousin appear a little unnerved. He had seen Ryder joke and laugh on rare occasions but nothing like what he was seeing now. The light mood in the room helped him to further heal from the loss of his father. In fact, he could not even remember laughing like this with his own family. He really liked having Myra at the base and was glad that Ryder rescued her. "So did you Shadow Slide out?"

Myra nodded. "Not until we were several leagues from the city. My grandson is a fair runner with admirable endurance. He took me to a cave not too far from here." She nodded towards Ryder before turning back towards Onyx. "Shadow Slide is probably the most useful technique we Shadowborn can use in our lives though as I am sure you have been told, you must be careful. Use it too much or stay in Shadow Slide too long and you risk your life. Many things such as physical injury or a shattered mental state can affect the strength of a slide."

Haven and Onyx nodded, both having heard that warning in their lives. Ryder kept quiet. She glanced at Ryder and gestured towards the empty seat with a plate of food waiting. He rolled his eyes in response before coming over to sit down. Haven switched her seat to sit beside Ryder at the head of the table. She squeezed his hand and smiled. It took him a while to respond. He then wrapped his hand around hers.

"Though you did not tell me what you were doing, I am glad

that it was for something noble and for love of your family. I still want to box your ears for not telling me that you were leaving though," Haven sweetly said with a slight grin.

"That was not proper of you if she is your partner. Secret or not, you should have told at least her what you were doing. Especially if you intend to marry her," Myra admonished. Ryder paused in eating a piece of bread. "My question is why haven't you yet and don't you dare blame Kaiser!"

Ryder swallowed hard as everyone stared at him. Only Onyx's expression appeared to be curious and not judgmental. He pulled his hand free from Haven. "Way to put me on the spot, Nana."

"Life is not just about war, Ryder. Eventually, wars end and fighters must return to their homes to rest. You have been with Haven for most of your lives. You have been by each other's side since you two met at Umbra's Winter Solstice Ball," Myra started to say. "Such a beautiful couple you two were that night."

"He did actually leave me for a century," Haven said curtly. She sat back in her seat. "I think it is time you tell your grandmother the truth and I am sure that your cousin deserves to know as well."

"The truth about what? Why I left? I thought that I already made that clear. Why do we have to keep talking about it?" Ryder asked in a tight voice.

Haven popped the back of his hand. "Because you have yet to make your reasons clear. Yes, you are afraid of Kaiser. Everyone is. That is not a good enough reason to leave your home and those you love behind without a word."

Ryder pushed back his seat and stood up. He pressed his fists on the edge of the table. "As my grandmother said, fear is a powerful prison and it is also a poison. I could win this war against Kaiser but he will always be a part of who I am. I cannot escape his name or his reputation for as long as I live. The thought consumed me one hundred years ago and I needed to know if I could rise above it on my own. I had intended to return after a few years but rumors reached me of Kaiser's increasing acts and the Daylord's continued absence. At first, I had the mind to increase my own knowledge and power to eventually challenge Kaiser. But as I trained, I came to the realization that he knew me better than I could know myself. He shaped me from the very beginning. I could be called Kaiser light if you really think about it. How could the Spirits bless me in any way such as becoming the Shadowlord or having a normal family? In a way, I became a poison like him."

"You are not Kaiser. You will never be Kaiser," Myra stated with conviction. "And I refuse to believe that you allowed such thoughts to separate yourself from those you love. Unlike me, you chose to leave. Now, you must pay for those choices. Earn back the love of your life and of your family truly and honestly." She stood up and grabbed Ryder's chin. "You are afraid of your destiny but you don't know what that is. No one can tell you what path to take and where it will lead."

Myra jerked her hand back and Ryder sat back down. He looked completely flabbergasted. "Now tell me, Peredur. What are you truly afraid of? Why did you really leave?"

It took a long time for Ryder to answer. "I was afraid that I would fail everyone's expectations. Haven included. Onyx, your grandfather tried to keep me from leaving as he did not want the throne any more than I did." He turned to look at Haven. "Being a war hero is easy enough but eventually your actions become a distant memory. To be a husband and father is a greater challenge. Normal life for me doesn't exist and it never will. I don't want to fail you, Haven. I do not want to promise a future and not be able to deliver on it."

Onyx had been silent through the entire exchange, seeing it more as part of the continued spat between Haven and Ryder. He could tell that Ryder was uncomfortable with confronting the reality of his decision. Many had already made it clear to Ryder that his decision to leave was a terrible one. At first, Onyx thought the same as everyone else. His cousin could have been the Shadowlord. He could have protected the Silvanus family from Kaiser's murderous intentions. Ryder could have even defeated Kaiser in a challenge. Living in the past and constantly questioning one's acts was a terrible poison, even more so than fear.

"What is done is done and cannot be undone," Onyx suddenly said, bringing all attention to himself. "All that matters is that Ryder is here now and you need to stop making him admit to things he has already spoken of. You do not have to agree or accept his words. Accept him for who he is now and be done with it."

Ryder smiled with a degree of pride as he leaned back in his seat with arms crossed. "Onyx is right. The past is done. It's the present we need to focus on. Nana, I have promised to marry Haven though I have yet to make my proposal formal. Haven, I am sure you are in no rush to wear a big frilly dress."

Haven immediately harrumphed at the thought. It was well known that she preferred wearing pants and armor. She grumbled and crossed her arms tightly. A strand of black hair fell in her face. Ryder patted her shoulder, chuckling softly. She batted his hand away.

"I remember when you two met. Both of you hated being

dressed up for the ball. You looked so handsome, Ryder, but I am biased," Myra reminisced with a smile. "Such a beautiful couple. I am sure that one day you will make beautiful children."

Ryder and Haven immediately sat up straight, looking shocked and embarrassed. Onyx had to laugh though he tried to hide his amusement by covering his mouth. Myra was confused by their reaction.

"You have not considered that possibility in all your years together?" Myra asked.

Haven smacked Ryder's arm to get him to answer. He turned to glare at her but she only glared back. The somewhat playful banter and teasing continued for several minutes as each nudged the other to respond to Myra's inquiry. Neither of them seemed willing to answer.

The small dining room filled with the nervous but delightful energy as Onyx laughed, Myra stared at Ryder and Haven in anticipation, and the pair continued to bat and poke each other. The half-eaten food became cold and forgotten until Haven tossed a bread roll at Ryder's head. It bounced off of Ryder's head and fell to the floor.

"Okay! Okay!" Ryder said as he held down Haven's left arm. She stuck her tongue out at him. "Only if the Spirits choose to bless our union with a child. Right now, I need to focus on wining this war before I try to learn how to be a father."

"Still, there hasn't been a baby in my family since you were born. Such cute little chubby cheeks," Myra mused as she moved to pinch Ryder's face. He batted her away. "This child, whenever it comes for I am sure it will, will be quite the warrior."

"Seriously, Nana," Ryder grumbled. He glanced towards Onyx. "First, I need to work with you and get you started on becoming a real warrior. Not whatever your prior teachers thought to teach you."

Onyx stiffened up. He wanted to defend the teachings of Sai with an extreme ferocity. He held a lot of respect for the old Saber Commander. Ryder seemed to have no respect for Sai. "Sai Parahazur was one of the best teachers I could have asked for."

Ryder chuckled. "He only became Commander because I refused the position. A little secret in how the Commanders are named. Those vying for the position engage in a no holds bar battle and the winner is the warrior still standing in the end. I had beaten him quite easily but deferred the victory. This war with Kaiser does not follow the rules that Sai taught you. You will have to take everything you learn from me and from others plus what you discover on your own in order to survive. Are you still up to it?"

Myra smiled with pride at Ryder. "The finest trainers can only do so much to shape you and your skill. In fact, only you can decide what kind of person you want to be. Fate may show you a path but you must make the decision whether or not to follow."

STUDENT AND TEACHER

"So tell me about your experience in Cross again," Ryder said as he brushed a handful of dirt between his palms.

Onyx shrugged, partially out of not wanting to revisit the fact that he had to kill his father. Even though the person he faced was his father only in appearance and not in mind, he still remembered the pained screams of his father trying to break free. Regardless of the fact that Iztal was possessing him, it was still a tough matter to deal with. "I guess I felt that I was fighting to free my father."

"That is not what I am asking. I am asking about the fight itself. What did you feel? With the odds against you, what kept you from giving up?" Ryder asked a bit more firmly. He moved to stand in front of Onyx.

The young Prince did his best not to look Ryder in the eyes. He glanced around the dirt yard, the same one where he and Ryder had had their first combat encounter. A few rebel stragglers paused to see what the two were doing but quickly grew bored and continued on. There were not many present at the base as Zoras had order the best scouts out to survey the region and determined Kaiser's movements. When Ryder had brought back the report that Kaiser was no longer in Cross, it had put a sense of unease in everyone.

"I don't really know. I was mostly fighting to defend myself. All that mattered was my . I did anything I could to make sure I lived and that my father lived," Onyx finally answered.

"So you battled out of desperation. Moderately effective but not so against greater opponents. You have to be smart and find a balance between three things: your body, your mind, and your heart. But I will say that you could have run once you saw Iztal and you chose not to. You have courage deep inside," Ryder stated placing a hand on Onyx's shoulder. "Courage in the face of fear. There is hope for you yet."

Onyx managed a small smile. He had always worried that being afraid made him weak. But he did worry about his fear overwhelming him and affecting his mid battle decisions.

"So why did I fail so horribly in a fight against you? Iztal was frightening to face and yet I managed to win anyway," Onyx asked looking back at his cousin.

"I suspect that you have not told me everything. Your heart was certainly strong enough but against the combined force of Iztal and your father's power, you should have died," Ryder said solemnly. "I'm sorry but that the truth."

It was hard to hear that, Onyx thought to himself. In reality, Iztal should have killed him but the Demon did not. Onyx told himself that he could not have won without the help of his parents' Spirits. He then told Ryder the full story.

Ryder nodded, scratching his chin. "The Spirits were looking out for you. That is always a good thing. As I am sure that you were taught, the Spirits come only sparingly to this world and only in the truest and greatest of need. Omu comes to guide the dead as dictated by the Covenant of Spirits. But to have the Spirits of our loved ones come to us, it is when our hearts have called to them and our minds have not. That is true need."

"I still don't understand," Onyx stated.

Ryder thought for a moment. "Put it this way. Spirits are extremely unpredictable." He scratched his chin. "Well to be honest your opponents in both situations had complete control of the fight from the beginning and could have killed you at any point." He laughed when he saw Onyx's worry and slapped his shoulder. "You are entirely predictable. You are also very emotional and lack control. Like I have said before, let your emotions guide you, not rule you."

Onyx still felt confused. What was Ryder trying to teach him? He did know how to fight like a Saber, one of the best in the land of the Shadowborn. He had to admit that in his fight against Ryder, he was upset that Zoras had called him a Prince. His jealousy caused to think irrationally and affect his decisions. In his battle against Iztal, he was horrified and saddened about the long time fate of his father. He did feel that he was more successful against Iztal but maybe it was just because his parents' Spirits were helping him. He grabbed his head in frustration.

It suddenly dawned on him and his hands dropped from his head. He felt bound by what he was taught. That what he learned was the only way. To stray invited confusion and his mind could not accept that. "I should not be afraid to bend and adapt. In Cross, I think I started to see that even if I did not know what it was at the time."

"Bingo. If you refuse to change and accept new things, you will always be defeated. The fight is not bound by the people involved. The environment and movements of energy can also affect your senses and physical prowess," Ryder answered, pleased that Onyx had worked it out himself. "Now, look around you and tell me what you see."

The question felt a bit strange but Onyx acquiesced. He let out a deep breath as he studied the dirt patch the rebels called a yard. It was an irregular circle in shape with a diameter of sixty feet across. There were sporadic patches of dry grass. He turned his head to the left. The entrance to the base, doors of stone, metal, and wood stood closed with a pair of guards making small talk nearby. He heard the splashing sounds of the small waterfall that was out of sight. On a low hanging branch that was void of leaves perched a white barn owl. It quickly rustled its feathers and clacked its beak.

"I see an owl," Onyx said after describing each detail of the yard. He tilted his head to the side to study the creature.

Ryder came up to him and set his hand on Onyx's shoulder. "You have had a chance to see this environment with your senses but you have focused too much on what you see. Now, see that owl? It uses more than one sense to read its surroundings. It doesn't just see a mouse on the ground. It uses its hearing to detect its movements. The beat of its heart. The flow of blood in its veins. In a fight against one or sometimes more opponents, you must use more than your sight." Ryder pointed to his ears. He then put his hand over Onyx's heart. "Just remember. What makes a Spiritborn great is in their heart, the center of their energy. We use it to interpret the world with every sense we have as one. Just like the owl uses all of its senses as one."

Onyx nodded before Ryder stepped away, giving him space to apply what he said. He settled his senses and focused them into one. He closed his eyes and breathed deeply. Sparks of energy erupted before he found the flows of energy only an Earthborn could see. Opening one eye, he looked over at Ryder.

"You have been taught that your focus in a fight is your opponent. While correct, you must not ignore your environment. At a moment's notice, a simple observation could prove the turning point towards victory. If your emotions have control, your focus will be gone and you will be overwhelmed. If you have control of your emotions, you will have the focus needed. In our fight, you were blinded by jealousy. In Cross, you fought to free your father, no matter the cost. You were guided by love," Ryder explained.

"But I was focused on besting you and proving that I deserved to be called Prince. I wouldn't say I was blind," Onyx pointed out.

Ryder scoffed and pressed his hand over Onyx's heart. "You were not focused here. You can't let your center become blinded, regardless of what your mind is doing.

Now it made sense. He must never lose his Spiritual center for he risked cutting himself off from his Spirit energy when it could be needed most. Things like pain and anger were weapons that could be used against him. Realizing this made Onyx feel like that he had reached a breakthrough.

"So how do I make sure that I don't lose my center?" Onyx asked.

"Spirit Anchor. You must have something or someone in your heart that you put before yourself above all else. Something you care about deeply. With that Spirit Anchor, you will be hard pressed to lose your center," Ryder stated proudly. He was pleased to be seeing some progress in Onyx's thinking.

"How will I know that I have the right Spirit Anchor?" Onyx asked.

"It's not really something you know. It is something you feel strongly about. As soon as I met Haven, I knew that I had found mine. You do not necessary have to have romantic feelings. It could be a family member. A favorite teacher. I am sure that you were Soja's Spirit Anchor. Sabers will always have the royals as theirs. What would you give your life for is the question you need to ask yourself," Ryder explained.

Onyx looked down at his feet. He scraped the dirt with the toe of his boot. "Does Kaiser have a Spirit Anchor? Is that why he is so hard to beat?"

"I would imagine that he does have one and I have a good idea on what it is. Right now, let's focus on you."

Onyx was surprised about how little he knew about reading the environment with Spirit energy. He listened and hung on to every word Ryder said, his cousin guiding him through various small exercises and tests. He was especially pleased to learn more about how to sense and read the energy flows in the earth. It was more than just through the ground at his feet. The energy flows were in the trees and the wildlife to varying degrees of strength. One of his more challenging tests was using his Earthborn Spirit energy to follow a Shadow Slide. Ryder did not make it easy on him either. He gave the instruction only once before repeatedly jumping into Shadow Slide and disappearing from sight. Onyx found it hard due to Ryder's speed being amplified while in Shadow Slide.

After what felt like the umpteenth pass of Shadow Slide, Onyx collapsed to his knees. Keeping his mind so singularly focused was exhausting. Never had he been pressured like this in his sessions with Sai. Ryder was both firm and forgiving, even making small shifts in his slide to show Onyx what to look for. But still, the skill escaped him. His chest heaved from the effort. Sweat beaded on his brow and dripped down his face. Despite this, Onyx was happy and determined to succeed.

"Using Spirit energy can exhaust you. Use it all or use it without the proper training and you will end up dead," Ryder said as he stepped out of Shadow Slide.

"No kidding," Onyx replied as he fought to catch his breath.

"It would not be so bad if you solely used your connection with the earth and not the energy in your body," Ryder pointed out. He tapped his foot on the ground. "The world holds a near infinite amount of Spirit energy. Your Spirit Anchor can help you with this. That will keep you connected to your body when you go to use the Spirit energy present in the world."

Ryder's words sounded easy and yet there was a mystery within them. If using the Spirit energy of the world was something everyone could learn, why was Kaiser still in power? He wanted to ask Ryder this outright but decided to challenge himself to find the answer. He could not always demands answers for every question. He had to challenge his mind and way of thinking. Becoming a well-rounded fighter was more than combat skills. Onyx could see that Ryder was trying to teach him that albeit in a roundabout way. Ryder was going to be a teacher like none other. To many, Ryder was one of the strongest and most skilled warriors on Terra. Now, Onyx was getting the chance to learn from a master. Onyx smiled with excitement for the future.

The two cousins bid each other good night and Onyx returned to his quarters. He washed and cleaned the sweat from his body. Slicking his wet hair back, Onyx dressed in clean clothes. He glanced at himself in the new mirror that had been brought to his room. A mantra of confidence repeated in his mind. Yes, he could do this. Onyx laid back on his back, hands behind his head. His mind settled on the Spirit Anchor question without prompting.

How was he supposed to know who or what his Spirit Anchor would be? Would he have a feeling or would he be told when he saw it? Based on what Ryder told him, it would be something that gave him complete focus and something worth giving his life for. The idea of dying entered his mind and he shuddered. Death was not unfamiliar to him, having lost his grandfather and parents. Kaiser appeared to be the very essence of death walking the earth, his mind a deadlier weapon than the Demon Rache at his side. He was more afraid of him than he was of dying. To Onyx, Kaiser represented a finality. He was an enemy and a danger to all. It saddened Onyx that his people had to suffer for so long under Kaiser's reign of terror, He was prepared to do anything for them so that they would no longer live in fear.

There it was! His Spirit Anchor! Onyx smiled as he thought about the love he had for the Shadowborn. It was only right that as their Prince, he would do anything to protect them. If that meant he had to die, he would gladly do it. Onyx wondered if Ryder felt the same about the Shadowborn people. He cared deeply about them and their wellbeing. Using these thoughts, Onyx closed his eyes and focused all of his Spirit energy into his core. He slowly let out a series of deep breaths to center his mind. The only mental images he let through were of the various Shadowborn he had met over his life. He smiled as he remembered romping through the markets and the pleasant greetings of the vendors. His final memory of Kader entered his mind and he reflexively clutched at his chest where the old pendent gift used to lay.

The fate of his beloved teacher was unknown to him but Ryder seemed to hint at Kader living amongst the Earthborn, unable or unwilling to cross the border. At one time, Onyx would have pressed for a direct answer. He laughed at he thought about his lack of patience and deep sense of curiosity. Remembering his Spirit Anchor, he refocused his thoughts. This time, he made sure to include Kader. He was filled with a powerful sense of love and devotion. Yes, this was his Spirit Anchor. He wondered if he was supposed to share what his Spirit Anchor was or was it something that should remain private. Ryder had gladly told him that his was Haven but he wondered if he only did it to further the lesson. He began to think that Spirit Anchors were supposed to be private. Kaiser could surely take control of a Spirit Anchor to threaten someone into obedience. Onyx gritted his teeth and hardened his resolve. If Kaiser tried to destroy the Shadowborn, Onyx was only going to fight harder and harder. He couldn't wait for his next lesson with Ryder to show his improvement.

*****

A WHITE MORNING

Gyr was happy when Charon finally returned from the mysterious town of Meras. Before the half breed had left, he had taught the Gryphon about the stars of the Southland skies. It had given him something to do while he waited for Charon's return. Charon had also made sure to leave a supply of meat so that he would not have to over exert himself for hunting. At first, Gyr had a hard time. His injuries restricted him greatly in the beginning. It annoyed him that he could not stretch out his wings after a good sleep. He couldn't wait to fly again. Each day that passed, Gyr felt himself getting better and stronger. He even got pretty skilled at working with fire. He joked with himself that he was becoming Dragon like when he snorted and puffed his breath to bring a fire to life from the wood scraps. He found that scrapping his talons on the flint rock was more effective in starting a fire than the tools Charon showed him. It allowed him to be more careful and delicate with his limited wood supply. He couldn't wait to demonstrate his talon on rock fire starter routine.

He was finally able to walk, albeit with some pain, a week after Charon had left. His right front leg pained him as the arrow had pierced the right side of his chest. He took his time and moved slowly out into the open. Being mostly white, the Gryphon blended in to the snowy environment. Of course, the beige colored blanket he used as a cloak made him conspicuous. He eventually ditched it to let the cool air on his healing wounds. When his wounds felt hot, he would pack some snow on them to cool them down. He developed a daily routine during Charon's absence to keep himself busy and to avoid boredom. Each day, he would test the limits of his returning strength, pleased with even the smallest of progress. He was determined to be flying by the time his new friend returned.

The mountains provided a perfect haven and private flying ground. Gyr did not venture out too far from the cave as he was not familiar with the Southlands. He also did not others to know that he was there. It had taken a while to get over the experience with the hunter. Also, any ground bound Gryphon felt vulnerable if he or she could not fly. He knew that he should not push himself too fast or too hard. When he was finally able to lift his wings without pain, Gyr felt that he could have taken off right then and there. Patience, he reminded himself. He began the same exercises he had done when he was a branching nestling all those years ago. Gyr was determined to build up his strength and fly for the first time when Charon returned.

The half breed man appeared on the horizon, a heavy pack on his back. Gyr watched with eager anticipation as Charon trudged through the snow. It took a great deal to keep his feet firmly planted on the ground. He rustled his wings and shook his tail. The combination of fur and feathers on his body had grown thick during his convalescence. It would take some time to get his body looking slim and prepared for rigorous flying. He stamped his feet. He was ready to fly.

"Wow, I did not think you would be outside," Charon called out as he came within shouting distance.

Gyr could not wait any longer and burst into the air in a great rush. Leaving the ground gave him an instant sense of freedom. He cried out with a joyous whistle as he ascended into the clouds. Screeching loudly, he popped out of a puffy cloud and zoomed towards the ground. He tucked his wings in and dove with increasing speed. Sending his body into a twisting spiral back upwards by quickly opening his wings, Gyr chawed with delight. With two hard flaps, he rocketed forward and flew over Charon's head. He spun around and came in low, flapping his wings to stabilize his body. He landed like an old pro and approached Charon with a big smile in his eyes.

"I am impressed," Charon said once Gyr came close.

"I tried to wait until you came back before I took my first flight. I am just glad I did not forget my skills," Gyr stated proudly.

Charon smiled back, happy that the Gryphon was no longer despondent. He had worried about leaving Gyr in his wounded state but he had to report to Meras. The Meras tax collector pushed on another job, keeping him away from Gyr longer than he had anticipated. His thoughts never left the Gryphon in the mountains though he told no one about him. No one questioned why he was returning to the north as he was from Garhune. Of course, many people were wary of him and his half breed status. Unlike the people of the Southlands, Gyr accepted him without much fuss. Being around the Gryphon made him feel that he was not so strange and different. Maybe Gyr could help him find out the identity of his Shadowborn father. In return, he might be able to help the Gryphon find his king.

"Is Meras a big city?" Gyr asked, cocking his head.

"It's not the biggest in the Southlands but it's a decent size. Meras sits at a crossroads on the other side of the forest you probably can see in the distance," Charon answered. He gestured towards a dark line on the horizon. "But it's a massive forest that takes a few days to cross."

"You could probably clear it in much less time if you used Shadow Slide," Gyr said after he studied the line of trees in the distance. He bobbed his head up and down.

Charon shook his head as he dropped his pack just inside the opening of the cave. He rolled his shoulders and stretched out his back. "You talk about this Shadow Slide like I should just instinctively know everything about it. What is it?"

Gyr smirked. "I'll show you."

In a burst of motion, Gyr ran forward and flipped Charon onto his back. Before Charon could protest, the Gryphon took off at top speed. Charon cursed as he managed to wrap his arms around Gyr's thick feathery neck right before the Gryphon took a hard turn.

"Shadow Slide is how you can fly as fast as me!" Gyr cried out over the rush of wind. He cackled when he heard Charon groan. It only made him twist and turn faster and harder.

When Gyr finally landed, Charon slid off the Gryphon's back and hit the ground. His head swam and his stomach churned. He pressed a fist to his forehead as he closed his eyes. Gyr stood over him, chuckling. Charon swatted at him to back away.

"Don't ever do that again," Charon said haltingly as he rolled onto his side.

"Though I have never been in Shadow Slide, I have been told that it is fast and agile. I'd like to think that it is like flying, just closer to the earth," Gyr described as he sat down on his haunches. He wrapped his tail around his feet. "If you come to Crossroads, I am sure that I can find you a proper teacher."

Never had it crossed his mind that going north was an option or a flicker in his future. Charon's stomach twisted with uncertainty. "I can barely get off the ground and you are talking about flying up over the Wall of Crossroads into the Northlands?

No way!"

"You're not the least bit curious about the Northlands? It is the land of your people," Gyr exclaimed. He then crouched down, snorting in Charon's face. "A little ginger root will help settle your stomach if that is the cause of your hesitation."

Charon managed to sit up after a minute. He ran his hands over his face. His hair was a straggly mess after the flight. Once he opened his eyes, he was looking directly into Gyr's gray eyes.

"I am a half breed remember? I am between worlds and the farthest north that I am willing to go is the bottom of your huge Wall."

Gyr sat back, giving Charon space. "Do people treat you differently just because you are not completely Mortal like them?"

Charon nodded. "When it comes to Immortals and anyone from the Northlands, Mortals are wary and easily scared. The Northlands represents the mysterious and unknown. About the only Northlands associated person Mortals like is Bane, your Daylord I suppose."

It was curious to hear that, Gyr thought. How could the Southlands know Bane well enough to have that high admiration and respect? And if he really had not been seen for many years, how was he supposed to find him? Gyr sighed as he wrestled with his doubt. He watched as Charon got to his feet, swaying slightly. Charon slowly made his way to the cave mouth, leaning on the stone.

"So what now for you since you can fly again?" Charon asked.

"I go to find my king," Gyr replied, looking over his shoulder. He then shifted his position to look at Charon straight on.

"Why are you even bothering trying to find a guy that is either dead or doesn't want to be found?" Charon asked as he finally got his bearings.

Gyr proceeded to tell him about the brewing war in the Northlands. He spat and cursed when he described Kaiser, gripping the snowy ground with his claws in response. "I must keep my belief that Bane is still alive, no matter his feelings or his hesitations. I believe in my king and I refuse to lose hope."

Charon let out a deep breath, looking down. "I doubt that there is much I can do to help you. There is no one alive who can say that they have seen your king. People only tell stories around the fire or over a mug of ale these days."

"Come with me," Gyr said, standing up on all fours.

"What?" Charon asked.

Gyr came forward and looked Charon in the eyes. "I can help you discover the heritage you do not know and you can help me navigate the Southlands that I do not know. Consider this as that I am hiring you as a guide. Gryphons do not exchange metal coins or paper bills for payment. In return for your service, I can give you answers that no one else in the Southlands can give you."

Usually, Charon ran from such hires. He needed money to buy supplies, bribe people for information, and give to those that dared to help him. Money was a driving force in the Southlands. But the chance at discovering his Shadowborn heritage was tantalizing. He always honored an honest business deal and usually thumped those that tried to swindle him. And he genuinely liked the Gryphon.

"So how do Gryphons close a deal?" Charon asked after a very long pause.

Gyr smiled. "Bad deals are closed with a peck and a slash but good deals are closed with a simple bow of the head and shake of the wings. So bow your head and shake your wings."

Charon laughed as he bowed his head and shook his arms. He nodded again when he made eye contact with Gyr. "The thing I want to know most of all is who my father was. Help me with that and I will take you anywhere in the Southlands I know."

*****

DEADLY TOUCH

"My dear, sweet Myra who escaped me not too long ago. Do I need to remind you of the day we met for you to come back to me? So many years have passed us by since you came to dance for the royal court. I remember that day well. You had travelled far, excited for the invitation. You and your group of dancers who were all dressed so finely in cloth of gold and silver. You danced with such grace and sensuality that I could not help by desire to speak with you once your show was done," Kaiser mused as he twisted the silver ring on his left index finger. He chuckled softly to himself

At first, it had made him laugh when Rache brought him the news that Myra was nowhere to be found in Eclipse. He could not believe that the woman had finally plucked up enough courage to leave. When he investigated her secret home, he immediately picked up on Ryder's trail. He had laughed again, impressed at his grandson's boldness to exit the city via the sewer system. He was not about to try and follow him. The stench was vile and stomach churning, especially now that blood ran thick in the streets. The boy would do anything to protect the people he loved. Of course, Kaiser had asked himself why Ryder would delay the inevitable.

He frowned at the chorus of noise happening outside of his tent. Wooden carts rumbled past, splashing in the puddles of melted snow and mud. Horses snorted in protest or neighed with delight. Booted feet marched in rhythm, the sound diminishing quickly. Soldiers grumbled about the wait and reason for their journey. He could even hear his faithful Demon servant, Rache, crouched down in front of the tent, picking at the sparse grass. The Demon mumbled about the thick cacophony of heartbeats and pulsating blood vessels.

"You were so wide eyed and young at our meeting. Here I was, a wealthy power player in the grandest court in the Northlands. A true example of intelligence and strength. A man worthy of respect and power. You had to have me as I had to have you. And now, look at where it has brought us."

A fist fight broke out to Kaiser's left. He growled at the disruption but was pleased when he heard Rache shout at the revel rousers to cease. His followers were hungry for more action. Unlike himself, they did not understand the concept of a patient hunter. The careful, unseen stalking. The calculated strike. They knew that their next target was east and not west of Eclipse. But Kaiser had more important ideas to address before he could consider his next step. He was not about to waste energy charging into battle or waste even more energy correcting a failed charge. It was just too time consuming and unnecessary.

He laughed softly to himself when Loran got involved in stopping the struggle. Loran's voice went from deep and threatening to high and raspy. Obviously, the once famous sea pirate expected an immediate response of cease and desist, more comfortable to shouting through high winds and rough seas. Kaiser thought about intervening just to show Loran how to command proper respect. He reset the silver ring on his hand, stretching his fingers. Reminiscing would have to wait for another time.

His tent was small but luxurious, possessing more furnishings than the usual meager tent of a foot soldier. The bed cot was made of ebony wood with silver details. The mattress was, to Kaiser's surprise, remotely comfortable. He preferred his plush feather bed in Cross with his three, young courtesans. He had a small side table with a mirror and wash basin. On the left side of the tent, Kaiser had a small table that was cluttered with books, papers, quills, and an inkwell. A simple rug covered the dirt floor.

Kaiser stood in front of the mirror, pausing to stroke the black and gray stubble on his jaw. Usually, he kept a clean face but now, he liked the idea of facial hair. To him, it reflected age and change and this was a time of change. His hair was a tousled mess, streaked with gray and in need of a good wash. He picked at his shirt collar, feeling the rough spun wool fabric beneath his fingertips. He dipped his hands in the steaming water. He rubbed his hands together, stroking the back of his right hand with his left thumb.

"You will answer for your insults against Lord Kaiser, you

pathetic waste of life," Loran snarled from outside the tent. The sound of a body hitting the ground with a loud thump followed. "Rache, will you take care of this filth?"

"I do not take orders from you," Rache snapped. He growled in warning.

From the hushed silence outside, Kaiser could tell that Rache's response was unexpected. It was unexpected. The Demon was his great executioner, always eager for the kill. In a way, the response of the crowd amused him but Rache's quick reply angered him. In declining the order to kill, Kaiser could see that Rache undermined himself and his fearsome reputation. He tried to remember if he had ordered the Demon to save his blood thirsty rage for the next battle. Either way, something would have to be done.

Everyone fell completely silent when Kaiser threw back the door flap and stepped outside. They all watched as he sauntered forward, dragging his hand across Rache's left shoulder. The Demon remained crouched and only scoffed in response to his touch.

"My dears. Why is there all this noise?" Kaiser asked sweetly. His smile was warm but his eyes were cold. He looked around at the crowd of soldiers. "Would anyone like to volunteer an answer?"

It took a long time for someone to answer. "This soldier insulted your great name by questioning your command," Loran stated.

Kaiser looked down at the soldier in the dirt. He was a thin youth with a shorn head that was starting to grow back black hair. His left eye was bruised and swollen and blood dripped from the corner of his mouth.

"Dear child. Who has done this to you?" Kaiser asked as he bent down to the soldier's eye level. He cupped the soldier's chin in his right hand. "You can tell me."

The soldier gulped. "Captain Loran, my Lord."

Kaiser looked up and locked eyes with Loran. "And what did this child say to upset you so?"

"He demanded to know why you were leading the soldiers instead of a High Commander or the Shadowlord. He asked what qualifies you to be here and why are we marching away from Eclipse," Loran explained.

"I see," Kaiser replied, nodding his head. He returned his attention to the soldier before him. "You are young. I can forgive your ignorance. You see, I was the son of a very famous general. A High Commander in fact. I would have succeeded him had my heart not been so terribly broken by his death." He paused and bowed his head. "Forgive me."

Only Rache did not feel sympathy for Kaiser's act of pain and sorrow. He snorted.

"Yes. I may not be the High Commander in name but I am in Spirit," Kaiser said, managing a hopeful smile. "And someone must step up and lead our people in this time of trouble."

"But is that the duty of the Shadowlord to lead our people?" the soldier asked.

"It is the duty of the Shadowlord but as you well know, Lord Aku is weak in body and cannot lead the Shadowborn as he wishes. He cannot even defend his throne from a war between heirs. That is what he had charged me to face and that is why we cleansed Eclipse. Rebels to the Shadowlord's rule must be dealt with swiftly and we must free his Shadowlord's loyal subjects from their twisted rhetoric. I must free them in the name of truth," Kaiser calmly explained. He lifted the soldier to his feet. "There now."

The other soldiers rose to their feet, uncertain of how to act. In their minds, all of their senses were muddled in a tangled mess. Sounds mixed with blurry vision where the only clear thing was Kaiser. They wanted to talk to each other but no one could find the words to speak. The world around them echoed their confusion. No breeze blew through their entire camp. The horses had fallen silent. Even the light of the sun appeared dim and hazy.

"But the Demon," the soldier said, looking over Kaiser's shoulder at Rache. He shivered.

Kaiser grinned as he forced the soldier to look him in the eyes. "Not all is what it appears. Now, let me heal you of your hurts so that you may understand our mission better."

Everyone watched with fevered anticipation for they all knew of Kaiser's great healing power. A few of the foot soldiers, dressed in an assortment of leather and steel armor, gasped when a twisting black mark appeared on the back of Kaiser's right hand. Even Rache stood up at attention. Loran shook his head, more from understanding what was actually going on than a desire to stop Kaiser. He knew better but was no less amazed.

It did cross Kaiser's mind that the soldier's injuries were minor and not worth his attention. What he was about to do was, however, worth everyone's attention. He slid his right hand to touch his thumb to the corner of the soldier's mouth and the tip of his finger to the side of the soldier's eye.

The youth looked back at Kaiser like he was a comforting father. He smiled as tears welled up in his eyes. Kaiser smiled back.

"Look into my eyes and you will see understanding and

truth," Kaiser murmured.

To the crowd, the sight of Kaiser being warm and kind despite his formidable reputation was awe inspiring. At his age, Kaiser represented a glimpse into the ancient past and the age of noble heroes. Perhaps, they all thought, he was a noble hero like the legendary Daylord. He had to be if he could perform such miracles of healing. Every last soldier pulled off their helms and skullcaps in respect.

The youth's minor wounds began to fade under Kaiser's healing touch. His left eye twitched as the swelling dissipated, leaving behind pristine skin. As the bloodied lip healed, the youth expected Kaiser to pull away.

What happened next horrified the entire assembly of soldiers. Kaiser's hand latched on to the youth's skull with a sickening crunch. The black mark on his hand shifted from its dark color to a haunting silver glow. Kaiser smiled as the soldier's eyes began to bulge in horror. His mouth gaped open in a wordless scream, blood vessels throbbing on his face. The vessels pulsated towards Kaiser's hand in a draining action. Kaiser appeared completely calm as the soldier's skin began to tighten over his diminishing frame. Musculature disappeared and the chainmail appeared heavier and heavier. The only change to Kaiser was his deepening smirk.

It seemed as if several long agonizing minutes passed before Kaiser let go with a pop. The youth's dried body collapsed to the ground, bones snapping from the force. No one dared to speak. They had just watched their commander kill one of their own with just a touch of his hand. At least seven retched and turned away from the sight. Rache snickered and slowly clapped his hands.

"See? I have healed him of his hurts. I took away his pain and confusion of the truth. He is at peace," Kaiser announced in a cold voice. He looked down at the dead soldier, nudging the body with his boot. In a sudden motion, Kaiser crushed the skull, causing more soldiers to turn away. "Pity."

Kaiser stepped over the body, moving past Loran with his hands latched behind his back. He slowly paced around the circle, chuckling softly with soldiers stepped back from his presence. He continued his silent trek until he had reached the center of the circle. "Death awaits those who refuse to see the truth. To those who pretend that the world cannot touch them. That they are safe from ruin and despair. Well I will tell you this now. The world is a vile and cruel place, filled with nothing but lies and hate. There is no love and no peace."

Rache shuddered when Kaiser turned his powerful gaze upon him. He swallowed hard as a chill crept into his bones. The chill spread, taking his breath and turning it into puffs of frost. The Demon shivered as he looked away, his chest stiffening. He coughed hard.

"But there is courage and great loyalty that can transform your life into a better one. I have seen such a transformation deep within my own being that tells me I must help others like you to feel the same. First, we must unite against those who claim to be the truth for I will allow no one to take what is rightfully yours to have: truth," Kaiser declared. He loosened his posture and put his hands out to the side.

Wonder and fervor replaced horror as Loran led the crowd in a round of chanting and cheers. The soldiers could not believe that one of their own doubted their grand leader. They came to believe that Kaiser saw the youth for what he must have been: a traitor and a coward. They roared and beat their fists on their steel plated chests. Kaiser was right to lead them for who else was great enough to do so? They were on a noble quest to free their homeland, the first step in reclaiming their lives. All in the name of truth. With Kaiser leading the way, the rebels could not possibly withstand them.

Kaiser reveled in the cheers and attention, turning about so all could see him. He gestured towards Loran with a twitch of a finger. Immediately, Loran began issuing orders to the officers, shouting at the soldiers to get back to their posts and tasks. A rousing song of battle broke out.

"That was quite a speech but you have done better," Rache said as he came forward. He studied the body on the ground, nostrils flaring. He snorted.

"Yes, I have done better. Perhaps I should have added a few more bodies for stronger impact," Kaiser mused as he watched the goings on of the camp. "I should not have to waste my energy doing what you should have done," he growled harshly.

Rache was taken aback. "The soldier was barely worth even Loran's time yet you do not accuse him and choose to accuse me instead."

In a heartbeat, Kaiser had his left hand gripping Rache's pale throat. "You know full and well that I can do to you what I did to the soldier. This was not just a show for them. It was also for you." He snarled and gripped Rache's throat tighter. The Demon gasped. "People tell stories about the dangerous Rache. Killer of the noble Begin Anu. Well , I am going to do one better. I will show the world how deadly a killer I can be. That I am more than a horror in the shadows and that Eclipse was just the beginning."

Rache try to swallow but was unable to get past the lump in his throat and Kaiser's tight grip. Kaiser smirked at him before forcibly throwing the Demon to the ground.

"You are growing soft during this time of idleness. Be careful, my dear Rache, or you will become as weak as your prey."

Rache coughed and rubbed his throat. "Then take off my chains and set me loose."

Kaiser shook his head. "Not yet. Not just yet."

ALL EYES ON UMBRA

"Do you know why we are here?" Kaiser asked Rache and Loran who stood several feet behind him on the path.

The shadows of the trees danced over the pair, branches creaking in the wind. They stood under the eaves of the forest while Kaiser was on a small hill in front of them. The light from the sun was dull and left everything in a gray haze. Loran gulped while Rache tried to study the environment in front of Kaiser. There was a small valley with tall snowcapped mountains in the distance. Just a few footsteps in front of Kaiser was the shore of a blue water lake. Rain heavy clouds loomed overhead. The Demon did not see anything of note. He shrugged.

"Look harder and you will see what I am talking about," Kaiser stated, waving his arm in a wide gesture.

The storm clouds parted and sunlight beamed down to a dark spot on the other side of the lake. A series of broken and weathered stone buildings were revealed. A flock of blackbirds lifted off of the roof of one building just before it crumbled down in a cloud of dust. They cawed and cackled loudly.

"The ruins of Silver?" Loran asked.

"You know this place?" Kaiser inquired.

Loran moved to stand closer to Kaiser. "Pirates talk about the ruins of Silver as if they hold a great treasure. Where that rumor got started, I have no clue."

"I do," Rache stated as he started walking towards the pair. He stepped past them to stand on the shore of the lake. "During the first Dominion War, Demon blood poisoned the lake and thus the city fell to ruin. The stones were left as a reminder of what happened."

Kaiser shrugged. "I suppose that is one story but let's test that theory. Loran?"

"If you are expecting me to drink that water, you are out of your mind," Loran immediately refused. He cringed under Kaiser's furious glare. Still, he was worried. What if the story was true and the lake water was poisoned with Demon blood? The blood would poison him and burn him from the inside out.

Kaiser did not wait and stomped over to Loran. He grabbed him by the tunic collar and dragged him over to the edge of the lake. He pushed him down to his knees. "Drink," he coldly ordered.

Loran gulped and swallowed hard. He had to quickly decide what was worse: poisoned water or Kaiser's wrath. There was no contest. Loran dipped his hands in the water. In a swift motion, he brought his cupped hands to his mouth and drank. The water was cold and tasteless. Though he had never tasted Demon blood, he expected the water to be warm and bitter.

"See, Rache? Just a story. Just an old fireside tale made up to prevent people from exploring the ruins. Now why would someone make something like that up?" Kaiser proposed. "Or more importantly who would make something like that up?"

A light breeze brushed by, creating small waves on the lake's surface. More sunlight beamed down through a break in the clouds. In a way, the valley appeared beautiful. It was as if the world was trying to show them that there was a treasure hidden in the ruins. Kaiser smiled as he looked at the stone across the lake.

"I have heard that story since I was a small boy though my father issued it like it was a warning to never come here. He used to tell me that my ancestor Adonis Anu was the first to tell of the poisonous lake water. Who would doubt Shadow Night's Chancellor and the son of Begin Anu? Our dear Shadow Night even issued a proclamation that the ruins were off limits in the interest of safety. Considering how anything Demon was taboo, no one thought to question them," Kaiser explained. He started to move into the water, arms out to the side. "Of course, the curious would investigate and discover that it was all hogwash."

Rache and Loran watched Kaiser walk into the water up to his waist. They fought the urge to whisper to each other for though they had comments and questions, neither liked the other enough. The only thing they had in common was their connection with Kaiser.

"One interesting thing is that Sage Silvanus was not seen

after his father's return from Silver. Once again, no one questioned the Shadowlord when they should have. Another rumor spread that Sage was dead and the Shadowlord buried him in Silver. Out of respect, no one thought to disturb these hallowed grounds. I feel that the Shadowborn did not question their leaders enough and took him too quickly at his word. Well I am of a mind to question everything. The lesson here is do not take anything at face value," Kaiser explained. He briefly looked back over his shoulder at Rache and Loran.

"What is he doing?" Loran whispered to Rache.

Rache could not answer for he had no clue what Kaiser was doing. His master did not speak to him about his search for the vaults in Eclipse. He did get a heavy scent of old paper and dust when he found Kaiser at the citadel. It was not too long after that when Kaiser had ordered Loran to settle the army and pass his command to a selection of officers. Rache had what he felt like was the privilege to see Kaiser meet with those officers and put the fear of death in their eyes. He had thought that Kaiser was angry at him for his actions outside of Eclipse. His master had made a point since then to demonstrate how to command respect and obtain absolute obedience. How the four men held it together without wetting themselves boggled Rache though he was sure that they threw up from nerves later. He had done so himself when Kaiser had discovered that Ryder had left the Shadowborn lands. He had never seen Kaiser that angry before. Rache shook his head to remove the image from his mind.

"Pay attention," Rache growled. He smirked when he saw Loran lean away from him.

Kaiser chuckled at the exchange before returning his attention ahead of him. What he did not tell the pair was that he stopped due to the invisible energy of a Shadow Mirror. It pulled at him, inviting him to interact with it. It also pushed him away as if to ward him off. Typical of a Shadow Mirror, Kaiser thought. He dug at his belt for a small knife. Finding nothing, he dug at the meat of his thumb, tearing it open. Blood slowly pooled at the wound, dripping down his hand to his palm. He pulled up his sleeve with his left hand, revealing his thinly muscled forearm.

Rache and Loran stepped back when they saw the wave of silver energy pulsate up to the sky. It was if it was alive and reacting to the presence of Kaiser's blood.

"Shadow Mirror. Genius," Loran smiled.

"You know about Shadow Mirrors?" Rache asked, lifting an eyebrow in question.

Loran pulled out his blood seal with the Adonis family crest. "I may be a pirate but I am no idiot. I use this little thing to help cross the one at the border."

Rache rolled his eyes and cross his arms tightly. He did not think Kaiser bestowed such knowledge to his new idiot follower. This one was smarter and more vicious than his unlucky cousin. But not by much. Morin was the stupid dog. Loran was the cunning wolf. He pursed his lips and pushed out a puff of heated breath.

Kaiser pressed his right hand forward, finding resistance in the energy field of the Shadow Mirror. He spread out his fingers, allowing the blood on his hand to connect. A web of red threads slowly spread out. Kaiser grinned as he watched the flow of energy, feeling the ancient power familiar to him. He watched with eager anticipation as the vessels beneath his skin began to glow with silver light. He basked in it, ignoring the influx of repulsive energy building up beneath his palm.

With a loud thunderous crack, Kaiser was thrown backwards. He crashed on the edge of the shoreline, mud splashing all over him. He coughed hard and shook his head, spitting out a globule of blood. Loran came to his side, offering to help Kaiser to his feet. Kaiser slapped him away, coughing again.

"If memory serves me correctly, only blood relatives can cross a Shadow Mirror," Rache said as he scratched his head.

"I know that!" Kaiser snapped. "Adonis Anu, my direct ancestor, helped Shadow Night to summon this Mirror. Why did it reject me?!"

"Well, you are kind of evil and your ancestor was kind of not," Rache pointed out. "My question is why did it throw you and not me if our bond is meant to protect you from harm?"

Kaiser got to his feet and sneered at the Demon. "Go throw yourself at it if you must insult me. Test your theory."

Loran snickered, trying to hide his mirth behind his hand. Forgetting any retribution against Rache, Kaiser stomped over to Loran and grabbed him by the collar. Loran shrieked in protest as Kaiser dragged him into the lake and up to where he had contacted the Shadow Mirror. The contact point still pulsated and sparked with a sense of living anger. Kaiser stopped just short of the Mirror.

"You are an idiot who has no idea how powerful a Shadow Mirror can be! Do you want to know what that little piece of metal protects you from?! Well here!" Kaiser snarled before shoving Loran's head forward.

The effect was immediate as the Mirror and Kaiser did battle with Loran caught in the middle. The right side of Loran's face bubbled and burned from the intense energy. He screamed in pain but Kaiser was unrelenting. He roared in some unintelligible language, cursing at the top of his lungs. Loran continued to scream and thrash his limbs. It was shocking how physically strong Kaiser was despite his lean body.

"This is the power of the Shadow Mirror!" Kaiser shouted before he let go of Loran.

Loran was thrown back and splashed in the water, swallowing some in a great gulp for breath. He shook his head and coughed hard. He kept coughing, spitting up water tinged with blood. The right side of his face oozed and smoked from the powerful energy. His lips and mouth were too swollen to allow him to speak in protest.

Rache came forward and dragged Loran out of the water by the shoulder. He bent down low so Loran could hear him. "You see, a Shadow Mirror rejects those not of the bloodline. A quick touch throws you back. Extended contact will eventually kill you. You are lucky that you just got an energy burn. If you are nice enough, Lord Kaiser might offer to heal it for you," he said with a mocking tone.

Kaiser's chest heaved from the effort of facing the energy of the Shadow Mirror. He sneered at Loran blubbering like a small child. The Mirror's energy was blinding as it illuminated Kaiser from behind. He looked unholy covered in mud and soaked to the bone with blood dripping from his clenched fists and splattered on his face.

"There is only one reason that this Mirror rejected me. Shadow Night helped Adonis to raise it. I need a Silvanus to unlock the Mirror with me. Then I will get my hands on Sage, snap his neck, and make sure that he is dead," he growled in a low voice.

"What makes you think that Sage is still alive after all this time?" Rache asked. "Hasn't it been like a thousand years?"

"Why else would a Shadow Mirror be here if he was dead? Why use it to protect a worthless corpse?" Kaiser reasoned as he pointed towards the ruins of Silver.

Rache squinted his eyes. It did make sense. A dead body offered no information. "Then I hope that if he is alive, he saw the power that was trying to break through and is afraid." The Demon did not mean his words but he hoped it would calm Kaiser.

"I need a strong son of the Silvanus bloodline otherwise the Mirror would destroy the key. I need my stupid grandson," Kaiser snarled in realization.

"Aday is older. Why not call him back?" Rache suggested. Loran continued to whimper softly nearby.

"He is a broken soul. I need someone who is whole. The boy Prince is worthless and weak but Peredur is strong. Of course, he will not come willingly. I will need to convince him," Kaiser reasoned with himself. He walked back to the shore and came to stand beside Rache. He kicked Loran when he cried too loudly. "Help him up. We must leave Silver for now until I can get Peredur to come."

"Back to Eclipse?" Rache asked.

Kaiser chuckled. "No. Eclipse is no longer worth anything to me. It is time to move on and destroy Umbra."

"Why Umbra? I know that Eclipse was the original home of the Silvanus bloodline. Umbra has nothing to do with them," Rache asked as he picked up Loran holding him under his left arm.

"Umbra is both my home and that of my grandson. I will destroy it to back him and his rebel followers into a corner. I will drive him down until there is no other choice but to come with me. If he is as noble as he pretends to be, he will do anything to protect what and who he loves," Kaiser stated before he mounted the back of his horse. "Loran!"

Rache helped Loran onto the back of his horse, guiding his hands to the pommel of the saddle. Loran groaned and leaned heavily to one side. "Yes," his voice rasped.

"Take the army to Umbra and destroy it utterly. Rache and I must return to Cross to work on a little project," Kaiser ordered.

*****

OLD SOULS

"Ever are your eyes looking towards the northwest, my old friend. What troubles you this time?" Vorin asked as he flapped his broad leathery wings to land on the rooftop observatory.

The rooftop observatory was Proto Avis' favorite place in all of the Northlands. As a Gryphon, he loved the openness of the sky. But at his advanced age, he could no longer fly as he used to. His joints pained him daily. He was having trouble seeing through his cloudy eyes. It seemed as if his fur and feathers could no long hold a clean shine. He kept his feet bandaged to cushion them as he walked. Though age had taken its physical toll, Proto's Spirit could not have been stronger.

"I worry since little news has reached us in the last few weeks. If only I could fly as I used to in my youth," Proto said, dropping his head. "If only he would come home."

Vorin shifted over to Proto's side and laid a wing over him in comfort. He bowed his serpentine head and closed his eyes. "I miss the Daylord too but I have hope that Gyr will succeed."

The old Gryphon let out a deep breath that hinted at despair. He leaned against Vorin's wing, comforted by its warmth. "I feel as if nothing I do will change the tide of war. I have failed in my duty to watch over Bane's throne."

"Proto, I will not let you bear this burden alone. I am also to blame for failing in my duty, not only as Lord of the Dragons but as a Lord of Crossroads. In fact, the entire Northern Alliance has failed to uphold the Truth in the Daylord's absence and now we are suffering for it." Vorin bobbed his head once. "We have been idle for far too long."

Proto had fallen silent and appeared to be having trouble breathing. He then stamped his right front paw. "I cannot take it much longer. Will you fly to the Shadowborn lands? I must know what is going on there."

It was an idea that Vorin had not stopped thinking about since he heard of the Spirit Song from the Earthborn scout Haro. He wanted so desperately to fly to Cross. If he had the strength to fly to Tempest and Cascade, why couldn't he go to Cross? His pride would not let him admit weakness but ever since the writing of the Immortal Truth, his power had not been the same. His strength ebbed and flowed in unexpected ways. It was if his life and Spirit had been bound in the stone along with that of his kin. What affected the power of the Truth affected him. To risk his life in war meant potential harm to the Truth. Its tenets dictated the very foundations of life in the Northlands. Vorin also felt diminished by the absence of the Daylord and a proper Shadowlord. For this, he was angry with Bane.

"The Spirits would tell us if something good or bad has happened. That is one thing Kaiser cannot control no matter how hard he tries," Vorin said encouragingly. He opened his eyes to lock his gaze with Proto. "We must have hope that the Spirits have not abandoned us and our cause.

"I will never lose my belief in the Spirits," Proto stated with great conviction. He held his head up and nodded. "The day we lose our belief is the day that the great evil succeeds."

Vorin nodded back and smiled by turning up the corners of his mouth. Smoke tendrils slowly rose from his nostrils. "I have been thinking. If Kaiser is so intent on war, why don't we bring the war to him? Assemble all of the Northern Alliance as we once did before the Immortal Truth was written. Take back the Shadowborn lands and cast him into the Spirit World!"

"I do not think even the Spirits want him," Proto laughed halfheartedly. He shifted the weight on his hips to the right. "But you are right. Let us bring the war to him."

"Of course, only the king can call the Northern Alliance to a War Council. I know that Evander will argue that fact when our message reaches him. His lack of," Vorin started to say before shifting to speaking in his native Dragon tongue. He hissed, growled, and spit a small jet of flame. "His lack of passion for the rest of the world beyond his borders infuriates me."

It was well known to many that Evander was resistant to doing anything that risked his people. The Lightborn had suffered heavy losses in the last Dominion War. When Bane had left the

Northlands, Evander had vowed to fight for no one but him. Vorin thought him foolish to make such promises on absolutes. It was also insulting to the Dragon that the Lord of the Lightborn did not think him worthy enough to obey any of his orders. He was the eldest being on Terra. That alone demanded respect. Very few people were brave enough to outright oppose a Dragon in any way.

"I want to send a messenger to him first. If the fool wants to sit and stay then we will do nothing to oppose his wishes. We will also do nothing to protect him and those that follow him. Only those that see the Truth will receive the protection of the Northern Alliance," Proto said firmly. "But it must be the right messenger."

"It does not help that Ryder once broke his arm because Evander will immediately refuse to do anything that helps him. I can remember it now and exactly what Evander said: The royal bastard has earned no respect from me. Even if he crawls on his knees, begging for forgiveness, and asks me to help claim the throne, I will not give in. Let his abandoned throne crumble for the chance is gone," Vorin imitated as he twisted and turned his head in mockery.

Proto thought long and hard. Most Gryphons loved Ryder and had accepted him as one of their own. Lord Stellaris himself had been the one to tag Ryder with the traditional mark of respect for an outsider. Usually, it was the sitting Lord of Peace but Stellaris took the responsibility instead. The Gryphon Lord of War recognized Ryder's might and power. Proto had been present at the ceremony and remembered the Lord of War's strong words of hope and promise.

"Lana. We should send Lana," Proto suddenly said. He then shifted his position to face Vorin.

"Why her? She is not of a high rank among the messengers though Savanna speaks highly of her," Vorin asked, pulling his head back and folding his wings over his back. His red scales glittered in the sunlight.

Proto chuckled deep in his chest. "I have taken her under my wing. She came to me upon her return to Crossroads after the Coal mission seven years ago in search of understanding. She told me that her heart was conflicted in a way that she could not explain. I have seen a transformation in her since then and I believe that she is the best choice to fly to the capital of the Lightborn. Trust me on this."

*****

Lana scanned the talon scratched lines of ink on a page of

parchment before turning her attention to another page on its right. On the second page were words of the common tongue, a direct translation of the original Gryphon written page. She mouthed the words on the second page before saying them out loud. She repeated the exercise two more times before deciding that she had mastered the list of words.

In the few minutes after Proto's request reached her, Lana furiously went over her language study papers. This time, her skills had to be perfect. She would accept nothing less. Proto Avis and Vorin had named her to be a war missionary, one of the highest messenger ranks for a Gryphon. It was a position of honor that earned after many years of service. To have been named by the Lord of Crossroads and the Dragonlord, Lana could scarcely wrap her mind around the idea. She was going to make everyone proud. She promised herself that she would succeed.

"Evander, Lord of the Lightborn. I am here. No. That won't do," Lana said as she tried to practice a speech. "The Lords Proto Avis and Vorin. No. That doesn't sound right either."

After going through several variations, Lana was still not happy with her speech. She pushed away her papers and fell on her back in a huff. Her swishing tail created a further mess but she did not care. Her front paws came to rest on her feathery chest.

"How do I convince a pacifist leader to go to war? I am asking him to go against his heart," Lana told herself. She sighed deeply.

"You can start by telling him the truth."

Lana rolled to her side and held her head up. Savanna, the beautiful pale Falcon Gryphon, sauntered in and sat down in front of her.

"I thought that you had a flying lesson over the Wall," Lana wondered. She folded her wings on her back, rustling the feathers.

"There was not a fair enough wind and the younglings are not yet ready for such conditions. Their flight feathers are still very new," Savanna said with a shrug. "And a little birdie told me of your new rank. I wanted to come and congratulate you."

"A little singer or a Gryphon like us?" Lana asked with a chortle. Savanna nodded. "I suppose that nothing stays secret for very long in Crossroads. We messengers are a chatty bunch."

The two Gryphons chatted and reminisced about menial things. Lana started to believe that Savanna was there to get her to relax about what was to come. They whistled and laughed about the silliest memories, rolling on the floor when their mirth overtook them. The pair managed to break for long enough to eat a small evening repast.

"How do you convince a pacifist to arm himself and march for war?" Lana asked the older Savanna.

"That's like asking a Gryphon to stop flying and start swimming," Savanna replied before snapping up a piece of roasted venison. The juice splattered over her gray beak.

Lana nudged a cloth napkin over to Savanna with her paw. "Lord Avis believes that I am the one to do it. I am not just delivering a message. I am negotiating on behalf of Crossroads. What I do could change the future!"

"You are thinking too much. You should not be so rehearsed. You need to be natural. Be a Gryphon and not one of the Spiritborn." Savanna paused to wipe her beak clean. "That was always your problem."

Lana shrank down in embarrassment and looked away. She had to admit that she did worry too much about appearance and presentation. She always wanted to appear perfect with exceptional manners. When that view was challenged, it sent her into a state of confusion. It took a special Spiritborn to make her realize that it was what was inside that counted for who she was. That dinner in Coal had been life changing for her. The Silvanus bastard had taught her the greatest lesson. She paused and twisted her head in thought. Lana had not seen Ryder in seven years and wondered how he was getting on.

"Guess I have not completely changed my ways," Lana halfheartedly laughed.

Savanna stood up and rustled her body from beak to tail. She shook her wings before resettling them on her back. "Be true to your heart, Lana, and always keep to the Truth."

*****

SURPRISE ATTACK

Kader bent over to the side table to pour himself another cup of mint tea. He poured the hot steaming liquid and dropped in a single sugar cube. He stirred briskly before picking up the cup to drink. The scent tickled his nostrils. He always enjoyed a few cups of tea as he read. During most evenings, Kader sat by the fire with a pile of leather bound tomes by his feet. Sometimes, the books were pieces of satire or comedy. Earthborn poetry was something he had developed a special fondness for. This evening, he had started to read the second volume in a six volume poetry series.

His little sitting room was warm with a crackling fire in the stone fireplace. A pile of chopped wood sat in the corner while the fire poker leaned up against it. Books were stacked and stuffed onto all the shelves and some on the floor. His reading chair and side table were positioned in front of the fire. To Kader, this was comfortable and pleasant. He did however miss his life in Cross and his fellow Shadowborn people. A day never went by where he did not think of his young Prince Onyx, now surely a grown man. He often wondered why he did not try to contact Onyx though the thought that he was protecting him crossed his mind soon after. Kader let out a deep breath and leaned back in his chair. Yes, he was protecting Onyx and himself from Kaiser.

A rush of activity burst through his front door, the source hidden by the crooked wall and entrance back into the small foyer. He screeched when he spilled his hot tea on his lap, dropping the cup and his reading book in the process.

"Hit the skies, Arik!" Haro called out to his Barn Owl Gryphon companion.

"What in the Spirit's name is the meaning of this?" Kader demanded as he stood up. He grimaced at the tea stain on his clothes, pulling at the ruined fabric.

"You have to leave Agin at once. There is no time to ask questions," Haro stated firmly as he darted over to check the window. He looked up and around, searching for something.

Kader could barely form the question in his mind before Haro tossed a travelling cloak at him. The way that Haro moved and spoke was worrisome. He knew the Earthborn scout well and this was completely out of character. He pulled on the cloak and instinctively strapped on a long knife to his belt.

"We must hurry. They will be here soon," Arik urged, poking his head in the front door. The Gryphon's shoulders pressed against the frame, too wide to enter.

"Wait. Who will be here?" Kader asked, the question slipping out.

Haro came in close, speaking low. "A message reached my Lord Palani not but two nights past from Crossroads. The Lords Proto Avis and Vorin have called the Northern Alliance for a War Council to respond to Kaiser's threat of war."

Arik shoved his way in, hissing at his stinging shoulders. He locked eyes with Kader. "The winds coming from your homeland have revealed that the traitor knows that you are alive. He has ordered your assassination." The Gryphon hissed again, this time from anger. "He sends the Dark Spirits after you."

Every sense of warmth left Kader's body in that instant and a cold sweat broke out on his skin. It would be no Saber coming after him this time. It would be Dark Spirits. They would be numerous and single minded. Their touch could drain the warmth right out of his body and kill him. "Then let us hurry."

To clear the way back out, Arik kicked hard at the door frame. It broke in two from the force. He squeezed through the opening and rustled his wings in instinctual response. His head darted up in alertness, turning about in all directions. Haro directed Kader to go out in front of him while he covered from behind. The Earthborn scout held his long knife in his right hand and kept his left hand ready to summon his innate Spirit energy. It was odd to Kader that the city was so quiet. He pulled his hood up over his head and shivered from fear.

Arik held his wings up in ready position, his body tight with tension. His leonine tail flicked back and forth behind him. Haro placed a hand on Kader's shoulder and pointed at it. He held up four fingers. Just as he put his arm down, four large shadows descended out of the night sky. The shadows landed in front of Arik and Kader expected him to jump up and attack. Instead, the Owl Gryphon bowed his head.

"My Prince and Princess. It pleases me greatly to see you," Arik chawed in the Gryphon tongue.

"Out of respect for Master Erebus, we should conduct our business in the common tongue," Palas said, standing up tall and proud. The young male Osprey Gryphon's golden eyes shined brightly in the darkness.

The three other Gryphons nodded their heads in agreement. Kader could only recognize Pala, the twin sister of Palas. She was smaller in size and sleeker in frame than her brother.

"These are the Captains Voci and Harper, son of our General Nova," Pala introduced. Voci was the brown and white Eagle Gryphon, slim but powerful in frame. Harper was the larger grey Eagle Gryphon with a black tipped crest of feathers on his head. Kader made eye contact with each Gryphon and bowed his head in respect.

"I will fly you, Master Erebus, to Cascade. My sister and Voci will protect you from the front. Harper, Arik, and Scout Haro will protect you from the back. Should the enemy win through, I will protect you with all of my being," Palas explained with great formality.

It was an honor to ride on a Gryphon's back. To ride on the back of the heir of a Gryphon Lord was even greater. Kader looked back at Haro who mounted Arik's back. The Earthborn whispered something to his partner. Palas bent his limbs slightly so that Kader could more easily get up on his back. Kader gulped once he was in place, feeling the tight muscles in the Gryphon's body through his legs. His feathers were surprisingly coarse.

"Trust me to carry you true, Master Erebus. I will not let you fall," Palas reassured him before he rocketed off of the ground.

Kader threw his arms around Palas' neck. He slammed his eyes shut as the group ascended into the night sky at high speed. The wind was loud rushing by his ears, his hood blown off his head and flapping loudly on his back. Without the distraction of his surroundings, Kader's thoughts drifted to the city of Agin. The townspeople were likely now discovering that five Gryphons and a scout had blown through like an errant wind, taking their sole Shadowborn resident with them. He wondered if more scouts had come with Haro to bring the news to them.

Palas suddenly dipped and Kader's stomach churned with uneasiness. "Arik has detected movement coming up fast. I ask you to be prepared with your strongest Spirit energy to help support Scout Haro. I will ready my talons for whatever comes."

"Arrow formation! Talons at the ready!" Harper called out before he dropped down. As the biggest of the group, he would take the brunt of the attack to ensure both Kader and his royals survived. Pala immediately positioned herself on her brother's right side and Voci flew in to be on Palas' left.

Kader's nerves kicked into overdrive. How did Kaiser find out that he was alive and that he was in Agin? Who could have told him? There was only one Shadowborn that knew where he was. Soja would have never betrayed so great his Saber loyalty was to everything that was good. Regardless of how Kaiser found out, was it Rache that was leading the Dark Spirits coming to kill him? Kader wept as he thought of the powerful Demon tearing the five Gryphons and Haro apart. They could not possibly survive a fight with him. In his current state, he was of no use to summon his Spirit energy to help. His heart hammered in his chest.

"On your left!" cried Arik in a shrill voice.

Voci snarled and darted, talons spread wide for the attack. A cold shadow burst up through the tree tops, a white hot blade in its right hand. Sharp red claws erupted out of its left hand. Voci zipped out of reach of the sword, slashing at the shadow's back with incredible agility and speed. The shadow twisted around, roaring with a guttural sound. Harper rocketed up from below and slammed into the shadow with great force. To the two Gryphon's surprise, the shadow dissipated.

"It's a Dark Spirit!" Kader shouted. This was not good.

Before the Gryphons could respond, two more Shades sped in with their white blades raised. Arik shrieked, giving Voci and Harper just enough time to avoid getting their wings cut off. Palas rolled towards his right to avoid a strike from a third Dark Spirit.

"If you know how to combat this power, do so now!" Palas ordered.

Two more Dark Spirits joined in, bringing their numbers to five. Each Gryphon was beset by their attacks with the agility and speed managing to protect them. Kader could not admit to the proud Palas that Dark Spirits were projections of the respective summoner, complete with their power and skill. If Kaiser willed it to be so, the Dark Spirits could be as powerful as him. He did not have the strength to contend directly with Kaiser.

Palas flapped his wings hard to increase his altitude. He screeched an attack cry before diving back down. Kader held on for dear life, slamming his eyes shut again. He felt the Gryphon suddenly roll to the right, leaving one wing up for balance. Palas' muscles surged beneath him. "Die, you foul beast!"

Kader's stomach churned as Palas twisted and rolled beneath him. He could feel the great Gryphon's limbs slashing and tearing at their dark foe. The Gryphon's wings beat and flapped in an irregular rhythm, shifting his body in the air in all directions. Kader imagined it like a bird fighting, attacking with wings and claws to defend its territory. Only a Gryphon was much bigger and more fierce. Palas had been well trained in combat maneuvers and moved surprisingly well with the weight of Kader on his back. He grunted only once when Kader held onto his neck too hard.

He managed to open his eyes in time to watch Arik swoop down towards the ground, Haro shouting a war cry from the Owl Gryphon's back. Arik twisted and darted towards the ground, tilting to the side. Haro shouted again as he swung his arm swiftly. At his command, pillars of stone rocketed up from the ground. The first of the six pillars knocked into a Dark Spirit with a loud crack. The Dark Spirit's sword had been broken in the attempt to cut at the rock. Arik shrieked a victory cry before he and Haro rushed in for the kill.

Further ahead, Harper was engaged with two more Dark Spirits. He slashed with his talons and beat his wings furiously to keep himself in the air. The Eagle Gryphon was something to behold in his fury. A third Dark Spirit joined the fight, swinging its sword at Harper's back. Like a lightning strike, Voci sped in to knock the Dark Spirit away. He grasped the white blade in his talons and wrenched it from his enemy's grip. He flew away with the disarmed Spirit in pursuit.

Pala was enchanting in her game of chase with the final Dark Spirit that kept going for Kader. Every time it drew close, she zipped in between it and her brother in a rush of wind, knocking the Dark Spirit off balance. After one more pass, the Dark Spirit changed its strategy and arced its sword to hit at Pala's flank. Kader reacted quickly, summoning his Spirit energy into Shadow Shock. The black bolts shot out from his hand and slammed into the Dark Spirit, knocking him away. Before he could celebrate, a sixth Dark Spirit appeared and ripped him from Palas' back. Palas shouted in the Gryphon tongue to his sister. She quickly brought her wings up before rocketing into a steep dive after Kader.

Kader struggled to free himself from the black ghost's grip, trying to summon more Spirit energy. The bolts of Shadow Shock shot out in erratic directions, none hitting his captor. The Dark Spirit's grip on him tightened to where he could barely breathe. Kader coughed hard and the Spirit's grip became even tighter. He started to black out, his vision disappearing down a long tunnel, the light of his world fading. Inside, his heart screamed for salvation.

"Unhand him!" Pala screeched in anger. She slammed into the Shade, knocking Kader loose. Feathers and fur were sent flying into the air as she slashed and kicked the Shade.

Palas swooped in at the last moment to catch Kader in his claws. His back slammed into the hard ground with a crack. Palas was not worried for once he was taught how to fly, he learned how to fall. His left wing stung from a row of broken flight feathers but he knew that he would be okay. He stood over Kader, hackles raised. Pala was soon at his side, favoring her right front leg. She snapped at her brother when he showed concern. She snarled fiercely at the approaching pair of Shades.

"They just keep coming. I thought ghosts were incorporeal. These things have weight and substance," Pala pointed out to her brother.

Palas slashed his left paw in warning and raised his wings in a threat display. "Kader said these were Dark Spirits. Something different than our beloved Spirits. Something dangerous."

Voci tumbled into view, looking worse for the wear. His white neck was streaked with blood and there was a gash across his left flank. Arik and Haro soon followed. The pale Owl Gryphon was splattered with mud and plant debris. He was missing three primary feathers on his right wing and the spot was stained with blood. Haro's right shoulder had been torn open. Harper kept up the aggressive defense, using his bulk and strength to keep the Shades at a distance. The large Eagle Gryphon took up position in front of the royal Osprey Gryphons, wings flared.

The group of five Gryphons and two Spiritborn were surrounded by a slew of Dark Spirits brandishing white hot weapons. Their mouths dropped open in taunting laughter and jeers.

"By the great Spirits of this world, I will stand and fight you all!" Harper challenged.

"You cannot fight what you cannot see for there is a greater power in this world yet unseen," the Dark Spirits collectively said.

A booming and earth shaking roar rocked the trees and silenced everything. The Gryphons and Haro looked about in confusion and worry. The Dark Spirits muttered amongst themselves in a singular voice. It was strange to hear them talk for they only spoke in one voice as if they were the projections of a single attacker's mind. Arik glanced at Haro for an explanation but the Earthborn shrugged. A curious look appeared in Arik's dark eyes and a smile crossed his face.

"What is it?" Haro whispered, worried about speaking too loudly.

Before Arik could answer, an even more powerful roar erupted from what felt like everywhere at once. The Dark Spirits all grabbed their heads and screamed. In an instant, they shattered and left no trace behind. The desperate sense in the air wavered for a moment before everyone let out a deep breath.

"It must have been Omu," Arik finally said as Palas bent down to inspect the unconscious Kader.

"Could he have summoned the Great Wolf?" Voci wondered.

Palas and Harper shrugged as they relaxed their wings. Arik lowered his right wing for Haro to inspect his wound while Haro picked at his flank injury.

"We must not delay. Though I trust in the power of Omu, I do not doubt that the great evil will rise up quickly to strike again," Pala urged. She was the only Gryphon who kept her wings raised up high.

Palas nodded. "Scout Haro, where is the nearest station for your order?"

"About two hours as the Gryphon flies to the northwest of our position," Haro answered. He pointed in the direction of the scout station.

Palas turned to Harper. "Use your strength to ensure safe passage for our injured kin. The Earthborn will show you the way. Tell our kin present that darkness flies and to be on alert. We will continue on to Cascade. I will send word when we have arrived."

"Fly true my Prince and Princess," Harper stated with a bow of the head.

Haro helped to get Kader onto Palas' back, taking his belt to help secure him. He stepped back and bowed his head. "In my homeland, we would say at a parting to stay strong like the stone and to bend like the tree and always keep the Truth."

Before the group split up, Palas and Pala pressed their brows to that of Harper, Voci, and Arik. Even Haro was granted the honor. Palas and Pala were soon airborne and flying east towards Cascade. Harper called up from the ground in the Gryphon tongue, waving his wings. He soon disappeared from sight as the royal pair flew further away.

They remained on high alert for further attack but the feeling started to dissipate when the sun peaked over the horizon. Pala let out a deep breath and embraced the wind fully with her wings. Even Palas was able to relax ever so slightly. They were surprised when Kader started to stir.

"What happened?" he weakly asked.

"The Great Wolf watches over you, Master Erebus," Palas stated, not wanting to frighten him with the dark details of the attack.

Kader sighed deeply and smiled. "Then the Spirits have not abandoned us. Not yet."

"So as long as we believe in the Truth and in the goodness of Spirits like Omu, we shall be safe on our journey. Fly true, my winged kin," Palas said with a bow of his head.

*****

THE WOUNDS OF THE PAST

"Well that achieved nothing," Haven griped as she, Ryder, and Hayden walked across the dirt yard of the base. All three were covered in mud and plant debris as a form of camouflage.

"I think that it achieved a great deal. Even the lack of movement tells us what Kaiser is doing," Hayden stated. He glanced over at Ryder who had been quiet since their return. The Saber noticed that he seemed to favor his right side, periodically placing a hand over a spot on his torso. Ryder dropped it quickly when he saw that Hayden was watching him.

Hayden had been watching Ryder closely over the last few days of their mission, noticing that something was physically bothering him. Despite his size and obvious strength, Hayden could see that Ryder was in pain and did not want others to know it. Hayden had seen the pained look in his eyes and the tension in his mouth as he gritted his teeth.

"Go on and give Zoras our report without me. I need to get some sleep. I'm exhausted," Ryder finally said.

Haven turned around to face her lover, putting a hand on his shoulder. "You do need to get some rest. You haven't slept well since before we left. I'll smack anyone that wants to bother you with something trivial."

Ryder managed a smile. "Not even if I bother you for some tea later?"

She patted his cheek. "Maybe. Now go."

"I can make sure this tired soul finds the way," Hayden

suggested. Haven smiled and seemed pleased at the suggestion while Ryder shot him a dirty look. "I am a Saber. Forever bound to assist the Silvanus bloodline in any way possible," Hayden faked a laugh towards Ryder.

"Can't blame him for his sense of duty, Ryder," Haven said with a shrug. She spun around on her feet and headed towards the right hand hallway, disappearing around a corner.

Ryder leaned back against the wall, seething as he gripped his side tightly. He pulled his hand away, his fingers and palm stained with blood. He did not fight Hayden when the Saber moved to support him.

"Nothing escapes a well-trained Saber. You should be Commander with your attentiveness," Ryder admitted with a tired smile.

"Is that a recommendation?" Hayden asked, fighting the urge to say my Lord. He knew how Ryder hated the honorific title. To Hayden, Ryder was his Lord and Commander. His Shadowlord. There was nothing that could change that. "Let me help you to the healers."

"No," Ryder grunted harshly. "They talk too much. If you must insist upon helping me, my grandmother's quarters are not far."

Hayden let Ryder lean upon him as they slowly walked towards Myra's room. He could feel the fever in Ryder's body through their close contact and wondered what else Ryder was hiding. Hayden had to wonder how serious Ryder's condition was for it to affect him. Usually, Ryder kept injury close to the heart and revealed very little if anything at all. Their mission had not consisted of any combat. To Hayden's knowledge, Ryder's last major combat mission was in Cross two months ago. A mission where he fought Rache, Kaiser's powerful Demon servant. Ryder had more courage than most in facing a Demon and dealing with Kaiser. Hayden had a suspicion as to why.

Myra was returning to her room as she spotted Hayden and Ryder. Her face paled slightly upon seeing her grandson's condition and quickly opened her door to let them in. Hayden thanked her. She closed the door behind him and locked it.

"What happened?" she asked with worry.

Hayden helped Ryder to lie down on the bed. Without hesitation, he began pulling off Ryder's light armor with precision and speed. He dropped the pieces to the floor before he took his hands and ripped open Ryder's tunic. Myra covered her mouth and nose once she saw the festering wounds on Ryder's right side. The largest gash, where Ryder had been impaled by a spike on Rache's back, had torn open and oozed a blackened liquid. The smaller cuts were red and the skin around the entire area was a deep purple.

"When did this happen? I thought that you three just went on a scouting mission!" Myra shrieked with concern.

"Not so loud, Nana," Ryder said, pressing a fist to his forehead. He seethed as the air hit his wounds. "My head hurts."

Hayden quickly wrapped his hands in preparation. He gestured towards the wash basin. "He has a fever. See if you can help cool him down while I clean this mess up."

Myra picked up the basin and a nearby cloth. She settled by Ryder's head. Dipping the cloth in the water, she soaked it through before squeezing it to remove excess moisture. She sighed as she laid the cloth on Ryder's forehead.

"When did this happen? Was it Kaiser?" Myra demanded.

Ryder shook his head. "Remember how I told you that I went to Cross with Onyx to try to rescue Aku. I had to confront Rache to keep him from killing Onyx while he went into the castle for his father."

"You went into battle against him? Are you an idiot? He could have killed you," Myra admonished. She shook her head.

Hayden did his best to remain focused on cleaning up the blood and mess but could not help but hear the banter between grandmother and grandson.

"You know he won't kill me. Not yet at least," Ryder mumbled.

"But you can't trust in that," Myra replied as she dabbed his forehead with the soaked cloth. She paused as she realized that Hayden was paying attention to their conversation.

Ryder did his best to hide his pain but he could not help but wince and seethe every time Hayden scrubbed his torn skin. Myra worked to soothe the heat in his body, rubbing the cloth over his forehead and cheeks. It hurt to breathe due to his pain and he wondered how he was able to keep himself composed for so long. Ryder knew what was going on. Rache's Demon blood had poisoned him and it was only due to his strong constitution that he had survived this long. He eyed Hayden's careful work.

"You are quite skilled. Not many know how to treat Demon wounds," Ryder commented.

Hayden let out a deep breath as he paused to rewet his cleaning cloth. "I have learned a great deal as a Saber just by watching my betters work. Being watchful is key for my order."

"The art is not common in these days. Who did you learn from?" Myra asked.

"I learned by watching Kaiser each time that he treated Lord Aku. The man may be evil incarnate to many people but he is frighteningly intelligent and a very skilled healer. My combat trainer always said to learn from my enemies," Hayden replied. "And a true Saber is prepared for anything."

Hayden pulled a small first aid kit from the pouch on his belt. He lifted an eyebrow as he set it aside. "I'll be right back. I need to go get some fresh salves to pack the wounds." He disappeared into Shadow Slide and slipped out under the locked door.

Ryder and Myra only had to wait a few minutes before Hayden was back, carrying two small jars. They were amazed at his speed. The Saber smiled with a degree of pride as he settled back by Ryder's side. He pulled up a footstool and sat down.

"I am glad to see Sabers of your skill are still with us in these times. The order has become perverted since Kaiser took over," Myra commented as she smoothed back Ryder's hair from his face.

"You would certainly do a better job than your grandfather if you were on the throne," Hayden said as he finished packing a deep gash.

Ryder and Myra froze. How did Hayden know? Ryder did not think he had told the Saber. His thoughts raced through every conversation that included him revealing the secret.

"Do not be alarmed for no one told me but my own observations. I have been around Kaiser for a long time and I know you well enough to see the resemblance. You share the same brow and your eyes are both powerful and striking. Most would say it is the Silvanus in you but I know better." Hayden paused for a moment as he packed another gash. "Even the way you move. You both walk and move in a manner that is not entirely Spiritborn."

Ryder wrenched his face in confusion. He had never thought that his movement was anything strange. He then hardened his expression. "I am nothing like him." Myra nodded in agreement.

Hayden looked up from preparing a bandage strip he had soaked in a warm green liquid. "And you are not your father either but you look like him too. We cannot choose our blood. We can only choose who we are and who we become. The Spirits have a plan for all of us."

"And here I thought Sabers were superstitious about Spirits," Ryder commented. He pressed his fists to his forehead as Hayden dressed the wounds with medicine soaked bandages.

"The younger members of my order are. Those that joined during the reign of your great grandfather are less so," Hayden replied as he continued his wound care.

"You became a Saber under Sin?" Myra asked curiously.

Hayden nodded. "The Crowned Prince Aday was still at court when I joined. I did not much care for court life so I became a field Saber. I sadly missed the downfall of Aday and it still hurts me after all these years. I never did believe that he did the things they say he did."

A silence fell upon the trio except for Ryder's occasional pained sighs. Aday was the dirty family secret for the Silvanus clan. No one dared to speak of him and he had not been seen in centuries. He was presumed dead. Aday was considered taboo among the Shadowborn.

"Whatever became of Aday?" Ryder asked when he felt brave enough to break the taboo.

Hayden sighed deeply. "Dead or lost. Either way, he is never coming back to the land of his ancestors." He set down another layer of bandages before sitting up. "All done," Hayden said with a smile.

Myra helped Ryder to sit up and pulled off the ruined tunic. She smiled and shook her head when she saw the Gryphon talons on his right shoulder.

"If the Gryphons accepted you into their society, then you really are something special," Myra mused.

Ryder got to his feet, feeling a bit better though the poison still stung. He rolled his shoulders and stretched his arms. "Thank you, Hayden."

The Saber stood up tall, put his right arm across his chest, and bowed. He came back up to face Ryder. "You should not be ashamed of who you are. If I were you, I would not hide your kinship to Kaiser. People would see you as Kaiser's own blood rebelling against him and they would have hope."

"It is not that simple. I was already vilified for being a royal bastard. How would telling people that Kaiser is my grandfather make things better?" Ryder sighed deeply.

"Because I have known that you are his kin for quite some time and I do not think less of you. Even if you were not a Silvanus, I would still say the same thing. You carry yourself with honor and respect for others. You are not perfect and you have made decisions that others do not like. But you came back and that is what matters. Now, I have a decision to make," Hayden said with great conviction. "Lady Myra, if I may ask you to bear witness."

"What are you doing?" Ryder nervously asked.

"As the senior living member of the Silvanus bloodline, you are by right the head of the family and acting Shadowlord until one is named. That is the law of the Shadowborn. I ask you for permission to leave my position as a field Saber and become a court

Saber in direct service to you. I also ask this of you: accept the fact that you are connected to the throne, the throne of your ancestors, and that you may be called to sit upon it someday. Zoras has his ideas about your future and I have mine. Mine is service regardless of what happens," Hayden stated. He bowed again, waiting for permission to rise.

Ryder looked back to his grandmother, an expression of confusion on his face. "This is something you have to deal with on your own, Peredur. Your heritage, your destiny," Myra said with encouragement.

"Look. I'm not one for decorum. Stand up," Ryder said, gesturing for Hayden to rise. "I do not want a guardian or a servant who is blinded by loyalty. If you feel that this is the best path for you, take it. You do not need my permission to follow your heart."

This time, Hayden bowed his head. He glanced over at Myra. "Lady Myra, I extend my offer of protection to you as well as I am sure that your grandson would wish it."

"I accept, Captain Abendroth. I hope to one day see you as Commander of your order," Myra replied with a bow of the head. "Maybe you should seriously consider the throne, Ryder."

"First, let's win it from Kaiser before we start talking who should sit upon it and wear the crown," Ryder grumbled.

*****

GARHUNE

Gyr rippled with excitement and anticipation at visiting his first Mortal settlement. He had only heard stories and read sparingly about the short lived people of the Southlands. Most Immortals only spoke of the Mortals as a flight of whimsy with their innocence. They seemed more like fairytales than actual living beings. To Gyr's knowledge, only three souls had ever met a Mortal: Charon's mysterious Shadowborn father, the Farlander hero Begin Anu, and the Daylord. Among the three, the Daylord had been the only one to spend any real time among them. Gyr had to think for a moment. How could the people of the Southlands know the Daylord as Charon seemed to indicate? He did not think the Mortal people capable of understanding the power of a Spirit Song, the likely vessel to have spread his story. He decided to find an elderly Mortal to get his answers.

Charon was however not as enthusiastic about going to Garhune. He preferred the vast wilds, wandering the paths of the forest or climbing tall mountains. Or to be more precise, he preferred his own company. To the people of the Southlands, he was something to jeer at and be wary of. No matter the love the Mortals had for the Daylord, anything Immortal was considered dangerous and evil. He pulled his hood down over his eyes and dropped his shoulders in dread. The sooner he was out of Garhune, the better.

The pair climbed up a hill, the last before a lush grassland opened up before them. Gyr resisted the urge to jump into the sky for a flight. They stood together on top of the hill.

"There is Garhune, a little village by the Last River," Charon said halfheartedly.

"Last River? That is its name?" Gyr asked, cocking his head.

Charon looked in the direction of the distant Wall of Crossroads. "The people call it the Last River as it is the last before the Dominion of the Immortals. I am sure the scholars in Arken keep an official name."

"What is this Arken?" Gyr asked. A part of him hated not knowing the land like he did back home.

"It is the capital of the Southlands. Some say it is where the Farlanders first landed thousands of years ago," Charon stated. He then looked towards Gyr. "Or so the stories say."

Finally! Something he knew well. Gyr was a finely educated Gryphon and had learned all he could about the Farlanders in his youth. The Farlanders were as mysterious to the Northlands as the Immortals were to the Southlands. Begin Anu was the most well-known Farlander whose bloodline was rumored to remain alive to this day.

"I would like to visit Arken. My Lords Proto Avis and Vorin would enjoy the knowledge of the Mortal scholars. They would be sure to enhance the library in Crossroads," Gyr mused as he sat down on his haunches. He took a deep breath, taking in the scent of the tall grass and wildflowers. "It must have been lovely growing up here."

Charon scoffed. "I am a half breed bastard. There is nothing lovely about that."

Gyr turned to face him. "I know a bastard in the Northlands who has risen beyond his birth to become something great. My kin say that he is the rightful Lord of the Shadowborn and has been since the death of his father. Even now, he leads the Shadowborn in their rebellion against the great evil."

"What is this bastard's name? Is he full blooded Shadowborn?" Charon asked. He ran his fingers through his hair though the breeze was quick to mess it up again.

"His birth name is Peredur Coba-Silvanus. His mother was a woman named Aylin and his father was Lord Akakios of the Shadowborn. To my knowledge, he is full blooded but no one really knows his mother's origins. The Lords of my kin speak very highly of this man," Gyr proudly answered.

"Then why are you searching for a king that does not want to be found when you have him? He sounds capable of facing the evil you have told me about," Charon asked as he readjusted his travel pack.

Gyr stood up and shook his body from beak to tail. He rustled his wings again. "If you knew the entire story, you would not think to ask that question again. My people need their king and I will do anything to find him. In a way, I must unite the Daylord and the Shadowlord again. Together, they would be a force to be reckoned with."

"I'm sorry. I place more faith in what I can see and touch than what I hear in rumor and stories," Charon admitted with an exacerbated sigh. "Mortals love a good story and some will believe all of them to be true without any proof. Be careful what you say around them. Garhune will be better than most as the town sits within sight of your Wall."

"Then the sight of a Gryphon will not alarm them too much. Flying lessons are held for new messenger recruits over the Wall. Even the Lord Vorin will join in on occasion," Gyr described. He picked at a stray feather.

Charon chuckled softly. "I remember the first time that I saw a Gryphon. It was a big gray creature," he stretched out his arms to emphasize size. "Huge wings that spread out like this."

In response, Gyr unfolded his wings to their full length. Charon stumbled back to avoid being knocked over. The Gryphon kept his wings raised high enough so Charon could inspect them. Charon lifted his left arm up to one of the primary flight feathers, measuring the length.

"Likely you saw an Eagle Gryphon that day. Sturdy fliers and a bit too proud for my tastes. I prefer speed and agility over strength. Eagle Gryphons are the easiest to spot over a distance. Their flying lacks finesse and style," Gyr commented as he refolded his wings on his back.

Charon sighed deeply as he looked back towards the Wall of Crossroads. A sense of longing stirred in him but he quickly squashed it. His eyes turned towards the town of his birth. He was not happy about it but Gyr insisted on stopping to ask around about the Daylord. Charon also did not want to admit that though he claimed to know the Southlands well, there were still places he was unsure of. He intended to find a good map while the Gryphon talked with the people.

Gyr descended from the top of the hill first, his leonine tail swishing behind him. Charon slowly followed, becoming more reluctant with each step. He lagged further and further behind until Gyr turned around and noticed their distance.

"What is the matter? This is the home of your birth," Gyr stated.

It took a long time for Charon to answer. "I don't know how people treat your bastard rebel leader but here, I am pretty much a leper."

"What is a leper?" Gyr asked in confusion.

The question made Charon laugh heartedly for it was unexpected. "It means diseased or untouchable. You don't have things like leprosy or plague in the Northlands?"

Gyr shook his head. Charon listed several more diseases and biological catastrophes to the same result. "The kin of the Northlands are especially long lived and hearty. The greatest killer of Immortal kind is each other. Ailments such as you have described and time are just passing thoughts."

"I am sure that Immortal kind would be more accepting of me than Mortal kind," Charon said, imitating Gyr's manner of speaking.

"We have our share of purists but those are the Immortals of the greatest age and closed off from the world. Like Lord Evander of the Lightborn. Do not ever present yourself to Lord Evander. He and most of the kin care for nothing but themselves and it is harder to convince such people of your worth. Lord Aves of the Airborn is more accepting but he can be rather cold and emotionless," Gyr explained. He gestured with his head for Charon to come to his side. "But it can be done with them and it can be done with the Mortals."

He could see that Gyr was trying to encourage him but the Gryphon was completely oblivious to the harsh treatment. It wasn't enough to tell him that Mortals treated him differently. The words could not encompass the wariness and hate he experienced. He suspected that even Gyr would not be spared though perhaps his comments would be less hurtful. Part of him felt sorry for the Gryphon and his cluelessness. Was the Gryphon really as intelligent as Charon originally thought? He was an animal after all. Charon thought to voice his comment but decided that calling a Gryphon an animal was an insult.

"Well I am ready. If people do not like me then I can just fly away," Gyr stated. He started walking towards Garhune.

Charon took a deep breath and let it out slowly. He reluctantly followed behind the Gryphon. He kept checking his hood to make sure his eyes were covered. He wanted to be confident and walk into Garhune with his head held high. He tried to follow Gyr's example. Gyr appeared confident and ready to face anything. It seemed as if the Gryphon ignored the fact that he was a stranger walking into the fires of Mortal society.

Gyr led the way, his wings raised slightly and head up straight. He was determined to represent his Lords with honor and respect. Being the first Gryphon south of the Wall was also a responsibility that excited him. He was an emissary and representative of his homeland. A thought crossed his mind. He hadn't had a bath since he left Crossroads! Tension spread throughout his entire body.

The pair approached the road that led into Garhune. Charon glanced down the road in the opposite direction. The road passed through fenced in farmland before disappearing in the distance. He let out a deep breath. Gyr ignored the road that led away from town completely. The Gryphon's attention was on a stone and wood bridge that stretched over the river. A gate house had been built on the left and right sides of the bridge. A trio of men were crouched over the ground, tossing small stones on a dirt drawing. They shouted and jeered at each toss. One man looked up and started furiously slapping the shoulder of his neighbor. Gyr slowed to a halt before them, lifting his brow.

"It's a... you're a..." the smallest of the three men stuttered. He looked young with a clean face and radiant blonde hair. He was dressed in brown wool pants and an off white tunic that had been tied in at the waist with a dark brown leather belt.

"It's a Gryphon, you knuckle head," a blonde haired man dressed in light leather armor that clung to his lean frame. He appeared to be the smaller man's brother as he smacked him across the back of the head. The small man squeaked and rubbed the spot.

The last of the trio was a tall, brutish looking man who glared over Gyr's shoulder at Charon. He too wore leather armor but his hair was a dark mahogany and he sported a full beard. "Got yourself some different company there, half breed."

Gyr moved to stand in front of Charon. "Were you a fledgling, I would give you a tongue lashing for your greeting. Yes, I am a Gryphon," he snapped.

The fact that the Gryphon could talk and speak clearly in the common tongue shocked the three Mortals. It was to Gyr's advantage that he was taller than they were. His sharp beak and claws also helped him to appear more fierce and imposing.

"I am Gyr of Crossroads, emissary for the Lords Proto Avis and Vorin, and I and whoever I travel with must be shown the proper respect. You should be ashamed. What if I had been your Mortal king? Would you have greeted him as you have greeted me? Where is your commander? Your town leader?" Gyr scolded. He gripped his talons into the dirt.

The two guards apologized profusely though they weren't sure why. The blonde youth looked at Gyr in wonder. He stepped around from behind his brother.

"But we don't have a king," the youth said in confusion.

Charon stepped forward to whisper in Gyr's right ear. The

trio of Mortals backed away in response. "The Southlands is ruled by a council of representatives in Arken with a head minister. No kings or queens." He stepped back.

"Then my traveling companion and I wish to meet with the leader of your town. I also wish to learn more of Garhune so that I may have a proper report for my masters upon my return," Gyr stated firmly. He was not going to take no for an answer.

"Of course. Little brother, can you lead these two to the inn? I will go get the mayor," the blonde guard stated.

"Perhaps you will learn some manners along the way. I hope that my first Mortal experience will be more pleasant than your greeting," Gyr chided with a toss of the head.

Charon hid a snicker when he saw the trio gulped and shiver in Gyr's presence. When he followed Gyr past the big brunette guard, he resisted the urge to snort and scare him. Maybe Garhune would not be so bad this time.

THE HALF BREED

Gyr followed behind the blonde youth, nodding every time he turned around to look at him. It was clear than the Mortal boy was amazed by the snow white Gryphon. Gyr had expected a more extreme reaction since he was a large beast from the Northlands. Out of the corner of his eyes, he spied people pausing in their daily routines to gape and point at him. They also stopped to whisper about Charon, some jeering at him like he was unwanted trash. That upset Gyr. Being a bastard and an Immortal half breed was no cause for insults in his eyes. He started to wonder if Charon was young like his Mortal kin or if he was older. More questions flooded his mind about Charon's exact identity.

Garhune reminded Gyr of Agin, a small town in the western reaches of the Earthborn territory. It was small and rustic in appearance. All of the buildings were made of a combination of stone, wood, slate, and thatch. The main streets were laid out in an irregular pattern, slightly raised so that any rainwater would roll right off into an embedded trough of stone on either side. Bright green grass grew in abundance, leaving no space uncovered. There was no town square for a market so many people sold their wares in stalls in front of their homes. The sole inn in town was the largest building and had a large yard where farmers had assembled to sell various vegetables, homemade sausages, and other such foods. There was a livestock auction as well with a lively crowd.

The crowd silenced at the sight of Gyr and Charon. Only the crates of cackling fowl and the snorting of a pig could be heard.

Gyr looked around at the crowd of Mortal people, seeing men and women of various ages mixed together. He saw that they looked like the Spiritborn and yet their eyes held a different kind of brightness and energy. While a Spiritborn's eyes were deep and mysterious, a Mortal's eyes were full of innocence life and wonder. Gyr expected that a Mortal of nefarious constitution would display a different energy in their eyes. They weren't as tall as some Spiritborn. Gyr's mind drifted to Ryder Coba who was described as six and a half feet tall. Ryder would have towered over the Mortals before him. Gyr fought the urge to tell the people to stop staring.

"I would be careful with what you say. Mortals are superstitious and wary of any Immortal," Charon whispered under his breath.

"I know that now," Gyr growled in response. He dug his talons into the ground as the youth bounded off, leaving them before the inn doors.

This time, Charon took the lead to which Gyr was grateful. He did not possess the necessary dexterity to open a door. He was used to the openness of Crossroads' buildings and that a simple tap on the door would grant him entry. Gyr stepped back to give Charon space. The right hand door creaked loudly as Charon pulled it wide open. He stood to the side to allow Gyr to pass. The Gryphon pulled his wings as tight as he could to his body. He took a deep breath and wiggled his way through the door.

Gyr immediately regretted going inside as the inn was not accommodating to a Gryphon of his size or Gryphons in general. Charon led him to a space to the left next to the window. Charon settled at the table while Gyr sat on the floor. Gyr glanced around and decided that it must be a performance space for nighttime bands and plays. He rather liked the homey interior, seeing a pile of orange coals in a fireplace on the other side of the room. He let out a deep breath, embracing the warmth.

"We will wait for the mayor here. The inn also serves as the council hall for Garhune. Nothing fancy and the mayor likes the ale that is served here. Just so you are aware, the mayor does not like me at all and wants to banish me from Garhune and its territory," Charon said, hunching over the table.

"Does anyone like you here?" Gyr whispered.

"The town treasurer tolerates me. He likes to hire me when it's time to collect taxes every year. He says I give off a creepy vibe that makes people more willing to part with their money," Charon answered.

"That sounds insulting. It ill becomes one of your heritage," Gyr grumbled. He eyed a barmaid that had nearly stepped on his tail. He wrapped his tail around his feet and glared in her direction.

Charon shrugged. "That is just the way things are here. I was my mother's shame when she was still alive. Sometimes I think she only pretended that the insults and jeers did not affect her but they did. As a child, I had no idea. I thought that I was just like everyone else. As I grew older, the adults in this town warned their children to stay away. That I was cursed by my father's blood."

"Blood may make you but it does not shape you," Gyr stated with conviction. He thought for a moment. "Gryphons respect those with great heart even if evil blood taints them. I am not sure how to properly translate that from my native tongue."

Charon managed a halfhearted chuckle. "Do the Gryphons have a name for someone like me?"

Gyr thought long and hard, contorting his avian face in deep concentration. "Man of the Short Shadow."

"And how does that sound in your tongue?" Charon asked, becoming interested in learning the Gryphon language.

Gyr whistled and chawed out the words, laughing when Charon tried to imitate it. The man failed horribly. Gyr started to direct Charon in how to move his tongue and adjust the muscles of his face. He tapped Charon's throat with a gentle talon. Charon only chortled and laughed.

A barmaid finally came over with a visible expression of reluctance. "I have been told to give you a message. The Mayor of Garhune will not meet with you until," she paused to point at Charon.

Gyr furrowed his brow and waved her off. "Perhaps it is best if we do not stay in town tonight. I have a mind to bite a few heads off if you are insulted one more time."

"Don't worry about me. I am used to it," Charon said. He gestured towards the west. "My old house is on the edge of town. The roof is leaky but it will be a decent place to sleep in."

"Good. I will need another day to build up the right insult. Gryphons can and will curse if needed. I am quite good at it," Gyr promised with a devilish look in his eyes.

Charon led Gyr out of town to an abandoned farmhouse complete with a small barn that was crumbling. The roof had fallen in and the plant life had taken over. The farmhouse was just four walls of moss eaten stone. The grass was waist high on Charon and Gyr had to keep his wings raised. Charon went ahead of Gyr towards the barn and shoved the door away. It creaked and fell to the side. Inside the barn was relatively bare in the middle with vines covering the walls. Charon dug in a corner for some firewood, ripping a few pieces free from the vines. Gyr scratched out a small pit before searching for a stone. Charon assembled the wood in a pile.

"What are you doing?" Charon asked when Gyr came close to the wood pile with the stone in his paw.

"Starting a fire. I will scrap my talons across this stone like so and a spark," Gyr said with a grin. The sparks came off the stone and landed on the wood, lighting it. "Learned this trick from my survival skills trainer. It's better than what you taught me back in the snowy mountains."

Charon leaned in to watch but kept a careful enough distance to make sure stray sparks did not touch his skin. He watched as Gyr scrapped his talons in rhythmic strokes, building up a stream of sparks. Gyr put down the stone and bent down low enough to blow a puff of breath to encourage the sparks to grow. A snap and crackle answered him and he sat up smiling. It was slow but soon the pair had a small fire to warm themselves by. Charon dug into his travel pack and pulled out some dried meat. He handed a large strip to Gyr who snapped it up with his beak. He threw it in the air, tossed his head back, and let it fall into his mouth. He chirped and smiled, licking his beak.

"How can you do that if your talons are not made of steel?" Charon asked. Gyr put his left paw forward so that Charon could inspect his claws. He gingerly tapped the largest one. It was hard and cold.

"Like metal but still a part of me," Gyr proudly said as he drew his paw back and set it on the ground. "It is an old Gryphon tale that the first Gryphon had claws like fire forged steel, a gift from the Dragons."

Charon sat back and leaned against a stone post that held up a part of the remaining roof. He rested his head against it and closed his eyes. He let out a deep breath. "My mother used to tell me stories by the fire to help me fall asleep. When I was ridiculed for being a half breed, she would distract me with more tales so I would not know what the insults and jeers meant."

"Are Mortals really that cruel?" Gyr asked as he laid down and crossed his paws.

"I'm sure they can be as cruel as any soul on Terra. Beings with the ability to think and reason what to do with their will can be cruel regardless of their Mortality or Immortality. Even if I was not a half breed, I am still the product of a non-wedded couple. People here think very highly of marriage and of courtship. What Mortals leave behind after their short lives are done consumes their thoughts on a daily basis. How can I better the world? How can I make sure that I am remembered?" Charon explained.

"Sounds like they are trying to make up for the fact that

they are not Immortal. That they view Mortality as a curse and Immortality as a gift," Gyr commented. "Immortality is not forever. We can still die as I already told you."

Charon's eyes shot open and he sat up straight. "Really? Immortals can die?"

Gyr nodded. "It is true that Immortals can have very long lives. But we age and we feel the burdens of the world in our endless days. You have heard me speak of Kaiser."

"The great evil Shadowborn," Charon quickly said. He moved closer to the fire.

The Gryphon cleared his throat and spat into the fire. "I know only sparingly of his origins so bear with me. He is the son of an ancient Shadowborn house that is no more for the last of it fell during the Second Dominion War. He emerged as the sole survivor. At first, the world was full of sorrow for him. He had lost everything and everyone. Personally, I would have wept and lost myself in the wilds if something like that happened to my family. Kaiser, as I was told, held his head up high and people praised him for his strong constitution. The court at Cross, that's the capital of the Shadowborn, welcomed him into their circle. He flourished as a man of knowledge and proved himself to be an adept healer. But one must not forget that his mighty father trained him in all things war.

"Kaiser refused the post formally occupied by his father, that of High Commander. He contented himself with court life and eventually made his way to the Shadow Council as official representative of Umbra."

"I'm guessing he was born in this Umbra," Charon commented. He poked a stick into the center of the fire.

"He was. Somewhere along this path, Kaiser became dark and twisted. Frightfully so. Never will you meet a smarter man, Mortal or Immortal. The things he is reported to be capable of with his mind. Ah, I am too scared to repeat them." Gyr shuddered and shook his head.

Charon let go of the stick and watched it burn and turn into ash. He brought his knees up and wrapped his arms around them. He let out a deep breath. "Is this because he is an Immortal?"

The Gryphon nodded. He nudged his lightning stone out of habit. "Since he is Immortal, his evil will last beyond centuries if he is not stopped now. He will kill and he will burn anything and anyone in his path. The Mortals are not safe here in the Southlands for eventually his evil will spread. It will take us all united together to stop him. The peoples of the Northlands need their king to lead them once again."

"The Mortals know of Bane but not of Kaiser. I can tell that you do not approve of their treatment of me. But you can't undo their prejudices and long held thoughts for all Immortals and things Northlands simply by yelling at them. That will only enforce their opinions." Charon sighed deeply and looked away. "Maybe they know something I don't about my father and they hate me just like they hated him," he stated. He leaned back against the post.

Gyr sighed deeply and looked up at the coming night sky. "Then I will just have to tell them the truth."

THE WORDS OF A GRYPHON

Charon woke first, having slept only a few hours. He looked across the cold fire to see Gyr on his back, feet in the air. The Gryphon's feathered chest slowly rose and fell with each breath. It then became apparent that Gyr was snoring. He resisted laughing out loud. Gyr kicked his left rear leg, snorting loudly, before calming down. His tail thumped on the ground with a soft thud. Charon then spotted a yellow winged butterfly slowly floating down through the open roof. It seemed curious by Gyr's presence and unafraid of his claws. The butterfly landed on the tip of Gyr's beak and resorted itself to taking a rest before flying again. Gyr's face twitched, slow at first. The Gryphon then let loose a wild and loud sneeze, blasting the butterfly back through the roof. Charon fell back in shock.

Gyr rolled over on to his stomach and shook his head. He smacked his mouth, his beak clacking loudly. Sleep was still heavy in his eyes. He slowly got to his feet, stretching dramatically and flapping his wings. He shook his entire body from beak to tail.

"That was hilarious," Charon snickered.

Gyr frowned. "Have I laughed when you sneezed? Honestly, why do people find Gryphons so funny when we sneeze or take a dust bath? The Earthborn scouts always seem to laugh when their Gryphon partners do what comes natural to them. Well I find it rude and not as entertaining as you might."

"I'm sorry. It was just that before you sneezed, a butterfly had landed on your beak. You, a big fearsome creature, and this delicate little bug," Charon said with a mischievous grin. He demonstrated the difference in size with his hands.

"Wingless two legs," Gyr said with an exacerbated sigh. "I wish to put this judgmental town behind me as soon as possible. But first, I want to talk to the mayor. Someone needs to set him straight. Before you try to run and hide, you are coming with me."

The pair left the run down barn and headed towards the center of Garhune. The sun beamed down through the clouds, casting a golden glow over the land. Birds and an assortment of bugs flew in and out of the grass. They chirped and whistled at Gyr with delight as he passed. A hummingbird flitted around in front of the Gryphon before speeding off in a twisting spiral.

"Does that happen a lot? Can you understand them?" Charon asked as he trailed behind him.

"Gryphons hold a close connection to nature, more so than the Earthborn. Their feet are rooted to the ground like a high mountain. A Gryphon lives and breathes the world," Gyr emphasized his statement by taking a deep breath and slowly releasing it. "As for bird speech, I could tell that the hummingbird was happy to see me. She greeted me with a welcome to her home and expressed hope that I would find it pleasing. What you call beasts and creatures are quite complex and not as simple as one would think."

Their journey back to town was short. Garhune's people were already at work preparing for the new day. Farmers were out in their fields, inspecting their crops and pulling weeds. Shepherds were tending to a collection of livestock, dogs stalking the field and waiting for their masters' commands. Boats lingered on the river bank, knocking against each other with the current. Horse bound riders galloped out of town on various missions that ranged from hunting to going to other cities in the Southlands. Charon believed that the one headed south was going to Meras to tell them about Gyr.

Gyr strode into town with absolute confidence, Charon trailing behind him with his hood drawn. He kept his wings slightly raised to emphasize his importance and size. He ignored the whispers and pointing of the curious townsfolk who had not seen him yesterday. Finding the inn on their own was easy for it was the largest building in town. The doors had been thrown open for a delivery of produce. Gyr approached a man with a parchment and quill.

"I desire to speak with your mayor and I will not take no for an answer. If the mayor denies me an audience then Crossroads will withdraw all interest and protection of Garhune. If you must wake him, wake him for I will not let him refuse me again," Gyr said sternly. He towered over the short, stocky man with a gray mustache and bald head.

The man gulped at the sight of the fierce eyes of Gyr. Gyr flinched his brow and the man took off running. The delivery continued on with hesitation. No one felt comfortable with Gyr watching their every move.

Charon leaned in close to Gyr to whisper. "He's not a part of the council or the mayor's retinue. You just scared the piss out of an innocent man."

Gyr snorted. "So?"

"Would have been better to talk to the owner of the inn. He is good friends with the mayor," Charon replied in the same soft voice.

"The half breed is right. What is the meaning of this? Is this how your Immortal emissaries treat other? With such harshness and demands?" a tall, brown haired man asked as he set down a wooden crate of legumes. He wiped his dirty hands on his striped apron.

"His name is Charon and my name is Gyr," Gyr growled. The feathers and fur along his spine bristled with restrained fury. "Forgive my ignorance of your people and their ways but I was under the impression that Mortals were kind and full of wonder. I was sadly mistaken," Gyr exclaimed. He looked around at the small crowd that had paused to watch the exchange. "Strong souls with good hearts denied simply because they are different. In this town, you are lucky to have someone of such noble constitution willing to defend you from acts of war."

"What war? There hasn't been a war in generations. There has only ever been peace in my time," a gray haired woman cried out.

Gyr lifted his right wing up, revealing the scar on the right side of his chest. "I was attacked in the Sol Mountains and would have died if not for the intervention of the one I seek. And the war I speak of? It is creeping in the shadows here in the Southlands while it rages in the Northlands. The Wall of Crossroads cannot protect you forever. Not from the enemy I know. This enemy sent an assassin to kill me so that I would not reach a great hero that roams in the mists and dark forests. I seek Bane Arlis, Daylord and High King of Terra, so that I may bring him home to get rid of the great evil that would seek to consume us all."

The mention of Bane's name sent everyone to whispering and talking. Gyr listened carefully to each word, seeking any concrete evidence of Bane's presence or location.

"Bane Arlis has not been seen since my grandfather's grandfather's childhood. If he lives, he walks this land unseen," a tall man with a white beard and head of hair. He had a golden pendent hanging from his neck and carried himself with great importance.

Gyr turned to face the man he assumed had to be the mayor of Garhune. "The earth speaks in ways that you cannot hear. Ways that you refuse to hear. Bane came to my aid in the Sol Mountains. I believe this with all my heart and being. He may be unseen but he is here with us. Watching and keeping us safe. And he certainly would not have insulted Charon as you have."

The mayor paused and held his hands in front of him. "Does the earth tell you that the man named Charon is worthy of our trust and respect?"

"He is worthy of mine and I have not known him as long as Garhune has. Whatever you think to blame him for, he is blameless. Like I told your people, there is a war coming and soon, it will spill over the Wall of Crossroads. The Southlands is defenseless unless you accept help from people like Bane and Charon," Gyr growled.

"So you want us to pretend like Charon is not an abomination, that Bane is a living legend who walks as the eternal guardian, and that there is a war coming. I see nothing in your claims that is worth risking my people. I deal in facts, not fantasies," the mayor replied.

Gyr shoved his face close to the white haired man's face. He growled. "Do you fancy death sooner than the eternal laws of the Spirit World dictates? I had spent most of the night thinking of the gravest curses that I could throw at you for your ignorance of the Truth. Yes, the Immortal Truth which I know that all of Terra has heard of. In the days following its writing, a copy was brought south to Arken and sits there to this day. Now tell me. Why do you bear such hate for Charon?"

The mayor swallowed his breath but kept a stern expression on his face. "Because of his alleged father. I know that he is half Shadowborn and only one Shadowborn has ever been seen in the Southlands. Wherever that nameless Shadowborn has walked, fear and despair follow. His spawn is a beacon for the father to come home, seeking his blood. We may live under the shadow of your Wall but none of us feel safer. Those of Immortal blood have been nothing but trouble. Only the Daylord has been kind to the Mortal people. We pray that he will come to rid us of such troubles."

A nameless Shadowborn? This immediately set Gyr's thoughts to racing. He glanced over his shoulder at Charon before quickly returning his attention to the mayor. "A beacon for evil you say? Did you ever once think that maybe keeping a man of Immortal blood around would bring Bane to you too? Perhaps that is why Bane has not come to heal your hurts. You have insulted him by shunning Charon for no other reason than an assumption that has not been proven."

The mayor looked over at Charon with a renewed sense of curiosity. Charon only pulled the hood further over his face. Others now shared the same curiosity. "Gryphon, may I speak to you in private?"

"Now you want to speak to me in a manner befitting our respective stations? After you have insulted me and my friend? No! You will speak to me plainly. Right here. Right now." Gyr adamantly said.

"Fine, Gryphon. The Shadowborn I speak of is mad and uncontrollable. In the days of my grandfather, Garhune was attacked by this Shadowborn for no reason. Many were killed and those that survived passed on the painful memories of that night. My people trust no one touched by him. I have also heard of this war you speak of. Every time this Shadowborn has attacked, he speaks very few words but he always says this: Kaiser is coming. There is no escape," the mayor described in a low hissing voice.

It was a small relief to Gyr that the Mortals were not completely unaware of the goings on of the world. He squared his shoulders and shuffled his wings.

"If you will not trust Charon then trust me. I have looked into his eyes and I can see that he desires nothing but knowledge. He fears the Northlands as you do but that he is strong enough to help defend Garhune from another attack," Gyr explained. He bobbed his head once. "But I need to find Bane my king. My people need him home to fight this war so that the Southlands and all of Terra can be at peace."

It took a long time for the white haired mayor to answer. He let out a deep breath. "He was last seen in Sawn a little over two hundred and fifty years ago, disappearing into the mists east of the city. Some say he was hunting the Shadowborn I told you about. Others say he walked away, haunted by something or someone he saw. All I know is that he has not been seen or heard from since."

Gyr was a bit disheartened by what the mayor had told him. An insane Shadowborn wandering the Southlands unchecked and mounting attacks against innocent people. Bane literally disappearing into memory. Charon was nothing more than the target of the people's anger and fear from something that preceded his birth. It was all very confusing to him. Either way, his direction laid south.

"I will not linger in Garhune any longer. I hope to return to a town in sight of the Wall of Crossroads more accepting of those that had no control over what their father did. Perhaps then we can renew a proper relationship between the Northlands and the Southlands," Gyr said before turning around.

Charon was grateful when Gyr started walking towards the main road out of town. The people of the town had been completely silent and had stared at him while the Gryphon was talking to the mayor. Gyr strode forward a few more paces before stopping and raising his wings.

"Is your travel pack secured?" Gyr asked as he waited for Charon to catch up. Charon jogged to his side and nodded. "Then hang on tight."

In a rush of motion, Gyr slipped under Charon and flipped him onto his back. He rocketed into the sky, pumping hard with his wings. Charon wrapped his arms around Gyr's neck, his head swimming.

"Can we just walk?" Charon cried out over the rush of air.

"We need to put Garhune behind us as quickly as possible. They have been poisoned by their own thoughts and need to heal without lingering and walking into the distance. Now which way to Sawn?"

*****

CONSUMED BY MEMORY

Kaiser's mind was an endless field of pulsating energy, some areas dark and others blinding and bright. The energy moved in streams. He could see everything that he wished to see. All of memories played out before him, flashing in and out as he scanned through them one by one. His childhood rushed by as he watched himself grow into a man. He sneered at his childish stupidity and beliefs. The ignorant innocence and senseless lack of desire for freedom. Kaiser wanted to yell at his younger self to open his eyes and see the world for what it really is. The energy streams around him turned blood red in response. They swirled around him faster and faster until they suddenly disappeared. He was plunged into absolute darkness.

A scream of rage cut across the silence, soft and low at first before building into a blast of sound. It brought with it explosions of rainbow colored energy. It felt as if his mind was shaking violently. He felt his soul ripping from his body. He quickly pulled it back in to protect it from the force. As soon as he felt his soul close to him, it was quickly rushed away into the most horrible memory imaginable.

It was the worst memory that Kaiser could have ever had in his eleven hundred years. It was one he always shoved into the depths of his mind and yet it would rise up to haunt him. It would tear at him, ripping his essence to shreds at every waking moment. He snarled with anger, the energy rushing by him flashing a deep red. The energy sparked with black bolts that reaching out for him.

His throat throbbed with burning pain and his back felt like it was on fire. Each surge of pain transformed the memory, making it clearer to see. He tried to shut his eyes in an attempt to shut the memory off but it was still there.

The memory consumed him utterly, bringing him back to that terrible time. Kaiser fought with every ounce of his being to free himself for he did not want to die again. Every struggle, every thought of resistance made the memory's hold on him even tighter. He knew that he had to escape but he couldn't. He just could not anymore. He was now trapped inside of it.

His throat was ripped open and all warmth left him yet he still tried to scream. Tears were in his eyes, the pain going deeper than his wounds. He gasped for breath only to gargle a fountain of blood and choke on it. He flung himself at his foe with what little strength remained, tearing his right arm in the process. He felt himself falling down a dark tunnel, falling away from the light. He remembered screaming until his heart burst in his chest. His strength returned to him the further he got away from the light. It became greater and greater, burning through every fiber of his being.

The strength was an explosive rage that could not be contained. It commanded him to fight back and fight back hard. It told him to resist all sense of containment and that he must break free no matter what. He thrashed and fired his Spirit energy uncontrollably in all directions. The spiraling world around him shook. It only made him angrier. He ripped anything that resisted him into shreds with his bare hands. He was rage incarnate and nothing was going to stop him.

The world around him was frightened. What had just happened? What force had entered their world, a force not seen since a much darker time when all was new and vulnerable? They had to get rid of it. They had to stop it before it tore down the very foundations of the world. They did the only thing they thought they could. A shadow struck Kaiser across the back, slashing at his being. The moment the shadow pulled back, Kaiser felt a rushing sensation.

Waking up had been an absolute nightmare. He was whole and yet he was broken inside. But he had learned a powerful lesson: trust no one. His heart hardened and iced over. His mind sharpened into a powerful weapon. Slowly, Kaiser felt himself being released by the terrible memory into the energy filled blackness of his mind. The slow moving streams had returned and everything was calm. He no longer felt pain or heart. Nothing at all. He just was.

Kaiser opened his eyes. Sweat had beaded on his brow and

dripped down his face. His eyes hurt and his throat was cracked. Nothing new or unexpected. The deep forays of concentration into the depths of his mind were always exhausting events that drained every bit of the stolen Spirit energy. He never dared to use his own for he viewed it as a waste. Perhaps using another's Spirit energy for his own ends made his mental journey more difficult. He did not care. He found too much joy from taking the Spirit energy. It was almost as much fun as taking a life. He laid back on the stone floor, the coolness a comforting sensation to his bare back. He laid his arms over his head and stretched out his legs. His limbs were stiff from sitting for so long.

The room had changed very little since Kaiser had claimed it for his own from the Shadow Council. His ebony wood chair remained against the wall, a black velvet cushion upon its seat. He did however add a footstool that was made in a similar fashion. All windows were filled in with stone and mortar. The only light source was a trio of candles that Kaiser had brought. They flickered nearby, half melted by the flames.

He laid on the floor for a long time, breathing deeply and slowly. The ceiling provided no distraction from his thoughts and he growled. He thought about carving an angry design, ready to trace it with a fire licked finger. Effort, he reminded himself. He sighed deeply and put his hands behind his head, feeling his matted black hair. Out of reflex, he briefly reached with his left hand to stroke his throat. He found the familiar scar hot but cooling quickly. His right arm still felt sore. He closed his eyes again.

The immense depths of his mind twisted and swirled at various speeds. It was if he never lost sight of his surroundings when his eyes closed. He was hyper aware of everything at all times. To a simpler person, it would have driven them insane but he was nothing of the sort. Kaiser made sure that he could never be blind of the world and was on constant alert. It had taken centuries of practice to get to this point. Every dawn and dusk, he would delve into his mind, facing his darkest memory to make himself stronger. He took several deep breaths, releasing them slowly. With each breath, his mind grew calmer until everything flowed in a steady rhythm.

His mental training done, now Kaiser turned to his physical training. Despite his hate of it during his youth, he realized the importance of it now. Kaiser did not have a heavy muscular physique but every inch of his tall frame was compact with muscle. Even after a thousand years, he was as fast as lightning and as strong as thunder. He pushed himself off of the floor, sitting up and leaning forward. He ran his fingers through his hair and scratched at his straggly beard. He stroked his jaw wondering if he should shave it off. Laughing softly, he pushed the thought away and got to his feet.

Kaiser stretched his back by reaching for the ceiling and then bending over to touch his toes. He rotated his spine by moving side to side. He shook his arms and rolled his neck, cracking the vertebrae. Now, his body felt loose and ready to train. He stepped over to his ebony chair, tossing back his bed jacket to reveal a pair of thin curved swords. The swords were sheathed in black leather. Kaiser kept his eyes on the swords as he wrapped his hands and wrists with strips of white cloth. Once he was done, he swiftly ripped the swords free and stepped back, spinning them slowly.

The swords had been buried in a trunk that he had stowed away in a closet. The trunk contained an assortment of mementos from his early days in Umbra. Normally, the trunk lay forgotten and unwanted yet Kaiser could not bring himself to get rid of it when he did bother to remember it. When he did finally decide to dig through the contents, he found the truck covered with a thick layer of dust and several cobwebs stretching across the outside. He pushed past everything else in the trunk to pull out his old combat swords. Even though it had been many years since he last held them, the fit of the hilt to his hand was perfect. The comfort gave him a renewed sense of strength.

Kaiser slowly strode around the room in a circle, spinning and striking with the swords in mock play. The weapons felt like extensions of his being. He smiled as he held up the left sword in a straight line. He looked down his arm and the blade to the very tip. The sword glinted in the low light and Kaiser could see the face of the last person he killed with the weapon. A part of him was pleased to see the horrified expression and the wordless scream. Yes, these weapons of death would taste blood again.

"You thought that you had to end me to get rid of the embarrassment you had as a father. Well look at me now. Knocking on the door of greatness. But a son has to ask: what secrets did you keep for your mighty Shadowlord?" Kaiser mused out loud. He began to slowly move through a series of poses and combat patterns. He paused to chuckle softly. "You were his great Commander, defender of Umbra and son of the Anu line. You were proud and yet subdued. Deadly but also gentle and kind. The perfect balance."

Kaiser turned towards the trio of candles, smirking. The light illuminated his face in a frightening way. He puffed once, his breath taking command of the miniscule flames. The fire rose up like a wild inferno, red hot and bright. In it, he saw the same face that he had seen in his sword.

"Look into my eyes! Look at what you have created!" Kaiser challenged the face in the fire. "This is the face of a true son of Begin Anu, one who does not hide and submit himself to others!"

Kaiser slashed his swords in a decapitating motion, extinguishing the flames. He hung there in the darkness, breathing heavily. Anyone else would have been uncomfortable but Kaiser embraced the shadows. They did not blind him or leave him defenseless. He was in his element. And yet he was reminded of his failure to cross the Shadow Mirror of Silver. The flames roared back to life to replay the scene. Kaiser gritted his teeth as he was forced to watch. He knew the power of Shadow Mirrors inside and out! Even if someone else had raised the Mirror, he knew how to break them! Kaiser growled, baring his teeth like he was a rabid wolf.

It was as if the memory was insulting him, reminding him of his weakness and inability to break the Mirror. Kaiser slashed at the fire, splitting the flames. The flames quickly reformed. Kaiser cut again, this time using both swords. The fire reacted with the same result.

"I will break the Mirror of Silver! I will raze it to the ground! I will kill Sage Silvanus! I will win!" Kaiser roared as he furiously tore at the fire.

The fire finally retreated back into the trio of candles, the light flickering. Kaiser watched for a moment before snorting. "You cannot hide forever, Sage. Every Shadow Mirror has a weakness and I will find yours."

FANNING THE FLAMES

Kaiser strode through the long hallway towards his private quarters, ignoring the portraits of past Lord's Chancellors. It angered him how his ancestor left that legacy behind, submitting himself to the Silvanus family and retiring to Umbra. He was sure that in the old laws it stated that should the Silvanus family fail, the crown would pass to Adonis Anu and his descendants. Was that true or was it just a lie? Would the Silvanus family had really turned their throne over to a Farlander bloodline? Everyone always spoke of how Begin Anu refused to rule in the Spiritlands. Even Rache had said this to him on several occasions. But why? He was a Farlander, a being of greater power than the Spiritborn. Kaiser sneered at the thought. Ruling to him was more than lording over subjects and telling them what to do and how to act. It was about ordering the world so that it would last for an eternity.

He looked up to see the tallest and oldest of his three courtesans leaning back against the door to his quarters. Her long black hair was draped over her shoulders in loose waves. A thin silk bed cloak had fallen open revealing her slim body. She was still wearing her nightdress, a fine piece of black silk with silver threaded flowers stitched near the hem. Her skin was milky white and soft. She turned her head to look at Kaiser.

"Where are Raye and Zee?" Kaiser asked as he stopped. He

put his hands against the door, pinning her beneath him. He bent in to smell her neck.

Cora pushed up a wax sealed letter between their faces before he could kiss her lips. "I sent them away for breakfast when this was handed to me to give to you."

Kaiser frowned at the interrupted moment and snatched the letter from her hand. He stepped back and quickly broke the wax seal. His eyes quickly scanned the inked lines. "It is a notice from the Shadow Council. Wonder what was so important to deliver a message so early in the morning and when it is out of session?"

"Would it be best to read such a note in private?" Cora suggested.

Kaiser scoffed as his eyes scanned the letter again. "If anyone seeks to disturb me and my peace, I will simply snap their necks. I may not have a big muscular frame but I am deceptively strong."

"Murder in the capital? Sounds dangerous and intriguing," Cora commented as she pulled her bed cloak closed. She tied the belt around her waist. "Perhaps the Council thinks there has been too much of it as of late. Maybe they finally decided to get off their asses and notice what is actually going on?"

Kaiser burst out laughing. "I mean, how many cities do I have to destroy and how many people do I have to kill to get noticed around here? It took them only a thousand years. It took my father far less than that to notice my true nature."

Cora chuckled softly as she crossed her arms. She leaned lightly on her feet, subtly shifting her weight back and forth. "Still this note seems rather odd. Was the Council not brave enough to send for you in person? I think the action they chose shows that they are afraid. Already you have asserted your domination over them." She snaked in close, teasing him with kisses. Kaiser pressed a hand on her chest to get her to stop.

"I am sorry, my dear lady. As true as your words are, that is not how the Shadow Council actually works. In all my years as a council member, I never lowered myself to delivering my own messages. I will say my handwriting is far better than this scribble." Kaiser tapped Cora's forehead with the paper.

She made an attempt to take the paper to no avail. She pouted and Kaiser chuckled softly. "Who do you think wrote the letter?"

"By this scratchy line of words, I would say Teralin. He has never been one for elegance or subtly. Much like Rokar. But without a Lord's Regent or Shadowlord, Teralin and the other councilors have decided to become bold in Rokar's absence," Kaiser stated once he folded the letter. "I have been summoned to an emergency meeting."

Cora took the letter from Kaiser and stepped to the side so he could open the door. She followed him inside, dropping the letter onto a pile of previous messages. She glanced down at the pile of paper. "Should we burn these?"

Kaiser waved her off as he pulled off his bed cloak and threw it over the back of a reading chair. He then stepped over to the windows and threw open the curtains, letting sunlight pour into the room. "I care nothing for the whims of the Council even when Rokar was still a part of it. They have become an annoyance to me."

"Then they are truly bold to summon you," Cora said as she sat in the reading chair. She continued to watch Kaiser carefully. "Your back is red again. Shall I massage it for you?"

Kaiser paused to consider the sight of his red marked skin. She was not old enough or smart enough to recognize the specific pattern of scars. He smirked. "Maybe later, my dear. I must prepare for council."

Cora stretched out her long legs, resting her feet on the soft foot stool. She gripped the armrests and tapped her toes together. "What is the point of a Shadow Council when there is no Shadowlord to summon them? I was taught that only he could get them together out of session."

"I am sure it is a decision they fought over for many weeks. Calling a council without the Shadowlord is disrespectful and threatens the balance of power. It would be as if they claimed his right to govern as they saw fit for themselves. That is not how the Shadowborn do things here," Kaiser explained as he stood before a window. "But surely rumors have reached them that have caused them enough concern to challenge that."

"Like Rokar spreading lies about you?" Cora asked as she glanced over at him.

"At this point, it does not matter. I will deal with them soon enough," Kaiser said. He took in a deep breath and released it slowly. "The system they believe in is heavily flawed. It would be best to cleanse it and wipe the slate clean."

Cora got up from her seat and stepped over to Kaiser. She wrapped her arms around his neck, resting her chin on his left shoulder. "Then you should kill them all and set up your own council."

Kaiser chuckled softly as he reached up and stroked her intertwined hands. They stood together in silence for a long time. Kaiser eventually unlocked Cora's hands and pulled them apart. She frowned cutely as her arms dropped to her sides. He put a finger under her chin. She made to bite at it when he pulled away.

"I like the way you think, Cora, but I must disagree with some of what you said. I do not need a council. Not yet at least," Kaiser stated as he turned his back. He walked to the left and entered a washroom, leaving Cora outside.

Inside, Cora could hear the sound of running water. After a while, Kaiser was whistling a tune that she did not recognize but it sounded happy. It was several long minutes before he came back out, his skin glistening with moisture. She handed him a wash towel and he began to dry his hair. She followed him into the bedroom and watched him sit down in front of a mirror and vanity table. He handed back the damp towel. Cora then worked to dry his hair and style in the manner that she knew he liked.

"What was the song you were whistling?" Cora asked as she combed his black hair.

"Something I used to sing in my youth when the court had a better view of me. Back when I thought that I could have a Silvanus princess for a bride," Kaiser mused.

"You mean the Princess Mali?" Cora asked as she ran her fingers through his hair. She combed back the mess in even strokes.

Kaiser's mind drifted briefly to his early memories of Mali, the proud daughter of Sin Silvanus. He remembered how blindly he thought of her grace and beauty. She was considered the greatest beauty in the land with her long midnight hair and bright silver eyes. Many thought her a worthy queen in the making though she refused any but a Shadowborn to be her husband. Of course as the daughter of a reigning Shadowlord, her husband would have to be great and worthy in his own right. Kaiser had thought himself both of those things and he wanted her badly. But he had failed to see how the fall of his house from power in Umbra had made him look. Some had sympathy for the deaths of his family but many suspected him of dark deeds and thoughts.

"Her father was a fool to deny me. He could have saved his family from destruction had he accepted my proposal. It is too late now," Kaiser gritted his teeth.

"If he had then Ryder Coba would have never existed," Cora said as she brought him a hand mirror.

"Well we cannot turn back time. We can only continue on looking forward into what will be instead of wondering what if," Kaiser stated. He nodded in approval at her work. "Though I wonder what the world would have been like."

Cora did not say it but she decided how what had happened was in the world's best interests. She had not been deaf to the whisperings of the Shadowborn in regards to Ryder. Many brave enough to think so believed him to be Shadow Night's spiritual heir and the rightful Shadowlord. A vision of salvation from something darker. That maybe the Spirits engineered the chain of events that had played out. It was enough to give her hope.

"I may not be able to read your mind but I can tell what you are thinking. You are thinking of something that gives you hope. Why?" Kaiser asked firmly.

"I was just thinking of the world you promised to give me. I can barely contain my excitement for your success," Cora answered with a coy smile. She laid a hand on his shoulder. "To see you rise to greatness gives me the hope I think of."

Kaiser smiled in response. "Ah, a fine twisting mess of flattery. Be glad that I do not feel up to unraveling the puzzle of your words." He stared into the mirror, studying the lines on his face. "But where does that leave the young Onyx Silvanus? He is a child pretending to be a man. I do not have room for him in my golden future nor do I want him there."

"You could order an assassin to kill him," Cora suggested. She stepped back as Kaiser stood up.

"I could but he is not even worth the honor of assassination. He will simply be collateral damage. Maybe I will give a prize to the soul that kills him and brings me his head," Kaiser stated with a shrug. He stood up and faced her, lifting one eyebrow in question. He snickered when he saw Cora shiver and look away.

"Then what of Ryder?" Cora asked as she handed Kaiser a white linen shirt. She was careful not to make eye contact.

Kaiser pulled it on after putting on a fresh pair of trousers and boots. "I have orchestrated his life in every way since I learned of my daughter's condition. I have shaped him into the man he is today. The last of the great Silvanus sons all thanks to me. The prize of Sin's denial."

"The last of your line as well," Cora said, holding a richly decorated jacket in her hands.

He waved off the item and picked up a plain black coat. "That jacket is too tacky and gaudy. I do not care to be covered in jewels from head to toe."

Cora put the jacket away in the closet and came out holding a chain made of silver. The silver had been shaped into a pair of owl wings holding a creamy white moonstone. She helped Kaiser to set it around his shoulders. She picked and pulled at it to make sure it was straight.

"I have always admired the fact that you do not dress like many here at court. Simple and dignified," she smiled sweetly. "You do not need to drape yourself in cloth of silver to show that you are noble and mighty."

"You are too sweet, my dear," Kaiser said, holding her

chin. He then kissed her lightly on the lips. "Do you think to make yourself my queen?"

Cora startled at the question and stammered for an answer. Kaiser chuckled at her confusion, stepping past her to pick up his sword belt. He held the weapons for a moment, considering if he should walk into council fully armed with his old swords. He scoffed. Such weapons would be superfluous when he could slay a man so easily. He did not want the council to know his intentions until the very end of the game.

RED COUNCIL

The careful, calculating gaze of Kaiser's eyes swept over the dimly lit council room, counting the number of chairs that surrounded a large rectangular table. He lightly tapped the top of each chair's back with his slim fingers before turning to face the ornate seat at the head of the table. He smiled, revealing a flash of white teeth. With the open door of the council room behind him, the sunlight poured in, throwing his shadow to the ornate seat where the Lord of the Shadowborn usually sat. Where he would sit. He wrapped his hands around the edge of the Lord's Regent's chair that sat across the table from the Lord of the Shadowborn's chair.

"Too bad, Zoras. You are not here to witness my moment of triumph," Kaiser mocked out loud before tossing the chair to the right. It hit the stone wall and cracked into several jagged pieces of wood, the pieces held together by the cloth of the cushion. "For I do not need a Lord's Regent."

He moved to go sit at the head of the table. He immediately hated how hard the cushion was and resigned himself to stretch his legs, propping his feet up on the table. The heels of his boots clicked together.

As soon as Kaiser settled himself in his new seat, seven councilors dressed in robes of black, crimson, and silver wandered into the room. They mumbled amongst themselves as they took their respective seats, eyeing Kaiser with disgust at his lack of decorum. They especially did not like the fact that Kaiser was seated in the Lord's chair.

"Good morning, gentlemen! Isn't this a fine day to make history?" Kaiser greeted. "I see that we have a few council members missing."

"This is an emergency meeting, Master Adonis, regarding your conduct and some of us are so disgusted by the rumors that they could not bear to be in the same room as you," Master Teralin said as he glared at him. He sneered at the sight of Kaiser's feet on the table.

Master Teralin was somewhat portly man with the edges of hard muscle in his shoulders and limbs. He was the big and burly Master of Justice and one of Zoras Rokar's allies. Kaiser glanced over at the Master of Trade and the Master of Roads, two men who had been afraid of him before but now sat with a renewed sense of strength. Kaiser frowned. They were encouraged by something unknown to him.

"And what of my conduct?" Kaiser growled. He smirked when he saw the two men shuddered.

Teralin pulled out a stack of papers covered in writing. He picked up the first sheet. "Where do I begin or would you prefer to own up to what you have done?"

Kaiser swung his legs off of the table and pulled his seat forward. He set his elbows on the table and rested his head in his hands. He lifted an eyebrow.

"Some of the supposed acts," Teralin started to say.

"You see? Supposed! What evidence do you have if all you have to present is a pile of papers filled with rumors and insults to my name?" Kaiser stated as he sat up straight. "I am not blind to the fact that there are those that hate me and my proximity to the throne but I only do as the Shadowlord commands. If he orders me to be at his side, I will not refuse him."

"Yes. There are those that hate you. Most of Cross cannot stand the sight of you," Teralin snapped. He crumbled up the sheet of paper in his hand. The other councilors nodded in agreement though they did not dare to say anything more.

Kaiser leaned back in his seat, resting his hands on the armrests. "Is it hate or jealousy, Master Teralin? Anger that I survived the fall of my house?" Kaiser paused to laugh softly to himself. "Why should the house of Adonis be considered fallen and lost to the shadows of time? It is the house of Begin Anu's son, his blood running through my veins as surely as it did his. Don't look surprised that you and your ancestors have forgotten that fact. I think it rather obvious that the origin of my surname comes from the first name of my ancestor. By the heavens, the world has grown fat, idle, and stupid."

Teralin and the others stammered for a response. They

looked back and forth amongst each other as if to silently encourage anyone brave enough to speak. Eyes kept darting over to Teralin who lingered with his lips parted. Kaiser waved his finger in a mocking manner.

"I am old, Teralin. In my long lifetime, I have acquired a vast wealth of knowledge of both the good and the bad in this world. I understand a great many things. This supposed hate you speak of? I do not understand it at all. Is it because of distrust over my knowledge and the expanse of my aged mind? Or is it fear over the fact that I could crush you and everyone within a thousand leagues with my command of Spirit energy?"

The seeds of doubt were being sewn but Teralin shook his head to avoid being taken by them. He took the remaining pile of paper and slapped it right in front of Kaiser. "Read this then and see the answer for yourself."

Kaiser picked up the top sheet and began reading. His eyes skimmed the lines quickly before he set it back down. He pressed a finger to the center and set the papers on fire. The sudden flame shocked the seven councilors and they leaned back from the brightness.

"These words mean nothing to me so why should I waste my time reading them?" Kaiser coldly asked. The papers smoldered before him, quickly turning to ash.

"You should have a care to what others say if you wish to continue in service to the Shadowlord," Teralin snarled.

"Aku is dead so I see no reason to care," Kaiser fired back.

The revelation that their beloved Shadowlord came as a complete shock and at least three of the councilors started crying. Even Teralin was rendered speechless, unable to find the words. His mouth gaped open.

"Slain by his son near on three months ago upon the Heights and by the command of the royal bastard," Kaiser stated with apathy. "Terrible things happen when the council decides to take a vacation away from their precious Lord. In these times, you must always be ready. Always on alert for any danger."

"And you did not think to tell us?" Teralin managed to ask as he tried to catch his breath.

Kaiser shrugged before he stood up. "I am still shocked myself that a son would kill his father under the command of a man who would surely kill him to open the path to the throne."

"Ryder Coba is noble and great. He would never do such a thing and I have a hard time believing that Onyx would kill his own father," the Master of Trade exclaimed. Kaiser shot him an angry glare and he immediately silenced, sinking into his seat.

"The royal bastard may be a bastard but he has never

shown us such evil tendencies. Only poor decisions and the fate of his illegitimate birth to a man unfit to rule," Teralin said, finding some strength.

Kaiser started to walk around the table, dragging his hand over the backs of the chairs. Each of the councilors shuddered when he drew near. They breathed a sigh of relief when he stepped away. Kaiser made his way to the open end of the table where the Lord's Regent's chair once stood.

"He may yet. He is of my blood after all so who knows what he will really be like in the coming years," Kaiser said. He was beginning to like the shock in their eyes.

Again, another revelation shook the seven men and women. Teralin shot out of his seat, the chair falling backwards to the floor. He pointed accusingly at Kaiser. "Enough of your lies. It's time that you started telling the truth."

Kaiser continued the path back to his original seat, stopping behind the Master of Trade's seat. He set his hands on the councilor's shoulders. "What? Is it so impossible to believe that I, Kaiser Adonis, fathered a daughter that took the Lord Akakios' heart and bore him a son? That my blood could sit on the beloved throne of our people? How impossible of a thought! I am sure you are thinking what woman would want to come to my bed? Rest assured, that very woman is still alive and in hiding. But not for long."

Everyone gulped when Kaiser snapped the Master of Trade's neck. The now dead Master fell face forward, his forehead cracking on the hard table. Blood slowly spread out into a small pool. Kaiser bent down next to the body. "He is going to have the most awful headache when he wakes up."

The Master of Homeland turned to the side and threw up, her carefully coiffed hair falling loose. She could not bear to look at the body lying next to her seat. Kaiser made to pull back her hand and she slapped him away. Tears streamed down her face. Kaiser smiled back at her before he smashed her head into the table, cracking it open. He wiped his head on the back of her elaborate dress. The body slumped to the side and slid free of the table. The table had been crushed from the force and everyone knew that she was dead.

The wiry Master of Roads leaped up from his seat and ran for the open door. Kaiser lifted his left hand and the door slammed shut, locking with a twitch of a finger. He smirked with delight as he watched the councilor struggle to open the door.

"A lesson to the wise. Never seek to challenge me," Kaiser said before he moved on to the next councilor. "Because this might happen to you."

Kaiser slapped his right hand on the side of the Treasurer's head. Lightning flashed brightly as Kaiser initiated Shadow Shock. The Treasurer began to convulse and blood spewed from his mouth. His eyes then exploded with a loud pop. Kaiser released his grip and the body slid down in the chair. He shook the gore from his hand with a look of disgust.

The Master of Roads continued to struggle and pull at the door as Kaiser drew close. He could not even breathe a sigh of relief when Kaiser stopped coming towards him. He renewed his battle to pull open the door to his freedom. He swallowed bile and vomit when Kaiser struck again.

"You murderous," the Master of Shadowborn Affairs squeaked as Kaiser had his arm pressing tightly on her small throat. He pinned her to the back of her chair.

"Go ahead and say it," Kaiser snickered in her ear in a low and dangerous voice. He pressed down harder until her windpipe cracked. He brought his lips in closer. "Tell them how the Shadow Council let a monster into their midst."

By this time, it was clear that Kaiser was going to kill them all. Four councilors were dead, slumped over in their chairs. Teralin dragged the Master of Education from her seat and pulled her to the far corner away from Kaiser.

"Shadow Slide out of here and warn Zoras as fast as you can," Teralin whispered under his breath, praying that Kaiser could not hear him. The Shadowborn woman nodded. She disappeared in an instant in what seemed like she was escaping.

Kaiser knew from the start what was happening and stomped his foot on the ground. The woman was thrown out of Shadow Slide and crashed into the Master of Roads. The two fell in a tangle of cloth and limbs. Kaiser walked over to them, looking down at the pair with an evil grin on his face.

"Go ahead. Shadow Slide out of here. No matter where you go, I will hunt you down and kill you," Kaiser warned. He straightened up, throwing his shoulders back. "Do not think that I have forgotten you, Teralin. You have the same offer of escape but do not take too long to decide. I am not feeling very patient today."

Kaiser slammed his foot down on the Master of Road's head, crushing his skull. Brain matter and blood splashed on the Master of Education's face. She shrieked with fear as Kaiser turned to look down at her.

"I never did like you," Kaiser stated. He locked eyes with her. She started to tremble violently, her body no longer under her control. She convulsed and gasped for breath, blood vessels swelling from the invisible pressure. Her eyes rolled back into her head just as blood began to pour from her mouth. She gurgled and choked on the blood before falling still.

Teralin slipped into Shadow Slide as soon as Kaiser turned his back to him. He sped around in the room in a wide circle, aiming for the door. What he did not realize was that Kaiser was aware of him the entire time. As soon as he reached the door, Kaiser unleashed a devastating blast of Spirit energy. The door flew open and shattered while Teralin was torn apart into a red cloud of gore. It rained blood as Kaiser walked through the opening and descended the stairs. The people in the streets immediately fell to their knees in a bow of submission. They kept their foreheads pressed to the ground as Kaiser passed them, too afraid to look up into his fierce eyes.

He paused by one shivering guard and looked down. "The Shadow Council has been suspended indefinitely."

*****

RYDER'S TEST

"Hey, wake up."

Onyx grumbled as he shoved his face into the pillow. He pulled his legs up and tried to appear small. A heavy hand shook his right shoulder. He groaned again and untangled an arm to slap the hand away. His effort was weak and he rolled over on to his back. He squinted his eyes when a bright light shined in his face.

"Go away," Onyx mumbled as he rubbed his forehead. He brushed his bangs away.

"Come on and get out of bed," Ryder said, holding a small flame over his open hand. It illuminated his face but left the rest of him in shadow.

"Are we under attack?" Onyx asked. As soon as he asked the question, it did not make sense. If the base was under attack, Ryder would not have been so calm and polite in waking him. But why was he waking him up so early? It was not even close to dawn by his reckoning.

Ryder sat back on the edge of the bed. He wafted his flame wielding hand around to shrink it. The light dimmed and Onyx blinked several times. He rubbed his eyes before he sat up.

"No, we are not under attack," Ryder chuckled. "It is time for your first evaluation under my tutelage."

Onyx twisted his face in confusion. He had never had a test from any of his previous trainers at such an hour. They had always let him sleep. Ryder's earlier comments about his former teachers roared back into his head. Despite his status as a student, he was the heir to the throne and needed to be whole and well at all times. They did not or would not treat him as a regular student, afraid of the Shadowlord's wrath. Ryder was going to be a different kind of teacher. Part of him was worried and the other part was excited. He needed a firm and knowledgeable teacher like his cousin. Right now however, Onyx just wanted to go back to bed and sleep until the sun rose.

"Do you even sleep? It's so early," Onyx said, still trying to rub the sleep from his eyes.

"When I can get it. The war keeps me busy and Haven keeps me awake at times," Ryder replied.

Onyx's eyes opened wide at Ryder's implication of his love life. Ryder laughed at his horrified expression and slapped his shoulder.

"It's not what you are thinking. Not all the time at least," Ryder stated with a big smile. "She tends to snore when she has had a little ale. She normally doesn't drink but we were celebrating your birthday after all last night."

The birthday celebration had been an enjoyable one where everyone at the base came to wish him well. A fine meal had been served and Myra had made a cake for him. Onyx's mouth watered as he remembered the fresh wild berry flavor. He had even gotten to try his first real mug of ale courtesy of Ryder. The taste was rather sour to him and he did not much like it. Donovan and Hayden had refrained from drinking but Hayden did tell him that he would get used to the taste of ale. The Saber Captain also added that he preferred Shadowborn wine for its rustic and fruity flavor.

"You must have had a whole barrel by yourself," Onyx stated, remembering how much Ryder had drank.

"I have a high tolerance. Sorry for leaving early but a little ale makes my lady amorous," Ryder shrugged. He chuckled softly.

"When is your birthday?" Onyx asked as he swung his legs over to the side, putting his feet on the floor. The stone was cold to the touch and he drew his feet back.

"All Spirits Day. Same day as Kaiser," Ryder answered. "I'll be two hundred and fifty one in two months."

It was still strange that Ryder was as old as he was. Even then, Onyx was now nineteen years old and had celebrated his first birthday without his father. It did make him sad but he was glad for the company of Ryder and the others. Ryder's grandmother provided him with a motherly figure to admire and look up to. She also loved telling stories, good, bad, and embarrassing ones of Ryder, which amused Onyx.

"Now get dressed. I'll be waiting for you outside," Ryder said, slapping Onyx's knee.

Onyx quickly pulled on a pair of black wool pants. He stumbled and fell against the bed, bruising his right knee. He slid to the floor to put on his leather boots. He rolled to the side and jumped up to his feet. In one swift move, he grabbed a white linen shirt and a belt from a nearby chair, putting them on. He smoothed down his hair and tied it back with a small strip of cloth. For a split second, he contemplated whether or not he would need a sword. The royal blade had been refitted with a new hilt though it had yet to mold to his grip. Certainly his cousin was capable of defending him from danger.

No! That was not the point of his training. He had to be able to defend himself and others if called to for his more powerful cousin would not always be there. With that thought, Onyx attached the sheathed sword to his belt. He made sure to move quietly away from his room and out to the open yard of the base. Ryder was waiting, dressed in a similar manner as Onyx but his shirt sleeves had been ripped off. His cousin certainly seemed proud of his physique. Ryder had his twin swords strapped across his back.

"Remember what I taught you about the specifics of tracking in Shadow Slide and follow me," Ryder said.

It had amazed him how little Sai taught him in regards to Shadow Slide. The old Saber Commander had stressed that Shadow Slide was a way to escape attack and to move quickly. He had only briefly hinted at tracking auras in Shadow Slide but did not dwell on the subject. Ryder had laughed when Onyx related the lesson to him. At first, Onyx was embarrassed that his skill was so paltry but he had dedicated himself to learning from his cousin. Now, he could follow other Shadowborn in Shadow Slide regardless of knowing the area he was in. Focal point, Ryder had called it.

It was not long before Ryder came out of Shadow Slide and Onyx soon followed. They were now in a small clearing before a cave, surrounded by tall pines. He turned about on his feet, looking up at the sea of stars. A light breeze rustled through the tree tops.

"This is the Site of Ascension. It is where our ancestor Shadow Night was named the Shadowlord and leader of his people. It is only fitting that I give your test here," Ryder said as he turned his eyes on Onyx.

Onyx gulped, feeling suddenly unprepared. He wiped the nervous sweat from his brow. "So what do I have to do?"

Ryder took a few steps back and put his hands out to the side. "Your task is simple. Knock me off of my feet by any means necessary. Physical force or Spirit energy. Your choice. I want to see how you use your environment and react to change. Remember, the world is alive and can transform at a moment's notice. It is not static. It will not be the same going to sleep as when it wakes."

"I thought this was going to be a test, not a lesson," Onyx commented.

"Just do as I have asked and you will see."

Under normal circumstances, that seemed like an easy enough request. Onyx rolled his shoulders and shook his arms to loosen the tension in the muscle. He had to remain focused and not let frustration and anger take over. He took in a deep breath and let it out slowly. This was it. This was his moment to prove to both his cousin and to all who had come before him. That he was worthy to be a Silvanus. He looked back at Ryder and pulled out his sword. He was ready.

Onyx rushed forward, jumping into Shadow Slide at the last second to slip under Ryder's feet. He spun up and out of Shadow Slide, swinging his sword. Ryder was prepared and twisted around to counter the strike. Onyx's sword slammed into Ryder's sword with a loud steel clang. In an instant, Onyx shifted the earth beneath him to throw him up into the air. Ryder's sword followed as Onyx flipped over head. Onyx twisted his body in a spiral so that he could land spinning. His left foot hit the ground first and he swung his right foot. At his command, a web of cracks appeared in the earth and shot out towards Ryder.

Ryder smirked before he kicked off into the air. The force of his launch sent a responding quake to dispel Onyx's attack. He landed several feet behind the crashing cracks. He swept his right hand sword in a parallel line to the ground. The broken ground quickly reset, leaving no trace of the damage. Onyx jumped into Shadow Slide again. Instead of charging forward, Onyx rocketed to his right. While in the cloak of his Spirit energy, he sheathed his sword. At the last second, he dove into the ground by Ryder's feet.

He had used a version of this technique before when he fought Iztal. Shadow Quake Line he had called it when he had a chance to mull it over. This time he was going deeper into the ground, utilizing the smallest of shadows to move through the earth. He felt the chill of an underground water source and knew it was time to turn around. Using the pressure of his surroundings, he shot upwards at high speed.

"Good. You are not giving in to the unexpected. You are living in the moment," Ryder mused as he kept his eyes on the ground. He could feel the burst of Spirit energy coming up beneath him and stepped to the side.

Onyx burst through the ground and out of Shadow Slide,

expecting to have knocked Ryder over. He spied Ryder smirking back at him. In a split second decision, Onyx spun and kicked several stones with great force. Ryder reacted in the blink of an eye, swinging and spinning his swords to deflect the stones. One stone the size of a clenched fist shot back at Onyx and hit him hard on the jaw. Onyx cried out in response and forced himself to push through the pain. His jaw throbbed but he could not worry about that.

The momentary pause was all Ryder needed to overwhelm Onyx and put him on the defensive. He rushed forward at high speed, swords held back behind him. Onyx was astounded at Ryder's short distance speed and barely got away before he could strike. Ryder slammed his swords forward, cutting across the back of Onyx's shirt and ripping open the fabric. Onyx squeaked at the cool air on his skin but quickly held his breath. He dove back into the earth and out of reach of the swords. This time, he initiated the same stone pillar raising technique he saw in Crossroads.

Stone pillars shot up out of the ground, one right after the other. Ryder proved nimble enough to avoid being hit by one before leaping up to the top. He bounced from pillar to pillar, counteracting with his own power to send them back into the ground. He kicked particularly hard at the sixth pillar to send off a shockwave. The shockwave threw Onyx from the safety of the earth and sent him sprawling. He slid ten feet before coming to a stop. Before he could move, Ryder was on top of him, swords crossed beneath his chin.

"I failed you," Onyx grumbled, turning away.

"No, you didn't," Ryder said as he sheathed his swords. He offered a hand to help Onyx up. He pulled his younger cousin to his feet. "I gave you a task so that you would focus. I wanted to see how you reacted to conditions changing from what you expected. In our first little fight, you let anger and frustration determine your decisions. This time, you jumped from one plan to the next with very little hesitation. To me, that is improvement."

Onyx brushed the dirt from his knees. "I still feel like I should have done more."

Ryder patted Onyx's shoulder. "You are nineteen. I am two hundred and fifty. I have much more experience than you and a few more tricks in my arsenal than you. I am not training you to be as good as me. That takes years of personal experience and learning. I am teaching you how to think and analyze. I am sure that Sai said Sabers graduate somewhere around age twenty eight. Personally, I would have done things a bit different and ensured a potential Saber's skill before declaring them fit, regardless of their age."

"You never seem to say anything nice or decent about Sai. He really was a good Commander of the Sabers," Onyx commented.

"More that he does not care for me. I thumped him several times in my youth and he never got over a younger Shadowborn beating him in a brawl," Ryder chuckled. "Sai was a good man for at least he taught you some decent morals. Be proud of that."

Onyx sighed deeply. "What does it mean to be a great warrior? How can I be seen on the same level as Shadow Night?"

"It is about your heart. Shadow Night was a leader during a dark time and he did not let that stop him from fighting to protect who he loved," Ryder stated. "You could be the strongest warrior in existence but your life will be empty if you do not have heart and a sound mind. You can only be the best version of you."

It all made sense. Physical strength was not the only power a great fighter had. Onyx knew that though he did not have the same physicality as his cousin, he possessed a heart that was endless. It made him think of how there were times where he wanted to give up but did not. Even if the path was bumpy, he always managed to keep moving forward. He and Ryder both looked to the sky, seeing the coming of the dawn.

THE SPY FROM CROSS

The sky started to turn from a dark purple to a pink orange dawn, the clouds wispy in shape. The stars faded and the moon disappeared. A light breeze rustled the trees and a pine scent filled the air. Ryder breathed in deep, closing his eyes. For a moment, everything was peaceful and pleasant. His eyes then shot open.

"What is it?" Onyx asked, seeing the sudden change.

"Energy surge heading to our location. A strong and fast Shadow Slide," Ryder said in a low voice. "Draw your sword. I will take the first shot from whoever is coming out of Shadow Slide. Should they break free, you will take the second shot."

Onyx pulled out his sword, holding it tight in his right hand. "Is it Kaiser?" he asked with worry.

"I don't think so. If it is, run and don't look back," Ryder warned.

"What about you? Kaiser will kill you," Onyx squeaked. He was intensely worried about who was behind the energy surge.

"Onyx," Ryder said, sounding firm. "In a war, you will eventually have to face your enemy and determine the victor. You cannot run forever nor can you avoid the fight. I ran and look at how it has affected everyone. If this is Kaiser, then let us fight for the throne of our ancestors."

He still was not ready to face Kaiser but he also did not want Ryder to fight him alone. He tried to focus himself and search for the energy surge, remembering Ryder's lessons. His nerves were getting the best of him. Onyx wondered how Ryder could remain so calm. What was he able to read in the energy surge? Onyx tried to imagine that if it was Kaiser coming for them, he would be able to sense him. He gulped and held his sword in both hands. Sweat beaded on his brow. The thought then struck him. How does someone knock another out of Shadow Slide? That could be very useful to know, Onyx thought to himself.

"Incoming! Get ready!" Ryder shouted.

A whirlwind of motion followed as Onyx saw a familiar shadow speeding towards them. It was small and ordinary, nothing special about it. His cousin had described that the more powerful the caster, Shadow Slide would appear like a sparkling storm of energy. Ryder stomped the ground hard with his left foot, black bolts erupting under his boot. Immediately, the Shadow Slide broke and out came a thin Shadowborn in the dirty clothes of a commoner. Certainly not Kaiser. Onyx managed a sigh of relief as the Shadowborn slid to a stop at his feet. He put his sword tip on the Shadowborn's throat.

"No! Please! Please don't kill me!" the Shadowborn squealed. He strained to look down at the sword tip. The sight caused him to cry.

"I remember you," Ryder said. He gestured for Onyx to put away his sword. "It's Den is it not?"

Den nodded quickly before crab crawling away from Onyx. He sat up and coughed hard. "I never thought that I would be helping the rebellion but I am. I need to get to the base as soon as possible."

When Onyx reached for his sword, Ryder shushed him and gestured for him to stop. "Den is a former student of Master Erebus. He is a healer and not a fighter like you. He would not hurt a fly." Ryder bent down to Den's eye level. "You are among friends. Trust me and I can Shadow Slide us all back to base in the blink of an eye."

"I can Shadow Slide," Onyx immediately said. He pouted his lip. Ryder glared at him and he dropped his shoulders in shame.

"This is not the time to have an attitude, Onyx," Ryder admonished as he lifted Den to his feet. Den clutched onto his arm as Ryder held out his hand towards Onyx.

As soon as Onyx touched Ryder's hand, the world disappeared around him into complete black. He felt that he was being flung across a great distance, his body squeezing and pulled tight. He felt bile bubbling in his stomach. He fought back the urge to vomit just as Ryder took him and Den out of the Shadow Slide. He fell forward to his hands and knees, gasping for breath. Den's grip slipped and he stumbled back, rubbing his head. His chest heaved as he fought to catch his breath. Ryder popped him once on the back and Den burped loudly.

"Thanks. I needed that," Den weakly said.

"I thought you would be long gone from the capital city territory. Being of Kader Erebus' order did put a target on your back," Ryder suggested. He glanced over at Onyx.

Den cleared his throat. "First rule of being a healer: never abandoned the sick, weary, and downtrodden. The last time I saw you, I saw a sign from the Spirits. I saw Shadow Night with Omu at his side and I knew that there was more that I could do."

"Then why did Master Erebus run?" Onyx asked Den. "Maybe he would still be here..."

Ryder let out a deep breath as he listened to Onyx's voice trail off into a faint whisper. He knew of the love that his cousin felt for his old teacher and friend. He thought back to one of his last conversations with Soja. The Saber had warned him not to reveal anything he told him. Times had changed however.

"Onyx," he started to say.

Ryder spotted Donovan and Hayden coming towards them with Haven leading the way. His conversation about the fate of Kader Erebus would have to wait. As soon as Haven drew in close, she raised up a hand to slap him on the face. He caught her wrist and scowled at her. She struggled against him for a moment before ripping her arm free. She harrumphed loudly.

"You left me again. Imagine my shock when I woke up and you were not there beside me," Haven growled.

"Not now, Haven. Donovan, tend to Onyx. He is a bit sick from experiencing his first Shadow Jump," Ryder ordered.

Haven frowned and looked to Den. Hayden was already checking him over for injuries but Den pushed them both away. "I need to talk to the person in charge."

"You can talk to me. What is it?" Ryder asked. He spotted Zoras pausing to help Donovan with Onyx.

It took Den a few minutes to respond. "Kaiser had destroyed Eclipse. Leveled it to the ground and killed everyone within its reach. There is nothing left but the bones of the dead. How I came by this information, I will not say." He shook his head and swallowed hard. "The remnants of the Shadow Council sought to confront him and he slaughtered them. He killed them like they were ants!"

Ryder saw Zoras flinch when Den had mentioned the demise of the council. "You are brave to bring us such news and I am glad to hear of at least one person in Cross willing to be our ears."

"He's marching on Umbra! He's going to destroy Umbra! I

just know it!" Den wailed. He was never a brave soul.

Haven gripped Ryder's forearm tightly and looked into his eyes. "My family."

"Den, how do you know that he is marching on Umbra? I have travelled the area and seen no army or hint of one on the move," Hayden stated.

Haven gripped Ryder's arm tighter, digging her nails into the muscle. "It does not matter. We have to go to Umbra and bring my family here. I will not let them get killed," Haven declared with conviction. "Please, Ryder. It may be nothing but it could be something."

"Umbra is Kaiser's city but who knows what feelings he harbors towards it. I agree with Haven. We have to know if and why he would be targeting Umbra in the first place and we cannot let innocent people remain at risk without knowing. One city has already fallen. I do not need another to follow Eclipse's fate," Zoras exclaimed. "Lady Ombre, I charge you with the mission to Umbra. Find out what Kaiser's army is doing and bring your family back. Your father is a master sword smith and his skill would be greatly appreciated and needed here. Your eldest sister's husband is also a valuable soldier that the rebellion could find use for."

Haven nodded, releasing her grip on Ryder's arm. He gasped and rubbed it. "I am taking Ryder with me. You might not like to admit it but he is the strongest one here and the only one capable of facing Kaiser and his Demon."

"Then I will go too," Hayden said as he helped Den to his feet. He pulled Den's left arm across his shoulders.

Ryder bit his lip and clenched his fists. Thankfully, Zoras answered for him. "Hayden, I need you to go to Cross and see to the truth of these rumors. Take what people you need to search the city but keep yourself hidden. Donovan, head west to Eclipse and assess the damage. Bring back any survivors. May the Spirits have spared a few souls from Kaiser's destructive wrath."

The two Sabers did not argue with Zoras though Hayden glanced back at Ryder. The glance was momentary before Hayden returned his attention to Den, speaking to him in a low voice. Donovan was tending to Onyx who was sitting down. He dabbed his clammy forehead with a wet cloth. The yard had fallen silent with news and any discussion had turned to Zoras' orders. A quiet but determined pace filled the rebels. Everyone went about their business in preparation.

*****

Onyx joined Haven and Ryder in their shared quarters. Ryder's grandmother had offered a passing hello before going to the infirmary to help with tending to a terror stricken Den. Onyx fiddled and picked at his sword hilt while Haven rattled on about the reasons to go to Umbra.

"Ryder, why aren't you answering me?" Haven asked.

Ryder had sat back on the bed and leaned against the wall with arms crossed tightly. He shrugged.

"This is serious and you are acting like it is nothing!" Haven accused.

"Kaiser is only targeting Umbra to get to me. I go there. I risk everyone with him following," Ryder stated.

"But it does not help just to stand by. You told me once to stop worrying about the what ifs. Well now I am reminding you," Onyx argued. He felt a sense of duty fill his heart. His hands dropped away from his sword hilt.

Haven slid down on the bed beside Ryder, sensing that there was something deeper. She laid a hand on his muscled shoulder. She rested her other hand on his knee. Onyx watched the two, trying to decipher what Haven was muttering. It was clear why Haven was ready to run to Umbra: she wanted to protect her family. Umbra was also Ryder's home and yet he seemed willing to watch it fall. Rumor or not.

"I am sure that I can beat Rache but we cannot defeat Kaiser without getting rid of the Demon. I cannot face them both at the same time. Also, think about it. The rebels do not have the forces necessary to combat an entire army to defend a city the size of Umbra. It is nearly as big as Cross," Ryder explained.

"With what you can do, I am certain that you could tear apart his army on your own," Onyx confidently said. He shrank when he realized that Ryder had not even looked up.

Ryder was deep in thought, a web of complex emotions running through his mind. First and foremost, Umbra represented a dark place full of terrible memories. It was where his mother died. But what was really getting to him was that he could face Kaiser or that the rebels believed him the only one capable of facing his evil grandfather. Kaiser's power was unimaginable and he had barely scratched the surface in showing it to the world. He could not be outsmarted and as such it was near impossible to overpower him. Ryder was one of the rare few to know the truth for rumor had the ability to inflate the truth. He let out a tense breath.

"I am but one man and I cannot do this alone. We cannot do this alone. We need to find a way to break the Shadow Mirror and get the Northern Alliance to help," Ryder said. Haven wrapped her arms around him, feeling his fear. She laid her head on his shoulder. "I will fight in Umbra if I must but my goal will be to find out the true secrets of the Shadow Mirror. Surely in Kaiser's city, there will be some tome or old letter from the Adonis family about the Shadow Mirror."

"I will take care of my family," Haven stated as she sighed.

"I want to come and help in any way I can. I have learned a great deal from you and I want to prove that your tutelage is not for aught. I want to help the people of Umbra," Onyx declared proudly.

Ryder managed a halfhearted smile. "Then you have more courage than me. Your people should be honored to have such a Prince fighting for them."

"It's not about courage. It is about doing what is right," Onyx replied with a shrug. "Den was terrified and he came to us in spite of his fear. That inspires me to go on."

*****

GRYPHONS IN CASCADE

Kader shook his head as his insistence to walk was ignored by Palas. The Osprey Gryphon laughed in a low chaw, pumping his wings harder. Kader groaned and leaned forward, pressing his head into the crook of his left arm. Flying on the back of a Gryphon had been exciting at first. Flying a long distance with the rare stop on the ground was unsettling. Kader relished their stops on the ground. Once he had recovered more of his wits from the attack, he assumed that the Gryphons would stop to rest when the sun went down. He was surprised that Palas and his twin sister Pala chose to fly at night. It was clear that they wanted to get to Cascade as soon as possible.

The Shadowborn had lost track of their progress, unfamiliar with the territory from the air. He tried to read the patterns in the shadows but Palas flew too fast. He stopped after a while when he kept getting dizzy and lightheaded. Kader knew that he should feel privileged to ride on the back of a Gryphon, especially on a royal heir.

"Feel the air, Master Erebus. You would feel that it is quite relaxing to stretch out your arms and let the cool air wash over you," Pala chirped. She had been flying above her brother since dawn."

"I was not blessed with fur and feather, my lady. This cloak only protects me from so much," Kader said. He shivered and pulled the old cloak closer around his body.

Pala chirred as she surged forward. She was a beautiful

sight to behold with her graceful form and contrasting black and white colors. She was lighter in frame than her brother and faster in flight. While Palas flew straight and steady, Pala never hesitated to dart around in elegant loops and spirals.

The forest ended beneath them and opened up into wide grasslands of green grass and golden wheat. Up ahead rose the rooftops and towers of Cascade, capital of the Earthborn. Kader breathed a sigh of relief, more so from the anticipation of finally setting his feet on the ground for good. He was not a young soul and his body ached like he had been on the back of a horse. He knew immediately that he should never openly say that thought. A Gryphon was not a horse or any beast of burden.

"How many of your kin came to Cascade?" Kader asked over the rush of wind. He could tell that Palas was eager to get to the city, feeling the increase in the Gryphon's speed through surging muscles.

"When word reached my father and Lord Stellaris, there was no discussion or doubt. We knew that we had to fly as fast as our wings could carry us. For Crossroads to call a War Council is a truly serious matter. Councilor Bubo laughed and asked my father what took him so long to decide that the war against the Shadowborn Kaiser was real. Oh, I had never seen my father so mad," Palas chuckled.

Pala flew in closer. "Father always knew it would come to blows with Kaiser but as we have all seen, he is no ordinary man. Our elders seem to think there is something beneath the surface that only the Spirits know."

"I shudder to think of what that is. We have had powerful Spiritborn and even people like Begin Anu. But then, Kaiser is a descendant of Begin Anu," Kader mused as he pushed back the hair from his face.

"So he has Farlander blood? That may explain some of his power. Farlanders throughout history have proven to be stronger than any Spiritborn. Still, something doesn't add up and I fear what that could be," Palas stated.

The royal twins dropped in altitude to move closer to the ground for better visibility. Pala moved to fly point in front of her brother. She whistled loudly as they crossed over the road. Kader looked over Palas' right shoulder to see the streaming crowd. He watched as they raised their hands and cheered in response. Kader noticed that the road travelers were a mix of Earthborn and Airborn, all armed and carrying battle supplies.

"So many questions," he muttered to himself as the Gryphons soared over the land.

Pala led the way, whistling of their approach and from what

Kader thought, was giving glad tidings for the Lords of the Northern Alliance. Cascade had been chosen for the War Council, a great honor though Kader knew it was more for proximity's sake. The source of their strife was in the west and if the armies were to unite against Kaiser, it was better to start together in strength. The sight reminded him of the stories he used to hear about the First and Second Dominion Wars. The Northern Alliance always marched west. He was repulsed by the thought that his homeland was a source of evil or at least where evil took root. It certainly was a strange coincidence to consider.

Out from behind them rocketed Arik, Voci, and Harper. Haro rode upon Arik, shouting an Earthborn battle cry with his fist raised in the air. The three Gryphons cried with him. Voci was the loudest but Harper had the deepest tone. Arik's screech was unpleasant on the ears and Kader quickly covered his.

"Down with Kaiser! Down with Kaiser!" Haro shouted, pumping his fist up and down in the air. He threw both of his arms up and shouted the Earthborn battle cry again.

Kader was glad to see Arik doing well. He smiled as soon as he caught Arik's dark eye. The Barn Owl Gryphon bowed his head before letting loose another screech. Kader cringed at the sound, trying to hide it from Arik. The Gryphon did not seem to notice or care.

More Gryphons of different sizes and colors came into sight. Many were perched upon the walls and rooftops, laughing as only they could. Kader watched as an Earthborn farmer and his family offered up food and drink to a trio of red headed Vulture Gryphons. He personally thought that their featherless heads were strange to look at but the Earthborn farmer seemed to delight in their presence. The farmer gestured towards his fields and laughed. A pint sized Kestrel Gryphon zoomed by, carrying something in his talons.

"That is Amke, one of Father's messengers. Father trusts him with many important messages," Palas pointed out.

"He is Lord Stellaris' favorite when it comes to talking war with Father. I suspect that Lord Stellaris is upon the fields somewhere," Pala said as she swooped in to fly beside her brother. "The Gates of Cascade are ahead."

Palas took the lead in landing the group before the gates. As soon as the Osprey Gryphon touched down, Kader slid off his back. He fell to his knees, feeling dizzy. He wanted to kiss the ground but quickly decided that it would be disrespectful. He managed to get to his feet as the burly Captain Oaken came forward.

"Greetings to you all. I am glad to see that your rescue was successful," Oaken said, first addressing the group before turning his attention onto Kader.

"The Gryphons are mighty and true of heart. Though I was afraid at first, I was glad to see this fine group come to my aid," Kader said. He coughed and cleared his throat. "I suspect that I am the only Shadowborn present in Cascade. As such, I will do my part to represent those of my people with good and gracious hearts."

"Kaiser may have claimed the title of Lord's Chancellor but that was never accepted here. You are here as representative of the Shadowlord whom Lord Proto Avis says responsibility falls to the eldest living Silvanus son," Oaken bowed in respect.

Kader's thoughts immediately turned to Ryder, bastard though he was. Akakios' son had already denied the crown once but that had been a different time. A much different time that could have changed the current state of events. He remembered the long talks and arguing between the eventual Lord Shiloh and the royal bastard. Ryder listened to very few people back then and only a few years would pass before he left the Shadowborn lands entirely.

"The matter of who sits upon the throne is solely the concern of the Shadowborn. I will gladly listen to counsel but ultimately it is the will of my people. Let me represent both Peredur and Onyx," Kader said after some thought. It was the sensible path to take.

Oaken bowed his head. He stepped to the side of the opening gates, gesturing for the group to enter. Palas led the way with his head held high. Pala fell in behind him, nodding towards any Gryphon or Spiritborn that shouted well wishes. Kader came in behind her. Voci and Harper followed with Arik and Haro bringing up the rear. The scout and Owl Gryphon spoke to each other animatedly about being recognized by strangers.

"When exactly did the Gryphons arrive? I know that I have lost some track of time so you must forgive me for my lack of memory," Kader asked.

Pala glanced briefly over her shoulder at him. "About two moons before we came to rescue you. Organizing Gryphons in our homeland is easy. Organizing them in that of the Spiritborn is decidedly more difficult."

"Two moons? From what I do know, that seems a bit early. You came before the arrival of the message from Crossroads by my reckoning," Kader tried to figure out. He twisted his face in thought.

Pala chuckled. "Gryphons are more apt to listen to Spirit Songs than some think. In my culture, a Spirit Song is the truest kind of message and my Father and Lord Stellaris knew what was coming. The time has come to rise up and fight."

Indeed it was time. Kader had long believed that Kaiser needed to be stopped before it was too late but the world seemed to tarry around in deep fear. Fear was a powerful weapon indeed and Kaiser used it to his advantage. What was even worse that he barely had to do anything for the fear to spread. Rumor proved stronger than truth and spread faster than the wind could blow. What was scary to Kader was the thought that Kaiser's power was as great and terrible as the rumors said. It seemed inconceivable for one man to be so strong. Certainly the Spirits had abandoned Kaiser a long time ago and Kader believed that even Demons feared him. But why? How? Kader hoped that the War Council would answer his questions. As he thought more about attending a council with the collection of Lords and dignitaries, he doubted that they would come to an agreement in one session. Rousing the entire Northlands to war after one thousand years of peace was not going to be easy.

Kader continued to appear stately by keeping his head up high and his shoulders back though his mind raged with questions. He tried to distract himself by studying the various Gryphons and Spiritborn. As the capital of the Earthborn and chosen rallying point for the Northern Alliance, many of them were present in varying states of armor. He quickly spotted several Airborn in their light leather armor and war paint on their faces. Their white and black hair floated in the breeze whenever a nearby Gryphon beat its wings. Their look was quiet and deadly, almost snooty Kader thought with their upturned noses and squinted eyes. It appeared that they were studying the lone Shadowborn with a sense of distrust.

The Fireborn were quick to bow their heads in respect. Kader had always appreciated their lively nature. They were a people who usually wore their hearts on their sleeves, letting others know how they felt. They were also quick to anger and feel offended. Kader immediately decided that he did not want to get on their bad side and feel their burning power. They were at least more gracious and welcoming than the Airborn had been.

Kader continued to look around, searching for any Waterborn and Lightborn. He did not see any. "Did the Lords Evander and Marinus receive the same message from Crossroads? Are they coming?"

Palas' twitching tail slapped his sister's leg. She hissed at him. "Sorry, dear sister. You are following too closely," he told her. Pala hissed again but slowed her pace. "Lord Marinus has asked for time and Lord Evander has not responded. Time is what we do not have anymore and they cannot ignore the summons of the War Council. All Lords must heed its call."

He knew that he could count on the Gryphons and their dedication to helping others without question. It was the likes of Lord Marinus and Lord Evander that caused him worry. Kader let out a deep breath, pushing the thought to the back of his mind.

TOO MANY LORDS

"You are a fool, Palani! Where has your mind been? I cannot always do your job," Oren shouted at his son.

"I seem to recall that you abdicated," Palani seethed in a vicious voice. "Which means you do not have the power to make orders without consulting me!"

"Am I just supposed to ignore a direct command from Crossroads?!" Oren fired back.

Kader sat in silence, watching the explosive argument between father and son. He gathered that Palani thought the War Council summons to be premature with the Shadowborn border still impenetrable. Oren on the other hand was ready to attack with full strength and was tired of waiting for an excuse. Kader had often wondered how the balance of power was between Palani, the current Lord of the Earthborn, and Oren, the previous ruler. He had believed that Palani's father relegated himself to the role as chief advisor but it was apparent that the former Lord still wielded influence and power.

"We can't get through the border. Am I to waste energy trying to bring down what can't be brought down? Kaiser will slaughter us in our weakened state. We must wait," Palani yelled.

"Wait for what? We have waited long enough and I will not let my fear keep me from doing what we must. We must fight," Oren replied with great conviction.

Kader crossed his legs and sat back with arms folded against his chest. He looked around the throne room, now being used as the War Council room. Aves sat across from him between Lord Paladon and Lord Stellaris. He was dressed in a white cloak that had a Gryphon feather collar that spread over his neck and shoulders. His ice blue eyes were haunting and cold. A feather and jewel ornament was woven into his black streaked white hair. He rested his hands on his lap, fingers laced together.

Argos was equally quiet though his left foot was twitching and tapping on the floor. He sat to the left of the massive Lord Stellaris, dressed in cloak that had been cut and colored like a fire. The lion's mane spread over his shoulders, its hair a shining gold. His bare and brawny arms were crossed tightly.

"I agree with Lord Oren. We must not tarry any longer," Paladon said calmly. He always referred to any leader, current and former, as Lord.

Even if it was the Gryphon's habit, Palani did not like hearing what Paladon had said. The golden haired Earthborn gritted his teeth, resisting the urge to curse. He paced the floor, the only one standing. Kader had to wonder what was going through Palani's head. He watched carefully and resisted the urge to shudder when Palani turned his eyes on him.

"What arcane curse wraps the borders of your homeland? How did you get through when so many others have failed," Palani said in controlled voice.

"In all honesty, I never had trouble crossing the border except for one time. Even then, I had help from the Spirit World," Kader said defensively. He held up his silver crescent moon whistle that hung from his neck. "I was given this most precious gift by Sin Silvanus. It is a Spirit Whistle. Where my Lord Sin had acquired it, I do not know."

Aves sat up a little straighter in his chair. "I have seen that Spirit Whistle before. It belonged to Shadow Night Silvanus. From what he told me, he received it from Bane Arlis in the aftermath of the Second Dominion War. The whistle has the power to summon a powerful Spirit from the Spirit World."

Kader nodded. "Omu the Great Wolf came to my aid and brought me across the River Shadow. My memory is hazy of that night but I do remember Omu being quite angry about something. He shook his head and shivered. He then looked up. "It can only be one thing. A Shadow Mirror," Kader stated. "A power very few can summon and control. My best guess is Kaiser raised the Shadow Mirror to prevent the intervention of others in his schemes."

"A power that can only be broken by the one who raised it or someone related to him," Aves said, breaking his quiet deep thinking. As the oldest in the room, everyone immediately fell silent at his voice and gave him their full attention. "People only call it a Shadow Mirror since it was Adonis Anu who first displayed the power. It is Farlander in origin, not Spiritborn."

"Well, I doubt that Kaiser will bring down his wall and he has no descendants. What woman would have wanted to lie with that vile creature anyway," Palani snarled.

Kader resisted the urge to say that Ryder was Kaiser's grandson. He wanted to tell them, the revelation on the tip of his tongue. Would they even believe him? "The man is over a thousand years old. My guess is that there is at least one person out there that shares his blood. He has never struck me as the celibate type."

"Well we cannot waste time searching for someone we have no proof exists. We must act and we must act now," Oren urged.

"This is not a proper War Council for the Lords of the Waterborn and the Lightborn are not present. If we intend to make war against Kaiser, we must do it united or not at all," Aves coolly said. He glanced over at Kader knowingly.

"Well we certainly have to figure out the mess Crossroads has made. There are Gryphons all over my city. I cannot house and feed them all. Then there are Fireborn and Airborn. We do not have the resources on such short notice!" Palani cried. He threw his hands up in the air.

"You underestimate the vitality and resourcefulness of your people, Lord Palani. And we Gryphons do not come unprepared. Myself and Lord Stellaris have ordered our kin to not harry the livestock and impede on any hunting lands," Paladon stated with a bow of the head.

"Besides, I prefer hunting bear to a cow or sheep," Stellaris commented. "Much better sport." His brown feathered chest rumbled with a deep laugh.

"I am glad that you find amusement for I don't," Palani snapped. "Why are the Lords Proto Avis and Vorin not here?"

Kader listened as Argos spoke up. The Lord of the Fireborn spoke of the old Gryphon and Dragon's arrival in Coal. The fire haired Lord glanced briefly to Paladon and Stellaris before describing that Proto's age has given him many infirmities and pains. It was true that the Gryphon sage and sitting ruler in Crossroads was not a young soul by any sense of the word. Vorin was even older but Dragons did not suffer from the same pains. Kader wondered if Aves did as the senior Spiritborn in the room. Kaiser was also among the oldest Spiritborn still alive but Kader doubted that he let his aging affect him.

"So you must have respect for Lord Avis. His mind is great but his body does betray him from time to time. Vorin is gracious in his aid," Argos finished.

"In truth, we cannot have a War Council without our king. A king who abandoned us long ago," Palani grumbled. He swept his forest green robes around him. The voluminous fabric threatened to tangle around his legs in his haste.

"Bane Arlis will come. One of my kin's best fliers is currently in the Southlands looking for him. I trust in Gyr to find our king and bring him home," Stellaris stated. "He is both strong in body and true in heart. Gyr will not give up without a damn good fight."

Palani held up a finger. "One thousand years, Stellaris. One thousand years have we been without the king our ancestors have named. That you, Aves, helped name," he said, gesturing towards the Lord of the Airborn.

"Are you questioning my judgment?" Aves asked. Kader cringed at the brewing frustration in Aves' voice.

"Both the Shadowlord and the Daylord are gone. What power does the Immortal Truth have? What power do we have?" Palani questioned before he finally sat down. Oren smacked his shoulder and glared at him.

"It saddens me when I see someone lose faith in the Immortal Truth. You cannot begin to understand what the signers went through to craft its power and I refuse to believe that our end is near. Kaiser is one man. Just one single man. Our Daylord is still out there, lost and wandering. The Shadowlord is alive but not named. They are here and just like them, we need to unite as one to face this war," Aves preached. He rose up from his seat and strode to the center of the room.

The throne room was a large circular space with long windows arranged side by side. The windows took up a majority of the space available in each of the four walls. As such, the room was very bright. The columns were made from large trees whose carven branches twisted together to form a ceiling. Woodland creatures decorated the stone branches, brought to near life by the delicate detail.

"Master Erebus, of all of us here, you have spent the most time in and round Kaiser's presence. What can you tell us of his power?" Aves asked after he finished his speech on loyalty and faith.

Kader shifted uncomfortably in his seat. "His mind is a potent weapon as is his command over Spirit energy. His Anu bloodline gives him the ability to use all six disciplines though I do not know to what degree. We certainly weren't close enough to be friends. I would say that the one that knows him best and is still alive is Ryder Coba."

"If only we had him and my grandson Onyx safe within the walls of Cascade," Oren said, leaning back in his seat. "I would feel more confident marching against Kaiser with them out of his reach."

"Well we can do nothing until that Mirror falls," Argos stated. "Wait. Couldn't Lord Vorin blast the Mirror with Dragonfire? Dragonfire is one of the strongest powers on Terra and surely can do some serious damage."

The suggestion became the hot topic for several minutes as Argos went through a series of ideas with Vorin in the lead. He animatedly acted out several different attack plans, stimulating Dragonfire with his Spirit energy. Kader was mesmerized by the display of power. Stellaris had been more than happy to help act beside Argos, pretending to be Vorin when directed.

"A Shadow Mirror is a Shadow Mirror. No one but Kaiser can bring it down. If Lord Vorin thought he could have brought it down, he would have done so already," Aves said, taking the wind out of Argos' excitement. Even Stellaris deflated and returned to Aves' left side.

"Like I tried to tell you, this Council is pointless. All we can do is assemble and wait for destruction to come to us," Palani started to say.

"I once thought the same way. That my silence and inactivity would protect my loved ones. It turns out that my silence only made things worse. I refuse to cower as I used to. If you will not use your crown properly and lead the Earthborn, I should just take it back," Oren dared.

Even Aves was visibly shocked by the suggestion of Oren. Palani was dumbstruck. His mouth dropped open and he struggled to find any words for a response. Argos appeared to be laughing, pressing his lips together to hold back the sound. Kader agreed with what Oren said as Palani, though capable, had done very little to advance the Earthborn.

"Perhaps we should wait for the remaining Lords to arrive before we continue," the sensible Paladon said, trying to act as a peacemaker. He mumbled something in the Gryphon tongue to Stellaris who nodded in response.

*****

Kader could not decide what was more infuriating: Palani's lack of real leadership or the inconclusive results of his first War Council. To him, the direction was obvious. How could it be any different? The long ignored war was knocking on their door, threatening to break it down. Kaiser was no longer an annoying insect. He was a full force swarm of destruction. It was almost too much to bear. He leaned against the wall outside of the throne room, still hearing the argument going on inside. It was clear to Kader that Palani was refusing to see sense and Oren was trying, what sounded like desperately, to make his son open his eyes to the world.

"From what I have been told, this argument has been going on for over a decade. I am sure that Oren had his reasons for stepping down but it seems his earlier faith in Palani was all for naught."

He looked up to see Aves, startling at the majestic Lord of the Airborn's presence. His mind became scattered and his thoughts rushed from bowing to not bowing. He managed a head tilt in Aves' direction.

"Forgive me, Lord Aves, but I did not hear you coming. I had thought myself to be the only one in this hallway," Kader stammered as he fought to gather himself. He closed his eyes and took a deep breath, releasing it slowly.

"Such is the gift of an Airborn to move silently if they wish. Like the wind, we can choose to be heard or unheard," Aves replied. He had his feathered cloak wrapped tight around his shoulders. He gestured towards the closed doors with a toss of his head. "Though it is easy considering the volume of their argument."

Kader briefly looked in the direction of the doors. "I may never understand completely why Oren abdicated and gave his throne to his son. It sounds like he is regretting the decision."

"The responsibility is not to be taken lightly. Palani has all the necessary tools and gifts to be a good leader to his people but perhaps he does not have the same metal of his ancestors. To lead during peace has its difficulties but to lead during war invites greater strain both physically and mentally. The Gryphons have mastered the art of leadership for no evil or ill will can survive amongst them." Aves looked away for a moment as if considering a vexing thought. "Unity. Yes, unity is what the Earthborn and the peoples of the Northern Alliance need."

Kader could not help but think that they also needed time to see the truth. United, the Lords of the Northern Alliance could rise. Divided, the entire world would fall into ruin.

*****

UNDER THE STARS

"Roasted meat is always good on the stomach after a long day of travelling," Gyr mused as he laid on his back, his wings stretched out. He smacked his beak and wiggled his front paws in calm delight. "The addition of that wild onion was a wise choice. Added good flavor."

Charon chuckled as he patted his full stomach. He had eaten his fair share. "What would a Gryphon say when a meal pleases him?"

Gyr first spoke in his native tongue before translating. "Good hunting, good eating. Shall I teach you the proper words and pronunciations?"

"I think that I would fail just as badly as I did the last time you tried," Charon laughed. He laid down on the grass and looked up to the night sky.

The pair stretched out in the grass under the eaves of the forest. Their small campfire flickered by their feet in a small dirt pit surrounded by stones. The sun was setting, casting an orange glow over the land. A light breeze wafted through the tree branches, knocking a shower of leaves loose. Gyr sneezed and wiggled his nostrils. He scratched at his face.

""We are not too far from Meras now. Maybe a couple of days give or take," Charon commented as he put his arms behind his head. "You may have been able to push the people in Garhune around but not so in Meras."

Gyr rolled to his side to face Charon. "How so?"

Charon let out a deep breath. "The people in Meras have seen their fair share of monsters and strange powers over the years. They trust no Immortal or Spirit save one."

"The Daylord?" Gyr asked.

Charon shrugged. "In the Southlands, the Daylord goes by many names: Daylord, Lord Bane, Wanderer. The list goes on depending on where you ask and who you ask. The people here know that he exists for their ancestors have told them tales by the fire. Why would dear old grandfather lie about something like that? In this day and age, no one has seen his face or knows the sound of his voice. All they do know is that he comes in times of great need. He is both a sign of hope and an omen of doom."

"Like the Shadowborn the people of Garhune spoke of? Has this Shadowborn been seen recently? Has there been any signs? Anything at all?" Gyr asked. He was intensely curious about the Shadowborn. It was too strange to have one wandering the Southlands. Especially one that was described as powerful and dangerous as this one.

"I think it was thirty years ago but a powerful being attacked Meras. Some say it was the Shadowborn who they say was not of sound mind and others say it was a terrible Demon. People refer to it as the Dark Night. Anyway, this being wreaked havoc and killed many true hearted defenders with deadly ease. It made to attack a child that was clinging to her dead mother when a Spirit appeared in a white haze," Charon paused to take a deep breath. "I was not in Meras at the time but I spoke to the child afterwards. She told me that this Spirit immediately made her feel safe and that she did not need to worry anymore. The Spirit never spoke a single word but the attacking being immediately cowered in his presence. He brought out a great sword, a claymore of some sort, which shined with a bright light."

Gyr watched as Charon made the attempt to mimic the slow action of pulling out a large sword from across his back. The details sounded very familiar and yet, he did not want to believe it.

"He pointed his sword at the invader in a manner of challenge. The dark being ran in fright. The little girl said that she turned around to thank the Spirit but he was gone in a rush of wind. She described as if he had never been there in the first place," Charon finished.

"In the Northlands, all of us believe that the Spirits come to us when our hearts call to them. I can't just get up and ask them to come. I have to mean it with all of my being. The Shadowborn experience this with their beloved Omu the Wolf Spirit for example," Gyr described.

"Do the Gryphons have a Spirit they believe in?" Charon

asked. He leaned on his elbow, facing the white Gryphon. "Do you have gods you worship?"

Gyr chawed in a low laugh. "We do not worship beings such as gods. My kin's relationship is to the world around us, to nature, and to life itself." He pointed a claw towards an emerging star in the sky. "Gryphons believe that our ancestors use the stars to communicate with us and through our ancestors, the Spirit World."

Charon studied the star that Gyr had pointed to, seeing its blinking light. He had always used the stars to navigate and pinpoint his location but he had never thought of them as the eyes of Spirits. It made him shudder. If what Gyr said was true, would the Spirits judge him harshly? He did not think that he had a dark heart but he had certainly made bad choices in life. Or maybe they could see darkness in his blood that he had yet to discover.

"Do you think they could tell me who my father is?" Charon asked solemnly.

"The stars can tell you anything you want to know. The trick is knowing how to read the signs and patterns. The best star reader in my homeland is Lord Proto Avis. He is a great sage and wise leader who rules in my king's stead in Crossroads. Even the Dragonlord Vorin cannot boast the same ability," Gyr replied. "Reading the stars is a rare ability and according to some, can make you go blind."

"Blind? Is it like staring into the sun for too long?" Charon asked. Part of him felt more exposed under the stars than filled with wonder.

The Gryphon shook his head. "It is like gazing into the Spirit World and you become lost within it."

A part of him was too frightened to ask for Gyr to continue but Charon desperately wanted to know more. He guessed that Gyr read the stars in the same way as he did, for navigation purposes. The Gryphon appeared practical and reasonable with no penchant for believing in the unknown. He believed in truth and honesty. It made Charon question what he believed in.

Silence fell upon the pair as the golden orange sky changed into varying shades of purple and black. Stars littered the cloudless sky. Their fire had died down to a pile of red coals. Charon wiggled his feet and pushed off his boots, stretching his toes in his gray wool socks. He debated on adding another piece of wood to the campfire.

"You said once that moon was important to the Shadowborn. Is it the same as the stars?" Charon asked.

"I cannot say for certain as I am not Shadowborn but from what I do know, they believe that the moon is a symbol of guidance. The Shadowborn only bury their dead when the moon is full so that the deceased's Spirit finds its way to the Spirit World without incident," Gyr explained. He let out a deep breath. He rested his front paws on his chest.

"I have always felt more at peace with myself when the moon is full though I could never say why," Charon commented. "Maybe it was my Shadowborn blood speaking to me."

"Much as the movement of the wind speaks to me," Gyr stated. "The world is just as alive as you and me. It has thoughts, feelings, and memories. At one time, this world and that of the Spirit World was one single place. During the First Dominion War, the two were separated into what they are today by the power of the Covenant of Spirits. It is a time that few in my generation wish to know for it was very dark. It was the Second Dominion War where history shines. The coming of the Daylord. The writing of the Immortal Truth."

Gyr had told him the story plenty of times since they first met. At first, it annoyed him how much Gyr spoke of it in his fervor to find the Daylord. It was just a story after all wasn't it? But his heart stirred every time the Gryphon told the story. It was a deep feeling in his core, distant but present. Was his Immortal blood trying to remember and tell him something? Was it the Spirit Omu that Gyr had told him about trying to wake up his power? He shivered at the thought of a Spirit trying to influence him. He turned away from looking up.

> *Fly high, sky high*
> *Soar among the stars*
> *Your loved ones are watching*
> *Love them, honor them*
> *Show all your heart*
> *Your legend is beginning*

The song had the sound of being translated from an old Gryphon melody. Its tone was that of a soft whistle. Charon imagined an older Gryphon singing it to an egg or a chick. He could feel the love and hope in the words. He listened quietly as Gyr continued his son in the Gryphon tongue, whistling and chawing softly.

*****

THE CITY OF UMBRA

The journey north to Umbra had been usually quiet for the trio expected to see signs of a large army. The ground was undisturbed and free of footprints. The trees and grass were whole and unbroken. The streams were unsullied by the stink of a latrine. Even the air was clean of the smell of horses and sweat. Onyx did his best to investigate and study their surroundings, hoping to find some sign. He searched for the remains of an animal killed by arrow and for old fire pits. Nothing.

"Shouldn't we have seen some sign of a massive army by now? I highly doubt that so many soldiers could move without leaving behind evidence," Onyx questioned after realizing the footprints he had been chasing were his own.

"The beauty of a well-trained Shadowborn army is that they don't leave physical signs of their presence. Because of that, we have to focus on a different set of signs. It is about tracking auras and Spirit energy," Ryder explained as he stood by his chestnut horse. The animal was busy chewing on a stretch of grass.

Onyx could have slapped himself for forgetting about Spirit energy and tracking auras. Even Sai had stressed the various signs they could leave behind. He did not want to admit that he had not been paying attention. His shoulders dropped in reaction.

"Do not worry. General Coba has kept his eyes and mind open," Haven teased. She sauntered past Ryder and tapped the center of his forehead with her thin fingers. "As have I."

Ryder batted Haven away, grinning. "It would be helpful if

we had a Gryphon with us. They can see signs that even we can't see with our senses. A Gryphon's connection to nature and the world goes deeper than anything a Spiritborn can feel."

"Well we don't have one. They are all east of the border so we must depend on our own eyes," Haven stated as she adjusted a saddle strap. She pulled on it and patted her horse on the neck.

"Have you ever met a Gryphon, Haven?" Onyx asked.

Haven nodded before she turned around. "Just a few times in my childhood when they used to fly these lands. But none of any real rank or worth. The last one of rank came to Umbra before my time. A Gryphon councilor named Bubo visited the city when it became known that Akakios had a child. Owl Gryphons are always so curious and sometimes won't believe things until they look upon it."

"Bubo came in good faith but was really spying on me for Lord Paladon and Lord Stellaris. My father's reputation was not a strong and noble one when compared to that of his predecessors. They were warriors and he was a scholar. Bubo wanted to see if I was worth the blood I had in my veins. To see if I would be capable of returning the Silvanus bloodline to its former glory," Ryder stated as he crossed his arms tightly.

"It sounds like you do not like him very much," Onyx commented.

"The idea that I was being judged for my worth before I could even walk is not one I am fond of. Only trueborn sons could bear the honor of the Silvanus name. Unlike you, I was expected to fail since I was a bastard. Child of a whore according to public opinion. Even Mali, my father's mother, did not think much of me and wished that my father would not recognize me as his child. She was in Umbra when Bubo arrived." Ryder scoffed. "She convinced him that I should be forgotten to the shadows and he agreed."

"That sounds horrible," Onyx exclaimed.

Ryder shrugged. "Imagine Bubo's surprise when I arrived in Ornith a full grown man. He wasn't the first to perpetrate the tale that I was Shadow Night reborn but it definitely spread like wildfire after that. He kept a close eye on me the entire time that I was in the Gryphon capital, trying to figure me out. Now Owl Gryphons might just be the smartest beings on all of Terra. He saw in me the blood of my mother's family before many others did. He is not my biggest fan but he is respectful enough to keep secrets. I think his exact words were that one day, I would have to choose what kind of person I wanted to be. Noble like Shadow Night or dark like Kaiser Adonis."

Haven patted her horse's neck and stroked its cheek. It

snorted loudly at her touch. "Don't let Ryder say that Bubo hated him from the start. From what I've been told, Bubo was already in a foul mood for being sent so far from his beloved forest home to investigate a bastard baby. Umbra doesn't have a lot of trees. Owl Gryphons prefer the forests to the mountains and valleys."

Onyx's horse nudged him in the back. He turned around to pet its soft pale muzzle. It snorted with delight. "I'm sure Umbra has changed since he visited. It had plenty of trees the last time that I saw the city."

Ryder swung himself onto the saddle and gripped the reins in his right hand. Haven and Onyx followed suit. Haven directed her horse to Ryder's left side, jerking on the reins to keep it from nipping the other horse's flank. Onyx fell in behind them.

"Umbra is just over the hill," Haven said, directing her attention to Ryder.

He sighed deeply. "I haven't looked upon it in one hundred years. I wonder if I will even recognize it."

Haven reached out and rubbed Ryder's muscled shoulder. "It was your home. I'm sure you will."

"Think that house you wanted to move into is still standing?" Ryder asked with a devilish smirk. Haven dug her fingernails. "I get it. I get it. You want to be proper."

Onyx was confused by their conversation. It hinted at the couple's once future plans when perhaps their world was less chaotic. He wondered if those plans were abandoned in the wake of Akakios' execution and when it became possible that Ryder could take the throne. It must have been such a tumultuous time for them. In a way, Onyx felt that he was starting to understand more of the pressure his cousin was under.

"I know that our mission to Umbra is important but you better not forget your promise. Ask my father for my hand in marriage. I won't let a war stop us," Haven teased as she pulled her hand back.

Ryder rubbed his shoulder. "You are starting to get pushy."

"Someone must be," Haven stated, throwing her shoulders back.

She urged her horse forward and took the lead. Onyx directed his horse to follow and came up beside Ryder. The trio of horses plodded along slowly. They crossed a small stream before beginning the climb up a large hill. Their path appeared to have been trodden many times over as no grass grew upon it. It did not take them long to reach the top.

"There is Umbra with not a sign of a hostile soldier to be seen," Haven declared. She glanced over her shoulder at Ryder. "The only soldiers I see are the city guard."

"Good," Ryder said as he pulled his hood up to obscure his face. He motioned for Onyx to do the same.

"Don't you think they will see past the hoods and lowered gaze? I'm certain the city guard is well trained to recognize a Silvanus when they see one," Onyx pointed out. He hesitated to follow Ryder's direction.

It was Haven that answered. She snickered. "There is more than one way to get into Umbra unnoticed. My eldest sister's husband is a captain on the south watch. He will let us pass without question though I am sure that he will have something to say about it later."

"I still owe him money," Ryder said with an exacerbated sigh.

"What for? A gambling debt?" Onyx asked.

Haven snickered even louder. It took her a while to gather herself. "My brother in law made a bet that Ryder would not propose before a number of circumstances. Some serious and others quite silly. As your cousin is a man of honor in some circles, he owes my brother in law a sizable amount."

"Do I look like I carry around a ton of gold and silver on me?" Ryder snapped.

"Ryder, people would just give you stuff if you asked. I doubt that you have suffered in poverty for the last century," Haven teased. She laughed when Ryder grumbled under his breath.

Onyx had to smile and laugh along with Haven. His cousin always seemed so serious and lacked a sense of real humor. He could see why he and Haven made such a good match. She helped him to face things and relax. He felt a stirring in his heart and wondered if he would find a partner such as her. Back in Crossroads, he had attempted to court Luna to disastrous results in his mind. She was sweet and lively with a dance in her steps. But in the end, it felt more like a friendship. He later realized that he should not expect to find his soul mate so easily or force a connection when one may not exist. Onyx had not seen Luna since Crossroads and he wondered if she still remembered him. He reached up to touch his lips, remembering their brief kiss.

Umbra rose up before them, a behemoth of a city that Onyx thought could rival Cross. Since it was not backed up against a mountain, it was spread out over the grasslands. Onyx lost count of the number of farm houses and cultivated fields of grain and vegetables. Fences divided the land into individual plots and kept out the voracious livestock. Onyx even spotted a farmer in a straw hat, beating away a flock of crows and another chasing a runaway sheep. There was such a sense of vitality that filled Onyx with wonder. Umbra was more a true capital city than Cross. Onyx was prepared to argue that point with anyone that said differently. Cross was wonderful but it was dark under the shadow of the Heights. Umbra had a vibrant charm that he fell in love with. He could not wait to see the city properly.

The inner city was surrounded on all sides by a high wall that reached for the sky. Turrets and towers were regularly spaced upon it where watchmen paced in their duties. Banners with the Silvanus crest flapped in the wind. The sight pleased Onyx and he sat up straight in his saddle. He was proud to be a Silvanus and it made him feel good to see the banners. Beyond the wall, he could see the roof of a massive citadel. Its spires rose even higher into the sky.

"Had Kaiser not been the evil bastard he became, he would have lived in the citadel as a ruler of Umbra," Ryder pointed out when he saw Onyx staring. "I lived there for a few years after I was born with my mother and grandmother. He claimed it was because I was the Shadowlord's son and that I deserved such lodgings."

"Are we going there first?" Onyx asked.

"We are going to my family home. I haven't seen my family in a few years and for Ryder, it has been over a century. They will be excited to see all three of us. They are incredibly loyal to the throne and the Silvanus family," Haven proudly said. "And no one cooks better than my mother."

Onyx caught a brief smile on Ryder's face before it disappeared beneath a veneer of quiet strength. As Haven started to put some distance between them in her eagerness to reach the gate, Onyx came in close to Ryder's side. "Does her family know that you are Kaiser's grandson?"

Ryder shook his head. "Haven didn't until a few months ago. They just thought Kaiser's attention was due to me being the son of the Shadowlord."

"Why would Kaiser have hid your blood identity a secret? He seems like the kind of person to shout that from the rooftops, claiming it like some kind of victory," Onyx suggested.

"My father's mother would have made sure I had all royal rights stripped from me. She hated Kaiser and if Kaiser wanted me on the throne, he would keep my identity a secret until it suited him to tell the world," Ryder explained.

It made sense that Kaiser would keep secrets to strengthen his own position and to act when he was ready to. The man lived in a sea of rumors regarding his past and his character. There were so many things said about him that no one knew what to believe or trust as the truth. In a way, it was a perfect weapon for no one could predict his next step. If he took one at all. He could create chaos without lifting a finger.

The road into the city was clogged with carts, horse riders, and travelers. People shouted, chanted, and sang, creating a storm of sound. Onyx tried to pay attention to the words exchanged in case someone spoke of a travelling army. The most interesting thing that was said was how produce prices had stabilized after the implementation of a new law. In reality, the tidbit was rather boring. Onyx refocused his attention on directing his horse to follow Ryder and Haven. As Haven had promised, a well-dressed guard with shining armor nodded towards them and let them pass without question. Now, they were entering Umbra and for Onyx, into uncertainty of what would be ahead.

THE OMBRES

Haven led Onyx and Ryder to a well to do section east of the citadel. Onyx started out with a nervous hunch in his shoulders but before the end of their journey, he held his head up high. The merchants and people greeted him warmly, ignoring Ryder in his darkened garb. Onyx had already prepared a lie to cover Ryder, deciding that he would name him as his Saber guard. Haven also sat up proudly, well recognized by her neighbors. She exchanged careful words regarding her absence and ignored all comments about her missing in action boyfriend. Onyx resisted the urge to snicker and laugh when some of Haven's younger female neighbors commented about the handsome and strong royal bastard. He could feel Ryder rolling his eyes from beneath his hood. Onyx let out a small chuckle.

The trio halted and dismounted. Onyx's horse shook its head vigorously and snorted. He patted its side, the horse twitching from the contact.

"Thank you. Now get a good rest and I hope the stablemen give you an apple as a treat," Onyx spoke softly to the horse. "If I have to slip them a few extra coins, I can."

"Don't you worry. The stables in Smiths' Alley will treat our faithful steeds well," Haven said as she pulled off her travel pack from the back of the saddle. She shouldered it before unbuckling the saddle bags.

Acting like he was a servant, Ryder took the reins of all three horses. He kept his head low and nodded when Haven reminded him about the neighborhood stables. Their conversation remained at a murmur for several minutes. Onyx was surprised that he could not hear their words for as an Immortal Spiritborn, his hearing was sharp and sensitive to the tiniest of sounds. When their voices increased in volume, albeit slightly, he was able to hear them.

"Promise that you won't run off," Haven said under her breath.

"Why would I run off?" Ryder asked in the same quiet voice.

Haven grabbed the collar of Ryder's tunic and pulled his face close to hers. "Just don't ok?" She let go once Ryder nodded.

Onyx found the statement odd and immediately jumped at the opportunity to ensure that his cousin would come back. "It would be improper to announce ourselves with one person in the party missing." He made sure that he was heard.

Ryder cringed but otherwise maintained a quiet demeanor. He led the three horses away and anticipated walking to the stables with a shudder of his broad shoulders. A pair of eager grooms greeted him before he could disappear from Haven and Onyx's sight. Ryder gave the grooms his instructions and coin for their help. The two grooms bowed their heads and thanked him as they took the reins to lead the horses away. Soon, the trio was left alone to finish the short walk to the Ombre home.

It was a modest house made of gray stone and timber. It had two levels and was capped by a slate roof. The first level had two windows, one on each side of the front door. The third level had three windows. A lantern hung to the right side of the door. Haven strode up the small stretch of stairs and pulled the iron door knocker. It banged loudly on the thick wood.

"Now, Onyx. My family can be a bit boisterous and as I said, they are extremely loyal to the throne. I know that you and Ryder have come to an agreement about titles but they will still call you Prince and show you proper respect. They will be excited to meet you. But you might want to cover your ears when they discover who else I brought home," Haven explained in a low voice.

"I think I can handle a little bit of bowing and your Highness," Onyx replied. He brushed his pants to smooth out the wrinkles.

"Well I am serious about covering your ears. I have two sisters and my oldest sister has two little boys who absolutely worship Ryder even though all they know of him is stories. They will scream when they see him and I mean scream very loudly. This will be the first time they meet him," Haven urged. She quickly jolted up straight and faced the door when it started to open.

A woman appeared, her dark hair pulled back in a messy bun. She was wearing a simple navy blue dress with the sleeves rolled up to her elbows. She wiped her hands on a tattered white apron. At her side was a tall and burly man with a full beard and silver streaks in his hair. He was dressed in dirty brown wool pants and a stained linen shirt.

"Haven!" her mother greeted as she embraced her daughter. "It has been too long, my dear child."

Haven returned the embrace before jumping over to hug her father. She held her breath and frowned at his state. "What have you been crafting in the forge that smells so?"

"I spent my time cleaning it today. I was about to wash up and change," her father said laughing. He hugged her tighter.

Haven stepped back. "Mother. Father. May I present to you, his Royal Highness Onyx Silvanus."

"It is a delight to meet you," her mother said with a deep curtsy. Haven's father crossed his chest with a clenched fist and bowed. "I am Nora Ombre and this is my husband, Ivan Ombre."

"Pleased to meet you. You may call me Onyx," Onyx said with a bow of the head.

Haven turned towards Ryder and lifted an eyebrow. At the silent command, he pulled back his hood. Nora covered her mouth in shock and fell back against her husband. Ivan only smiled as he held her up. Onyx stepped back to give them space.

"It's you!" Nora managed to say after she composed herself. She separated from Ivan and approached Ryder with caution. Ryder stood still, watching her carefully. Nora poked his torso as if to prove that he was real and not an illusion.

"I'm not a Spirit. I am alive and very real," Ryder stated, a sense of warmth entering his voice. He opened his arms in invitation. Nora immediately embraced him. Ivan came forward and shook Ryder's hand.

"Good to see you again after all these years, Ryder," Ivan greeted.

"RYDER'S HERE?!" came the chorus of voices from inside the house.

Onyx nearly fell back as two small boys rushed past him, sliding to a stop before Ryder. Ivan chuckled as he and Nora stepped back. The boys then leaped forward and tackled Ryder to the ground.

"It's really Uncle Ryder! It's really him!" they shrieked with delight while Haven's two older sisters came outside. They embraced Haven, all the well laughing at Ryder's predicament. They watched as the boys playfully wrestled with Ryder in the dirt.

"Can they teach me to do that? I have yet to knock Ryder to

the ground myself," Onyx inquired. He glanced towards Haven. She tried to hide her laughter, completely focused on Ryder.

The two boys laughed and asked Ryder dozens of questions as he tried to free himself. Ryder tried to roll over and flip himself up only to be pulled to the ground again. He started laughing heartedly as he joined in their game. Haven eventually came over with her older sister to extricate the two boys.

"Riven. Garett. Please calm yourselves. I am sure that Ryder will tell you stories of his travels later," Haven's sister said as she pulled her sons away.

Ryder flipped himself up to his feet much to the delight of the boys. "Didn't realize that I was an uncle, Sabrae," he said as he brushed the dirt from his legs and arms. Haven busied herself with removing the dirt from his back.

"You are a member of our family. You are my sister's husband," Sabrae said.

Haven hid her face against Ryder's back, gripping the cloth of his shirt. Ryder stiffened and clenched his fists. He then reached back and pulled Haven forward. "What have you been telling them?"

She shrugged. "It just seemed inevitable so I did not deny it. I kept your memory alive because I believed that you would return."

"Don't pout like that," Ryder groaned as he ran his hand over his face.

"Let's go inside. I have dinner cooking and I do not want to burn the meal for the first time in ages," Nora suggested. She clapped her hands in a motion for them to hurry. "Chop, chop!"

Onyx was amused by the display of affection towards Ryder though he found it odd that they were not angry at his century long absence. Maybe it was for show and that later, they were going to confront him. Did Haven inform her family ahead of time? He did not think so. Haven's other sister held the door open, curtsying when he passed. She looked like Haven except that her face was a little rounder. He tried to not cringe when she batted her eyelashes at him. He did chuckle to himself when he heard Haven admonish her second older sister to show respect.

"Tara, he is a Prince! And whatever happened to the soldier you were chasing?" Haven reprimanded.

"You mean the Earthborn I met in Branch? He told me that he had his duties to attend to and a kid sister to mind. I do hope to see him again someday. Him and his Gryphon friend. Such a beautiful creature," Tara replied sheepishly. She pouted at her sister before she went inside, flipping her hair as she passed.

"Sorry about that. She has pined after this Earthborn for

years. She is a hopeless romantic but I think her heart has decided that this man is the one for her," Haven apologized.

Onyx was about to reply when Ryder chuckled. He felt a nudge in his side and looked to see his cousin smirking back at him. It took a moment for Onyx to realize what Ryder was hinting at. Ryder had witnessed his encounter with Luna at the cliffs of Crossroads. His face flushed red.

Ryder hooked his right arm around Onyx's neck and pulled him along. "She was cute. Don't let a little thing like class rank stop you from courting her."

"You've been with Haven for so long. How did you court her in the beginning?" Onyx asked as they crossed the threshold.

"He courted me like a gentleman. He actually asked my father's permission to do so. Ryder's a bit rough around the edges but at heart, he is a hopeless romantic," Haven teased, patting Ryder on the chest.

The inside of the house was warm and inviting with a hodge podge of portraits and swords on display. Haven and Ryder left him to stare at the various decorations. His eyes looked towards the sitting room which had a large window on the back wall, looking over a small yard. A large gold framed painting hung over the fireplace on the right hand side. Onyx stepped up to it and studied the painting closer. It was the Ombre family tree. He scanned the many names, finding one that he did recognize: Torin. He remembered hearing that name in a story Kader Erebus had once told him about his famous ancestor. He struggled to recall the exact words but remembered that it was about the ultimate sacrifice.

"Ah yes, the ancestor of my family. Torin Ombre is remembered with great respect and honor for what he did. Had I had a son, Torin would have been his name," Ivan stated, coming up to Onyx's side.

"Master Erebus used to tell me stories of many famous Shadowborn. He always said there were more than just the sons and daughters of the Silvanus family that were great and noble," Onyx stated when Ivan directed him to sit.

Ryder sat down beside Onyx, looking nervous and tense, while Haven chatted with her two sisters in the background. The boys had disappeared into the kitchen with Nora.

"So it has been a little over a century since I last saw you , Ryder, and now you appear on my doorstep with the Crowned Prince. I know that this visit is not for pleasure and that Zoras Rokar likely sent you here," Ivan sighed. "I am not blind to what is going on."

"Then you have heard of what happened in Eclipse," Ryder

suggested quietly.

Ivan nodded. "Umbra may be Kaiser's city but we citizens despise him. Some openly, others more privately. What happened to our friends in Eclipse brings us terrible sorrow. What if Umbra is next?"

"We won't let that happen," Onyx interjected. He shifted in his seat. "Not so long as we sons of Shadow Night draw breath."

It took a long time before Ivan offered a reply. "Some say a little too late. Ryder, I am grateful that you are back but you have a great deal of explaining to do for leaving my daughter like you did. For leaving the Shadowborn for parts unknown and without so much as a word," Ivan said in a serious tone. He leaned forward, resting his elbows on his knees.

"Maybe I should go," Onyx said uncomfortably as he made an attempt to move away. Ryder pulled him back down, ignoring Ivan's shock. Ivan still saw Onyx as the Crowned Prince and heir to the throne, a person worthy of respect.

"There are not enough words that I can say to take back the pain I caused Haven and all of you," Ryder started to say. He let out a deep breath. "But I am done apologizing for something that cannot be changed. We must look to ensuring the future before we lose ourselves dwelling in the past. I know that your heart lies with those that oppose Kaiser Adonis."

Ivan nodded. "I do my best to supply the rebellion with good weapons and information when it comes."

"We came here to investigate reports of an army marching on the city. But we have found no physical or Spiritual evidence. What can you tell me of your observations? Have you noticed anything out of the ordinary?" Ryder asked sternly.

"I have not left the city boundaries in quite some time. I would ask Jarod. He tends to scout the valleys and mountains, rarely coming home. You two used to pal around back in the day, right?" Ivan asked as he sat back in his cushioned reading chair.

It was interesting to hear that Ryder had a childhood friend aside from Haven. Onyx wondered what kind of person Jarod was and why Ryder had not mentioned him. He thought about asking but decided against it for the time being.

"I doubt that Jarod would want to talk to me. Perhaps after some rest, you can take Onyx here to speak with him," Ryder suggested. He nudged Onyx's right shoulder.

"What will you do then?" Ivan asked. He caught eyes with Haven as she sauntered over.

Haven came over and draped her arms around Ryder's neck. "Ask him." When Ryder hesitated, she tugged his ear and repeated her command.

"Though I have my obligations as a soldier and son of Shadow Night's bloodline, there is another matter that Haven wants me to address. Your daughter wants me to be proper and formally ask for her hand. Ivan Ombre, I humbly ask for your permission and blessing to wed your daughter," Ryder said after a long silence.

Ivan smiled and nodded. Before Ryder could stop him, he shouted the good news. Squeals of delight came from the kitchen. Onyx lurched from reach as Haven's mother and sisters descended about the pair with hugs and kisses. He snickered as he saw Ryder's face flush red with embarrassment. Haven laughed when her two nephews rushed in shouting Uncle Ryder over and over. To Onyx, this was the closest he had ever seen Ryder in a family setting. The idea of a wedding in the middle of their great war was starting to grow on him.

AYLIN'S GRAVE

Haven's eyes fluttered open and she reached out her hand reflexively. Her fingers dragged down Ryder's bare right side. She smiled at the touch of his warm skin. She pulled herself to him and draped her arm over his torso. For a moment in time, nothing else mattered but having him sleeping next to her. With the silver moonlight beaming down on them through the window, Haven felt at peace. He was to finally be her husband and she his wife. She shivered with delight. His right arm slid down to caress the curve of her back.

"You awake too?" he asked, his deep resonant voice sending shivers down her spine.

"A little bit," she cooed. She rested her chin on his chest and looked up into his silver eyes. "What are you thinking about?"

Ryder let out a deep breath. "Getting married in the middle of a war I am expected to lead against my evil bastard of a grandfather. You know, he wanted me to marry Argos' younger sister. Fireborn girls are nice but not my type. A bit too spirited for my tastes."

"Then what is your type, sir," Haven teased. She tapped her fingers down the front of his chest.

He let out a deep breath and looked up at the ceiling. He then returned her affectionate gaze. "She would be kind, strong of heart, tenacious, independent. Should I stop or should I keep on describing you?"

Haven chuckled softly. "Point goes to you then for marrying

who you want. Double points for me."

"What for?" Ryder asked.

"I get to stick it to Kaiser and I get you. Double points," Haven replied as she settled against him.

"You will have to wear a dress," Ryder snickered. Haven immediately froze. He knew that she did not like wearing dresses or getting dressed up. "I would like to see you in a beautiful sparkling gown and I am sure your family would too. Remember, I am of the royal family. I can give you the wedding of your dreams."

"I'd rather be on a dirty battlefield surrounded by soldiers under a parade of swords than in a stuffy chapel in an equally binding dress," Haven grumbled. She tried to pull away but Ryder kept a tight hold. He laughed at her struggling to get free.

An owl hooted from somewhere outside with a deep airy sound. Ryder turned to look out the window. His usually rugged face seemed to soften under the moonlight. For once, he wasn't the powerful warrior or the bastard royal Prince. He was just a man.

"I wish that my mother could see us now," Ryder said solemnly. "There is so much that I want to tell her."

"You could still tell her," Haven suggested. "I can come with you if you don't want to go alone."

Ryder looked into her eyes and smirked. "We will have to put some clothes on first. It's a bit cold outside."

Haven giggled as she pulled away. She sat up on the edge of the bed, her bare skin smooth in the silver moonlight. Her dark hair fell down in waves. She glanced coyly over her shoulder, batting her eyelashes at Ryder in a teasing manner. Ryder leaned on his side, admiring her slender shape with heated desire. She gestured towards his clothes piled up on a nearby chair.

*****

With each step towards his mother's grave, Ryder felt his shoulders burdened by an increasing weight. A mixture of emotions filled him that he could not begin to explain as a whole. He kept asking himself what he was feeling to only greater confusion. He half led the way with Haven towards the northern side of the city. The streets were empty of people save patrolling guards who only paid him and Haven a passing mind. Haven put on a spectacular act of them being lovers returning home late at night. She held onto Ryder's side and pretended to laugh at something he had said. She would pull at his hood, bringing it forward and tell him to mind the chill in the air. Ryder was grateful for her company and her acting skills. He did not want to draw attention to his real identity.

Ryder and Haven made their way through the quiet streets, passing into the semi abandoned northern section of Umbra. Here, they could see the lingering damage of long ago battles. Though there were several pristine stone buildings with smoke rising from their chimneys, much of the area was blanketed by a sea of headstones. It was where the people of Umbra buried their dead. Headstones of different shapes and sizes were laid out in rows with paths crisscrossing around them. The pair was cautious not to step on a grave out of respect. On the outside edge and closest to the scarred city wall was the final resting place of Ryder's beloved mother.

Ryder immediately fell to his knees before his mother's headstone. Haven rested a steady hand on his shoulder and bowed her head. She knew that Ryder had loved his mother very much and missed her terribly. Beneath her hand, she could feel him shaking.

"I do not even know what to say. There is so much on my mind that I scarcely know where to begin. I always believed that my mother's Spirit was with me wherever I went but now, it like I am facing her in person. Completely bare of any armor or defense," Ryder trembled.

"Speak what is on your heart. I am sure that she will listen," Haven encouraged. She felt him take a deep breath and release it slowly.

"I am sorry that I abandoned you and dishonored your memory by running," Ryder started to say in a quivering voice. He wiped his nose with the back of his hand. "You would have told me to face my fears head on. To not let my fear stop me from doing what is right."

It was hard for Haven to hear and feel Ryder's sorrow and guilt. He was physically strong in his appearance and in how he battled. Mentally, he was broken and lost. A man under pressure to live up to people's expectations and desires while trying to find his own identity in the world. He wasn't the leader of the Shadowborn and yet people treated him like he should be. That he was wrong to abandon them by selfishly running away. Though she was still dealing with the pain his leaving had given her, she could not help but feel sorry for him. She bent down and wrapped her arms around him, resting her chin on his left shoulder.

"Long have I fought with the decision that was once laid before me. Do I take up the throne of my father? Do I assume the mantle of my ancestors? What should I do? What is the best path to take? I know what others expect of me but I barely know what to expect of myself. Am I honestly and truly capable of becoming what the world wants?"

Haven certainly thought that he was capable of wearing the crown with power and dignity. She felt prepared to accept the role with him even if it meant giving up parts of her old life. She squeezed his shoulder.

Ryder closed his eyes as he felt comforted in Haven's presence. "Mother, I wish that you were still here to see what I have become. To see my life and witness my union with Haven. To pass on what you have taught me to my own children should the Spirits choose to bless us."

Haven smiled at the thought of a grand wedding and happy family life though she dreaded the idea of wearing a dress. Being all dressed up did not excite her. She preferred chainmail and armor to frilly dresses and primly styled hair. She had a feeling that Ryder was of the same mind when dressing formally.

"You told me once that fear was a disease and that it could weaken your being and destroy it. I am afraid of him. His mind is the deadliest weapon the world has ever bred. I am certain that I can physically beat him in a fight. I am bigger than he is. But I cannot overcome the power of his mind. How can I hope to succeed when so many expect me to?" Ryder let out a deep breath and looked away from the headstone. "I am just one man."

"You are not alone," Haven said.

"I know that," Ryder replied with a hint of annoyance.

"No, I mean look!" Haven said as she grabbed Ryder's chin and forced him to look up. "You are not alone!"

Ryder's eyes opened up wide and his mouth dropped open in shock. He gripped Haven's hand, shaking. Before them was the ghostly image of Aylin, a silver wisp that slowly transformed into a translucent Spirit. She was still wearing what Ryder remembered as her favorite battle dress underneath a set of shining steel armor. Her long hair floated in the wind in glorious waves. Like her father and son, Aylin had a raptorian gaze that was both warm and resolute. Haven could see the strong similarities between mother and son. She helped Ryder to his feet.

"My dear son. You have grown strong and true of heart," Aylin stated. "I am glad to see you free and not corrupted."

Ryder could not find the words though memories of his encounter with his father's Spirit crossed his mind. He had been so close to his mother that when she had died, there had been a literal hole left in his heart. To see her again, even in Spirit form, made that hole throb with longing for the past. Haven shifted to his left side, his hand falling limp from hers. She could not believe that she was seeing a Spirit.

"You still have not married the girl? Never has there been a truer match than you and her," Aylin chuckled.

"Well, um," Ryder stumbled to say, reflexively pulling Haven to his side. "There's a war to fight."

Aylin nodded. "All of us can see the changes in the world and desire to help against the darkness in any way that we can. The power is great." She turned her head and looked away, a tear streaming down her cheek.

Haven wanted to speak and ask questions, feeling a stirring within her. She looked to Ryder as if to ask permission. His gaze was only ahead but he nodded. "Do the Spirits really hear us?"

"We can hear all if we listen," Aylin stated. She held a hand over her heart. "I have seen so many try to break through the void only to fall deeper and farther away from this world. The power is so great."

Ryder found it curious that his mother repeated the phrase about great power. The wheels in his mind started turning. "What power do you speak of?"

Whatever the power was made Aylin intensely scared as her Spirit image quivered. Ryder wanted to rush forward to embrace her but knew that he would only just pass through. Aylin looked deep into his eyes with absolute conviction. "There are truly terrible nightmares in this world and we cry to see one walking the land of the living. It was fear that pushed such an irrational choice and left everything out of balance. It cannot be contained. It must be destroyed. Obliterated into absolute nothingness. All must fight."

Haven clung to Ryder, afraid of the steely look in Aylin's eyes. Ryder wrapped his arms around her in protection. He swallowed a breath, nearly choking on the lump in his throat. He was starting to feel afraid. A fierce wind ripped through the graveyard. The Spirit of Aylin was cloaked in a veil of angry fire that threatened to burn everything. Ryder shielded Haven against the force, holding her tight against him. A deep guttural roar blasted into their hearing. Aylin's eyes suddenly changed from harsh to gentle. The harsh display of power was gone with no evidence left behind to indicate its presence. She smiled sweetly, keeping her hand over her heart.

"The Spirits have blessed you and given you reason to fight even if you do not know it yet. They will continue to bless those that fight with true hearts and curse those that seek to dismantle the very foundations of the world. On this night, my dear son, many years ago, I was blessed with you. I will always watch over you and those you love. Fight on, my dear Peredur and you as well, my dear Haven. I am glad to see that you will be at his side. I give you this," Aylin preached before reaching out towards the pair.

A small circle of light lifted from her hand and floated over to them. Ryder reached out and grasped the light. As soon as he did, Aylin's Spirit disappeared. He slowly opened his fingers and saw that it was his mother's favorite ring, a gift from Akakios. It was a silver ring that had been carved into a tiny pair of owl wings. A shining and sparkling diamond was set in place where the carved wings met. Without speaking, Ryder took Haven's left hand and held the ring up.

"Will you bind yourself to me, body and soul? Through all the pains and hurts of the world, will you stand at my side?" Ryder asked, a broad smile crossing his face.

Haven's heart fluttered as Ryder set the ring on her finger. Tears of joy streamed down her cheeks. Once the ring was in place, she leapt up into his arms and kissed him deeply. He held her to him, keeping her in his arms when their lips parted.

"War will not stop us, Ryder my love. Together, we shall overcome."

*****

HAUNTED VOICES

The throne room was cold and empty of decoration. Cobwebs were strung between the stone pillars that held up the ceiling in thick nets. Dust coated every surface and floated down to the floor when a flying insect got trapped in a web. Moonlight streamed down through the sky window, its iron and glass structure sealed shut. The throne of the Shadowlord was equally derelict and in shambles. The ebony wood was splitting and falling apart. A layer of debris was scattered at the chair's base. It was if it was no longer worth the power and strength that once sat upon it. The entire room had been abandoned.

Kaiser stood before the broken chair, his head tilted to the side in thought. His arms hung loose at his side. He studied the chair and scoffed. He turned around, scratching his chest. Stepping away from the raised dais, Kaiser made his way to the center of the room. He threw off the heavy black robe with a toss of the hand, revealing an adorned set of black clothes. His sleeveless tunic hung loose from his shoulders. Kaiser briefly thought that had he been gifted with a bulkier frame, the piece would have fit better. He smirked as he slowed his stride, latching his hands behind his back and swinging his feet.

Coming to his desired spot, Kaiser stamped his left foot hard and released a wave of fire. The fire shot out in a series of ripples, climbing the walls and meeting at the sky window. Kaiser raised up his left hand towards the ceiling. The fire twisted into a tight spiral and raced for his open palm. It formed into a point and disappeared in a burst of light. Kaiser then spun around and threw the energy towards the throne, blasting it into cinders. The cinders floated slowly to the ground.

"May the space be cleansed of all memory," Kaiser stated in a haunting tone as he lowered his left arm. "The past is nothing. The future is uncertain. The present is now."

Kaiser took a deep breath and slowly released it, settling his mind into a single and unbroken entity. He closed his eyes in focus. His mind was a blank space, free of any distractions. He thought of nothing. A spark in the darkness of his mind brought everything back to life. Memories flooded every possible space, rushing by at high speed. Here was a millennium of life playing before Kaiser's mental eyes. When he was satisfied, Kaiser opened his eyes and smirked. The time had come and he was ready.

With the first wave of his left hand and then his right, all around him whispered distant voices. The haunted voices were unintelligible but they spoke faster and faster. They fought to be heard as Kaiser continued to spread the fire in a controlled design. Soon the voices started to shout in protest, crying out curses in desperation. Kaiser scoffed as he continued his methodical preparation. Once the fire had been sufficiently laid, he brought up his right hand and closed it quickly. The voices screamed as the fire formed the first stage of a Living Map.

The fire transformed into a replica of the world laid flat. Kaiser stood in the center of what was the Shadowborn lands in the exact spot of Cross. The fire around him was a lifeless black. He snapped his fingers and a small silver Spirit Fire formed above his right hand. He then twisted his wrist around once with his fingers spread out to transformed the small flame into a circular band. The circular band rested above his spread fingers, staying in place as he turned his hand over. He used one finger to turn the band around in one revolution. Four tiny spheres formed on the cardinal points of the band, representing the four directions.

"I, Kaiser Anu Adonis, have walked this world for one thousand one hundred and one years. I have seen, heard, and felt every part of it from both sides of the veil," Kaiser started to say as he pressed the spheres from north to south and east to west. Each sphere lit up like tiny Spirit Fires. He pulled his hand back and the energy design floated in the air at heart level. "I unleash every memory I have touched with unyielding force."

The voices clamored louder and louder in protest. A howling roar joined the voices, giving them the strength to be heard. "Stop this right now, you foul abomination!"

Kaiser chuckled to himself as he pulled out a small dagger from his belt. "I have set the boundaries, Omu. You can do nothing to stop me. I do not call to you. I challenge you! You and all of those greater Spirits who presume to call themselves gods!"

Omu answered him with an earth shattering roar. The room shook violently, jolting hard with Omu's rage from the other side. It was if the great Wolf Spirit was slashing his claws against the veil to break free. Kaiser laughed at each shake of the world. He pressed the tip of the steel dagger into the palm of his left hand. The blade sliced through the meat of his hand. Blood quickly welled up. Kaiser clenched his hand tight to avoid any blood from hitting the floor.

"What will you do now? Will you break through the veil and strike me where I stand? You have already tried before. If you have forgotten, I can show you the scars on my back," Kaiser dared. He gripped the dagger in his right hand. The entire weapon heated up until it was cherry red. "I can bend the world to my will and shape it to my heart's desire."

"EXILE!" Omu shouted. His angry voice echoed loudly in the room, bouncing off the walls and ceiling. "YOU HAVE BROKEN THE COVENANT!"

"I haven't yet, Omu," Kaiser smoothly said as the cherry red dagger turned white hot. "It is you who has broken the Covenant of Spirits. You who acted without thought and reason. You were not always the caretaker of the dead."

Kaiser threw the melted weapon forward. The congealed substance soared for a few feet before hitting an invisible wall. It spread over the wall, forming a snarling wolf's face. The face pushed forward, snapping its jaws. Kaiser wiggled his fingers in a playful wave. He raised up his clenched left hand, blood seeping from between his fingers.

"Your blood may be red but your soul is black and cold," the metallic wolf head snarled. "The veil can only hold me for so long before I am called beyond it."

Kaiser lifted an eyebrow in question. "Oh really? Who is strong enough to summon a powerful Spirit such as yourself? To truly call out to you. I am sure that you have heard the Shadowborn cry your name for years upon end. Maybe you have even crossed over a few times at the call of a Silvanus." He shook his head and laughed. "But it never lasts."

"You know nothing of the true power of the Spirit World! Even now from beyond the veil, I am speaking to you and my roar shakes the very room you are standing in," Omu growled. The metallic wolf head came within inches of Kaiser.

"Go ahead and stop me if you are truly so powerful," Kaiser said coldly. "I dare you."

The wolf head snapped and struggled, silver spittle spraying outward. Kaiser laughed at Omu's attempt to sink his teeth into his face. He raised his right hand and tapped the metal wolf on the nose. An earsplitting metallic screech erupted as the wolf's head shattered into a thousand pieces. The debris was consumed by the fire in the blink of an eye. Omu's roar came from a distant place, muffled and lacking in power.

Kaiser reached forward and set his clenched left hand over the circular band. "With my blood, I will ignite the deep flames of the world and with it, see all that passes."

"NO!" Omu roared with a throat splitting cry. "IT IS FORBIDDEN!"

Kaiser paused and looked up, seeing the repeated strikes upon the veil. Circles of light pulsated with each hit. He turned his head around. All around him, the Spirits on the other side of the veil fought to break through in their attempt to stop him. The fingers on his left hand began to twitch from being held so tightly for so long. "You cannot undo what has already been done. If you want someone to blame, look to yourselves and watch the chaos that you have created."

A single drop of blood broke free and fell from Kaiser's hand. It seemed to float down in slow motion, twisting and spinning in suspended animation. Kaiser opened his hand up a little and more drops of blood fell. Each hit the sphere of energy in the center of the circular band. With every drop, the sphere sparked and crackled. The band began to spin rapidly as the cardinal point spheres turned crimson red. Kaiser pulled his left hand back and gently touched the wound on his palm with the fingers of his right hand. The wound quickly closed and left a red mark behind.

Surrounding Kaiser was his Living Map and floating before him was his Spirit Compass. The Compass was powered by Spirit energy and his blood. Both were created in a profane and forbidden ritual. The ritual came from the time before the Covenant of Spirits and the separation of the world of the living and the dead. How Kaiser came across it, only he and the Great Spirits knew. But it was deadly and very dangerous to execute.

Rache watched from the shadows just out of reach of the Living Map. He knew exactly what Kaiser was doing but was too curious not to watch. Keeping a careful distance, the Demon studied the Living Map. The Spirit Compass made him nervous. Unlike the Map, it was free to float beyond the boundaries, going to where his master wished. It could take the memories and life of a person to further enhance the details of the Map. Kaiser was especially adept at stealing Spirit energy and bending the memories of others to his will. Rache watched his dangerous master waft his hands, directing the Compass.

What the Demon would not admit to anyone was that he was deeply afraid of Kaiser. That his master was more dangerous than the world realized. He had become an echo of the past living in the present with a desire to conquer the future. A man free from time's constraints. Though Kaiser had praised Rache's power and ferocity, the Demon knew that he was expendable. He thought about the profane bond that held him to Kaiser, going over every detail of it. Using blood sacrifices in combination with Spirit energy, a Demon could be summoned to serve as a sword and as a shield against death. At first, Rache jumped at the chance. Suffering endlessly in the Spiral ended as soon as he took his first breath. He was free to roam the world again and fight for Dominion. In Kaiser, he found the stability that the Demons lacked in a singular leader. They were a mindless bunch and he was so much more. Rache was happy.

As he watched Kaiser work, Rache revisited the feelings of regret that had followed him as of late. Kaiser's lone descendent had pointed out that the Demon was nothing more than a prisoner. Many had told him that fact over the years but somehow Ryder made him believe it. He was a prisoner, a slave. He was not free. This was not what he wanted. He too heard the haunted voices and he was prepared to listen to them. Rache watched as Kaiser commanded the Spirit Compass to release the first drop of blood. The crimson drop touched the Living Map with a bright flash of energy.

*****

SPIRIT WAKE

"What was that?"

Ira Shunga looked up from his reading to glance at his wife. She knelt down and ran her hand over the rug as if to feel the earth beneath their home.

"Baya, you are not an Earthborn. You will not be able to read the ground to tell you that it was just an earthquake," Ira grumbled as he returned to his book. He licked his fingertips and slowly turned to the next page.

The ground shook harder, knocking over a vase. The fragile item hit the floor and broke into pieces. The flowers slumped over in a mess of water and porcelain.

"That is not an earthquake, husband. Not a natural one," Baya said as she stood back up. She looked about in nervous anticipation. She gulped hard. "Maybe Cross is under attack. Rouse the troops!"

Ira dropped his book on to the seat of his chair. He hushed his wife with a finger to the lips. Baya scurried to his side and grabbed him around the waist. She shivered with fright. Ira wrapped his arms around Baya in an attempt to soothe her. The ground shook again and the temperature in the air dropped dramatically. Both Ira's and Baya's puffs of breath were frosting in the air.

"Spirit energy but what kind?" Ira wondered out loud. He jolted when the fire in the fireplace went out with a rush of wind.

Baya buried her face into Ira's chest.

The fire fizzled out into a thin wisp of smoke. The room darkened with only the outdoor torchlight streaming in. Ira looked about, trying to discern anything of note. Outside of the window, an owl hooted a low sonorous song before screeching loudly. The window burst open in a rush of freezing cold wind. Baya clung to Ira as he held her tightly. The wind screamed and hissed as it blew through the room and out the door. Glass shattered and furniture flipped over in loud thuds. Sticks and leaves blew into the open window, striking Ira across the face. He bent over in pain white Baya tried to dab the cut on his cheek with her sleeve.

Ira snarled as he looked towards the broken window. "Get all of the estate in the cellar as quickly as you can. Alert everyone in this house. I'll run to the stables and the out buildings. Let no refuse my order."

"And do not let yourself get hurt any further. I do not know what is happening but I know that it cannot be good," Baya said as she cradled Ira's face. "Be safe."

Shadow Slide proved to be a life saver when Ira moved outside. He had never seen or experienced a tornado but the world was reacting as if one was nearby. Debris was flying everywhere, crashing into barriers with brute force. Ira managed to dive inside the foreman's house as a huge uprooted oak crashed before the doorway.

"Master Shunga!" the foreman shouted in surprise.

"No time for explanations. Get everyone you can and Shadow Slide to the manor cellar," Ira coughed as he rubbed his chest. He had hit the floor hard and lost his breath.

"Yes sir. At once," the foreman replied. He quickly slipped into Shadow Slide, leaving Ira alone.

Alone, even if for a moment, Ira's thoughts descended into a dark place of confusion. The Shadowborn lands rarely had tornadoes and even then the storms occurred in the southern reaches. There were no Airborn men or women within the borders. All signs pointed to one cause: Spirit energy. There was only one person in the Shadowborn lands capable of such power. Ira slammed his fist on the floor in anger.

"Kaiser," he growled. He pushed himself up to his feet, strengthening his resolve. He spat out a globule of blood and wiped his mouth. His tongue was bleeding.

Ira pushed himself to his feet and looked back out the door he had just come through. Outside, the windstorm was raging but this time, he looked at it with a sense of determination. He was not going to let Kaiser push him around anymore. He was going to confront him no matter what. With a passing thought, Ira slipped back into Shadow Slide and raced back towards his house. He ignored the deeper cold and more tenuous grasp he had on his Spirit energy. All that mattered was going after Kaiser and stopping his madness.

Ira arrived at the cellar door and opened it without knocking. Inside, the room was full. Baya went around speaking to the retainers who in various state of dress. Some were still wearing their work uniforms such as the small team of guards in their armor. People of the house were wearing their nightclothes, their hair undone. Baya spoke to a worried house maid before she noticed her husband.

"We are under attack by an enemy that we have long known. This storm," Ira started to say as he gestured towards the door and the outside. "Is no natural event. It is the work of powerful Spirit energy."

"Is one of Aves' people to blame?" a stable hand asked.

"No. Aves would never allow one of his kin to do such a thing. The Airborn are peaceful," Baya reasoned. She looked again to her husband.

"Kaiser Adonis is to blame," Ira said harshly. He pointed downwards to emphasize his statement. "He will always be to blame so long as we let him."

"What more are we supposed to do, husband? Our own son fights with the rebellion and we give them as much resources as we can spare to support the effort," Baya asked.

Ira turned around in a circle, making eye contact with each person in the room. "I am sure that some of you are asking how a windstorm could be blamed on Kaiser. It is not like a windstorm hasn't happened before. But there is something about this event that steals the warmth from my body." He put his right hand over his heart. "All of you know the chill of being in Shadow Slide and you all know what that chill is. Take a deep breath and feel the air. Tell me what it reminds you of."

The room fell silent save for the deep intake of breath. Only Baya did not follow her husband's suggestion. She looked at him with an expression of growing fear and worry. She already knew what her husband was thinking.

"The world quakes when Spirits wake from their cold slumber. Life beware. Hearts prepare for the hunter," the house chamberlain stated. He was an older man with gray streaks in his hair and beard.

"Something dark has been unleashed upon the world. I can feel it in my bones even if I do not fully know what that darkness is. It is more than Kaiser being destructive and murderous. It is something much worse and I will find out," Ira addressed the room.

He turned to face Baya. "I leave command of the estate in your hands, dear wife. I go to confront our enemy."

Baya rushed forward and grabbed his arm in an attempt to stop him. "You cannot go alone. You should not go at all. You heard how he murdered the Shadow Council. He slaughtered them with his bare hands! He will do the same to you!"

"I have to agree, Master Shunga. Kaiser has proven to be far stronger in mind and command of Spirit energy. If he is truly behind this windstorm as you say, then we must take a different path," the house chamberlain stated. He came to stand behind Baya. Others stepped closer to encircle Ira and Baya.

"Fear is a great weapon so long as you allow it to control you. Courage is an equally great weapon and Kaiser must know that he will not win control of Cross or our homeland. The rebels depend on souls like us to fight no matter what. I will not cower or bow down to my fear of him," Ira argued.

"It is a fool's errand to go. We should all leave together and give ourselves wholeheartedly to the rebel cause," Baya cried. She held onto Ira's arm tighter.

Ira gently laid his free hand on hers. He looked deep into her wet eyes. She wept openly. He then reached to embrace her tightly and she buried her face into his shoulder. For a time, they remained together. The retainers of the estate came together and places their hands on their masters in a sign of solidarity.

Suddenly, the ground shook violently and all fell still. Ira looked towards the door, hearing a vengeful hiss. His breath frosted in the air as he watched the door begin to shudder.

*****

Vorin surged upward with a furious series of wing flaps. His wings stretched and pumped to the limit to help him gain altitude. He twisted and turned erratically to throw off his attackers. He quickly rolled to the right to avoid a wing shearing strike. Like a cluster of annoying mosquitos, the black winged Spirits darted around the massive red scaled Dragon. They screeched and hissed wildly.

"Dark Spirits! I shall burn you!" he roared before unleashing a blast of hot fire from his maw. He snaked his serpentine neck around in a circle and flew through the flame wheel. Two of the Dark Spirits burnt up quickly while others soared around the dangerous Dragonfire.

The Dragon had taken to the skies when he felt the first shudder of the earth. Something about it unnerved him and woke up a deep seated memory. He had always gone on flights to sort out his thoughts among the clouds. This time was different. No sooner than he had crossed through the first cloud was he beset by enemies. Each sight and sound of the Dark Spirits worked to clear the ancient memory. It also fueled his rage and awakened his wilder side. He cursed in the Dragon tongue, spitting out jets of fire. Though it had been ages since he last fought in any contest, Vorin was ready.

With each passing second, the Dark Spirits transformed into a more recognizable state. Their once hazy wings hardened into black articles of flight. Spikes grew out of their spines. Eyes of white glowed in their heads as their bright fangs flashed. Though the creatures were smaller in size, they were great in number. Their breath was icy, frosting in the air. They were frighteningly fast. Vorin folded his wings and dropped in altitude at high speed. Just as quickly, the Dark Spirits raced after him.

Vorin descended quickly through the clouds. He repeatedly released fire from his maw to cloak himself in a protective shield. He began to twist in a spiral, letting the fire shield extend out behind him. Transformed into a shooting star, Vorin sped towards the ground. He did everything that he could to outmaneuver the Dark Spirits who he now saw as terrors of the ancient past. As the last Dragon, Vorin did not want to admit that there were those of his race that gave themselves to the darkness. It was a story his forebears had told him since the beginning. A story that originated from the darkest of days. He shook his head, not wanting to think of that time.

The Dragon Demons as Vorin began to call his pursuers surged after him. Icy breath shot out of their maws. One of the creatures shot forward to take a bite out of Vorin's muscular tail. Vorin swung his tail and slammed it into the biting creature. The bodily form dissipated but left a cold burn on Vorin's tail. The pain was intense. Vorin roared in response.

His roar boomed across the sky. Beneath him, the tree tops of the forest came alive as a multitude of Gryphons took flight to the Dragon's defense. Leading the way was Aves on the back of a brown owl Gryphon that Vorin recognized from Crossroads. He let out a rallying cheer.

"To the skies, Togra! Fly high to your Lord's defense!" Aves cried out, his face decorated with war paint. The brown owl Gryphon screeched in response.

The sky battle commenced as the Gryphon battalion struck hard at Vorin's attackers. Aves proved to be a masterful warrior, utilizing the sky born speed of Togra to launch Spirit energy attacks. The Lord of the Airborn never lost his fervor for the fight even when his attacks failed to tear down the Dragon Demons.

"Fly upon me, Aves! Let us take them down as one!" Vorin roared.

Aves leaped from Togra's back as the Gryphon drew close to Vorin's side. He twisted in the air, executing a precise full body spin to land upon the Dragon's shoulders. He stood up tall and spun his steel tipped spear. He moved and shifted his weight, keeping perfectly balanced. Aves cried out in the Gryphon tongue with a commanding voice. The battalion split up into several companies and took positions around Vorin to defend him from the Dragon Demons. The companies fought off concentrated strikes from all possible angles but were unable to eliminate their spiritual enemy. Vorin glanced over his shoulder and locked eyes with Aves. Aves nodded. The Lord of the Airborn cried out again in the Gryphon tongue. The Gryphon companies quickly flew out of range and descended back towards the forest.

Vorin's chest rumbled with an explosive flame as he arched his neck in preparation. A roar built up in his throat. His red scales began to shimmer as steam rose up from his body. Aves, in the meantime, carefully spun his spear and moved his body in a precise and sharp formation. The cloud of steam began to move and take shape at the Airborn's command. Smoke poured out of Vorin's nostrils, the heat building up inside his body.

Together, Aves and Vorin shouted in the Dragon tongue, releasing their combined explosive power. The pair were bathed in fire and charged upon the dark Spirits. Faced with their wrath, the Dragon Demons erupted into chaos, losing their annoying confidence. Aves and Vorin fought as one to victorious effect. Six of the creatures rushed off as the rest of their kin were incinerated. The Gryphons below cheered with raucous whistles and cries. Aves issued one last command as the fire around him and Vorin dissipated.

"Ah to feel the heat of battle, it warms my soul," Vorin said once he had landed in an open clearing. Gryphons flew overhead, chawing their orders to each other.

Aves looked back at Vorin after watching the Gryphons. He held his spear tightly. "The Dark Spirits have not been within the confines of this world since the days preceding the Covenant of Spirits. Dragon Demons, you call them, have found their way across the veil. The veil is the strongest shield in all of existence and yet they crossed it freely. I suspect that you were not the only beset by such occurrences."

Now free from attack, Vorin had a chance to think on the details. The dark memory that had inspired his flight returned to him and he growled. The growl turned into a full throated roar of rage. "I cannot even begin to fathom how and why. All I know is that I want to tear that traitorous villain to shreds! This goes beyond the Immortal Truth! Beyond everything this world knows as true!"

"Then you have realized it too. Though I do not yet know how, Kaiser has used Spirit Wake. If we do not stop him now, then this world will be destroyed. I'll be damned if I stand by and let it consume all that I love and hold dear," Aves promised.

"We can wait no longer for Bane. We must fight this war on our own and we will win it together. May we of the Northern Alliance unite before the end and cast Kaiser down into the abyss."

*****

MERAS IS BURNING

Gyr did not like the fact that the sunset was blood red. Something about the sight chilled him to the core. He sniffed the air, catching a strong scent of something burning. He looked away and shuddered. He quickly rustled his wings in a wild rush.

"You have been quiet for quite some time now. Is something bothering you?" Charon asked as he readjusted the strap of his travel pack. It had been digging into his shoulder, causing him discomfort. "Is it because the night is coming?"

"I may be a day hatched Gryphon but it is not the night that unnerves me," Gyr grumbled as he stood up on all fours. He gripped the earth with his paws. It felt warm to the touch.

"Well Meras is just around the bend. I certainly would not mind sleeping in a bed instead of on the ground," Charon said as he started to walk away.

Gyr jumped in front of him, halting his progress. He kept his wings raised. "I do not know how to explain it but I have a very bad feeling about Meras. We should not go there so boldly."

Charon sneered in disgust. The Gryphon and his inexplicable feelings were starting to get to him. At times, Gyr's intuitions were insightful and other times they were infuriating. He tried to step around Gyr only for the way to be blocked again. He made another attempt to the same result. Throwing his hands up, Charon admitted defeat.

"Ok. We will do it your way. Again," Charon snapped.

"You would do well to heed when the world tries to tell you

something. My gut tells me to beware of Meras. You can go there foolishly but I will choose a different path," Gyr growled. He held his face within inches of Charon's.

The wind shifted ever so slightly, bringing upon it the scent of smoke and fire. Hidden amongst the invisible folds of air were hints of blood curdling screams. Both Charon and Gyr looked towards the east with worry. They then looked back at each other.

"What does your gut tell you now?" Charon asked.

"For you to hold on tight!" Gyr shouted.

In a flurry of motion, Gyr knocked Charon off his feet and slipped under him. Charon thumped onto Gyr's back, grasping at Gyr's neck as the Gryphon rose high into the air. Charon's stomach lurched and he swallowed hard. He was still not used to flying. Gyr flew with determination, climbing up above the trees of the forest. The Gryphon banked hard to the right.

The sight in the distance horrified the pair. The entire city of Meras was engulfed in flames. Not a building was spared from the destruction. The smoke was so thick that Charon coughed violently. Gyr flew around the clouds of smoke with careful ease. To Charon, the Gryphon appeared completely focused on his path. A part of him was glad for the Gryphon's confidence because he was scared. Fire had always scared him for its destructive power and unpredictability. A darker memory threatened to creep out from the depths of his mind but Charon quickly shoved it back down.

Gyr flew with a completely different mindset from that of his companion. He could smell the energy in the fire, telling him that this was no normal blaze. No untended fire pit or careless toss of a match was the cause of it. It screamed Spirit energy and the Mortal people of Meras would be hard pressed to suppress the fire. Even if they could control the fire, there was still the matter of who set it. They would never last against such a foe. He twisted and turned to avoid singeing his flight feathers.

"We must help them. Summon your Spirit energy," Gyr started to say in a commanding voice.

"I can't! I do not know how and you know that! Besides even if I could, what good could Shadowborn power do against a fire as big and destructive as this?" Charon shouted back. He buried his face into Gyr's neck.

Gyr growled as he looked ahead. A flaming spiral arched ahead. He curled his wings and tucked in his limbs. "In your core, you are a Shadowborn and that ancient blood will see your will and answer your call. Look deep within and command the shadows like your ancestors before you."

It was an impossible task and Charon doubted that he

could do anything of worth. "I can't!"

"Charon!" Gyr tried to shout over the roar of the flames. He surged through the arch and threw out his wings. He pumped hard to gain altitude over the city square.

Beneath him, people ran in panic. They carried buckets of water to throw over the fire, shrieking when their efforts did little to squelch the flames. Children screamed in absolute fear, shouting for their parents to save them. It broke Gyr's heart to hear their cries. He snarled as he rocketed towards the ground. As soon as he drew close, he took a hard left and threw Charon to the ground. Charon tumbled several feet, losing his travel pack, before he slid to a stop.

"I do not ask you to do the impossible for it is within all Shadowborn to command the shadows to their will. Now, I do not care how you do it but use your power to help these people. Find where the fire is not so thick and show them the way to safety. The blaze is too large and far gone to stop it," Gyr said firmly. He looked over his shoulder. "I must find whoever started this fire and stop him from escaping. They can't have gotten far."

Charon could barely protest before Gyr leaped into the air. He still did not understand what the Gryphon was asking him to do. Even he could summon the Spirit energy, how could shadows defeat a fire? He got to his feet. All around him was heat and destruction. How could he make a difference? He gulped. A woman ran to him, tripping and falling. She lost her grip on a water bucket and it rolled to his feet. He watched as the woman wept, crying about the futility of it all. He started to back away, not wanting to get involved. Fear was getting the best of him.

He turned and ran from the city square. He hoped that Gyr would not see him and scream coward. Yes, he was a coward. He was not worthy of the blood in his veins. Even with that honest truth, Charon could not face his fear. There was no way that Spirit energy could save Meras. There was no way that he could do anything but die like the rest of them. Charon turned down a side street where the smoke did not seem as thick. He ran straight into a terrified child, sliding to a stop before he could knock him over. The child screamed at him, tears streaming down his face.

In that instant, Charon saw a reflection of the terrible childhood memory. This time it refused to be ignored. He shook his head several times to remove the image of the dark shadow with glowing white eyes, framed by a burning fire. He had screamed and begged for his mother, not knowing where she was and if she was still alive. Fear of the past and fear for the present threatened to overwhelm him. He looked down into the child's eyes, seeing a ghost of his memory. He thought about how he wished that someone had come to save him back then.

"Come with me. I will lead you to safety," Charon said as he whisked the little boy into his arms.

The boy howled and screamed for his parents. Charon kept the child tight against him as he raced through the streets, looking for an opening in the fire. The focus of finding an opening overwhelmed his senses into a singular force. He made it his singular mission to get the little boy to safety. Unbidden, the churning Spirit energy took control and whisked him away into Shadow Slide. The heat of the flames diminished as a coolness crept into his body. He could still see the light until suddenly it was not there anymore. He fell forward and collapsed into the dirt, free of the fire. He looked over his shoulder in confusion at what had just happened.

"You saved him!" shouted a woman's voice. Charon did not even register the child being pulled from his arms.

"What just happened?" Charon asked though he did not intend to voice his question out loud. He looked about, scraping his hands on the stone beneath him.

The woman who had pulled the child away, cradled him in her arms. She repeated over and over about how the mysterious black haired man would also save his parents. Charon finally turned his gaze towards them, pulling his eyes from the fire. The woman looked at him not in fear as he expected when people saw him but in gratitude and hope.

"Please help us," the woman begged. Ash covered his face and Charon could see that she had wrapped her hands with a dirty white cloth.

Charon wanted to say that he did not know what to do but his heart was telling him a different story. He had the power. He had just used it, brought it forth like Gyr had said. He could help Meras. He looked down at his hands and wondered if he could summon Spirit energy again. Was it Spirit energy that had helped him run right through the burning fire? He looked back up towards the path that he had just come from. Yes he could do it again. Charon looked towards the woman, smiled, and gave a thumbs up. It took only that confident thought to draw him back into Shadow Slide.

His confidence surged as he fully trusted in his instincts to guide him. He returned to the square, searching for the woman that he had abandoned. Jumping out of Shadow Slide caused him to stumble but he managed to catch his footing in time. The woman was nowhere to be seen. Charon looked around for a fountain or a water pump. He spotted a copper faucet over an empty watering trough. He rushed over to it and ripped it from its bearings in a single motion. Water sprayed out and soaked him. It continued to gush.

"Over here!" Charon shouted to a group of four men. He waved for them to see the flowing water spilling quickly from the pump. They ran to his side and began filling their buckets. "Where are the others?"

The man began pointing in all directions, shouting over the roar of the fire. Charon did his best to follow their instructions and ripped three more faucets from their bearings. A flood of water began to spread, filling the open square with a cloud of steam. Charon kept looking for anything else that he could do or a chance to use his churning Spirit energy to help.

Suddenly, Charon was thrown from his feet. He flew through the air and crashed twenty feet from where he had just been standing. He slammed down hard on his back, knocking the wind from his lungs. He coughed violently to the point that he was spitting out blood. He felt his limbs refusing to obey his commands to move. An instant later, another mysterious attack slammed into him. His whole body jolted like he had been struck by lightning. His chest burned and he could barely see.

On the edge of his hazy vision was a tall, black shadow. It moved slowly towards him with what appeared to be a hand raised at him. Charon fought desperately to recover his vision, blinking his eyes in rapid succession. As the shadow drew closer, he felt an overwhelming sense of fear and darkness take control of his being. His dark childhood memory was playing out before him as he faced the same shadow that had plagued him for decades. His body refused his commands and he laid helpless before certain death. There was no escape this time.

PAST COMES ALIVE

Gyr shoved his shoulder against the beam, throwing the broken wood to the side. He stuck his head inside the doorway and looked around. He spotted two women clutching each other and covered in ash. "Come on!"

The women both screamed in fright, frozen in fear. Gyr was about to shout an unkind word when another roof beam collapsed. He leaped forward and caught it on his back. His limbs shuddered from the weight but his strength held. He issued his order again, speaking as clearly as he could in the common tongue. Still they refused to move. Gyr wondered if they were afraid of him. His shoulders started to bend under the weight of the beam and he looked away.

"I will not let you die here!" Gyr roared as he threw back his wings. The beam fell back with a heavy thud, tearing a hole in the roof. Through the hole, the fires reached higher and smoke began to clear the room. Gyr then started to beat his wings in an attempt to clear it faster. He then looked back at the doorway and kicked hard. His well-placed strike opened up a bigger space for the women to escape. He locked eyes with them, conveying his ardent desire to save them and that he was not going to give up. He breathed a sigh of relief when the women got to their feet. He jumped forward and covered them with each wing and lead them outside.

"Thank you," both of the women said. They resisted the urge to touch Gyr's feathers.

"The only thanks I need is to see you both in the morning alive and well. Now go!" Gyr replied before leaping into the sky.

Gyr pumped his wings, now sore from the effort to hold the heavy beam. Some of his flight feathers had been singed and now caused him to be slightly off balance. He gritted his beak and powered through the exhaustion. This is what he had trained for. This is what he was born to do. He repeated the thoughts over and over to himself to give him stronger motivation. Soaring back towards the square, Gyr spotted the courageous efforts of the villagers, carrying bucket after bucket in an attempt to put out the fire. The sight pleased him greatly to see the people working together. He then turned his head towards the right and all warmth left his body.

*****

Charon slammed into the ground with a heavy thud. He managed to roll over and avoid a sword strike to the head. Blood spewed from his mouth as he groaned in pain. It took every desperate thought within him to use Shadow Slide again. Just as soon as he descended into the power, his attacker ripped him free and lifted him high in the air. Charon gasped and tried to cough, grabbing the attacker's wrist with both hands to free himself.

"I must kill him. Must kill him. Master's orders. Must not anger Master," the shadowy attacker repeated over and over in a quick voice. His eyes were wild with madness.

He recognized those eyes. There were the same ones from the memory that had worked its way out of the depths of his mind. He scratched and pulled at the hand holding his throat. He then kicked hard, slamming his foot into the man's chest. The grip slackened and Charon was able to break free. He fell to the ground, unsteady on his legs. Before he could dwell on what his attacker was doing, he flipped backwards four times and picked up one of the pipes he had ripped free earlier. He swung it around and got ready for the counterattack.

"Ok. I can do this. I can face down fear and a madman determined to kill me," Charon told himself. He rolled his shoulders in an attempt to keep loose. "He is only a Shadowborn many times older and stronger than I am."

Fear was threatening to take complete control again but Charon fought the urge to run. It was clear that the Shadowborn could tear him out of Shadow Slide and could run him down with his unnatural speed. There was no other choice but to fight back.

Charon held up the pipe like it was a sword, gripping the ridged end with both hands.

"Silly boy. Silly silly boy," the Shadowborn cackled. He took a threatening step forward, brandishing his sword in quick twisting circles.

"I am not afraid of you. Not anymore," Charon declared as his knees threatened to buckle. He swallowed hard.

The Shadowborn grinned in such a way that all warmth left Charon's body. Even the burning fire did little to keep the chill of his fear at bay. The Shadowborn stepped forward in a zig zag pattern, shifting his weight from foot to foot.

"Nowhere to run. Nowhere to hide. Nothing can stop the fear inside," the Shadowborn murmured.

All of his prior training and perfected skill seemed like a distant memory and Charon felt like a child before a master swordsman. He knew how to fight. He knew how to defend himself from trouble. But this was different. His foe was nothing like he had ever faced before.

*****

From above, Gyr saw the exchange and took no further thought than to help Charon break free. He screeched a Gryphon attack call and brought out his talons as he dove down towards the ground. He screeched again with greater fury. An updraft suddenly shot up before him and he flew through it before he could shift direction. Instead of coming to Charon's aid, Gyr crashed onto the ground. He rolled quickly to put out the flames.

"No one can save you. No one can save me," the Shadowborn hissed.

"I'm not finished yet!" Gyr shouted as he threw himself at the attacker. He ripped Charon free from the tangle of weapons and tumbled head over tail. Using his claws, Gyr gained traction and skidded to a stop. His feathers had been blackened and darkened his snow white body. Blood seeped from the corner of his beak and out of his nose.

"Foul beast of the North. You are nothing. You are nothing to my Master. He will kill you all," the Shadowborn rambled. He seethed for a second and spat to the side. He pointed his sword at Charon. "He will die."

"Not while I am still standing," Gyr snapped.

The Gryphon bounded forward, using his injured wings to scoop the air and give him some lift. Despite his size, Gyr was agile enough to avoid the Shadowborn's sword. He darted to the left and right, forward and backward, up and down. He kept his weight light to push his agility to the limit. In one pass to the right, the Shadowborn's sword cut his left shoulder and Gyr immediately faltered. The Shadowborn kicked him hard, sending him flying. The Gryphon crashed into a crumbling store building, disappearing in the rubble and fire.

"All must die. No one fights Master. No one wins against Master," the Shadowborn spat out quickly as he approached Charon.

The approach was slow enough to allow Charon a proper look at who was beating the life out of him. The man's clothes were worn and ripped, stained with dirt and blood. His black hair was a tangled mess. He was tall but thin and deceptively strong. Charon believed him to be from the Northlands for there was no one in the Southlands as powerful as his attacker. The crazed man was toying with him, rambling on about a Master and orders to kill all that tried to stop him. The man's eyes were the most frightening feature. They were completely void of life and self-control. They were so silver that the entire eye appeared white.

Charon began to worry about Gyr who had yet to rise out of the rubble. He worried about the fate of Meras and whoever this monstrous man was before him. Was this the deadly Kaiser Adonis that Gyr had warned him about? Unable to look away, Charon studied the sunken features of the man's face. Lines hinted at the man's great age and Charon felt that he must have been someone else in a past time. He gulped hard and closed his eyes, not wanting to see his death approaching anymore. However, he could not help but open his eyes at the touch of the cold steel under his chin.

"You are alone. Forever alone in the void. There is no coming back. No coming back," the man said. It sounded like he was on the verge of tears. "Save me," he whispered in a voice so soft that Charon was not sure he had heard it in the first place.

Charon's head jerked to the left when he heard pieces of stone and wood fall to the side. He was relieved to see Gyr though the Gryphon was badly injured. He watched as Gyr crawled out, fighting for every step. What surprised him the most was the look of utter determination in Gyr's eyes. Nothing was going to stop him but death itself.

The dark man stumbled back a few steps, a look of confusion on his face. He raised his sword towards Gyr, pointing it directly at the Gryphon's heart. He snarled. "You will die first."

A blast of wind rushed through the area, moving so hard and fast that it ripped away every inch of fire and drew it high into the sky. Everyone turned to look up at the orange and red spiral as it raced for a thick cloud. The spiral of fire quickly disappeared into the cloud with a thunderous sound. All three turned to look back towards the city square. Standing in the center was a cloaked man with his great sword pointed towards the night sky. His eyes glowed a haunting blue from the shadow of his hood.

Charon watched as the Shadowborn charged at the newcomer, screaming wildly with his sword raised. What followed was awe inspiring. The newcomer remained frozen in position until the last possible moment before engaging Charon's attacker. He moved with grace and absolute power, dodging errant attacks and blocking head cleaving strikes.

"I will kill you! Kill you for Master!" the Shadowborn shouted at the top of his lungs.

The Shadowborn swung his sword as hard as he could. It collided with the newcomer's sword and held him in place. He narrowed his eyes and was then overwhelmed with fear. He began to shake and tug at his sword. It would not break free.

"Your Master must be a cruel man," the newcomer said in a resonant and deep voice.

Gyr immediately stood at attention, feeling that he recognized the voice though he did not know from where. He wracked his mind for an answer. He strained his eyes to see under the newcomer's hood. It surprised him that with his sharp Gryphon sight, he could not discern the newcomer's identity. Was there a power blocking his ability to see? The more he tried, the more his mind began to wonder to that other possibility. He shivered with excitement at the thought.

"Watch out!" Charon shouted as he painfully leaped to knock Gyr down. Just as the two hit the ground, an errant black bolt of lightning shot over their heads.

"Shadow Shock or I am a chicken pecking on a farm," Gyr uttered as he glanced at the space where he had just been. The air was still popping. "Whoever attacked you is a Shadowborn of great power and age."

"Then who is the guy with that body cleaving sword?" Charon pointedly asked.

Just as soon as the words left Charon's mouth, the newcomer slid back and his hood fell from his head. The man's face was fierce with a strong jaw and furrowed brow. His eyes were ice blue and his hair was a deep mahogany brown. Charon thought that he was a rather seemly fellow with an air of authority about him. While he was confused about the newcomer's identity, Gyr was trembling with excitement. It no longer mattered to the Gryphon that he was injured and bleeding. He was sure in his heart that the Daylord had come to save Meras.

"You! My Master told me about you! You are him! You are the one called Bane!"" the Shadowborn shouted as he pointed at the newcomer. His arm shook and he dropped his sword. The weapon clanged on the ground. "The King of All!"

"I am no one but a wanderer awakened from the mists to the sight of a red sky and to the ramblings of an insane man. The question is who are you to command such destruction on the innocent," came the newcomer's reply.

Gyr could barely contain himself. His Lord and King was standing right in front of him. Bane Arlis was alive! He had found the Daylord! Was this even real? Charon did not share his excitement, more focused on the gaunt man in black. The man appeared deathly afraid. In the blink of an eye, the man was gone into Shadow Slide, leaving his sword behind.

"Your Majesty!" Gyr finally shouted with delight.

The man called Bane slowly turned to look at Gyr, holding his great sword down. He let out a deep breath as locks of his hair floated in the breeze.

BANE THE WANDERER

Gyr had Charon check his wings again, trying his hardest to find evidence of his injuries. It all seemed too amazing and surreal that he was completely healed and felt no pain. He extended his wings when directed, rotated and stretched each limb, and though he did not like it, had Charon examine every inch of his gray tufted tail. It tickled when Charon inspected his furry belly and he chortled with laughter.

"Hold still or I won't be able to see!" chided Charon as he tried to hold down Gyr's right wing. Gyr gave an involuntary jerk and his wing clipped Charon under the chin.

"Oops," Gyr offered when he saw Charon rubbing the injury. "Can you check my wings again? I want to make sure they are perfect before I try my flying exercises again."

Charon groaned and rolled his eyes. He waited until Gyr relaxed his wings. For the second time, he pushed and prodded through each feather and shook his head.

"I have never seen anything like it. He just touched you and poof! Every single cut, bruise, and burn is gone!" Charon exclaimed. "He must be some sort of miracle worker."

"That is my one and true king," Gyr said proudly. "A kind healer and living legend!"

"People always talked about how powerful of a warrior he was. To be a healer as well, I am quite impressed. I certainly would have been dead had he not intervened and there would have been nothing left of Meras," Charon commented. He reclined back on the grass, savoring the warm sunlight. "The only injury I have now is the bruise on my chin from your wing."

"Once again, oops," Gyr replied.

The Gryphon stretched out his body and laid his head on his front paws. "The sense of community among Mortal people is inspiring. It has only been a few days and already much of the debris has been cleaned up. I think that I even saw the walls of a barn already being put together."

"I would think that the presence of the Daylord has inspired people to come together and work hard. Has he even taken a break or slept since he came?" Charon asked as he looked over at Gyr.

The Gryphon shrugged. "The Immortal kin can be tireless."

"Have you had a chance to ask your king about your mission?" Charon asked. He sat up and brushed the grass from his hair.

"Not yet. As you suggested, he has kept himself busy helping the townspeople. But surely, he has to take a break sometime," Gyr declared. He hopped up on all fours. "Let's go find him!"

Charon jumped up to follow the eager Gryphon. Neither of them had had a chance to talk to Bane. The people of Meras had kept Bane busy with their requests for aid and healing. The self-professed wanderer worked without rest, never ignoring a request no matter how big or small. He did not speak unless spoken to, giving others the chance. He acted as if he was one of the people and did not place himself above them. Charon could now see why Gyr held Bane in such high regard. But one nagging thought kept him from falling under the same spell. Why had Bane disappeared from his home, seemingly bound to never return? What kind of king would do such a thing?

They first went to where the new barn wall was being raised and found that the task was completed. A team of four men hammered and secured the wall in place. Gyr asked them if they had seen Bane and were pointed south towards a large oak. It did not take long to find Bane sitting under the tree. His sheathed sword rested up again the trunk, his fur lined cloak and leather armor draped over the pommel. He sat beside his possessions, leaning back against the thick gnarled trunk. He rested his left arm on his knee while he held a bread roll in his right hand. His tunic collar sat loose around his neck. His brown hair was a tousled mess. He opened his eyes once Gyr and Charon approached.

"Your Majesty," Gyr said as he bowed before Bane. He slid his front paws forward and lowered his head, keeping his wings tight on his back. Gyr glanced side eyed at Charon and gestured with a twitch of his head for Charon to do the same.

Bane chuckled as he watched the silent banter between the two. Charon shrugged and mouthed that he did not know what to do. The Gryphon grumbled and repeated his bow, showing Charon each position he needed to adopt in order to show proper respect. Charon threw his hands up in the air and turned away. Gyr immediately hemmed and hawed in the Gryphon tongue, clearly frustrated.

"My deepest apologies, your Majesty. He does not yet know the ways of his father's kin," Gyr said, bowing his head several times.

"He was not born among his father's kin. I find no offense in his actions," Bane said. He tore off a piece of bread and popped the morsel into his mouth.

"You can tell?" Charon asked in surprise. He furiously inspected himself for some giveaway. He looked to Gyr for an answer. The Gryphon only shrugged.

Bane chuckled softly. He ate another bite of bread as he watched the nervous exchange. "Do you see me in cloth of silver and gold with a jeweled crown upon my head? A scepter in my hand or a throne to sit upon?" He pulled at his tunic. "This is my cloth. This tree is my throne and this bread is my scepter. At least while it lasts. Sometimes things are not what they appear except to the trained eye."

"I am sorry. It's just Gyr here weaved such a masterful image of this mighty commander and king," Charon apologized. He tried to look contrite. "You are not entirely what I expected."

Bane finished off his bread roll and gestured for the pair to sit. "Some would say neither are you. Like any true Shadowborn, you are mysterious. Hard to figure out. Given your Mortal blood, the line becomes even murkier."

"What of me, your Majesty?" Gyr asked, cocking his head to the side.

"What of you?" Bane countered. He lifted an eyebrow in question. "Gryphons are dedicated and loyal to kin and country. Never can a Gryphon's heart be swayed towards thoughts of evil. They respect the sanctity of life better than anyone."

Gyr sat up tall and turned up the corners of his beak in a smile. He turned to look at Charon. "See? We are not wild animals like the beasts of the forest."

"Forgive my ignorance then. I spent one hundred years without ever knowing a Gryphon beyond stories and distant sightings need I remind you," Charon replied. He rolled his eyes. "Still friends?"

"Friends," Gyr stated. He nodded once before returning his

gaze to Bane. "I am glad and deeply honored to have this opportunity to speak with you for I have much to say."

"You and everyone else in Meras. How can I sleep when all I hear are their thoughts and voices? Might as well keep busy lending my strength to rebuilding homes and healing the pains of the wounded," Bane said. He let out a deep breath. "Do not think that I have not heard your needs. I suspect it is something of great importance so speak your piece."

Gyr cleared his throat. "Your Majesty, I am overjoyed to have found you and cannot wait to share my success with the Lords Proto Avis and Vorin in Crossroads. I did not come to the Southlands on a trip of leisure nor did an errant wind push me off course. I come under order from my Lords to find you and tell you of the troubles besetting the Northlands."

Bane let out a deep breath and the mirth in his expression disappeared. His face hardened and his eyes turned cold. By all appearances, Bane had transformed from the welcome hero to the fierce commander in the blink of an eye. "What of it?"

"Kaiser Adonis, a Shadowborn of terrible power, has ignited the flames of war, seeking Dominion over the lands. Every day, he spills the blood of our friends and family for nothing more than pure enjoyment. He is a plague that has infected everyone with fear and sorrow. No one can stand against him save you. The Lords Proto Avis and Vorin beg you to return home and rescue us from our hopelessness."

It took Bane a long time to answer. "I knew Kaiser at one time. He has to be one of the most two faced individuals that I have ever met. There is not a charitable bone in his entire body. He may say that he can heal and untangle the unknown but he would just as sure stab you in the back. And now you tell me that the Lords of the Northern Alliance have allowed such a man to thrive and grow in power."

Gyr stammered for a moment. "But, but!"

"You are young, Gryphon, and you come to me with a true and open heart. But there are things you do not know nor can understand. I left my instructions with the Lords of Crossroads to deal with such threats with no mercy and no hesitation. Anu bloodline or not, Kaiser should have been dealt with a long time ago."

Charon was surprised at the harshness in Bane's voice. He was speechless though he wanted to say something. Gyr was equally taken aback. He was stunned to see the harshness in what had been his perfect image of Bane. No one ever spoke ill of him or said one negative thing about him. Did Proto Avis and Vorin know the truth? Did they know what Bane was really like? It took him a moment to recover.

"But he has broken the Immortal Truth! Kaiser has committed the most heinous of crimes and will continue to do so unless you help us," Gyr pleaded.

"You mean to tell me that Shadow Night has failed in his duties too?" Bane asked, lifting an eyebrow in question.

"Shadow Night is dead with only a few left of his bloodline still alive. Only two that I know of," Gyr immediately replied. He was shocked that Bane did not know.

It was clear that Bane was taken aback by the revelation. He cast his eyes over Charon, looking him up and down in a critical manner. Charon gulped hard under Bane's powerful gaze. Bane frowned and mumbled something to himself under his breath and out of hearing.

"So there is no Shadowlord?" Bane asked flatly.

Gyr stumbled for something to say. "Well it is said that a bastard of the royal family is Shadow Night reborn though he himself has yet to accept it. The Lords of Crossroads think quite highly of him."

"He is no Shadow Night. It is a shame that my old friend is gone. He would have handled Kaiser Adonis," Bane scoffed.

"But it was Kaiser who killed him," Gyr admitted.

Something was bothering Charon about Bane. While he was sure that Gyr was blinded by the legend of the mighty Daylord, Charon was not so deceived. He watched as Bane tightened his jaw, a blood vessel twitching in response. Was it possible that Gyr's admiration and very presence was making him nervous? Charon felt that he would have been a bit perturbed being formally addressed at every turn. In a way, he saw Bane more as a person than an ideal. He felt like he understood Bane better than Gyr could.

"Your Majesty, the Northlands is without a commander that can stand up to Kaiser. He will destroy us and the entirety of this world if he is not stopped. I fear that he will do something truly terrible," Gyr cried. The Gryphon was desperate.

"He already has otherwise you would not be here. Kaiser should have been destroyed by Vorin's Dragonfire a long time ago. Why do you think that I could be better than a Dragon?" Bane challenged Gyr. "Or perhaps Aves should face Kaiser as my instructions to Crossroads said. He is both wise and strong, older than me. Why does it have to be me to rescue the Northlands after they have ignored my orders?"

It was a question that Gyr had not prepared for and yet it seemed so obvious. Charon tried his best to console the confused Gryphon to no avail. Gyr kept turning away and pulling out of reach. When he could take it no longer, Gyr leaped into the air and took off over the tree tops. Charon watched him disappear. When he looked back towards Bane, he shuddered.

"Gyr never mentioned that you left instructions behind. He constantly told me that you left the Northlands without a word," Charon cautiously stated.

"It is likely that he did not know. After all, he is what? One hundred? Two hundred years old?" Bane suggested with a shrug of his shoulders.

Charon sheepishly looked away. "I don't know his age. He has not told me."

"Why are you traveling with the Gryphon?" Bane asked.

"I don't know," Charon shrugged, suddenly at a loss for the reason why he joined Gyr. He looked away briefly. "Maybe I am searching for answers like him."

"You are of Shadowborn blood. Unusual for anyone in the Southlands considering how far their homeland is. I too am far from home and my blood comes from an even farther place," Bane stated. He appeared to relax as he returned to his earlier calm demeanor.

"Gyr knows who he is. He knows where he comes from. I don't. Maybe there is a reason but I want to know where I come from and who my father is," Charon admitted, feeling open and honest with Bane.

"Then you are a wanderer like me. We are the souls in search of why life has dealt us the hand we were given. But you and I know that we do not have all the answers. Hopefully, your Gryphon friend will figure out that he doesn't have all the answers either."

*****

SILENCE

It broke Vorin's heart to hear Proto Avis sobbing. The old Gryphon cried as only a Gryphon could with high pitched whistles and long drawn out screeches. He wailed for long hours, refusing anyone to be in his presence. Vorin made sure that Proto's privacy was respected though he desperately wanted to talk to his friend and comfort him. He rested in the courtyard outside of Proto's quarters, willing strength to his friend by his sheer presence. He hated to see Proto suffering so terribly and not understanding why. He let out a deep breath as he laid his head on his paws.

He was one of the few that knew of Proto's poor vision that bordered on complete blindness. To make up for it, Proto had developed a way of seeing the world through Spirit energy. It wasn't perfect but it made Proto capable of seeing things that others could not. The self-taught skill gave him the gift of reading the stars. Vorin was constantly amazed by what the old Gryphon could see in the night sky. He himself could only use the stars to navigate and determine his position.

"How is he?" Aves quietly asked from the edge of the courtyard.

Vorin looked up to see the noble Lord of the Airborn standing in the shadows of a vine wrapped arbor. "He is no better. He refuses company or food and drink. I doubt that he has even slept since we told him of our concerns."

"The Dark Spirits are a terrible omen that even I thought lost to my deepest memories. I have tried to consult with the Eagle

Spirit Halia to send a message to the All Spirit." Aves paused and looked away, the hint of uncertainty and despair in his eyes. "My connection is so weak and tenuous that it seems like it is not there. Even in the presence of the Immortal Truth, my power is diminished."

"Spirit Wake was banished for a reason by the Covenant. I fear to think that even Bane Arlis is not enough to overcome it. Though he is great and mighty in our eyes, his youth is a hindrance."

Aves looked up quickly. "Never lose faith, my friend. If we do that now, then Kaiser has won and all is lost."

He approached Vorin, his feather lined white cloak wrapped tight around him. His black tipped white hair was slicked back on his head and draped over his shoulders. Of all the Spiritborn Lords present in Cascade, Aves was Vorin's favorite. He respected Aves' stoic and quiet nature. The Lord of the Airborn was a pacifist at heart but he also recognized the importance of war. He was among the deadliest warriors in the Northlands that possessed a balance of strength and agility.

"I am sorry. I should not lose faith so that Proto can feel my strength." The Dragon let out a deep rumbling breath. "I fear that my old friend can no longer see and is now completely blind," Vorin stated as he looked up towards where Proto was residing. He shook his head and closed his eyes.

"Then it is true. Spirit Wake has been used and now the veil has cracked. How long will it hold before it comes crashing down and the dark days of Terra's birth returns?" Aves mused. He looked to Vorin. "We are among the last souls to have seen such days. Echoes of a lost time and even then from the final years of the Dark Dominion."

Vorin opened his eyes. "I do not want to believe this newly risen power to be Spirit Wake but I cannot ignore the signs before me. But how? How!"

"I have my suspicions and I do not like a single one," Aves stated. He thought for a moment. "No. Not one bit. If I could just speak to the All Spirit, all would be sorted out."

Both Vorin and Aves cringed when they heard Proto cry out in the Gryphon tongue. The old Gryphon's voice was shaky and losing strength with each whistle. He spoke of failure to secure the world and loss against a powerful foe.

"We have not yet lost this war though it does not bode well if Kaiser has Spirit Wake at his command," Aves stated. "I fear that even the Daylord will not be enough to win if he does not return home. Perhaps I must face Kaiser in his place after all. He has yet to test himself against me as he did you," Aves suggested.

"No. Kaiser will rip you apart as he did Shadow Night. If he can kill the Shadowlord, there is no hope for any of us," Vorin urgently warned.

Aves let out a deep sigh. "Perhaps we are to blame in all of this. We allowed our fear of the dark days, of darkness itself, to control us. Now we must pay for our actions. In a way, I understand Kaiser. I bet that if we looked at all that has happened since the writing of the Immortal Truth, a great deal of our suffering could be explained by us allowing uncertainty and lies to become reality and truth."

"Surely you would not blame death and war on poor decisions that we might have made," Vorin challenged. He shook his head, trying to understand the idea.

"Our silence has destroyed us," Aves stated solemnly.

For a long time, Aves and Vorin remained in the courtyard. Neither spoke or moved. A light breeze moved through the area as the sun was starting to set. The sky had turned to an orange and red color, the clouds a light purple. A flock of pigeons flew overhead, the multitude of beating wings creating a loud but calming noise. Aves watched the birds as they passed by. Vorin contemplated spitting out a jet of flame to cook himself a snack from the birds.

"Maybe we thought by not doing anything that we were keeping the peace. Well, what's done is done and now we must act. Since I am not Spiritborn, what do they say of Spirit Wake?" Vorin asked. He felt some relief that he had not heard Proto cry out in a while.

"It is a power that originates from the Spirit World, not from the world of the living. To use it in this world, you must either be a Spirit who has escaped the Spiral or be someone who has been resurrected," Aves explained. He paused to think more deeply on the matter. A knowing look crossed his face. "It makes sense now."

Vorin put his snout in front of Aves' face. "What is it?"

Aves paced around Vorin as he fought to sort out his thoughts. He turned to face the Dragon. "He must be a Spirit Walker. It all makes sense now."

"You mean like the Daylord? But he is good and kind while Kaiser is blood thirsty and evil," Vorin asked in confusion.

"I cannot say with certainty for I do not have all of the details," Aves stated. He waved a finger. "I doubt there is anyone but Kaiser who knows the truth."

Vorin at first resisted but couldn't any longer. "His grandson might know."

It was Aves' turn to look confused. He looked the Dragon

up and down. He was having a hard time believing or even understanding what Vorin had just said. His face twisted in thought and doubt. "What are you saying?"

"I am saying that Kaiser has a relative out there. One of his own bloodline and another descendent of Begin Anu. One with a noble constitution and a strong heart. One that could equal if not surpass the great Shadow Night Silvanus," Vorin said in calm praise. He arched his neck and looked down at Aves. He lifted a scaly brow.

"So whoever this grandson is, he has the blood of a Spirit Walker in his veins. Perhaps he shares the touch of darkness too?" Aves suggested.

Vorin shook his head. "No soul is perfect but this man has something special in him. Even Proto believes the same thing about him."

"So you know who this man is? Care to tell me?" Aves asked. He stared hard at the Dragon as he waited for an answer but none was forthcoming. "Keep your secrets then, Lord of Dragons. I trust in your judgment of this man and know that you will burn him with your flame if he proves as dark as his grandfather."

"Thank you. You are certainly the most sensible of the Lords here in Cascade," Vorin stated with a bow of the head.

Aves chuckled. "I am smart enough not to anger a Dragon for I have known many in my lifetime. As sensible as you are, you are still many times my size with an arsenal of weapons at your disposal."

"What say you of the proceedings? Of Palani?" Vorin asked as he settled his head back down on his paws.

"Palani is the youngest of the Lords present. Yes, he has seen hardship in the loss of his two eldest children. No parent should ever have to experience the loss of a beloved child. My own children are my dearest treasures and I would do anything to protect them. What Palani has done is refuse all action and seems content to be as unmoving as a mountain. It will be difficult for him to overcome his deep seeded sense of fear," Aves explained after some deep thought. "I much prefer Oren's character and intelligence. He is wiser than his son."

Vorin tilted his head and glanced back towards where Proto was crying. The volume of the Gryphon's screeches had become raspy and breathless. He sighed deeply and contented himself to staying put.

When Vorin refused to leave, Aves said his goodbyes and left the Dragon in the courtyard. Much had been said and he needed the peace and quiet to sort his thoughts out. He walked in silence through a small alleyway between two out buildings that served as greenhouses. Overhead was a crisscross wooden frame covered in green ivy. The shade was a relief from the hot sun. Small songbirds flitted in and out of the ivy, tweeting and singing with delight at his presence. Aves had always had a special connection with birds and loved them dearly. A bluebird with a cream colored belly flitted down in front of him, hovering and cocking its head to the side. Aves paused and extended his hand for the bird to perch on. It gladly did, singing a bright song in response. He stroked its chest with a finger.

The sweet and tender moment allowed Aves' mind a chance to settle and calm down. It was like a small oasis of peace while the city was a hotbed of activity for the coming war. It was frustrating to see how negative and angry Palani was about the orders from Crossroads. The young Lord of the Earthborn was impetuous but above all, he was scared. Aves did not doubt Palani's dedication to the wellbeing of his people or the love he had as their leader. Maybe Palani felt that he had to do his absolute best to be a good leader despite feeling vastly inadequate for the job. Almost like he was not ready for the role given to him. The circumstances surrounding his rise were of course tragic and likely Palani had never gotten over the deaths of his two elder children. Aves was beginning to think that perhaps Palani should give up the throne until he was mentally strong enough to lead. It was not his decision however. He could only advise the Earthborn in what path to take should he be asked.

The bluebird flew away and Aves continued on his path towards the palace gardens. The smell of flowers in the air was pleasant and relaxing. In the distance, Aves could hear the collection of bubbling fountains. It was such a beautiful combination for the senses. Aves breathed in deeply. His thoughts drifted to the destruction that Kaiser threatened to bring upon the world. It made sense that the man was a Spirit Walker. Spirit Walkers carried the burden of seeing the other side of the veil and becoming a vessel for the whims of wandering Spirits. Spirit Walkers were so rare that most details about them were rumors and opinions of what they should be. Aves knew that Bane had gone through something prior to his arrival in the Northlands that hinted at this burden. He had begun to believe long ago that whatever happened had caused Bane to run from his newfound notoriety.

He entered the gardens, passing under a stone arch. The dirt path split off into three directions, the left and right paths curving around large rose bushes. The straight path lead towards the first of what Aves was sure to be many fountains. It was a small fountain, only ten feet in diameter. A statue of a stag rose up in the center, spitting out water from its crown of stone roses. The sound of falling water was relaxing to Aves. He swept his hand on a bench to clear it of debris before sitting down.

Facing a possible Spirit Walker in battle was daunting to Aves. He could no longer avoid the idea that Kaiser was more than a passing lunatic who would eventually fall to an assassin. Kaiser was here to stay and was not going to go away by simply avoiding him. Aves cursed himself for his now irrational thought of avoiding a problem being a good solution. He should have taken Kaiser more seriously when he first heard the rumors of his dark tendencies. Everyone should have listened and acted. Now the world was faced with another Dominion War that could have been stopped before it started. Now, Spirit Wake had been unleashed and the veil was threatening to break. They needed Bane now more than ever. Silence was no longer an option.

*****

UNLOCKING THE PAST

"It still doesn't seem right that we have had all of these rumors about an army without a single sign or sight of one. Not even a single soldier. Do you think Kaiser could have been lying just to scare us? Are we sure that the city watch is doing their job properly?" Onyx asked as he stood up. He brushed the dirt from his hands on his pant leg.

"My brother in law is trying but there are only so many people he trusts and knows. Do keep in mind that some people are too afraid to talk," Haven retorted. She looked away.

"I was not blaming him," Onyx said defensively.

"Stop the bickering. I am trying to listen," Ryder snapped from the other side of the room.

Haven leaned back against a broken stone column with her arms crossed. She watched Ryder in the distance, sorting through the debris of the house. She turned her attention to Onyx. "It is odd. We have already been here in Umbra long enough for an army to cross the distance from Eclipse and back several times over. My father has checked with his marketing contacts and they haven't seen anything either."

"If one really thinks about it, we three are targets for Kaiser and his allies. Him especially," Onyx said gesturing towards Ryder. He then pointed to himself. "I am a Silvanus Prince. You are Ryder's partner. And he is the rebellious grandson."

Haven waved her hand, the ring on her finger sparkling in the light. "Guess I was doomed from the start."

214

Onyx chuckled as he thought about the excitement brewing at the Ombre household. Despite the threat of war, the family was happily planning a wedding. Nora, Haven's mother, and her two sisters focused on deciding what kind of dress Haven was going to wear. The younger of the two elder sisters, a flirtatious girl named Tara kept emphasizing that Haven was marrying a Prince and stressed the importance of fine cloth and jewels. When asked for input, Ryder just rolled his eyes and said that he was not a true Prince. He repeated his only request that Haven wear a dress and look her best.

"Are you excited to be getting married?" Onyx asked her.

"We have had our ups and downs in our long years together but I think we both knew that this would happen at some point. A wedding just makes it official according to the law," Haven replied. She looked down at the ring and smiled. "I am excited and happy. Maybe even enough so to wear a dress."

Ryder chuckled softly. "Not that I haven't seen you without one on." A pebble hit him in the back of the head. He glanced over his shoulder to see Haven wiggling her fingers in a sarcastic wave.

Onyx turned red after he caught the underlying meaning of Ryder's comment. "So how is it going to work out while we are fighting this war?"

"Like I told my future husband over there, I would prefer a small ceremony in my armor under raised swords. I once thought that he would agree but no, he suggested the big fancy ceremony. The one time you actually accept your royal blood and claim you need to celebrate according to your station," Haven rolled her eyes.

"I can dream too can't I?" Ryder said as he stood up. He turned to face Haven. "I am a man after all."

Haven sneered at Ryder before giggling softly. "Have you found it yet?"

"Found what?" Onyx asked. He had been watching Ryder inspect the floor of the run down house for quite some time without any result.

"An old trap door that leads to a safe room. My mother kept some of her things in a chest that my father gave her. Things such as jewels and letters," Ryder stated. He swept his foot over the spot he had been inspecting. He tapped his foot and nodded.

Onyx strained to see a design etched into the wood. It was faded. He still didn't understand the point of coming to this house that was in ruins. The roof had caved in and nature had already taken over. Vines and various plants covered much of the walls and stretched out over the floor. A layer of dirt and debris covered much of the floor, broken up only by their footprints. Onyx was sure that this house must have been a fine place in its heyday.

"So how is this chest supposed to help bring down Kaiser?" Onyx asked as he watched Ryder pull a floor panel loose and toss it aside. He then jumped down through the hole, disappearing from sight.

"Nothing," Ryder said, his voice distant. He tossed the chest up and it thumped on the floor. A second later, Ryder leaped up through the hole and landed right beside it. He twisted around and replaced the floor panel. He picked up the chest, fiddling with the lock until it broke open. He then stepped forward and opened the lid.

On a black velvet cushion was a luxurious set of jewels. Haven's breath caught in her throat and she covered her mouth to hide her shock. Even Onyx was amazed by the sight. He knew the jewels from a portrait of Mali Silvanus from her wedding day long ago. The neckpiece was made up of several chains of silver with drops of moonstone and diamonds. It appeared to look like a ghostly owl in flight amongst the stars. The earrings were like stars with diamonds set in silver. In the middle was a gorgeous crown of diamonds and silver shaped like a moon in the sky surrounded by stars. The jewels were stunning and worthy of a queen.

"My father gave these to my mother when he learned that she was pregnant with me. He promised to marry her no matter what everyone else thought. He also declared to the Shadow Council and his parents that he would not marry anyone but my mother. She gave them to me for safe keeping for when I chose to get married. I want you to have these jewels, Haven, so that you will look like the queen you are to me," Ryder said as he held the chest open before her.

Onyx was impressed by the offer for the jewels were extremely valuable. Though he never doubted the love that Ryder had for Haven, it amazed him that Akakios had honestly thought that strongly to marry Ryder's mother. He wondered why they ultimately didn't. Why didn't Kaiser claim Aylin as his daughter? By all accounts, she was an intelligent and noble woman worthy of a royal. He watched as Ryder peeled back a corner of the cushion to reveal a set of folded papers.

"My mother's birth was registered with Kaiser's name attached though it was not submitted. My grandmother kept the parchment and eventually gave it to my mother for safe keeping. There are also a few letters between my mother and my father along with several from Kaiser. There is even my father's will though I have yet to open it," Ryder explained as he closed the chest.

"Why haven't you?" Onyx asked.

"Ryder is afraid of what it says," Haven stated. She took the chest from Ryder and held it under her arm. "The contents of

Akakios' will has never been made public and there are people like Zoras who believe that he declares Ryder as not only his heir but his successor. In the eyes of Shadowborn law, that would mean that he would have come to the throne as a legitimate son. Considering what happened to Akakios, no one pushed to open it and find out. It was Ryder's right as Akakios' only descendent anyway to make that decision," she further explained.

"An old friend of mine tried to steal it and bring it to the Shadow Council. It wasn't the first time I knocked Jarod senseless," Ryder chuckled. "There was that time he tried to kiss you. You hit him and then I hit him harder. I am pretty sure I knocked out several of his teeth."

The idea of a romantic rival made Onyx wonder if Luna had admirers at the Earthborn court. He puffed out his chest and squared his shoulders. Suddenly he lost the confident posture and sulked. Their only encounter had been so awkward. Plus, could she really see him as anything but the bumbling Prince. He was determined to at least cultivate a friendship with her. He shook his head to free himself of the confusing feelings.

Haven and Ryder exchanged various stories about the Shadowborn man they named Jarod. Haven laughed particularly loud when Ryder described a time when he and Jarod pranked a messenger from Cross.

"You know? Jarod was supposed to be my first dance at the Winter Solstice Ball since we were of the same social rank. But then in walks the mysterious son of Akakios. All the ladies forget their senses and fawn over the handsome would be Prince." Haven then snickered when Ryder rolled his eyes.

"I was nearly fifty when my mother finally got me to attend. She told me that it was important as then there was talk about me be legitimized as my father's heir. Represent the Shadowlord she told me." He smoothed down his tousled hair. "Our visit here, while not important in the grand scheme of Kaiser's war, is important to my future and that of Haven."

"Whether or not if he sits on that throne, I am finally marrying the man of my dreams," Haven giggled. "I am sure that Jarod will not be pleased even though marriage has been inevitable since that night."

"Guess I will have to thump him again," Ryder suggested.

Ryder was suddenly flung backwards as a Shadowborn man tackled him to the ground. The two rolled around until Ryder managed to throw his body weight and knock the man loose. He flipped up to his feet and swiftly drew out his sword. His attacker was equally as fast on the draw. Haven pulled Onyx back just as the two charged each other.

217

Onyx watched as Ryder was on the defensive until he realized that his cousin was just trying to tire out his opponent. At first, he thought this was strange. Surely if this man was an assassin or enemy, Ryder would have dispatched of him quickly. Ryder knew this man and he wondered if Haven did too. He glanced at her just as she shielded her eyes in disgust. She knew the man too.

"Seriously, Jarod! Give it a rest!" Haven shouted.

The man called Jarod looked up in his direction only to be socked across the jaw. He tumbled to the ground, dropping his sword. Ryder stepped on the weapon just as Jarod reached to grab the hilt. Jarod snarled as he looked up at Ryder.

Onyx was shocked as the furious cursing erupted from Jarod's mouth. The man attacked Ryder with a verbal tirade that would have made even the nastiest of pirates blush.

"Enough!" Haven yelled. She dropped the chest into Onyx's hands and stomped over to the two men. She then drew her arm back and slapped Jarod hard across the face. "I already told you to leave well enough alone!"

Jarod finally seemed to get the hint though he shot a sneering glare at Ryder as he stood up. He was two inches shorter than Ryder with a similar build and frame. His black hair was cropped short against his head. He had a full but neatly trimmed beard and mustache. On his body, he wore a leather cuirass and skirt. He looked every bit the soldier. Haven stepped in between the two men and put her hands on their torsos to keep them separate.

"That was uncalled for," Ryder grumbled.

"Oh it was more than called for and there is certainly more that I can give you," Jarod threatened. He glared harshly.

"Enough! Can't you two talk like civilized men instead of fighting?" Haven demanded. She shoved Ryder when he stepped forward. He stumbled back rubbing his chest. "Will you two behave or do I have to knock you two senseless?"

"Fine but he needs to start talking," Jarod snapped. He pointed at Ryder in a threatening manner.

"I take it that you did not part on friendly terms," Onyx suggested as he held on to the chest. Jarod look at him in surprise and dropped to his knee in a subservient bow.

Haven kicked at Jarod for him to stand back up. "These two used to be friends until this fellow decided to make a pass at me. Repeatedly. This other fellow had been drinking and stupidly started a fight." She turned swiftly to glare at Ryder.

"He grabbed your," Ryder started to say until Haven tapped his chest in warning. He quickly fell silent.

"What you did before pales in comparison to abandoning the supposed love of your life for one hundred years. Leaving home and country for spirits know where," Jarod growled. He narrowed his eyes.

"And you thought attacking me in my ruined home would make your anger just disappear. I ought to knock your teeth out for that," Ryder replied, rising his fist.

It was silly that the altercation between Jarod and Ryder was over Haven. Considering the more serious situation of the war against Kaiser, the matter was trivial. Onyx felt that he had to do something but he could not figure out what. He held on to the chest tighter, keeping his arms wrapped around it.

"Jarod, I am not the same person you think I am. I have changed. We all have. We used to train together and I know that you are one of the best fighters in Umbra. The rebellion could certainly use someone of your skill amongst the ranks," Ryder said with an exacerbated sigh.

Jarod looked Ryder up and down. "So you really are a rebel commander. I had heard rumor but did not want to believe them. Who would follow you anyway?"

"I do," Onyx said firmly. "You should too, Jarod. We need every good soul we can get to bring down Kaiser."

Jarod pointed at Ryder. "Then we have a lot of talking to do and a lot to catch up on. You have a lot of explaining to do."

STRANGE

"Enough with you too! Let bygones be bygones!" Ivan shouted as he kept himself between Jarod and Ryder. He held his hands up at each man in a threatening manner. "We have more important matters to think about than a past squabble over my daughter!"

Haven slapped her forehead, shutting her eyes in embarrassment. She let out a tense breath.

"Squabble?" Onyx covertly asked her. He glanced at Ryder holding up a ready fist.

"Before I debuted at the Winter Solstice Ball, Jarod and I were close friends. He had a crush on me but I only saw him as a brother. I met Ryder at the ball and I felt a spark with him. I had never experienced such a feeling with Jarod. He blames Ryder for stealing my affection when he believed himself to know me better than a bastard Prince," Haven explained. She opened her eyes and let out a deep breath of frustration. "I may want to beat Ryder over the head sometimes but I know that his love and desire comes from deep within him."

"I have a hard time thinking of him as sentimental," Onyx commented. He crossed his arms tightly.

Haven smiled sweetly. "You do not know him like I do."

They both looked back towards the trio of men. Ivan was tangled in between Jarod and Ryder. The trio of men pushed and shoved against each other. Jarod stumbled back and threw his hand forward fully expecting Shadow Shock to erupt from his palm.

Nothing happened. He jerked his hand back to inspect it, a look of confusion on his face. Jarod tried again to no effect. He held out his hand as if it was a mysterious and unknown object.

"What is going on?" Jarod demanded. He looked towards Ryder in a search for answers. "I did everything I was supposed to. Why did it not work?"

Ryder stepped around Ivan, deeply concerned. Jarod did not protest when Ryder inspected his hand, turning it over and studying it carefully. Ryder let go and Jarod pulled his hand back as if it hurt. "Were you trying to use Shadow Shock?"

"Yes. This has never happened to me before. I know how to summon the power and direct it. You taught me the technique!" Jarod exclaimed with a degree of horror. He held his hand, massaging his palm. "I felt the charge. I felt the energy. Why didn't it work?"

"Maybe you did not pull the energy in the correct way," Ivan suggested as he offered to check Jarod's hand. Jarod did not protest.

"I did! I swear I did! Ryder, you try it," Jarod cried. He was becoming panicked and his face lost all color. To be so sure of something only for it to fail horrified him.

Everyone paid close attention to Ryder. He stepped to the center of the yard, creating some space for him to work. The yard was rather small and surrounded on all four sides by open breezeways and walls. The grass and potted plants were dry and in desperate need of watering. Ryder settled his breath and collected his thoughts into one cohesive vision. It wasn't a struggle to find the flow of Spirit energy but somehow it felt different. His connection was present but strained. He pulled the necessary energy into his right hand and the strain became greater. He lifted up his hand, seeing the familiar black bolts of Shadow Shock. The entire effort had been exhausting.

"Something is different," Ryder declared. He wiggled his fingers as the energy dissipated. "You didn't feel the strain on your Spirit energy connection?"

"I don't know. I was kind of hoping to blow your head off," Jarod admitted halfheartedly.

"Onyx, try an Earthborn power. See if it works," Ryder suggested as he directed Onyx to the center of the yard.

The young Prince gulped as he approached his cousin. Suddenly, he was afraid that his abilities were not going to work. He came to Ryder's side and let out a tense breath. "What should I do?"

"Raise a stone pillar. Not a big one. Just enough to test out your Spirit energy," Ryder said in encouragement. He patted

Onyx's shoulder and stepped back.

Onyx tried to calm himself, managing to do so after a minute of deep and slow breathing. He found his center and pushed his senses into the ground beneath his feet. He manipulated his Spirit energy but found it extremely difficult to focus long enough to complete the task. He pushed again, pressing his right foot into the ground. Instead of shaping his energy like he should, he studied the strain on his power. He found that despite his direction, it did not know where to go or what to do.

"I can't. It doesn't feel like it's supposed to. No warm pulse to draw upon. The energy is there but it is like it is too far away to grab hold of."

"Bastard's done it," Ryder mumbled under his breath. He thought that he had spoken low enough only for Haven to hear.

"What do you mean the bastard's done it?" Jarod demanded. He stomped over to Ryder and pointed at him accusingly. "Do you know something we don't? How could you summon Shadow Shock and I couldn't!"

"Kaiser has broken the Covenant of Spirits like he always said that he would," Ryder stated.

A light bulb went off in Onyx's head. "The Demon Iztal said something about the Covenant of Spirits. Damn, I can't remember the exact words. But you told me that it was nothing good. Why is that?"'

"The Covenant of Spirits is a power enacted to separate the world into two distinct places of being. The world of the living and the world of the dead. It created the veil that must not be broken or crossed or so the tales say," Ivan explained. He looked towards Ryder. "For the dark days of Terra's birth was a time of energy unbound and danger. The Spiral is considered the last vestige of that time."

"No one knows that for sure. No one has ever come back from imprisonment in the Spiral. Only the Daylord is known to have walked in the Spirit World and come back to this world," Haven stated matter of fact. She set her hands on her hips.

"Rache was imprisoned in the Spiral. He would have stayed there if Kaiser had not called him back," Ryder whispered to Haven. She nodded.

His words were not lost on the others. Onyx was the only one aware of the facts and kept his silence. Ivan appeared surprised but Jarod seemed angry.

"Keeping your secrets again I see. How does the likes of Zoras Rokar and Hayden Abendroth stand working with you as a commander? Why should anyone trust what a bastard says? I can't use my Spirit energy but you can. You can read the energy field and can tell that something has happened to it but I can't," Jarod snapped. He growled in anger.

"It's not my fault that I know more than you. I have travelled the Northlands from shore to shore and learned from the masters of power and knowledge. Ask any Gryphon or the Lord Vorin about what I just said," Ryder immediately said, put on the defensive.

"No. I want you and only you to be honest. If I am supposed to help the rebellion and weed out this secret army of Kaiser's, I want to know the person who is giving commands," Jarod demanded. He made a threatening move towards Ryder.

"Are you seriously threatening to hinder the rebellion?" Ivan dared to ask. He was too flabbergasted by Jarod to say more.

"Look. All I know is that something freaky is going on. Ever since you showed up in Umbra, Ryder, things have not been the same. The Spirit energy, the faces of people I think I recognize but don't." Jarod stumbled back, grabbing his head. He babbled on about the different strangers he has seen.

As Onyx listened to Jarod's various descriptions, a thought occurred to him. He tapped Ryder's shoulder. "I think I know why we haven't seen the army. They are already here. They have infiltrated Umbra. Jarod, have you seen a man with a diagonal scar across his face?"

*****

"Why haven't they struck?" Ryder asked himself as he leaned over the dinner table. He ran his hands over an old tattered map of Umbra to smooth the wrinkles. "If his army is here, why haven't they attacked?"

"Know your target," Jarod said as he stood in the doorway, leaning against the wooden frame. He crossed his arms.

Ryder did not even look up to acknowledge Jarod, keeping his focus on the map. After a moment of thought, he relented. "Based on intelligence, Eclipse was openly attacked and decimated within hours. Kaiser marched on the gates himself in full war regalia. Why make the effort to infiltrate a city he already knows? What game is Kaiser playing at?"

"I think you know better than most," Jarod said as he approached. He stood on the other side of the table. "Your royal cousin so much as hinted at it."

Ryder sighed deeply. "Jarod, you are a good warrior, and the rebellion needs people like you on the front lines. We cannot sit and move in the shadows as we used to. War is upon us and it will consume everything if all who stand for what is right are not united. Work together and let bygones be bygones. Protecting this world and all we love is the most important matter now."

"Spoken like a true Shadowlord ready to lead his people to the end. I just wish that I could trust you," Jarod stated firmly. "You don't just up and leave without good reason. I am glad that Haven seems to know but now, I want to know."

It took a long time for Ryder to work up the nerve. He told Jarod about his carefully constructed childhood. The pride that turned to fear that turned to courage. In his story telling, he revealed his deeper than blood secret. "I did not choose to be born of Kaiser's line and I wish that I could tear his blood from my veins. But I cannot undo what already has been done. I have made mistakes. I have made decisions that could have changed the future had I chosen differently. The world may never know those possibilities. So I have to take what I have been given and use it to my advantage and to better the world."

Jarod took his time to process Ryder's answer. "You could have been the Shadowlord. Is it because you are an Adonis that you chose not to be?"

"Yes. Also if legends be true, the kin of Begin Anu were not meant to rule and I do not belong on the throne. That is not the path I see before me."

"Ryder, sometimes life chooses for us. It knows what we are supposed to be better than we do. We need to trust ourselves fully and honestly that the right path will lead us to our destiny. If it is my destiny to fight beside you, then maybe I will. I do still love Haven and will do anything to protect her," came Jarod's thoughtful reply.

"Don't tell her that. She might thump you over the head," Ryder chuckled softly.

Jarod chuckled. His face then became serious. "So what did Kaiser do to break the Covenant?"

Ryder let out a deep breath. He looked away briefly. "Kaiser's servant," he started to say. He looked up at Jarod. "Rache once said a long time ago that Kaiser knows of powers no living person should be able to command. Even he, an ancient Demon, expressed fear of what Kaiser was capable of. He cited himself as living proof."

Ryder then explained the summoning ritual to the best of his knowledge. He chanted the words of rising and binding. He talked about Kaiser and Rache's profane connection for a long time, indicating that it affected him as well. Jarod listened intently with only the occasional comment until Ryder finished.

"I never did like that servant but it seems Rache has more sense than Kaiser. I did not think that I would ever think of a

Demon as sane," Jarod remarked. He loosened his arms and shuddered.

"He was the one that told me about Spirit Wake. What it does it put a break in the veil that the one who cast the power has control over. The powers of the living world and the powers of the Spirit World mix together and distort. Rache was not certain of all the details, either out of wanting to withhold information or pure ignorance. The biggest problem with Spirit Wake is that Kaiser can summon Dark Spirits to do his bidding. You know, the nightmares of the Dark Days of Terra's birth. The ones that mighty Spirits like Omu fought against.

"The longer Spirit Wake is in play, the bigger the break in the veil becomes. Kaiser may think himself powerful now but if that break gets too big, the veil will come crashing down and the Dark Days will come again."

Jarod nodded. "So how do we stop it?"

"Kaiser must be destroyed."

*****

TARGET: RYDER

Loran watched the group of men and women packing horses and rambling on about trivial matters. He kept his hands steady as he held the crossbow. His eyesight moved down the line of the loaded steel bolt, waiting for his desired target to move within range. He stifled a snicker of delight. He did not want to be discovered before the right moment. It had taken everything to remain hidden. He had been following Ryder and his crew since they left the hill before the city, taking the road into Umbra. He was sure that Kaiser would be pleased that he and the army had infiltrated the city so perfectly to take it from within. Eclipse had almost been too loud for his tastes though Loran enjoyed decimating it. Revenge was sweet. But Umbra was his master's prize or more to the point, the moth to Ryder's flame.

He overheard the man called Ivan declare that several others will leave the city for the wilds. The sword smith gestured in different directions. Another man with a short black hair cut nodded and stated that he had similar success in convincing more people to leave. Loran listened more carefully, catching the man's name as Jarod. The woman he knew as Haven stood between Jarod and the true target. They were both in the way of his shot. He wanted a clean strike. The point of the bolt shifted between Ryder's head and heart at Loran's direction. His patience was starting to wear thin.

The signal to the army for the attack to begin waited on Loran's steady hand. He had a flare ready to shoot into the sky once he fired the steel bolt. But first, he actually had to fire the bolt. Kaiser's orders had been clear: capture not kill. It was easier said than done. Loran wondered why Kaiser did not send Rache to capture the wayward grandson. The Demon was strong enough to compete with Ryder, more so than himself. Loran ultimately knew that in a real fight, Ryder was very capable of killing him. This shot was important. Very important.

Loran raised his crossbow, taking aim. Now the shot had to present itself. He watched as Ryder stood beside a horse, the woman called Haven at his side. The woman tenderly touched Ryder on the left arm, whispering what Loran thought was a sweet nothing. She smiled as she stepped away. Loran squeezed the trigger, releasing the bolt. He quickly reloaded as the bolt soared through the air and embedded itself into the back of Ryder's left shoulder.

*****

Ryder lurched forward from the force of the bolt, falling against the side of his horse. He slid and rolled towards the right, seething. Blood seeped from his mouth after he bit down hard on his bottom lip. Before he could even shout, another bolt struck him in the chest. Haven rushed back to his side as he slumped to the ground. Onyx jumped to grab the scared horse's reins. The beast whinnied and screamed, fighting Onyx as he pulled it away from his cousin's side.

"Ryder!" she screamed. She pressed a hand around his chest wound, trying to stop the flow of blood. A third bolt flew in and struck Ryder on his left side just under his rib cage. "Onyx, help me!"

Onyx rushed in and quickly began ripping his cloak into pieces. He and Haven worked swiftly to wrap Ryder's wounds and staunch the bleeding. "We need to get out of here now."

The once organized group erupted into chaos. Ivan, Jarod, and Haven's brother in law immediately pulled out their swords. They assembled around Haven, Onyx, and the injured Ryder. Nora, Sabrae, and Haven's other sister Tara drew their own weapons. Sabrae pushed her two boys behind her, holding her short sword.

"Look!" the older of the two boys said, pointing to the sky.

Everyone looked up to see a red flare shooting into the sky above, burning brightly. Ryder was the only person who didn't look up. He seethed in extreme pain, feeling the grating sensation of steel on bone. He could feel the blood bubbling inside his chest, impeding his ability to breathe. He flung his right arm out of reflex to grab on to something for stability. His mind acted fast to gather

Spirit energy from the earth but the effort proved too much. His heart rate skyrocketed. His skull pounded with every heartbeat. He refused to be defeated like this.

"We need to get him to base as fast as possible but its days away on horseback," Onyx stated, feeling a bit hopeless.

"We can use Shadow Jump if we pool all of our energy together," Jarod suggested quickly. His eyes scanned the rooftops for further attack. He was completely on edge.

"Too risky. We can't cross into that space without endangering his life," Ivan argued.

In the distance, screams and blasts split the air. Soon columns of smoke rose up into sight. The clanging of steel swords rang out. The attack had begun. Before anyone could stop him, Jarod snarled and leapt up towards a nearby rooftop.

*****

Loran stood with a smug look on his face, pleased at his three clean shots. He tossed the crossbow aside and turned around. There before him was Jarod, sword raised and pointed in his direction.

"And here I thought you hated the guy that stole your lady love. A smart man would let his rival die to reclaim a lost prize," Loran said as he pulled out a steel bolt from his belt. He waved it around aimlessly.

"A man can change and realize the truth. Ryder is my friend. Haven is my friend. You are my enemy," Jarod stated. He shouted a war cry before charging forward.

Loran pulled out his own steel sword just in time to block Jarod's attack. They pushed against each other, snarling and spitting curses. Jarod gave a good shove, trying to knock Loran off balance but the experienced fighter was prepared. Loran planted his back foot and leaned away. Jarod stumbled and lost his own balance. Loran then slid to the side, letting Jarod fall and hit the ground.

"I spent much of my life upon the unruly waves of the sea. It will take more than that to knock me down!" Loran gloated as he swung his sword in a circle.

Jarod laughed as he grabbed Loran's right ankle and pulled. Loran fell hard on his back, barely maintaining a grip on his weapon. Jarod rolled and flipped up to his feet just as Loran did and the sword fight began again. They exchanged heavy handed blows, shifting their feet in a careful but deadly dance. Loran moved fluidly, his balance and agility honed from his days as the Mirror Sea Pirate. Jarod was more hard hitting and direct in his movements, reminiscent of his training days with Ryder.

At first, Loran enjoyed the contest. Jarod was a well-trained and formidable opponent not unlike Ryder. Their fight was going to be good practice for when Loran finally faced Ryder. He needed to know how to outwit or at least out pace his master's grandson. Even shot with three steel bolts, Ryder was still deadly with his command over Spirit energy. Of course, Ryder could not compare to Kaiser. No one could. As he remembered the power and fury of his master, Loran had a realization as to Jarod's actions. He was trying to keep him distracted from the true mission. That angered Loran.

"You are no super soldier and you cannot stop me!" Loran roared as he swung his sword. The tip caught Jarod and sliced down from his left shoulder across his chest. The wound was superficial but enough to allow Loran to get away.

Jarod stumbled a few steps but managed to keep his balance. In a swift motion, he kicked up Loran's discarded crossbow and loaded it with a bolt that he found nearby. "See how you like being shot in the back." He roared and pulled the trigger.

*****

"More water!" Onyx ordered. Someone tossed him a canteen and he immediately bathed Ryder's wounds. "Come on. Summon the Waterborn healing power you once told me about. Just enough for us to get back to base. To get you back to base."

Ryder was barely coherent, doing his best to conserve his energy. With the water he had been splashed with earlier, he was able to cool his body down enough to slow the bleeding. It was a desperate technique he had learned from the Waterborn. It left him functioning at a bare minimum and practically mute. Had he gone deeper, he would have placed himself in a self-induced coma. The pain in his body was dull but still very present. Haven guided his horse, constantly looking at him in worry. She fought the urge to reach out and touch him.

"He can't keep this up. We have to Shadow Jump. We have to try," Haven pleaded. She quickly wiped a tear away.

"I hurt but I will live," Ryder mumbled before his chest heaved. He hacked up a small fountain of blood and grabbed his chest as if to contain the pain.

"You Silvanus bloods are hardier than most. No wonder your family won the throne," Ivan commented. He glanced at Onyx. "It was always said that Shadow Night Silvanus was a warrior like none other in his day. Him and the Daylord were on such a different level."

Onyx acknowledged the comment but couldn't help but see how Ivan looked at Ryder. He too glanced at his cousin. Yes, he was powerful and stronger than himself. The big thing was that Ryder was much older and more experienced than he was. At one time, Onyx would have been jealous. Now, he began to see how people saw his cousin as the return of Shadow Night. But of course there was something more. Ryder was a direct descendent of the revered Farlander Begin Anu. Onyx began to wonder if there was a limit to Ryder. He hid a smile of admiration, not wanting to draw attention to himself.

A set of hooves thundered in the distance and over the hill rode Jarod. He kept up the pace until he drew close, slowing to a slow walk beside Haven. He glanced at Ryder. "Loran fired the crossbow so I had to get a little payback. Shot the would be assassin in the back. Should put him out of commission long enough to complete the escape."

"How about the other families leaving Umbra? What about the city itself?" Haven's brother in law asked.

"Property can be replaced. Lives can't. I think we acted just in time to leave. The loyal of Umbra got out safely. We can rebuild Umbra once Kaiser is taken down," Jarod stated. He nodded his head. "Loran said that Kaiser commanded him to capture Ryder and he failed. We now know his target."

"Why Ryder and not Onyx? Onyx is the legal heir to the throne," Nora asked.

Ryder was not offering any answers so Onyx took the floor. He tightened his hold on the reins. "We cannot trust anything Kaiser says or does. We can only trust in ourselves and our movement to get rid of him. By my account, we are all targets."

*****

FUN AND GAMES

The city had not been the same since Kaiser had summoned the power of Spirit Wake. Even Rache was beginning to feel bored by the fearful silence. He sat, perched on the rocky edge of the Heights, looking down on the streets below. There were a few street lanterns lit but most of the city was cast in darkness. Smoke rose from a single tavern chimney. Rache sniffed the air. Some sort of sour meat was been roasted over a fire. Resources were becoming scarce, even for the blood hungry Demon. People were more fearful than ever and afraid to move and act as they once did. Where would Kaiser strike next was the thought on every mind. Rache only knew this after his last blood meal and his reading of the victim's Blood Memory.

The people were scared into silence though Rache was certain that their minds were still loud and active. He had yet to hear hints of rebellion but it wouldn't be long until someone dared to speak in support of Kaiser's enemies. Rache wondered if Kaiser could see into the minds of the people as he once claimed. Or more to the point, could his master see into his mind? Unlike the weak minded people of Cross, Rache was powerful and could resist such attacks. Surely if Kaiser had seen his flights of switching allegiance, he would have done something about it by now.

Rache had been harboring thoughts about breaking his unholy bond for quite some time. He could not exactly pinpoint the moment such thoughts entered his mind but they were growing stronger. He was thinking more clearly than he had in a thousand years. More than when he was young and reckless. Back when death and destruction was just fun and games. Rache could see that he was becoming more logical and wise. He wondered if it came with age but he could not think of a single Demon that had acted in a similar manner. He was changing into something more, more Spiritborn.

He had never paid attention to Terra's ancient history. He did not even know where the Demon race came from. Were they related to the Spiritborn or were they a race all their own? He was starting to question his very existence. In a way, Rache welcomed the questions. Finding the answers gave him more of a purpose than being a slave to Kaiser. But there was still the matter of the bond. The profane ritual had brought him back to life. He was in debt to Kaiser and his blood. Breaking the bond in the truest sense meant death for the Demon. The only way he could still live was to somehow become bonded with Kaiser's lone descendent.

Rache liked Ryder. The man was a victim of circumstance and yet retained his nobility and good sense. People looked to Ryder as the undeclared leader of their hopes. Bearing the hope of the world was certainly a great weight to carry but he did it just the same. Rache then looked at himself. He was nothing more than a fearsome memory. Now Kaiser was the great destroyer and killer. He was practically a Demon in everything but blood and Spirit. He was going to destroy Terra.

A part of Rache wanted to see that happen but a deeper part roared about changing that. It struck him as odd that he wanted to see Terra survive. But he couldn't change the fact that he was a Demon with a dark reputation. There would be no place for him in a world of peace. Where would he live? Where could he go? Who would welcome him? Could there be such a thing as a good Demon?

He looked up towards the night sky, seeing the scattering of stars. As old as he was, he could see no patterns or signs of something worthwhile. He was no star reader like the decrepit Proto Avis. The air was cold and it cooled the heat in his body. Closing his eyes, Rache took in a deep breath and released it slowly. His mind settled into a quiet state of being.

For a moment, he wished the city still had a semblance of life to it. It would have given him more to distract his thoughts from the current state of affairs. He was still jealous that Loran was given the task to destroy Umbra. Unlike Loran, Rache could have decimated the city on his own power. He could have slaughtered every soul within its borders. And yet, it did not have a lasting appeal to him. He wanted more to his life than destruction. He wanted to act on his own will and decisions. He wanted to be free. He wanted to break the chains.

Rache rose to his full height, his flame colored hair wafting in the breeze. He eyed the tavern that he had noticed earlier, the smoke still rising from the chimney. He pulled up his hood, covering his head. A part of him wondered how many people were at the tavern. What they were talking about if they were talking at all? The city held no interest for him anymore. He was bored of Cross and longed to leave it. His eyes drifted back to the castle that Kaiser now claimed as his own. His master had rarely stepped outside of its walls since the Living Map had been created. In return, the bond only allowed him to go so far. He growled the longer he thought about it.

*****

"Where have you been?" Kaiser asked as he walked around the edge of the Living Map, hands latched behind his back.

"I was just off thinking," Rache replied. He kept his distance. He did not like the Living Map and what it could do.

Kaiser scoffed. "Since when do you think so deeply and so alone? Are you still hung up over Loran's command in Umbra?"

"You know that he will never be able to capture Ryder and hold on to him long enough to bring him to you," Rache accused, pointing to Umbra's location on the Map.

"Maybe so but it was certainly fun to watch him try. My grandson is tougher than most and won't be brought down so easily. I mean a crossbow? That is how he wanted to capture him?" Kaiser laughed out loud.

He stepped within the borders of the Map and it lit up at his touch. It was if it welcomed him and embraced him within its power. He wafted his left hand in a commanding gesture. The Map responded by swiftly moving from Umbra to Cascade. Once it settled over the city, little sparks of light appeared over it. The sparks took the shape of Gryphons.

"Such a pretty sight. So many Gryphons taking flight like the old days when a neighbor could trust his neighbor. Gryphons used to fly all over the place. The great messengers of the Northlands. Free and unbound by the Spiritborn though they faithfully serve the likes of Aves and his Airborn kin," Kaiser mused as he watched the Gryphon shapes. A larger shape rose up from the city, taking the form of a massive Dragon. "But no Gryphon can command the skies like a Dragon. Vorin. The last of his kind. The oldest living soul on Terra. The last vestiges of raw power."

"Your point? You have already proven immune to his Dragonfire. Why not kill him and get it over with?" Rache asked as he crossed his arms tightly.

Kaiser wiggled his fingers, drawing the Dragon shape in. "Why should I make death so easy? So simple? Has Vorin earned the dignity of a clean death so that he may join his kin in the Spirit World?"

Rache shrugged. "Enlighten me."

"Dragon Spirits are more apt to listen when one of their kin still lives. Right now, he is more useful alive and far more entertaining," Kaiser stated as the Dragon shape landed on his open palm. He let it sit for a moment before blowing the shape from his hand. It resumed its flight over Cascade.

"Killing a Dragon is easier said than done. Their power is more ancient than that of the blood that runs in your veins. And I'm pretty sure you did not kill all of those Dragons who gave their power to the Immortal Truth," Rache reasoned.

"You are confused about what the truth really is," Kaiser growled as he turned and snapped his fingers.

The Map transformed into a field of flames. Kaiser stood in the center. The flames took the shapes of Dragons, roaring and spitting fire from their maws. At first, the Dragons appeared fearsome and strong. Soon they began to cry out in pain and sorrow. In the midst of the fire rose up the tablets of the Immortal Truth, a spark of light carving runes across the surface. For a moment, Kaiser was hidden by the brightness. He snapped his fingers and the entire display disappeared.

"You're right. I did not kill them. They chose to die and took their own lives. Words can be so destructive," Kaiser snickered knowingly. "The right word can cut as deep as a sword."

What exactly happened at the creation of the Immortal Truth and Kaiser's role was a mystery to Rache. He wondered if Kaiser was deliberately hiding the truth from him. Only five other people could possibly know the details: Vorin, Proto Avis, Bane, Evander, and Aves. "So what is the point of all this?"

"Oh Rache. How little you understand of how my world works. Death is a game. One I have already won once," Kaiser said. He patted the space over his heart. "I believe that everyone should be in on the fun. The betrayal, the anger, the revenge."

Kaiser stepped towards Rache menacingly, his eyes full of rage. He exited the boundaries of the Living Map and it returned to its sedate form. Rache pushed himself back against the wall he had been leaning on. He dropped his arms to his sides. He swallowed hard as he imagined Kaiser invoking the bond. Did Kaiser see what was in his mind? Could Kaiser read his deepest thoughts? Rache shivered. He for the life of him could not read what was going on.

"I do not make my decisions lightly, Rache. I do not move without reason. There may be times where you think that I am doing nothing. Well, I am always doing something. Acting does not always require me to lift a hand or take a step," Kaiser stated. He pointed to his right temple. "This mind never sleeps. It is always awake. Always aware of the turnings of the world."

"Don't I know it," Rache stated. He gulped. He was so afraid of him invoking the bond.

Kaiser poked Rache in the chest. "I am not completely blind to the conflict that is raging within you. You are distant and uncertain. That much I can tell."

Rache gathered his resolve. "I am a Demon in your world. A scion of the past that has long since died. I feel trapped in this city. I want to run free."

Kaiser's twisted face of rage quickly turned into a patronizing smile. He patted the side of Rache's face. "Your time will come. Your time will come."

THE COURTESANS

Cora gingerly stepped across the green grass, feeling the prickly touch under her slippered feet. She pulled her shawl tighter around her shoulders. Her long black hair tumbled down her back in loose waves. Her tall lithe body swiftly moved around the unkempt garden. The plants were still thawing out from the cold winter. Cora missed the lush well-kept garden of old where flowers bloomed around every corner. Birds and other such creatures called the royal gardens their home but not anymore. The garden was practically devoid of life and warmth. She paused by an old rose bush and sighed. She reached out and touched an icy bloom only for it to shatter into pieces. It made her sad and she quickly pulled away.

Around the corner and in the very back of the garden was a secluded alcove. Green vines coated the stone and held it tightly. Two tall and thin trunked trees rose up and created a canopy of shade with their tangled branches. Beneath the canopy were Raye and Zee, sitting upon a blanket. Raye had her hair pulled tightly back in a bun. It made her look harsh and unforgiving. Zee was picking at her loosely styled braid, appearing nervous.

"What if he sees that we are gone?" Zee asked as Cora sat down on the blanket.

"Of course, he knows we are gone but not from the city. I told him that I wanted to survey the gardens so that I may restore them. I also said that you two would be with me, helping me to determine where to start. It is better to be direct with Kaiser and not secretive," Cora explained.

"But surely he is not so foolish as to believe we are doing a simple garden survey," Raye suggested. "He can read our minds."

Cora shook her head. "Rather than being a fool, he thinks we are fools. That we are too simple minded to warrant anything but a passing and heated thought. I can assure you that he does not keep us around for our intellectual prowess."

"Cora's right. We are just here for Kaiser's physical pleasure. Nothing more. Nothing less. We are here to feed his self-serving ego," Raye stated as she nodded her head. She rubbed the nervous Zee's shoulder. "It will be ok."

Zee picked at the hem of her dress. "How do you know that? All of Kaiser's enemies say his mind is the most powerful and deep the world has ever seen. Nothing escapes his notice. Nothing!"

Cora and Raye slid closer to Zee and embraced her. They tried by their very touch to convince her that she was safe. Zee began to weep softly. She was truly terrified of Kaiser. For a long time, the three girls remained in their positions. As the eldest, Cora tried to comfort Zee as best she could.

"Do you want to know how Kaiser found me? He didn't. I found him. I claimed to be seeking the truth, one that I was sure only he could give. I doubt that he believed me but he has kept me around," Cora started to say. She took Zee's hands in hers. "Sometimes a rebel must do terrible things in order to achieve the ultimate victory."

With her words, Cora hinted at something deeper. Or more to the point, suggested something more sinister than spying on the Northlands' greatest enemy. It was stepping into truly dangerous territory. All three of the girls had been enlisted years ago by the rebel faction to infiltrate Kaiser's inner circle and gain access to his person. Zee had been the most nervous of the bunch, having barely escaped from Kaiser's vicious wrath and losing her brother in the process. At times, she was indifferent and fully immersed in her role, dedicated to avenging her brother. But Kaiser truly frightened her. It was a hard thing to get passed the sight of watching him slaughter her brother.

"You are doing this for him. For Lysander. He died trying to protect you," Raye said as she held Zee while she wept.

For a long time, the girls comforted each other about their fears. Each of them revisited their first encounters with Kaiser, going over every detail until the fear appeared as an afterthought. Cora revealed her past as a would be Saber who left the program to take care of her family after her father was killed by pirates. She told the girls that when she saw Loran, she was reminded of her loss. Raye stated that she was a lost orphan that Kaiser had found upon the road. He had rescued her from a trio of road bandits that had come dangerously close to raping her.

"Kaiser doesn't act without reason. In every situation, he looks for personal benefit. If there is none, he does nothing and leaves it for others to act in his stead. I do not think his actions that day were heroic. Why protect a nobody?" Raye supposed. She shrugged.

"It makes me wonder how Ryder has remained relatively untainted by his grandfather's evil. Kaiser's blood flows in his veins and as such, Kaiser has declared him his heir," Cora suggested. "Ryder is never going to join Kaiser no matter how hard he tries to push him."

"Then we will have to help Ryder push back harder. We will have to help the rebels more than we already have," Raye said with confidence.

Zee leaned away, wiping the tears from her eyes and drying her face. She sniffled. "Ok."

They went through various methods of assassination, Cora providing a great deal of input. She revealed the many stories that Sabers like Donovan Shunga shared regarding the sheer level of threats against the throne.

"The best story occurred after the execution of Akakios and when there was no declared Shadowlord. The Sabers had been sorely divided in who they wanted to serve. The more conservative faction threw their support behind Lord Shiloh. The more liberal faction wanted Akakios' son on the throne. Then there were the radicals who wanted another bloodline on the throne. They claimed that the Silvanus family was failing in their duties to serve and protect the Shadowborn. You can guess who defected to Kaiser first," Cora explained. She lifted an eyebrow. "Before now, that was the closest our people have come to falling apart at the seams. Ryder had remained in the capital at Shiloh's behest. Neither of them wanted the throne!"

She waved for the two girls to lean in closer. Their foreheads were touching. "Some say that Kaiser was preparing to put his own name forth as a candidate for the throne based on his Anu blood. When Ryder revealed that to Shiloh, Shiloh rushed home to Cross and claimed the throne."

"I am sure that it made Kaiser angry," Zee suggested.

"Who can say? No one really knows if he truly intended to take the throne for himself. Maybe he said those things to draw Shiloh in to his dangerous net," Cora replied. "Like Kaiser, we need to draw the moth to our flame so that we may knock it out of the air."

"But how?" Raye asked.

"Listen carefully and I will tell you," Cora whispered.

*****

Delighted with their carefully constructed plan, Cora skipped back to the castle. She danced past the guards who paid her no mind. She let her shawl slip from her shoulders, holding onto the fabric and letting it stream behind her. Her pleasant mood was a stark contrast to the relative dark and brooding atmosphere. She leaped and pirouetted through the halls towards the royal library. She rounded the corner and was immediately pinned to the wall by Rache's strong hand.

"And what on this fine day makes you so happy?" Rache growled. He had his hand wrapped around her throat.

Cora did not lose her composure. "And what did Lord Kaiser say about laying a hand upon me?"

Rache frowned. He loosened his grip but did not let go. He leaned in and sniffed her neck. He snorted loudly. "You stink of nature. Why do you people find such pleasure in it?"

"Let go of me," Cora snarled.

"I am no idiot, whore. I can smell the confidence oozing from the heat of your skin. What are you and your little whore friends planning?" Rache smirked. He tightened his grip and lifted Cora from the floor. "Tell me or I will pull it from your blood with just one bite."

She tried to wrench Rache's thin bony hand from her neck to no avail. She held on to his wrist with both of her hands. "Go ahead. What purpose will it serve you? I can be replaced just as easily as a guard or a kitchen cook."

Rache drew in close, sniffing her neck and lightly touching his tongue to her skin. He snickered as he felt her tense up. He then dropped her and stepped back. She fell to the floor, coughing and rubbing her throat. She pressed a hand to her chest to steady her breath.

"Of the three, you are the least of all idiots. Given your incomplete training as a Saber, I am surprised that Kaiser has even the least bit of trust in you. Some Sabers are hard to break of their loyalty to the throne. They are so fun to rip apart though," Rache gloated.

"Then why are you wasting your time? Tear me limb from limb and explain to Kaiser why you did it," Cora warned as she got to her feet. She brushed the dust from her dress with a few swift hand motions.

Rache got in her face and studied her closely. "You are not

as blind in your loyalty as I once thought. I do not sense the hint of Shadow Blind on your like many close to Kaiser's inner circle. Consider yourself lucky. Enjoy your freedom while it lasts."

"Then if I am not bound by Shadow Blind, what does that make you? Why do you follow Kaiser like a stupid dog?" Cora challenged.

Rache snarled in warning and true aggression. His eyes flashed blood red. "Don't make me kill you."

"Go ahead and make me one more casualty for the rebels to fight for," Cora dared. A smirk played across her face.

It was hard to tell what the courtesan was getting at. Rache had never paid her much mind before though of the three, she appeared to have the most sense. Maybe she would prove useful to his aims. Could he turn her away from Kaiser to serve him? The Demon stepped back. "I think that we might be useful to each other. You are not as stupid as I originally thought."

"Then Loran wasn't kidding. You do hate Kaiser," Cora pointed out. She brushed back her hair from her face.

"Yes. Very useful," Rache said with a smile.

THE EVER WATCHFUL EYE

"So Bane has finally decided to show himself after all this time. One has to wonder why," Kaiser said as he scratched his chin. He looked back into the flames. "Any thoughts, Axum?"

The bald Demon in the flames looked back at Kaiser inquisitively. Black tattoos coated his bare left shoulder and neck. Claw marks disfigured his face, leaving him blind in his right eye. He had a permanent sneer and darkened eye bags. A tattered black cloth was wrapped around his right shoulder and torso. The rest of him was obscured by the flames.

"It is odd that after a thousand years, the Daylord seems to have woken up from his delusional stupor. It might have been better if he had stayed asleep. Now he will have to face the death and destruction of the last thousand years," Axum stated as he crossed his thick arms.

"I do wonder what he has been doing all this time. It's not like I cursed him when I drove him south. Pity. I should have killed him," Kaiser supposed. He shrugged as if the thought was an inconvenience.

"The Daylord is preoccupied with something that weighs him down. Should be fun to terrorize him and force him into a hole so deep, he won't be able to climb out," Axum laughed.

Kaiser wafted his hand and the flames disappeared. He turned around and walked out of the Living Map, deep in thought. It disappeared with another twist of his wrist. Axum had given him a troubling report of the activity in the Southlands. It did not

241

bother him that Bane had reappeared. That the Gryphon Gyr had escaped his assailant and joined forces with Charon. No, what bothered him was that Aday was showing signs of resistance. He thought hard about every encounter he had ever had with Aday after his exile. Kaiser was proud of that one. A twist of events and words on his end got the Crowned Prince exiled from his own homeland and his inheritance stripped away.

The look of betrayal on Sin Silvanus' face had hidden his fatherly pain. Kaiser laughed out loud at the image. He braced himself on a nearby column, holding his stomach. He rolled over and slid to the floor, sitting down. The emptiness of the throne room gave him all the space he needed to think. He looked up and waved his left hand. Immediately, the Living Map appeared like it had been hung on a wall. He watched the flashes of red where his blood had broken the veil. In his mind, Kaiser had never intended for the simple Dark Spirits that were likely to break through into the world of the living to do much more than annoy and harry his enemies. He had a better plan for those Spirits. He needed to back his enemies into a corner.

At some point, his cavalier attitude and playful strikes would have to become deadly and serious. He hated the idea of leaving his fun behind. It brought him joy to cause chaos but as anyone knew, chaos would have to end. Kaiser now had to start thinking about his new world order. What was he going to do? Where would he make his capital? Who would serve him? The only thing that Kaiser knew for certain was that Ryder would be his heir. He smirked at the thought. All he had to do was break his grandson of his softness.

A wave of red rippled towards Cascade. Kaiser considered it for a moment before snapping his fingers. The wave halted and bubbled in place. His eyes looked towards the lands of the Waterborn and he smirked. He pointed towards the southwestern part of their territory and the red wave responded at his command.

"Let's see how Marinus handles the dark power of the Spirit World," Kaiser laughed. He wiggled his fingers to speed up the red wave.

He leaned back against the column and let out a deep breath. He turned his head, looking towards the bright light that was Crossroads. Lifting his right hand, he twisted it in a circular motion. The Map zoomed in to the edge of the city with its high cliff wall, a waterfall spilling down into the Southlands. Though it had not been long since he was last in Crossroads, it had been many years since he stood upon that cliff. He laughed as he thought about how the youth of the Northlands used the spot for cliff diving, completely unaware of its dark history. The spot was where Bane

Arlis last looked upon the Northlands before he abandoned it.

*****

Kaiser sauntered through the last of the maze of buildings to reach the cliff's edge. As he drew closer, his steps slowed. He dragged his left hand along a white stone wall before stepping out into the open. His coat flapped in the breeze. The breeze tousled his shoulder length raven hair. He chuckled softly as he approached the man on the edge. Dressed in his typical rough fare, Bane seemed to pay him no mind.

"What brings you to this place?" Kaiser calmly asked. He latched his hands behind his back. "Was the council meeting that strenuous?"

"The politics of this land are so twisted and muddled," Bane said as he kept his eyes on the distant rolling grasslands. "I question how such a system has survived for so long."

Kaiser shrugged sheepishly. "Perhaps I can offer some aid in deciphering the ways of the Northlands."

Bane turned to look Kaiser in the eyes. "I think that there are those better than you to best serve me in that capacity. But thank you for the offer."

Kaiser bit back a curt reply. He took a moment to calm himself. "Maybe I am not as old or experienced as my gracious Lord Shadow Night. That is true. But I am here on my Lord's behalf to answer any questions you may have."

"Really?" Bane asked, lifting an eyebrow. He crossed his arms tightly.

"Well I too have Farlander blood in my veins. I know what it is like to live in this land with origins from another. I have questions of my own that I would like answered," Kaiser asked, trying to sound contrite and inquisitive.

Bane was not completely fooled by the act. He turned his attention back towards the grand view. He took in a deep breath and let it out slowly. "They say that those who have walked where I have can see it in others. The strain such a walk has on one's mind. The burden of the experience and the realization of eternity. I would not wish it on anyone."

"Is that what you see?" Kaiser asked, genuinely interested in what Bane had to say.

Bane looked Kaiser up and down. He then pointed towards the scars on Kaiser's throat before tucking his hand back under his arm. "The Spirits have told me about a man with black scars upon his throat. A man that was murdered by his own father. Such a tragedy they said. A terrible tragedy."

The bold statements rocked Kaiser to the core. He was almost ready to weep but he hardened his heart. His reaction was not lost on Bane. However the noble hero did not offer to comfort him.

"I do not know what you are talking about," Kaiser forced himself to say. He clenched his jaw.

"I think you do. You think that you are alone in your suffering. That no one can see the burden only a Spirit Walker can bear. That I do not see what you really are. Don't come to me offering charity or wisdom. I can see right through you," Bane warned. He dropped his arms. "Never have the Spirits expressed such deep fear when speaking about you."

Kaiser clenched his fists and frowned. "They lie. They know nothing of what I suffered and what they put me through. My own father." He could not even verbalize his raging thoughts.

"One can only hope that you are strong enough to overcome what life has given you. To earn the honor that is a Spirit Walker name," Bane stated with no emotion. He strode past Kaiser without saying another word.

*****

"Fool," Kaiser scoffed. "They are all fools."

He waved his hand, the Map disappearing at his command. He got to his feet and pulled on the hem of his jacket. He looked about, feeling that the Spirits trapped on the other side of the veil were watching him. He stepped towards the center of the room and held his arms wide open. It was a posture that dared the Spirits to act against him. He did not have to hear their screams of rage and frustration. He knew that they were angry.

"The almighty Bane thought that he saw the monster within. Your precious instrument of justice! Little did you realize that I had the power to drive him away! He is nothing! I am everything! Everything you feared!" He laughed out loud as he spun slowly in a circle.

Kaiser always got a high from openly challenging the Spirits. Now he was starting to feel a bit amorous and wondered where his three courtesans had gotten to. The eldest Cora had said something about surveying the royal gardens. He smirked as he thought about the dirty task. He paused and tapped his chin. Yes, he would head to the baths first.

*****

Rache watched as Kaiser strode out of the throne room, apparently not noticing his presence in the shadows outside the doors. He kept his eyes on Kaiser who seemed to walk with a skip in his step.

"I should go," Cora said as she leaned up against the wall beside the Demon.

"Why? So you can service a man that you want to kill? I can't imagine a more disgusting task," Rache asked in a condescending voice.

"Sometimes one must do things they don't like to get ahead," Cora replied with a roll of her eyes. "I must always be watching for the right opportunity. Searching for a weakness. The moment to strike."

*****

A DARK MYSTERY

Night had fallen and the city of Meras had settled down for the evening. Bane rubbed his left shoulder, sore from lifting stone and raising newly framed walls. He readjusted the leather strap of his travel pack and continued out of the city. His great sword had been strapped tightly across his back but not out of reach. Bane considered the weapon his constant and unwavering friend. It did as asked and never complained. Like him, it was capable of deciding one's right to live or die. He hated that it was an instrument of destruction in his hands and yet, he could not cast it away. The long steel blade was as old as he was, a relic from a distant time and faraway land. Only he knew its true power and could wield it. He was also glad that it kept its silence, never asking him questions.

The thought made his mind turn towards Gyr, the white Falcon Gryphon from the Northlands. The messenger was young and certainly dedicated to his Lords. Bane had to admire Gyr's loyalty but the Gryphon was blinded by it. It was really a shame, Bane thought. Gyr had promise to be someone great. He sighed deeply as his feet plodded on the dirt path. Bane had once heard those words about himself a very long time ago but it was a time lost to memory. Only he was left to tell the tale.

Coming to Meras felt like a mistake to him personally. For countless years, he had drifted away into memory as he had wanted. Bane paused and shook his head. Now was not the time to become burdened by such heavy thoughts. He needed to focus on his path and where he was headed. As far from civilization as he could get.

A twig snapped behind him and in a flash of movement, Bane had drawn his sword. Out of the shadows, Charon fell backwards onto his rear. He coughed after breathing in a cloud of dust. Bane held the long sword towards Charon with his left hand, the weight causing his sore shoulder to throb again.

"What are you doing out here?" Bane asked in a quiet but firm voice.

Charon remained frozen in place, looking down the length of the blade. The point was within inches of his face. He swallowed hard. "I was worried when I saw that your bed was empty."

"You need not worry about me. There is little I fear in these woods," Bane stated as he sheathed his sword. He noticed Charon breathing a sigh of relief. "You have much to fear in these woods and should be back within the city sleeping like the rest of your mother's kin. Even the Gryphon is smart not to leave the city at night."

"Is the one who burned Meras," Charon started to ask. He gulped, unable to finish his question.

Bane scoffed. "Like I said, go back to Meras. You are safer there." He turned around to leave.

"Wait!" Charon called out as he got to his feet. "Where are you going? What if he attacks again?"

Bane paused and turned to look over his shoulder. "Of course, he will attack again so long as you remain in Meras. The city and its people is not what he is after. It is you."

The statement chilled Charon to the core and stole all warmth from him. It reminded him of what the people of Garhune believed: that he was an omen of trouble. His face paled and he felt dizzy. It took Charon a long time to recover enough to speak. "Why me? Is it because I am a half breed?"

"You are not strong enough to handle what I am capable of telling you. But his master commands him to kill you all the same. Why do you think this to be so?" Bane challenged. He turned to face Charon full on.

"I don't know," Charon admitted. He stumbled back and leaned against the trunk of an old oak tree. He rubbed his forehead, looking confused and pale. "Please tell me."

Bane let out a deep breath. His sore shoulder burned underneath the weight of his travel pack and he longed to set it down. "Come on. Let's get you back to Meras first."

Charon did not object and in fact, he felt himself regain a little courage. He wondered if this was a part of Bane's mystical allure and power. Bane walked slowly for him as if he was sympathetic to his diminished state of mind. The idea that someone was out to kill him was frightening and Charon could not help but think of every word the man said and the horrible look in his eyes. It boggled his mind as to why someone would want him dead. Who was this mysterious master? Did he know him? Have they even met?

"I feel like my head is going to explode," Charon admitted. He grabbed his head with both hands. "What if he attacks us?"

"He won't," Bane reassured him.

"How can you be so sure?" Charon quickly demanded. His fear was getting the best of him. "What if he is watching us right now?"

Bane watched out of the corner of his eye as Charon looked about nervously. "Keep acting like that and he will."

Whatever courage he had completely drained from his system. He felt vulnerable and wanted Bane to say something. Anything to make him feel better. The dark trees felt like they were closing in on him. He found it hard to breathe and a sweat broke out on his brow. He looked about, fearing that each little shadow was his would be killer. Bane then popped him across the back of the head, startling him.

"Open your senses and stop focusing on the what if," Bane admonished. He tapped Charon's head. "Think with this and not this." He pointed to his heart to emphasize his words.

Charon tried to pay attention. He really tried but his mind was focusing on one insane thought. What if his attacker was his father? Garhune's mad Shadowborn. People had always told him such horrible stories of murder and destruction. They accused him of terrible acts just by association. He had never taken a life nor burned someone's house down.

"So why did you really come looking for me?" Bane asked.

Charon knew that Bane could see right through him. "Earlier, you looked at me as if you recognized me. As if you knew something that I did not."

"You think that I know who your father is. I don't but I can guess at who he might be related to. That is what I saw," Bane replied. He kept his eyes on the path through the trees. "You ask a lot of questions. You are what? A century old?," he asked as he side eyed Charon.

"A hundred and one next month," Charon sheepishly answered. He shrugged.

Bane chuckled softly. "To be that young again. I came north for the first time when I was your age. I was a different person then. Much has changed. You will learn as the years pass that to endure is more painful than it is to die."

"I just wish I did not have to endure it alone. I have seen so many people die. Some I did not even know and yet I felt pain at their loss. Will I always feel like this?" Charon asked Bane. He honestly felt scared of that possibility.

It took a long time for Bane to answer. "Some pain always stays with you no matter the count of years. You try to run. You try to hide but it is still there."

"Is that what you have been doing all this time?" Charon asked without thinking. He kept walking while Bane stopped in his tracks. Charon finally realized that Bane was no longer walking beside him after thirty feet. He turned around to see Bane with a frozen expression on his face. It seemed shocked and yet angry. "What is it?"

Bane snapped to at the sound of Charon's voice. It was if the curious expression had been a figment of Charon's imagination. He quickly strode forward to reach Charon's side. "A thought occurred to me that stole all of my senses for a moment."

A part of Charon was relieved to have arrived safely at Meras but another part realized that Bane seemed more open to talk away from others. In particular, away from Gyr. It was a mystery to him that Bane would seem so standoffish. Yet, he understood him in a way. Bane had spoken to him about a deep kind of pain that can last long after its cause. Charon had to wonder what happened to Bane to cause him to run far from home and country. He reached for Bane's shoulder but hesitated. What if the mighty Daylord drew his sword again? He risked it anyway and grabbed Bane's shoulder. Bane paused and turned around as Charon drew his hand away.

"If you are intent on leaving, then answer this one question for me. Who do you think is related to my father if you cannot name him yourself," Charon asked.

Bane let out a deep breath. "The name may not mean much to you now but your features remind me of an old friend of mine who I now know is gone. If it is true, you should be proud of your heritage. Do not let others make you think less of yourself because you are a half breed. The people of Garhune should consider themselves lucky to call you one of their own."

Bane's last words surprised Charon and made him smile. He watched as Bane pulled up his hood and disappeared around a corner. He resisted the urge to follow the Daylord. Instead, he returned to where Gyr was sleeping. The Gryphon was out cold, his back left paw twitching from some dream. Charon smiled and shook his head as he quietly got under his blanket. He pulled it tight around him, settling comfortably on the straw mattress. He looked out of the window, the glass broken in the wake of the city burning. Outside, Charon could see the moon and stars. A sense of peace began to settle over him. He did not know his father's name but Bane had hinted at his Shadowborn heritage. Finally, the pieces were coming together.

*****

AXUM

"Master is not very happy with you. You did not do as he asked and he is very angry," Axum said in a cold voice. He stood over the shivering Aday with knotted arms crossed tightly. His big and brawny form gave him a threatening and powerful look. "What do you have to say for yourself?"

Aday whimpered as he remained at Axum's feet, curled up in a ball. His chest heaved and he kept his eyes away from the fearsome Demon. Hot tears streamed down his cheeks. He yelped sharply when Axum kicked him in the back. His limbs untangled and he turned to pressing his brow onto the dirt in an act of complete submission. He mumbled something unintelligible.

"Did you not hear what Master said? He asked you. No, he ordered you to kill them both. Why are they not dead?" Axum demanded in a more forceful tone. He drew his left foot back as if he was making to kick Aday again.

The thin Shadowborn froze in place, smashing his face into the ground. He waited for the inevitable strike, trembling. He sneezed, spewing out a mouthful of dirt.

"Look at me," Axum growled. He reached down and pulled Aday up into a sitting position. He grabbed Aday's chin and forced their eyes to lock.

"He wasn't supposed to be there. He was there," Aday gulped.

Axum sneered before forcibly tossing Aday's head to the side. He turned around and took a few steps away. He paused and tapped his chin. "What makes you think that Bane would not come?"

"I do not know," Aday admitted, sounding clear and sound in his mind.

The change did not go unnoticed. Axum peered over his right shoulder, studying the sniveling Shadowborn on the ground. It really had been a shame watching the once tall and powerfully built warrior deteriorate into an unstable shell. Axum did not know Aday's past well but he did know that Aday had been the Crowned Prince of the Shadowborn and Kaiser's rival. Or so Kaiser had told him. Sometimes, he was not sure that he could believe everything Kaiser had said. He scoffed and turned back around.

"Well the stakes have changed for me but not for you. If you do not kill them, I will. Then I will kill you and end your suffering," Axum said casually with a toss of the hand. He ran his hand over his smooth head. "I do not much like this game that Kaiser is trying to play but I am indebted to him for his uncanny abilities such as raising the dead, cause widespread destruction with a single pass of his hand. A worthy master. My life now has purpose again."

Aday's breathing became more unsteady and erratic. Amidst the torrent of thought and emotion, he knew that what Axum said was not true. Kaiser could not resurrect the dead. Only the Spirits could. It just could not be possible for a single man to thwart death in such a way. It was an abomination. The concept of resurrection was just too great of a subject for Aday's fractured mind to handle.

Axum watched Aday's mental struggle, seeing the pain and desperation in the Shadowborn's haunted eyes. Such was his weakness. Kaiser may have had no qualms about killing his loved ones but Aday certainly did. The Demon was moderately surprised that his fatherly love was so strong. He did not understand the emotion. He could barely begin to explain it to himself.

The dark woods creaked as a fierce wind ripped through the tree tops. A flock of songbirds rose up out of the branches, squawking loudly at being disturbed from their slumber. Aday remained rooted to the ground while Axum watched the birds fly away.

"Will not make Master angry again. Will do as he says and kill them," Aday muttered, bowing repeatedly towards Axum.

Axum listened as Aday rambled on, continuously repeating the same words over and over. He rolled his eyes in annoyance. He decided to leave Aday, bored with his caretaker duties as stated by Kaiser. He started to walk out of the clearing but Aday wrapped his arms around his legs.

"Don't leave me here! The dark scares me!" Aday begged. He held on tightly to Axum's muscled legs.

"You are a Shadowborn. You should embrace the dark," Axum sneered as he kicked Aday off. "If you want something to be afraid of, fail to kill your bastard children and I will peel your skin off with these."

Aday squeaked when Axum flexed his hands, claws erupting from his fingertips. The bones cracked and twisted with a sickening sound. Blood dripped onto the ground. Axum shoved his scythe like claws in Aday's face, wiggling them and flicking blood onto his face.

"In fact, why don't I give you a taste now?" Axum chortled as he grabbed Aday's face with his right hand.

*****

Axum mulled around in thought. He glanced towards his left, watching the tunnel of broken trees with great interest. An hour earlier, a bruised and battered Aday stumbled off into the darkness. The Demon scoffed as he fully turned in the direction of Sawn, looking southwest through the forest. He thought about following Aday. Maybe he should make sure that the unbalanced Shadowborn actually completes the job that Kaiser had laid down for him. He shook his head and looked back towards Meras.

The city sat in the distance, building frames dominating the skyline. Only a few streetlights had been lit. Axum narrowed his eyes and spotted a few light armored guards pacing the perimeter. The guards did not seem as nervous as Axum remembered. Of course they wouldn't if the Daylord was still present in the city, The mighty hero and guardian gave the Mortals an abnormal sense of courage. Even the presence of the beastly Gryphon added to the feeling. Axum crossed his arms tightly and frowned.

Why did Bane appear? Why now? That was the biggest question of all to Axum. Bane had been missing in action for so long that the Mortals believed him to be a wandering Spirit. Axum had heard the Mortals talk about the wandering Spirit, describing him as a bringer of hope and aid when it was needed most. In a way, it was a genius move on Bane's part. No one could know or remember anything about him but praise and good things. He laughed at the thought. Bane was controlling his legend by living as a hermit. Some king and leader he was.

Axum thought back to when he had first heard of Bane the wandering king. A wandering soul himself, he had escaped the senseless assault on the Northlands, wanting more for his life. He had never agreed with the full frontal attack on the Spiritborn. It was doomed to cause more damage to his kin than a subtle take over from within. Even a victory would have drained the Demons to the point that the defeated Spiritborn could rise up again and take back their Dominions. He remembered laughing when he heard that his kin had failed in their quest for he had seen the mysterious Bane before his fame. Granted, the Bane he saw was a lost soul that appeared shell shocked from some unknown trauma. That was not the Bane that became the legendary Daylord and King of Terra. A happy accident, Axum thought, and it made him laugh out loud.

Staying near Meras now seemed pointless. The city no longer was a desirable target. It had never been much of one in the first place but Axum did not feel like questioning Kaiser's motives. He stopped trying ages ago. For what Axum knew, Kaiser delighted in creating chaos even if it did not benefit him. Maybe Kaiser was more insane than Aday. And yet, Kaiser was dangerously smart. Mad and intelligent was a volatile combination. Axum wasn't sure how long he wanted to treat with Kaiser. At least he wasn't trapped in service to Kaiser like his kin Rache. Axum took one last look at Meras and turned away.

*****

FAME AND INFAMY

"Where's Bane? I haven't seen him all morning," Charon exclaimed as he entered his and Gyr's shared bed quarters. He leaned against the wooden door, glancing all around for some sign or indication.

Gyr yawned and stretched before standing up. He rolled his shoulders, shaking his wings. The hay barn had been a warm and comfortable space. He was glad that it survived the fire that nearly razed Meras to the ground. He was also happy that Charon refused to stay in the inn. He stepped down from the ledge of a platform where he had been sleeping.

"How should I know? I sleep. He doesn't," Gyr grumbled as he bent down and stretched his front legs and toes.

"Even the Spirits rest sometimes," Charon commented as he entered the room.

"At least it is finally a nice day. I could use a good flight," Gyr said. He gestured with his head for Charon to open the barn shutters. Charon strode across the space and unlatched the wooden shutters. "Thank you."

Charon watched as Gyr took off through the opening, crying out with delight at being able to stretch his wings. He considered lying down on his bed roll and catching a few restful minutes of sleep. But his curiosity at finding Bane was keeping his senses awake. After their last conversation, Charon felt certain that Bane was not going to leave suddenly. As time went on though, he was not so certain anymore. Bane was after all over a thousand years old and well within his power to resist anyone that tried to stop him. Charon certainly wasn't strong enough. He started to wonder if perhaps, Bane was tracking the mad Shadowborn during his long absences.

He fell backwards onto his rear when Bane slid into view. He flipped down from the edge of the roof, landing perfectly balanced on the wooden floor. By all appearances, Bane was dirty and mud stained. A fine layer of stubble covered his face and it looked like he had not bathed since Charon had last seen him. His blue eyes pierced through the dirt and muck. Bane dropped his gear to the floor with a loud thud. Charon did not know what to do or say in response. He gulped hard.

"You look like you just saw a ghost," Bane commented as he stretched and rolled his shoulders.

Charon got to a seated position and rubbed his lower back. He brushed the slivers of hay from his pants. "Gyr and I just haven't seen you for a few days. We got kind of worried."

"You worry too much. You need to learn to focus on the path ahead, not the fixed path behind," Bane shook his head. "Had you been remotely trained in tracking, you would have proved useful on my search. But then what I found would have terrified you."

Charon managed to get up to his feet and brushed the hay from his legs. "So you were searching for the mad Shadowborn?"

Bane pulled off his dirty leather armor and dropped the set upon his travel pack. He set his hands on his hips and turned around. "I am not concerned about the mad Shadowborn. It is his handler that draws my worry."

There was a second monster out there? Charon stumbled back and nearly fell down. "There's another one?"

"Not a Shadowborn. A Demon. Surely, I do not need to tell you about them and their ilk," Bane said. He rubbed his wrists after removing his deep red leather bracers. "He has been hiding himself well, using this Shadowborn like an attack dog."

"Is he the Master that the mad Shadowborn was talking about?" Charon swallowed hard. He did not like the idea of a Demon in the Southlands. Demons were well known as characters in nightmarish stories from Arken to Garhune.

"I cannot be certain for my findings proved fruitless. The Shadowborn I can easily deal with. The man is only a shell of his former power, more like a starved cat than a mighty lion. You are the starved cat's prey," Bane pointed at Charon.

Being the mouse to the Shadowborn's cat was not a position that Charon wanted to be in. If there was a Demon hunting in the wilds, what if the monster considered him just as desirable a target as the Shadowborn. The two had to be working together. There was just no other way around it.

"It seems that I can't leave you until I figure out what those two want from you. You are not exactly an Immortal blood of note. Perhaps they are interested in you as a half blood. In that, I am also interested," Bane stated. "But the fact that you allow fear to so easily take control is a hindrance and a self-imposed death wish. Do you have any skills? Any worthwhile training in self-defense?"

"I taught myself. Most people here in the Southlands will have little to do with me. Ever since I joined up with Gyr, I have had more attention in the last few months than in the last fifty years." Charon frowned, feeling insulted. He crossed his arms tightly and hunched his shoulders.

"You need to refine what skills you have and utilize your Immortal blood more. I cannot count on the Mortals being able to stop your Shadowborn hunter or a Demon. I also can't leave the Southlands unprotected like Gyr wants."

"I do not think that Gyr would want to leave such a state of things behind him. He has an honest and pure conscience," Charon quickly said in defense.

Bane turned away from him and stood at the opening he had just come through. He leaned against it as he looked out over the yard below. Chickens clucked and mulled about, scratching in the dirt. When one found something, the others quickly converged and squawked loudly with excitement. The sight made Bane smile. He let out a deep breath.

Charon was not sure what to say though there were many things that he wanted to ask. He still felt offended that Bane questioned his combat skills, albeit his direct statements were true. In fact, everything Bane had said was true. He was terrified of the mad Shadowborn and he had always been afraid of Demons.

"You don't have to be so harsh. I know that I am not perfect," Charon mumbled.

Bane scoffed. "Nobody is. Not even me and don't let the Gryphon convince you otherwise. I know that I have done things that have upset many."

"Like leaving your people in the Northlands for a thousand years?" Charon blurted out before he could stop himself. He swiftly put his hands over his mouth and stepped back.

"I am not from the Northlands. I was not born there. I hail from a small town called Norsov in the Eastlands though it is no more." Bane then fell silent and seemed to look off into the distance.

Charon was familiar with a very old fireside tale known as the Fall of Norsov. It was a story that originated from the town of

Koa, the closest settlement in the Southlands to the Eastlands border. Countless years ago, supposed refugees from the east migrated to Koa looking beaten and downtrodden. Many soon died after their arrival from injuries sustained in a terrible battle where a Demon destroyed their beloved home. Though Bane was not mentioned by name then, Charon wondered if he was one of those survivors in the tale.

Bane untangled his arms and clenched his fists tightly until his palms bled. He suddenly was angry and full of vitriol. "This Demon is master of nothing but causing pain and suffering. Now that he has shown himself, he must be dealt with. Tell your Gryphon friend that if he wants me to return north and face his great evil, he will help me kill this Demon first."

Charon was confused by what Bane said for it seemed as if there was a great deal that he was hiding. The wording of his coarse demand indicated that Bane knew exactly who this Demon was and that they shared a history. More and more questions flooded his mind and he grabbed his head in a desperate attempt to calm his thoughts. "What about me?"

Unexpectedly, Bane laughed. It took him a moment to control his mirth. He covered his mouth to muffle the sound. His hand then dropped from his face. "I'll answer your question with a question. Do you honestly want to go after a Demon that is older than I am? Stronger, more ferocious, and not above killing anyone or anything in his path? What you know of Demons is paltry and a hindrance."

He had to admit that Bane was right. If there was a Demon in the Southlands, what could he possibly do? "Then teach me what I can do to help," he requested without thinking.

Bane faced Charon straight on, lifting an eyebrow. The request was bold. Incredibly bold. Bane found himself intrigued by the idea, a flicker of a past memory flashing in his mind. It made him smile. "The Demon's name is Axum and I know him well for reasons I will not tell you until you have earned the right. Like your fireside stories say, a Demon can be in the guise of a man or change into a beast like form born out of the deepest abyss of the Spiral. That is a place in the Spirit World meant for the darkest of souls."

Was Bane actually agreeing to train him? Charon was not so sure but it certainly appeared to be that Bane was willing to educate him on his Immortal roots and all the ensuing details. "Spirit World. Spiral. Got it," Charon said, bowing his head.

"No you don't. Until you have walked within the Spirit World, you will never understand its power to the fullest extent. People tend to think it is black and white. Kind of like life and death. Well, there are a lot of gray areas hence the crap we are dealing with today. If you honestly want me to teach you anything, you must understand that first," Bane explained. "You must also let go of your crippling fear. It might even help you find out who your father is."

Charon looked away in shame and shrugged. He did not much like Bane's way of speaking and how his words tore him down. Yes, he was afraid. He shuddered when Bane placed a hand on his left shoulder. Letting out a deep breath, Charon forced himself to look into Bane's eyes. The expression was surprisingly warm and comforting.

"I will not force you to follow me or even leave Meras. That choice you must make on your own. But I am leaving and there is no guarantee that you or your Gryphon friend will see me again. I depart in an hour," Bane stated before pulling away.

*****

When the people of Meras learned that Bane was leaving, they were very reluctant to let him go. A crowd formed by the southern gate. Bane was right in the center, pulling on the straps of the saddle. His horse snorted in protest and turned back to nip at Bane's hand. Bane chuckled and pushed the horse's snout away. He readjusted the fastenings of his travel pack to make sure it would not break free.

Gyr soared into view and landed awkwardly in the midst of the crowd. "You're not leaving without me!"

Bane chuckled softly. He spotted Charon coming forward, leading a chestnut horse behind him. "I go where he goes," Charon stated. His horse nudged him in the back. "Plus, that horse is this one's friend. I would hate to separate them."

Before Bane could respond, a pair of children nervously approached him. The little boy held the even smaller girl's arm, acting protective. The straw haired girl carried a crudely assembled bouquet of yellow and white flowers, held tight up against her chest. She looked down and shivered. Bane squatted down to the children's eye level.

"Please stay, Mr. Daylord," the little boy begged. He wiped a tear away and sniffled. The little girl at his side nervously handed Bane the bouquet.

Bane gingerly held the honest gift. "I wish I could. Nothing could make me happier than to help you rebuild your home and bring Meras back to life. But I am called away to bring justice to the one who took your family from you. That is what I do. Fight the bad guys so good people like you can live in happiness and peace."

"I'm scared," the little girl cried.

Bane immediately took the children in his arms and embraced them tightly. He wanted to reassure them through his strength that everything will be ok. Their fear and sorrow touched on something buried deep within him. Something he had not visited in many years. It opened a raw wound and he felt himself wanting to weep. He held the children tighter.

"Don't be scared. Know that I am watching over you. I will protect you," Bane promised, a slight quiver in his voice.

Charon heard the quiver, finding it uncharacteristic of the Bane he knew. To see Bane in such a state was new and it begged questions. The mighty Daylord admitted to being well over a thousand years old with a past left to memory. Even Gyr had not been able to tell Charon much about what Bane was prior to his arrival in the Northlands. But something seemed clear to Charon now. Bane once had children for what he saw was a father's pain, not that of a benevolent king. This pain appeared too raw and real to be anything else.

The crowd was oblivious, clapping when Bane rose to his feet. They cheered for him and wished him well. Gyr proudly strode over to Bane's side, his feathered chest puffed out. Bane mounted his horse as Charon did while Gyr took to the skies. The people continued clapping and cheering, wishing the trio safe travels and safe return. Gyr whistled loudly, singing a Gryphon song in a joyous tone.

Charon was too focused on the very poignant moment before Bane and the two children. Yes, he had to have been a father at one time. It was just too real and unlike the stoic Daylord he knew. The idea of losing one's children would explain why Bane was so closed off about his past. Perhaps he did not want to revisit the pain. Maybe it was the reason why Bane avoided associating with the Northlands. Charon glanced at Bane who was riding ahead of him. The Daylord's shoulders looked bowed under an invisible weight. If that weight got any heavier, Bane was surely going to break.

*****

CHANGE OF HEART

Lana stood before the doors of Evander's great hall. She had cleaned and picked through her feathers until they gleamed. She had shined her claws and beak and brushed her furry flanks. She was ready to meet with the Lord of the Lightborn. She held her head up high, looking proud and confident. Inside, she repeated her prepared speech, first in the Gryphon tongue and then in the common tongue. On her flight to Prism, the capital of the Lightborn, she practiced her speaking skills. At first, she was desperate to make sure that her accent was nonexistent but now, she was ready to embrace it. The speech she was about to make was going to be the most important in her life. Lana was determined to not fail the Lords of Crossroads.

On both sides of the heavy and richly carved white wood door were guards. They were dressed in bronze scaled armor that wrapped around their shoulders and torsos. The metallic pieces were worn over white leather and cloth, creating a mystical allure. Like many Gryphons, Lana thought armor to be a hindrance to true physical power. She knew that her talons were sharp enough to rip through the protective outfit. She side eyed the guards' long spears and tapped her talons lightly on the stone floor.

In her opinion, Prism was a bright but cold place. Everything had been built too perfectly and the streets were too clean. It had disturbed her that the people were so quiet and barely acknowledged her. She had to wonder if the Lightborn were so deep in their thoughts that they ignored all else. In a way, the

Lightborn appeared oblivious. It was such a contrast to the Airborn who bowed and spoke to every Gryphon like they were dear friends and family. Even the Waterborn had more of a personality. But Lana had to put that behind her.

The doors cracked open and a thin Lightborn man dressed in rich robes of white and gold satin appeared before Lana. His cornflower hair was slicked back from his face and cascaded down to the middle of his back.

"Lady Gryphon, my Lord Evander is ready to see you now," the Lightborn man said.

Lana frowned. "My name is Lana of Ornith."

"Yes. My apologies," the man said, tapping the side of his head to acknowledge he had forgotten. "Lana of Ornith, I am the Lord Evander's chief chamberlain. My name is Rayn of Prism."

Lana cocked her head back. She felt offended by the Lightborn's manners but chose not to pursue the issue. She had more important matters to attend to. "Lead on."

Rayn gestured towards each guard with a bow of the head before turning around. The guards worked in sync to pull open the doors, never dropping their spears. Light poured in from the great hall. Rayn started to walk forward and Lana dutifully followed. The great hall was dominated by a massive sky light made of glass and iron. In fact, the entire ceiling was made of clear glass that shimmered in the sunlight. It cast small rainbows everywhere on the white stone floor and walls. There were so many windows of multicolored stained glass that the room was flooded with color. At the other end of the hall was a throne of white wood and gold trim. Upon that chair sat Evander.

The Lord of the Lightborn leaned to his left side, whispering to a fully armored man with white eyebrows and shorn golden hair. The man had a deep scar on the left side of his face. It was the first hint of imperfection Lana had seen on anyone since she had arrived in the capital.

"My Lord Evander. Commander Solar. This is the Gryphon Lana of Ornith," Rayn introduced. He gestured back towards Lana. "You may speak to my Lord now."

Lana waited for Rayn to step back before she came forward. She bowed in respect towards Evander as a Lord of the Spiritborn though she loathed to do so. She glanced at Commander Solar, glad that the soldier was present to hear her words.

"I hear that you have flown all the way from Crossroads. Where is your Feather Whisper or parchment with the words of Lord Proto Avis and Lord Vorin?" Evander asked as he sat up straight in his chair.

"I bear their words on my tongue," Lana said, proud to hear

that her accent was very slight in the common tongue. Her practice had paid off.

Evander opened the floor for her to speak by waving his hand before him. "Speak then."

Lana cleared her throat. She had prepared herself for this moment. "The Lords of Crossroads implore you to take up arms in the new Dominion War against the aggressor Kaiser Adonis. Those of the Northern Alliance are commanded to assemble in Cascade so that we may march united to the lands of the Shadowborn. Within the lands of the Shadowborn, a rebellion fights alone against Kaiser and we are duty bound to help them."

"Says who?" Evander curtly asked.

"By the laws of the Immortal Truth and the command of Crossroads whose authority was given to them by the High King of Terra," Lana replied. She did her best to ignore Evander's lack of empathy for the situation. "The War Council has been called and you have been summoned."

Evander let out a deep breath and rapped his fingers on the arms of his chair. He remained silent for a long time. Lana felt uncomfortable under his uncompromising stare. "You have been given a heavy burden to carry and far you have carried it. A noble mission for any Gryphon messenger. You should be proud."

Flattery was an unexpected response and Lana was not prepared. It took her a minute to recover. "Lord Evander, I am not here for pleasantries. We are at war. People are dying and we are facing an enemy like none other. You may think Kaiser is one man but he is one man with many dark talents."

"Do not presume to tell me what to think! I know what goes on in this world!" Evander snapped. He leaped up from his chair and pointed accusingly at Lana. "I will not have Crossroads tell me what to do and how to command my people. If I deem it worthy to fight then I will fight. I will not risk the Lightborn with obliteration in a pointless war."

"Pointless? You think that Kaiser believes what he is doing is pointless? All who have died in the cause to defeat him? Were their lives pointless because they chose to fight and you did not?" Lana immediately challenged. She did not care if she offended Evander. In fact, she wanted to. "We have all sat long enough and now we must pay the consequences. "If we do not fight, this world will be torn apart and collapse. The Dark Days will return and the worlds of the living and the dead will be as one. Is that what you want?"

Evander furrowed his brow and clenched his fists tightly. "You..."

Lana interrupted him before he could finish his curse. "You

are a coward, Lord Evander. You do not deserve your high office if this is how you are going to act. I hope that when the Daylord returns, he takes it from you and gives it to someone more deserving!"

That instantly silenced the room. Solar pulled out his broadsword and came towards Lana threateningly. Lana hissed and postured in an aggressive display with wings flared. Only Rayn did not react. In fact, he had no expression of all, appearing blissfully unaware of the severity of Lana's insults.

"Get out of my lands!" Evander shouted.

"No! I will not! Someone needs to tell you the real truth so you can no longer hide and let the world fall apart around you! If you continue to refuse the call then you are just as terrible as Kaiser Adonis! You have become the enemy of hope!" Lana cried out, her accent heavy in her fury.

Evander was completely taken aback by Lana but Solar was more than prepared to strike her down. He ran forward with his sword held high. Lana growled and hissed, whipping her tail back and forth. She was prepared to fight the Lightborn Commander with all of her might.

"Enough of this!" Rayn shouted, the most emotion he had shone since Lana had first met him.

Solar stopped in his tracks and turned to face the chamberlain. His expression was one of shock. He slowly resheathed his sword and glanced over to Evander for guidance. The Lord of the Lightborn was still speechless. Rayn walked with quiet confidence, coming to stand before Evander. He waved him back. Evander sat with a heavy thump on the throne. Rayn nodded once before going over to Solar. The chamberlain tapped him on the shoulder to get his attention. As soon as he had it, he pointed to the left hand side of the throne. Solar's shoulders slumped and he plodded over to the spot.

"Lady Lana of Ornith, I apologize for the abhorrent behavior of my Lord and Commander," Rayn said with a polite bow. "Your mission is true and I have at least heard your words with an open and honest heart. I can only pray that my Lord Evander will do the same." Rayn glanced over his shoulder at Evander.

Lana turned up the corners of her beak into a smile. She now realized that she had misjudged Rayn after their initial interaction. "Do you speak for the Lightborn?"

"I speak for myself. If the Lords of Crossroads will have me, I will return to Cascade with you," Rayn declared.

"No. I forbid it," Evander barked.

Rayn turned to face Evander. "My Lord, you asked me to be honest in my role as chamberlain to your household. I believe in this Gryphon and what she has to say. And I certainly don't want to be remembered for standing by as the world fell apart. You should be ashamed of yourself for thinking that could solve the problem. Ignore a fire and it can burn your house down."

"Thank you," Lana said softly. She turned her attention to Evander. "I want to be remembered as the Gryphon of the Shadowlord who I believe in with all my heart. The past must be set aside for us to save the future."

Everyone waited for Evander to speak. The Lord of the Lightborn slowly rose from his seat and stepped down the dais. He paused at the bottom, keeping a respectful distance from Lana.

"Never has a soul spoken to me as you have, Lana of Ornith. Not even the Dragons of old dared to do so. Were you one of my people, I would have you jailed for your disrespect and boldness. For questioning my authority, I would have you banished for treasonous words for a length of time of my choosing. However, you are not of my people. You are a Gryphon and hail from a land where individuals are allowed to question authority and you are also under the protection of Crossroads. But your claims of being the Shadowlord's Gryphon? Are you trying to assume the mighty Bellico's place?"

"Bellico was my ancestor so it is only right. Were he still here, he would be proud of me," Lana replied with a puff of her chest.

"Ah a daughter of Bellico?" Evander questioned. He looked her up and down. "Yes I see it now. His fur and feathers were not the brightest of pelts but his Spirit was noble and fiercely loyal. The role you claim to assume is premature though. There is no Shadowlord like Shadow Night Silvanus."

Lana flared her wings and tossed her head. "He may not have named himself but I have named him through heart and power. Peredur Coba-Silvanus is my Shadowlord and I will follow him and protect him with all that I am."

Evander briefly turned away, having a private conversation with himself. Occasionally he locked eyes with Solar before dropped his gaze towards the floor. After a few minutes, he let out a deep breath and looked up at Lana.

"I did not want to admit it at the time, considering the bastard broke my arm, but he is like the Shadow Night of old. The one before the Immortal Truth. The brash but true hearted warrior," he muttered to himself. He then straighten his back and squared his shoulders. "What you ask of me, Gryphon, is to undo centuries in a matter of moments. I cannot do that. I will need time to think. Time to prepare. Time to consider all that you have said to me."

Lana nodded her head. "That is all I and Crossroads asks. At least progress had been made for the sake of salvation of the world. We do not ask for you to change everything you are. We only ask that you remember your promises to the Immortal Truth and to Terra."

*****

PUSHING THROUGH THE PAIN

"What are they working on now?" Myra asked as she sat down on the wooden bench beside Zoras.

Zoras sat in deep concentration, closely watching the training match between Jarod and Onyx. Ryder paced around the pair, directing Onyx and giving him pointers regarding his posture and forms. Haven sat on the opposite bench, interjecting her own commentary. She giggled at every misstep, holding her stomach to avoid laughing out loud.

"How to disarm and disable a more powerful opponent with the least amount of physical energy," Zoras answered without looking away. "My boy Soja was quite good at it. Sometimes all it took for him was clever wordplay to throw an opponent off their guard."

"I am sure that you miss him terribly. I feel the same way about my daughter every time I look at Ryder. I see his mother's eyes and smile in him," Myra said, trying to offer some comfort.

Zoras sat back and crossed his arms tightly. "At least you have your grandson. I am the last of my line."

Myra rubbed the old Commander's left shoulder. "You must not think of it that way. Your legacy will live on long after the world ends. You have done what few were brave enough to do: oppose Kaiser and lead a war against him."

Zoras scoffed. "In reality, it is your grandson that leads the Shadowborn. They look to him and his royal cousin for guidance and hope. That is the role of a descendant of Shadow Night."

"You are still important in all of this as was your son. Symbols of loyalty and strength in these trying times," Myra encouraged with a smile.

"I know that there is nothing I can do to bring my son back but I can at least honor his memory by winning this war," Zoras sighed. He turned to face Myra. "I am not a heartless soldier. I am a father who lost his only son. Soja lived the life that I wish I could have. One of happiness and duty. Now that is lost to me."

Myra had not seen this side of Zoras since she had been brought to the base. She glanced down as Zoras twisted something in his hands. He crunched up his hands.

"It would have been Soja's birthday today," Zoras sniffled, holding back a sob. He choked down the tears. "Excuse me."

"There is absolutely no need to apologize. Not to me or anyone else here," Myra comforted.

It took Zoras a few minutes to recover his strength. He studied Ryder and narrowed his eyes. "What did you see in Kaiser?"

The question was off putting considering how just moments ago, Zoras was close to breaking down in sorrow. Myra felt herself at a loss for words. She mumbled to herself, looking at the dusty ground beneath her feet. "Kaiser is incapable of true love and compassion though he makes play at it. Every word that passes through his lips could be a lie or could be a truth. Looking back, I did not see what I do now. As terrible as Kaiser is, he did give me a precious gift: Aylin and through her, Ryder."

"If only Mali had wholeheartedly accepted Akakios' love for your daughter. She would have been an extraordinary queen. But I doubt that would have done anything to save us from the war we are fighting now. We cannot change what has already been done," Zoras mused as he pocketed the crumbled up piece of black cloth. "Soja always said he did not like to focus on the past and chose to live in the present. Do not worry about what has been and what is to come, Father. All that matters is now."

They both turned their attention to the training session, seeing that Ryder now stepped in. Onyx sat beside Haven on the wooden plank bench while Jarod gloated about an old battle memory. Zoras chuckled softly and shook his head.

"Seeing this brings back so many memories and reminds me that there is still light in this world," Zoras smiled. "When Soja was a small boy, he used to boast to all of his training comrades about my accomplishments and tell them that he would exceed me with little effort. Oh the many tests I put him through to keep that attitude in check. I was so sure that at one point, he would declare that he hated me. He never did. He never gave up. Given the chance, I am certain he would have been a great Commander."

Myra gestured towards Onyx. "The Prince could certainly use a wise instructor's touch."

"You doubt your grandson's skill as a teacher? I think he is doing quite well considering," Zoras asked. A hint of laughter was in his voice.

"As equal as Jarod thinks himself to be, he is no match for my grandson. You are at least a bit closer and better trained. I believe that Onyx could learn more from a match between you and Ryder," Myra said matter of fact.

Zoras pushed himself up from his seat on the bench. He looked back at Myra and winked. He then strode towards Jarod, tapping him on the shoulder. Jarod immediately slid to the side.

"If it pleases you, your Highness. I would like to challenge the one known as Ryder Coba to an exhibition match. I hope that by witnessing our contest, you will better understand your lesson and learn about Shadow Touch," Zoras presented formally with a bow.

"What is Shadow Touch?" Onyx asked in confusion. He glanced to Haven. She shrugged.

Ryder crossed his arms and rolled his eyes. "It's not a technique that uses Spirit Energy if you are wondering. It's an advanced Saber skill where you strike the pressure points to disable an enemy."

"Indeed. Especially useful if the Shadowlord wishes to question an offender. Use enough force and you can kill with it. It is about restraint and control of your physical power," Zoras explained as he straightened his posture.

"I still don't get it. How can such a skill be more useful than a weapon or Spirit energy?" Onyx asked.

"Watch and learn. If my son could learn to use it, you can too," Zoras smirked as he looked at Ryder. He nodded.

Zoras threw the first punch at high speed towards Ryder's right shoulder. He fully intended to stun him and render the limb useless. Ryder acted in the blink of an eye, catching Zoras' clenched fist. Zoras gritted his teeth as Ryder twisted his left arm to the outside. The action put tremendous strain on his elbow.

"Are you sure that you want a rematch? My grandmother did say I was better than you," Ryder smirked.

Ryder suddenly pulled Zoras in close and kneed him under his chin. Ryder then drew his left hand back and struck Zoras hard on the center of his chest. Zoras slid back and stumbled ten feet before coming to a stop. The old Saber Commander balanced himself with his right hand before looking up with an eager expression.

"Now it begins. Hold nothing back, Ryder. Your cousin needs to see Shadow Touch in action," Zoras declared before charging forward.

To Onyx, it seemed as if his cousin was more powerful without a weapon in his hands. He watched as Zoras and Ryder exchange calculated blows. His thoughts drifted to a memory of their last match. No one was in the proper mind back then, himself most of all. This rematch was more than showing him a Saber technique though Onyx was not about to ignore the lesson. He leaned forward over his knees, his eyes darting back and forth. He followed Zoras and Ryder's quick movements with increasing cheer. Despite the war and the seriousness of his training, Onyx was enjoying the moment. He glanced over to his right to see Jarod crouched down and watching the match with keen interest.

Myra settled beside Onyx and bowed her head. "I remember when Zoras tested Ryder during the reign of his father. Akakios had requested the then Commander Zoras to evaluate his son's combat skills. He did so before the entire court."

"What does Ryder say of it? He has never mentioned that to me," Onyx said as he twisted his face in confusion.

It was Haven that answered. "A word to the wise. Do not ask Zoras what happens when a sitting Saber Commander is defeated in open combat in front of the Shadowlord. It took Zoras a long time to come to terms with losing."

A cloud of dust rose up around Zoras and Ryder as they scuffled back and forth. Zoras swung his right arm forward in a forward punch. Ryder immediately leaned back, the would be attack passing inches over his nose. As Zoras moved to fire another shot, Ryder flipped backwards with one hand spring and dropped to the ground. He swung his left leg in a sweeping arc, knocking Zoras off his feet. In the blink of an eye, Ryder was on his feet and had elbowed Zoras in the chest. Zoras collapsed to the ground in a breathless heap. Instead of cursing at his misfortune, the old Commander smiled and sprung back up to his feet.

"You would have made the best of all Saber Commanders," Zoras commented as he and Ryder squared off again.

"And here I thought you preferred me on the throne instead of in its shadow," Ryder laughed. He bounced back and forth on the balls of his feet.

Ryder prepared a difficult set of maneuvers to counter Zoras' renewed attack but he suddenly paused. It was if he sensed some form of danger for he looked back over his shoulder. Zoras slammed his clenched fist hard on Ryder's right side. Ryder crumbled to his knees, clutching the spot and gasping for breath. Zoras' face immediately paled. Ryder rolled onto his back, his left hand slipping from his side. His palm was covered in dark red blood.

"Geez! I cannot have hit him that hard!" Zoras stumbled to say. Zoras knelt down and reached for Ryder's hand in an attempt to examine the blood. Ryder batted him away and groaned softly.

"No. It's not that," Ryder said through gritted teeth. "Just old wounds slow to heal."

Just then, Donovan raced past with tears streaming down his face. His Saber leathers were dirty and disheveled. What was most shocking was that his front was stained with blood. He disappeared beyond the darkness of the base entrance before anyone could stop him. Hayden came out into the yard, charging after Donovan. He quickly slid to a stop.

"Onyx, with me now. You might be the only person he will listen to," Hayden said with a hurried tone. He kept glancing in the direction where Donovan had disappeared.

Onyx rose to his feet and caught the sheathed sword that Hayden had tossed at him. He fumbled as he struggled to belt it on, dropping it twice.

"Wait. What is going on?" Zoras asked sternly.

"A runner arrived from the Shunga estate with dire news, dying soon after he delivered this message: Kaiser is on the march. I need to stop Donovan before he does something stupid and I need Onyx's help," Hayden reported. He shoved Onyx before him once he came close. Onyx stumbled a few steps. Hayden glanced down at Ryder. "I will bring your cousin back. You have my word."

"I'm coming with you," Jarod said as he spun a sword around and sheathed it at his left hip. "It may take the three of us to bring Donovan back if what awaits him is truly something he does not want to face."

The trio rushed away after Donovan, disappearing beyond the mountain base gates. Zoras helped Ryder to his feet, throwing Ryder's left arm over his shoulders to support him.

"If Kaiser is on the march, then we need to prepare swiftly to meet him," Ryder suggested once he was steady on his feet.

"What about you?" Haven asked. She gestured towards the blood stain on Ryder's torso.

"I'll live. Right now, we need to get prepared and gather together our combined forces to meet Kaiser on the battlefield. We do not have much time either."

*****

ONYX TO THE RESCUE

"Damn. Where could he have gotten to?" Hayden grumbled not for the first time. The Saber Captain kept a ready hand on his sword hilt as he looked around.

Onyx wiped his brow and rubbed his palm on his pant leg. He grimaced at the smear of dirt and sweat. "Surely Donovan was running for his family estate. Even I know where that is."

"That is not the point. We need to reach him before he gets to the estate. Who knows what is waiting there?" Hayden said as he stepped up onto a moss covered tree stump. He turned his head about. "If only our Spirit energy was working properly. I could have tracked him better.

Both jerked their heads behind them at the sound of a snapping twig. Jarod came through the brush, kicking free from an ivy vine. "We might as well go to the Shunga estate or what is left of it. We are never going to catch him before he makes it there."

"I am just worried about him. He has been quiet and unsteady as of late and I fear that he might harm himself. Call me selfish but we can't afford to lose another warrior. We need him alive," Hayden said as he jumped down from the stump. Mud splashed on his already travel stained boots.

"Hayden, if the runner's news was as dire as you said, Donovan may be facing the fact that Kaiser executed his family. I know what that is like," Onyx said in Donovan's defense.

A silence fell over the group with only Onyx appearing confident and ready to proceed. Hayden's head drooped in shame and his hand fell from his sword hilt. A clap of thunder sounded in the distance. The sound reverberated through the trees, shaking the canopy above. Clumps of wet pine needles rained down. Jarod batted one away that fell on his head.

"Perhaps we should let Onyx lead the way now. Of us three, he is thinking most clearly about the entire situation," Jarod suggested. He shrugged when Hayden gave him a hardened look.

Hayden eventually gave way after a tense minute and stepped to the side. He waited beside Jarod. Onyx squashed any nerves that he had and took the lead. He led the way down the wet green hill, weaving around massive pine tree trunks. After treading through the thick woods for another hour, the trio came upon a dirt road that had turned to mud with the recent rain. Onyx paused to look up and down the road before crossing it. Hayden and Jarod followed dutifully behind him and into the next patch of trees and underbrush. Another four hours passed and it started to drizzle. The rain was light and refreshing.

Onyx had everyone pause before an eight foot tall fence that had been coated in ivy vines. He took seven calculating steps to his right, running his hands over the vine. He stopped and smiled.

"Donovan told me of a break along the eastern fence of his family estate. He said he used to climb through it and go on adventures in the woods when he was a child," Onyx said as he worked to pull apart the thick vines. With a little effort, he revealed the opening.

"Let me go first. Jarod, you bring up the rear. Everyone, stay vigilant. We do not know what we will find," Hayden ordered softly. He put a finger to his lips to indicate that silence was a good idea.

Hayden carefully passed through the fence opening first, a steady hand on his sword hilt. After a few seconds, he reached through and waved his hand for the others to proceed. Onyx came through next followed by Jarod. The land opened up before them into a wide space. To the distant left was the main entry way with an ornate iron and steel gate. Both sides of the gate had been ripped free of their moorings and lay on the ground. Onyx dreaded looking towards the right. He closed his eyes and took in a deep breath. He let it out slowly before he opened his eyes to look.

A fizzle of smoke rose up from the stone and wood ruins of a once sprawling estate. Outer buildings smoldered while the remaining wall of the central house still standing crumbled in a cloud of ash and dirt. There was no life to be seen and nothing worth saving.

"This would surely be Cross' fate if the Heights did not protect it," Hayden commented as the trio cautiously began to cross the wide grassland towards the ruins.

"I don't think a thick mountain wall can stand against whatever dark power Kaiser poses," Jarod pointed out.

"Just look for Donovan and forget about Cross for the time being," Onyx barked. It pained him to think that way but he told himself that a city can easily be rebuilt. A life could not be restored.

They cautiously approached the ruins. Hayden and Jarod pulled out their swords and looked about for any sign that would indicate an impending attack. Onyx, though concerned of an attack, focused his thoughts on finding Donovan and praying that he had not done himself harm. Donovan had admitted to Onyx on multiple occasions that he would not fail his Prince as he failed his royal father. What had happened to Aku had been an unforgivable burden to Donovan though Onyx had tried to convince him otherwise. Onyx wondered what drove Donovan to such desperation to make amends. Was this the downside of Saber loyalty? That failure to serve the Shadowlord in anyway resulted in deep depression? Onyx could only hope for the best as ideas for transforming the Saber Order danced in his head.

The scent in the air was a mixture of burnt wood, rain, and hints of decay. Onyx twisted and rubbed his nose as he stepped over a large broken piece of stone. He slipped as the stone pitched forward. Hayden quickly reached out a hand to steady him.

"Thank you," Onyx whispered. He did not feel comfortable speaking any louder. Something about the ruins urged him to have respect for the dead. He sniffled again as the scent of decay grew stronger.

Jarod reached forward and held Onyx back. He put a finger to his lips and pointed towards their left. Both Hayden and Onyx looked to the left, seeing Donovan on his knees with shoulders bent forward. Onyx nodded and indicated for them to stay put by pointing at the ground. Once he had their silent word, Onyx proceeded with caution towards Donovan.

Donovan cried and sobbed loudly, seemingly unaware of Onyx's approach. His Saber cloak spread out around him like a black cloud, one that reflected how dark his thoughts had become. Tears streamed from his eyes and mucus bubbled from his nose. He could hold nothing in, feeling that he was on the edge of breaking down completely. All that he had known and the people he loved were gone. Gone!

"I have failed you!" he shouted towards the sky. "I could not protect you!"

It was heartbreaking for Onyx to hear Donovan's cries. Every word and syllable spoke of his deep pain. It was obvious by now that Kaiser or even his terrible Demon had come to the estate, obliterating everyone and everything. He was the last of the Shungas much as Zoras was the last of the Rokars. Onyx paused, clenching his fists. Just like how he and Ryder were the last of the Silvanus bloodline. Kaiser was wiping out entire families just for the sake of sadistic joy and chaos. Never more in his life did Onyx want to kill Kaiser but an often pushed away mental voice spoke up. Ryder had more of a right to Kaiser's death than anyone else on Terra. If there could be such a thing.

"You have not failed me, Donovan," Onyx cautiously said as he bent down by Donovan's left side. He was not sure if in his depressed state that Donovan would be volatile.

His fear of such disappeared when Donovan reached out to embrace him tightly, still sobbing profusely. Onyx slowly put his arms around the Saber. For a long time, the pair of them remained in position as Onyx let Donovan cry. Hayden and Jarod soon joined them but Onyx bade them back.

"You have not failed me in the slightest for you have faced the truth more than any of us. You have seen the true depravity of Kaiser and have chosen to continue on. You chose to serve my father and myself. You chose to rebel against Kaiser when doing so risked certain death. You are strong, Donovan," Onyx soothed.

Hayden fell to one knee and bowed his head. His heart swelled with pride and love for the young Prince, seeing a glimpse of a leader within. Jarod also followed suit, sheathing his sheath before bending to one knee. Together, Hayden and Jarod reached out and placed a hand on each of Onyx's shoulders.

"They are gone and I will never see them again!" Donovan cried. His chest heaved as he tried to catch his breath.

"But you will. In the Spirit World and there is nothing in all the world that Kaiser can do to stop it," Hayden said softly. "Omu is watching over them and he watches over you."

"The Great Wolf watches over all of us," Jarod added in the same soft voice.

Donovan's cries continued strongly for countless minutes before it seemed he ran out of strength. His cries became raspy and his voice cracked as he spoke. "I am broken and lost with nothing left."

"You have me. You have Ryder. You have all of us who fight to bring down Kaiser. We are family and we always will be," Onyx declared. "You are not alone in your suffering."

The sky slowly turned deep shades of red and orange, signaling the approach of sunset and the coming night. Though it was imperative that they return to base as quick as possible, Onyx forbade it until Donovan had rested. Hayden and Jarod set about securing of the still standing buildings which turned out to be a hay barn. The now group of four settled in for the night, lighting no fire. Jarod volunteered to take the first watch though no one was in a mood to sleep save Donovan. Onyx kept close to him while Hayden joined Jarod by the broken door to the barn.

"I don't know what happened to my family. They disappeared one hundred years ago, not long after Ryder left. I'd like to think that they are in hiding somewhere just waiting for it to be safe enough to come out," Jarod admitted as his eyes scanned the ruins and forest's edge. "But who am I kidding? Kaiser probably slaughtered them in his fury."

"My nephew fell under his spell and lost his life. At least that is what my heart tells me," Hayden said as he leaned against the doorframe. "Rothe was always a foolish and ambitious sort but I had thought him above believing in such traitorous people such as Kaiser. What do either of us have left now?"

Jarod shifted his weight and looked at Hayden. "We still have hope and the courage to fight. The Shadowlord and the Daylord will reveal themselves when the time comes. I can only pray that it will be soon."

The orange red sunset darkened to a dull shade of purple as storm clouds rumbled in the distance. Hayden looked back over his shoulder at the holes in the roof and sighed. It was going to be a long and wet night.

*****

BLESSING IN DISGUISE

Ryder let out a deep breath as he stepped into his quarters, feeling mentally and physically exhausted. The battle plan meeting had gone on through most of the night but he was at least pleased that progress had been made. Still it saddened him that Donovan had yet to recover any semblance of strength. In his current state, Ryder was considering leaving Donovan behind at the base. Donovan just wasn't in the right state of mind for a pitched battle. There was no time to wait for him. Ryder leaned back against the closed door, closing his eyes. He wondered if he could even sleep in his current state.

He looked over at Haven who was already under the covers and facing away from him. He had missed her presence at the meeting, one she would have normally and eagerly attended. Of all the people currently at the base, few were more eager about combat. Ryder stepped over to the bed to his left and sat down on the edge. He started to rub her back in slow circles. Haven stirred but did not turn over to face him.

"I missed you at the meeting. Were you able to rest?" Ryder asked.

Haven shrugged her shoulders. "Not very well. I worry for Donovan. It cannot be easy losing everything like that."

"Onyx is doing his best to comfort him but I worry too. My cousin told me that Donovan feels he has nothing left to fight for with his family gone," Ryder said with an exacerbated sigh. He ran his fingers through his hair.

"The love of a family gives many something to fight for. But family does not have to be one of blood. Donovan needs to see that he is still loved and that he is one of our brothers. A beloved son," Haven expressed in a soft voice. She sniffled loudly.

Ryder took the hand that had been resting on her left side, giving it an encouraging squeeze. "Have you been crying?"

Haven sniffled again and pulled her hand away to wipe her nose. "Only a little."

"Why?" Ryder asked.

"I am scared," Haven quietly admitted. She let Ryder take her hand again.

Ryder smiled sweetly. "You have no reason to be afraid. I am here with you."

Haven took in a deep breath and let it out slowly. "I am with child."

With a heavy thud, Ryder hit the floor after falling off the bed in shock. Haven laughed as a tear streamed down her cheek. She wiped it away before sitting up. She laughed again as Ryder slowly climbed back onto the bed. He rubbed the back of his head and swallowed hard. He examined his fingers for any trace of blood. Haven waited, keeping her hands on her lap.

"What did you say?" Ryder managed to ask.

Haven wiped another tear away. "I am with child."

"Mine?" Ryder stupidly asked.

She nodded. She then picked up his left hand with both of hers and guided to her belly. At first, Ryder resisted any movement but slowly, his hand moved about. His head jerked back in further shock as he felt the small but obvious roundness of a child growing inside. His rough hand continued to move over her belly as if to confirm the truth.

"I put that there?" Ryder struggled to ask.

Haven laughed. "Surely your mother told you how things work when a man and a woman lie with each other in such an intimate manner. The Spirits have blessed our union and given us this gift. Our very own piece of light in these dark times."

"Who else knows?" Ryder asked. He was starting to get back some of his clarity and ability to think.

"Your grandmother first suspected it," Haven admitted. "And my mother knows."

"No wonder my grandmother was looking at me funny and giggling," Ryder said. He let out a deep breath. "A baby. Wow. You're going to be a mother."

"And you a father," Haven stated rather proudly. She caressed her small belly as if to emphasize the point. "I was at first afraid. I mean we are in the middle of a war. How can we think to bring a child into this world? But my mother told me and I have to agree. This child gives me something to fight for. Something for us to fight for."

*****

Ryder felt a combination of butterflies and nerves as sleep continued to escape him. Haven was sleeping peacefully beside him, her back to him. He was looking up at the stone ceiling with both hands behind his head. He found it impossible to sleep when his mind and heart were so active. A baby! His baby! A part of him fluttered with excitement and growing love. It would be at least six more moons before his son or daughter would arrive according to Haven. He wondered what this child would look like. Would it favor Haven's looks, his looks, or be a combination of them both? Would it be a warrior or a scholar? The idea of having a child made Ryder think more about the Shadowborn throne. The question of should he rise up and take it flashed in his mind and refused to be shoved away.

As he thought about the throne, the war against Kaiser raged in his mind. He sighed deeply, careful not to be too loud and wake Haven back up. He looked over at her peacefully sleeping. It was not just her that he had to protect. As soon as he thought about that, he grinned. Haven would have smacked him for thinking that was the only one that needed protection. To Ryder, she was strong and a very capable battle partner. He would surely miss her at his side and he knew that she would not be pleased at being told she could no longer suit up for battle. Ryder wanted her to be safe especially now that she was carrying his child. It wasn't enough to keep her safe. Ryder knew that he had to stay alive when Kaiser seemed so hell bent on killing him. He was going to have to win the war before the baby arrived.

Unable to sleep, Ryder carefully got out of bed and pulled on a long sleeved shirt, leaving the front untied. He ran his hand over his right thigh, tugging at the fabric of his pants. He pulled on his leather boots and quietly left the room. Making his wall through the twisting tunnels, Ryder found his destination.

"Did you ever manage to get some sleep? I couldn't," Zoras admitted as Ryder entered the refurbished war room. A map of the Shadowborn lands was stretched out over the table top. Various instruments were placed on strategic points to indicate the rebel forces and Kaiser's armies. Zoras stepped back and scratched his chin.

"Have you had a response from the rest of the rebel bases?" Ryder asked.

Zoras wiggled his fingers briefly. He gestured towards Dusk. "They will meet us in Dusk and join in the defense of the city. Perhaps with all of us together, we can protect the way east."

Ryder leaned over the table, studying the map carefully. He reached forward to pick up a chipped moonstone. He set it back down on the small diagram of Cross. "As far as I am concerned, Cross is lost. At our current numbers, we cannot hope to take the city while Kaiser marches on Dusk. He can break the Mirror and continue to march across the Earthborn lands. We have to stop him in Dusk."

"What if we don't? We cannot enter this battle and believe that there is only one possible outcome. Such thoughts breed desperation and lead to poor decisions," Zoras admonished.

"I know that," Ryder grumbled as he lowered his head.

"Well here is what I think," Zoras said reaching across the map. He pushed several tiny soldier models to the outskirts of Dusk's diagram. "You and I need to keep Kaiser and his Demon on us. Let the rest of our forces engage Kaiser's army. Hayden can take on Loran here." Zoras pointed to a spot on the diagram's southern border. He dragged his finger to the northern border. "If Kaiser's forces split as I am sure they will, Jarod and Haven..."

"Not Haven," Ryder interrupted in a firm voice. He gripped the edge of the table.

"She was trained by you! Among those of the captains, she is best suited to lead with Jarod as her second. I do not think that she will be happy if you keep her from the battlefield," Zoras argued in Haven's defense. "She is a great warrior and you know it."

Ryder let out a deep breath. "She has greater concerns to attend to."

It boggled Zoras' mind as to what could be more important than a battle that could change the outcome of the war. He threw his hands up in the air and turned away. He kept his back to Ryder as he crossed his arms tightly. He fumed for a moment until it dawned on him. A smile slowly crossed his face and he dropped his arms as he turned around. Ryder had not moved from his head down position over the table. Zoras mimicked his posture and waited for Ryder to look up.

Ryder eventually lifted up his head and his eyes met Zoras' joyous expression. He shrugged as if to say what. He stood up straight as Zoras rounded the table to stand before him. He leaned back, feeling uncomfortable. "You're not going to kiss me are you?"

"Congratulations, Dad!" Zoras said exuberantly as he slapped Ryder's right shoulder. He held his hand in place. "Now I understand why you couldn't sleep."

"What was your reaction when your wife told you that she

was with child? I nearly fainted when Haven told me," Ryder admitted once Zoras' dropped away.

"If Soja's mother was still with me, she would tell you that I jumped and twirled around like a court dancer and went running through the streets of Cross telling everyone the good news. I actually ran and told your great grandfather Lord Sin Silvanus. I just so happened to tell everyone that would listen along the way," Zoras chuckled as he set his fist on his left hip and leaned on the table. "The Silvanus bloodline lives on."

Ryder stood with arms crossed, his expression a bit more solemn and serious. "Put on your Lord's Regent hat for a moment and get serious. The idea that I will be a father scares me. It scares me even more that this child will be born in the midst of a war that I may not survive." Ryder paced back and turned away from Zoras, running his fingers through his tousled black hair. He put both hands on his hips. "Recent events has forced me to consider things that I do not want to consider. Do not get excited for I must speak to Onyx first as the rightful heir to the throne."

Zoras' heart leapt with even more joy than being told that Haven and Ryder were to be parents. Was Ryder considering taking the throne of the Shadowborn after all? Either way, this child was a blessing from the Spirits and he was glad for it.

*****

LINE OF SIGHT

"We have been sitting here, staring at the godforsaken hovel for eight days! When are we going to destroy it?" Rache roared with pent up frustration. He stood by the tent opening, leaning back against the support pole with arms crossed.

Kaiser stood with his arms held out straight. His eyes were closed and a smile was perched on his face. All around him were his three courtesans dressed in plain knee length dresses and slippers. He himself only was only wearing black wool pants and a pair of leather boots. Cora, Raye, and Zee were sponging his bare upper body clean of any sweat and filth. Each took a turn to caress the curves of his lean muscles.

"Patience, my friend. All is going according to plan," Kaiser mused as Cora massaged his skull with gentle swirling motions.

"Well what plan because attack Dusk seems to have been forgotten," Rache grumbled. He mashed his teeth together.

Kaiser chuckled softly once Cora had finished combing his hair back. Raye and Zee helped him to pull on a white linen tunic. He batted them away to let Cora in close. She set a silver pendent around his neck and bent in to kiss him. "Not now, my dear. I must focus upon the coming battle."

Cora snickered. "Then may your enemies quake when they hear your voice and weep when you raise your sword," she teased as she held the folds of his shirt collar. She giggled as he playfully nipped at her nose.

"You are such a tease," Kaiser said as he shook his head

slowly.

"And why did they have to come? You are more than capable of dressing yourself," Rache sneered. He glared at Cora who nodded back.

Kaiser ignored him as he closed his eyes again. Cora pick up the padded leather shirt and with Zee's help, put it on over the tunic. Raye came forward with a shirt of fine chain mail. She too tried to seduce Kaiser but he ignored her advances. He flicked his left hand for her to hurry. Over his head went the chain mail. Kaiser smiled as he reached in to smooth the tiny metal links with a brush of his hands. He gestured for the girls to begin piecing on a set of gleaming silver steel armor.

"No, little child. Leave the cloak for last," Kaiser said when Zee picked up a supple fur lined black cloak.

"Oh, I see you brought the good armor," Rache said with a roll of his eyes.

"I am meeting with the envoys of Dusk and I must look my very best," Kaiser stated with a dark smirk.

"Why? You are going to destroy the place regardless," Rache sneered. He harrumphed and looked away when Kaiser did not answer. He then glanced over to see Kaiser with his broad smile and eyes closed.

"Death is such a glorious thing is it not?"

Rache dug his fingers into the meat of his arms. "It would be if I could kill someone instead of sitting on my ass doing nothing."

Kaiser let out a deep breath once the cuirass had been latched on and secured over his torso. "The people of Dusk must think that I want to treat with them. Why rush such death and destruction anyway? I intend to put on a show. One so bloody and dark that will show my enemies what will happen if they act against me. This is not just for the Shadowborn. This is for everyone beyond the Mirror."

"But your enemies include your grandson. A powerful warrior in his own right. One that you helped shape into what he is today," the Demon said matter of fact. "He will not go quietly into the night anytime soon."

Kaiser sneered, curling his lip. He forcefully stepped away from the courtesans once his cloak was secured around his shoulders. He got right into Rache's face. "Do you think me incapable of undoing what I created?"

The Demon stumbled for words, suddenly worried. Kaiser leaned to whisper into his ear. Rache blanched when Kaiser threatened to invoke the bond. He wondered if Kaiser could see straight into his mind, analyzing every thought. He had certainly had some dangerous ones as of late.

Loran pulled back the door flap and startled. His sword banged against his armored hip, the sheath swinging from his belt. "The envoys from Dusk have arrived."

"Good," Kaiser said flatly as he tore away from Rache and stepped out of the tent.

Rache looked back at the three courtesans, catching eyes with Cora again. She nodded and starting ordering the others about. Satisfied, Rache turned around to follow Kaiser.

The dead sunlight provided little warmth and there were still patches of snow on the ground. Rache did not like snow but had learned to get used to it. The chill of a lingering winter reminded him of deep and dark memories. He shuddered from the thought. His own battle gear consisted of a set of light armor that could be torn off at a moment's notice. He had not utilized his monstrous form since he had fought Ryder in Cross months ago. Part of him even wondered if the beast had buried itself within his being and never to return.

In fact, ever since he had acted as Ryder's prison guard, Rache had felt changes stirring within his mind. He had once viewed the world as merely a plaything and something to destroy at his whim. Now, he was seeing substance and value in it. Rache looked at Kaiser who was walking confidently ahead of him. His master had been born a Shadowborn, one with Farlander blood flowing in his veins. He wanted to believe that there was Demon blood in there too but if that was the case, wouldn't Kaiser's grandson also have Demon blood? Rache did not know much about the origins of the Farlanders but perhaps there was some darkness deep within the ancient race. Someone had certainly been eager to eliminate them into nothing but a few individuals. The more he thought about it, the more it opened his mind to the world around him.

The camp of tents along with a restless army was usually quiet. All assembled to witness the parley between the envoys of Dusk and their beloved Commander. When one foot soldier dared to clap, Kaiser halted immediately and stared down the offender until he fainted from fright. Kaiser scoffed and continued on like the pause was a mere inconvenience. Loran led the way from the center of the camp towards the edge, following the great East Road. One hundred feet from the first farm house was the envoy of Dusk, surrounded by three masked guards.

"Ah, I see that you have brought a welcoming committee with you," Kaiser greeted pleasantly. He directed Loran to stand on his right side while Rache came to stand on his left side.

"As did you. I question why an army of Shadowborn sits

upon my city's doorstep," the envoy growled. He was a stout man dressed in steel plate armor, holding his wolf's head helm under his left arm. His short cropped black hair had heavy streaks of gray.

Kaiser thought for a moment. "I am a very important man that needs protection. You can never be too careful."

"Perhaps," the envoy replied. He looked about with suspicion. "So shall we get to business or would you prefer to bulldoze Dusk to the ground first?"

"Hold on a moment. What makes you think that I would do such a thing? Ever have I labored in Cross and spent time in Umbra, never in Dusk. Dusk is the city that guards the East Road and the way to the border of our land. Why would I want to destroy it?" Kaiser asked innocently.

The envoy pointed towards Loran and Rache. "I am no fool. At your sides are the Mirror Sea Pirate and a Demon."

Kaiser looked back and forth between Loran and Rache. He shrugged. "I see an opportunity for unity, cooperation, and forgiveness between one time enemies. My father always taught me that there is good in everyone."

The leanest and shortest of the three tall guards stirred. Standing on the envoy's left side, he moved his hand towards his sword hilt. The tallest guard who stood in the center shook his head. The envoy looked back, gesturing with his hand to wait.

"It seems that one of your party disagrees with me. He seems young so I will forgive him," Kaiser commented. He rested his left hand on the pommel of his sheathed sword. "Weren't we all a little quick to judge in our youth?"

"You speak kindly, pretending to be a friend, when all I hear are curses and lies," the envoy snarled. "So what does the world's most terrible soul want from me?"

"Hey, have I insulted you yet? Why have you insulted me and continue to treat me so poorly? I have come here to talk like civilized men," Kaiser leaned back in feigned shock. He made to act as if he was complaining to Loran before smirking with a dark gleam in his eyes. He pointed towards Dusk. "I am going east with a few friends and your city is in my line of sight. It is too much trouble for me to go around it or through it. I mean the logistics of moving so many people and supplies is just taxing and I am not a young man anymore. I am hoping that you can help me."

Rache had to admire how Kaiser was dancing around the fact that he was going to raze Dusk to the ground regardless of what the envoy said. This meeting was just a show. He seen grew bored with the conversation and turned his attention to the three guards. The guard on the left of the envoy was certainly young based by his constant twitching and readiness to launch. The guard on the right stood like a statue, arms held tightly at his side. The one in the middle drew his interest the most. He tilted his head slightly as he attempted to discern the faces behind the black cloth masks. The guards' attire resembled that of the Sabers but more heavily armored. All wore their battle gear as well. They were bound to give good sport.

"Well it seems we are getting nowhere and I am already behind schedule. I had hoped to reach the border by night but it seems I will not get there in time. I have no choice but to as you say, bulldoze Dusk to the ground," Kaiser said with a shrug.

"Not without a fight, Kaiser," the middle guard said.

All three guards pulled back their hoods and masks revealing Zoras, Ryder, and Onyx with fierce expressions on their faces. Onyx ripped his sword free from its sheath and snarled. Zoras held up his right hand, ready to give a signal. Ryder stared directly at Kaiser with nothing but rage in his eyes.

Kaiser returned Ryder's stare before putting on his helm. "So be it. We shall fight."

He turned away and headed back towards the camp with Rache and Loran in tow. His fists were clenched tightly and his jaw tight.

"What are your orders?" Loran asked, leaning in to make sure no one else over heard.

"Ready the troops for attack," Kaiser said through gritted teeth. He suddenly stopped and turned around. He jabbed a finger at Loran's chest. "But leave Ryder Coba to me. If anyone of you so much as think to attain glory and fight him yourself, I will tear your very soul apart until there is nothing left for even history to remember." Kaiser slowly turned his dangerous eyes on Rache who shuddered under his terrible gaze. "I will only give this warning one time or it will be the end for you."

*****

BATTLE OF DUSK

Onyx had long ago stopped worrying about whether or not he was doing exactly as Ryder had told him. At first, he had entered the battle with a fool proof plan in mind, detailed from beginning to end. But as soon as he engaged his first enemy soldier in combat, that plan went out the window. He realized very quickly that he had to be flexible to his environment and the circumstances. He had to be aware of everything and focused. Finally, all of Ryder's lessons about keeping his mind centered and open made sense. It just took a deep cut to his left arm to make him truly learn the lesson.

He had joined Hayden in covering the southern boundaries on Dusk though he had not been given a command. When he had complained to Ryder, Ryder swiftly told him that he has to prove himself first a capable battle leader. His cousin's words reverberated in his head. A desperate fight against his Demon possessed father, though admirable, was not enough to prove himself capable of real leadership. Ryder had ended their conversation with a very serious question: was he truly prepared to die for his people and their cause. The manner in which Ryder had said those words made Onyx believe that his cousin had given the question a lot of thought. Ryder was prepared to die. He wasn't. Not yet at least, he told himself. Onyx wanted to believe it body and soul before he would admit to it.

It scared him at first that Hayden bolted off, leaving him alone in the streets to fight. In his mind, he had done well enough

287

on his own with four of Kaiser's soldiers collapsed and bleeding from his deft sword cuts. He had even managed to swallow the vomit that threatened to shoot out after he cut through the first soldier. The nausea of his first kill lingered on the edge of his senses but it grew weaker and weaker with each sword stroke. Onyx did not like that he was killing Shadowborn. Kaiser's soldiers were his own people and yet they weren't, possessed of a primal ferocity to survive and please their powerful master.

The streets in southern Dusk twisted around and crossed each other at irregular intervals, giving Onyx a sense of confusion. Dusk was nothing like Cross with its grid like street patterns. All around him, the battle raged with shouts of rage and pain mixed in with the clash of steel weapons. He wished that he knew where Hayden had gone. He wasn't given a chance to consider that thought further as two steel clad soldiers rushed at him with their swords raised.

With a seamless transition, Onyx's thoughts transformed into a sense of determination and focus. He blocked the first solder's attack, the strike jolting his right arm. Thankfully, his grip on his sword held as he shoved his weight forward, knocking the soldier off balance. The second soldier, a flap of leather hanging from his left side, leapt over his stumbling comrade. He spun at full force and high speed. Onyx managed to dodge the attack, sliding to the side. He struck hard at the soldier's left side, cutting through the last of the damaged cuirass and slicing through flesh. The second soldier squeaked in pain and stumbled back. Onyx thought he had bought himself a momentary reprieve but the first soldier rejoined the battle.

Onyx exchanged heavy handed blows, keeping the second soldier in sight. He did not think that he had cut him deep enough to keep him from fighting. His thought proved true as the second soldier joined his comrade. Together, the two soldiers backed Onyx up against the wall of a ramshackle house. But Onyx was far from trapped. He leaned towards the left as the first soldier stabbed his sword. The weapon stuck deep into the semisoft wood. Onyx ducked under the second soldier's attack and kicked hard at his torso. The second soldier went flying back and slammed hard onto the stone street. He quickly drew his long knife and stabbed it up at an angle into the first soldier's right side. He ripped it back out as the man crumbled, gasping for breath. A swipe across his pant leg cleaned the blade and he resheathed it. Onyx then pulled the stuck sword free and stepped forward.

The second soldier got up to his feet, coughing and spitting out a mouthful of blood as Onyx came forward, spinning both swords in wide circles. The soldier gritted his teeth and prepared himself to meet Onyx's attack.

"You would dare attack your Prince?" Onyx challenged boldly. He stopped, standing ten feet away from the soldier.

"There is no Prince. No Shadowlord but Lord Kaiser," the soldier sneered.

Onyx had hoped that his words would have elicited a different response, one of surprise and regret. But Kaiser's soldiers proved too deep in their dark master's control to remember who were the rightful rulers of their shared homeland. Offering salvation would surely give him the same result. A spit and sneer. Onyx then renewed his attack. He aimed his assault at the soldier's sword arm, slashing the muscle deep enough for the soldier to drop his weapon. With his right hand sword, Onyx cut across the soldier's left side again, digging deeper. The soldier crumbled to his knees. But Onyx halted. His morals raged forward. He did not want to kill this man. He was the Prince and this man was a Shadowborn, one of his own. The feelings he had experienced during the fight against Iztal came back and made his decision for him. Onyx slashed open the soldier's throat and he collapsed face first on the ground.

"In death, I set you free from him," Onyx mumbled. He looked up in time to see more soldiers pouring into the street where he was standing. He let out a deep breath and readied himself.

*****

Hayden wiped his face with a quick motion, flinging the blood and gore away. He spat on the ground. His sharp eyes darted around the small courtyard, each side surrounded by a three story stone building. The second and third floors were open to the courtyard but the railings had fallen to the ground below. An archer leaped out of the darkness, jumping over the pile of rubble. He quickly fired a series of arrows. Hayden smirked and swung his sword, twisting his body to meet each shot. He expertly deflected each arrow until he had caught one and threw it back with great force. It struck the archer in the chest and he collapsed backwards on to the stone with a heavy thump.

To his left and right, two more archers appeared, protected from their place upon the third floors. Before they could even load their bows, Hayden had swiftly launched two throwing knives to cut their bow strings. One archer took a knife to his exposed right shoulder while the other over corrected and fell over the railing. He was dead before he hit the ground, a throwing knife buried in his lightly armored chest. Hayden then burst up from the ground, leaping up to the archer he had wounded and quickly dispatched him with a single sword strike to the throat.

A battalion of steel clad soldiers streamed into the courtyard, looking around for a target. Hayden swiftly and quietly restrung the bow before throwing the dead archer's quiver over his shoulder. He took one deep but quiet breath, letting it out slowly. In the blink of an eye, he jumped up to his feet and began firing, sending deadly arrow after deadly arrow into the crowd of twenty. He dropped ten of the soldiers before he ran out. He sneered before quickly throwing the useless bow away and jumping back down to the ground.

"For Truth!" Hayden bellowed as he spun and twisted around, slashing with deadly precision in the crowd of survivors.

Despite facing a stronger and faster opponent with greater odds, the ten surviving soldiers fought back with equal ferocity. The idea that facing Kaiser's wrath was more terrible than death in combat flashed in Hayden's mind as he sliced off one soldier's sword arm at the elbow. Despite the injury, the soldier still kept coming for him. Hayden snarled and swung his sword, decapitating the wounded man. A stream of blood splattered across his face as he turned to cut down the next one in line.

Many minutes later, Hayden dispatched the last of the ten, a fresh cut across the left side of his face actively bleeding. His chest heaved from the exertion. Out of sight, Hayden could hear more soldiers stomping towards him. Not wanting to be cornered, Hayden bolted from the small courtyard. He leapt light footed up and over obstacles, taking out the occasional enemy that had come too close. Up ahead, he saw some of the rebel soldiers being cornered by Kaiser's forces. He charged forward at high speed, spinning his sword. At the last second, he slid down, passing by the back of three soldiers that had come closest to his allies and sliced open the back of their legs. He stomped his left foot and spun himself around into a standing position. Seeing the brave Saber, the rebels rallied and charged forward.

Hayden smiled with pride for a brief moment until suddenly twisting around, swinging his sword. It collided heavily against another.

"I am not like the fodder that Lord Kaiser sends to battle, mighty Saber. Are you prepared to fight me now?" Loran teased with a devilish smirk.

"Gladly!" Hayden shouted.

The Saber shoved his weight forward to knock Loran off balance, much as he had done against Loran's cousin Morin on several occasions. Loran was not so easily fooled and planted his feet, pushing back with equal force. They shoved against each other in hopes of breaking the hold of their swords. Hayden snarled and immediately slipped his sword down towards the cross guard of Loran's weapon. Loran managed to pull away but not in time to avoid a deep cut to his thumb. Loran quickly tossed his sword to his right hand, flicking his left hand and swearing. Hayden kicked him hard in the chest, knocking him to the ground.

"Is this all the Mirror Sea Pirate has? You are weaker than I thought," Hayden declared.

Loran kick flipped back up to his feet and charged forward, his right hand holding tight to his sword. Their blades met in a clash of sparks and steel screeches. They focused on nothing else but each other. All around them, the battle raged as flames leapt into the night sky. Battle cries and screams for salvation melded into a singular song. But Hayden heard none of it. All that mattered was ridding the world of Loran Win and ultimately Kaiser Adonis.

*****

What Onyx and Hayden could not tell, though Onyx suspected, the battle for control of Dusk was going badly for the rebels. The western boundaries of the city where the two armies first met lay in smoldering ruins, the streets strewn with bodies. They just did not have the numbers. The rebels would tire faster before Kaiser's forces gave up. They had the fear of Kaiser's terrible wrath that drove them to extremes.

Onyx managed to escape and hide from yet another battalion. He slipped into a crumbling house just in time as a group of twenty soldiers rounded the corner. He pressed his back against the brick and mortar, biting his tongue when a ceiling beam fell and struck him on his right shoulder. Reflexively, he reached up to rub the spot, feeling the bruise already forming. As he sat rubbing the muscle, Onyx could not help but feel utterly alone. Sure, he had managed to survive relatively whole. With that thought, Onyx assessed his physical condition. The knuckles of his left hand stung mercilessly. He seethed as he tried to flex the individual joints. He doubted that he would be able to see a healer before battle's end. Hell, Onyx still was not certain that he himself would see the end.

"Hey, let's check over there! Loran said he will reward anyone who brings them the royal brat!" a crass voice declared. It was soon followed by a round of laughter.

"Like Aku's boy is worth anything these days," another voice snickered. More laughter followed.

291

Onyx sneered. All sense of pain was shoved aside as he leapt from his hiding place. He bounced off the broken wall and slid into the street before the soldiers. There were five dressed in heavy steel armor, better protected than the previous soldiers he had come across.

"See for yourself what my worth is. I am still the blood of Shadow Night but no prize to be won," Onyx growled. He spun his sword into an upward attack position.

A man stepped forward, pointing his broad sword at Onyx. His steel chest piece bore three deep scratches. "Lord Kaiser has deemed you expendable. I would say that makes you nothing."

"I may be nothing to you but I am everything to those I fight for," Onyx boldly declared. "And I will continue to fight for them so long as I draw breath!"

The five soldiers laughed heartedly. "Well tell them goodbye for you do not have long," chuckled the man with the scratched armor.

Onyx gritted his teeth and grabbed his sword with both hands. He turned slightly to the right and planted his feet. He shuddered when he felt a hand on his shoulder and turned his head to see Ryder, covered in gore, but looking at him proudly.

"Then neither do I for I shall fight at my cousin's side. Just pray you do not forget your master's orders," Ryder taunted. He brandished his sword that was slick with crimson blood dripping from the tip. He turned and looked at Onyx. "Together?"

"Together," Onyx nodded.

*****

Kaiser stepped over the tangle of bodies that had mounted up before him. He sheathed his clean sword at his hip and threw back the folds of his cloak. The motion exposed his glittering silver steel armor, pristine without a speck of dirt or blood. He descended down the pile of bodies and landed lightly on the stone ground. Glancing over his shoulder, he scoffed and smiled.

Walking towards him was Rache, a contrast with his appearance. There was not a single inch of his body that was not stained with gore. His flame red hair was a matted mess. He reached up and wiped away a smear of blood from his fanged mouth. His blackened eyes swiftly changed back into his normal pale gray color.

"I do not even know why they are trying to put up a fight but they do give good sport," the Demon commented.

Kaiser immediately slapped him hard across the face and

knocked him to the ground. He drew his hand back as if to threaten another hit. Rache cringed in response.

"I told you to keep Ryder in your sight and you are wasting your time with the fodder!" Kaiser shouted. He ripped Rache up from the ground by his chain mail collar. He snarled in Rache's face. "Where is he?"

Rache stammered for an answer and was only saved by the roar of a battle charge. Kaiser rolled his eyes and threw the Demon to the ground. At the other end of the square moving at a full run were fifty rebel soldiers. Each wore steel plate armor and brandished an assortment of weapons. Rache watched as Kaiser took a few steps before pulling out his sword. He paused to examine the weapon. With a sudden burst of energy, Kaiser leapt high into the air. He came down hard, stabbing his sword through the stone and landing with one knee on the ground.

Like a massive rolling wave on the ocean, the stone surged forward in a great rush. It rose up to a height of twenty feet, clearing the rooftops. The stone wave slammed into the rebel soldiers, tossing them around like dolls. Those that managed to shriek did so in great fear before slamming back to the ground below, shattering every bone in their body. The wave of destruction sped off towards the east.

Kaiser turned his back to it, acting as if to rub his hands free of dust. He came back to Rache's side, not looking at him. "I could have laid waste to this city the instant I set my eyes on it," he said before looking down into Rache's eyes. "But where's the fun in that?" Kaiser snickered as he looked away. "The world should consider itself lucky that I rather enjoy toying with it."

Rache gulped, wondering if he should get up. For a while, it seemed like Kaiser was ignoring him so he stood up. He did not attempt to brush any filth away. He stood like a whipped dog, his shoulders bent and his eyes averted in submission. He jolted when Kaiser patted his cheek.

"There, there, my Demon. Do not be troubled. I do not intend to drag out this war forever. There will be light at the end of the tunnel as a golden age awaits us. But first," Kaiser said, his voice going from kind and warm to dark and terrible. He gripped Rache's chin tightly. "Bring me my grandson."

ZORAS' LAST ACT

"How much longer do you intend to fight this battle because at this rate, there will not be any souls left," Jarod commented as he bent down over the bloody body of a dead rebel. He scoffed and smiled. "At least you did not go down easy, my friend."

Zoras stood a few feet away, arms crossed with a tight expression on his face. Every so often, his eyes would dart around the wreckage of what used to be a stately manor and its out buildings. Five rebel soldiers moved with heavy dejection as they sorted through the bodies of their comrades. Though he watched the scene, feeling sad at the loss of life, Zoras could not bring himself to admit defeat. Not just yet. His fingers dug into the meat of his arms, tightening down on the muscle through the armor. No, he was not going to admit defeat and retreat. He was going to make a stand.

"So long as I breathe, I will fight. I will not let Kaiser and his black army win," Zoras snarled. His head jerked up to meet Jarod's doubting gaze. "I will not abandon Dusk to obliteration."

"At this point, there is not much left to Dusk save the ruins and the dead. I spent enough years as a border soldier, learning when to back away and move forward from a place of strength," Jarod said as he stood up. "We of the faithful cannot do this without the Northern Alliance."

Zoras snarled. "Border soldiers know how to hunt beasts and are as flighty as birds when it comes to real danger. I have commanded child Sabers braver than you."

Jarod was immediately put off by Zoras' attitude and seemingly foolish outlook on the battle. He had heard of the ex Saber Commander's fanatical zeal and one track dedication for his beliefs. He clenched his fists, wanting to knock some sense into Zoras. The plates of his steel armors scraped against each other as he took a step forward. He tossed his head, flinging sweat from his brow. His midnight hair clung tight to his forehead. He snarled as he locked eyes with Zoras.

"Zoras, there are more important enemies than those you consider allies," Hayden admonished as he climbed over a large pile of broken stones. He jumped down to the ground and rolled his neck with an audible crack. "We could spend day after day killing our kinsmen when their spaces would be filled with Kaiser's fiendish black Spirits. The Spirit World is endless. If you truly want to win against Kaiser, we will need the full might of the Northern Alliance and hope that the Daylord will come."

"Is this what I am hearing? That you have given up hope? That you balk in his presence?" Zoras demanded. He turned around to see everyone's eyes on him. Even the body collecting soldiers had paused in their work.

But Zoras' declaration was not the reason for everyone's pause. Onyx had appeared from the same path that Hayden had arrived from, battered and bloody but otherwise sound. There was an audible sigh of relief from the small crowd. Their young Prince was still alive. Not far behind him was Ryder, wiping the blood streaming down the left side of his face from a cut over his eye. It smeared across his forehead. Onyx welcomed his cousin at his side, patting his right shoulder and smiling.

"You fought well," Ryder whispered to Onyx.

"As did you. Our ancestor would have been proud," Onyx replied. "Do you still think this path is the best one? Will Shadow Night think that we are abandoning our home?"

Ryder let out a deep breath. "Not every path is straight and easy to follow. Do you remember what we talked about?" Onyx nodded as they continued walking towards Zoras, Jarod, and Hayden.

Other rebel soldiers streamed in, all bearing an assortment of injuries. It appeared that their forces had been whittled down to a couple of hundred. The rebels had never been that numerous to begin with, starting the battle with five hundred souls. If anyone asked Zoras about numbers, he would swear that each of the five hundred that marched with him were among the best and bravest. To have joined the rebellion against Kaiser meant to many that they would not let fear and doubt about the future rule them. That they would stand for those too afraid to. But the two hundred, including Ryder, Onyx, Zoras, Hayden, and Jarod, still had a long battle ahead of them

"I am glad to see you alive. I would have thought that Kaiser would have made sure to kill the two of you first," Zoras admitted with great relief.

"Killing a son of Shadow Night would have a negative effect on those driven by fear and not loyalty. Though we all know that Kaiser is behind many of the deaths of the Silvanus bloodline, he has yet to admit it openly to the Shadowborn people. All he has said is that the bloodline is failing. Of course, do remember that the Shadowborn agreed to the execution of Akakios," Hayden explained. He gave Ryder a side-eyed glance.

Everyone expected Ryder to have some sort of reaction to Hayden's comment. None was forth coming. In fact, no one dared to say anything further on the topic.

"As sons of the crown, we look to you to decide what we do next. We cannot hope to continue this battle at our numbers," Jarod said, breaking the silence. He had been at Ryder's side when Akakios had been executed.

"So you have finally realized that all of your efforts to save precious Dusk proved useless," Rache mocked.

Everyone looked up and spotted the flame haired Demon perched on the top of a crumbling wall. He held a pole with a white flag waving in the breeze. He balanced it against his left shoulder, keeping a tight grip with claws tapping on the pole. His tattered clothes were stained with blood. A fresh cut on his right cheek bled slowly and dripped down his chin.

"I did not even think that Kaiser carried a flag of truce with him. It looks like a torn bed sheet or pillow case," Ryder stated, unafraid at the Demon's presence.

"Then a soldier will be cold when he sleeps tonight," Rache replied. He licked at the blood by his mouth.

Zoras stepped in close to Ryder's right side. He leaned in even closer to whisper. "I would trust nothing he says. Kaiser does not intend to be fair in this truce."

"And how would you know?" Ryder quietly asked. He locked eyes with Rache and smiled. "I trust this Demon more than I trust my grandfather."

"You can't be serious!" Zoras hissed. He jerked his head back.

Ryder chuckled. "Let's see what he has to say first before we judge him."

"Indeed you must hear what I have to say. My master in his graciousness has decided on a truce. Let those in command come and speak with him," Rache gloated. He then laughed out loud.

"We will parley with Kaiser only when he pulls back his armies from Dusk and lets those still living to leave in peace," Zoras immediately declared.

Rache lifted the flag pole and turned it to point at Ryder's chest. He snickered for a moment, exposing his white fangs. "Lord Kaiser will do so if he comes with me... alone."

Immediately, Zoras, Onyx, Hayden, and Jarod leapt in front of Ryder, drawing their swords and snarling. The remaining rebel soldiers also assembled in preparation for attack. Ryder remained stoic, his sword safely at his side. He let out a deep breath and laid a head on Onyx's left shoulder. Onyx turned to look at Ryder with a mixed look of determination and confusion.

"You can't go with him. Kaiser is sure to kill you. We need you. Haven needs you," Onyx pleaded before lowering his voice. "Your child needs you."

"If there is one thing I am sure of, Kaiser does not want to kill me. I am his sole descendent and heir." Ryder then paused and chuckled softly. "Well not anymore." He cleared his throat. "I need you to go with Jarod and Hayden and take the soldiers away from Dusk."

Zoras quickly turned to face Ryder. "If you intend to send me away like the rest, I will not go. I refuse to go!" He slammed his sword back into its sheath.

There was a great deal of protest at the turn of events. The very idea that Ryder was considering Rache's proposal inflamed every soul within sight. Those standing closest to Ryder were even more upset. Onyx refused to budge and he was gripping his sword hilt so hard that his knuckles had turned ghost white. Zoras continued his verbal tirade, joined in by Jarod. Hayden only looked on in silence, his eyes holding an expression of sad acceptance. It was clear that he was the only one, albeit reluctantly, agreed with Ryder.

"You do realize that I said alone. As in just him," Rache pointed out. He spat down to his left and readjusted the flag pole to rest against his right shoulder.

"Alone or not, I will not leave a son of the throne unprotected and at the mercy of a man who can never be trusted," Zoras snapped. "He would just as soon murder him with our backs turned."

Rache scoffed and shrugged his shoulders. "Then you go at your own peril. Let us parley as proper enemies in war. I shall wait for you to say your last words to your beloved followers."

"There is nothing left to say for they know my love and loyalty without me telling them so. I fight for them and all Shadowborn with the fullness of my being and I will continue to do so long as I live and beyond," Ryder stated with great conviction. As soon as the words left his mouth, he took a step towards Rache. Zoras quickly followed after him.

*****

"Are you so sure that Kaiser will not up and decide to kill you?" Zoras asked doubtfully. He laid a hand on Ryder's right shoulder as they walked.

"He had his chance when I was a newborn and he had me in his arms. Why wait until I was a fully grown adult that was taller and heavier than him?" Ryder asked as he brushed Zoras's hand away. He did not offer any further explanation.

Rache, who was walking several feet ahead of the pair, chuckled loudly. "What glory is there in squeezing the life from a squalling babe especially one of your own bloodline?"

"Considering your murdering prowess, I am surprised that you do not speak with more delight," Zoras said flatly.

"Oh believe me. I wanted to kill this screaming infant that became your precious Ryder," Rache started to say. He then paused as if considering how to phrase what he was about to say.

It was Ryder's turn to smirk. "The bond between him and Kaiser prevents him from killing anyone whose blood flows in their veins. He might as well be bonded to me."

That was a curious possibility, Zoras thought. He was not fully aware of the intricate threads of Rache's and Kaiser's bond but an idea occurred to him. He wondered if Ryder had already thought about it himself.

The Demon turned a corner with Ryder and Zoras at his heels. They were back before the western gates of the city, this time on the inside. Kaiser stood alone with the heavy gate doors shut tightly behind him. He rested his left hand on the pommel of his belted sword. His cloak swept down to his ankles and laid open, revealing his pristine silver steel armor. How he had managed to stay clean through hours of battle was a mystery. He reached up with his right hand to sweep his tousled midnight hair back. Though he was not physically imposing with his lean frame, he stood with a great sense of gravitas that came with his eleven hundred years of life. With silver eyes that could stare straight into a person's soul, Kaiser was quiet power incarnate, ready to explode at any given moment.

"Is this how our battle shall end?" Kaiser mused.

Ryder and Zoras halted and stood with fists clenched while Rache sauntered to his master's side. Kaiser snorted and the

Demon immediately backed away. He kept a careful distance with the gates at his back.

"This battle will only end with your death," Zoras snarled as he reached for his sword. He ripped it free from its sheath.

Kaiser held up a staying hand. "Please. I have asked to speak with you under the flag of truce. I haven't drawn my sword so why should you?"

"Pull back your forces and let us end this battle once and for all," Ryder said firmly.

Kaiser waved his finger back and forth. "Have you learned nothing from this war? It will take more than asking nicely for me to back down." He pulled out his sword in the blink of an eye and swept it before him. "Peredur, the fate of Dusk is in your hands. When it falls, the blame will solely be on you. Defeat me and maybe you can save what is left of the Shadowborn."

It was then odd when Kaiser started to laugh, low and soft at first before bursting into a loud booming sound. It was maniacal in its tone. It took him a long time to calm and regain his battle composure. He reached up and wiped a tear from the corner of his right eye. "Oh, I needed that."

"And just what was so funny?" Zoras demanded.

Kaiser took a deep breath and exhaled slowly. For a moment, the mirth of his laughter remained. Just as suddenly as it had appeared, it disappeared. A dangerous expression manifested on his face. His silver eyes glinted like the light coming off his steel sword. He was a weapon ready to be unleashed. He pointed his weapon towards Zoras. "Why are you here?"

"Like you, I understand the meaning of treachery but unlike you, I understand the meaning of loyalty. That oath I took when I first became a Saber did not end when I retired. I will fight for the Silvanus bloodline that I swore to protect all those years ago," Zoras declared with a great deal of confidence.

"Kill him," Kaiser ordered.

Rache immediately jumped to attention, claws extended. He snarled ferociously, saliva dripping from his lips. He leapt towards Zoras.

"To the blood loyal, no hand will slay. All will obey," Ryder chanted.

Kaiser's eyes opened up wide upon seeing Rache collapse to the ground at Ryder's chant. He watched as Rache writhed on the ground in the tangle of the ancient power but unlike his invocations, the Demon was not in agonizing pain. And he did not like what he saw. His eyes narrowed as he locked eyes with Ryder.

The movement was so fast that Ryder barely had time to react. Kaiser bore down on him with lightning speed that far exceeded his age. Even for an Immortal, his attack came faster than the beat of a heart. Red spilled into Ryder's vision and he found himself falling backwards under a heavy weight. He hit the ground, his skull slamming against the solid surface. His head swam. He wished that he could see what had happened and what weight was crushing him. Did Kaiser cut open his chest? Were his ribs tearing into his lungs and were they filling with blood so that he couldn't breathe? But he could breathe. In fact, the only thing that was hurting him was his back and head. He then saw what was on top of him.

Zoras' gargled breath was horrific as a fountain of blood squirted out of his ripped open chest and dribbled out of his mouth. He tried to gasp but choked each time. His sword laid on the ground four feet away in two pieces. Kaiser had sliced him from across his throat and down his chest towards his left side, nearly cleaving him in two.

"So dies the last of the Rokar bloodline! Another family gone because you refused destiny and ran away like the stupid fool you are! Not only did you run from your Silvanus blood, you ran from mine! A true son of Begin Anu would have welcomed the chance to rule but instead you cowered before it!" Kaiser roared in anger. He kicked at Rache and cursed at him in the darkest of tones. The Demon screamed in agony.

Ryder wanted to scream as a powerful surge of Spirit Energy rushed through him. Every fiber of his being burned like a hot fire. The world around him exploded with white light, smothering Kaiser's violent roar. The light blinded him and he slammed his eyes shut, keeping his arms wrapped tight around Zoras. He started to scream just before being thrown out of the white light.

*****

The city of Dusk had been replaced with a dark expanse of pine forest. Beams of moonlight struck the ground all around him. A pair of wood owls hooted in the distance. Ryder had no idea where he was. As soon as Zoras coughed with a heavy wet noise, Ryder forgot everything else.

"I'm..." Zoras gurgled. His chest heaved and blood squirted and squelched underneath Ryder's hold. "...coming,,, Soja."

With that last declaration, Zoras died in Ryder's arms. Ryder wept as he held the man, a wispy beam of moonlight falling down upon him.

THE RIVER TOWN OF SAWN

At first, the influx of complex emotions were easy to ignore. Bane had enough trouble dealing with his own inner turmoil even before he first stepped foot in the Northlands. The burdens that stemmed from his past was his alone to bear. But for the last few weeks, everything inside was a torrential storm that whispered of something he hadn't felt for a thousand years. It was if a long dormant power had been awakened in the world. One that hinted at a deep and unbreakable promise that had been made in blood. He unclenched his right hand, seeing the faint white scar that stretched across his palm.

"He's doing it again," Gyr whispered to Charon.

Charon sat with his back against an old oak tree, the dry leaves crunching under his boots as he tapped his feet. He glanced over at Bane who stood ten feet away by the edge of a trickling forest stream. Charon shook as Gyr snorted out a hot puff of air through his nostrils. He knew that it meant the Gryphon was thinking. Gyr did it again and Charon put up his hand to push the Gryphon away. He jerked his hand back when Gyr nipped aggressively at his thumb, clearly annoyed.

"He keeps looking at his hand. Big deal," Charon grumbled as he returned to cleaning and tending to his sword. He picked up the whetstone and gently moved it up and down the edge of the blade.

Gyr let out a low growled and pressed a talon to the back of Charon's hand. "I can forgive you only so many times for forgetting the history I have taught you. If you paid any attention, the Daylord's right hand holds the scar for the Immortal Truth's blood promise."

"Okay, okay. Can you take your claw out of my hand?" Charon implored. Gyr furrowed his brow before pulling back his taloned paw. Charon immediately shook his left hand and rubbed the back of it.

"If I am correct, the blood promise is waking up. A great binding power has been lifted and I believe my king is hearing the call of the Shadowlord," Gyr exclaimed with delight.

"Wait. You said Shadow Night was dead. Even he was surprised to hear that," Charon pointed out as he put his whetstone away and resheathed his sword.

Gyr squared his shoulders as he sat up straight. "Shadow Night is dead. His bloodline is not."

The Gryphon had been immensely excited by Bane's statement in Meras. The hope that his exalted hero and king would return to the Northlands had given him a renewed sense of strength and determination. He jumped at Bane's every word with an intense eagerness. He went out of his way to please him. At least that is how Charon saw it. It was like Gyr had become a stupid puppy too excited to see that Bane had withdrawn more into himself.

Charon watched as Bane rubbed the scar on his palm, studying it intently. "For all you know, he could be suffering from arthritis. I mean he is a thousand years old."

"What is arthritis?" Gyr inquired with a tilt of his head.

Bane's sullen mood was momentarily forgotten as Charon became the teacher to Gyr. It was a role he alternated with the Gryphon ever since they met in the snowy mountains northeast of Garhune. As they drew closer to their next destination, Gyr pestered Charon with a stream of questions about Mortal society from dawn until dusk.

"Ah ok. We Gryphons have such an ailment joint rot. Rarely do the oldest of my race complain of pains like that though," Gryphon stated. "My father once spoke of an ache in his right wing..."

Bane's sudden movement towards the pair silenced Gyr immediately. The Gryphon nudged Charon to stand up as he did so himself. He bowed his head as Bane came to stand before them.

"Sawn is not far. Mount up and take to the skies," Bane said, addressing Charon and Gyr with an unreadable expression. It was if he was just going through the motions, withholding any sign of what he was thinking.

He was right in that Sawn was not far, just beyond the

stand of trees that they had stopped to rest in. They were approaching the city from the north. It was still early in the morning and the road was empty. However the heavy wooden gates remained shut tight. A man with a thin mustache and carrying a leather folder stuffed full with papers in the crook of his left arm was conversing with a pair of soldiers. By all appearances, the trio was preparing for the day's activities and knew each other well. Nothing was out of the ordinary or indicated that Sawn had faced any recent danger.

Charon led the way with Gyr plodding along at his right side. Bane hung back with his hood drawn up to shield his face. It was hard not to notice Gyr, who was as tall at the shoulder as Charon's horse. He was also a Gryphon and to the trio of Mortal men at the gates, a stranger and possibly dangerous monster.

"Stand back!" the two guards shouted together as they jumped forward with their halberds pointed in a threatening display. The third man stood behind him, his folder clutched in his arms.

Gyr growled, a low rumble deep in his throat, and expressed his unhappiness with a warning threat display. He lifted up his wings, flaring the tips of his feathers. His leonine tail whipped back and forth. Even Charon laid his hand on his sword hilt.

"Who are you and what is your business here?" the guard standing to Charon's left demanded.

Both Charon and Gyr were preparing an equally surly response. Bane harrumphed and cleared his throat. He urged his horse forward, coming between the pair. Charon's horse sidestepped towards the left while Gyr stumbled towards the right. Their deference towards him was clear to the Mortals and it put them on further edge.

"Bane Arlis, Daylord of the Immortal Truth and High King of Terra," Bane said as he pulled back his hood. The cloth dropped to his shoulders, his brown hair a tousled mess. He was relaxed but held himself in a noble manner.

The three Mortals immediately dropped to one knee and bowed their heads in shame. No matter how rumored Bane was or how rare his appearances were, no one would dare claim the title of High King of Terra but him. Even the Mortals of the Southlands knew the name of Bane Arlis the High King.

"We beg forgiveness at our pathetic welcome that was not worthy of your person," the man carrying the leather folder cried in remorse. He mumbled more under his breath.

"I seek provisions and safe lodgings within Sawn for myself and my companions. Charon of Garhune and Gyr of the Gryphons," Bane said before gesturing to Charon and then to Gyr.

"If none can be provided, then we shall move on and leave your city untroubled."

With those words, the three Mortal men scrambled to heed Bane's request. The guards worked quickly to pull open the gates while the other man rushed away into the city.

"Sometimes it pays to travel with a king," Bane smirked.

The moment of amusement delighted Charon and Gyr, having travelled with a sullen Bane for many leagues. In fact, Charon did not think that Bane had a sense of humor. He glanced over at Gyr who was soaking it in with a stupid smile on his animal face. The Gryphon, though powerful and majestic, was utterly deluded. To Charon's eyes, Bane appeared uncomfortable with his legendary status, hinting to that in the few conversations he had without Gyr around. He often wondered if Bane even liked having Gyr following his every move.

"Shall we?" Bane suggested as he guided his horse towards the gates. Gyr was quick to follow, folding his wings on his back. Charon nudged the flanks of his horse with his heels, directing the animal to follow.

The people of Sawn were still waking up for the day and had yet to realize the identity of their new guests. A pair of lamp lighters was out with their extinguishing sticks, systematically snuffing each ten foot tall iron street lamp. Both of them were tall and thin with brown hair though one sporting a full beard. The clean face man gestured towards his companion, pointing at Gyr with an expression of wonder. Gyr caught their glances and arched his neck and tossed his head back with pride. Being a Gryphon and thus a strange creature to the Mortals, Gyr garnered the most attention. It was not too long before people started whispering about Bane.

People started to crowd the market square before the Mayor of Sawn's house, whispering and pointing at the trio. Vendor carts laid half unpacked, a produce seller actually dropping a head of cabbage. Another's cart fell open completely, spilling potatoes and assorted root vegetables on the street. Bane paused and dismounted from his horse. In a swift motion, he pulled off his great sword and cloak, hanging them from the saddle. He bent down to help the vendor collect his wares.

"Here. Let me help you," Bane suggested politely as he gathered an armful of potatoes. "Shouldn't let your hard work and delicate farmer's hand go to waste with your wares in the gutter."

"Thank you," the farmer replied.

It wasn't long until all of the produce had been picked up and set up at the farmer's wooden stall. The farmer continued to thank Bane profusely. Bane smiled and bowed his head before stepping away. It was then that the Mayor of Sawn approached, his blue and gold robes flapping in the breeze.

"So it is true. The legendary Bane Arlis has come to my city on this day," the Mayor greeted. He bent down in a deep bow.

Bane gritted his teeth from the resultant shouts and exclamations. Charon shuddered in brief shock from the sound while Gyr continued his proud posturing. The normal market crowd swelled around them and the Mayor, everyone talking and a few begging favors of Bane. There were shouts for stories. Others for display of his mighty power. Several asked for healing from a physical ailment and a rare few begged to stay the death of a dying relative.

"Come now, my people. I am sure the Lord Bane is very tired from his journey and needs his rest. He and his companions are welcome to my home. I certainly delight in talking to the Gryphon," the Mayor exclaimed as he turned about on his feet. He stopped before Bane. "If it pleases you, I open my home for your stay."

"A rest before a warm fire would be nice. I look forward to getting to know the newest Mayor of Sawn," Bane forced out with as pleasant of a smile as he could muster. He took the reins of his patient chestnut horse in his right hand.

Gyr's sudden hesitation did not escape the Mayor. "Do not worry, Master Gryphon. My home is accommodating to all Gryphons no matter their size and wingspan. It has been standing for well over a thousand years since the mighty Bellico the Traveler first visited. Albeit some renovations have been made during that time span."

"Bellico the Traveler! My egg parents told me many stories about his grand adventures!" Gyr squealed with delight.

*****

Bane sat in silence by the fire with a still full flagon of mead. He traced the rim of it with his finger before setting the cup aside.

"Perhaps I can have a better drink brought for you," Chane asked. The Mayor had introduced himself by name as soon as they had settled in the sitting room.

"He's not much for talking once he gets thinking," Charon pointed out. He picked up another blueberry scone and tore into it.

Each of the four had situated themselves in the sitting room with only Bane sitting by himself. Chane and Charon sat on either side of a small table that was laden with pastries and a pitcher of mead. Gyr stretched out on the floor to Charon's right, his back to a window that overlooked the rear gardens. He pecked at the scone that Charon had handed to him.

"A thousand years of life with many thousands more ahead can burden a man's soul," Chane started to say. He cleared his throat.

"I do not partake of such drink and never have since my earliest days. It addles the mind and turns good men into scoundrels," Bane interjected. "But to many, it is the drink of good cheer and good friends."

"Rightly so. Sawn has claim to the best mead in all the Southlands though Meras seeks to take that from us," Chane said, raising his own flagon. "What about you, Gyr?"

Gyr nudged the scone away with his paw. "Given enough cheer, a Gryphon is known to sample some mead and wine. Never whiskey. It's too hard on the stomach."

"It sounds like you speak from experience," Charon laughed before taking a sip.

"Never try the forest brewed whiskey of the Earthborn. Vile drink and leaves your head in a vice for days," Gyr grumbled, mashing his beak.

The talk of drinking and descriptions of various brews continued for several minutes. Bane seemed content not to participate in the conversation even when asked about what his own home had to offer. In fact, he ignored Chane's question completely as he stared into the fire. Talk eventually turned to events of the Meras attack with Charon and Gyr giving vivid descriptions of the event. When they got to the point when Bane appeared, Chane turned towards him.

"What of this Shadowborn man? Does he pose a danger to Sawn?" Chane asked in a serious manner.

Bane took in a deep breath and let it out slowly. "There are many dangers in this world, Mayor of Sawn. Some known and unknown. It is the unknown that gives me concern. But this town is strong as many Mortals are when driven to defend what they love."

Chane bowed his head. "That we are. I know that the Lord Bane has been to Sawn before but what about you Charon? And you too, Gyr?"

"I would love to see your city," Gyr excitedly said before Charon could answer.

NOT WHAT IT SEEMS

"It is too bad that the Lord Bane is not with us for things have changed greatly since his last visit to Sawn," Chane said as he gathered his robes to step over a stone ledge. He grimaced when his feet splashed in a muddy puddle.

"Somehow I get the impression that he has been here more often than you think. Just not always announced," Charon commented. "Gyr here considers him his king from every depth of his being. Even though the blood of the Northlands runs in my veins, I have yet to decide."

"He is my king through and through. Even a thousand year absence cannot diminish my loyalty. Are we almost to the docks yet?" Gyr asked. He rolled his shoulders in an attempt to relax his tight muscles.

Chane chuckled softly. "Just around the corner here and you shall see what makes Sawn thrive."

The Mayor of Sawn spoke true as he led Gyr and Charon to the riverside docks. Though Gyr commented that they did not compare to the ships of the Waterborn, he still expressed amazement at the array of river boats. Chane pointed out a ship called the River Runner. The man admitted that it wasn't the most creative name but that it was the fastest and most nimble ship to navigate the rivers of the Southlands.

"With the river, the sails and masts have been designed to optimize for speed and maneuverability. Two masts with boons pointed back towards the stern with triangular sails. A strong keel and mid height deck. Not likely to run into large sea waves," Chane described. He gestured wide with his arms towards the River Runner. "Not an overly large vessel but it is sturdy and strong. Take a good look for it is due to set sail for Arken very soon."

"As soon as Captain Howe arrives, we shall weigh anchor. I suspect he will be here within the hour," stated a scholarly looking man with midnight hair. He nodded politely towards Chane.

Charon looked at the newcomer with a sense of déjà vu. The young man bore a striking resemblance to himself though he had a bit more muscle on his frame. They were the same height and general build. Even their eyes, silver and gentle in expression, were the same. About the only difference in their physical appearance was that his own hair was longer and he was sporting a rough mustache and beard.

By now, the pause was noticeable enough that Gyr came to stand between the pair. He looked back and forth with increasing curiosity and then confusion. "Charon, he looks like you. A slightly younger you but you."

"Odd," Charon managed to say. He resisted the urge to reach forward and touch the man's face.

"Yes, it is uncanny. Perhaps you are a long lost relative," Chane chuckled. "Meet Ferran, scribe of the River Runner, and occasional scribe at the city council."

"Charon of Garhune. Are you from Sawn?" Charon asked Ferran, ignoring everyone else.

The man named Ferran gulped, glancing back and forth from Charon to Gyr to Chane. "Yes, I was born here as was my mother too. She said my father was from the north though she knew not where," he said cautiously. "Um, I have work to do."

Ferran could not run fast enough to get away, clearly uncomfortable. He glanced over his shoulder several times while attempting to talk to a portly looking fellow.

"Sad thing what happened to his mother. Murdered fifteen years ago by the man most believe was the boy's father. Hates all thing to do with fighting and weapons. A peaceful fellow," Chane stated as he watched Ferran. He let out a deep breath as he scratched his chin.

Charon was still processing how closely Ferran resembled himself. He was certain that Ferran was not a long lost son for though he was a century old, he had yet to bed a woman. Sure, he had entertained the idea many times but most people were wary around him. Only the bravest of streetwalkers dared to approach him and they repulsed him. The resemblance was too strong for Ferran to be a distant relative. One thing that stuck out to him was that they both had mysterious and missing fathers but did not share mothers. Could Ferran be his half-brother?

"Do you think that Bane would say he is Shadowborn too? Like me?" Charon asked Gyr.

"The resemblance is uncanny. Is that what the Mortals say when things look exactly alike and are yet different?" Gyr asked as he sat on his haunches.

"Indeed we do. How would a Gryphon say such a thing?" Chane inquired. He turned to look at Gyr.

The two launched into a lengthy conversation about differences between the Gryphon tongue and the common tongue. Chane became rather animated and in time, Gyr was becoming amused, excited to learn new phrases. Charon could barely begin to follow their conversation, too absorbed into studying Ferran. After a moment, he squared his shoulders and strode over to where Ferran was standing.

"I'll finish with you later, Quartermaster," Ferran lamented once he spotted Charon. The portly man nodded and stepped away to speak with another boat scribe. "What do you want?"

"What do you know of your father? Did your mother refuse to speak of him?" Charon quickly asked.

Ferran held up his hands in a vague attempt to defend himself from the uncomfortable situation. "I know nothing of my father because my mother refused to speak of him. There is nothing more you can learn from me."

"Come with me. I know someone that might be able to help us," Charon said as he reached to grab Ferran's wrist. Ferran quickly jerked out of reach.

"I have business in Arken to attend to. Captain Howe is expecting me," Ferran blurted out before rushing away.

Charon let out a huff of breath, disheartened by how his last attempt at conversation went. He wanted to get to know Ferran. He wanted to know if they could be brothers. A part of him desired to have someone who could share in his half breed misery. He was fully prepared to wait on the docks until the River Runner's return from Arken.

*****

Bane had not moved from his place by the fire, his sky blue eyes still staring deeply into the flames. He did not even flinch at the sound of Chane tripping over the front threshold and cursing loudly. He did however allow himself to smile at the silliness of it.

"I must be going blind in my old age," Chane grumbled once he entered the sitting room. "That or I need these boots resized. I told that cobbler that my feet were small."

"Oh to worry about the little things in life again," Bane chuckled. He fingered the end of the chair arm with slow circular motions.

"I would say that I understand the burden of leadership but I lord over a city. Not an entire land of Immortals," Chane said as he eased himself into the chair facing Bane's. "Pardon my infirmities."

Bane held up a hand in pardon. "No matter how big or small your charge is, the burden is the same."

It was not long before Chane had a pot of tea brought to them. He took the task of pouring out two cups. The brew had a slightly orange scent to it, steam rising in small clouds. Chane quickly described the origins of this particular tea, a treasure from Arken's port.

"There are a brave few in Arken willing to test the dangerous reaches of the Eastlands for this delicate fruit and its leaves," Chane described.

Bane however laughed. "The fruit you speak of comes from the east, yes, but only slightly east of Koa in the Southlands. Only a fool would venture into the Eastlands."

"An outlandish story to ensure the high price," Chane supposed with a roll of his eyes. He took a sip of his tea. "But it is quite delicious."

They sat in silence for a long time, politely sipping tea and listening to the songbirds outside. It was Bane who spoke first.

"What do you know of the Shadowborn said to wander the Southlands?" he inquired after setting his still full tea cup down. He dropped two cubes of white sugar into the liquid.

Chane cleared his throat. "I have never seen him myself and I am almost seventy, nearing the end of my Mortal years. I do find it highly unusual for any Immortal to be south of the Wall of Crossroads. Your kind tend to keep to themselves and their affairs. According to the history my kind keeps, the Southlands has not seen such might and war for more than a thousand years. Maybe even two. But the Gryphon told me of a terror, a man that now wages war upon the Northlands. He warned me that this man's evil could spread to encompass the world."

"Kaiser Adonis," Bane uttered almost as an afterthought.

"Yes, that was the name. As dangerous and powerful as Gyr described him, I cannot fathom how one man could cause such fear and terror," Chane wondered. He shook his head in doubt.

Bane sighed deeply. "Sometimes it takes a single man to tip the scales and change the course of the future," he said as if from a distant place.

"And so he came from a distant land unknown. A warrior like no other who bore a great sword upon his back and a magical fire on his hands. None could stop him. None could oppose him. Side by side, he fought with the night and into the dawn," Chane began to recite.

He had heard the Mortal version of his legacy many times before. A story mixed with truths and falsehoods but he did not feel like wasting his energy trying to tell the correct story. Let them talk, he thought. It will keep them distracted. He leaned back in the velvet cushioned chair, crossing his arms tightly.

"What rumors or dark tales have you heard these days of late?" Bane asked, breaking his silence.

Chane appeared to think for a long time, muttering to himself. He ran a palm over his thinning white hair and twirled the end of his short beard. He nervously patted his knees, inadvertently smoothing out the wrinkles that his gray robe had cast over his legs.

"Yes, I have heard talk of this Shadowborn for many years. Mad and dangerous like wild animal but seemingly fearful of something far more dangerous. If I may, let me speak plainly," Chane stated. He waited until Bane lifted a permissive hand. "This Shadowborn has been attacking Mortals for as long as I can remember. My father and his father have been warning me about traveling through the darkness of night, fearful that it would draw the Shadowborn's ire. In fact, my grandfather's only brother was found slain with wounds no earthly beast could have caused."

"A Demon," Bane said flatly after hearing Chane describe the wounds. "Named Axum. He is the only one I know that has ventured south of the Wall of Crossroads."

Chane shuddered in his seat. "I dare not even think of this dark beast. Demons have not roamed the Southlands for..."

"A thousand years. It seems that a millennia ago was the culmination of a peaceful world," Bane interrupted. He sighed deeply, looking into the flames. "The Immortal Truth is failing and it's my fault. My fault for letting the guardian bonds break."

The last of Bane's words were uttered at a whisper but Chane still heard them. A nagging thought sat waiting on the edge of his tongue to be expressed but he bit it back. What he desperately wanted to ask was why Bane had abandoned the Northlands and all but disappeared from the Southlands. Why was he here now in what felt like out of the blue? He thought of Gyr and wondered if the Gryphon awakened something in his king. Was it a long buried power or was it guilt? Who was Bane truly?

"Why did you leave?" Chane dared to ask.

Bane held his breath for a moment. "A story for another

time when the right to the truth has been earned."

*****

LIGHT FROM THE EAST

Lana let out a deep breath that was filled with pride once she crested the hill and spotted Cascade in the distance. She halted and rustled her wings, shaking them vigorously. She stretched her entire body from beak to the tip of her tan furry tail. Arching her neck, she stared at the capital of the Earthborn. From the east, the lands before its high walls were dominated by the extravagant estates of the nobility. Wide green fields were dotted with finely bred horses in a rainbow of colors. But one thing stood out among the sight: the many tents and camps for the armies of the Northern Alliance. She stretched her neck and spotted the flaming red tents and banners of the Fireborn, likely the first to come to the call. Towards the eastern edge of the land were the white tents of the Airborn, some as large as a house for the Gryphons. Scattered amongst the many camps were the Earthborn who have comes from the distant reaches of their territory. Missing were the Waterborn and the Shadowborn for obvious reasons. The Waterborn were reluctant to support the cause of the Shadowborn rebels and the Shadowborn were trapped beyond a mysterious shield. At least the Lightborn would soon join them.

The idea that she had succeeded in convincing Evander to take up arms made her feel light as a feather. Only duty and decorum held her to the ground and kept her from flying into the air with delight. She cleared her throat and steadied herself. She wanted to lead the Lightborn into Cascade with dignity and restraint. But the longer it took in their trek to the city, the less Lana felt that she could keep herself firmly on the ground.

"I do not see the likes of the Waterborn among the assembled," Evander commented as he pulled on his white horse's reins. The beast stopped beside Lana and eyed her with wariness.

Lana thought about teasing the horse with a heavy snort and flash of talons but decided against it. It would not be in good taste despite all the harsh words and actions she had said and done to get Evander to listen. Spooking his horse was not a good idea.

"What say you, Gryphon, or do you intend to go to their capital and give them a good tongue lashing too?" Evander inquired. His tone still bore a hint of embarrassment and irritation.

Lana slowly turned her head to lock eyes with Evander. "They will come. I have faith."

"You do realize that the Waterborn will not so easily throw their support behind Ryder Coba considering how his father killed Nereus," Evander pointed out, lifting an eyebrow.

"Some would have said the same of you and yet, here you are. People can change," Lana fired back. She smiled when she say Evander's chamberlain Rayn approach on his own mount. She nodded towards him.

More mounted Lightborn, including Commander Solar, slowed to a stop behind Lana, Evander, and Rayn on the hill top. Behind them pushed the assembly of foot soldiers, supply carts, a scattering of followers, and a team of workmen in charge of everything from cooking to weapon repair. As Lana had learned, the Lightborn army was an organized parade with no detail left forgotten. They all followed Evander without question, at least ones that could not be heard. Especially since Lana's verbal bashing and near fight with Evander in the throne room. She was certain that she saw a few smiles of approval. Perhaps Evander did not command the unquestionable loyalty of his people as many thought.

"My Lord, you are marching into a new history of the world. What you do from now on will be remembered forever," Rayn placated. He reached forward to pat his horse's neck, shushing it with a soft breath when it whinnied loudly.

Evander sneered. "You are lucky that the Gryphon spoke for you."

"I thank the both of you for my rising as speaker for the Lightborn in Cascade. I am sure the new chamberlain will handle the affairs of your house in Prism with great dignity and love," Rayn said with a wink towards Lana.

Thus had been Evander's general attitude since leaving the

Lightborn capital. He wanted to be angry at Lana for her harsh words and acts of disrespect. In fact, he never ceased to express his thoughts about Lana, both behind her back and in her presence. He regularly insulted her beast like appearance, increasing the severity of his words when she laughed. Lana could not help but laugh. Evander had assembled his army and followed her to Cascade despite his negative opinion of her. The Lord of the Lightborn had released Rayn from his chamberlain duties as soon as the first meeting ended and Rayn joined Lana's growing group of followers.

Lana learned one very important thing about the Lightborn during her time in Prism. Very few actually agreed with Evander, following him as their Lord due to a long held sense of loyalty. Some people she spoke to said that Evander had been their leader for so long that none of them could imagine a world without him. She learned from the oldest of the Lightborn that Evander had been a much different person before the Immortal Truth and even in the days of Begin Anu. Why and when he had changed, none could tell her. Whatever it was, Lana felt that she had awakened Evander to the world beyond.

Ignoring a still fuming Evander, Lana launched into the air. She did not go too high off the ground but high enough to be seen from a distance. Once she had risen three times her body length, she twisted around and flared her wings. The undersides were a bright cream color, speckled with brown. She flapped her wings in a rhythmic code known only to the Gryphons to signal that she had arrived.

"Could you not have flown to the city and told them that we were here?" Evander moaned. His horse stuttered back a few steps before he tugged on the reins.

"And leave you here to turn around like a coward? I do not think so. You will face this war like everyone else: head on," Lana retorted with a toss of her head.

"I will have a word with your Lords about your abhorrent behavior towards a sitting Lord of the Spiritborn!" Evander threatened with a growl.

She could not tell him that both Paladon and Stellaris would never go against the word of Proto Avis who had sent her on the mission in the first place. Though they were the leaders of the Gryphons, Proto Avis was the representative of the High King of Terra, the top power in the world. She knew exactly how each would respond. Stellaris would tell her that he would have done the same in her place. Paladon would have said he would have chosen different words to get the same message across. She chuckled to herself as she sat down on her haunches, the grass smooth beneath her.

"Why did Ryder come to your lands?" Lana inquired, realizing she had not yet asked the question. It was something she had been wondering about since she first left Crossroads for Prism.

Rayn thought for a moment. "Many things are said of it. Some say he came to learn as the Lightborn are known to hold truer to the ways of peace than of war like the Shadowborn. Others say he was searching for something. Lord Evander accused him of trying to escape reality after the execution of his father and using his lands to hide. He actually ordered him to leave," Rayn explained, half serious and half with humor. He shook his head.

"Ordering someone to leave does not seem like a reason to break an arm," Lana commented.

"It is when one calls the other's mother a whore. Ryder did not take too kindly to comments about his mother who had only recently passed on to the Spirit World. I was there. He told Evander that he knows nothing of his life and affairs and what had driven him to leave. Evander demanded answers, saying no Prince of the blood of Shadow Night would have abandoned the Shadowborn and then Ryder struck him," Rayn described.

"Now that was a fight to remember," Solar stated as he came to Rayn's side. "My Lord Evander, despite his misgivings of combat and aggression, is a great warrior. But young Ryder is absolutely breath taking and deadly. I have never seen a Shadowborn command such power like that before and not just his native Spirit energies. How Ryder does it at his age is a mystery."

Solar's comment spiked Lana's interest. She turned around to face him. "What do you mean in regards to not just his native energies?"

"He is Shadowborn by birth and blood on both sides. That means he should only have command over the Shadow Spirit energy. But I saw the might of the Earthborn, the ferocity of the Fireborn, the agility of the Airborn, and the grace of the Waterborn against that of the Lightborn. He commanded those powers like he had been born of those nations. That is just unheard of but then, Evander was right. We do not know much about his mother's background. Perhaps she was not preborn after all." Solar shrugged his shoulders.

"Or she had Farlander blood," Lana suggested after some thought.

The suggestion of such surprised Rayn and Solar. They spoke amongst themselves in low voices for a long time before looking back at Lana. By then, the graceful Falcon Gryphon Savanna, had begun her descent from the air. She landed before Lana with a smile in her eyes. They too whispered to each other in the Gryphon tongue.

"The Lords of the Council have asked that I escort you to the city of Cascade. Lord Evander, your army may be settled beside that of the Airborn," Savanna stated, addressing Evander. The Lord of the Lightborn's sneer slowly softened, apparently pleased to be addressed so politely by a Gryphon. "Lana? Shall we take to the skies?"

Lana was glad to be flying again with one of her own kind though she wanted to learn more about the confrontation. She wondered what Savanna would know. She thought about asking her but decided against it. She glanced over her shoulder at the Lightborn, seeing Solar going back to assist Evander. Rayn had already distanced himself from his kin, pushing his horse into a fast canter. At least, she told herself, she could be focus on the success of her mission. Now, she just had to wait to see what Paladon and Stellaris would truly say of her behavior.

*****

A DRAGON'S WORDS

He should have been in a thousand other places but this
one. Well maybe this one since it held such great importance to
many but for him, it held a deep sense of sadness and regret. What
his people had decided, was it the best idea? Was it really the only
idea? Why would such brave and noble souls choose to do what
they did? Why did he choose his fate if he did at all? Vorin closed
his eyes and shook his head. There was no use worrying about
something that could not be changed. There was no way to go back
in time without upsetting the entire balance of the world. But the
old red Dragon could not help but wonder what could have
happened if he had.

Vorin clawed his way closer to the cavern opening, trying to
remember the old magic. He snorted out a puff of black smoke as
he sat on the mountain ledge. A burst of thought and he
remembered what to do. He sucked in a great puff of breath like he
was preparing to shoot out a jet of flame. Instead of drawing the air
deep into his chest, he held it briefly in his throat. He then snaked
his neck towards the cavern opening and following the frame of
stone, blew out a cloud of white smoke. Once complete, he backed
his head away. The stone began to crackle without any piece
breaking. It was the sound of the old magic being awakened by the
only one who could now wake it up. Dragon magic was unlike
anything on Terra and the secrets of it were never shared to anyone
who was not one. Not even Vorin's dearest friends, Proto Avis and
Bane Arlis, knew how the power worked.

It took several minutes but the cavern opening had expanded to a large enough size to allow him inside. Vorin shook and rolled his massive frame vigorously to remove the snow that had accumulated on his wings and back. Normally he would have just built up enough heat in his body to melt it but he had to conserve his energies for more important things. His long talons gouged the earth beneath his paws as he pushed himself up. The now size appropriate opening loomed before him. The sacred stones inside were waiting and he did not hesitate any further. With a last strengthening of resolve, Vorin entered the tunnel. The opening shrank back to normal as soon as the tip of his tail passed.

Vorin remembered the time he had asked the Earthborn to seal the entrance from him. Outwardly, he had said it was for protection of the sacred stones. Inwardly, Vorin just did not want to face what the space represented to him. He did not want easy access to a place that would induce such a powerful sense of mourning. This was the first time in centuries that he had entered the mountain. To cover his hesitation to visit the stones, Vorin had suggested that the Immortal Truth be celebrated in Crossroads every turn of the century. He had said that more people could come together and remember the writing of the Immortal Truth. The event had evolved since its beginnings and many but the eldest of the Spiritborn and Gryphons could remember what it used to be. To remember why they really celebrated.

The sacred cavern was as he remembered with its moat and pillars of white stone. He briefly glanced up at the small opening high above. A thin beam of sunlight streamed down to illuminate the space. Golden light suffused the cavern, motes of dust floating in the air. Vorin liked the sun. It was warm and comforting. He preferred it to the moon. He still respected the moon like he did the sun though as he was not a fool. Each had its own power like many things in the world. He took a deep breath, not to expel fire, but to take in the scent and consciousness of the space. To him, it was alive with power and memory. Every carved line, even that of the runes on the stone tablets of the Immortal Truth, had been made with Dragon blood. Not his own, he quickly reminded himself, save for his signature at the tablets' end.

He looked up at the ceiling, seeing the intricate murals of a time long past. It was a writing of the beginning of the world that he knew now. He closed his eyes in appreciation. He remained in the stark still position for a long time. A shift in the air woke him back to his senses. He glanced back at the sunny window, the magic of the space keeping the snow out. Good, he thought. He wasn't too keen on snow either. At least it had not been a blizzard outside when he had arrived. Just a quiet morning snow fall, the ice crystals falling from the higher peaks in the mountain valley whenever the wind blew.

"My brothers and sisters, do not think that I have forgotten you. You are never far from my thoughts," Vorin mused in a soft voice. "Not a day goes by where I do not think of you and remember what you have done for Terra."

It was true. Vorin felt the sacrifice of his race in his bones and very essence every moment of his life. Some days, the thought was more powerful and threatened to break him. Other days, it was a quiet ripple in his mind. Sometimes, Vorin wished he could convey what he truly felt. But he was a Dragon, an ancient beast of great ferocity and wild power. At least he once was. He smiled at the thought of how his friendships with other races had transformed him into a more understanding and emotive creature. He was endlessly fascinated by the Spiritborn and the Gryphons. He understood the Gryphons better as a fellow member of a beast race. All in all, his life was fulfilling on the outside.

On the inside, Vorin was troubled. His thoughts turned quickly to the apparent rise of Kaiser Adonis. His mind raced with a thousand questions, unable to latch onto one long enough to try and come up with an answer. He snarled loudly and froze the endless stream of questions. In that moment, his mind grabbed one before it could disappear in the mass. Why had he stood by and let Kaiser's dark power happen?

The answer immediately came to him. He was the last Dragon and to risk himself in true open war risked the end of his race entirely. He was afraid of dying. That fear made him angry. Yet, he could not break himself free of that endless cycle of fear and rage. It made him even angrier as he tried to figure out why. He was a Dragon! He could tear down mountains and set fire to the land, burning everything! He was not supposed to be afraid of anything! Especially of a single Shadowborn man!

But Kaiser was not an average Shadowborn man. He commanded powers that he should not even know. Powers he should not be capable of summoning. He simply did not have the physical mass to channel the massive amounts of Spirit energy or whatever magic it was. Vorin mashed his teeth together and gripped the stone floor tightly. He thought that his ancient age would grant him a sense of all knowing in regards to the powers of the world. But it did not. That made him even angrier. An inferno raged within him.

He jerked his head up towards the murals. His eyes darted from the assembly of pictures and writing, trying to discern an answer. Why was the most powerful space in all of Terra being so silent?

"Show me!" he roared at full volume. The cavern shook from the vibration but held together. "Show me what I cannot see!"

He half expected for a rush of voices shouting back at him what he wanted to know. But he was foolish to think so. Vorin bowed his head, closing his eyes. It was pointless for him to have come here.

"What is made can be unmade. What is done cannot be undone," spoke a distant but unmistakable voice.

Vorin's eyes shot open and he looked about for the source. He could not see anything but he was certain that he had heard the voice of Ogon, the last Dragonlord before the Immortal Truth had been written.

"Ogon?" Vorin shouted back. "I cannot see you. Are you near?"

It was foolish. Ogon was dead. The ancient white Dragon with ice blue eyes could not possibly be in the cavern with him. But he was so sure he had heard him speak.

"What is made can be unmade. What is done cannot be undone," Ogon's voice repeated.

For the love of all life, Vorin could not figure out what Ogon was trying to tell him. If he had allowed Proto to come with him, the old Gryphon would have told him that the Spirit of Ogon was trying to help him. How, Vorin was not sure.

"I hear you! What is made can be unmade. What is done cannot be undone. What does that mean?" Vorin begged. His voice echoed off the walls.

Everything fell silent and Vorin waited for a painfully long time for Ogon to speak again. Was the voice just an echo of a lost time? His heart fluttered with anticipation. He shifted his weight as he turned about, uselessly looking for a source to draw answers from. His eyes fell on Ogon's picture in the mural. He half expected the lines of it to be glowing, giving him some indication that Ogon was present in the cavern. Only the eyes were shining white. Vorin slumped in disappointment. The eyes were only two embedded pieces of moonstone reflecting the sunlight, not some mystical force emanating from the picture.

It would have been easy for him to dismiss this trip to the sacred cavern. He did not experience a Living Memory or feel some great revelation of knowledge that had been hidden from him. No, his visit only reminded him of his sadness and fear of death. But the voice of Ogon refused to be quieted in his head. Even if he had only imagined it, the words were powerful. What is made can be unmade. What is done cannot be undone.

A thought occurred to him as his mind fought to decipher Ogon's hidden meaning. Those were the last words the former

Dragonlord had told him before the sacrifice and when he had passed on lordship of the Dragons to him. Maybe it was his own memory that had woken up in the sacred space, not a spontaneous Spirit event. Of course, it could not be a Spirit talking to him. Spirit Wake had been used and the living world's connection to the Spirit World was now tenuous. The free use of Spirit energy in any of its forms was rarer than a Dragon on Terra. If a Spiritborn had managed to summon up a modicum of Spirit energy, it was unpredictable in its strength and direction.

Even if it was a memory, Vorin could not ignore it. Why now? Why would Ogon's words, ones he admittedly had forgotten, come to him? Had he truly not lost them to the depths of his mind? He was not sure who he could ask for the last words of a Dragon were sacred and meant for only Dragons to hear. But he was the last of his kind. Who would he tell his own last words to? Who would continue to share the Dragon legacy when he was gone? Who was worthy enough for him to break a tenet of his race?

*****

UNRAVELING

"I do not see the reason for this council if Lord Vorin is not even here. He is the eldest of us all. Why isn't he present to discuss matters that you all claim are world shaking and life altering," Evander griped. He sat on his carved golden wood chair with his head in his hands. He shook his head before looking back up.

"None may command a Dragon even if that Dragon is considered a friend," Oren said after grabbing Palani to prevent him from jumping up and agreeing with Evander. He pulled on Palani's sleeve and forced him back into his seat. Palani glared back at him. "I personally do not fancy being cooked by Dragonfire."

Ever since Evander had joined the council, by all appearances against his will, the discussion had only been a stream of insults and past hurts from everyone. The assembly of eight sat in a circle in the castle throne room. Oren and Palani sat at the head of the room, with Palani sitting upon the Earthborn throne. Of the two, Palani sat uncomfortably, constantly tapping or massaging the arm of the intricately carved chair. Oren sat up straight with more confidence. To Oren's right seated on their haunches were Paladon and Stellaris. Stellaris was busily arguing with Evander while Paladon sat, mumbling under his breath about his kin's behavior. On Palani's left sat Kader who was the only non-royal in the room. Argos was the most animated in the room, gung ho for going to war. Evander was out of his seat and pacing the center of the room.

"It would seem to me that those the Northlands considers to be our leaders in times of trouble are absent. In fact, who is truly in charge of this council if those like Lord Vorin and even Bane Arlis are nowhere to be found," Evander pointed out. He gave an exacerbated turn and sat down on his seat with a heavy thud. He gestured towards Kader. "Why is he even here? He is not a Lord nor has he been."

Kader gulped under the sudden attention. He looked about to see if someone else was about to comment about his presence. He let out a deep breath and strengthened his resolve.

"He is here at these proceedings as per the Immortal Truth and at my request. Why should we decide the fate of a nation without a member of its ranks amongst us?" Aves said firmly. He stood up slowly, keeping his eyes locked on Evander. "As stated by the Immortal Truth and tradition, the eldest Lord has the right to call council and mediate it. So hold your tongue!"

To see Aves show the slightest semblance of anger was a shock. The Lord of the Airborn was known to be famously calm even in battle. Everyone who had been standing or talking loudly immediately sat down and closed their mouths. Aves strode towards the center of the room and looked each person in the eye. Only Paladon held his gaze without twitching or turning away.

"By our inaction, we Lords and great minds have failed to uphold the Immortal Truth. We must face that now or perish. We must face the fact that we have failed to protect Terra from darkness in the most abhorrent way. I count myself among those who have failed," Aves started to say.

"If you are as great a warrior as many claim, why did you not step up sooner to slay Kaiser and stop this war? You could have saved thousands including that of the Shadowlord. You could have stopped Bane from abandoning us!" Evander accused Aves.

Aves rounded on Evander with fury in his eyes, his very gaze on fire. "You among everyone have seen a world without the Immortal Truth! You who have lived to see Begin Anu die in battle! You who have seen a war that should only have existed in our deepest nightmares! I will be the first to admit that I was terrified and battle weary."

Aves' voice fell as he turned about towards each and every soul in the room. He fiddled with the silver eagle broach that held his white feathered cloak in place. With an audible snap, the garment fell to the floor in a heap. Underneath, Aves wore light gray boots with white wool pants, a gray waistband, and a white sleeveless tunic. Contrasting with the stark white color of his clothes, his knotted arms were covered in black script like tattoos. Everyone held their breath in surprise.

"These Spirit Marks are a testament to my experiences during both Dominion Wars. Perhaps I was foolish in believing that a person like Kaiser and his ideas would simply die out over the years. I was wrong and now our enemy has become something too terrible for the likes of me. Which is why we must come together and make our stand. I do not know why the Lord of the Waterborn has yet to come or even our King. Without the Lord Proto Avis here, I am by law the final say in what is decided here. Judge me not for what I have done or not done. It will not solve things," Aves explained, ending his speech by looking Evander in the eyes.

Outside of the throne room doors, everyone could hear a scuffle going on. Muffled voices escalated into all out shouts. Aves looked towards Palani before turning his gaze back to the door. It was if he was accusing his fellow Lord with a mindless interruption.

"But I must see my Lord Aves!" came the first discernable shout.

"Open the doors!" Aves commanded with a booming voice.

As he thought, Eru came through the doors as soon as he could fit through the crack. He slid to a stop before Aves and dropped to his knee. "The Lord Vorin has returned and wishes to speak with you at once."

"Take me to him," Aves ordered before grabbing his cloak.

*****

Aves told Eru to wait inside the castle before hastening out to the courtyard before the gardens. It was a massive space decorated with carefully laid stones. A large fountain forty feet across sat in the center. Two statues, one a stag and the other a doe, spat out rain of showering cold water. Another twenty feet beyond the opposite side of the fountain was the entrance to the gardens, framed by tall green hedges.

Vorin stopped his pacing, slowly letting his thick tail fall to the ground. He breathed a sigh of relief. "Thank you for coming so quickly."

"One does not make a Dragon wait especially when he is a friend," Aves replied as he came to stand before Vorin.

"At least some of you still remember," Vorin chuckled to himself. He turned his head away briefly. "You have always had a deep understanding that can only be obtained with age. That is to be admired."

"Vorin, I am sure that you did not send my own man to pull me away from a council of the Lords without good reason," Aves stated, getting straight to the point. He pulled his cloak close around him.

Seeming to remember himself, Vorin shook his head to settle his senses. He mumbled briefly under his breath as if he was arguing with someone. The behavior spiked Aves' interest. Vorin ended his silent conversation with a huff of breath and a puff of gray smoke that trickled from his nostrils. He then recounted his experience in the sacred cavern in full detail. His fast paced delivery started to slow down as he reached the part in the memory where he faced a dilemma. He took a deep breath and let it out slowly. He then proceeded to tell Aves the last words.

"What is made can be unmade. What is done cannot be undone. A curious statement from Ogon and I know that he never spoke of such things lightly. I know a little of the ways of Dragons. For you to trust me enough to tell me his last words, I am deeply honored. Rest assured, I will not share this knowledge with anyone," Aves commented.

"No. You must tell all who will listen. If I shall be the last of my kind, let all know of the might and majesty of the Dragons. I will appoint a Memory Keeper to pass on my knowledge sometime in the near future," Vorin quickly said. He bowed his head. "But what do you think of them? Ogon's words."

Aves thought and ran over every word in his mind for a long time. He turned away from Vorin briefly, his eyes closed. Vorin studied his every move, waiting for an answer. Aves paced away to the point that Vorin thought he was leaving.

"A simple answer comes to mind but I know that it will not answer the question Ogon's words raise," Aves said as he turned back around. "A sword can be made by the hand of a smith and melted in a hot fire. Thus the sword is no more. A man can die but his death cannot be taken back. To break that cycle is to break the foundations of the world. It makes sense and yet it doesn't."

"Then you have gotten no further than me. Maybe if I had paid attention more," Vorin mused before falling silent.

Aves came forward and laid a hand on Vorin's wing. "We may not know the exact meaning of the words but the timing of your memory of them makes me think it relates to our war. I will meditate on this." He paused and raised a finger as a thought occurred to him. "What do Dragons say of Spirit Walkers?"

"Souls who managed to return from the Spirit World. Same as the Spiritborn. Bane is the only one I have ever heard of, even in legend," Vorin replied with a curious tilt of the head. His eyes then widened. "Are you suggesting that Kaiser is a Spirit Walker? What is done cannot be undone. One who has died and returned cannot do so again."

"The nature of a Spirit Walker is that they exist in limbo, capable of powers originating from both planes of existence. I first saw this with Bane, admittedly a nobody who changed the tide of the last Dominion War. A curious occurrence that few sought to question considering how much we desired peace against the Darklands," Aves explained.

"We were all tired of war," Vorin commented. "I did not think it was possible to use up all of my flame and energy but I certainly did. It took a very long time to feel the heat in my belly again."

Aves nodded with approval. "A Spirit Walker can be unmade though they cannot be destroyed. Damn, if only Bane were here after all. He could face Kaiser with all of us Lords and people supporting him. Bring our combined power full force at Kaiser."

It was easier said than done considering Bane had been gone from the Northlands for a thousand years. Even then, thoughts of doubt permeated both of their minds. What if Kaiser was stronger than Bane? Was having the Daylord any help at all if he could not guarantee victory? What if Kaiser was defeated and returned with greater power? Were they about to enter an endless cycle of war?

*****

DECEPTION AND POISON

"Are we seriously going to do it?" the tiny Zee asked, feeling smaller than her short stature showed. She wrenched a white napkin in her hands.

Cora nodded as she pulled out a small glass vial filled with a dark red liquid. She first looked over at Raye who was setting silverware on a tray. Raye paused as she set her hand on the stalk of a silver goblet.

"Yes, we are. We always were going to," Cora said as Raye pushed forward the decanter of crimson wine.

Zee sat down on a nearby wooden bench, looking nervously at her slippers. She crossed her feet back and forth. She repeatedly smoothed out her dress. "I'm scared."

"You have every right to be," Raye said as she set a plate of roast chicken and vegetables on the tray. The hot food smelled like garlic and crushed black pepper. A small bowl holding several rolls was added along with a small thimble of yellow butter. "Be glad that Kaiser does not employ us as food tasters. Likely our attempt is not to be the first but hopefully it will be the last."

"But it will be the last because we will succeed," Cora stated firmly as she set up the tray of wine. She paced over to the ebony wood cabinet and pulled out four additional goblets.

"How can you be so sure that the Demon is on our side? I trust Kaiser more than I trust Rache?" Raye asked. She snatched the napkin from Zee and folded it, slipping the napkin ring on the cloth.

Cora clutched the vial in her hand, careful not to break it. She rubbed her forehead in frustration. "Because I would not be standing here if he was still on Kaiser's side one hundred percent. That alone tells me what I need to know."

The thought that Rache may be rebelling against Kaiser had been the topic of the three girls' conversation for a long time. Even prior to the Battle of Dusk, Cora had suggested to Raye and Zee that Rache was not so loyal to his master as before. She gave her observations and Raye believed her first. Zee was too terrified of Rache to believe anything she said about the Demon.

The three courtesans continued their prep of Kaiser's dinner in the small servants' waiting room. It was the size of a large closet but had no windows. The walls were dirty white above the dark wood waist high panels. A dining cabinet laid open to the left of the door. Another cabinet, full of table and meal linens, sat on the opposite side of the room. A single table was placed in the center where the girls prepared the tray of food and wine. Cora directed Zee to picked up the candelabra while she picked up the wine and Raye the food. Zee led the way out of the closet like room with Raye and Cora behind her.

Cora could see that as they got closer to Kaiser's quarters, Zee shivered with fear. She mentioned it to Raye who put a comforting hand on her shoulder. Zee let out a deep breath and her shivering appeared to calm.

"Zee, I know that you are scared but you need to try to stay calm," Cora whispered.

"He can read minds! What if he already knows?" Zee frantically asked. Raye gripped her shoulder tighter.

"He can't read minds so stop your worrying," Raye stated firmly. She glanced back over her shoulder and shrugged.

It was a worry that dwelled in Cora's mind. Kaiser was so intelligent and acutely aware of his surroundings that it would be difficult to fool him. But maybe that was his weakness. Perhaps he was too smart and focused on other things to notice something small and trivial. Like a little more bite to a normally strong wine. She had crafted this meal as a distraction to her goal.

*****

"Come in," Kaiser said, not looking up from his book. He quietly turned the page.

In walked the three courtesans. Zee set the candelabra down on the table Kaiser had perched his feet on. Raye and Cora set their respective trays down. All three stepped back and curtsied low. Kaiser harrumphed and swung his legs free from the table. He closed his book and handed it back to Rache who stood by the nearby bookshelf. The Demon set the book down upon a short pile of tattered tomes. He then clasped his hands before him and kept his head down.

"What did you bring me?" Kaiser asked as he leaned back in the chair waiting.

Zee attempted to light the candelabra but her hands were shaking too much. Raye took over and quickly lit the five candles and mumbled an order under her breath. The frightened girl nodded and gulped loudly.

"Oh do not be upset, my sweet. I am here to stay with you," Kaiser cooed as Cora laid a napkin across his lap. "I know that we have not spent as much time together due to events beyond my control. It upsets me that these foul rebels seek to destroy the world that I am trying to create."

"They do not understand your vision, sir," Cora said as she stepped away from his side.

Kaiser chuckled. "Of course they don't. Most are too young to see and those old enough are too senile to realize. The world needs change and I will lead it into a new future."

"As you should for it is your right," Raye commented as she pushed the tray of food towards him.

The two other girls set about pouring out the wine. Zee held the individual goblets as Cora dispensed the deep red drink. The full goblets were set back down on the table in a straight line. Kaiser sat up and reached forward. He wiggled his fingers before grabbing the centermost cup. He leaned back in his seat, holding the goblet by the rim.

"Do you think that I took victory in Dusk?" Kaiser asked, gesturing towards Cora.

"I cannot see it any other way. Zoras Rokar is dead," Cora replied as she passed out the remaining goblets. Rache sneered when he took the cup from her, scaring Zee in the process.

"Do not frighten her. She is fragile and needs some tender care to make her well again," Kaiser chuckled. He put the goblet to his lips but paused before attempting a sip. "But still, I would not say Dusk was a complete victory. I learned things that vex me terribly. Gives me such a headache."

"You mean like Ryder escaping you when Spirit Wake should have prevented it?" Rache commented.

Kaiser growled audibly and Rache immediately silenced and became stiff. "You know my thoughts on that. Do I have to repeat myself again?"

"No," Rache quipped.

"Good. I am sure that you do not wish to feel that pain again though I will gladly remind you of it," Kaiser threatened darkly. "Drink, my ladies. It would be rude of me to partake first when you have worked so hard to prepare this meal for me."

Cora and Raye started to raise their cups to their mouths when Zee spoke. "My Lord, if I may ask, what shall you do next? You have conquered the Shadowborn lands with great ease. What is your plan for the future?"

Her sudden confident words pleased Kaiser and appeared to distract him from the other two girls not taking a sip. He chuckled softly before taking a deep draught. He smacked his lips and set the goblet down beside the silver meal tray. He picked up a bread roll and leaned back in his seat to pick at it. Watching the three girls, it seemed like he was waiting for something.

"I told you that you could drink. Now drink," Kaiser said firmly before popping a morsel of bread into his mouth.

Zee was the first to raise the cup to her lips but Raye put a hand on her wrist. "My, Lord. I think we should first have a toast to your victory. I do not feel it is right to drink until we have done so," Raye stated. She raised her goblet into the air, the other two girls quickly following suit. "To the victory in Dusk and future victories by Lord Kaiser."

"To victory," Kaiser mused before draining the contents of his cup. He smacked his lips and ran his tongue over them. "Perhaps a little more to truly toast my victory."

Cora quickly set her cup down and reached for Kaiser's glass. His left hand shot forward and grabbed her wrist with enough force to break it. Cora yelped in pain and tried to pull away to no avail. Zee dropped her cup in shock, bringing her hands to her mouth to muffle a scream. Raye froze in place, gripping her goblet so tightly that her knuckles were white.

"I said. Drink," Kaiser growled, locking Raye in a deadly gaze.

It was if she was no longer in control of her actions. Raye raised her full goblet to her mouth and drank deeply. The cup had barely left her lips before she collapsed into a seizure like fit. Cora and Zee watched helplessly as Raye's body convulsed. A bloody foam spilled from her mouth. Her eyes rolled back into her head. Where skin was visible, blood vessels bulged, swollen with a blackish colored liquid. The convulsions increased in severity until finally Raye stilled.

Kaiser finally let go of Cora and she fell beside Raye. He chuckled as he spotted Zee glancing quickly back and forth between him and the others.

"I suppose your attempt to poison me should be considered

admirable and brave. But you forgot one very crucial thing," Kaiser said as he reached forward and refilled his goblet. He took the full cup and leaned back in his seat. "I am not a fool."

Cora, despite her broken wrist, stood up boldly on her feet and stared Kaiser down. "No. You are the biggest fool of all. So long as there is one soul to oppose you, you will not win."

Kaiser smirked before he burst out laughing. The sound was slow and soft at first but quickly grew into a boisterous noise. It took a long time for his mirth to calm. He returned Cora's strong glare with his own.

"Again, you forget another crucial fact," Kaiser admonished. He set his full cup on the table and stood up slowly to his full height. Rache stepped up behind him on his left side, having remained silent during the horrific death of Raye.

"I do not care if I die so your threats mean nothing," Cora snarled. She gritted her teeth as she clenched her fists, ignoring the searing pain.

"Oh really? You really should have care about your death. There are dark and terrible things that await you in the Spirit World. Of course, the process of death itself will be much worse."

It was that statement that made Cora's courage start to break.

A GAME OF CHASE

Zee huddled in a corner of the damp stone cell, arms wrapped tightly around her bent legs. Her chest heaved from continuous sobbing. Her nose dripped and tears streamed down her cheeks. Her eyes were red and puffy and her hair was a matted mess. She no longer wore the fine trappings of her station, now dressed in a simple canvas dress and slippers. Her new clothes were already stained with dirt and muck.

"Will you stop crying?" Cora grumbled, sitting on the opposite side of the cell. She too wore a canvas dress and slippers.

"We are going to die! He is going to kill us!" Zee sobbed before pressing her forehead to her knees.

"So?" Cora snapped. She did not intend to be so mean in her tone but it was her way accepting the inevitable.

Perhaps it was part of her old Saber training though she had never graduated to the ranks. Sabers, though a superstitious bunch by nature, accepted death when it came to them. Dying was just another part of their service in protecting the Silvanus bloodline. Such a statement was part of the graduation oath. She mumbled the words she knew to herself, cringing every time Zee sobbed loudly.

They sat in the cell, a single window just below the ceiling letting in a thin beam of sunlight. The space was small, six feet by six feet. Cora sat in the corner furthest from the iron bars of the door while Zee leaned against the wall right next to the door. The stones that made up the walls, floor, and ceiling were coated in patches of green and gray moss. It was a holding cell, hidden somewhere in Cross. Cora had visited the city prison many times before but she could not place her and Zee's location. Were they even in Cross?

"Do you think he will torture us?" Zee asked, finally in control of her emotions.

"I don't know. We may not be important enough to waste his grim talents on us," Cora replied. She leaned her head against the wall.

"Then our death will be quick?" Zee gulped.

"Probably but who's to say? Kaiser is both predictable and unpredictable." Cora let out a deep breath. "I guess we should have believed the old adage more strongly. Often what he doesn't say and do is worse than what he does say and do."

All of a sudden, the cell door unlocked and creaked open. Cora stood up slowly and stepped towards it. Zee quickly got to her feet and grabbed Cora's elbow. Her expression urged caution. Cora put her hand on Zee's and gave it an encouraging squeeze.

"We might as well try to see what this means. Perhaps we are so worthless, he does not deem us worthy of death," Cora suggested. "Together?"

Zee swallowed hard and nodded. "Together."

The two girls took their first cautious steps out of the cell and into the hallway. It was devoid of light save for the window of their own cell and the light emanating from an open door at the other end. They held on to each other tightly as they walked towards it. With each drip of water and distant creak, they flinched but kept going. It was odd that there were no other cells and even more so, no other people present. As they got closer to the open door, they could feel the warmth of bright sunlight. It seemed as if they were walking towards salvation.

"What if we are already dead and do not realize it? Are we about to walk through a door into the Spirit World?" Zee suddenly asked.

It was a legitimate question but Cora already had an answer. "We are not dead for if we were, Omu would be leading us home. Beyond that door, we would see our lost loved ones again. Including Raye."

Her answer appeared to calm Zee and she started to walk with more confidence. The light beaming in through the open door was blinding white. Both girls raised a free hand to shield their eyes as they stepped through it. For a moment, they could not see anything. As their eyes adjusted, it was not what they expected. It was a world of fire and ruin. Once proud buildings were engulfed in flames, upper floors crumbling and failing to the streets below.

A thick black smoke blanketed the sky. The heat of the raging inferno was unbearable.

"What is this?" Cora demanded.

"This is your death," crooned a dark and terrible voice.

The girls stumbled back as a black figure stepped out of the wall of fire before them. As soon as it left the flames, they instantly disappeared. The figure then transformed into a living nightmare: Rache with black eyes and long white fangs. His crimson hair wafted in the breeze. He wiggled his thin fingers, sharp black claws growing from the tips.

"Run," Rache laughed.

Zee scrambled towards the door that they had just passed through only to be stopped by another wall of fire. She turned around, looking at Cora for help. Tears streamed from her eyes. Cora rushed forward to grab her and get her up. All around them, the fire and ruin had returned. Cora held tight to Zee's left arm and dragged her as she ran.

Neither of them recognized where they were. Zee was too terrified to say anything but Cora was certain that they were not in Cross. First thing that she noticed that the grid of the streets was completely different. Cross was nowhere as steep as this mysterious place. Despite her athletic body, her chest was heaving from the effort of climbing so many hills and stairs as well as keeping Zee on her feet. Why were there so many hills? Instead of feeling frightened, Cora was starting to feel angry. She did not like what was going on and not knowing how to deal with her environment. The memories of her old Saber trainee days roared back to the front of her mind.

A sudden screech woke Cora up from her thoughts. She felt herself being dragged back just in time to avoid being crushed by a burning roof beam. They kept each other balanced just long enough to run towards the left. Neither could say if they were running deeper into the mysterious city or heading towards the outskirts. All that mattered was that they keep away from Rache and the death that awaited them.

The heat became more intense and the girls were coated in sweat. Their lungs burned from the effort of breathing. Zee constantly rubbed at her eyes while Cora coughed over and over. Very quickly, the physical effort went from one of ease to one of desperation and exhaustion. Each girl took turns helping the other to keep running. But it seemed as if they were running in circles and getting nowhere. Cora wanted to pause to get her bearings but the fire was racing to catch them.

Zee fell, dragging Cora down with her. They both hit the ground hard enough to lose grip on each other. Cora shook her head and immediately scrambled to latch on to Zee's arm. Her entire body froze as she saw a wall of utter darkness that her Shadowborn eyes could not penetrate. Zee groaned but was suddenly snatched up and dragged back towards it. She screamed bloody murder and clawed at the ground, digging furrows with her fingers. In the effort, she ripped off her fingernails, bloodying her hands. She shrieked one last time before she disappeared into the darkness.

"Zee!" Cora cried out. She reached for her despite knowing it was too late. A sob built up in her chest.

The darkness surrounded her on all sides. What little light she had came from a small fire an arm's reach from her. It was odd. It was a pile of burning flowers, the first plant life she had seen since the moss in the cell. What was even stranger was that a single rose remained untouched. She reached for it and everything went black.

*****

"Are you sure it's working?" Rache asked as he leaned over Cora. He watched as Cora twitched and groaned.

Kaiser stood back from the heavy wooden table where Cora and Zee lay. He ran his hands over a collection of sharp metal instruments, the multitude of tiny candlelit alcoves illuminating his face. He let out a deep breath as he turned back around.

"I took many souls within an inch of their life in this room. Including two Silvanus Princes. I know what I am doing," Kaiser growled.

Rache pointed to the still Zee. "Well, this one is dead."

"And I am supposed to care?" Kaiser asked flatly. He turned around and approached the table, coming to stand by Cora's left side. He glanced over at Zee who laid to her right. "A pity. She made me laugh."

"And what about her?" the Demon asked, pointing to Cora.

Kaiser looked over Cora with a curious expression. It was not one of love or fond memories. He had the look of a predator about to make the final strike. He raised his left hand over her faces with fingers outstretched. A strange twisting mark covered the back of his left hand and wrapped around his wrist. It glowed with a silver light.

"Another Spirit Mark? How many do you have?" Rache mocked as he crossed his arms.

A deep throated snarl let the Demon know that he was crossing into dangerous territory with his question. He immediately clammed up and stepped back. Rache knew a great deal about Kaiser, more than most, but one thing he could not get Kaiser to talk about was his time in the Spirit World. How he honestly felt and not just what he told others if he told them at all. It was best to keep his mouth shut for the time being.

"You were always the strongest in mind and staunchest in heart. I can see why you chose to train as a Saber. I never did learn why you never joined the ranks," Kaiser mused. He kept his outstretched hand over her face. "No matter. Every Saber, whether in leathers or not, will break. They always do."

*****

LORAN'S HORIZON

Loran grunted as he pushed off the body of his most recent victim from his fatal sword thrust. He kicked the mutilated man and jerked down threateningly. Though the would be city defender was dead, Loran wanted complete mastery over him. Kaiser would expect nothing less from him. He had to destroy everything, kill everyone, in order to save his own life. Even though he was leagues from Cross, Loran was not so sure in the safety of the distance between them. He had heard rumors of a Living Map, conjured with blood, that sat in the throne room. He had to believe that Kaiser could be watching him right now through that mysterious entity. The Living Map could see all and thus Kaiser could as well. Loran suppressed a shiver before stepping over the body.

Another angry soldier, dressed in light steel armor with blue and black livery, charged at him with a spear. Loran paused and rolled his eyes. Though he currently fought with a sword in hand, he could not think of anybody among the Shadowborn that was a better spearman than him. He could not see the soldier's eye through the thin opening on the helm but it did not matter. He had his orders. Loran side stepped the thrust and gripped the shaft of the spear with his left hand. He jerked it towards him, knocking the soldier off balance. With a quick swipe, his sword split the weapon in half. He spun the sharp end around and shoved it forward, digging it into his adversary's stomach. He then swung his sword around and decapitated the man.

It was odd that there were still souls left in the Shadowborn lands that had allied themselves with the rebels. In reality, few people were brave enough to join their ranks. Most stayed put with the insane belief that someone else will take care of what threatened them. For Shadowborn, a historically war trained nation, to see such hesitation bordered on stupidity. Loran had always taken chances. He did not wait for danger to come to him. He gladly took up arms to meet it head on. That attitude had done well when he was still active on the seas as the Mirror Sea Pirate. He was well on his way to be a legend when Shiloh Silvanus managed to defeat him. He was not going to let that embarrassment happen again. He was going to make Lord Kaiser proud.

He wiped his mouth with the back of his head, doing little to clean the blood from his face. All around him, he could hear the screams of the desperate and dying and it pleased him. He turned around to look back towards the city of Horizon. He had fought his way to the sea side edge, leaving behind the jumbled collection of lower class houses. Many of the houses that he could see shared a common wall with at least one other. Laundry lines were strung up in their yards though the wash had been forgotten and burned. Roofs had fallen in and all shrubbery and plant life were reduced to blackened stumps. Beyond the ruined homes were the taller buildings of the inner city with the citadel dominating the skyline. The main tower of the citadel had been pulled down by chains and the many windows had been blown out. He vividly remembered the showering of glass.

Loran chuckled. The sight of the ruined city reminded him of his old raiding days. He was certain that many of the smaller villages along the coast still feared his name. He thought about taking to the seas again once Kaiser had his victory. A part of him wished he could do so now but Kaiser believed too strongly in the power of his impenetrable Shadow Mirror. He did not think a navy was necessary. Kaiser had also told him that his previous attack against the Waterborn had rendered the entire nation into recluses in matters of war. Even Loran had to admit that the plan had been brilliant. The Waterborn were not war minded by nature, though still able fighters, and preferred diplomacy to outright war. But Loran knew that once driven to fight, the Waterborn raged like their beloved sea.

He strode up to the edge of the seaside cliff, setting his right foot on a small stone. Stretching out to the horizon, hence the name of the city he had just destroyed was the Mirror Sea. On the edge of his vision were the mists that surrounded Water's Eye, a Waterborn island territory. He had sailed to the island long ago under the command of a now dead captain. Back when he was still an innocent youth in defiance of his family's desire for him to be a soldier in Cross. His father did not approve of a life at sea when glory could be found on the battlefield and in service of the Shadowlord. His cousin Morin had been convinced. He had not. If Loran could have seen his family again after all these years, he would tell them that following what he wanted made him great. He was going to be a part of a new world order.

The surface of the water was spotted with the white caps of rolling waves. A brisk wind brought up the strong scent of salt and fish. Loran breathed it in deep, savoring the memories it brought on. He stepped back from the stone and turned back to the city, cleaning his blade on the leg of his pants. He looked up in time to see one of his underlings approaching.

"Report?" Loran commanded as he sheathed his weapon.

"The city has fallen. No further resistance is expected unless someone can raise the dead," the mustached Shadowborn officer said with a bow of the head.

"Good. Lord Kaiser will be pleased," Loran stated as he strode past the man.

The man did not follow. Instead he turned around to face where Loran had gone. "Is the south ours now?"

Loran stopped in his tracks and turned back towards the officer. "Be glad that I am too weary to reprimand you for your stupid question. Yes, the south is ours. More to the point, this nation belongs to Kaiser and Kaiser alone. We are just tools in his conquest. Forget that and he will kill you faster than you can blink."

His reaction was unduly harsh but Kaiser had given him a similar answer when he had been brave enough to ask a question. In Kaiser's regime, asking questions was grounds for punishment. It all depended on what was said and who heard what was said. The biggest worry was if Kaiser would care enough to react and no one could predict that. There was only one guarantee: if Kaiser was in a foul mood, one was sure to die. Loran stifled the shiver that threatened to go up his spine.

"I am sorry for my insolence," the officer said, dropping his head and keeping his eyes looking towards the ground at his feet.

He had no time to act sympathetic. It could be interpreted as weakness and easily reported back to Cross. Loran could lose his command and his life. But then, nothing seemed to stop Kaiser from killing who he wished, even if they had not wronged him in anyway save for existing. At least, Loran could be glad that Horizon was no more the shining jewel on the southern coast.

"Send a runner for Cross and let Lord Kaiser know of his victory. Tell him his loyal soldiers march shouting and praising his name and power," Loran ordered as he walked past the officer to take one last look at the water.

By now, Loran could see dark smudges in the mists around Water's Eye. This was new. He knew the coast around the island as well as any Waterborn and there were no hidden pillars of stone or small rocky islands baring the way to shore. The officer noiselessly joined him and fished out a small eyeglass from within a pouch on his belt. Loran quickly snatched it out of his hands and made a threatening lurch forward as if to remind the officer of his orders. The officer scrambled away, tripping once, before running off into the ruined city.

Loran raised the eyeglass up and squinted. It took a moment but a billow of mist cleared and revealed what the dark smudges were. Loran dropped the eyeglass from his eye before quickly raising it again. He could not believe what he was seeing. Battleships with banners raised and sails billowing in the distant breeze. The telltale blue flags on the masts told Loran that the Waterborn were marshalling for war. This was not good news though Loran believed that Kaiser would be excited by a sea battle.

What the Waterborn could not understand was that Kaiser was just as skilled if not more skilled than they were at commanding the waves to his whim. Loran had witnessed it first hand in Eclipse when Kaiser had used Spirit energy to send a surge of water into the city. On another occasion, Kaiser further proved his power by twisting his right hand around and clenching his fist. Loran could now saw that he never seen the castle fountains freeze so quickly in the middle of summer and that he had never felt so cold in his life. What worry that had come with seeing the ships transformed into evil delight. The Waterborn had no chance if Kaiser decided to destroy them utterly.

Loran left the seaside cliff and made his way back towards the western gates of the city. All around him, buildings were crumbling from the destructive fire his forces had set to start the battle. It had been Kaiser's command to do so. Loran paused to look up at the walls where a cloud of black shadows had perched. He knew that the shadows had been the dark Spirits that Kaiser had summoned forth with his mysterious power. They were dissipating after serving their purpose to cause terror. They were the kind of enemy that could not die though they were inherently weak to injury. Loran had to admit it was a brilliant move on Kaiser's part. Fear was just as great a weapon as a fully armed soldier.

Fear was a weapon and a disease that had enabled Kaiser to gain control over most of the Shadowborn nation. Only a brave few banded together to openly oppose him. Soon, those traitorous rebels would not matter. The thought made Loran smile. So long as he served Kaiser, he was guaranteed a place in his new world order. He just only hoped it would be back on a ship. He began to imagine being named Commander of the Shadowborn Navy, a title he would gladly welcome. He would no longer be the Mirror Sea Pirate. He would get the glory he deserved.

*****

THE BREAKING WAVES

"You will not go! I forbid it!" Marinus shouted.

Alton looked back at his father, holding his helm in the crook of his right arm. He was fully dressed in shining steel armor engraved with fantastical marine designs. Upon his chest was a great sea serpent, the coils of its body wrapped around a bright blue jewel and a long spear.

"I will not disobey an order from Crossroads. It would be as if I disobeyed the will of the High King and that I will not stand for," Alton snapped back. "I refuse to be a coward like you!"

The air in the white marble throne room was heated as if a massive fire had been lit. The gold trim around the columns and the windows glittered like flames were reflecting off the shiny decoration. The Waterborn courtiers that had been in the throne room conducting business quickly scurried away. The arguments between father and son were famous and not something to linger around and witness.

"How dare you call me a coward!" Marinus roared. He nearly knocked over his golden chair as he stomped down from the raised dais. "Not only am I Lord of the Waterborn, I am your father! You will respect me!"

Alton fought the urge to throw down his helm. He furrowed his brow. "A wise man once taught me that respect is earned, not given freely."

Marinus stormed over to Alton, his ice blue eyes ablaze. He pointed accusingly at him. "At least you listened to one thing I have said. But I will not let you go and throw yourself into a war that is not of our making. That is not our way."

"Then the Waterborn need to change or otherwise be destroyed. I will not let them be destroyed. I will not sit idly by when I can help stop the madness," Alton argued as calmly as he could.

His father threw up his hands and spun around, his ocean blue robes swirling around him. A white cape, held on by a pair of golden seashell broaches and chain, fell down his back like a waterfall. A golden circlet dotted with blue gems held back his white streaked blue hair. On any other day, Alton would have thought his father lordly in his presentation and bearing. Now, his shoulders were hunched over and his head bent in thought.

"Grandfather helped to write the very laws that Crossroads is using to call us to arms," Alton started to say.

"Your grandfather was killed by those very laws," Marinus sneered, clenching his fists tightly. "The Waterborn were foolishly led to believe that the Immortal Truth bound the nations in friendship. Well, where were our friends when the Shadowborn attacked us! Where were the fires of Argos' kin and the strong power of the Earthborn? The Immortal Truth failed your grandfather and for that, he was killed by a son of Shadow Night! The bloodline of the Immortal Truth's Shadowlord champion!"

The events that Marinus spoke of were near taboo topics of discussion amongst the Waterborn. Over a century ago, Akakios, the then Lord of the Shadowborn, led an attack that resulted in the death of Nereus. Marinus had been the first to demand that the Shadowborn pay for their crimes, putting all blame on Akakios. Despite his heinous crime against the laws of the Immortal Truth, Akakios took his punishment with dignity. Even Akakios' bastard son watched his father being executed with calm. Alton had been present too at the execution, standing in close proximity with the royal bastard. Ryder's eyes never left those of his father and great uncle Shiloh who wielded the executioner's blade.

The sight had never left Alton, constantly on the edge of his thought. How could a son show no emotion for the death of his father? One thing that he did remember was that once the blade had dropped, Kaiser, who had been at Ryder's side the entire time, leaned in to whisper something. Ryder swiftly threw his shoulder to remove Kaiser's hand from his right shoulder. The look in Ryder's eyes towards Kaiser was vicious. It was the only emotion Alton had seen in him that day. Alton could not help but be angry towards Ryder though he was not the one to have killed his grandfather. His blood was tainted. Alton was sure that Ryder could be just as terrible as his father.

He looked at his own father. It was not within him to sit idly by as his father seemed intent on doing. He was different. Though he understood his father's fear to some extent, it saddened him that the once proud man had been reduced to fear controlled recluse. Deep in his heart, he was not afraid like him.

"Father, often the truth is the last thing that we want to hear but it is what we need to hear the most. Here is my truth. I believe in the Immortal Truth. I always have. I believe in its every word and those that wrote it believed in it too. I trust in the authority in Crossroads to lead us. I will answer their call to arms and I will bring with me every Waterborn willing. Banish me if you wish for disobeying your authority but I go to save the future."

Alton put his helm on his head and did an about face. He marched out of the throne room and down the exterior steps. He was quickly joined by four others, three men and a woman dressed in light leather armor and wearing the royal seal. It was the same seal that adorned his chest plate and signified the commanding officers based on where it was placed. Upon the right shoulder were those of the army and on the left shoulder were those of the navy. All four wore their seals on their left shoulders.

"Admiral Marina. Are your ships ready to set sail? Did you locate the last of your captains?" Alton asked the woman on his immediate left.

The tall broad shouldered woman with her short blue hair tied back in a ponytail nodded. "Yes, your Highness. It took a little convincing but he is ready to sail at your command."

"He has always been a staunch supporter of my father but I knew that deep in his heart, he would do anything to make sure that the seas stay wild and free," Alton said.

"We all would, your Highness," the stocky man behind Marina stated with conviction. "We are your Admirals after all."

Marina and the three men were among the finest commanders the Waterborn had to offer. All had lived aboard a ship since early childhood and rarely set foot on dry land. Each of them came from a long line of able bodied sailors. They had been assigned to his command once he had come of age. It had taken him a while to be comfortable but now they were among his closest confidants. The differences in their ages did not matter. They trusted each other.

"Have any of you heard from the Water's Eye? How are preparations there?" Alton asked.

"Stores are being loaded as we speak. By the last report, fifty ships have assembled. Forty passenger ships with ten battle ships. Three battle ships per ten passenger ships and the last as the commanding vessel. Sir Myst may be a music master in his retirement but he has not forgotten his old sailing ways. He will command the fleet like the days of old," the weathered man to Alton's immediate right said with confidence.

Alton knew that Admiral Storm, for he preferred to be called that, spoke true. Storm and Myst had sailed together for many years. They were legends that he had looked up to as a child. Storm had in fact been his first sailing teacher.

"What of the rumors that there is a Shadow Mirror surrounding their borders? What if we cannot evacuate the innocent?" the thin white haired Admiral asked. He was a bit of a worrywart at times but was crafty when unexpected situations arose.

The question made everyone stop in their trek towards the docks of Lough. They were still within the palace walls and had a ways to go.

"Shadow Mirror? What have you heard?" Alton asked cautiously.

The thin man cleared his throat. "My contacts along the River Shadow speak of an impenetrable barrier. Even the scouts they had spoken to confirmed it. It was a Gryphon that first suggested it was a Shadow Mirror at work."

"I am glad for your contacts then, Admiral Titus," Alton thanked. He bowed his head once.

"I can only hope my own contacts can reach the Gryphons and ask for the assistance of a Sea Brigade. We could sure use their far superior sight and hearing," the stocky man beside Marina exclaimed.

"We will have them, Warren. I'm sure of it," Marina said encouragingly. She set a hand on his shoulder and nodded.

The discussion of the evacuation plan continued as the group of five made their way to the docks. Alton offered a quick bow of the head to those Waterborn people that greeted him and shouted good tidings for his voyage. It seemed as if everyone made point of wishing them well. Such a thing was normal before so many ships took to the waves. Some dared to asked what they were sailing for but Alton was not about to offer an answer. He loved his people but he could not trust everyone. It pained him to think that way but he had to protect his mission.

Alton's plan was for an evacuation fleet to assemble along the Shadowborn coast. He and his four admirals would lead smaller fleets up the network of rivers that led inland. Another fleet entirely would be left behind to protect the Waterborn territory. He could only hope that his father would come to his senses in time. Surely his mother would convince her husband to act in the best interests of their people. Alton could only pray.

He let out a deep breath once they reached the docks and saw his favorite ship. He always loved the smaller and faster river runner vessels. He had once raced Ryder during an official state visit by Kaiser. Thinking of Kaiser made him shudder. His first meeting with the shrewd man had given him a wary feeling. He still did to this day. The idea that his hate was misplaced grew on him even more. He thought again of the call to arms from Crossroads as he boarded the ship.

*****

A FRIEND GONE

Ryder slowly paced around Zoras' office in a profound silence. He paused by the black wooden chair, holding the back of it with both hands. The entire room was still in a form of organized chaos. The war table as his cousin had rightly called it had a map stretched from edge to edge. But one could scarcely tell that there was still a map on the surface. Piles of unfurled scrolls and crumbled parchment were strewn about, three leather bound tomes left open. A single inkwell sat in front of the black chair. Feather quills were scattered, their inked tips long since dried up.

"This is not my place and yet I now find myself in it," Ryder solemnly mused. He bent over the back of the chair. "I do not want to be here."

For a long time, Ryder wept. Though in later years, he had come to despise Zoras' ideas for the future, the man had been a mentor. He had been a kind if not firm teacher and one of the few who was openly at odds with Kaiser. Zoras was brave beyond measure when pushed. A man truly dedicated to what he believed in. A man who would have gladly served him and did until his last breath.

"Three. Three commanders have died for me. And how do I honor them?" Ryder fought back more tears. "By running!"

He threw the chair back and it crashed against the far wall, shattering into many pieces. He pressed his right hand to his forehead and fought back tears. Stumbling back, he hit the wall and slid down to the floor. The cold stone chilled his bones though after Zoras' death, he could no longer feel any warmth in his body. It perplexed him at first why Zoras' death affected him so strongly. Zoras was not his father nor were they close friends. But as Ryder said that to himself, he did not believe it. The man had been a different kind of friend and mentor to him all throughout his life. That made his death hurt worse.

Ryder jumped when a framed document hit the floor beside him. The glass cover shattered into a fine sparkling dust. Ryder reached over and pull the aged piece of parchment free from the mess. On the front was an official declaration dated from his father's first day on the throne.

"I hereby recognize the resignation of Zoras Rokar from the Sabers and name him the Lord's Regent of the Council," Ryder read softly. He laughed at it though he did not know why. He let the parchment fall to his lap.

He looked at the elegant curving lines of his father's signature, stroking the long dried ink. His own handwriting was crude and messy at best. It had been a constant sore point according to his mother and grandmother. Both of them had excellent penmanship. Sure, if he tried hard enough, he could write just as beautifully. But as a child, Ryder preferred combat training to scholarly studies. His father's opposite as it were. He also examined Zoras' signature, messy but still mildly elegant.

On a whim, Ryder turned the parchment over. He was surprised to find a block of handwriting. He quickly recognized it as Zoras'. At first, it appeared to be a letter. Ryder brought it close to his face to examine it before pulling back to read it.

"The matter is secret but not for long. Word has reached Lord Akakios of Master Adonis' growing obsession into the care of his bastard son. Even the Lady Mali and Commander Coba are beginning to protest. They say that based on law of blood, Kaiser has no say and has no right to keep the Shadowlord's own child away from him. But Kaiser refuses to back down in his own mysterious way. The Lord Akakios has asked me in private to remember my old ways and keep watch over the young Peredur. And I will. I promised the Shadowlord that I will protect his son from all dangers, even if it means my life. Every time I look at this document on my wall, I will remember what it says on the other side. I will keep my promise."

By reading the words, Ryder felt as if he was there when Zoras wrote them. All before him, he could see the flashes of memory. The way his father expressed his concern. The manner in which his own grandmother, who he knew at first did not approve of Aylin, fought for the protection of her only grandchild. Even his grandfather Madhuri Coba agreed with his wife and was the first to suggest that perhaps there was a darker secret at play. The flashes continued for a moment longer before finally disappearing into nothingness. He looked down at the parchment in his hands and wondered why Zoras chose the back of it to write his personal promise.

He could not say if it made sense but it was certain to him that Zoras had never forgotten his Saber oath and the promise he made to Akakios. "Once a Saber, always a Saber."

Ryder looked up when he heard the door to the office creak open. He got to his feet as Haven peeked in. He did not have to wait for long before she entered the room and closed the door behind her.

"They said that you would be here," Haven revealed in a soft voice.

Her condition could no longer be denied. The roundness of her growing belly showed more day by day it seemed. She had of course fought the suggestion to wear a dress, claiming that she will wear armor and chainmail regardless of the child growing in her belly. For once, Ryder could not talk her into it. He smiled as he remembered how his grandmother, Haven's mother and two sisters, argued with her for hours. Despite her discomfort, the sight of Haven carrying his child now gave him joy. He needed it badly so he would not be consumed by his dark thoughts.

"I was just thinking," Ryder admitted.

"You have been doing that a lot since you came back from Dusk," Haven pointed out. She came to a stop before him, picking at her fingernails with her head down.

Ryder reached forward and gently lifted her chin so that she could look at him. "I am trying to make sense of what happened and what was left behind. What the next step should be."

Haven pulled his hand down. "Nothing has made sense for a long time. But we can no longer pretend to wish we had acted sooner or differently. We cannot change the past."

He let out a deep breath. "But we can change the future. We both have something very precious to fight for."

Haven's hands drifted down to her belly. She caressed it gently. "What are you going to do?"

"I am going to make a promise that I intend to keep," Ryder grinned. He put his hands on her shoulders. "You are right. I cannot change the past but I will seize control of the future that I want to see. Now, tell those who are waiting in the hallway to come inside."

Haven chuckled softly. It amused her that Ryder had expected the gathering of people to accompany her. She called back towards the door. Myra, Onyx, Hayden, Donovan, and Jarod came inside the office. Myra came forward and embraced her grandson, kissing his forehead as a gesture of love and reassurance.

"He was a good man to the end but do not hide away in sorrow," Myra whispered to him. Ryder embraced her and mouthed a thank you.

Ryder released his grandmother and looked up to the others. "How many of those loyal to the rebellion are left in these lands?"

"By last count, though it is not confirmed, three hundred including all in this room," Jarod stated. "Kaiser's grip is tight."

"But it can be broken though we can no longer do it alone. We will have to do as our noble ancestors did and call for the Northern Alliance to help cast him down," Ryder stated.

"I am sure that they are already trying. But with Spirit Wake in play and the Shadow Mirror blocking the way, there is nothing they can do to help us," Jarod pointed out. "What are you thinking?"

Ryder thought for a long time before answering. "First, call those loyal three hundred. There is something I wish to say."

*****

The entire yard was packed full with the assembly of rebel survivors, all in some state of injury and healing. Ryder stood where he had a year ago when he had asked them to follow his battle command. Onyx was again at his side with Hayden, Donovan, and Jarod standing a short distance away to their left. Haven and Myra stood to their left, arm in arm. All were silently waiting.

"Much has happened since the rebellion first gathered together under Zoras Rokar. Much still awaits us now that he is gone. We are still fighting a war against Kaiser Adonis, a war that Zoras gave his body, heart, and soul to. He was greater than I think many of us realize. He was a Commander of Sabers and a Lords' Regent. He was a revolutionary and brave warrior. But first, he was a father and friend to us all. He believed that no matter the odds, he would see the rebellion succeed. He would see Kaiser cast down. That he promised you," Ryder spoke loud and clear. He cleared his throat. "I want to follow his example and fight with all of my being, open to all and with no secrets."

His last statement caused several people to whisper amongst themselves. Ryder could see a few bent heads and furtive glances in his direction. A part of him resisted but he knew that he had to do it. He had to tell them. He just wondered if they would believe him.

"I wish to tell you my true name," Ryder started to say. He paused, suddenly afraid. He then heard Myra whisper for him to go ahead. He swallowed hard. "My name is Peredur Adonis Coba-Silvanus. So named for the blood that flows in my veins. I am the grandson of Kaiser Adonis and I freely reveal it to you all. Judge me not for the actions of my grandfather for they are not my actions nor my beliefs."

Even Onyx had expected an uproar from the crowd but they were silent. Shockingly silent. Were they stunned from the news? He could not tell. He looked to see that Ryder was surprised from their non-reaction. The crowd then began to talk amongst themselves but their tone was positive.

"So flows the blood of Begin Anu in you. The blood of the most noble Farlander to ever walk the land. The only one greater than the Daylord," said a thin man with silver hair. Others around him nodded. "It would do us no good to cast you out just because you bear the blood of our enemy. You have given us no cause to see you as we see him."

"I also agree," Onyx declared, stepping forward to put attention on him. "What makes a great leader is first admitting the truth. That is what Lord Shiloh taught me. What makes a Shadowlord is a soul that will fight for the Shadowborn in times of trouble. Whatever authority lays within me as Crowned Prince, I name Peredur Adonis Coba-Silvanus the war leader and Shadowlord for the Shadowborn."

The cheers came slow but the noise grew into a joyous roar. Many pumped their fists into the air and shouted Ryder's name.

"For Truth!" Ryder shouted with them. "For Zoras Rokar and all who gave their lives! What we achieve in the coming days, we fight for them all! Let not their memory die! It is time that we honor them! Together and our hands raised in victory!"

DECLARATION OF WAR

Kaiser stood in the midst of his Living Map, the energy undulated around him. He stared hard at a small trio of mountains northeast of Cross. Mists rolled around the space as if to signify that it was hidden and unapproachable. Kaiser knew better. Whatever the mysterious power was around the space, Kaiser knew what was beyond it. Or he at least had a strong suspicion. He had been watching this space for a long time. The feeling he always got from it was that of resistance. At first, he associated the resistance to the mists. Usually mists on the Living Map indicated a place that was supposed to be hidden to any but those of the nation's bloodline. Kaiser would have understood it better had it not been within the lands of the Shadowborn.

One thought that occurred to him was that the space was the true Site of Ascension. Sure, there was the clearing to the north of Cross that anyone could visit. The place that everyone said was where Shadow Night Silvanus took command of the Shadowborn and was named king. A silly tale, Kaiser thought. He scratched his chin and crossed his arms. A tale to keep prying eyes and thoughts away from the true sacred space. The space he knew was now occupied by the rebels.

For a long time, he had debated an attack on the rebel base. Was it worth his effort to crush them so early in their conflict and deprive himself of the excitement? Kaiser was no fool. He knew of the rebellion as soon as the first words of the conspirators were uttered. At first, the rebellion was something to brush off. It posed no real threat to him. It was just whispered words. Even when the rebellion started gaining some real power, it was still a thing of little concern. The ideas behind it though intrigued him. He had done nothing personally to the growing group of followers. But he would later make them regret their thoughts against him. And now, Kaiser stared at the misty trio of mountains with a battle hungry stare.

He frowned as the mists started to swirl around, lighting from inside as if it was a growing thunder storm. Little bolts of lightning spread out of the tiny clouds in increasing frequency. The center then lit up with a glaring white light. Kaiser watched as a thin stream of what appeared to be smoke rise up from the bright center. It climbed up until it reached his height, pausing for a moment before rising up four more inches. A snarl formed on his face. Something or someone was trying to use his Living Map from beyond. There was only one other person who could and who shared his blood.

Ryder appeared before him, dressed in some of the finest armor that Kaiser had ever seen. Armor that was reserved for those of the highest rank on the battlefield. It then occurred to him that the black and silver armor resembled that of Shadow Night. He knew that it was not the exact same set for the long dead man was buried in his war regalia. Also, a different seal was emblazoned on the front of the chest plate. It was an eclipse with the moon in front and the sun in back. Two swords were crossed beneath it.

"So you have discovered the uses of our shared blood. I commend your intellect though frown upon your lateness of it," Kaiser glowered. "It seems I have taught you perhaps a little too well."

The Spirit like Ryder stared back at Kaiser with a fearsome expression. He held his shoulders back. His posture spoke of great physical power and a commanding presence. A silver glow surrounded him, casting brightness over his entire body. Kaiser's eyes drifted from Ryder's face down towards the floor before moving back up. It had never bothered him before but now he hated the fact that Ryder was taller. His grandson was physically bigger than him but he could never have the same deep intellect.

It felt like a painfully long time before Ryder spoke. "Or that I know you better than you think."

"One of the few that I have left alive that can claim that and, quite possibly, actually mean it. Consider yourself lucky," Kaiser replied.

Astral projection was difficult to maintain for very long, a fact that Kaiser knew well. He did not particularly like it himself.

He described the sensation of the technique to be like ripping his soul from his body. He studied Ryder for the telltale signs of strain. His eyes swept up and down in the span of a heartbeat. Nothing. He clenched his jaw and bit the inside of his cheek. A slow trickle of salty blood filled his mouth.

"I suppose that you have come here in your strange new finery to beg for a retreat or to accost me for killing dear Zoras. I never did like him much. He was too bold and blindly dedicated to the false ideal of the Immortal Truth," Kaiser said in a smart mouthed tone. He spat out the small mouthful of blood. It hit the map within inches of Ryder's feet. The Living Map sizzled and sparked from the contact, causing Kaiser to chuckle deeply. "Do not anger me too much. My blood has a nasty effect on the Living Map and thus on the world."

Ryder then snarled and stamped on the bloody spot. As soon as his foot made contact, there was a bright and loud explosion. He swung his foot from side to side, pressing down hard before drawing back. "Then my blood will do the opposite."

The statement made Kaiser laugh. It was an impossible notion for so many reasons. But he was going to allow his grandson the delusion. As soon as that thought came to him, he hesitated. Was there something that he did not know? The very idea made him angry. He only wished that Ryder's physical being was before him so that he could tear the desired answers free. He snarled, flashing his white teeth.

"Why are you here and not with those traitors you call friends preparing to take Cross by force?" Kaiser snapped. He dug his fingernails in the muscle of his upper arms.

"The only traitor I see is standing before me," Ryder replied. His voice remained calm and even keeled.

"Are you still harping on the worthless idea that the Immortal Truth is the order of the world? That because I blaspheme its name, I am considered a traitor?" Kaiser asked in rapid fire fashion.

"The Immortal Truth is more than can be explained and I will not waste my time doing so on someone who will not listen. Reason and good sense do not exist for people like you. People who refuse to believe in anything but their own arrogance," Ryder countered harshly. He clenched his fists tightly.

The newfound confidence, if it could be called that, perplexed Kaiser to a small degree. He had seen Ryder accuse him of such before but there was something in his manner that was different. There was an air of command about his grandson that demanded respect not as a highly skilled foe but as an equal on the playing field. As a leader.

"The Immortal Truth was broken from the start and I made sure of that. You will never begin to understand how or why. As it seems that I cannot break the world of its belief, I will just settle with breaking the world of its very essence!"

"The Covenant of Spirits cannot be broken by an act of war and the deaths of thousands of true souls," Ryder interrupted. He pointed at Kaiser. "Neither can the Immortal Truth. So long as there is a heart that believes in its words, it will live forever."

Kaiser roared out loud with laughter. He bent over, holding his stomach. He then stood up straight after several minutes and wiped a tear from his eye. "Are you daft? Anything and everything can be broken if one knows the way. A tree can be ripped from the ground. A river diverted. A mountain torn down by a quake of the ground that holds it up. I can do all of those things. Can you?"

Ryder's brow furrowed. "I do not need to nor do I want to for I love the world and do not seek to destroy it."

"Then why fight me? Did you ever once think that your resistance and that of the rebels is doing more damage than healing? No, it does not look like you have," Kaiser mocked. He then dug a knife from his belt and set the blade over his right palm. "With the blood from this hand, I can heal the world of all its hurts." He switched the blade over and rested it over his open left palm. "With this hand, I can destroy it."

"Go ahead. Do as you have promised all these years and destroy the world. Leave nothing left but ash and memory. Just like the Darklands."

"Now hold on a minute. The destruction of the Darklands was not my doing. I was not the one who set the fire and burned everything in sight. I did not raise the Mirror that seal it from the rest of the world. That was the Daylord's doing," Kaiser waved the blade around in a twisting motion.

"And yet you feel inspired to follow the example. Well, I will not stand for it. We may share blood but you will always be my enemy and I will always be yours. So long as you seek to cause chaos and threaten the Immortal Truth, I will be here to oppose you. I, Peredur Adonis Coba-Silvanus..."

Kaiser roared. The Living Map was set ablaze and the fires raged around the both of them. They locked eyes and stared each other down. No one was going to yield.

"You have forsaken the name of Adonis by forsaking me!" Kaiser shouted with rage.

"No. I have not forsaken the name of Adonis and I never will. People must know it for what it used to be: that of Begin Anu's son. By right of birth, I claim it and I shout it to the world. By that name, I declare war upon the enemy of Truth and thus forth dedicate my life to destroying you. You are nothing to me but my foe."

Kaiser twisted his face into an expression of disbelief and confusion. He could barely form a dark enough insult to shake his grandson. He was honestly stunned for the first time in a very long time. "And just who do you think you are?"

Ryder smirked as his astral form began to fade into the illusion of fire. "I am the Shadowlord."

*****

ECHO OF A LOST TIME

He fell back, his ever reliable sword knocked too far from his reach. He looked up at the massive dark form that had blazing red eyes. It was a Demon beast too terrible to describe and whose name that he would never remember. The Demon cackled with delight as it loomed over him. It wiggled the talons on its right hand while gripping a wicked looking blade in its left. The cackle turned into a vicious snarl following by an intake of breath. He watched as the Demon raised its sword high above its head. He shut his eyes, unable to see his death coming.

A rush of powerful energy flattened him to the ground. At first, he thought it was his being passing into the Spirit World. He sniffed. No, he could still smell the burning battlefield and the heavy stench of blood. He listened carefully and realized that he could still hear the sounds of battles. Yet, they were not as loud as before. It was if they were slowing down or stopping altogether. He gripped the ground, feeling the wet blood soaked dirt. Gathering his courage, he opened his eyes.

Before him stood a glowing man in a powerful stance. The newcomer had a massive battle sword raised up before him, blocking the Demon's blade. The newcomer's cloak rippled and undulated from the energy's windfall. It slowly settled down his back as the brightness dissipated.

"Who are you to raise your weapon against me and prevent me from killing my prey?!" the Demon demanded in a deep masculine voice. He pushed forward to no avail.

The newcomer was not budging. It was rather shocking considering that the Demon was twice as big. The Demon tried again in rapid succession. Still, he was denied. The Demon roared and spat, saliva spraying from his fanged jaws. It was clear that he was not going to back down despite his failures to move the deceptively strong newcomer. He pressed forward with all of his weight. He snarled in his tongue. There was a pause and a look of confusion crossed his face.

"You will do no such thing," the newcomer finally spoke.

The Demon was prepared to counter but slowly realized something. The newcomer held his battles word with only his right hand. His left hand was pressed against his chest. He looked down in horror. How? Who was this strange man? How could he know? There was no one left alive that knew of the ancient power or was capable of using it. Was this newcomer some sort of a deluded fool? The Demon began to lose all sense of battle fury, a powerful feeling of doom overwhelming his body.

The newcomer then shouted some strange words in a booming voice. Immediately, a blast of energy tore the Demon to shreds, his body disappearing in the white light. The resulting shockwave rippled across the battlefield with a violent quake.

"Who are you?" the man on the ground asked.

"My name is Bane Arlis and I seek the one called Shadow Night Silvanus. Are you he?" the newcomer asked, looking over his right shoulder.

"I am," Shadow Night said as he got to his feet. He had no clue why a man as powerful as Bane would be looking for him. Was he an assassin hired by the Demons to kill him? He wished he had his sword.

Bane turned around and looked towards the left. He raised his hand and Shadow Night's blade slammed into his palm. Bane then flipped the weapon around to offer towards Shadow Night hilt first. "It seems you have a Demon problem."

The statement made Shadow Night laugh. The two of them stood on a small hill top surrounded by a huge crowd of soldiers and Demons too stunned to move or speak. Of course, he had a Demon problem. He had been fighting them and the might of the Darklands for so long that he could not think of a time without them being a problem. He laughed again.

"Perhaps I can help you," Bane offered.

Shadow Night gripped his sword and took a step forward. He felt intimidated by Bane. He took in a deep breath and released it slowly. "Then let's finish it, Bane Arlis, and I will help you with whatever it is you need." He stepped forward again until Bane put a hand on his shoulder to stop him.

"There is no need to sacrifice more of your people's lives. They are weary and not long for this world if they continue to fight," Bane said with an air of command.

Shadow Night did not need Bane to verbalize it. He stepped back to give him a wide space. He watched as Bane uttered more strange words, his voice increasing in volume. Bane then flipped his sword around and stabbed it in the ground. A blinding flash of white light exploded.

*****

Bane broke through the surface of the water, throwing his head back. His brown hair slapped back against his neck as his bangs clung to his forehead. He planted his feet on the soft underwater river bed to avoid being taken by the current. There was really no reason for it as the small cove he had chosen was well protected. He stood firm with only the top half of his body exposed to the air. He ran his hands over his head, slicking his hair back. The water dripped down his lean muscled body.

He wondered why the memory of his first meeting with Shadow Night had come to him while he was swimming. It seemed that within the last few days, it visited him with increasing frequency. It never varied in what was shown to him. Each time his mind cleared from it, he felt an increasingly stronger sense of coming together. He was not sure how he could explain it to someone like Gyr or Charon. In fact, he was not sure if he should even discuss it with them at all. Whatever was going on involved people and power more ancient than their young minds could understand. He was having a hard enough time understanding the purpose of the memory.

One thing he did notice with the arrival of the memory was that he was feeling reinvigorated. More awake and aware than he had been in a long time. He set his hands on his hips and looked away from the shore. The water slowly flowed around him, oblivious to his internal conflict. The twittering song of two cardinals brought him out of his trance. He looked up to see the red feathered birds in the branches above his head.

"Your song reminds me of things I once thought long forgotten. Do you feel it too?" Bane asked them.

The cardinals paused in their chirping and looked at him inquisitively. They tweeted to each other, pausing to study Bane. With a flutter of motion, they took flight and disappeared into a tangle of distant limbs.

"What is it that I feel?" Bane asked as he put his left hand over his heart.

His thoughts then drifted to the name that Gyr had told him: Ryder Coba. The Gryphon did not seemed so taken with him as he had described of his kin. He had said that Proto Avis, among many, thought Ryder to be Shadow Night's spiritual heir and was like his famous ancestor in many ways. Gyr readily described all of the living Silvanus family members when asked. Bane chuckled as he thought of how Gyr reacted to his statement that the young Onyx was more like Shadow Night. He had quickly told the Gryphon that Shadow Night never ran away from his people. That was the last they had spoken of the matter.

Bane got out of the water and lay back on the grass to dry his soaked pants in the sun. He let out a deep breath as he put his hands behind his head. He closed his eyes and savored the warmth of the sunlight beaming down on him. In the distance, he could hear the pair of cardinals singing again. He whistled softly along with them. For a time, his mind was clear and at peace.

It would not be that way for very long. Memories from all across his lifetime flashed in his mind. Some of them, he was glad to see again. Others, he wished had stayed buried. A moment like this was not the first time in his life that his age bothered him. The snap of a twig caused him to look quickly to the right.

"I used to come here when the pressures of my position became too overwhelming. The waters help to calm the mind," Chane said as he stepped over a small patch of white flowers. He looked back and settled down on a stone seat.

"The waters do little to a mind as old as mine," Bane commented as he closed his eyes. "It is always awake and aware of the world."

Chane chuckled softly. "I did not think so." He looked about once he heard the singing cardinals. "What do you think they are singing about?"

"They say that I am not human like the people from around here. They are right. I am not a Mortal human," Bane stated. "I am of Farlander blood if the world still chooses to remember."

It was a long time before Chane replied. "Your legend has not been forgotten. Not by me and I am sure not by those your deeds have touched."

Bane opened his eyes. "So that is what I am now? A legend? A tale meant for the fireside?"

"Surely you knew that already. Time cannot diminish the great works you have done," Chane exclaimed.

He did not have the heart to tell the Mortal man that he had done some terrible things too. What kind of king abandons the land that crowned him? What kind of hero doesn't come when he

needed most? He clenched his jaw and bit the inside of his cheek.
A small trickle of blood coated the inside of his mouth. He
swallowed hard. He shot up to his feet in the blink of an eye,
surprising Chane with his sudden movement. He walked over
towards the tree branch who he had hung his tunic shirt. He
paused with his hand on the branch.

"Time may diminish memory but it can never get rid of it.
The length of my life has taught me that. What has time taught
you?" Bane asked before he pulled on his shirt.

"To never stop believing in the good of the world no matter
how dark it becomes. It doesn't take an Immortal god to know
when someone's heart is troubled by heavy thoughts. Though I do
not know what troubles you, I will tell you something that my
father told me and his father before him. Time may be a destroyer
but it is also a healer. There is always hope."

Bane paused just as he finished pulling on his boots. He
spoke in a voice too low for Chane to hear. "Yes. There will always
be hope." He smiled.

*****

REFLECTIONS

Aday sat on his rear, arms wrapped around his legs. He rocked back and forth as he chewed on a thumbnail. His hair was a tangled mess. He was covered in dirt and grime with blood staining the right side of his face. The blood had come from a cut above his eye. He snorted but mucus still dribbled from his nose. He mumbled to himself in unintelligible words.

"Shut up," grumbled Axum. He swiftly kicked at Aday's back, knocking him over. Aday whimpered as he laid sprawled out on the dirt floor of the cave. "I said shut up. Should I kick you again?"

Aday shook his head no. He managed to crawl over to the nearby wall and pressed his back against it. He resumed the same position he had before only this time, he kept silent. A tremor rolled through his body every few seconds. He watched as Axum paced just beyond the sunlight coming in from the cave opening. His eyes followed the Demon's every move. He shuddered and squinted his eyes every time Axum drew close.

"I tire of this waiting game. Why should I have to wait to attack Sawn? I could take the city now," Axum argued out loud. He crossed his arms tightly. "What say you?"

He did not speak for fear of Axum striking him again. He had come to learn that to speak, even when spoken to, meant pain regardless of what was said or done. Aday swallowed hard when he heard a sharp intake of breath.

Axum was at his side in a heartbeat, grasping Aday's chin

and forcing him to look in his eyes. "I asked a question. I expect an answer," the Demon hissed.

"Daylord," Aday managed to say, his mouth restricted by Axum's tight hold. He fell over when Axum released him. He rubbed his chin and jaw. "Because the Daylord is there."

Axum scoffed. "He may have scared you off but he does not scare me." He tapped his foot. "The Daylord is not invincible. I know that and Kaiser knows that."

Aday had a hard time believing that the Daylord was not invincible. He remembered how his father had described first meeting Bane on the battlefield. The explosive power he wielded. His mind felt clearer as he thought about his memories of Bane. His first one stood out the most: when he met his father's new friend. Bane was unlike any Shadowborn or Spiritborn he had ever known. Once he had displayed his power on the battlefield, the Demons went into immediate retreat. Aday remembered his father describing how Bane knew what a Shadow Mirror was and how to raise it. There were so many wonders about Bane that Aday's mind threatened to explode. He took a deep breath and his mind calmed.

While Axum continued to stare out of the cave, Aday was left to peacefully mull over his first memory of Bane. His father had brought Bane to a meeting of the Lords of the Northern Alliance just after the end of the great battle. Everyone was bruised and battered. Even Ogon the Dragonlord was breathing heavily. Aday thought about first spying his father approaching with the stranger at his side. His father had been proud to introduce Bane to the other Lords and they were gracious to receive him. Bane and his actions had been awe inspiring for no one else, even with their forces combined, thought that they would live to see the dawn. Even in that time, Aday saw Bane as a mythical hero. To him, he was invincible.

It made him wonder how or why Axum was not afraid of Bane. Surely, word of Bane's power bringing down the might of the Darklands would have frightened him. It frightened Aday. He shivered at the thought.

"The sun is hot. You cannot be cold," Axum pointed out.

Aday gulped and stilled his body. The Demon had not expressed the thought out of concern. He must have known what Aday was thinking. Was Axum expecting him to speak and comment? Aday clenched his jaw to fight the urge to reply.

"Good," Axum snickered.

Aday was grateful when Axum closed his eyes. He knew that this was how Axum liked to study the unseen forces of their surroundings. Sight can be deceived, he had always said, and Aday never forgot it. And yet, whenever Aday had a chance to look upon his sons, his sight made his mind clearer and less unstable. Charon looked so much like him and yet, he had his mother's softness in his features. In the back of his mind, Aday heard Kaiser's voice screaming his dark command and suddenly, his mind erupted into turmoil. He grabbed his head in response.

"I often wonder what it would be like to face Bane in battle. How epic of a match that would be," Axum mused. He appeared oblivious to Aday's condition. "We have both grown stronger since the days of the Second Dominion War. Where I have always been who I am, he has not. He was a simple farmer, a man of no notoriety. He tended his fields, minded the livestock, and went home to his family at the setting of the sun. This was all he was before he earned the title of Daylord and King. King? How foolish of the Spiritborn lords to name such a man as king. They do not know him. None of them do. Not even your idiot father."

Aday stiffened. Even his erratic mind froze. He could not decide whether to reply or not. Thankfully, Axum turned away from his train of thought and focused on a possible fight against Bane. He listened as Axum waxed and waned about their various talents and shortcomings, focusing more on Bane's than his own. Some of the statements, Aday agreed with but he could not believe that Bane had been broken of his old Spirit. In fact, he refused to believe it.

A burst of red and gold fire exploded within the sunlight coming through the cave opening. Axum stepped back and shielded his eyes from the brightness. Aday pressed his face into his knees and covered his head.

"My Lord," Axum said as he dropped to his knees and pressed his forehead to the ground.

Kaiser frowned as he stood in the flames with arms crossed. A vein throbbed on the left side of his forehead. He clenched his jaw so tightly that it appeared ready to break. He let out a hiss that brought Axum slowly to his feet. He jerked his head towards Aday. At the silent command, Axum strode over to Aday, grabbed him by the shoulder, and pulled him to his feet. He dragged him back over to stand before Kaiser. Aday gulped as he looked as Kaiser's less than pleased expression. This was not good.

"To what do we owe the pleasure of your presence?" Axum asked.

Kaiser snorted and Axum stiffened. "A new development is vexing me in a manner I did not expect."

This was definitely not good. Aday swallowed hard, unable to look away from Kaiser's face no matter how much he wanted to. All color had disappeared from his skin. He was terrified of the powerful Shadowborn. He had seen Kaiser commit acts so dark and heinous that the very memory of them caused great fear in him. He could not help but shiver in terror from the inside out. His mind began to split again as a result and all sense of sanity left him. He began to move his lips in a silent conversation. Every so often, his left eye twitched.

"But I will overcome it in time. I always do," Kaiser said with a sigh. He briefly looked towards the low stone ceiling before returning his gaze to Axum. "But what do I do with you? Do not think that distance keeps me from hearing of your frustration."

"I do not doubt your plan. I only eagerly await the fight so that I may please you," Axum stammered to say.

"Stop with the flattery for I can see right through it. I know your history and of every secret that you pretend to hide. Do not think to use my orders to your advantage and attain glory for yourself or for your fellow Demons," Kaiser viciously snarled. He dropped his arms and clenched his fists. The flames around him grew hotter and reached out towards the Demon. "I see all."

Aday dropped to the ground, perched on his feet with arms wrapped around his legs. He rocked back and forth and chewed on a thumbnail. "He sees all. Master sees all. Must please Master."

"See?" Kaiser pointed out, gesturing towards Aday. "He gets the idea."

Axum clenched his jaw and stiffened his posture as Kaiser slowly approached. Kaiser walked with his hands behind his back until he had his face inches from Axum's. He scoffed. All of a sudden, Kaiser gripped Axum's throat so tightly that the Demon's face turned bone white from lack of blood. Axum's eyes bulged, transforming into a blood red color while his fangs flashed. His skin bubbled in rippling waves. Kaiser snarled. The blackened Spirit Marks on his right hand glowed silver. The silver color extended over Axum's swollen blood vessels.

"I may not have brought you to this world like I did Rache but I can take you from it in the blink of an eye! Forget your past as a witless wandering fool! Forget everything you know! I need you to be at your best and I need you to keep Bane from going north!" Kaiser roared. He then ripped his hand back. "At all costs."

Aday's frantic mumbling faded into a whisper while Axum coughed and spat out blood. Kaiser sneered at them both before turning around and disappearing into the flames. Soon, the fire that had brought him disappeared as well. Axum fell down beside Aday, rubbing his throat and coughing hard.

"You know the legends of the north. Why should I keep Bane away from there?" Axum asked honestly.

It surprised Aday enough to clear his mind to think for a

short moment. Axum had never spoken to him in such a confused tone. Of course, there was only one true reason Kaiser would not want Bane to come north. Someone powerful had claimed the title of Shadowlord. Someone with a true claim. Aday knew that it was not him and could never be him. Even if he was who and what he used to be, he still believed that he could never be a Shadowlord like his father had been. He thought of the various members of the Silvanus bloodline, focusing on those still living. For a split second, he worried about his two sons but quickly dismissed them. Kaiser's worry was about Bane going north. There were two sons of his younger brother Sin's line. Based on what he knew, it had to be the elder of the two. Before his mind wandered back into the minefield of insanity, Aday promised to help Bane return north in any way that he could help. He had to somehow save the Silvanus bloodline from extinction.

*****

CHAINS OF DARKNESS

Gyr flapped his wings twice to regain height as he soared over the tree tops. He liked the feeling of the sun on his feathers and twitched his leonine tail with delight. The air rippled and rolled across his wings. Though he preferred pleasure flights over grasslands and in the mountains, the forest beneath him provided a plethora of sights, smells, and sounds. He was supposed to be studying the forests around Sawn for any sign of danger. He had gladly taken Bane's order to heart and soared over the northern and eastern reaches of the territory surrounding Sawn. Though he had Bane's order, he made a point of looking for the ship that Ferran, Charon's newly discovered brother, was returning on.

Charon had been desperate to get to know Ferran and sent Gyr out constantly to search the river when Ferran was on a trading trip. The much younger man was fearful of Charon though Gyr did not have the heart to reveal that observation. It did not help that Bane did little to help the two brothers. In fact, Bane seemed distant and kept away from Sawn for long stretches of time. Gyr shook his head. He let out a deep breath and flapped his wings again.

In the distance, he spotted the river runner ship that he had seen Ferran hastily board over a month ago. Gyr had stopped counting the days a week in. As a Gryphon, he recognized the importance of ships but his kind did not use them. Why sail on a ship when one could fly? He loved flying and the feel of the air passing over his body. He shifted his weight towards the right and banked westward. His path went right over the top of the ship's mast, eliciting a few cheers and greetings. The sailors of Sawn had gotten used to seeing him in the skies. They knew of his powerful senses and welcomed his protection.

He continued his turn, heading back towards Sawn. He wanted to pass the northern road just one more time before landing to rest his wings. The city quickly passed beneath him as he soared north. Flapping his wings in quick succession, Gyr moved higher above the trees as the buildings disappeared in the distance. He took the chance to ride the crests and troughs. It was a simple flight exercise meant to prepare for flying during rough weather. He went through the warm ups, imagining each twist and turn of the air to be a vicious current. He started to whistle to himself a Gryphon song in praise of the sky. He continued to dance on the air currents, rising higher and flying further away.

Gyr lost himself in the soothing currents, happily swinging back and forth with the slightest of wing flaps. In his opinion, this was the most enjoyable flight he had had in ages. It certainly was the best one he had experienced in the Southlands. He hummed as he crossed into a slow moving air stream.

A cold shiver passed through his body and Gyr immediately flared his wings to slow down his speed. He fanned his rump feathers. He looked about quickly, looking for the source of the unnatural chill. Gyr knew the air and how it functioned. What he felt was not normal. His eyes darted back and forth as he hovered in the air. They narrowed as he spotted a wave of dark forms slowly creeping through the woods. The misty creatures kept to the shadows, halting only when the sun broke through the canopy. The road turned towards the east and blocked their way. It was too bright and open to cross. Gyr could tell that the creatures seemed uncertain but he started to suspect that it wasn't the sunlight they feared. He watched as all of the strange creatures halted at once. It was as if they had reached the end of invisible chains for Gyr saw a shudder rippled from the front to the back of the crowd.

He immediately turned tail and sped back to Sawn as fast as his wings could carry him. Being a Falcon Gryphon, Gyr was as fast as the wind but even then, he felt that he was not going fast enough. He cursed himself for his absentminded flight of leisure when he had orders to follow. The muscles in his body from beak to tail began to burn and protest with growing throbs of pain. Why hadn't he stretched properly? That was not the least of his worries. What were those dark misty creatures that he saw?

Gyr soared into Sawn and quickly landed with a skidding stop in the middle of the market square. He knocked over a stall as he clumsily folded his wings. He muttered an apology before bouncing off towards Chane's house. He could still hear the angry stall owner shouting at him. When he did reached Chane's house, the old man was already outside talking to none other than Bane.

"You mean to tell me that those tablets in Arken are glowing?" Chane asked in a low voice, clearly not wanting to be heard by prying ears.

"Such are the rumors in the southern reaches of this land. To be sure of this, I concealed myself and snuck into the Arken Vault of Truth. Now the tablets may not be the originals but they still reacted to my presence so I had to leave quickly. But the runes were glowing. The Lord Mayor of Arken was heard to have stated that due to the changes in the Immortal Truth tablets, he was going to organize a team of Truth acolytes to bring word to the other cities in the Southlands." Bane paused to think deeply for a moment. He turned away, muttering to himself.

Chane took a cautious step forward and whispered in a nearly inaudible voice. "Does this have to do with the mad Shadowborn? The Gryphon Gyr? Charon and his half-brother?"

"So they are half-brothers. I thought so myself when I saw Ferran and then Charon. The resemblance is too uncanny. It is like looking upon Sin and Sage all over again." Bane stopped and then gestured towards Gyr with his eyes.

"Well you are in a right state," Chane commented with a jovial smile once he looked up.

Bane did not share his mirth and looked Gyr up and down. "Gryphon ears are sharp so I am certain you heard what I just said. I trust that you keep what you heard to yourself. Now, what did you see on your flight?"

Gyr was glad to see Bane as he did not think Chane capable of facing the enemy that was marching towards the city. Pushing the overheard conversation out of his mind for the time being, he squared his shoulders and puffed out his chest. "I saw something that gave me a frightful chill. It followed a wave of shadowy creatures that I have never seen before. Well not since I entered the Southlands."

Chane looked between Gyr and Bane with utter confusion. He did not know the Gryphon tongue but he could at least tell that Gyr was concerned about something. He looked to Bane for an answer. "Do you understand what he is saying? Is my city in danger?"

"You should not speak in your native tongue in front of the Mayor if what you say means danger to Sawn," Bane admonished Gyr in the Gryphon tongue before turning to Chane. He quickly translated Gyr's words into the common tongue.

Chane gulped but kept his cool. "What should I do? My

people have never faced such foes before."

Both Chane and Gyr stared at Bane, watching as he started off towards the north and the direction of the coming threat. "I do not have authority over your people but if you wish, I can help them prepare and fight. If you wish for orders, have Charon meet the coming ship at the docks in your place. The harbor master should be able to assist him. In the meantime, Gyr can assist your officers to gather all able bodied men and women."

"Women? You expect the women to fight too?" Chane blurted out. He shivered when Bane glared back at him.

"I expect them and any man or woman to contribute to the protection of this city whether it be in combat or to deal with the wounded. Defense of Sawn will be a collective effort. Does the city have a defense plan?" Bane said in a tone that Gyr thought was rather harsh.

"For repelling Mortal foes, not Immortal foes," Chane replied. He leaned away from Bane, seeing a glimpse of his fearsome side. Even Gyr stepped to his side and put a wing protectively around him.

Bane turned his back to them in order to think in a degree of privacy and silence. He then turned back around after several minutes. "I do not think this attack will occur soon but it will happen. The manner of these creatures that Gyr described to me tell me that their greater power comes from darkness where they cannot be unmasked. Sunlight will be our protector for now and firelight will be our guardian later. Activate your defense plan and secure what you must. We have precious little time to prepare and I fear that their terrible master is on the move."

*****

Bane stood with his arms crossed and his back to the northern gate of the city. He was dressed in his leather cuirass, pauldrons, bracers, and boots. It was the only armor he had on. He also had his two handed battle sword strapped across his back. In comparison to the collection of steel armored soldiers that had assembled before him, he did not appear to be physically well protected. But no one could doubt his powerful presence. The Mortal soldiers all knew that Bane had abilities beyond wielding a sword in battle.

"I have told you of your foe and of the creature that commands them. Those of you that are standing here before me will be on the frontlines under my command. Do not fault your kin for choosing not to stand with you for I have asked a great deal. You are Mortals facing Immortals. However what manner of creature you are preparing to fight is no true Immortal like myself or those of the Northlands. They are dark Spirits of little power but great numbers." Bane pulled out his sword in the blink of an eye and held it before the crowd so that they could see its full length. He also showed them that he was strong enough to hold it with only his right hand. "Take out your weapon of choice."

The group of one hundred and twenty soldiers pulled out an assortment of weapons ranging from swords to pole axes. They stood at attention, waiting for Bane's next instruction.

"You must strike before they can touch you. Their touch will freeze wherever they make contact. The longer they have hold of you, the deeper the chill of their touch. Let them hold on long enough, you will find yourself looking upon the doors to the Spirit World. Should you find yourself with a dark Spirit at your head or heart, consider your life forfeit in that instant. That is reality for Mortals and Immortals. I will do what I can to protect you from the Spirits but I cannot stop death. The best way I can protect you is to kill their commander. That is a foe best left for me. Do not engage him for any reason unless it means to save the life of an innocent." Bane then stabbed his sword forward. "To dispatch a dark Spirit, strike the chest or the head. That is where they are most corporeal. Do note that it will not kill them. It will just send them back to the Spirit World where they can be summoned again. Questions?"

A red bearded man slowly put his left hand in the air. Bane nodded, inviting him to speak. "What are Dark Spirits?"

Bane lowered his sword until the tip touched the ground at his feet. He let out a deep breath. "Remnants of the Spirit of Destruction from the days of Terra's birth. They exist within the Spiral of the Spirit World. Under the Covenant of Spirits, our world was separated from that of the Spirits and thus the boundaries were drawn and the Spiral created. The Spiral's purpose was to contain the Spirit of Destruction and all he has touched. Here in the Southlands, the story is called Chains of Darkness."

Several of the assembled soldiers murmured amongst each other in low and quick voices. It took them a few minutes to collect themselves and return their attention to Bane.

"Demons are the race created by the Spirit of Destruction. Mortals were made by the Spirit of Creation. Though Immortality was gifted to the Farlanders and races of the Northlands from the Spirit of Time, you have your own gifts and powers. They have helped your kind endure all of these many years. Now, we all come from the same place but Mortals were chosen to walk first on Terra.

Be proud of your vitality and bright strength. Do not let the power of others deter you from living your life to the fullest. You are important. You are special. I am honored to be standing here before you as your teacher, your commander, and your friend. I believe in you and together we will win the night!"

Bane directed the crowd through a series of combat stances and attacks, focusing on building their confidence more than anything else. He walked amongst them, correcting posture and providing a strong and dependable presence. When asked, Bane gladly demonstrated the maneuvers again.

"What can we expect from these Dark Spirits? How do they move?" the same red bearded man asked as Bane assisted him with a particularly rigorous finishing move.

"Imagine facing a pack of rabid dogs, starving and desperate for their next meal. A single dog is easy to dispatch with a single stroke but ten? Twenty? The strength of the Dark Spirits is in their numbers. They are fast but not especially so. You can defeat them we work together."

He knew that they were nervous but tried desperately not to show it. They were good and honest souls with brave intentions. He knew that he could count on this group to fight with all of their beings despite their supernatural opponent. He thought about giving them an unofficial name, managing a smile. The smile did not carry over into his physical expression for he remained fierce and imposing.

*****

To the side of the open square where Bane was training the soldiers, Chane stood watching with a degree of wonder and pride. He was in awe of Bane's knowledge and sheer courage but he was more impressed by his own people's courage. Here were Mortal men facing creatures that had crawled out of their nightmares or so he told himself. He certainly was afraid. He thought that it was fortunate that Bane was in Sawn and even the noble Gryphon Gyr. Gyr had proven a valuable resource with his far reaching sight and tracking ability.

Still one thing bothered him about the whole affair. There had been many times before when Sawn was beset by terror and the presence of the mighty Daylord could have been useful. Most recently was the attack from the mad Immortal, for it had to have been an Immortal, fifteen years ago that took the life of young Ferran's mother. Even then, his people cried out for help for many days and nights until something unseen drove the Immortal away. Chane was not certain then if it had been Bane for if it had been him, why did he not show himself? Why has he kept himself hidden, keeping to the wilds? He had become the living legend that was more legend than living. Chane started to believe that Bane's presence was not mere coincidence and neither was that of the advancing supernatural army. What had called Bane to Sawn?

BROTHERS

Charon sat upon a wooden barrel, hands on his knees and heels bouncing together. He had tied back his raven hair into a ponytail that had fallen loose. Strands of hair dangled down his forehead. He brushed them away and sat up straight. He was not feeling very patient as he had already been waiting several hours for Ferran to finish with the harbor master. He did not think that cargo sorting on a ship took this long. It was not like spices, bales of spun cotton, bolts of silk, or whatever mysterious things were stored in the hull were important enough to warrant this kind of attention. Charon was glad that he did not work in the trade industry. It was infinitely boring and tedious.

He jumped off the barrel, feet hitting the hard street with a sting. He harrumphed but did not have long to consider his soreness when he saw Ferran walking away. Charon jogged after him to catch up.

"How was the trip?" Charon asked in polite conversation.

"You were watching the harbormaster and I. Certainly one of your sensibilities could have heard all that transpired," Ferran curtly replied. He did not look at Charon as he packed up his leather folder.

"There is no need to be rude. I was just trying to make polite conversation," Charon retorted. He held his hands up in the air as Ferran stomped past him. "I want us to be friends."

Ferran whirled around and looked at Charon with an annoyed if somewhat pained expression. "Well you have been trying for weeks and it is not working. Why don't you just leave me alone? I think that I have made it clear that I do not want to get to know my long lost brother."

Charon felt hurt and watched as Ferran walked away. He clenched his fists tightly. "Why?"

Ferran halted in his tracks and slowly turned around. "Do you ever give up? Like I have said, you have been trying for weeks to no positive result. And I am doing just fine without a brother. I am sure that you were doing just fine too not knowing I existed."

"If you would bother to talk to me for more than a few minutes, you would learn that my life was quite empty before I met Gyr. Now, I am discovering things about myself that I never knew about."

"Good. You do not need my help if you have the Gryphon," Ferran snapped before turning back around. He took a few steps forward before Charon grabbed him by the arm. He quickly ripped his arm free and snarled at Charon. "Stay away from me. Do not follow me. Do not try to talk to me again."

"Why?" Charon demanded with more force than he had intended. He watched as Ferran stared back at him with an expression of hurt in his eyes.

"Because you look like him! You look like the man that killed my mother! Now leave me alone!" Ferran shouted. He stomped off down a small side street and disappeared from view.

Charon stood as if he had been slapped in the face. He did not notice the swarthy harbormaster coming up behind him until he felt a hand on his shoulder. He glanced back towards the man.

"He hasn't been right since his mother died though he tries to hide it. Give it time. I'm sure he will come around and see the truth," the man stated with a warm fatherly tone.

"You believe that he is my brother?" Charon asked.

"It's not every day that you run into someone that looks just like you," the harbormaster replied. He bent down to pick up a heavy coil of rope. He whistled as he walked back towards the River Runner ship.

Charon could not help but feel upset that Ferran had rebuked him. He was very excited at the idea of having a brother. Why wasn't Ferran just as excited as him? Was it because he looked like their father like Ferran had said? Somehow that did not seem right to him. He harrumphed and followed the direction that Ferran had just gone. It was quickly apparent that he had no idea where he was going as he turned into a dead end alley. He startled just as a scrawny gray cat did. The cat jumped up to the high fence, hissed at him, and then jumped down the other side out of view. He let out a deep breath and turned back around.

Sawn was deceptively big for a river town as buildings were laid out in a tight grid like pattern. This seemed especially true close to the docks. Each block looked like one large building instead of ten houses squished together and sharing common walls. The second floors loomed over the street, the angle getting progressively less visible as Charon got further away from the docks.

He stepped into a wide rectangular plaza. Despite the threat of attack, it was still crowded with horse drawn carts, street vendors, and an assembly of townspeople. He side stepped a man leading a black draft horse by the reins, splashing in a puddle of dirty water. The water stank and Charon turned up his nose, pressing his arm against it. He held his breath as he slinked his way through the crowd. After a dozen feet, Charon was able to breathe easy again. He took a deep breath and let it out with a sigh of relief.

Leaving the plaza behind, Charon headed back towards the large market square. A feeling of failure began to creep over him. Ferran was nowhere to found and anyone he asked said they had not seen him. Most people could talk of nothing but the legendary Bane. In fact, Charon realized that no one appeared openly nervous or scared so high was their confidence in Bane. Charon wanted to share in their feelings but every time he tried, he thought of what happened in Meras.

"The battle has not been won yet," Charon murmured to himself as he passed a group of four men fantasizing about Bane's power. For those that noticed him, they pointed and whispered with a similar sense of wonder and hope. Did they not know that he was nowhere near as powerful as Bane and that he was just as scared as they should be?

When Charon could no longer take the stares and whispered comments, he ducked into the open door of a modest house, closing it behind him. He put his back to the door and slid down to the floor.

"What in the heavens and hells are you doing in my house? I thought I told you to leave me alone!" Ferran shouted.

Charon ducked to avoid being hit in the head by a ceramic mug. It crashed and shattered, the pieces raining down on him. "Woah! Just hold up!"

"Get out!" Ferran hissed as he reared his hand back, ready to throw another mug at Charon.

Charon's hands shot up to shield his face. He waited for a painfully long span of time until he realized that the mug was not coming. He lowered his hands just as Ferran relented and set the mug down on a nearby table.

"It would do me no good to hurt you when Sawn needs you so desperately," Ferran acknowledged with a sense of defeat in his voice. His expression then sharpened dangerously. He pointed at Charon. "This doesn't mean we can be friends or brothers."

"I thank you for not hitting me in the head but why not? If what you said earlier is true, then perhaps you should look in a mirror too," Charon pointed out as he got to his feet. He brushed the ceramic dust from his shoulders.

"Look, I have a good life. I like it as it is. I don't need people like you or Bane in it. I don't want to be a part of your world," Ferran half pleaded. He swept his raven hair back and let out a tight breath. "And now, you have brought your world to my home."

"That was not my doing by any means," Charon quickly said in defense. He watched as Ferran appeared to pace about and mutter to himself, hysterics increasing subtly. "I'm from the Southlands too, born in Garhune to a Mortal mother."

Ferran's posture tightened and he clenched his fists. "And how did your mother die? Did she know the identity of your father?"

Charon leaned back as if to ward off Ferran's instability. He half expected him to lash out. He looked about for potential weapons and projectiles. The unused mug caught his eye. He tensed up in preparation to defend himself. Ferran instead leaned over the edge of his dining table with the design of the front window shadowed across the surface. Beyond him was the darkness of a kitchen that was unlit by anything but fading sunlight.

"Our father. You know it to be true even though you won't accept me as a brother. It is not like I expected to find someone like you in my lifetime which is already longer than most Mortals can imagine," Charon pressed.

"How old are you?" Ferran asked, tears in the corners of his eyes.

"A hundred and one next month," Charon replied. Normally he was proud of his age. Now, it seemed like a burden. "My mother died of infection over fifty years ago."

Ferran chuckled softly to himself. "Long before my own birth."

Charon approached Ferran and dared to lay a hand on his shoulder. He gave it a comforting squeeze when Ferran did not immediately brush off the gesture. "Chane told me what happened to your mother. I am sorry that she was taken from you. Like me or not, you deserve to know the truth."

"You know what? Bane said something similar the night she was killed," Ferran revealed as he turned to face Charon.

"You've met Bane before?" Charon asked in shock.

Ferran nodded. "I was holding her in my arms, watching her gasp for breath when he came. It was like a dream passing through the mists. He bent down and laid his hand on her forehead. I can remember exactly what he said and I remember feeling a sense of peace. A sense of knowing that where my mother was going, she would no longer feel pain and fear." He paused to wipe a tear from his cheek. "With someone like him, how could the Southlands see Immortals as bewitched monsters? And yet, that is all I see and feel when I am reminded of him."

"There are those in my neck of the woods that see me as such. I am barely welcome back in Garhune though Gyr gave the Mayor quite the verbal lashing." Charon chuckled. He recounted the tale to Ferran who managed to laugh as well.

Forgetting the danger outside of the house, Charon sat down with Ferran at the wooden dining table. He spun tales of his travels since meeting Gyr. Ferran could not get enough of the stories about the Gryphon, expressing great interest in the strange language of the race. Charon gave his own account of Gyr trying to teach him his native tongue to disastrous results. It was clear that Ferran preferred scholarly pursuits and greatly enjoyed his work as a scribe and trade duty officer. When prompted, Ferran gladly told Charon about his time in Arken and gave an account of his own life story.

"My mother was married to a kind man who raised me as if I was his own son. For fifteen years, I believed him to be my father. He taught me everything he knew about the river trade, took me on ships to Arken as soon as I could walk and talk. I loved sailing with him. When my mother was killed by the mad Shadowborn, he changed and fell into a deeper sense of melancholy than I could have ever felt on my own. Before he died a year later, he revealed the secret that I was not his blood born son and that the man who was my father was the Immortal that had taken her life. He also revealed that most of Sawn already knew the truth but did not speak of it to me. My mother wanted to protect me, shield me from the blood that flowed in my veins. It was if that not talking about it would make the Immortal blood disappear and that I would be as Mortal as her."

Ferran looked away and sniffled loudly. "But I knew that something was different from an early age. I could see the most minute of details and hear things such as the flutter of a songbird's wings over the roar of a thunderstorm. There were so many times I frightened my mother and her husband by leaping off of high places only to land like a cat and walk away like nothing was wrong. As a result, they encouraged my studies in language, math, history, and science as opposed to more physical activities like other children in

Sawn. Fortunately for them, I took to reading like it was my greatest love."

"Then you are better than me for I was never a good student. My mother taught me at home. I preferred exploring the outdoors. You are lucky to have had the life you had. People in Garhune treated my mother like she was a whore and me like I was a parasite. What ever became of her family, I will never know. She never spoke of them even when I asked. I suspect that they were perhaps from Meras," Charon shrugged.

Ferran then plied him with questions about his early life, focusing on his knowledge of the mad Shadowborn. They ended up speculating about their mysterious father. Charon recounted his encounter in Meras again, not leaving out any detail.

"This Shadowborn sounds strong. I wonder who he was before he went mad," Ferran supposed. "Bane said he was reminded of someone when he looked upon him?"

"It is hard to figure out what a man who is a thousand years old is thinking. I am also a little afraid of pressing him too hard for answers. I mean, we all know the tales of the mighty Daylord, and Gyr has waxed on endlessly about his power," Charon commented. He leaned back in the thin cushioned chair, arms draped over the sides. "Gyr has his orders from his Lords in Crossroads to bring the Daylord home to the Northlands."

"Gyr's mission is one of great importance. This Kaiser does not seem to be someone who will just go away if ignored. I'd hate to say that if nothing is done now, it will be too late," Ferran finally said after Charon told him the details of Gyr's orders.

"Then Sawn will need to survive the coming nights. I am no Bane Arlis but I will do what I can. That I can promise you." Charon paused, hesitant to finish his thought.

Ferran reached an open hand forward. "Brothers."

"Brothers," Charon smiled as he shook the outstretched hand.

*****

BREAK THE MIRROR

Onyx and Ryder were surrounded by piles of books, stray pieces of parchment, and clouds of dust. Open books were spread out on every available surface, including the two wooden chairs. Ryder sat on the floor, a heavy black leather bound tome open on his lap. Onyx perused the shelf behind him. He made to grab a book's spine but pulled back to think about it.

"The library at Cross would serve us better. It's ten times as big as this room," Onyx commented.

Ryder harrumphed. "And the library at Crossroads is even bigger but we must work with what we have."

The rebel base library was really nothing more than a small square room. Except for the door, there was no wall space as the book shelves stretched from floor to ceiling. A worn rug that was thread bare in places was stretched out under the heavy wood table. The only light source was a five candle iron candelabra that Onyx had brought with him. Being Shadowborn, they did not need much light to be able to see though they both expressed their preference for a brightly lit library.

"I have a sneaking suspicion that Zoras may have taken a few of these books from the royal library," Onyx said as he pulled a thin book from the shelf. He tapped the gold lettering on the front cover. "This was my father's favorite book of poetry."

Ryder held his hand out. "My father wrote it as a profession of love for my mother. I'm surprised a copy still exists."

Onyx handed the book to Ryder and watched as he flipped

through the pages. "But the author is Shadow Heart. Kind of a strange name."

"The way you can tell it is him is that his first poem is titled 'Aylin.' My mother's name," Ryder pointed out by tapping on the page. He quickly flipped to the last entry and directed Onyx's attention to the title. "The Light of my Life. He wrote this after I was born."

Taking the book back from Ryder, Onyx read the poem and smiled. "He really did love you."

Ryder scoffed. "My father, though born with the blood of warriors, was an artist and scholar. He loved books, not swords. I appreciate a good book myself but I much prefer the feel of a sword in my hand. What about you?"

"Sword or a book about swords," Onyx laughed. Ryder chuckled softly before setting the book in his lap aside. "Nothing?"

"Nothing. I doubt that Zoras would have known any texts about the ancient powers. If he did, I doubt that he would have thought them important enough to steal away from Cross."

"Surely with the Shadow Mirror at the border, he would have," Onyx suggested as he held the book of poetry. He did not want to put it away to be forgotten. He wanted to read it during a quiet moment.

Ryder stiffly got up to his feet and stretched his lower back. "Even my own knowledge is limited and I share blood with the guy that raised it. I'd like to think that Kaiser does not know much more than me."

"Well, what can you tell me?" Onyx asked. He leaned against the shelf.

"The Shadow Mirror is an ancient power that is Farlander in origin and not Shadowborn. It involves calling upon the Spirit World and essentially raising a veil that only Spirits can cross. However, anyone that shares blood with the person who summoned it can cross through," Ryder explained, gesturing towards himself. "I know that Kaiser created blood seals for people to carry so that they may cross it. I myself can act as a blood seal."

"So the Mirror can be tricked but can it be broken?" Onyx wondered. He shrugged. "Can you conjure a Shadow Mirror?"

Ryder set his hands on his hips and let out a deep breath. After a long moment of silence, he nodded. The gesture surprised Onyx and yet he had the idea that Ryder could all along.

"I know how but I never have. To delve into the power of the Spirit World and bring it to the world of the living is dangerous. Yes, we can use Spirit energy but we summon the residual energy from the environment and within our bodies as Spiritborn. Not directly from the Spirit World. For lack of a better term, the

Shadow Mirror is a Spirit Power," Ryder explained. "You mean a power that originates from the Dark Days when the worlds of living and death were not separate?" Onyx inquired.

"Correct. A time where energy was wild and uncontrolled. When the Covenant of Spirits was created, the worlds were separated into what we know today. Only those of Farlander blood, the blood of the Covenant's scribe, can use and control that energy. Guess that makes me his descendent." Ryder scratched the back of his head and laughed. "Who am I not related to?"

Even Onyx laughed though a part of him was jealous. Ryder had more impeccable breeding as a bastard than he did as a trueborn son. However the more he thought about it, the more he believed such a background to be a burden. In that, he felt pity for Ryder. One thing that quickly became apparent to him was that Ryder did not boast about his ancestry unlike himself.

"So how do you raise a Shadow Mirror?" Onyx asked, not wanting to focus his thoughts on ancestry anymore.

Ryder picked up books from the floor with Onyx's help while he thought of a proper answer. He reshelved ten books before replying. "First let me warn you to never try to do it yourself. The Shadow Mirror is an extension and manifestation of your will. The older you are, the more powerful this extension can be. The more you know of the world, the more you can control it. Even if you were of Farlander origin, your age and lack of worldly knowledge is a hindrance. The power would kill you before you could take your next breath." He took a deep breath and let it out slowly. He lifted up his left hand and pointed out a scar on his palm and on each of his fingertips. "You first cut your left hand on the palm and fingertips. Not deeply but enough to shed blood. With your right hand, you bathe it in Spirit Fire. You press your hands together, mixing the blood and Spirit Fire. The silver fire should turn red and then you extend your hands forward. You say a specific incantation and manipulate your hands and fingers accordingly. I will not repeat the incantation now. It fills me with too much dread and makes me feel naked."

Onyx was curious about the incantation for using Spirit energy did not require a spoken word or magical command. A thought occurred to him. "So if you did that backwards, would a Shadow Mirror come down? Does it really just boil down to the caster pulling back the extension of his will? But then if that is true, I don't think Kaiser will pull back his will if we asked him. It's why we are fighting anyway."

"Will can be challenged but you either have to be stronger than the caster or be too stubborn to give up," Ryder said as he returned to picking up books and stray pieces of parchment.

"Then maybe we should just attack the Mirror at one point and have my uncle attack at the same point but on the other side. Surely our combined powers would be great enough to break it. I mean, Lord Vorin is the eldest being on Terra. With him and the other Lords of the Spiritborn, I am sure that we would succeed," Onyx exclaimed, breaking the silence of Ryder's cleanup of the library. The idea got Onyx excited. He started bouncing on his feet. "We could totally do it!"

Ryder did not share his excitement. "A good idea but should we fail, the one accessing the Mirror for attack would die. I would die."

The excitement left as quickly as it came. Onyx felt a little deflated. He did not want Ryder to die. He knew as did everyone else that Haven was pregnant with Ryder's child and he did not want that child to grow up without a father. "Then we will do it together so that you won't die. If you are prepared to sacrifice yourself then so am I."

"Thank you. But now the matter is how do we tell your uncle where to be?" Ryder asked. He chuckled for a moment. "Even with my claim as Shadowlord, I doubt he will listen to me. He does not like me very much."

Onyx had to laugh at Ryder's statement. He crossed his arms. "Are there any Lords that you have not pissed off in some way? You broke Evander's arm. You nearly broke Argos' jaw."

"Vorin and the Gryphons seem to think highly of me. I can't be too sure but I think Aves likes me. The rest? Not so much," Ryder answered with a slightly devilish expression.

"Next challenge. How do we get a message through? We can't spare you to run all the way to someone who may not listen to you. Also, I am sure that Kaiser is watching the Mirror and that no one you send with a blood seal can get through," Onyx pointed out. He started to shelve the books that had been sitting on the table.

Ryder thought for a long time, crossing his arms and scratching his chin. He then lifted a finger. "Shadow Shot. It's small enough to escape notice but enough to carry a letter. If we work together like we did for the astral projection, I am sure that we will succeed. Since it is your uncle and he is blood bound to like you, you should write the letter."

"Just like Shadow Night and Adonis working together a thousand years ago. Their memory lives on through us. Through you as the Shadowlord."

"Thank you, your Majesty, for you are King as I am the Commander of your forces. That is what the Shadowlord is to me. The war charger to the leader," Ryder teased with a wink.

Together, Ryder and Onyx cleaned up the library. Neither were upset at the failure of their research. It was really the conversation and draw upon old memories that gave them their direction. Though Onyx had been given the task of writing the letter to his uncle, he discussed what would be said with Ryder. They went back and forth with the wording. At first, everything sounded emotionless and formal. Though Ryder had thought it fine, Onyx wanted to push for more emotion.

"Master Erebus always described my uncle as a man driven by his heart. By what he likes and what he fears. He needs to read this letter and feel our fear, our courage, and our hope. He and all the other Lords must feel inspired to truly risk it all because that is what this war is about now. We are risking everything for an uncertain future," Onyx pushed. He gestured with his hands as he spoke, "Can you trust me to write this on my own?"

Ryder nodded. "I put my faith in you, your Majesty."

"Thank you, my Shadowlord."

DREAMS OF A HAPPY LIFE

Ryder lay on his back, staring at the ceiling. It wasn't the first time that sleep eluded him and it was starting to drain his mental and physical being. He rubbed his eyes before switching to his temples. The persistent headache that had started days ago had dulled into a slow throb. No matter he did to cure his headache, it remained. He wondered if he was just imagining the pain. He closed his eyes and pinched the bridge of his nose. Even the bed, though soft and warm, was starting to feel uncomfortable. There was just too much to think about and the weight of his thoughts was pressing down on him. For a moment, he thought he was cold and considered putting on a shirt instead of leaving his torso bare.

He glanced over at Haven who was sleeping beside him. She slept on her left side with one hand under her head and the other wrapped around her round belly. The bed quilt had fallen away from her shoulder. He silently picked up the edge of the quilt and pulled it up over her shoulder. She stirred slightly just before he took his right hand away. The sight of her made him smile and the fact that she was carrying his child made him smile even more. He reached over again to push back a lock of her raven hair that had fallen over her eyes.

Haven and now his child were the reasons that he fought and kept going. They were why he finally decided to accept being the Shadowlord. He wanted to create a better world, one that didn't have war and bloodshed. Never had this feeling been stronger. But he was worried. So much had happened over the last few months and there was still a great deal waiting to happen. Most of all, his life was going to change forever and he was going to be a father. One thing that immediately occurred to him was that he did not want his child born in the rather tartan base they were currently occupying. The thought of abandoning the base immediately felt uncomfortable and yet it felt right. But where should he go?

Ryder sighed a little bit too loud and Haven stirred awake. She stretched and yawned before opening her eyes and looking back at him. Sleep was still heavy in her eyes.

"Awake again?" Haven murmured. She yawned and grumbled softly.

"You should be sleeping," Ryder commented as he crossed his left arm behind his head. He gently stroked her head with his right hand, brushing his fingers through her hair.

"You should be too. A lot of people are counting on you to be at your best," Haven said. "To be well rested and ready to act at a moment's notice."

Ryder let out a deep breath. "My mind is too awake to let me sleep. Kaiser suffers, for lack of a better word, from the same problem. That is why it is so hard to outsmart him."

"You should still try to sleep. You haven't had a good night's sleep since Zoras died," Haven pointed out, gaining more strength in her voice.

Ryder's right hand drifted down towards her right hand, giving it a squeeze. He then let go and she set her hand on top of his. For a long time, he kept his hand on her belly, savoring the contact between him and his unborn child.

"Remember what I said about Onyx's message?" Ryder asked softly. Haven nodded. "What do you think of it?"

Haven thought for a moment. "Our backs are against the wall with nowhere to go but through it. I don't think that we can bring the entire Shadow Mirror down but maybe just destabilize long enough to pass through. You are powerful, Ryder, but I think we need to get out of the Shadowborn lands and join with the full might of the Northern Alliance. I think the best place to do that is Twilight. Like you said yesterday, Branch is just over the river from Twilight with strong bridges connecting the two cities. It is also the most distant city from Cross and closest to the Daylord's Mirror. Surely that Mirror's power will help us in some way."

He appreciated her honesty even if some of what was said was tough to hear. "Do you have faith in me? Do you think that I can break the Mirror?"

"Ryder, there may have been times where I was angry and upset but I have never lost faith in you. I never will. There is something about you that is honest and true. Something noble. I almost can't describe it." Haven paused to think, looking away from Ryder. Her right hand squeezed his. A tear formed in the corners of her eyes.

Ryder knew what she was thinking about and to see the pain in her eyes hurt him worse than any sword thrust through the chest. He had warned her that if he failed to break the Mirror, he would die. He sat up and pulled her in his arms. He embraced her, emanating all sense of comfort so that she would not feel sad.

"If I had not run away, this war would not be at our doorstep. If I only had accepted the throne, a lot of our problems could have been prevented," Ryder murmured.

Haven sniffled. "Ryder, you know as well as I do that you cannot change the past. And I don't think you should for what you have done or not done has made you who you are today."

"You're right. I should listen to you more often," Ryder replied.

Despite the obvious need for sleep, neither felt they could rest without comforting each other. No further words needed to be said. In the silence, their thoughts turned to more lighthearted matters, one in particular that could no longer be ignored.

"I know that we have discussed names before but now we have to make a decision. What to call our son or daughter?" Haven proposed. She looked up into Ryder's eyes. "Every day, I feel him move more and more. Soon he will be so big that there will be no room left."

"How do you know that it is going to be a boy? The baby hasn't been born yet," Ryder retorted.

Haven chuckled softly. "I dream about our child being a little older and seeing the world. Last night, I saw you crouched down by the Wall of Crossroads and pointing to the distance with him glued to your side. I am standing further back, watching everything with a smile on my face."

"Torin right? That was the name you liked if it's a boy. Remember if it's a girl, I want to name her after my mother," Ryder pointed out. He teased her by tapping her nose with his finger.

"Regardless, this child will be loved," Haven replied as she leaned into him. She then cradled her belly and looked down. "It won't be too much longer."

"I just have to defeat the greatest evil the world has seen since the Dark Days so our child will not know such terror. Simple enough," Ryder commented. He leaned his head back and looked up at the stone ceiling. His eyes followed the irregular gouges and lines of the tan stone. "I miss fighting with you at my side. It is just not the same anymore without you watching my back."

"I know. I miss the thrill of battle too but I cannot risk the child. Especially now with my condition being so obvious," Haven stated. Her hands rubbed her swollen stomach. "Son or daughter, we will teach this child combat skills to rival our own."

"If he or she chooses such a life. I will support our child's desires, whatever they may be. Even if they choose to pick up a book instead of a sword."

They always seemed to be the most honest in the middle of the night with no one around to interrupt them. In the comfort and safety of their shared room, they could talk for hours until they felt too tired to continue. This they did though Haven was quicker to nod off. Ryder wrapped his arms around her and hummed softly. Soon, he too was feeling sleepy.

"Haven, would you ever consider raising our child in Crossroads?" Ryder asked. He yawned loudly.

"Why Crossroads?" Haven asked. She too yawned. She pulled away to lie down again on her left side.

Ryder slunk down to lie on his back. "Our homeland holds too many bad memories for me. It no longer feels like home. So long as I have you and our child, home will be where we choose it to be. Crossroads has so much to offer to a young family."

"What about being the Shadowlord? We can't abandon them for Crossroads," Haven asked, still hanging on to consciousness.

Ryder took in a deep breath and let it out slowly in a yawn. He smacked his lips twice and rubbed his eyes. "Onyx and I talked about what the Shadowlord really is. He is a leader to the Shadowborn in times of trouble and a champion of the Immortal Truth. I do not feel that the Shadowlord is the same thing as being the leader of a nation. Shadow Night just happened to be both King and Shadowlord when the Shadowborn needed him most. He only became King as it were when Adonis Anu declined the crown."

"Must be why Kaiser feels so entitled to seize power. He must see it as a birthright denied to him." She closed her eyes and shoved the pillow under her head.

It was something that Ryder had considered as to Kaiser's reasons for acting and igniting the war. Kaiser had decimated the bloodline of the Silvanus bloodline over the last thousand years. And yet, he had done little to grow the Adonis name. Ryder's mother had been an accident of a night's passion though he doubted that Kaiser had ever loved her. Ryder was Kaiser's only descendent. He briefly looked at Haven who had fallen asleep. Well, he and the child she was carrying were the only descendants that Kaiser could claim. Ryder found himself smiling. Kaiser may have ultimately damaged the Adonis Anu name but Ryder was determined to change that. He was going to bring glory back where it needed to be and he was not going to do it by ruling others. In his heart, Ryder did not feel that was his place.

He turned over on his right side to look at Haven. As he did, all sense of doom and dread left him. In that moment, he allowed himself to imagine a better, more happy life. His eyelids became heavy and soon, Ryder had fallen asleep.

A dream came to him that was reminiscent of the one that Haven had described. He was crouched down by the edge of the Wall of Crossroads, his lookalike son holding on tight to him. Looking at himself was odd enough but to see a small version of himself mixed with Haven's features was a wonder. The child had his eyes and Haven's smile. He would point to something out in the distance and the boy would repeat his gesture. Ryder wished that he could hear what his dream self was saying to his dream son. It had to be something delightful for the small boy giggled.

Just then, the sky turned red and his dream self and son transformed into his own father and himself as a boy. Dream Akakios, tall and lean, stood up. The child version of himself hung on to Akakios' leg. Ryder wanted to shout out to the both of them as Kaiser appeared as a disembodied face in the angry clouds. He watched as Akakios pushed the child behind him, a fierce expression in his eyes. Kaiser's disembodied face laughed out loud before lurching forward. The entire scene became dark.

Ryder opened his eyes. The room around him was silent save for Haven's soft breathing. To reassure himself of her presence, he glanced over at her sleeping form. He wished that he could convey to her how much she meant to him. He could not tell her that despite the optimism of others, he was worried about his future. Would he survive the days to come? He let out a deep breath and closed his eyes.

PACK UP AND LEAVE

Onyx held the tight roll of parchment pages in his hands, forbidding himself from twisting it from nerves. He was not sure how Shadow Shot would operate. Would the power alter the texture of the paper or jumble up the letters of his carefully written message. And yet, a few tears or creases might better serve to emphasize his feelings. He wanted the reader to feel his pain as their own when they perused the lines of ink. He wanted them to feel horror and sorrow at his desperate situation. His uncle Palani did not seem to be a sentimental man in the few times they had spent together. Instead, Onyx wrote the lengthy letter as if he was pouring out his heart to the world. He wanted the world to listen and decide what they wanted the future to be.

He glanced about his small room. His eye caught the sheathed sword hanging from the back of a chair by the belt. He stepped forward and reverently belted on the sword around his waist. The hilt felt cold beneath his touch. He patted it lightly before turning back towards the bed where his travel packed lay. He paused as he caught his reflection in the shards of the broken mirror. He cursed himself for breaking it again in the aftermath of the Battle of Dusk when so much effort was made to acquire a replacement mirror.

The rebel movement was not a wealthy one, funded almost solely by Zoras' estate and anonymous donations. So his broken mirror had not been replaced quickly. At first, it had annoyed him. He had grown up surrounded by wealth and was now living for the first time having to truly work for everything. Living such a life under the circumstances had humbled him. In a way, it made him a better person inside and out. On the outside, he had developed a strong musculature due to Ryder's training. On the inside, he had become someone who walked with eyes wide open. He was no longer the sheltered and scared boy.

Onyx studied the lines of his face, seeing the physical changes that had occurred over the last year. He gently touched a small scar on his right cheek. "I am not a boy but a man now. Father. Mother. I will make you proud to call me your son. I will win this war for you."

He left his room and walked down the hallway. The doors to the outer yard had been thrown wide open. The light outside was not bright but it was enough to see by. It was strange to Onyx not to see the forge fires of the smiths or the stream of soldiers going out on missions. In the center of the abandoned yard was Ryder. Onyx had half expected his cousin to be wearing his glorious silver steel armor. Instead, Ryder was dressed in a similar manner to himself. Ryder wore his old Crossroads Arena light armor in the form of a leather cuirass, bracers, and pauldrons. He had a travel pack slung over his shoulder and a sword on his left hip.

"Ready?" Ryder asked.

Onyx held up the roll of parchment that he had tied together with a thin leather strap. "As ready as I'll ever be. Where is Haven? I would have thought that you would leave together."

""She has already gone ahead with her family and Jarod. I trust that she is well protected." Ryder then held up a finger. "She might be pregnant with my child but she is still quite capable of pulling a bow and arrow or wielding a sword."

Onyx chuckled. He gripped the straps of his travel pack. Before he could comment, Hayden and Donovan slinked out of the shadows. Both were in flawless Saber leather armor with supple black cloaks. They had their hoods drawn up over their heads but kept their faces uncovered. The only distinction of rank between the two was that Hayden had a silver pendant hanging over his heart with Ryder's new sigil. Donovan had the Silvanus crest attached at his collarbone.

"We do not go without our own protection. Despite telling these two that we would be fine, these Sabers insisted. How could I deny them?" Ryder supposed with a shrug of his shoulders.

"I took an oath to protect the Silvanus family and I intend to honor it to my very end. I have had my failures but I will not fail you now," Donovan said after he dropped to his knee before Onyx.

Hayden had dropped to his knee as well before Ryder. He kept his head bowed with his right arm pressed across his chest.

His left fist was planted on the ground beside his foot. His breathing was steady and quiet.

"Hayden, I may have claimed a title but you are still a friend, not a servant," Ryder stated.

Hayden rose up to his feet and bowed his head. "I have been a Saber for a long time. I cannot forget or set aside my oaths so easily. War may threaten to tear me down but I will remain strong. Our people will be strong."

Ryder patted his left shoulder before turning to Onyx. He reached out for the parchment roll. Onyx gladly gave it to him.

"I know that you said that I should write to my uncle but I wrote to the person who could help us most. I used my honest thoughts and feelings to convey our need," Onyx stated proudly. He smiled when Ryder nodded. "My uncle can be a bit stubborn."

"Yes he can. He and I actually had a good shouting match in Crossroads before the Arena matches. He blames me for a lot of things, namely the death of your mother."

Onyx bit his lip but quickly quelled any feeling of sadness. "You did not kill her."

"Well your uncle seems to think that I might as well have wielded the murderer's blade. He also blames me for the death of his two elder children." Ryder sighed deeply. "There are a lot of people that blame me for things I had no hand in. Whether or not my presence in Cross or on the throne would have prevented them is best left for speculation."

A compulsion to yell at his uncle filled Onyx's core. He clenched his fists and gritted his teeth. He closed his eyes and took a deep breath, letting it out slowly. He needed to be calm and centered. He continued with a series of breathing exercises before he felt everything settled. He opened his eyes.

"Ok. Let's get this done. Everyone put their left hands in with palms up. Make sure you are touching your neighbors' hand. Good. Just like that," Ryder directed.

The four of them formed a four pointed star with their hands. They all leaned in slightly. Ryder then swung his right hand in and balanced the roll of parchment on their open palms.

"Normally Shadow Shot is performed by holding the object you wish to send in your left hand and placing your right hand six inches over top of it. Like so," Ryder began to instruct. Each person put their right hands in with palms down, replicating the same pattern of their left hands. "Now close your eyes and center yourselves like you were preparing for Shadow Slide. This time, focus on our need for help. Pour every emotion you can and every memory of this war."

Onyx closed his eyes first. Immediately, the words of the

message streamed through his mind. This time, he guided his complex network of emotions to his core, focusing on his desire for help. It was odd that Ryder had instructed everyone to center themselves like they normally would for Shadow Slide. The technique required calm and what he was doing now was the opposite of calm. But as he thought about it, he subconsciously was focusing his being. What was odd was that he felt the minds of Donovan and Hayden. The contact was faint but there. Donovan, who on the outside was a mix of guilt and desire for restoring his honor, was strangely even keeled. Hayden's mind was very much like his exterior: cool and focused. He felt a nudge from Ryder's mind and shied away. The force from his cousin's mind was powerful and commanding.

He started to feel an undulation that pushed and pulled at his emotions and memories. It was an odd feeling and yet, he welcomed the sensation. He felt his mind being opened up to the world beyond. It was clear that Ryder was taking the lead and Onyx was glad to let him. The open sensation grew in intensity. With a rush that he could not explain, Onyx saw himself walking among the stars in the night sky. It was an amazing sight to behold. He looked up and saw galaxies swirling overhead. Planets circled around burning suns. To his left, a comet rocketed by, leaving a trail of sparkling dust.

Suddenly, he was falling into absolute darkness. At first, he was scared. Where was he falling? The familiar chill of Shadow Spirit energy enveloped him and the speed of his fall slowed. His being was cushioned by a green mist. His feet lightly touched the invisible ground. Warmth began to grow around him that was both familiar and strange. What was even stranger was that mixed in with the earthy warmth was a shadowy cool. He reached forward and a light appeared over his hand. The ball of light hung in the air for a moment before slowly moving away from him.

A flash of white light blinded him. All of his senses were on fire. Memories filled Onyx with such a massive rush that he could discern no message from them. Images of his past swirled around in an erratic pattern as his vision began to clear. Just as quickly, everything disappeared and Onyx could no longer see himself.

"It is done," Ryder said.

Onyx opened his eyes, his head swimming. Hayden and Donovan appeared to be unaffected. He pulled his left hand back and rubbed his eyes. "That was the weirdest thing I have ever experienced." He described what he saw.

"I did not see anything," Donovan commented.

Ryder patted Onyx on the shoulder before giving it an encouraging squeeze. "You saw what you needed to see. Because you poured your soul out in your letter, the Spirits have blessed the message. They will make sure it is heard."

Onyx's head was still unsettled by what Ryder described as a mental and spiritual journey. It was something that he had never experienced before in all of his training and familiarity with Spirit energy. Even when he had helped Ryder with the astral projection, this was completely brand new. Maybe he did imbue the letter with some of his Spirit energy without knowing it. Was that why Ryder wanted him to write the message? He would have time to consider it on the way to Twilight.

"We should get moving," Hayden urged.

The two Sabers took the lead while Ryder and Onyx walked beside each other. The four men walked towards the open gate, leaving the base behind without a second look. Ahead was a journey to the northeastern Shadowborn city of Twilight. Ahead was a door waiting to be opened to an uncertain future.

*****

SHADOW SHOT

Kader stretched out on the lounge chair, the sun beaming down on him. He was surrounded by piles of books and papers strewn everywhere. A heavy leather bound book laid across his lap with his hands resting on top. On a side table to his right sat a cold bone china cup of mint tea. The tiny silver teaspoon had fallen to the floor. He snored with a low rumble in his chest, pursing his lips to expel each breath of air. He had exhausted himself, unable to deal with the stress of the arguing Lords. Of the Lords assembled in Cascade, only Aves seemed to have the most sense and consideration of the future. It had been Aves that told him to rest and recharge before the next council meeting.

He smacked his lips and turned over onto his left side. The book on his lap fell to the floor with a heavy thump. He snorted and rolled on to his back. He rubbed his eyes and yawned.

A shot of cold energy jetted over his shoulder and Kader shivered. He rubbed his eyes again. He pushed himself back against the lounge chair. Floating before him was a black ball of undulating mist. Fear welled up inside him that he could not explain. Was this some terror sent by Kaiser to kill him?

Unexpectedly, the mist disappeared and a tight roll of parchment dropped onto his lap. He wanted to leap up and throw it across the room. His breath caught in his throat. It was if the roll of paper was a poisonous entity for he felt that it was from Kaiser. The roll shifted forward, revealing a short line of letters.

"To a true Shadowborn," Kader read out loud.

He was not entirely familiar with the handwriting but reached forward anyway. The leather strap was not too tight that he could not pull it apart. He did so, albeit carefully, to avoid ripping the parchment. As soon as the leather strap was gone, the tight roll fell open and Kader realized that it was several pages full of handwriting that he knew very well. He picked up the first page and began reading.

My name is Onyx Shadow Silvanus, son of the Shadowborn Aku and the Earthborn Nuru. I was born a Prince of true royal blood but now I am something more. I am transformed. I am no longer the boy Prince of years past. I am a young man who has seen the truth and opened my eyes to the world. I am Onyx Shadow Silvanus, rebel soldier. This is my truth.

Kader could not have been happier to see that the letter was from Onyx. He had not seen his favorite student since he was the age of twelve. He thought for a moment, trying to remember the date of Onyx's birthday. Kader smiled. Onyx was going to be twenty years old in a few months.

At the age of eight, I lost my father to a Demon. I bore witness to his suffering and his near death like state. Never again would I get to feel his love with a warm embrace. Never again would I get to listen to his stories about his grand adventures beyond the borders. Never again. My father's soul was gone with only a shell left behind.
At the age of twelve, I lost my mother and grandfather within the span of a few months. I was made an orphan with no one to look to. Before I could see my grandfather as a beacon of light against the pain of loss, he was taken from me. Murdered in his own house with no one around to blame.
For six years, I had to quickly become a leader in waiting while the shell of my father suffered with unimaginable pain. All people that I could look to for strength were gone, either dead or in the wind. I had told myself that I will be the best Shadowlord possible so that I could honor their memory by my actions and words.

Kader had to pause to wipe a tear away. The sorrow that Onyx had experienced at far too young an age overwhelmed him. He remembered his own heartbreak over the loss of Shiloh, a dear friend and confidante. He took a deep breath before he returned to reading the letter.

I had thought that at eighteen, I was prepared to face the world. I was a man with the skills necessary to take my father's throne. Then I met the one person who exceeded me in everything from physical power to the respect he commanded from the great Lords of Crossroads: my cousin Peredur.

Here was the one person who could threaten my true born claim to the throne. It angered me. I was more determined than ever to prove that I was the rightful heir. The best and most loyal. I was prepared to take the crown and spare my father the burdens of leadership. But I was wrong. I was dead wrong.

I can scarcely begin to list every terrible deed that Kaiser has committed, both known and unknown to the world. I will begin with the one that has affected me the most. This great evil of our time had the shell of my father being possessed by a Demon named Iztal.

His hands shook as he held the paper. He had his fair share of tales regarding Kaiser's dark deeds but the possession of Aku horrified him. He dreaded reading the next few lines.

I dare not dwell too long for the hurt is still too near. To slay my father was the hardest thing that I have ever had to do. But I had to do it in order to set him free from Kaiser's prison like grasp. I would like to think that my father's Spirit is at peace but I do not think it will be until Kaiser is destroyed.

The pages went on, detailing every horrific act that Kaiser had committed. Kader held a hand over his mouth. Onyx had spared no detail about the bloodshed. The detail was so gruesome that Kader felt the urge to vomit. He swallowed the lump of bile in his throat. It burned on the way back down to his stomach. After nine pages, he arrived at the last one. He read it through once and immediately jumped to his feet. He scrambled for the bedroom door.

"Oops! I am so sorry!" Kader squeaked after he ran into a blond haired teenage boy and fell to the floor.

"My apologies to you, Master Erebus. I should have been more observant."

It was not the servant's fault. Kader had exited his quarters in such a rush that he did not see him. The boy helped him up to his feet and bowed his head.

"Wait. Where is the Lord Palani? It is urgent that I speak with him," Kader asked, stopping the servant before he got too far down the hallway.

"He is with his queen and heir upon the veranda. They are dining with his parents and have asked not to be disturbed," the servant replied cautiously. He looked Kader up and down, frowning at his disheveled state.

"Thank you!" Kader shouted as he took off down the hallway.

"But they don't want to be disturbed!" the servant cried.

The no disturb order did not matter to Kader as what he had was far too important to let wait. As he ran, he was surprised at his energy and nimbleness. He was not a young soul and yet he had been filled with enough strength and agility that he felt tireless. He began to wonder if his sedentary life had robbed him of such an invigorating sensation.

Kader practically flew down the foyer stairs that led towards the private quarters of the palace. He slid down the curving wooden bannister at high speed, leaping to the floor and landing perfectly. A cluster of maids and butlers did a double take as he rocketed past them towards the east wing. Kader blew through the tall open doors and disappeared from their sight.

He had made a small effort to learn the layout of the palace six years ago and knew exactly where he had to go. He quickly descended another set of stairs before reaching the lower level of the wing. This was where the servants congregated and it was the quickest route towards the veranda where the royals liked to dine. Servants of all duties and rank shouted after him, some cursing his rudeness and blaming his foreign blood for his strange behavior. He ducked and danced around them until he reached the desired door that led into a small, bright foyer.

The doors flung open at his push and Kader slid to a stop on the marble floor. He looked about quickly and saw the burly Captain Oaken by a pair of glass paned doors with equally tall windows on both sides. Kader paused to smooth down his flyway raven locks, running his fingers through like a comb. He pulled at his sleeves and adjusted his belt.

"You look affright," Oaken commented warily. His grip tightened on a long bladed spear. His leather and steel armor creaked from the slight movement.

"I must speak with Lord Palani at once," Kader said as he caught his breath. He did not know why he bowed to the Earthborn but did it just the same.

"He is not to be disturbed and I will obey his order," Oaken replied. He nodded to his right and left to two groups of four similarly dressed guards. They edged in closer.

"But it is imperative that I speak with him," Kader urged. He waved the crumbled roll of parchment in his left hand.

"You may be a guest here but even then you are Shadowborn and this is the Lord of the Earthborn's house. You will abide by his laws and commands as if you were his kin," Oaken frowned. The eight guards lined on his left and right, brandishing their own spears.

Kader snarled, a strange action for such a calm and collected man like himself to take. "I come bearing a message from the Lord's own blood! His nephew whom I love and serve with all my heart and being. Does he not have say here as the son of Lord Palani's beloved sister?" He waved the letter again. "I will speak and fight for my young master if I must to make sure his message is heard and you young souls will be powerless to stop me!"

It was a bold thing to say outside of the Shadowborn lands but Kader could think of nothing else. He had grown tired of Palani's foolish indecisiveness. Palani need to see the letter in his hand with his own eyes.

*****

"What is going on in there?" Willow asked as she set her fork down on her plate. She first looked over at her husband before looking to Palani for answers. "Perhaps it is a war message that must be addressed at once."

"I have already briefed Captain Oaken on what requires my attention and approval beyond that of my councilors. Also, am I not allowed a moment's peace even in this day and age?" Palani grumbled before shoving a large piece of buttered toast in his mouth.

Despite Palani's confidence in Oaken, the veranda doors opened. Kader stumbled but caught himself in time. He harrumphed towards Oaken and brushed off his left shoulder. Kader turned his attention towards the table.

"Lord Palani, Queen Avana, Prince Flynn, Lady Willow, and Master Oren," Kader greeted, bowing his head towards each of them. "Pardon my interruption but I come bearing a message that could not wait."

Palani dropped the half-eaten piece of toast on his plate. "Unlike people like Aves and Evander, you are not a Lord of the Spiritborn. You are only here as a representative for Shadowborn interests. You have also been a guest of my nation for the last seven years. Do not push for power that does not exist."

Everyone stiffened when Kader slapped the pile of papers on the table beside Palani. "You may not want to listen to what I have to say but you will listen to what your nephew has to say. The borders are not so sealed that Shadow Shot cannot be used to send a message."

Kader stepped back and went around the table to stand behind Oren. Oren gestured for him to bend down so that he could speak to him quietly. "The handwriting on the outside of that page. That is not my grandson's."

"No. I suspect it might be that of Peredur Coba. I feel confident in saying that your grandson does not know how to execute Shadow Shot and that his cousin does," Kader whispered in Oren's right ear.

"If the border is sealed and with Spirit Wake in play, how could Shadow Shot even be used? Enlighten me on the powers of your nation," Oren quickly asked. Only he was not watching Palani read the letter.

Kader was reluctant to answer but Palani did so for him. "Because the bastard of Akakios is of Farlander blood. Kaiser's own blood has declared himself Shadowlord above Onyx and has taken command of the Shadowborn after the death of Zoras Rokar. Master Erebus, how long have you known this?"

"I only just learned the truth moments ago when your nephew's letter came to me. The borders of my homeland are sealed even against my sight and power otherwise I would have seen fit to return home. I have had my suspicions about Kaiser's obsessive interest in Peredur for many years but had no evidence to make any substantial claims," Kader explained with a bow towards Palani.

Palani let out a deep breath and for the first time, he appeared completely transparent. He looked down and sniffled loudly. Avana reached over to her husband and clasped his right hand with both of hers. She whispered something to him.

"We must help him. For Nuru," Avana said just loud enough for her husband to hear.

It was clear that Palani was struggling to figure out what to think and say. He vehemently opposed open war, making it seem as if he did not want to risk failure. But those closest to him could tell that he was deeply afraid and unwilling to revisit the pain of his two elder children's deaths and that of his sister. He was so afraid of Kaiser and his power that he had decided that not acting was in his best interests. He looked up towards Kader, his eyes glistening with tears.

"We must print this letter for all to see," Palani stated, sounding clear for the first time in a long while.

Oren had picked up the last page and scanned through the lines. "Not this one. Though little escapes Kaiser's sight, we must do what we can to disrupt and delay him."

Flynn had gotten up and stood behind his grandfather's left

shoulder, reading the page. "Breaking a Shadow Mirror?"

"It is what Kaiser raised to seal the borders of my homeland, your Highness. He controls what comes and goes by the sheer force of his will. To break the Mirror, even if for a short while, will allow the Shadowborn survivors to reach shelter with us," Kader stated as Oren handed the page back to Palani.

"Master Erebus, can you perform the Shadow Shot power?" Palani asked.

"I can certainly try but with the Mirror and Spirit Wake, it will be nigh impossible," Kader admitted honestly.

"Then we must do everything we can to help you and to help my nephew and Peredur Coba. Call a War Council. In the name of the Shadowlord of the Immortal Truth."

MOBILIZATION

Palani waited for everyone to settle down, watching each Lord carefully from the comfort of his carved wooden seat. This time, he did not look at them with a sense of nervous trepidation. This time, he was ready for his voice to be heard. For the first instance in his reign, Palani felt like a true leader with a clear mind. The crown on his head was no longer a burden. Once the room was silent, he slowly rose up from his seat and walked towards the center of their circle. He had made sure to call the War Council to the gardens so that Vorin could attend.

"I want to begin this council by giving you all my sincerest apologies," Palani stated. He turned on his feet to look each Lord in the eyes. His opening statement had caught all but his father, Kader, and Aves off guard. He bowed his head. "I have done nothing to honor my exalted role as Lord of the Earthborn and as a Lord serving in the Northern Alliance. My pigheadedness, lack of dedication, and atrocious behavior has been unbecoming of all that the Earthborn represent. My people are courageous and loving. I need to be an example of that."

"Why the sudden change? Last council, you seemed prepared to fight your own father," Evander pointed out. He gestured towards Oren with a nod. He crossed his legs and set his hands on his lap.

"I should ask the same of you. You have yet to whole heartedly accept this war as reality," Palani retorted. He then reached into the inner folds of his robes and pulled out Onyx's letter. He waved it in the air for everyone to see. "It took the honest words of my sister's son to convince me that my old way was wrong and detrimental to the survival of Terra as we know it."

Kader bent down and picked up a basket that held nine tightly rolled scrolls. He went about the circle, giving a scroll to each Lord. Each time he handed one over, he bowed his head in respect. At Vorin's bidding, Kader unfurled the scroll and set it on the ground for him. He did the same for the Gryphon Lords before returning to his seat.

"Thank you, Master Erebus. Everyone, this letter came by Shadow Shot to Master Erebus not more than two hours ago. The author is my nephew and heir to the Shadowborn throne. And he had borne witness to horrors that only exist in our dreams. Yes, the Lords Aves, Evander, and Vorin have seen the Dark Days but nothing compares to what he describes," Palani stated before he took his seat again.

There was a long moment of silence as everyone read their copy of the letter. Vorin appeared to be the most visibly distraught and angry. The Dragon snapped his head back and cursed loudly in his native tongue. Beside him, Aves closed his eyes and cringed. After Vorin cursed, Paladon and Stellaris whispered amongst themselves in their native tongue. Argos and Evander mirrored the Gryphons' behavior, both apparently disgusted by something. The cool breeze that wafted through the garden courtyard did little to chill the rising tension.

"You mean to tell us that Akakios' bastard shares blood with Kaiser Adonis?! No wonder Lord Marinus is not here. He would sooner abandon the Northlands to ruin than fight beside," Evander fumed. He found himself unable to speak due to his fury regarding the news. He stuttered and spat before he found the words again to speak. "The Silvanus bloodline is dead if Kaiser has seen fit to mix his blood with it. It is finished! The Shadowborn have fallen! Shadow Night would be furious to see what has become of his name!"

"You speak as if only you know Shadow Night's mind. I beg to differ on that matter," Aves commented in his stoic and restrained manner. He stood up from his seat and stepped to the center of the circle. "What is clear to me is that young Onyx Silvanus, though faced with great fear, has risen beyond it to fight. Doing at his age what we custodians of this world have failed to do. We should all live by his example."

Evander shot up from his seat, his fists clenched so tightly that blood was seeping through his fingers. Before he could act further, Vorin growled in warning and the Lord of the Lightborn sat back down.

"Kaiser's greatest weapon through all of this has not been some secret power unknown to us. It is one we all know: fear. Fear of the past. Fear of war. Fear of death. Fear of sorrow. It has stopped us all from doing what we have been charged to do in life. Taking Onyx's example, I say no more. We must risk it all on this last chance. If we die, then we die knowing that we tried. If we do nothing, then we will be remembered as cowards. That is not how I want to be remembered. I want to be remembered for protecting this world, not for letting it die. The Shadowborn have suffered long enough without our help. We all have.

"Evander, what has happened to you over the last thousand years? You used to be noble and courageous and my partner on the battlefield. I used to consider you my friend, not this shell of your former glory," Aves faltered. He turned away and appeared to stifled a tear. "It is upsetting to see you this way: broken and distant."

All had thought that despite his presence, Evander had fought every step of the way against any real sense of action. He was argumentative and abrasive, usually ending each council meeting in an argument with one or more people. He had made it clear that he detested war in every sense of the word and had no direct conflict with Kaiser. His behavior confused everyone that knew him well enough to call him friend. Aves had been the first to openly express a declining relationship. But Evander refused to break.

"Why should we fight? All of this resistance has caused greater pain and suffering than Kaiser has done with his own two hands. Is open war the best option?" Evander challenged.

"Yes it is because Kaiser must be held accountable. He will not listen to reason. He is truly evil in every sense of the word. He will return this world to the Dark Days if he is not stopped. War is the only choice and I will gladly take up arms," Argos argued. He stood up and locked eyes with Palani. He nodded once. "I may not like Peredur a lot but I respect him. If he wants us to go to Branch and help him break the Mirror, then I will go."

"I will go as well. The Shadowborn will need my Dragonfire," Vorin declared.

Stellaris and Paladon spoke amongst themselves in low voices for a moment. Stellaris then looked up. "I will lead a battalion of Gryphons to fight and help ferry the survivors to safety. Paladon will remain here to delegate the messengers."

"The Earthborn will gladly go to help and I will lead them myself. My father will remain in Cascade with Lord Paladon. I recommend setting up a communication line with Crossroads." Palani sat forward on his chair. "Master Erebus?"

"I am not a masterful warrior like many of my kin. I wish that I could meet my people in Branch but I fear that Kaiser will sense my presence and send his Dark Spirits to finish the job. I suspect that he knows more that goes on than we realize and we must keep all semblance of secrecy for as long as we can."

Everyone looked at Evander who sat in his seat like a pouting child. His arms were crossed tightly and his brow was furrowed. His gold and white robes appeared dull instead of retaining their normal luminous sheen. His blonde hair had fallen free from the gold circlet around his head.

"I am not saying that I would ever ally myself with Kaiser but there are some things about him that I agree with," Evander admitted.

"Like what? Everyone he does is against your beliefs," Aves fired at him in a harsh voice. He contorted his face into an expression of confusion.

Evander let out a deep breath. "Kaiser once said, not long after the Immortal Truth was written, that we cannot exclude those we call enemy for even if they are our enemy, we can learn from them. Kaiser is our enemy and he is one with a vast degree of knowledge to be jealous of. To destroy him is to lose that wealth to the depths of time."

"If you are thinking that he is worthy of redemption." Kader became too flabbergasted to finish his thought.

"There is just something about him. A sense that he hides within the depths that fills me with a sense of pain and betrayal. I remember seeing it in Crossroads during the celebration. Your Dragonfire, Vorin, it should have burned him but it did not. Only someone who had suffered true pain can do that." Evander sighed deeply. "I see it every time I see him or hear him speak."

Everyone wanted to look over at Vorin but no one dared to. When they heard the great Dragon growl, they were glad that they did not. As usual, Aves did not react. Instead he quietly laid a hand on Vorin's left forelimb. It did little to still him.

"Dragonfire cannot harm Spirit Walkers," Vorin hissed. Smoke poured out of his nostrils in heavy puffs. He cursed in his own tongue under his breath.

It was if Vorin had cursed them all, rendering the crowd silent. For the younger members who had not seen the Dark Days, they were horrified by the idea that Dragonfire could be rendered powerless. For the Gryphons and Evander, the mere mention of a Spirit Walker stole all warmth from their bodies. Paladon and Stellaris immediately chattered back and forth in the Gryphon tongue with Stellaris becoming very heated in his manner. It took Aves saying a single curt word in the same language to silence them.

"The truth of that matter is best left unspoken for the time being. Myself, Vorin, and Evander know the tale and we do not want to horrify you with the details. Now, how to assist our new Shadowlord? Evander, stand up and show them," Aves firmly suggested. He nodded towards the Lord of the Lightborn.

Evander let out a deep breath and stood up. He appeared to be small and nervous than high and mighty as he moved to the center of their circle. He stood still and slowly pulled off his outer robe. His arms were so white with scars that his skin appeared to shimmer in the sunlight. He twisted and rolled his arms with a degree of difficulty.

"Only my people and Lord Aves know about these scars and how I got them. During the last battle of the Dark Days, I fought alongside many of your ancestors. You think this war is terrible now? Try living in a world where the dead walk among the living and their touch steals all warmth from you. The opposite of Demons who can burn you with their touch. I found myself assaulted on all sides by the Dark Spirits, the same ones that Kaiser has seen fit to summon. My life was only saved by Lord Aves," Evander gestured towards Aves. "And Cassiel Cipher, scribe of the Covenant of Spirits."

"Drako's Dragonfire drove the Dark Spirits away and while he rushed off to finish the job, I remained behind," Aves commented.

"Breaker of Dark Spirits. That is what my kind called the First Lord of Dragons," Vorin added to the conversation. He locked eyes with Aves and nodded.

"Cassiel had been in the path of the fire and was untouched by it. In fact, the Spirits, both good and bad, gave way to him. He was a Spirit Walker, born in the Darklands. That is the true origin of the Farlanders who later escaped to the land that gave them their name. Cassiel's blood lives on in the Anu line and that is why I am reluctant to face Kaiser. Spirit Walkers cannot be destroyed except by other Spirit Walkers. Cassiel is not here because he gave his entire being to the Covenant," Evander explained. He then threw his hands up in the air. "Why oh why did Bane leave us!"

The circle of Lords fell silent as Evander put his robe back on. Everyone seemed deep in thought, wondering the same thing. Why did Bane leave? Where was he? Was he even alive? Evander appeared to mope as he returned to his seat. He sat down in a slump, leaning to his right with his head in his hand. The sun seemed to dim as their Spirits did.

Aves then stood up and took command of the gathering. "Then we will just have to find a way to destroy a Spirit Walker ourselves. Perhaps together, we can combine our power and might and succeed in breaking Kaiser's Mirror. Then our real battle will begin."

THE WISDOM OF AVES

"What do you think that I should do to advise Ryder?" Kader asked as he followed Aves towards the Airborn camp on the eastside of Cascade.

"Peredur is under incredible strain. To attack a Shadow Mirror with such force and against a formidable will such as Kaiser, he will be hard pressed to succeed. Kaiser is eleven hundred years old. Peredur is two hundred and fifty. Even assuming the mantle of Shadowlord is no guarantee of success," Aves said over his shoulder. He was walking so quickly that the folds of his cloak undulated behind him. The feather detail on the fabric made appear as if he could take flight.

Kader struggled to keep up the pace. He was younger than Aves by many centuries and yet, he felt like the old soul. He ran over his various infirmities and pains in his mind. As he did, his right hip starting throbbing and he was reminded of the arrow that had struck him there seven years ago. He started to huff and puff.

Aves slowed his pace. "My apologies. When driven, Airborn can move quickly without realizing it."

"Thank you for your consideration. My body is not as whole as my mind is nowadays," Kader admitted with an exacerbated breath.

"Perhaps I should teach you some mediation and energy concentration techniques," Aves suggested with a grin. "Or perhaps how to refocus your pain?"

"That would be great. I do not think that my soul or energy

has been at peace since I started my career in Cross. Almost like I have been infected with a Mortal plague all these years," Kader replied with a sigh of relief. He wiped his brow.

He soon realized that Aves was not going towards his nation's camp as he turned towards the right and headed further east. He held back as Aves ascended a small hill that overlooked the camp. At the waving of his left arm, Aves elicited a chorus of shouting and cheers of praise. There was no doubt to Kader that the Airborn would do anything for their leader. They raised their voices up in love and respect for him without hesitation. He had to admit that he missed that in his homeland. It had been years since he had last seen and heard such widespread devotion from all walks of life. Those that lived in Cross were very quick to praise the royals while those further away were more divided.

The divide in the Shadowborn had existed since the death of Sin Silvanus. Sin had been a well-respected leader that was both firm and merciful in his rule. He was an experienced soldier and astute statesman. In the wake of his father's death, Sin was everything the Shadowborn needed. Then nothing short of chaos ensued after his death. Sin had exiled his eldest and former heir leaving his daughter Mali and second son Shiloh. It was thought obvious for Shiloh to take the throne but he was reluctant and stayed away from Cross. The people eventually agreed that the throne would go to Mali's son. Was it the best choice? Probably not but Akakios rose to the occasion when his uncle ran. History would tell a different story. Kader let out a deep breath as he pushed the thoughts away. It did him no good to dwell on a past that could not be changed.

Aves left the hill and directed Kader to follow. They walked along a well-worn path, the grass beaten down by the constant flow of foot traffic from days past. Every so often, Kader saw a dark patch where it appeared that a burning footprint had touched down. The sight sent shivers down his spine.

"Though we are not in a full scale attack, the Dark Spirits under Kaiser's command have seen fit to harass the brave souls of the Northern Alliance. I doubt that life will ever return to those spots. Let the blackened grass and soil serve as a reminder of what we face."

Kader glanced over at Aves who bowed his head briefly. The simple action made him wonder if an attack had killed one of the Airborn. Or was Aves just constantly reverent towards the lives of any lost souls?

"Come. Evander and Vorin are waiting," Aves stated.

Kader wanted to feel some sort of shock at learning that he was meeting privately with three great Lords instead of just Aves.

But in a way, this was what he wanted. A meeting with the three oldest beings on Terra. The three most likely able to decipher the power of a Shadow Mirror and figure out how to break it. He wondered if they had already considered how to break the Mirror. Maybe they figured out that all they needed was someone like Ryder to help. Or more to the point, challenge Kaiser's will with the likelihood of death if the effort failed. Was this something that they had already considered?

He did not have long to dwell privately on his thoughts. Vorin was stretched out across the meadow, folding in his left wing. Evander dodged the hard leading edge of the wing to avoid being hit in the head. He brushed his hands across his thighs to smooth out the golden fabric. Kader watched as Evander looked back to Vorin and say a few words that he could not hear. Both of the Lords greeted Aves with a polite bow of the head.

"Glad that you could join us so quickly after what we both decided was a very sudden council meeting. Vorin says it was our most decisive one yet," Evander suggested. He smiled. "It was very eye opening for me."

"Have you decided that this war is worth something after all?" Aves dug at Evander.

Kader thought that it was an insult but the three Lords started laughing.

"I still detest war on principle but as always, I understand why it is necessary," Evander responded. "Let us lose our fear to the winds and fire!"

Vorin snorted out a small burst of flame from his nostrils. He chuckled deep within his throat, creating a rumbling sound. "Save the celebration for later. We have a more important matter to discuss: how can we help break the Mirror?"

They all looked at Kader whose breath caught in his throat. He pointed at himself and immediately thought his response was stupid. He mentally told himself to calm down and realize that they were looking at him for input.

"Well, um, what remains of the rebellion within my homeland are going to Twilight. We should focus our attention on Branch since it is just over the River Shadow from their new base. I expect that our efforts will be quite bombastic to say the least and I recommend that the city be evacuated of civilians to avoid collateral damage," Kader proposed. It took him a moment to find his old diplomatic voice and confidence.

"Stellaris and the Gryphons will handle the evacuation with the Earthborn. The scout teams will also assist in the transport to safer grounds. Palani has already recommended a scout pair to lead the first leg of the evacuation. You might know them, Master

Erebus," Aves smiled. "Haro Artemis and Arik Barr."

Haro and Arik were a good choice, Kader thought. They had proven themselves in the skirmish near Agin and had been promoted as a result. They were now lieutenants of the Western Watch. The pair were rarely in Cascade nowadays much to Haro's sister's chagrin. Kader had bonded with the young Earthborn girl and had discovered her affection of Onyx. He enjoyed every moment he could get with her and often had her repeat the events of Crossroads. He could tell that both of the Artemis children were destined for greatness.

"But first, the Shadow Mirror. How do we help break it down? Attacking it directly will just waste our energy. We must unlock it," Vorin declared. He stretched out his neck and laid his head on the ground between the trio. "I think I know how but you must see it, not hear me describe it. If you will, lay your hands upon my head. I will impart a memory of when the Daylord raised his Mirror to seal the Darklands."

Kader, Aves, and Evander laid their hands on Vorin's head, focusing more on the crown of his skull. Kader stood on Vorin's right side with Aves while Evander stood on the Dragon's left side. All of them closed their eyes and settled their breathing. Even with Spirit Wake in play, the four connected their minds into one entity. Vorin's mind was the biggest and heaviest and the most wild. At its very core, it was savage and uncivilized, reminiscent of his bestial roots. He swept their minds through the noise of his thoughts towards the desired memory.

*****

Bane and Shadow Night stood side by side facing the ruins of the Darklands. In the distance, the land had turned gray with ash and the stones were black. The smell was that of death and decay. Amongst the desolation were the corpses of the dead.

"In a way, I find it cruel," Bane commented. He stared at a blast burned Demon skeleton with a broken banner pole through its chest.

"How so?" Shadow Night asked.

"To seal their land from yours is to give them up for lost. No hope of redemption for those who may not follow their race's darker ways," Bane replied. He bowed his head and closed his eyes. He put a hand over his heart.

Shadow Night looked over at Bane, perplexed by his behavior. "Do you have Demons where you come from?"

"A different kind of Demon that can destroy lives without shedding a single drop of blood. To seal such terror away is a fool's idea. But this is not my land so if it is what you wish, I will use my power to seal the Darklands away," Bane promised reluctantly.

Bane pulled a small knife from his sword belt. He turned over his left hand and made five small cuts, one on the meat of his fingertips. He then sliced open his palm. None of the cuts were deep but were deep enough for blood to well up. He put the knife away. He flicked his right wrist and a silver fire engulfed his hand. The blood on his left hand sparkled as he brought the fire close to it. He held his two palms a short distance apart. In the space between, the fire reached out for the crimson blood, turning red as soon as it made contact. Bane then pulled his hands apart and put them out before him.

Shadow Night listened as Bane began an incantation, twisting and manipulating his hands. When directed by Bane, he mimicked the same cuts on his left hand and pressed his hand forward. He tilted his head in confusion when it met resistance. The blood on his left hand did not drip and run down his arm but instead latched on to the invisible wall. A network of red veins extended out from his hand and connected with the webbing surrounding Bane's hands. The fire burned like a bed of coals, the size of it increasing with each of their heartbeats. Bane quickly dragged his right hand down and then ripped it upwards.

At his command, a massive and bright wall of energy erupted from the ground. The energy screamed like a chorus of distant voices, singing of something that was both jubilant and painful. Shadow Night wanted to pull away but he was completely paralyzed and locked in place. He could only watch as the wall spread out quickly in all directions. It shot to the west and east, all the while reaching for the sky. The wall was so bright that Shadow Night was sure that people could see it from leagues away.

Bane pulled back and Shadow Night felt himself able to move again. A hot puff of breath rustled their hair.

"Vorin, if you will," Bane said. He directed Shadow Night to step back and give the Dragon space. They watched as Vorin bathed the spot with a blast of white fire, the hottest he could generate from his core.

"So his fire is sealing the Mirror?" he asked Bane.

"No. His fire is warning both the Dark Spirits and the Demons that the wall will not come down until the ending of the world. Or the ending of our bloodlines," Bane explained. He chuckled lightly. "It would need both bloodlines working in reverse to break it. No other force will be able to breach its power."

"Then let our lines live forever for I do not want to see such war and destruction again. I am glad that you came to us in our hour need. The world will never forget," Shadow Night stated with great admiration.

Bane offered a polite nod. "So our legend begins."

*****

"Thank you for allowing us to see your memory but I still do not understand how we can help Ryder," Kader doubted. He bit his lip in nervousness for he did question a Dragon about his memories. He expected Vorin to roar his displeasure. The great Dragon did nothing.

Evander instead spoke up. "We must count on Ryder knowing how to raise and thus know how to reverse the process and bring it down. Because it was Kaiser that raised it, I don't think he will be able to get rid of it completely. Open a breach perhaps? Either way, he is far too young to attempt it alone. I will connect from the other side. Vorin? Aves? You should work to keep the breach open long enough for the Shadowborn to cross into Branch."

"I cannot use my Spirit energy as I wish. I do not see how I can assist Lord Vorin," Aves quickly pointed out.

"Then use your sword and spear to keep whatever Kaiser throws at Vorin and myself at bay. We three Lords will protect the break in the Mirror for as long as we can," Evander replied.

Aves nodded. "Then you have my hand and heart. Use your Spirit touched hands to connect Shadow and Light. Show Kaiser that to challenge the Immortal Truth is to challenge the sleeping giant in us all. He will learn that fear no longer controls us and that we will fight back. All of us."

*****

THE LIVING MAP

"Say that again. I wasn't listening," Kaiser grumbled as he pinched the bridge of his nose with his left hand. He leaned heavily on the left chair arm, acting as if he had a headache. In his right hand, he held the rim of a crystal wine glass that was half full with a deep red liquid.

Loran cleared his throat and started again with his report. "With the fall of Horizon, the last of the western strongholds are now under your control. Before I left Horizon though, I spotted in the distance several ships of the Waterborn preparing to set sail. I could not tell if they were armed..."

"How many?" Kaiser interrupted as he opened his eyes and dropped his hand. He took a sip of wine.

"Fifteen by last count. I have set a pair of watchmen to observe the fleet and a line of runners to make sure reports of their movements reach Cross as quickly as possible," Loran nervously stated. He was not sure how this conversation was going to go. Was Kaiser annoyed, tired, or did he just not care?

"I suppose you are looking for congratulations on your forthright thinking. Good job. You get a gold star," Kaiser mocked. His voice held no mirth and was utterly cold. He let out an exacerbated breath.

Loran gulped. He was certain that he had done everything right by Kaiser's command. He clenched and stretched out his hands several times in a row. "Where are the three ladies of your company?"

Kaiser scoffed and this time, a smirk spread across his face. He took another sip of wine and smacked his lips. "Disloyalty is punishable by death. Or in the case of your cousin, lack of power and stupidity. I certainly hope that you are not plagued by such troubles."

His words were as good as a threat to Loran. He was having a harder time figuring out where he stood in Kaiser's good graces. Even Rache appeared to be more openly nervous in their master's presence. His steel plate armor was starting to weigh down on him. Or was it his nerves that made his shoulders drop? He had already decided that he felt stronger and more at ease when he was away from Kaiser's presence. He had yet to decide if Kaiser's power overwhelmed his own into submission without even trying. It worried him as did the constant threat of death. Kaiser was sure to kill him without reason.

Loran watched in silence, waiting for Kaiser to dismiss him. He would not dare leave without being commanded to do so. But it seemed that Kaiser was content to slowly sip his wine. He then noticed a thin silver web creeping along the surface of the glass. The web spread out until the glass glowed brightly. He lifted his left hand to shield his eyes as he leaned away. Even with the seven foot distance between him and the dais, Loran was sure that Kaiser could send the pieces of glass out like jets of Dragonfire. He peered through his fingers when the expected shattering sound did not come.

The glass had broken apart but the hundreds of pieces floated quietly in the air around Kaiser's right hand. He twisted and waved his hand around in a trance like dance. The glass responded accordingly, floating away from his touch and swirling around his hand. Kaiser would flick a finger and a single piece would shoot away before being drawn back in. He chuckled softly as he swept his hand towards Loran. It looked like a sparkling battering ram aimed right at him.

"Are you afraid of me, Commander Win?" Kaiser laughed.

"No sir," Loran stated once he found his voice. He coughed a few times. "No sir."

"You should be. Fear is healthy. It means that you know your limitations before your betters. Now go. I have no more need of you at the moment," Kaiser dismissed with a wave of his left hand.

Loran stiffened and bowed so low that he could have kissed his knees. He did an about face and marched towards the tall ebony doors that led out of the throne room. He paused before them. With a loud creak, the doors slowly opened. Loran slipped through the opening as soon as he could fit. Just as he disappeared in the darkness beyond, the doors started to close. They shut with a heavy thud.

Kaiser got up off the throne and slowly descending the raised stone dais. He flicked his right hand and the glass pieces shattered into sparkling dust. He moved it in a circle. The cloud of glass dust streamed backwards to land upon the seat of the throne. It reformed into a solid crystal glass again. He put his palms together as he stepped to the center of the room. Kaiser quickly spread out his arms and the Living Map appeared at his silent command.

The Living Map was as he left it last: a transparent kaleidoscope of natural colors spotted with black. The opaque spots were also identified by the tiny streams of smoke that rose up from them. The once vibrant lands and waters looked diseased as if infected by a pox. The sight amused Kaiser as he slowly spun about on his feet. He had placed himself in the grasslands between the Waterborn and Fireborn nations. He sniffed the air, smelling the cold dew and earthy soil. Looking towards his right, he spotted the fleet of the Waterborn leaving the coastline of Isle.

"The most formidable navy of the Northlands." Kaiser scoffed. "Well second most once I have reformed that of the Shadowborn. We have great sailors in our own right to rival yours. We have already conquered the land. Let us conquer the sea."

He watched a small fleet of five ships heading towards the mainland. The royal banner of the Crowned Prince flapped vigorously in the wind. Still chuckling, Kaiser sliced open his left palm and let blood well up. The coin sized crimson pool broke into a web of crimson, following the lines of his hand. He moved and swayed to direct a stream of blood towards his innermost fingertip. The drop of blood hesitated for a moment before falling from Kaiser's reach. It hit the location of the fleet with a snap and sizzle.

Immediately, the seawaters turned rough as a fierce wind whipped up. The clouds above darkened and started to rumble. The sound grew in intensity. The first clap of thunder quickly followed the first sparks of lightning. The storm grew in size until it covered the fleet from all sides. Amidst the sound, a deafening roar boomed overhead. Kaiser watched as a large black Dragon shaped Spirit flew out of the thundercloud. It whipped around towards the first ship, flames spewing from its mouth.

"Not all Dragons are as civilized and cordial as Vorin. Some are savage and untamable, echoes of their violent beginnings with the Spirit of Destruction. Never underestimate the power of your enemy and assume that of their race will be kind," Kaiser mocked. He spat at the spot.

He could almost hear the screams but turned away towards

the east. In the east laid the lands of the Fireborn, hotheaded but great warriors. Adapted to a life in the desert and in the dry fields, the Fireborn were almost as hardy as any Shadowborn. Kaiser had to wonder how they would handle the attack of his Dark Spirits.

"Decisions, decisions. Being masters of a destructive force like fire, what is it that you fear? You venerate the Dragons like gods, even the destructive ones. You worship their great power and hot flames. Perhaps a little chill will do you some good," Kaiser stated.

He blew a puff of breath over his bloody hand all the while watching a patrol of Fireborn going north. The blood turned from crimson to dark blue. He raised his hand over the patrol and let a single drop fall. Faint screams erupted as dozens of Dark Spirits attacked. He watched as the Spirits ripped through the Fireborn. The sight of their suffering amused Kaiser. He pulled his hand back and began to consider where else that he could drop his poisonous blood. He laughed at the exciting thought.

"Come. Let us see how you fare alone," Kaiser murmured to a single Fireborn that had remained standing. He wafted his right hand over his left palm, bringing the image of the pitched battle to his hand. The Fireborn, a tall and brawny man, swung his spear around in a desperate attempt to keep the Spirits at bay. It wasn't long before a Spirit attacked from behind and ripped the Fireborn apart with its dark kin.

Another puff of breath made the image disappear. Kaiser traced the cut on his hand with the tip of his right inner finger. It quickly sealed at his touch. He wiggled his fingers and the blood faded. A sudden thump pressured his mind and he immediately knew that it came from the Southlands. He spun about on his feet and swept his left hand back to drag the map to Sawn. The river town was so bright with sparks of life that it would have been blinding to anyone but him. Kaiser could see through the light with no trouble, seeing the forms of Bane and a Gryphon speaking to each other. The Gryphon image then lifted up into the air and flew to the north. Its path brought Kaiser's attention to the blots of darkness. He snarled.

Axum's impatience for the lengthy wait brought Kaiser to a very dark place. He snapped his fingers and was set in the environment as if he was with them and not in the throne room. The forms of Axum, Aday, and the Dark Spirits were transparent due to the energy of the Living Map.

"So you are questioning my methods. Do you know nothing about how to hunt your prey? You do not rush in at the sign of blood. You wait and watch for the opportune moment to strike. You wait until," Kaiser started to say. He walked about the forest clearing and tapped every Dark Spirit's forehead. At his touch, their white eyes brightened and they roared, spittle dripping from their fanged mouths. "You wait until ferocity is at its peak and they are driven to kill anything and everything without hesitation."

Kaiser could see the slightly worried expression on Axum's face. He obviously had noticed the sudden change in the Dark Spirits. "Good. You realize that I am watching more closely than you previously thought."

He turned towards Aday who stood beside Axum like a nervous rat. The Shadowborn mumbled under his breath and wrung his hands repeatedly. In his eyes, Kaiser could see the conflict of interest and hints of humanity. Too bad it would not last for long. Kaiser pressed a finger to Aday's forehead, releasing a powerful madness in him. He laughed as he watched the struggle intensify and the madness strengthen.

"Do as your Master commands and kill them both. Kill them all."

*****

MEANING OF THE BOND

Normally, Rache watched Kaiser during his sessions with the Living Map but this time, he could not bring himself to stay. He had never felt this conflicted before. Everything within him was in turmoil. His senses were dull and his mind was numb. He felt physically diminished. Even the black cloak that he was wearing felt heavy. His shoulders slumped under the imagined weight. He let out a deep breath, his chest hurting him. It hurt in a way that reminded him of a pain that he wished that he could forget. He pressed his left hand over his heart.

A memory came to him unbidden as he steadied himself against the wall in the tiny alley. He covered his mouth with his right hand as soon as he felt the urge to cough. Cough! A Demon did not cough! Not like he was infected with some Mortal disease! The small physical action made him incredibly angry. He wanted to pound the wall behind him into dust. He wanted to scream out loud. As soon as he had that thought, his chest heaved and he coughed out a spray of blood on his hand. It was black and sticky. In a way, the sight was not unexpected. He had not drunk any blood in months though he killed many people in that time.

Why had he refused blood? That was not the way of a Demon. Blood was life. It was memory and power. It was everything to him. But as Rache considered how important consuming blood was to him, he did not miss it. Consuming blood was a way to take someone's identity. It laid a victim bare to his power and control. He could lose himself in the kill. Blood awakened the monster within.

Blood did not matter to him as much as it once had. It had been the crimson water of another that brought him back to life. The profane ritual that Kaiser had used thumped around his mind though he remembered very little of the moment. The memory of Kaiser's blood flowed in his veins like a constant chain between master and beast. Rache sneered at the thought. The mysterious bond was no way for a Demon to live. He should be free to roam the world as he pleased. Staying with Kaiser was just as finite as death and he almost preferred death to life as a slave.

Rache wiped his hand on the wall, smearing his black blood on the stone. He dragged his sleeve over his mouth to remove any residual staining. The coughing spell was over. He pushed himself to his feet and walked out into the street.

He wandered into the northeast section of Cross where the poor and destitute congregated. The main street was nearly empty of people. Two scrawny boys with sunken eyes scrounged around in the gutters. A hunch backed gray haired woman hobbled through a tavern door. Rache paused to look inside, seeing a roaring fire in the small common room through the dirty windows. He watched as the woman settled down beside it. A compulsion to follow her overcame him and he went inside.

The common room was tiny. Only three people were seated at the four available tables. Two men were huddled over a game of cards. A small pile of coins rested on the table between them. Rache brushed off the attention of the two men and chose to sit at the neighboring table next to the woman. He never carried coin and he was about tell the barman when the woman interrupted.

"Two ales good sir," the woman said. Her voice was aged and shaky.

"Of course," the portly barman said. He glanced over at Rache who still had his hood covered his face. He looked him up and down before going back towards the bar.

"Aren't you a bit old to partake in such an inferior drink?" Rache dared to asked.

"I should say the same of you or have you tired of the finest wines of the castle?" the woman fired back.

Rache slowly turned to look at her. Her face was heavily wrinkled and her hair was thin and gray. Her left eye was cloudy. Rache began to believe that at one point in her life, the woman was quite beautiful. She wore a patchwork dress and black long coat over her tiny frame. Rache could tell that he was twice as tall as her.

"You are the smallest Shadowborn that I have seen who is not a child," Rache commented.

The woman chuckled. "Cursed with short height but I am Shadowborn through and through." She thanked the barman as he set down the two flagons of ale. She glanced towards Rache and lifted her flagon. "Drink with me."

It was an innocent enough request and poisons did not affect him so he picked his up and took a big draught. The ale was light without any real body to it. A poor man's drink, he thought.

"It is not much but I rather like this ale. Does not leave one too inebriated to walk home. I have seen you with Lord Kaiser. Do you live in the castle with him?" the woman asked.

Rache had to wonder if this woman knew exactly who and what she was. If she did, she was not afraid. "I go where I wish."

She did not appear to notice his aversion to answer honestly. "I envy you then. To be free is the greatest gift of all that the Spirits can grant us."

"I do not think that Spirits think that highly of me," Rache admitted.

He had never bothered to familiarize himself with them. He only knew the name of the wolf Spirit Omu. The rest of the hierarchy was unknown to him. In a way, it was sad that a long lived being such as himself could not name the higher Spirits. The only reason he knew Omu's name so well was that the Great Wolf lorded over the passage of the dead. In reality, his education was rather poor. Kaiser was never interested in teaching him much of anything. Yet another prison.

"Even the All Spirit sees us, both good and evil, as part of the evolution of the world. We are the makers of change. The world is at our command if we choose to take control of our destiny," the woman mused in between sips of ale. She coughed once. "To destiny!"

Rache tapped the rim of his flagon to hers, drinking as she did. He set it back down on the table in front of him. "I wish that I could say I share in your optimism."

"Ha! This is not optimism. It is just acceptance that the fate of the world cannot be changed so long as it stays on its current path. Might as well raise my glass to that," the woman laughed out loud with a cackling sound.

"But it can be changed. Surely it can," Rache proposed in desperation. He wrapped both hands around the flagon.

The woman finished her cackling. "Let me tell you something. I was not always this shriveled or half blind. This hand." She lifted her right hand. "It once carried a bow. I could shoot a deer in the skull at a thousand paces. Sometimes even two thousand paces. But one foolish decision and I blinded my left eye. Now, I am withered and reduced to the chains of age and poverty."

"You do not seem like a fool to me," Rache pointed out.

"Oh but I am. I am a fool for allowing my infirmities to hold me back. I could have been great. Not if I had not injured myself but if I had chosen to live my life in a different way. Now I will become nothing more than a memory if I am lucky." The woman chuckled to herself, shaking her head. She traced a thin bony finger around the rim of her flagon.

She was such an odd character and yet, Rache was intrigued by her. He turned in his seat to face her more directly. "But you have seen so much. Is the path you ended up taking any worse or better than what could have been?"

"What could have been is a selfish dream. What could be is something greater if you are brave enough to take the chance," the woman replied. She kicked back and finished the rest of her ale. She smacked her lips. "Good as always."

Rache shook his head and laughed softly to himself. He turned back towards the woman to say something else only to discover that she had disappeared. Rache startled and leaned forward to study the space the woman had just been occupying. He pressed his hand on the wooden chair, finding it to be cold and lacking of warmth. He then investigated the flagon. It was full to the brim. He jerked his entire body back.

"The Gray Lady caters to the troubled. She comes and goes as she pleases for such is the nature of Spirits," the barman said after he witnessed Rache's confusion.

No wonder the woman knew who and what he was without saying a word. Any normal person would have been afraid of him. He checked his hood. It still lay heavy on his head and shielded his face. He looked at his pale hands. They did not look terribly unusual and different. He turned them over several times before glancing at the neighboring chair that had been occupied by the woman. He resisted the urge to inspect the chair and flagon again.

"Who was she?" Rache asked.

"No one knows save only the oldest of souls that walk Terra. Some say she was the mother of the Shadowborn people. Others say she was no one of great importance, just a soul looking for company," one of the card players stated as he looked up from his hand. He dropped a silver coin on the small pile.

His companion studied his hand of five cards before tossing two silver coins forward. "My grandfather told me that the Grey Lady was an old soothsayer from the Dark Days."

"Your grandfather is a drunken liar. Now are you going to hand me a card?"

The two men returned to their game without further word. It was strange that Rache had never heard of the Gray Lady.

Kaiser had never mentioned her. He was certain that she was not a figment of his imagination for the barman and the two men playing cards had seen her too. All of her words replayed in his head with a great rushing sensation. As he went over the words, he came to realize that they had been exactly what he needed to hear. He had to take control of his destiny if he was going to be anything more than a chained slave.

But what options did a Demon have in this world? Only one and it would mean going against everything he had known for the last thousand years.

*****

KING'S ORDER

Gyr flew one last circle over the city of Sawn before tilting his wings and twisting his body in preparation for landing. He shifted his weight and banked to the left. He flapped his wings once to maintain course. The wide walkway that wrapped around the top of the gate house was clear. With repeated short flaps, Gyr started to hover in an attempt to control his descent. His landing was clunky to say the least but Gyr was at least thankful that he did not fall backwards. The memories of his first landing attempt on the walkway made him cringe. He shivered in embarrassment and disgust. He was certain that if his friends back home watched him land, they would burst out laughing and whistling loudly.

Bane stood at the exact center point of the gatehouse with his arms crossed tightly. He was wearing his leather cuirass, pauldrons, and bracers for armor. His claymore was strapped across his back. To Gyr, Bane did not look any different than he had when they first met. The only thing missing was the fur lined cloak.

"Does the forest speak or are the trees silent?" Gyr asked quietly.

Bane reached up and scratched his brow. "It is a different silence now. The birds are quiet. The woodland creatures dare not move from their nests and burrows. Even they can sense the danger that is coming." He let out a deep breath and frowned. "And yet, the danger has not moved since you first spotted the Dark Spirits. It has been days, weeks, maybe even a few months, and still they remain frozen in place. What are they planning? Where are they going? Will they attack Sawn?"

"At least their pause has given you time to train the people here and for the Mayor of Sawn to send messengers to Arken," Gyr commented as he looked towards Bane.

"Still. This is not the nature of Dark Spirits. They are beings of limited intelligence. Once they have a target in sight, they attack until either the prey is destroyed or they are. They do not just hesitate. What is he playing at?" Bane mused. He shuddered once.

"Who?" Gyr asked.

"Axum the Demon controller and perhaps even the made Shadowborn," he replied.

Gyr looked in the direction of the northbound road. The trees loomed over the wide dirt path, casting dark shadows. Each time that the shadows moved, Gyr became tense and uneasy. A part of him dreaded the battle to come. It had oddly taken longer than expected for any sign of attack. Bane did not appear too worried but Gyr was always guaranteed to find him at nightfall in the same spot. The people of Sawn appeared anxious but ready with the soldiers trained by Bane to face the supernatural enemy. But perhaps that was the strength of a real leader, Gyr thought. A leader and certainly a commander in battle was strong in body and in control of their emotions. Gyr could not help but think that Bane was rather emotionless until he was pressed for a response. It was perplexing.

"Battles do not always happen as expected or planned. Right now, this is a waiting game. Danger is coming and stalking this city like a predator on the hunt. It wants to catch the people off guard before desperation kicks in," Bane stated, never taking his eyes off the road. "Tell me, have you ever been in battle before?"

His first memory of the Southlands replayed in his mind. Gyr shivered at the thought of the hunter that had tried to kill him during the blizzard. "I am trained in combat but no, I have never been in a true battle. The Northlands has been in relative peace for a thousand years."

"Save for the menace you named to me. Kaiser Adonis," Bane mused. He fell quiet for a moment. "Kaiser Adonis. It has been a long time since I last saw him."

"How well do you know him? Or know of him?" Gyr asked. He had put this question to Bane before but Bane had yet to answer him.

Bane let out a deep breath. "I know that he is older than me by twenty years." He paused for a moment. "Kaiser was acting as a healer when I first met him. A good one for his age. Of course,

I could see why his talents were so great. Spirit Walkers are capable of acts far greater than those of the Spiritborn, Gryphons, and yes, even the Dragons. There was instant animosity between us because he knew that I could see straight through him. I tried to warn Shadow Night against Kaiser's councils but he chose to ignore me. Thus, Shadow Night knew exactly what Kaiser was and when his eldest son Anu was killed, he looked to Kaiser as a way to bring his beloved child back. Shadow Night may have been my friend but even we fought and argued."

The statements shocked Gyr for he had always thought that Bane was older than Kaiser. And Kaiser being a Spirit Walker? The Shadowlord and the Daylord, two legendary friends, fighting? Maybe he had wrongly viewed Kaiser as an upstart child to what he believed to be Bane's authoritative adult. In a way, Bane's statement about age and Shadow Night punished him for his mistaken thought. He dropped his head sheepishly.

"Age is just a number. This Ryder Coba you have spoken of is proof of that. He should not be able to compete with Lords like Aves or Evander and yet he does. Kaiser should not be able to keep Vorin the Dragonlord at bay and yet he does. Thus is the power of a Spirit Walker."

"He keeps you at bay," Gyr blurted out without realizing what he had just said. As soon as he did, his eyes widened in horror and he shuffled away from Bane. He lifted his wings to shield his head and neck.

Unexpectedly, Bane laughed though it did little to ease Gyr's mind. Gyr peeked through his wing feathers. Bane held his head up towards the sky with eyes closed. His arms were still crossed and thankfully, his sword was still sheathed. The Gryphon breathed a sigh of relief. But still he wondered. Was Kaiser involved in Bane's abandonment of the Northlands?

"There are greater evils in this world than Kaiser Adonis. I suppose you do deserve to know why I left. Both Vorin and Proto Avis knew that I was leaving to tend to private affairs. I fully intended to return. They fully believed that I would be coming back after a year. But as the years passed, I am sure that they began to wonder what happened to me? Was I dead? No, I am certain that they refused to believe that. Your presence here is proof of that," Bane proposed solemnly. Bane turned to face Gyr. "Tell me. What do you think is the most powerful weapon of a war?"

Gyr folded his wings over his back as soon as he was certain that Bane was not going to strike him. Though it seemed like the Daylord was prepared to speak the truth, Gyr was not entirely certain he was going to get it. "Fear?"

Bane nodded. "Fear is a powerful weapon that can stop you

from making a decision or it can help you make a foolish one. It can do more damage to your courage and willpower than any physical weapon can. But fear can also make you desperate and wild. It can force you to seek the comforts of the life you know rather than to step into the unknown."

"What does fear have to do with you? The tales speak of your unshakable courage," Gyr cautiously asked.

Bane turned back to look upon the north road. He studied the environment with a careful eye. A thin branch fell to the ground with an audible thump. The falling of the branch spooked a rabbit out of its hiding place in the grass and it bounded away. It was the first sign of life that he had seen since he started his watch. He let out a deep breath.

"Once again, those of greatest age in Terra know a small truth of my origin. I am from the Eastlands, a man of no renown until my appearance in the Northlands. I went from a nobody to High King of Terra and Lord of the Immortals." Bane chuckled. "Me a king? If my kin were still alive, they would fall over laughing at the idea."

Now the mystery was starting to unfold! Gyr got excited and shuffled in closer to listen. He wondered if the Lords in Crossroads knew the story that Bane was about to tell him. Suddenly, he felt hesitant. Was learning the truth really this easy? There had to be a catch. Bane could not be undoing a thousand years of mystery just because he asked nicely.

"Though I wish to know the truth as much as anyone in the Northlands, I want to earn the right to know. I want to be able to show you that I am true to myself and what I believe in before you place that trust in me," Gyr put forth with a bow of the head.

"Then you are as noble and true as your kin are known to be. That is one of the things I miss the most about the Northlands. The honesty and purity of your race. The great love you bear for heart and home. I can say that I am glad to have a Gryphon such as yourself at my side in the battle to come."

Gyr shivered with delight and joy at Bane's words. What greater praise could there be? But the mention of the battle brought Gyr back down to earth. He listened to the assembly of soldiers on the ground that until this point had remained silent. They were undoubtedly nervous about the setting sun and fighting in darkness. Gyr managed to glance over his left shoulder to see torch bearers and street lighters darting amongst the crowd in their mission to provide as much light as possible.

"What are your orders for me?" Gyr asked, stiffening his posture before his commanding officer.

"Something tells me that Charon and Ferran's Shadowborn

father will make an appearance, fighting alongside the Demon Axum as his ally. I want you to keep all three of them alive. However, should this Shadowborn seek to kill his sons, you have my order to kill him."

"Certainly I would protect them. Charon is my friend and by extension, I will safe guard his brother," Gyr declared with gusto. He squared his shoulders and sat up straight.

Bane sighed deeply. "I know."

"Then why order me to kill when I will already do anything to ensure their safety?" Gyr was confused. Was Bane just trying to stress the importance of eliminating a threat?

Bane closed his eyes as if to reexamine a memory or ancient thought. After a long moment of silence, he opened his eyes. He turned his head to look directly at Gyr. "Because I believe this Shadowborn to be Aday Silvanus."

Gyr was struck silent. Aday Silvanus was alive? A Shadowborn royal fathered two half breed bastard children with two different mothers. But kill a Silvanus, a trueborn descendent of Shadow Night? Inconceivable! He could not do it. He would not do it! To do so would further breakdown the protective power of the Immortal Truth. No, he absolutely refused to do it. And yet, by refusing the order, he was dooming Charon and Ferran. Kill one to save two or let two die to protect one. It was a decision that Gyr did not want to make lightly.

"I know what I ask of you is difficult. It does go against the tenets of the Immortal Truth, a code that you have held dear for your entire life. But this is that tenet in full. Protect the bloodlines of the champions at all costs. Even if it means to bring harm to the bloodlines in order to protect the whole," Bane explained with a very serious voice. He nodded his head once.

"The true meaning of sacrifice," Gyr gulped.

It brought him back to his father's stories about the execution of Akakios. The Shadowborn leader had waged an unjust war against the peaceful Waterborn, killing Lord Nereus in the process. According to him, it was Kaiser that stopped Akakios from going further. The remaining Lords swooped in to clean up the mess and began criminal proceedings against Akakios. The prosecution lasted for months before a decision had been made. From what his father told him, Akakios took the writ of execution with great dignity and acceptance. His uncle Shiloh had been the one to deliver it to his hand. What Ryder thought about the proceedings, few knew.

"When the time comes, listen to your heart and let it guide you. I need you to do this for me for my efforts must be focused on the Demon. I need to be able to trust in you like you trust in me so strongly. What these people are about to face is most certainly be beyond them. You and I are who they are depending on to help them survive the night."

It took a long time for Gyr to reply. "Ok."

ANCIENT POWERS UNLEASHED

Bane's brow furrowed and he turned his gaze back on the road. He clenched his jaw tightly. He dropped his arms, stretching out his hands and flexing each finger.

"What is it?" Gyr asked quietly. He shuffled in closer to keep their conversation private.

"It has begun," Bane replied.

Gyr looked down at the roadway and spotted a black cloaked figure. The cloak was plain with no adornments. The figure was unusually tall. Gyr shivered with a sense of cold and dread. Whoever the figure was, they were an omen of darkness.

"Bane Arlis! High King of Terra and Daylord Champion of the Immortal Truth! Lord of all Immortals! I greet you most heartily!" the figure shouted with an undeniably male voice. He swept his left arm forward in an exaggerated bow before standing up straight. "And I see that you have a fine feathered friend at your side. What is your name, Gryphon?"

Gyr snarled and prepared a curse in his native tongue but Bane stayed him with a head shake. "Do not rise to his taunt."

"You are right to listen to your liege lord, Gryphon. A curse in your tongue would do little to frighten me or stay me from my path. I have my orders to attack this city and attack it, I will!" the figure laughed out loud. He lifted a finger to point at Bane. "But I much prefer battling for the fate of Sawn in single combat. Come on, your Majesty. Show us the true power of the Daylord."

"This has to be a trap. I advise you not to accept," Gyr

warned. He growled as he looked back at the figure. "I sense no good about this creature."

"Of course you wouldn't. He is a Demon. The one I must face," Bane laughed softly. He cleared his throat. "Axum! Long have you sat in waiting, waiting for the command of your dark master! Let us end it here tonight and determine who is stronger and master of the Southlands!"

The figure's cloak unfurled into hundreds of Dark Spirits. The Dark Spirits surrounded him, their eyes glowing white, gold, and red. They were an assortment of shapes and size but all had long claws and sharp teeth. Axum himself was not heavily armored, wearing dark gray pants, black leather boots, and a thick blood red waistband. His bracers matched his waistband. A breast plate, back plate, and pauldrons cover his upper body and shoulders over a shirt of chainmail. He held a thick broadsword in his right hand. A twisting black scar wrapped around the muscle of his left arm. The lower half of his left arm was visibly lighter than the rest of his body. He had no hair on his head or face, not even eyebrows.

Axum's entire appearance felt unnerving to Gyr but the Gryphon knew that he had to harden himself quickly. This was battle, a real battle where life and death was on the line. He glanced over at Bane and nodded.

"May the good Spirits bless and protect you, your Majesty," Gyr stated. He then frowned and turned his full gaze on Axum. A growl built up in his throat. He flared his wings and stood up tall.

Bane covered his mouth to hide his laughter. He glanced at Axum's shocked face. The Demon had clearly not expect a Gryphon to curse him in his native tongue. It was a well thought out choice of words though Bane was quite certain that Gyr's parents would have fallen over in shock. The words were definitely not polite conversation.

"That might be the best cursing that I have heard in a long time. And I thought the Mortal ocean sailors were terrible," Bane commented.

Gyr puffed out his feathered chest with pride. "My parents might be upset that my grandfather taught me that curse. He told me that it came from the Dragons."

"Then I am sure Lord Vorin would appreciate knowing that his kin can still upset a Demon long after their bones have become dust," Bane replied. He nodded once. "You know your duty and I have mine. If we both survive this battle, it seems that I have a bit of explaining to do."

"Before I go, can I ask one question? Why now when I have been begging for answers since we first met?" Gyr asked. He had half turned towards the back ledge, preparing to take flight.

Bane sighed deeply. He lifted his gaze towards Axum who was babbling and trying to come up with an equally damaging response. "I don't know."

That was going to have to do for now but Gyr at least felt that his mission was no longer foundering in uncertainty. He took one last look at Bane before launching up into the air.

*****

"Are you done with your shock or should the Gryphon come back and repeat his words?" Bane mocked.

Axum stammered for a bit before answering. He jabbed a finger towards Bane. "Words are merely words. What will matter is if a farmer from the Eastlands is ready to tell the truth to the people that worship him to godhood. You have waited a thousand years."

"Perhaps I realized things that I thought I could ignore. Turns out I cannot no matter how hard I try," Bane replied as he pulled out his great sword. He gripped the heavy weapon with his right hand.

The Dark Spirits moaned and spittle dripped from their jaws. Axum stayed them with a gesture of his hand. He then pulled out his own sword. "Whatever your reasons, I intend to finish the job that Kaiser Adonis asked of me. Say hello to the Spirit World for me."

As soon as Axum spoke his last words, the hundreds of Dark Spirits split apart and became thousands. They surged towards the city wall like a rolling ocean wave. Their outlines undulated and shifted as they banded together to attack. Bane needed only a second to cast a protective Spirit Shield with his left hand. The silver wall of energy pushed outward until stopping just before reaching the Dark Spirits. It then rocketed backwards, fading as it went into the city. Bane could only pray that the Spirit Shield would protect the Mortals fighting with him from the deadly touch of their enemy. He now had to focus on stopping Axum.

Axum leapt up to the wall, flipping over the stone railing of the gatehouse to face Bane. He roared a battle cry, gripping his black curved blade tightly with both hands. He charged forward to attack. Bane pulled his sword up in time to block. The collision between the two weapons was electrifying, metallic sparks shooting out. They pushed against each other for a moment before Axum pulled back and rushed forward for another attack.

All around them, the Dark Spirits rushed over the walls and

streamed into the city. Axum was exhilarated by their presence. However when one drew too close in an attempt to attack Bane, Axum cut it down. The dark energy dispersed with a deafening scream.

"Do not think that I did that as a favor to save you. You are mine and mine alone," Axum sneered.

"Then I won't thank you if that will ease your conscience. But then, you do not have one," Bane retorted sharply.

"No, I don't!" the Demon roared.

Bane flipped off the wall to avoid Axum's charge. He landed in a cloud of dust and quickly looked up. Axum was flying towards him with his sword raised over his head. Bane brought his sword up to block. The two steel edges screeched as they scraped against each other. Bane whipped around under the attack while Axum slid towards his right side. He swung and cut across Axum back. Axum lurched forward with a cry but immediately wheeled around to counter. Bane jumped back to avoid the slash to his stomach. The Demon kept swinging his sword about, forcing Bane on the defensive.

With his claymore, Bane needed more room to mount an attack. But he would never give up the weapon that had been with him through countless battles. One thousand years had done little to diminish its strength and sharpness. Bane had always made the effort to take proper care of the blade. Because of that, he knew it would never fail him. He launched himself up and over Axum to land behind his back. He swung hard, expecting to cut the Demon's chainmail shirt off. Axum, having predicted the maneuver, spun around to defend against it. The two swords met again with a metallic clang.

Both Mortals and Dark Spirits alike fled from the reach of the battling Bane and Axum. Each of their hits on each other shook the ground, knocking a few soldiers off their feet and scaring several small Dark Spirits into dissipating. Sparks shot out every time their swords met. Whenever they darted forward or swung their weapons, it was if their bodies commanded the wind to give them speed. Silver and black fires burned in their wakes before fading quickly. The fires left gouges on the ground.

The speed and strength behind their exchange increased the longer their battle dragged on. Bane moved with a rough but calculating sense of elegance. Axum's moves were more refined and sharp. Despite their differences in style, neither could land a hit on the other. Bane was either too agile or Axum was too quick in mounting a defense. Their shared failures to draw blood drove them even harder.

"For a self-trained warrior, I am surprised at the level of

your skill," Axum commented as they pushed each other. He gritted his teeth and snorted in Bane's face.

"Why should you be surprised? You and your master pissed off an already angry farmer from the Eastlands and helped shape who I became. The farmer is gone but the King of Terra has arrived!" Bane laughed. "We take heart and home very seriously where I come from."

Axum shoved hard and forced Bane back. Bane stumbled for a few steps before steading himself. "You say that you take heart and home seriously? If that were true, then why have you let a war brew up in the Northlands? One so big that it has spilled over to the Southlands! Its power before you now!"

"I am not from the Northlands. My home is in the Eastlands," Bane said without thinking. He immediately regretted it. The home of his birth was gone. And soon, the one of his true heart would be too. He could not let Axum win. He clenched his jaw. His grip tightened over the hilt of his claymore. No, he was not going to let Axum win. "No, I am from the Northlands and when I am done with you, I will return and destroy your master."

Bane leaned forward, his left crossed in front of him and his right holding his sword out behind him. He lifted two fingers of his left hand. A rush of silver fire engulfed the sword.

"You should not be able to use your powers," Axum growled. He flashed his pointed white teeth.

"Your master's attempt at Spirit Wake may stop the Spiritborn but it cannot stop me. I am Farlander, not a single drop of Spiritborn blood in my body. I am a child of the Spirit of Time's mind, Immortal and strong."

Axum snapped and snarled in the Demon tongue, saliva spraying from his mouth with each guttural syllable. "Then I am a child of the Spirit of Destruction, here to annihilate the children of the Spirit of Creation. Time versus destruction. Let us write a battle for the history books o mighty Daylord."

They charged at each other, fires in their wake. Nothing else mattered but each other. Bane swung his Spirit Fire licked sword at full force as Axum's wicked blade drove up to meet it. The entire ground shuttered beneath their feet from the collision of weapons. Axum and Bane slashed, cut, and stabbed at high speed, creating even more powerful quakes. The stone streets cracked and split, fissures rushing outward. The metallic sparks burned whatever they touched. When Bane spotted a fire starting to grow out of the corner of his right eye, he swiftly swung his sword through the air. The burst of wind snuffed the flames in a flash.

Seeing the split second distraction, Axum attacked Bane's left side. He threw himself like a battering ram and knocked Bane off balance. Bane stumbled, falling to one knee, his sword flush with the ground. Axum stood over him with his sword raised up high.

"It won't be that easy to kill me!" Bane shouted. In the blink of an eye, he fired a blast of silver light from his left hand directly into Axum's torso. The Demon flew back and crashed into a granite pillar etched with the date of Sawn's founding.

Axum flipped up to his feet and roared. He launched himself towards Bane but not before cutting through the stone. His sword sliced through the hard granite with ease. He struck Bane as soon as the broken piece hit the ground. The furious exchange of blows continued in a deadly twisting dance between Demon and Daylord.

*****

DRAWN TO THE FLAME

"Must do as Master says. Like Master says. Must kill them. Must set them free. Yes I must," Aday babbled as he stalked into the city in a hunched over manner. He ignored the weight of his old armor and thick cloak. His stringy black hair hung in his face.

Despite his erratic mannerisms, Aday skulked into Sawn undetected. The chaos of the attack helped to shield him from attention for as soon as someone saw him, a Dark Spirit jumped in and killed them. Aday did not pause to watch, focusing solely on his master's orders. Nothing else mattered to him but the end game. He repeated the words over and over under his breath.

He moved through the eastern section of the city. Trees grew thick and tall over the rooftops and casting the area in shadow. Yellow light streamed on to the dirt streets from where people, who had locked themselves inside, had lit fires in their homes. Aday could hear a mother and a father tell their two children not to worry and to believe in the Daylord. The father said that the Daylord would make sure that dawn would come and they would be safe. Safe. Aday briefly wondered if they knew the true meaning of the word. How many of their kin would have to die to ensure their safety?

The Mortals were a stupid short lived race. They physically resembled the Immortal peoples as they had hairless skin, walked on two legs, and had able hands to do a variety of tasks. The hair on their heads varied from yellow blonde to midnight black though the older a Mortal was, the more white their hair was. Mortals showed their age and in Aday's mind their frailty all too well. If Bane had thought to set up a guard around his sons, they would be no match for him. He would slaughter them before they could bat an eye. No one was going to stand in his way. He would kill them all. Stupid Mortals. They knew nothing. They made him angry. He snarled as he spotted a group of four soldiers running his way. They did not seem him yet. He was going to pounce on them and cut off their heads before they could even realize what had happened.

And yet, Aday paused. He remained in the shadow of a knotted oak tree's branches, his black cloak shielding him from sight. He watched as the four soldiers ran on by him. Why? Why did he not kill them? It would have been so easy for him.

Because that is not who you truly are.

Aday looked about to see who just spoke to him. It took him a while to realize that the voice was inside his head. He smacked his left temple and bent over as if to empty his ear. He wiggled his jaw.

Listen to me. You are not a killer. You are strong. Fight this. I know that you can do it.

Again the voice! Aday growled as he slapped both sides of his head repeatedly. He hated that voice. It was evil. He had to rid himself of it. But how? How could he get rid of it? Yes! His orders. He must kill his sons.

No!

"Master says we must and I will do as Master says," Aday replied. "Master knows what is best."

He pushed himself away from the oak tree with such reluctance that he wondered why he was moving in the first place. He paused just before he could step into a beam of yellow light. The yellow light felt foreign and yet strangely familiar. His thoughts drifted to the father who spoke to his children about the protective might of the Daylord.

Yes, the Daylord can help you. He can free you from this prison.

This time, the voice in his head did not fill him with a sense of anger. In fact, he welcomed the clarity of it. It reminded him of something distant and warm. The image was hazy but grew stronger the more Aday thought about the memory.

*****

"Grandfather, I am glad to see you well and alive," Aday greeted. He and Shadow Night embraced tightly.

438

"Alive yes. Well? My body has seen better days. My ears haven't stopped ringing since that one Demon struck me in the head with a rather nasty club," Shadow Night laughed as he tapped his left temple. Blood was caked in his hair. "What of you, my grandson? How do you fare on this morning?"

Aday grabbed his right shoulder and attempted to rotate his arm. He cringed and seethed in pain. "A dislocated shoulder. A fair share of cuts, bumps, and bruises but I think that I will live."

"Nothing that a healer cannot fix. Even that young Adonis boy could take care of your wounds. He is a fine healer in his own right," Shadow Night suggested. He set his hands on his hips and bent backwards enough to reset his spine. The vertebra cracked loudly. "This is going to hurt for a while."

"Grandfather, he is the one that nearly killed me. Do you not remember? I do not want to be anywhere near that monster of a man," Aday retorted.

Shadow Night patted Aday's left shoulder gingerly. "People can change, Aday. If you will not see him, perhaps your Uncle Sage can tend to your wounds."

He did not know why he laughed at this particular moment. But Aday felt relieved to see his grandfather in one piece. The battle had gone terribly wrong so quickly and the sea of Demons had separated them early on. Eight days had gone by since they had last seen each other and when either had a decent rest. As an Immortal, Aday knew that he could fight for a long time on little rest but this battle was beyond his physical capability. Many had died to protect him and keep him alive. He was their beloved Prince after all. It saddened Aday to think of those who fell.

Shadow Night put a hand on Aday's left shoulder. "Do not worry for the battle is over and we of the Northern Alliance have won. Your father and uncle have also lived to see the dawn and it makes my heart happy to see my family whole. Even your grandmother and mother, who both fought with amazing power and grace, will greet us when we return to camp. As well as one other."

"Who?" Aday asked. He quickly went through in his head all of his family members who participated in the battle. His uncle Sage was at camp as chief healer. His little sister was safe in Cross. He was certain that his grandfather would have mentioned one of the other Lords by name.

"Come and you will see," Shadow Night smiled. He directed Aday to walk with him at his side.

The pair snaked their way through the carnage and mixed crowd of soldiers. The Shadowborn soldiers leaped up and cheered the Silvanus name with their fists high in the air. The sound of their voices cheered Aday up. He offered a wave when he could for his left arm pained him from a long gash. He had ripped off strips of fabric from a fallen banner and bound the bloody wound days ago. It needed proper medical attention..

Aday was surprised to see Ogon, the white Lord of the Dragons, and a smaller wine red Dragon blocking the entrance to the Shadowborn camp. Both of them twitched with excitement uncharacteristic of such fierce creatures.

"I have never seen you before in the Northlands but I am glad to see you now," boomed the deep voice of Ogon. "You are most welcome among us. Vorin, go and tell the Lords of the Gryphons about our new friend and ally."

The red Dragon nodded once before stepping back. Aday watched as the still massive creature turned around, hit a running start, and lifted into the air with six deep wing beats.

"This new ally? Is that who you meant?" Aday asked his grandfather in a low voice.

Shadow Night nodded. A wide smile spread across his face. "Never have I seen such power and finesse from a single individual. Together, we were a sight to behold. Nothing and no one could stand before us. It seems that he brought out the best in me even though I had long thought it gone."

Ogon turned towards them with a bright light in his ice blue eyes. He flashed his teeth in a manner that Dragons considered to be a smile. Standing beside him and in front of the entrance was a brown haired man with fair skin and eyes as blue as Ogon's. He wore a dark brown leather cuirass with matching pauldrons on his shoulders. His pants were dark grey and his tunic was a brilliant blue. His deep red bracers and waistband matched the color of the red Dragon Vorin that had just left. A claymore was strapped across his back.

"May I present Bane Arlis, a hero who came in our darkest hour to bring our world back to the light of day," Shadow Night said as he gestured towards the man.

Aday suddenly felt compelled to bow before Bane. He glanced towards his grandfather for direction.

"Finally, I meet your grandson. He resembles you greatly," Bane greeted with a slight bow of the head. "Perhaps I can help you with that wound on your arm and draw out the Demon poison that is festering there."

He did not know why he did it but Aday extended his arm towards Bane once he came within reach. Bane gingerly took his injured arm and held it up with his left hand. He then carefully put his right hand over the bloody makeshift bandage. Aday then felt a strange tickling sensation that rippled from his fingertips up to his shoulder. He resisted the urge to pull away. The sensation then focused on the gash and Aday felt his pain diminishing. He looked up at Bane in confusion.

"What sort of magic is this?" Aday asked.

Bane chuckled. "It is mine. You need not fear anymore. The Demon poison is gone and your wound should now heal properly. I suggest the talents of your Uncle Sage to tend to your shoulder."

"But what of you? What happened to the poison?" Aday quickly wondered out loud. He did not mean to speak his thoughts for everyone to hear.

"So long as you are well, you need not worry about me. But if you should ever need my help again, do not hesitate to call."

*****

Help. That was what Aday needed. But what kind of help? He did not know and the very thought frightened him. The madness was too deeply ingrained in his being. He was broken and unfixable. Tears welled up in his eyes as he started moving forward against his will. He could feel the madness tightening its hold again.

No! I need more time!

Aday gritted his teeth as that same infuriating voice filled his head. He quickened his pace before breaking out into a full run. He easily leapt over obstacles. If any souls crossed his path, Mortal or Dark Spirits, he cut them down without a second thought. No one mattered. Nothing mattered. Nothing but fulfilling his Master's orders.

"I will not fail you, Master. I will kill them. Kill them both. Yes, Master. Must kill them all."

*****

CHARON STEPS UP

"Are you sure that this place is safe? I mean, Bane said it was Dark Spirits that were going to attack. I doubt that a stone wall would be able to stop them from coming in," Ferran nervously said. He sat in a chair by the fire place, his arms wrapped tightly around his knees. His skin was pale white with fear.

"Not to worry. Though the Southlands is largely known as the home of Mortal humans, it has a little Immortal influence. It is said that Arken was one of the first places that Farlanders landed with their ships thousands of years ago. They met the first Mortals who were very primitive and lived a hunter gatherer lifestyle. Some may disagree with me but Farlanders brought a sense of culture and civilization to our ancestors," Chane explained as he uncrossed his legs and rubbed his knees.

Charon stood closest to the front door, leaning against the wall behind Chane. He kept his arms crossed tightly. "Why would people disagree with you?"

"Some are of the mind that the Farlanders should have bestowed Immortality upon the Mortals but I do not believe that was in their power to give. So those same people believe that the Farlanders, though admittedly more wise, imposed their will and left without a trace when they decided that Mortals were too short lived and stupid to make any sort of progress," Chane replied. He reached over to a side table and offered Ferran a biscuit. Ferran shook his head and he put it back.

"And yet, Bane is a Farlander and the Mortals look to him

442

like some sort of god," Charon commented. He returned his attention to the front door.

"I cannot control what others think and I do not believe that Bane can either. Immortality left this land a very long time ago and thus transformed into distant and mysterious legends," Chane stated.

Ferran mumbled to himself for a moment before speaking up. "Then how does Bane think that Mortal people can fight against Dark Spirits. I ever heard that a Demon was coming too!"

"Because Mortals can be just as strong as Immortals. Just in a different way. Long life does not equal great power as short life does not equal weakness. Bane knows this and taught the people here exactly what they needed to do. As for the Demon..."

"Bane will face the Demon himself. Perhaps if he kills the monster, the Dark Spirits will disappear," Charon suggested.

"A wishful sentiment. I certainly hope that is the case." Chane let out a deep breath.

An uneasy silence fell between them. Outside, they could hear the creak of tree branches moving in the wind and the hushed conversations of the soldiers. Twenty of them had been assigned to guard the house and defend it against any attack. Ferran shivered as he could clearly hear what they were talking about. He had never thought about how strange his sharp hearing had always been. Now that he knew that he was a half breed from a powerful bloodline, it freaked him out. He slumped down lower in the chair, desperate to disappear.

Charon recognized the uneasiness in his brother. He wanted to comfort him and let him know that everything would be ok. He remembered his own struggle with his burgeoning senses and abilities. When Ferran looked up at him, he mouthed the words that everything would be fine.

"How do you know that? How do any of us know that?" Ferran demanded.

"Because Bane is here and so is the Gryphon Gyr. I promise you that we will survive this night and live to see the dawn. That is what my ancestors believed and that is what I believe," Chane stated. He stood up from his seat and stretched by pressing his hands on his lower back. He then excused himself from the room.

"Charon?" Ferran meekly asked.

"Yes?" Charon replied. He turned to face Ferran.

Ferran gulped and swallowed hard. "As strong as Chane's belief is, I just can't bring myself to feel as hopeful as him. Both him and the soldiers talk about how powerful Bane is but he is after all one person."

"One very powerful person if you were to ask Gyr."

"What about you?" came Ferran's quiet question.

Charon knew that he was nowhere near Bane in terms of power and skill. Explaining that to Ferran would only make his fear worse. He bit his lip, trying to figure out what to say. Only one thing came to mind. "I am as strong as I need to be."

Chane returned, adjusting a wide belt he had tied around his waist before sitting back down. He leaned back and savored the comfort of the chair. "These old bones are not what they used to be. My poor spine needs so much support these days."

The comment made Ferran and Charon nervously laugh for both knew that Charon was thirty years older. They were certain that Chane knew too but declined to comment. It was such a light hearted thing to say when things looked so dark for them.

Screams of death and metallic sword strikes alerted the three men to the pitched battle outside. All sense of peace and safety left them. Ferran moaned while Charon pulled out his sword and place himself before the front door.

"Hide!" Charon shouted.

Chane jumped up from his seat and went to pull Ferran out of his. Ferran refused to move. The scared young man shook his head vigorously.

"Go now!" Charon ordered sharply. He glanced over his shoulder at Ferran. "I will protect you but you have to move!"

"Come on. There is a cellar beneath this house. I will lock us inside. We will be safe there," Chane quietly urged. This time, Ferran did not resist when Chane pulled at his arm to get him up. He staggered on his feet. "Follow me."

Charon breathed a sigh of relief as he listened to the two leave the room. He kept his eyes on the front door. It shook after each heavy hit outside. He wondered if someone was trying to break in. His thought was answered as the entire front wall was ripped away. The stone dust was heavy in the air and Charon coughed hard.

Through the falling dust cloud came the mysterious Shadowborn from Meras. His eyes were glowing red and his wicked curved sword was slick with blood. He still wore the same tattered cloak but this time, the fringes of it were burning like embers in a fire. The Shadowborn's skin was a sickly white but he still appeared full of vigor for the fight.

"You will go no further," Charon mustered up the courage to say. He held his sword hilt with both hands.

"Master says we must. Cannot be stopped. Must do as he says," the Shadowborn stated. He snickered as he brandished his sword.

"You may have scared me in Meras but I am afraid of you no longer. I said that you will go no further and I meant it," Charon snarled. He tightened his posture until he remembered Gyr's lesson on remaining loose and ready. He relaxed slightly.

The Shadowborn burst out laughing. The sound was loud and maniacal. He then lifted up his sword and pointed it directly at Charon. "Master says you must die and die you shall. Master says I will be set free if the sons die."

At first, Charon was confused but then it dawned on him. And it made him angry. "You are no father of mine!"

He had grown up without a father figure but he knew that no true father would want to harm his children. Bane acted more like a father figure than the crazed Shadowborn did. Rage filled his entire body and he rushed forward to attack.

*****

Ferran huddled in the further corner from the cellar door. He kept himself out of reach of the candlelight, suddenly fearful of it. He chewed on a thumbnail as he rocked back and forth.

"Trust in your brother. He is stronger than he looks," Chane tried to comfort him. He reached out to touch Ferran's shoulder but he jerked away. "This is not the end."

"It sure feels that way. Ever since Bane arrived in this city, my life has been turned upside down and inside out. I do not know what to feel anymore or who to trust. Maybe Charon since he says we are brothers but still I do not know," Ferran blurted out.

He was such a shattered mess that Chane did not know what to do or so. It seemed that only the end of the battle would bring the poor boy some peace. He wished that he could give Ferran some of his confidence or figure out something to perk him up.

"Battles have been fought for thousands of years. People live and die. We will come out of this stronger than before. You will as well," Chane stated firmly.

Ferran sniffled and wiped his dripping nose. "My mother used to say that there will come a day. I never understood what it meant back when she was alive. Now, I think I do."

"What do you think it means?" Chane asked. He came to sit down close to Ferran. He rubbed his back.

"When life and death meet and that I must choose a path to take. Will I let myself die or will I fight to live? But I am so scared to do either!" Ferran cried out before he buried his head against his knees.

"That time has not come for you. Whatever decision you make, I hope you make it for the right reasons. You are a good soul, Ferran. Kind hearted and true. It will be as the Good Spirits and your mother say: there will come a day. In your heart, only you will know what that means for your life. Why don't we ask the Good Spirits for protection?"

Ferran slowly nodded. "Good Spirits, protect my brother so that he may live." He mumbled something under his breath.

*****

BANE VS AXUM

Blood trickled down the left side of his face. Bane tried to wiped the red sticky liquid from his brow only to smear it into his hair. He flicked his wrist, flinging drops from his fingertips. His head throbbed painfully as he shook it. Dirt and tiny shards of stone scattered over his shoulders. He had only a moment to savor the reprieve before the rest of the wall came crumbling down.

Bursting through the cloud of dust was Axum and the Demon slammed into Bane. They tumbled to the floor, crashing into furniture and scattering a terrified family of five. Bane pulled in his legs and kicked Axum hard in the stomach, throwing him back through the collapsed front wall. He flipped up to his feet and took a step towards the opening. He paused and looked over at the mother and father clutching their son and two daughters.

"Go. I will keep the Demon from following," Bane directed. He pointed towards the back door.

"Thank you," the father said before pulling his family away.

Bane turned his attention back towards the opening and jumped up to the pile of broken stone. He faltered for a second on a loose slab but quickly recovered. He readjusted his grip on his sword as he looked about. He coughed when he inhaled dust.

In the distance, he saw Axum struggling to get up on his feet. He watched as the Demon got to his knees and paused to steady himself. On the ground and out of reach was Axum's black sword. Bane rushed forward in a series of bounding leaps. He brought his sword high over his head. Axum managed to grab his

447

sword in time to meet Bane's attack. Bane pushed downward to keep Axum from standing up and gaining leverage.

"So I am the last obstacle to the mighty Daylord's return to the Northlands. An honor I will gladly bear."

"Brave words from a Demon at my feet," Bane laughed as he put more strength in breaking Axum's defense.

Axum threw himself to the right, knocking Bane off balance. He took the opportunity to slash at Bane's legs. His sword tip tore open Bane's pants above his left knee. Bane stumbled forward and toppled over Axum. He managed to tuck and roll, jumping back up to his feet. He lurched towards his left and nearly lost his balance. He glanced down to see a deep cut that was profusely bleeding. Suddenly, Bane was upended and he fell hard on his back. Axum loomed over him.

"Oh no. You are not getting away from me until you answer some questions," Axum shouted before stabbing his sword. The blade plunged into Bane's left shoulder, scraping the bone and tearing muscle. Bane clenched his jaw hard to avoid screaming out in pain. "Why did you leave Norsov? Why did you leave the Eastlands?"

Bane's left shoulder burned as a poisonous fire spread through his left arm. He glanced towards his sword, seeing the blade pinned beneath Axum's left foot. He was grateful that he had not lost his grip on the hilt. In fact, he felt the molded ridges of leather digging into his palm.

"Why does it matter to you?" Bane seethed through his teeth.

"I just wonder why a farmer of no reputation leaves his home for distant lands. How such an individual could become what history knows him as? How did you truly become the Daylord of legend?" Axum mocked as he twisted his sword.

Bane nearly bit his tongue in half from the pain and his chest heaved. But he resisted crying out. As he thought about his answer, his heart soared with strength. Pushing past his pain, Bane twisted his right leg and kicked hard at Axum's left ankle. The Demon stumbled back, pulling his sword free and cutting down the length of Bane's arm. Bane swung his sword with all his might and cut off Axum's left arm. Axum shrieked as his severed limb flopped onto the ground, the stump of what remained spraying a shower of blackened blood. The gore splattered across Bane's front.

Axum then roared and mashed his fanged teeth as his eyes turned blood red. His right arm swelled with thick muscles and a net of swollen vessels bubbling beneath his skin. His fingers transformed into scythe like claws. He spewed out a long line of ferocious curses before slashing at Bane's injured shoulder. It was clear that the Demon intended to deal the same injury.

His shoulder took the brunt of the attack as Bane managed to twist enough to avoid his arm being sliced off. Axum fell face first as Bane leaped up to a nearby rooftop. The Demon continued to curse loudly as Bane dropped down to the street on the other side of the building. He crumbled and hit the ground hard. He spat out a mouthful of blood before pushing himself to his feet and staggering towards a dark side street.

*****

"Where oh where did you go? Have you run again?" Axum's voice boomed. It was followed by a boisterous laugh. "A thousand years has done little to change who you truly are. You pretend to love war but in your heart, I know that you hate it!"

Bane grimaced as he heard Axum's taunting. He coughed in his left hand, spitting out a mouthful of blood. A thin stream of blood oozed down the left side of his face from a bad cut above his eye. The pauldron on his left shoulder had been ripped away and his tunic torn to shreds beneath it. His shoulder was a deep purple tinged with red. He flexed his injured arm, cringing in pain. Axum had slashed him with his Demonic talons. He was grateful that the limb was still attached and able to move. His right arm was no better.

His fight with Axum had started out evenly matched, each of them exchanging powerful blows. Their swords had slammed against each other so many times that the individual blades had become heated. The steel sparks that shot out whenever their weapons hit each other stung mercilessly. One had even struck Bane on the cheek. The spot on his face burned and oozed a red tinged liquid. But Bane was not the only one with injuries. It made him immensely proud to have cut off Axum's left arm. Axum roared more from rage at losing the limb again than actual pain. He screamed about the difficulty of reattaching severed body parts but the exact details did not matter. Bane laughed at Axum's misfortune when Axum first found in the dark alley. The Demon struck hard and fast, fully intent on tearing Bane in half. Axum had slashed his left side from knee to the top of his head before he managed to get away a second time.

"Come out, come out wherever you are! Don't you want to play?"

He refused to believe that his abilities were rusty after his long years of wandering. He was a bit too proud for that. It seemed impossible that Axum was so much stronger and far more resilient. He snarled and gripped his sword tightly with his right hand.

"No, I will not lose," Bane told himself. Each twinge of pain was ignored as he pushed himself from the stone wall of the dark alley. Each battle cry from a Mortal soldier and scream of death drove Bane out of the shadows. No, he was not going to fail them. Sawn was depending on him. A lot more people far beyond the Southlands were depending on him.

But a major part of him just wanted to give up and run away. Like he always had when things seemed too big and great to handle. He questioned why he should go on if those he loved were gone, never to return to this world. As soon as he had those thoughts, Bane felt as if they were wrong. Yes, his family of old was gone but in his travels, he had gained a whole new family. The diverse people of the Northlands looked to him as a father and protector and admittedly, he saw them as beloved children and friends. He sorely missed the delightful nature of the Gryphons in their honest approach to life. He missed the lengthy conversations with Vorin the Dragonlord. Most of all, he missed Shadow Night, a dear friend and companion that he could count on.

However, Shadow Night was gone. His memory lived on in the blood of his descendants. And if he was correct, that included the mad Aday and his two half breed sons. Bane felt a strange and new sense of obligation to them that he had not felt before. They needed him as much as he needed them. He needed to go back to the Northlands. He clenched his jaw and readied his sword.

"It's time that I earn back my title," Bane told himself.

Axum smirked as Bane stepped out of the shadows of a cluster of ruined houses. He snickered before leaping down from a nearby roof top. "So you finally decided to show yourself again. You never were one for unshakable courage. Even the Mortals are braver than you."

"Then I envy them for their courage, strength, and loyalty. We of the Immortal races should look to them as examples of how to live our lives honestly and to the fullest. I gave them an impossible task: defend their home from supernatural forces that were beyond their power. Rise up they did and I am proud to fight with all of them," Bane declared. He whipped his sword around and gripped the hilt with both hands. "You should be afraid."

"Why? I could shout boo and stop their hearts dead," Axum laughed. He freed his sword from the strap on his back.

"I mean of me. I am not the same Bane that was named Daylord and King a thousand years ago. I am stronger in body and heart," Bane challenged before he charged forward at high speed.

Their swords crashed against each other with a high pitched metallic screech. The sound had yet to dissipate before it was joined by a second and third. Bane and Axum exchanged furious blows that sent out shockwaves after each strike. They never stayed connected for longer than a few seconds, separating quickly to attack again. The pitched contest lasted for several minutes with neither side making any sort of progress. Axum fought surprising well despite the fact that he was missing his left arm. He twisted and angled his body to get maximum power. He always made sure to hit hard towards Bane's injured left side.

Bane quickly detected that it was Axum's new goal was to deal the same limb tearing injury to him. He had bit the inside of his mouth after each attack due to the pain. He was surprised his left side lasted for so long under the extreme stress. Maybe he was reinvigorated by his change of heart.

"Maybe that strength was always there and I let it fall to the wayside," Bane whispered to himself.

One thing that bothered him was that Spirit Wake was in play. Though it did not affect him as strongly as it would a true Spiritborn, it changed how the energies of the world moved. It was a terrible power that only the foolish attempted to summon. And he had a pretty good idea who had used the power: Kaiser Adonis. Kaiser had threatened him before Bane left that he was capable of powers known only to the depths of the Spirit World. Bane knew the power very well and how it would affect his energy. At times, his energy was strong and other times, it was weak. To use it properly, Bane had to bide his time and wait for the fluctuation to swing in his direction.

"Having an existential crisis or just finally realizing that you cannot win against me?" Axum taunted. He snickered loudly.

"Taking a breather or just trying to decide if your right arm is worth it?" Bane fired back. He flipped his sword back up into ready position.

Axum's attack came quickly. He zigzagged from left to right at high speed as he charged at Bane. He roared, saliva spraying from his mouth. The edge of his blade glowed blood red along with his eyes. A blackened vein pulsated across his forehead and down the right side of his face.

"I have to wonder, oh mighty Bane, if you have heard the screams of the Mortals fighting to save this stink hole of a city. Did you honestly think such a weak race could stand up against the power of the Spirit World just by teaching them how to fight?" Axum sneered. He spat on the ground before him. "Does it remind you of the screams of other people you failed to protect?"

Bane refused to listen to Axum for he knew that as soon as

he did, his memory would cripple him. But he could not ignore the desperate cries that surrounded him and the incredible sense of pain. His protective shield could only do so much. He needed to end the battle now. A plan began to form in his head but he needed time. He replaced his sword in its sheath before pulling off the strap and tossing it to the side. He put his arms out to his side and took a step forward.

"What foolishness is this?" Axum asked as he lifted an eyebrow. He looked back and forth between Bane and the discarded sword.

"Why do we fight with swords when our physical power is just as great if not greater? We are both beings from an ancient time and I say we fight as such. With our raw physical power," Bane calmly suggested.

"Hah! You think that I am stupid? You have two arms with which to hit me with while I only have one. I will keep my sword for it has served me well enough," Axum narrowed his eyes and snorted. He brandished the blade before him.

Bane laughed out loud. "No, I think that you are a complete idiot. Yes, I do hear the screams and I am sure there are those dead and dying at this very moment. But still the Mortals continue to fight. Not because they believe in me but because they believe in something greater." He pointed at Axum. "You are greater than your Master and you have allowed yourself to be chained up. How pathetic!"

That was the catalyst for Axum's fury. The Demon rocketed forward with wild abandon; feet hitting and lifting from the ground so fast that it appeared as if he was flying. He roared like a clap of thunder, his white fangs flashing like lightning in the sky. The length of his stride started to increase before he took a powerful leap into the air.

"Yes. A complete idiot," Bane told himself.

He needed Axum to be solely focused on him to the point of desperation. He also needed to be on his guard. A moment's hesitation could be the moment between life and death. The space between him and Axum quickly diminished. Axum swung his sword around a little bit too hard as he threw himself off balance towards the right. Bane was able to easily jump out of the way. Axum hit the ground on his back and skidded several feet before righting himself. He renewed his attack with even greater fury.

"Why not draw all of the Dark Spirits towards you?" Bane suggested as he dodged another botched attack.

Axum snarled, a wild expression in his red eyes. A web of blackened veins pulsated around his left shoulder and the stump of his arm. Black mist slowly surrounded the space where his arm

452

would have been, forming an exaggerated limb with long talons for fingers. The sharps edges of the talons glowed with an eerie white light.

Yes! He was drawing the Dark Spirits' power towards himself. Bane could not help but grin with delight. Just a little longer, he thought, as he glanced down at the damaged bracer on his left forearm. He ripped it off and threw the pieces of leather into the dirt. He stretched and wiggled his fingers. The silver Dragon tattoo that the bracer had covered was now exposed. It wrapped around his wrist, stretched down his arm, and ended just short of his elbow. Even covered in dried blood, the silver ink glowed brightly. He then ripped off his right bracer, exposing a golden Gryphon tattoo on his right forearm. Both marks glowed so brightly that even Axum halted in his attack. A look of shock and horror appeared on his face.

"Good. You see these tattoos for what they really are. Spirit Marks drawn by two of the greatest souls to walk the earth and fly amongst the heavens. You are right to feel fear for they were gifts from the mighty Drako the first Lord of the Dragons and Gia, the noblest of all Gryphons. Even with Spirit Wake in play, their power cannot be diminished. You foolishly called the Dark Spirits to your aid and now I can call on the power of mine," Bane declared for all to hear.

*****

All of the Dark Spirits halted in their attack. Several were destroyed as the Mortal defenders cut through their essence before they realized what had happened. The men and women looked around at each other in confusion. They had heard Bane's declaration but they did not know what it meant. Above them, the clouds parted, revealing a night sky filled with twinkling stars. Two streams of silver and gold energy swirled around, pushing the clouds further away.

*****

Bane put his palms up towards the sky, drawing in the streams of silver and gold. He looked up, putting his hands together above his head. He then brought them down in a position of prayer over his heart. He closed his eyes and bowed his head.

"Prayer will not save you. Kaiser watches all that goes on

and he will act to stop you," Axum quickly blurted out. His entire body shook and he tried desperately to still himself.

Bane's eyes snapped open. "If that is so, where is your master now? If he is so powerful, why did he send you? I say that he is too afraid to fight his own battles so he sends servants like you to die in his place. It is no loss to him whether you win or die tonight."

"I DON'T CARE! GLORY WILL COME TO THE ONE THAT KILLS YOU!" Axum roared at the top of his lungs. Blood foamed around his mouth.

"Well that's not going to happen. I am back and I am here to stay," Bane smirked.

He separated his hands, a twisting flow of silver and gold energy undulating between them. He twisted and moved his body from side to side before throwing his hands forward. The bright energy shot out like a Dragon and Gryphon flying around each other. Axum's eyes widened before he was engulfed and disappeared from sight. It was like an explosion of fire as the Dragon and Gryphon Spirit forms rose up into the night sky.

Sparkles of light rained down over Sawn. Dark Spirits scrambled to get away only to disappear in a puff of black mist. At first, the city was silent but soon loud shouts and cheers of joy rang out. Bane let out a deep breath and smiled.

*****

GYR TO THE RESCUE

Charon slammed back against the wall, crashing through the wood and stone. He had been thrown into a guest bedroom situated in the left wing of Chane's house. The bedding cushioned his fall somewhat but still his entire back stung. He managed to cover his head and face in time before the rubble fell on top of him. One small sliver of stone cut his forehead while the rest pummeled his body. He held on to his sword tightly to make sure he would not lose it in the mess. The rain of debris stopped, completely covering him.

It felt like a moment of respite which he sorely needed. Fighting against Aday was a lost cause. The older and pureblooded Shadowborn was far too powerful and his mental state too unstable. He did not know what he was thinking, challenging such an opponent. As far as he was concerned, it was a match to the death and he was the one who was supposed to die. He hurt all over and just wanted to sleep. But he knew he could not. He still had to protect Ferran and Chane. If that meant that he had to die, then he would accept his fate with an open heart and mind. Charon just wished dying did not hurt as much as it did.

Suddenly Charon was dragged out of the pile of rubble. He looked up to see Aday's back before the Shadowborn turned around. Aday grabbed Charon by his exposed chainmail shirt and lift up off the ground. He held him close to his face.

"Run," Aday's voice cracked. The look in his eyes was wild and scared. His left pupil was wide and dark while his right pupil was the size of a needle point.

Charon struggled to release himself from Aday's grasp, pulling free and falling back on the floor. He scrambled to his feet and shuffled back away from Aday. He was not sure why he hesitated.

"GO!" Aday shouted with a pained voice.

The half wild look in his father's eyes told Charon everything that he needed to make his decision. Aday's control was wavering back and forth between sanity and insanity. Sanity would protect him. Insanity would kill everyone in sight. Charon stumbled before he rushed out of the bedroom door and into the hallway. As he ran, he thought about where Chane and Ferran were hiding. Since Aday had yet to discover their hiding place, Charon wondered if it was secret enough that he could take cover there. His entire body throbbed in pain and he was sure that his left wrist was broken. He was certain that he would not last much longer without rest.

One thing that quickly occurred to him was that he did not know where the hiding place could be. He had no idea and Chane had not mentioned any such places in their conversations. Going outside of the house risked being attacked by a Dark Spirit. Staying in the house also seemed like a dangerous choice as well. He needed to make a decision fast. He did not have much time before Aday's moment of sanity deteriorated.

"Master says you must die!"

Charon's breath was knocked out of him as Aday tackled him. The pair crashed through a thick wooded door and tumbled down a twisting set of stone stairs. They hit the floor hard. Aday snarled like a wild animal as he held on tightly to Charon's throat. Charon gasped and struggled for air.

"Let my brother go, you monster!" Ferran shouted. He picked up Charon's loose sword and swung it at Aday's back.

Aday kept his left hand on Charon's throat while he ripped his sword free from its sheath. In the blink of an eye, he slashed upwards and cut Ferran open from his right hip up to his left shoulder. Blood streamed down the blade and stained his hand. He looked at the hot liquid, his pupils shifting from pinpoints to wide saucers. He released his grip on Charon's throat and fell backwards. He dropped his sword and shrieked.

Freed from Aday's tight hold, Charon coughed hard for several seconds. He only stopped when he heard Ferran's gurgling cry. He quickly righted himself and lurched over to his fallen brother. Chane pressed his hands on the deepest part of Ferran's wound. He swallowed hard, trying not to vomit as he felt the hard pounding of Ferran's heart beneath his hands.

"No! No!" Charon repeated to himself over and over again as he clumsily examined the deep gash. Blood squelched between his fingers.

Aday mumbled quickly under his breath before grabbing his head and screaming. "RUN!"

This time, Charon did not hesitate. Using Chane's outer robe, he wrapped it tightly around his brother's body. He then lifted up Ferran into his arms, cradling him carefully. He followed Chane, who now held his discarded sword, out of the cellar. They ran as quickly as they could through the destroyed house.

"We have to find Bane," Chane stated as they slid into the foyer. His shoulders dropped when he saw the door blocked by a massive roof beam.

Charon would not be deterred. Still holding Ferran in his arms, he summoned up as much strength as he could and kicked at the beam. The beam lurched from the force and the door fell open with a heavy thud on the front stairs. Chane crawled over the beam first, waving the sword before him as he waited for Charon. Charon easily leapt over the beam and landed beside him.

Now outside, both could see the ravages of the battle. The courtyard was strewn with the bodies of the dead and dying. Dark Spirits dashed about with wild abandon, attacking anyone that came within reach. The front gates had been torn free from their moorings and thrown to the side in a twisted heap of metal. Outside of the gate, a broad shouldered Dark Spirit with long arms and sharp claws paused. It appeared to smile, flashing its white fangs. By its actions, other Spirits were drawn in like moths to the flame. Four more Spirits crawled over the walls and soon, all five were stalking towards Charon and Chane.

"Trapped between the talon and the fang. That is what a Gryphon says about difficult decisions," Charon commented with a nervous laugh.

"No kidding," Chane replied as he looked over his shoulder into the darkness of the house and then at the five Dark Spirits coming towards them. "You will have to take the sword. I am too old and feeble to be of any worth. I can look after your brother."

Charon was reluctant to let go of the ailing Ferran but the man was right. He was the more physically capable of defending them all from the Dark Spirits. He struggled with the decision to release Ferran, feeling that if his brother was to lose contact with him, he would weaken even further. He looked down into Ferran's fluttering eyes, searching for an answer on what to do.

"For the Immortal Truth!" Gyr screeched as he rocketed into the courtyard. He blasted through the five Dark Spirits and flew over Charon and Chane. The Gryphon slammed into the leaping

Aday, talons first. He angrily chawed in his native tongue as he pulled Aday over him and flipped him onto the ground.

Aday snarled as he scurried from reach. He bent low over his feet like some sort of creature with his right hand pressed to the ground and his sword in his left hand. He held the weapon out to the side. Gyr screeched again as he reared up on his back legs and beat his wings furiously. He managed to kick up a wicked gust of wind that knocked Aday backwards. He then leapt forward with his talons extended and tackled Aday, pinning him to the ground and making sure he unable to reach his sword. Aday shouted at him as his left hand clawed at the ground between him and his weapon. Gyr bit at his face, snapping his beak within a hairs breath of his left eye. He snapped his beak again when Aday did not stop struggling.

"I WILL KILL YOU!" Aday roared as he attempted to kick the much heavier Gryphon off of him.

"Go ahead and try, you foul shadow! My talons will dig deeper and I will pluck your eyes from your head!" Gyr shouted back. He tightened his grip on Aday's shoulders.

"SKY DEMON!" Aday cursed with a ferocious snarl.

Gyr reared back and then head butted Aday hard on the forehead. With his thick Gryphon skull, he was able to knock out the mad Shadowborn with a single blow. He flared his wings and threw back his head to cry out his victory in the Gryphon tongue.

"Mighty Gryphon, your timing is most opportune," Chane stated as he helped Charon to steady himself.

Gyr looked over his shoulder, a smile on his face. The smile quickly dropped as he saw Ferran's weakened state. Not wanting to relinquish his grip on Aday, Gyr dragged the unconscious man over to where Charon was standing. Chane pressed the sword to Aday's exposed neck and nodded towards the Gryphon.

"Should he wake, I will cut through his neck," Chane said firmly.

"Should he wake, you must act quickly before he can overpower you," Gyr warned before turning his attention back towards Charon.

Ferran's condition had worsened with the extreme amount of blood loss. His skin was pasty white and his body cold to the touch. His chest fluttered with weak breath. Gyr closed his eyes and gently pressed his forehead to Ferran's.

"Please help him," Charon begged. Tears streamed down his cheeks.

Gyr snorted his hot breath over Ferran's face. Ferran stirred slightly. Still, his eyes did not open. He tried again only to get the same result. He pulled away from Ferran. "He is weak.

The blade has cut deeper and shed much blood. Bane cannot undo this wound."

"No! He must! My brother cannot die!" Charon pleaded. "Immortals cannot die!"

"Oh yes they can if the wound or poison is great enough. Immortality does not mean that we escape from death. It just means that death has a harder time finding us," Gyr quickly stated. He spoke with such finality that Charon fell silent.

"Then all we can do is pray for his salvation much as you came to ours," Chane said softly.

THE DAYLORD'S JUSTICE

It became apparent that when Gyr had dispersed the five Dark Spirits in the courtyard, they disappeared into puffs of black mist all over the city. Mixed in with the cries of pain and sorrow were cheers of victory. Many of the cheers praised Bane's name as the great savior of Sawn. Boisterous songs broke out from beyond the courtyard walls.

Victory to our king
He is the best that has ever been
He has pushed back the night
And brought us the dawn
He slayed the Demon monster
And rescued dear Sawn

Gyr loved songs under normal circumstances but he placed himself amongst those who felt terrible pain and sorrow. He glanced back at the suffering Ferran who had weakened even further. The poor man was dying and there was nothing that he could do. A sob built up in his chest. He barely knew Ferran and yet he had formed a connection to him. He wondered if it was the fact that Ferran was a Silvanus. No. It was because he was a new friend and Charon's brother.

His head shot over to Aday when he heard him stir. He stomped over to him, pushing Chane out of the way. He gripped Aday's shoulders with both sets of talons and snarled.

"Move and I will kill you," Gyr warned. Bane's command roared back to the forefront of his mind but he swiftly pushed it away. He wanted to make Aday suffer for what he had done. Aday did not deserve a quick death.

Aday started to whimper, tears welling up in his eyes. "So much pain. So much sorrow. All my fault. All my fault. I was not strong enough."

"You deserve it for what you have done," Gyr snapped in a low voice. He added a curse in the Gryphon tongue that made Aday shudder.

"Enough," Bane stated as he stepped over the twisted metal gates. "Leave him be now. The madness is broken and now the crippling weight of the last thousand years is laid bare."

Gyr was reluctant to release Aday, wary that the crazed Shadowborn would suddenly attack them. He only moved when Bane gave him a stern look. He settled himself beside Charon, extending his right wing across his friend's back like a shield. The tips of his feathers touched Chane's shoulder who promptly but slowly set the sword down on the ground.

Bane knelt down beside Aday's left side and grabbed his chin. He turned Aday's head from side to side before letting go. "Who is your Lord and Master?"

Aday gulped and swallowed hard. He looked terrified and ready to burst out into tears. "I do not know."

"Then let me help you. It is not Kaiser Adonis for he has not acted as a true leader should. A true leader does not use his people as weapons against his enemies and force them to do acts that go against their hearts. I knew you once, Aday Silvanus. If Kaiser had left well enough alone, you would have been home in Cross living your life as it should have been," Bane said with great authority.

"I had no choice," Aday wailed out loud. He was overcome with desperate sobs and tears. "He did this to me! He broke me!"

Bane frowned. "You had a choice once but it has long passed you by."

Aday's nose dripped and mucus bubbled from his left nostril. "I came looking for you but you were not there. My grandfather always said that the Daylord could make it right for he has powers no one else has."

It seemed as if Aday was partially blaming Bane for his wretched state. Gyr and Chane waited for his reaction to the jab. It was not as explosive as they had imagined.

"But I do not have the power to heal you of your hurts nor do I have the power to save the son you killed. I was a farmer from the Eastlands, not a great warrior or master over others. If I had the power that you think I have, I would have been able to save my wife and children from their fates and I would have never left my home. But fate has chosen a different path for the both of us and I am sorry for what has happened to you for it is my fault. Had I not abandoned the Northlands, I could have saved you and your family from Kaiser's destructive aims. As the Daylord and your King, I have failed in my duties to you and all that you once loved."

Bane put his left hand on Aday's forehead and bowed his head. Aday continued to weep until the strength of his sobs faded. He trembled and glanced over to look at Ferran. More tears welled up in his eyes.

"Can I speak to them?" he begged Bane. "Can I hold my sons one last time?"

Bane nodded and shuffled back to allow Aday to get up to his knees. Aday crawled over to Charon and Ferran like an unstable child. He stopped when Gyr shot him a dangerous look.

"Let him. He will bring no further harm," Bane ordered quietly. The reluctant Gryphon backed away and went to sit on the other side of Chane.

Aday bit his lip as he lifted his hand over Ferran's gaping wound, fighting back more tears. He mumbled to himself for a long time before he dared to pick up Ferran's limp hand. He cradled it like a precious and delicate thing. "I remember the last time that I held you. You were newly born and so tiny in my arms. I remember thinking that I could have a normal life if I could bring the two things most precious to me together. You needed to know your brother and you needed your father." Aday's wavering resolve broke and he wept. He clutched Ferran's hand in both of his before he looked up into Charon's eyes. "I loved you both so much."

Charon wanted to hate the man and resisted the urge to reach out and embrace him. But the pained expression in his father's eyes was like nothing he had ever seen before. It was if he was looking into Aday's broken soul.

"Is there anything you can do? Anything at all?" Charon asked, holding back tears.

Bane stood up and shook his head. "The damage is done and he is too far gone and broken to be healed. Even if I could, the memory of his actions would tear him apart. He will never be at peace."

All discussion stopped as Ferran shuddered for the final time and fell still. Aday threw himself on top of his dead son, crying profusely. He reached out a hand to pull Charon's head in and together they wept. Chane and Gyr bowed their heads, each whispering their own prayers. Gyr extended his right wing around Chane, closing his eyes. For a long time, the group wallowed in their sorrow as Bane watched over them.

"What is to become of me?" Aday dared to ask once his tears had calmed. He looked over his shoulder at Bane.

"You already know," Bane stated.

Aday lowered his gaze. "Then I am to die." He looked up again. "Thank you for letting me hold my sons. I only ask for an honorable death even though I have lived a dishonorable life."

"I do not relish what I must do, Aday Silvanus. Perhaps you will find your salvation from pain and peace in your heart within the depths of the Spirit World."

*****

Bane stood before the funeral pyres for those lost in the battle for Sawn. His cloak was wrapped tight around him and his great sword strapped across his back. Gyr stood on his left while Charon stood on his right. Each of them looked upon the pyres with a sense of sorrow for those lives lost. Charon had lost his father and brother and their two bodies burned side by side on the pyre in front of them.

"What now?" Gyr dared to ask.

"First, I will help the people of Sawn with the process of rebuilding. After that, I go to punish the soul responsible for all of this. Will you fly with me, Gyr, as your ancestress once did, and take me back home?" Bane turned to look at Gyr. "It is time that I go back to the Northlands."

"I want to come too," Charon suddenly said. Both Gyr and Bane turned to look at him. He had been silent ever since the fires had been lit.

Bane nodded. "Then we will all go and end the war that took those most precious to us away. Justice will be served."

*****

DEAD OR ALIVE

Kaiser snarled silently, his lips pulling back from his teeth like he was an angry wolf. The Battle of Sawn had not gone as expected. He stared at the tiny fires, black puffs of smoke rising into the air. A crowd of white lights surrounded the fires. Kaiser frowned and he wafted his hand. The Living Map zoomed in closer at his command. Multiple funeral pyres were burning in the market square of Sawn. There was a large one in the center with fifteen smaller wood piles surrounding it. The assembly of men, women, and children was thick but Kaiser only had eyes for one of the watchers.

The loss in Sawn was maddening. He had set up everything so perfectly. He had first attacked Meras to draw in Bane and reveal Aday. He had forced the decision that brought Bane to Sawn. Everything had fallen into place and yet, his plan failed. Bane was still alive and Axum was dead. The only consolation prize was that two Silvanus sons were dead

"You can have your victory for now, Bane Arlis. I will still win this war," Kaiser sneered. He flicked his left wrist and the Living Map disappeared.

"I told you that Axum is too hot headed to be an effective battle commander. Push him too hard and he will break. Well, he broke," Rache laughed. He leaned up against a nearby pillar with his arms crossed.

"Shut up," Kaiser snapped.

"I am just telling you what I see. The Daylord is coming

back to the Northlands. The game has changed. What are you going to do about it?" Rache challenged. He shrugged when Kaiser glared at him.

Kaiser chuckled softly and shook his head. "How little you understand. What happened in Sawn may have been a loss but it is not a setback. It just seems that I must kill the all mighty Daylord myself."

Rache could not figure out if Kaiser was angry or happy. The man paced around in an erratic circle, arguing with himself in a low voice. He waved his hands and stomped his feet for several minutes. He threw his arms up in the air and wheeled towards Rache with a crazed look in his eyes.

"I don't have to kill him! Ha! I mean I will eventually but I do not have to kill him at this moment," Kaiser stated with a laugh. He snapped his fingers and the Living Map reappeared. He swiped his hand back and the Map sped over to the seaside city of Twilight. A subtle twitch of a finger zoomed in even closer.

Twilight was a bustling city with an active port during peaceful times but now the docks were empty. The stone streets were mostly abandoned save for those on the eastern side along the River Shadow. Standing before the main bridge over the river to the Earthborn city of Branch was Ryder with his hands on his hips. Standing beside him was Onyx gesturing towards something.

"You wanted them in Twilight. What is your point?" Rache shrugged.

"Because I can kill him instead. Get rid of the Shadowlord or whatever it is he calls himself these days," Kaiser laughed out loud. He swung his hands apart to make it seem as if he was standing behind Ryder and Onyx. Kaiser reached out and swiped his hand through their heads. The energy parted briefly before reforming again.

"You do realize that he is your heir," Rache pointed out.

Kaiser rolled his eyes. "I can always make new heirs."

"But not like him," Rache said as he walked around to stand in front of the Ryder apparition. "Not only is he a descendent of your bloodline, he is also a Silvanus. In case you haven't noticed, there aren't any Silvanus daughters left to breed with."

"I have plenty of time to breed the perfect son and shape him to be something greater. But then, you are right. There will never be a soul like him. There will never be another Shadowlord."

"What about Onyx?" Ryder asked.

The Demon blanched when Kaiser turned on him with a dark look in his eyes and a snarl on his lips. He stomped through the two apparitions, breaking them apart. Rache started to back away until he hit against a pillar. He briefly looked up towards the ceiling before returning his gaze forward. The Living Map had disappeared.

"Onyx Silvanus will never be the Shadowlord no matter how hard he tries. He does not have the power or might and I could care less if he lives or dies. And that parasite in the whore's womb? A mere bargaining chip for my grandson's cooperation," Kaiser spat out in a harsh tone.

For the longest time, Rache had heard Kaiser wax and wane about how Ryder was his grandson and his only heir. There were very few days where his Master did not mention his power and how he was responsible for it. He praised himself constantly on shaping Ryder's foundation for combat. When it came to fighting Ryder, it was all about keep him alive. But now his Master was changing his tune and Rache did not much like it. Rache did not like that he found it unsettling and he could not understand why.

Suddenly, Kaiser had an accusing finger pointed in Rache's face. The look in his eyes was angry and full of betrayal. "Do not pretend that your rebellious thoughts are going unnoticed by me. I see each and every one. Stop thinking that my grandson can save you from your fate for this world will never accept you alive and free. Even I am incapable of making them see you as anything but a monster. That is something you brought upon yourself by killing my ancestor."

"I am no fool and I do not pretend that the world will change their ways," Rache angrily fired back. He got in Kaiser's face, flashing his white fangs in an angry snarl. "I am far older than you and only this profane bond keeps me from ending your life. Had I known what it would become, I would have gladly stayed in the Spiral for all eternity."

Kaiser smacked Rache hard across the left side of his face. When the Demon looked up in angry shock, Kaiser hit him even harder, knocking him to the ground. Rache coughed and spit out a mouthful of blood. Kaiser stood over him, looking down with his clenched fists shaking in restrained fury.

"The legends say that the infamous Demon known as Rache was even feared by his great Lord. Well, it is time that you learned to fear me as much as the world feared you. As much as the world fears me now," Kaiser said, his voice growing from a low growl into a furious roar.

Rache screamed until his throat cracked, spilling blood and making him choke. He clawed at his neck, feeling like it was being cut open repeatedly. His heart beat so fast that he thought it would explode in his chest. Every vessel in his body burned like he was engulfed in a raging inferno. He could see nothing. Hear nothing but his dying screams. He thrashed about in convulsions for what felt like hours until everything calmed. Yet the pain of the experience remained as did the claw marks on his neck and the blood in his mouth. His sight returned to him and he furtively glanced up at Kaiser. Kaiser had not moved from his spot but slowly withdrew his Spirit Marked left hand. He watched as the marks faded.

"There is a reason that the world fears me. Break my body? Fine, then I will not pick up a sword to attack. I will use my mind to destroy you instead. I will make you feel the horror of death a thousand times over without so much as the blink of an eye. I will bring the full force of the Spiral upon you for such is my gift as a Spirit Walker." Kaiser chuckled for a moment. "Spirit Walker. Such a tame title for one such as I. I prefer Spirit Destroyer for that is what I truly am."

He did not want to get up nor did he have the physical energy to do so. Whatever Kaiser did to him was worse than invoking the bond. He grunted when Kaiser kicked him in the stomach. His Master wanted him up. Rache gritted his teeth and held his breath as he slowly and unsteadily got to his feet. Immediately, Kaiser's left hand shot forward and gripped his throat. He wanted to resist but shoved the desire away into the back of his mind. He allowed himself to breathe, blood pouring from the corners of his mouth.

"Poor stupid child of darkness. Just because you are a Demon older than myself, that does not make you stronger or smarter than me. Because of this, I am feeling a bit charitable. I will release you from the bond if you do one last thing for me."

Rache tried to swallow but couldn't get the lump in his throat past Kaiser's tight hold. "What is it that you wish, Lord Kaiser?"

"Bring me my grandson," Kaiser said before he put his face closer. "Alive."

A thought occurred to Rache that he could not force away. What if Kaiser intended not to kill Ryder but to enslave him? Would that be a fate worse than death? To become a mindless killing machine? Would Kaiser force him to kill his own child as a proof of loyalty? In his youth, Rache would have gladly killed without any hesitation but such was the nature of Demons. Ryder was different and would likely not be so easily subdued. He quickly masked his last thought before replying. "As you wish."

"Good boy. As a reward for your success, I will free you from the bond. But should you turn traitor in heart, body, and mind, I will kill you on the spot. There will be nowhere in all of Terra and the Spirit World that you can hide from me. I will obliterate you from existence if your rebellious thoughts become reality. Got it?" Kaiser warned in the darkest of tones. The look in his eyes was absolutely terrifying.

"It shall be as you command. Should I earn the freedom I do not deserve, I will leave this world and become nothing more than a memory. I shall take my own useless life and return to the Spiral for all eternity," Rache replied in a submissive voice. He lowered his eyes.

But not without taking you down first.

*****

THE BRIDGE

"I thought that I might find you here again though I expected you to be at Haven's side," Onyx said as he stepped up to Ryder's side.

Ryder chuckled as he stood with arms crossed, staring at the connecting bridge between Twilight and Branch. It was a wide gray stone bridge that was thirty feet from railing to railing. It arched over the River Shadow, the water below splashing and rolling through the rocky rapids. Directly in the center was a line with runes on either side of it. On the Twilight side, it spelt out 'DOMINION OF THE SHADOWBORN' and on the Branch side, the words were 'DOMINION OF THE EARTHBORN.' The bridge stretched the entire three hundred feet from shore to shore with a gate house on each end and in the center. On this day, the bridge was deserted.

"I suppose I should be at her side considering that my child is due to arrive soon. Another moon cycle and I will learn if I have a son or daughter," Ryder smiled. He scratched his chin briefly. "She wants me to shave off the beard as she does not want the baby to feel like it is being kissed by the backside of a goat."

The comment made Onyx laugh out loud. It was just so silly that he could not help but be amused by it. "Just how would she know what that is like?"

Ryder smiled. "When we first were courting, I had a beard and she was afraid to kiss me. Her sisters dared her to kiss the back end of their family goat at the time to get an idea of what it would be like."

Onyx covered his mouth to avoid another outburst of laughing. He bit his lip and held his stomach. After a few minutes, he took a deep breath and let it out slowly to calm himself.

"Sounds like something Soja would have done. He may have been a Saber but I doubt that there was a better joke teller or prankster in Cross. Whenever I was sad, he would make me laugh again."

"He was a good soul that left this world far too soon. At least now, he and his father are together again and looking over us from the Spirit World," Ryder commented. The smile fell slowly from his face.

They both looked at the expanse that separated them from Branch. Invisible within that space was the Shadow Mirror. Even though the Mirror was invisible, they could still not see beyond it. Both were certain that the Earthborn and others of the Northern Alliance were assembling on the other side. No reply had come after the Shadow Shot message was sent nor did they have confirmation that it was received.

"I am sure that your uncle received your letter," Ryder quietly said. He nodded towards Onyx.

"I wish I shared your belief," came his sheepish reply.

Ryder directed his attention to the boundary line that had been drawn on the bridge. "Right there sits a part of the Shadow Mirror. I know that you cannot see it but every once in a while, it shudders like something is striking it from the other side. It is subtle so it is easy to miss. Concentrate and focus your sight upon that spot."

Onyx did as instructed and watched the boundary line carefully. For a long time, nothing happened. He was about to give up when he saw a small shudder that repeated over and over. It was odd for it made him think of a dog sniffing the crack between the bottom of a door and the floor.

"That was strange," Onyx commented.

"I suspect that Vorin is trying to sniff out any weak spots. Dragons are better at deciphering the weaknesses and strengths of Spirit energy than anyone else."

"If Dragons are as great as the stories say then why does Vorin not attack the Mirror directly? Everyone has always told me that Dragons are the most powerful beings on Terra," Onyx pointed out. He looked back towards the boundary line, seeing the same sniffing like shudder.

"It is a bit more complicated than you think. Yes, Dragons are the most powerful beings on Terra but this is a force of the Spirit World. The Spirit World has a different set of rules. Those rules are dictated by the Covenant of Spirits. Breaking the Mirror will be a fight where the reward for failure is death," Ryder explained as he unfolded his arms.

Ryder turned around and began walking away from the bridge. Onyx soon followed. The pair moved away from the open square before the bridge and into the maze of tight streets and buildings. Those buildings facing the river were stores with living spaces on the second floor. Wooden balconies stuck out over the street and signs hung over the storefront doors. Under normal circumstances, the river front would be bustling with activity. Earthborn would be coming over the bridge with wares to sell and trade. Now, it was practically empty. Ryder gestured for Onyx to follow him towards a store with needles and a spool of thread on the sign.

"What are we doing here?" Onyx asked.

His cousin did not answer him and instead opened the door and bid him to enter first. He did so, stepping into the darkened interior. All around him were bolts of fabric in a rainbow of colors and patterns. On the wall behind the counter were shelves of sewing instruments, spools of thread, buttons, and various clothing adornments.

Ryder popped the counter three times. "Hey Nana! You up for some visitors?"

"Ryder where are your manners? Is that how you speak to all of your elders?" Myra snapped from somewhere in the room behind the counter.

Onyx shook his head. "You know for a history making leader, you are rather brash."

A soft chuckle escaped from Ryder's mouth while he leaned on the counter. His back was towards the storeroom door. Soon, they heard a quick series of footsteps coming down stairs and the admonished mutterings of Myra. The silver haired woman appeared in the doorway, tightening a red wool shawl around her shoulders. Ryder slowly turned and smiled at her.

"Shouldn't you be with the mother of your child?" Myra asked, lifting one eyebrow.

It amused Onyx to see the same behavior he had seen from Ryder in his grandmother. "I said the same thing."

Myra gestured towards Onyx. "Finally. Someone with some sense in this city. Your Highness," Myra stated before curtsying. "Why aren't you with Haven?"

"I needed to see the Mirror one last time," he said as he stepped around the counter and embraced her.

The height difference between the two was staggering. Ryder towered over his grandmother and was at least twice as heavy in his frame. Even Onyx felt small next to him and he was four inches shorter. A year ago, Onyx felt threatened by his cousin's obvious physical power. Now, he had a healthy respect for it. Size was not everything when it came to being a great warrior. Soja was proof of that as the Saber was tall and lanky in life.

"Have you packed what you needed? I don't want you close to the bridge when I challenge the Mirror and Haven could use you at her side," Ryder said warmly.

"Good because I cannot wait to see that baby of yours when it gets here," Myra replied. She popped Ryder on the stomach. "My bag is in the back. Go fetch it for me."

Myra watched Ryder step beyond the doorway and into the darkness of the backroom. She then reached over under the counter and pulled out a brown paper package. She handed it to Onyx.

"I found this when I was searching for who had owned this shop. They had it in a trunk in their sleeping quarters," Myra said with a degree of reverence.

Onyx pulled at the tan string holding the package together. As soon as the string came loose, the paper fell open and revealed a heavy folded black cloth. Onyx let the paper fall to the floor and he held up the cloth. It was a beautiful cloak trimmed with silver embroidery. The Silvanus crest was emblazoned on the back. He threw it over his shoulders and attached the silver chain to hold it in place.

"I haven't had a cloak such as this since I was still living in the castle with my father. How would such a thing end up here?" Onyx asked. He rubbed his hands over the fabric. It was sturdy but refined.

"I suspect that it was repurposed from a banner. Perhaps the owners of this shop made the cloak and left behind for you. We may never know unless we find them. Until then, I think it best that you wear the cloak so people know that their Prince still lives and is with them," Myra suggested. She curtsied again.

"Then I hope to meet them and thank them for this. Thank you for finding it." He bowed his head towards her.

He heard Ryder grumbling about the weight of the bag before he appeared with it slung over his right shoulder. "What did you stuff in here?"

Myra grinned as she strode past Ryder, patting his chest. "Your child will need clothes, blankets, and of course diaper cloths."

"Diaper cloths?" Ryder asked.

"Yes. Diaper cloths. I remember changing yours when your mother needed a rest. You were such a cute baby. I expect your's and Haven's to be just as adorable."

Onyx always laughed when Myra told an embarrassing story about his cousin. It brought light into their dark situation. He followed Myra and Ryder out of the store, proudly wearing his new cloak. A part of him hoped that whoever was on the Branch side of the river could see him. He hoped that they were excited to see him and cheering loudly. Soon, he would be among them. He would feel safe for the first time in years. It all depended on Ryder breaking the Shadow Mirror and he was confident that his cousin could do it.

CONTENTION OF WILLS

The time had now come and what remained of the rebels along with a crowd of displaced Shadowborn surrounded the bridge. The collection of people were dressed for a long journey during the winter. On their backs, packed in carts, and laden on pack animals were their worldly goods and supplies. A team of guards had been assembled from the group of nine thousand refugees and were armed with an array of weapons. Many of the guards had eagerly volunteered when Ryder had asked for help. Four stood behind Haven and her family with Jarod as their captain. All respectfully held back, leaving twenty feet between them and Ryder. He stood on the bridge, a few steps from the boundary line.

Onyx stepped forward with Hayden and Donovan trailing behind him. He too was dressed for the journey, the royal blade sheathed at his left hip. He wore light steel and leather armor as well as his new cloak. Donovan and Hayden were dressed in their Saber uniform. Each had a different broach pinning their cloaks to their shoulders. Donovan's cloak was held in place by a silver Silvanus crest while Hayden had Ryder's crest as the Shadowlord on a silver chain.

"They refused to stand back and I could not deny them," Onyx apologized halfheartedly. He shrugged. "I could not as well."

"Then they are true Sabers and we should be glad to have their loyalty and service," Ryder commented with a nod. He laid his right hand on Onyx's left shoulder. "You also have a true and noble heart. The steps you took to discover it were painful and hard but such struggles shape you to be who you are standing before me today. You would make a good leader to the Shadowborn."

"Thank you for your training and willingness to show me how to be a better fighter," Onyx said graciously. He bowed his head once.

Ryder smiled. "There is more to life than war. What we do today is the next step towards a peaceful world. But this next step is very dangerous. Despite your growing strength," he started to say before he turned his attention to Donovan and Hayden. "And your unwavering loyalty, I cannot risk your lives when I challenge the Shadow Mirror. I order all three of you to stand back."

Onyx was shocked by the sudden change in their plan. He refused to move and was not surprised to see that the Sabers had remained in place. He stammered as he tried to form a response. In his mind, he begged Ryder not to push him back. He wanted to help. He gripped the hilt of his sword in an act of defiance.

"I can see that you do not like my order. Onyx, you are not my servant or my soldier to command. You are my cousin and my family. You are also the only other Silvanus left and the Shadowborn need a leader who is whole and true." Ryder came in close to whisper. "And should the Mirror prove too much for me, my child will need a guardian."

Did Ryder think that he was going to die? Onyx refused to believe that. He shook his head. "No."

"I am not asking you as the Shadowlord. I am asking you as a brother. Now please. Do this for me," Ryder softly pleaded.

It took every fiber of his being to force himself to turn away. Once he did, he paused to let out a deep breath. He nodded once towards Donovan and Hayden before walking off of the bridge. The two Sabers dutifully followed. Onyx took his place on Haven's left side while the Sabers stood behind him. Haven grabbed his hand and held it tightly. He stole a look at her. Her eyes were red from crying but she was otherwise standing strong and proud.

"Brothers and sisters of Shadow Night!" Ryder cried out with a booming voice.

Everyone stopped talking and turned their attention to him. Haven squeezed Onyx's hand tighter. He was surprised at how strong her grip was but resisted the urge to pull away. He could tell that she was upset and scared.

"It will be ok," Onyx mouthed. Haven did not react nor release her grip on his hand.

"We are here, standing on the edge of a precipice with nothing but destiny awaiting us. Do we turn back towards what we know or make a leap of faith towards the unknown? What we know is a world torn apart by fear of war and by war itself. We have experienced suffering and death. We have felt sorrow and anger. Many of us have lost a family member or a friend to this once silent reign of terror. Some of you are all that is left. Despite all of that, you are here today because you are ready to take that leap.

"I wish that all of our kin could be here with us so I ask you to lift up them up. I am proud of those who have elected to remain behind to rescue the innocent and bring them to Twilight so that they may join us in the lands of our allies. Lift all Shadowborn up and any who are feeling scared and oppressed."

The crowd muttered a variety of prayers, many bowing their heads and locking hands with their neighbors. Donovan put his left hand on Onyx's right shoulder. Hayden simply bowed his head and closed his eyes. Onyx glanced at Haven out of the corner of his eye. She appeared stiff and nervous, biting her bottom lip.

"I do not want you to feel like we are giving up. We are not giving up on our kin or our homeland. We are taking a different path to victory. We will return to reclaim this land and rebuild it into something far greater. Our cities will shine and reach high into the sky. Trade will flourish and our children will see a world of love and light."

Ryder paused to lock eyes with Haven. He nodded once and smiled. She wiped a tear from her cheek before running the back of her hand under her nose. Her hand then dropped to her swollen belly. The simple action made his breath catch in his chest. He took a moment to settle himself, letting out a deep breath slowly.

"Today, we will be making history. Our descendants will one day tell stories of the day that we chose to no longer live in fear. About how we chose to face terrible evil head on and with all of our might. What lies beyond the Mirror are souls that believe in us and will help us take back what is ours. United as one, we will take control of our destiny!"

The speech that Ryder had started on a somber and reflective note was building in strength. It ignited the fervor of the crowd to cheering.

"As your Shadowlord, I will join my power with that of the Daylord. Together, we will crush Kaiser Adonis once and for all. I promise that I will never surrender and that I will never stop fighting. So long as I draw breath, I will fight for the Immortal Truth and for the future of Terra!"

With the conclusion of his speech, Ryder turned around and stepped up to the boundary line. He reached forward and tapped the invisible Mirror. Immediately, it shuddered as silver ripples rolled out in all directions. Ryder reached into his belt and pulled out an old silver dagger. It was the one that Soja had given him in Crossroads over a year ago. To Ryder, he could think of no greater honor for the gift. He held it lightly in his right hands. He pressed the tip of the blade to each of his fingertips, slicing them open. He then cut open his palm before repeating the cuts on his right hand. Pocketing the knife, Ryder lifted his bleeding hands and examined the wounds. He paused as he flicked both of his wrists, bathing his hands in silver Spirit Fire. He let out a deep breath and pressed his hands forward.

The effect was immediate as red twisting lines shot out in all directions. They reached far into the sky, disappearing amongst the clouds. Veins of silver stretched from under Ryder's collar and spread across his face. His eyes glowed with a white light before transforming into bright silver. His entire body was rigid as he was locked in place with the Mirror. The contest of wills had begun.

A wind whipped up, emanating from the Mirror and Ryder's fight. Above, the clouds darkened to black and rumbled with claps of thunder. When Ryder turned his hands towards the outside, lightning shot out and struck him. An audible cry rose up from the crowd but Ryder remained standing. He was more determined to keep fighting. He shouted and a bright silver Spirit Fire erupted all around him. The red veins on the Mirror ignited in response. The invisible nature of the Mirror started to unravel as it became hazy and opaque. At first, the fiery veins and opaque haze was center around Ryder but it slowly spread out to surround the bridge. Lightning struck Ryder again and he stumbled for a moment but renewed his assault.

Hayden stepped up behind Onyx and laid a hand on his shoulder. He leaned in to whisper. "What you are seeing is a contest of wills. The question is not Ryder being more powerful than Kaiser. It is can he outlast the Mirror's response to his attack. Will Kaiser let him succeed or will he let him fail?"

"Kaiser wants to keep him alive so I have hope," Onyx quietly replied.

"Still, the Mirror is a powerful and ancient force that is little understood. We must prepare for if he fails," Hayden said. He glanced at Haven who visibly stiffened at his comment. "Do not worry, my lady. Your child's father is strong, stronger than I think many of us realize."

"Then may the Spirits be with him," Haven whispered.

Everyone in the crowd hushed when the Mirror shuddered as if struck from the other side. A cloudy yellow and orange light appeared and grew in intensity. The appearance of it filled Ryder with a greater sense of confidence. He pushed forward and felt a meeting pair of hands.

"When Shadow meets Light, dark becomes bright. I command with all that I am for the power to set the world right. No more will chaos stand for Truth is our might!" Ryder called out with a booming voice. "SPIRIT BREAK!"

*****

"There it is! Vorin! Hit it with everything you've got!" Evander shouted. "Bathe me in Dragonfire!"

"But you will be burned!" Vorin snapped his head back.

Evander shook his head. "I have connected with Ryder through the Mirror now. I am protected by him and through him by Kaiser's own power. Unleash your hottest fires!"

"Gladly," Vorin smirked. He curved his neck back as flames licked his jaws. He sucked in a massive gulp of air through his nostrils before opening his mouth. A bright yellow and orange fire shot out and slammed into the Mirror.

*****

A white crack appeared on the Mirror a hundred feet above Ryder's head. He did not look up to see it grow in size as he pulled his hands in. With great resistance, Ryder ripped his hands apart, spreading his arms out wide. Just as he looked up to see Evander's determined face, lightning struck him for a third time and tore him back from the breach. He was flung backwards, skidding to the foot of the bridge. His back stung unmercifully and he felt numb from head to toe.

Hayden was the first to break from the crowd and rushed to Ryder's side. He slid down to his knees as he reached him. He smiled as he saw Ryder laughing and holding his chest.

"That hurt," Ryder forced out in between hard coughing. Blood foamed at the corners of his mouth.

"But you are still alive and the Mirror is open. The first true victory against Kaiser," Hayden smiled with a sense of relief.

BROKEN SPIRITS

There was a palpable sense of relief in the air. Kaiser's Shadow Mirror had been broken and Ryder, though weak, had survived the effort. It was a double blessing. Onyx, Donovan, Jarod, and Myra helped to get the crowd going. Others passed the message along to those in the back and on the fringes. Everyone seemed more than ready to cross over the bridge and into the safety of Branch.

Hayden had pulled Ryder to the side, sitting him up against a post at the foot of the bridge. He reached down into a puddle, scooped up some water, and tossed it into Ryder's face.

"Are you still in there?" Hayden asked.

"Yea," Ryder gritted his teeth.

"Can you feel your toes? You hit the stone pretty hard," Hayden said as he looked towards Ryder's feet.

Together, they went through the health check basics. Hayden was surprisingly efficient and knowledgeable for someone without a healer's background. When questioned, Hayden stated that it had been a part of his Saber training. Ryder remained silent through the rest of the check. It was clear that he was beyond exhaustion and needed many hours of rest. His hands were still bleeding and there was a scent of burnt skin from the lightning strikes. Hayden tore strips of fabric from his own cloak and wrapped both of Ryder's hands.

"There. That should do until you get to a proper healer. You need to be able to hold that child of yours when it arrives,"

Hayden smiled, a twinkle in his eyes.

"You know? A part of me wishes that my child could be born in my homeland," Ryder mused. Hayden helped him up to his feet. Ryder leaned heavily on him.

"Your child will be born surrounded by love. That is all he or she will need," Hayden replied as he secured Ryder's left arm to hook around his neck.

Ryder grunted and stifled a groan with every movement. "Did you ever want children? I think it is silly that Sabers are forbidden to marry."

"I am married to the throne as a Saber. That is all I need for now though I intend to enjoy my time watching your child grow," he chuckled. "Son or daughter, this child will be a warrior like its parents. With your permission, I would like to help guide them."

"Permission granted until I am able to think straight. My senses feel so muddled and hazy," Ryder said with an exacerbated sigh.

*****

Aves stood on the north side of the bridge, helping to direct traffic. He bowed his head often and offered words of encouragement. Vorin and Evander stood on the Branch side of the river, keeping an eye on the breach. The broken edges of the breach burned fire red. Every so often, Vorin would snake his neck up to spit out a small jet of fire towards a questionable edge. He would curve his neck back down with a smug expression on his face. On the Branch side of the bridge, Earthborn, Airborn, Lightborn, and Gryphons worked together to address the greatest concerns of the Shadowborn refugees. Many were surprised that Ryder was going to be a father and welcomed Haven like a queen.

"Reminiscent of the Shadowborn ladies of old. I am glad to have met her," Evander stated after she passed by with Onyx.

"It stirs my ancient heart to think of such a blessing. Though my fate as the last of my kind makes me sad, I am glad to know that the bloodlines of old friends shall continue on. Dragons did not give gifts for the birth of a youngling. What do the Spiritborn do? Vorin asked Evander.

Evander chuckled before describing a Lightborn tradition to the Dragon. "I would like to congratulate the father. Think you can keep watch on your own?"

Vorin nodded. "The breach is holding strong. The power of the Shadowlord is as great as his noble ancestor."

The Lord of the Lightborn left the Dragon's side and made

his way towards the boundary line on the bridge. He felt light on his feet and resisted the urge to swing his arms. He still had to show decorum and proper manners befitting his station.

*****

Ryder looked up to see Evander approaching and managed an exhausted smile. He leaned against the bridge railing, still trying to catch his breath. His right side stung with pulsating pain leftover from his old Demon inflicted wounds. His back was no better and his shoulders felt like they had been stretched beyond their limit. He was hunched over with both hands resting against the railing. He really was not doing well but he did not anyone fussing over him. Hayden was already keeping a close eye, ready to help him if needed. The priority was getting the nine thousand Shadowborn over the bridge.

"I do not think even Kaiser Adonis would have thought someone could break his precious Mirror," Evander stated as he held onto his sword hilt.

"Pretty sure he has noticed but is debating on acting," Ryder exclaimed in a single breath. "He might have even let it happen."

"Have a little faith in your abilities. You are quite strong for your age. You did break my arm after all," Evander chuckled.

"Glad to hear that you have put that behind you," Ryder replied. His chest tightened and he stiffened. He waited as the surge of pain passed.

The crowd of Shadowborn continued their trek over the bridge with their array of carts and livestock. It was a mixed group with poor to rich walking in solidarity. Nobody was above helping another with their goods or in wrangling excitable children. It was a pleasing sight to Ryder. He had worried that his declaration about his heritage would deter many from following him. Nine thousand people was a lot but it was not the entire population of the Shadowborn lands. He could only hope that those who elected to stay behind would round up the rest.

A scream erupted from somewhere deep in the crowd. Others followed. The first scream put Ryder on high alert for he recognized it. Despite pain and exhaustion, he rushed into the throng of people. Hayden and Evander followed.

"Move!" Ryder shouted as he tried to push and shove his way through.

What felt like a painfully long time lasted only a few short seconds. Ryder broke free of the crowd and stumbled into an open circle at the foot of the bridge. In the center of the circle was Loran with his hood thrown back and holding a knife to Haven's throat. She whimpered and shrieked whenever Loran pressed the blade harder against her neck.

"It was so easy to sneak my way in and take my desired prey. Who would notice a man bent over with age in a dark and heavy cloak? Perhaps he hides his face due to a horrific injury," Loran taunted.

Vorin snarled loudly, flames licking his jaws. "Release her and I will burn you quickly."

Loran snickered. "A precious prize for a certain someone's cooperation. Go ahead. Bathe me in Dragonfire and risk killing your precious friend's lady love and child too."

"Let her go," Ryder ordered. He clenched his fists tightly. Blood dripped from his hands as his fingernails cut into his palm, reopening the self-inflicted wounds.

"Now why would I do that? Unlike you, I hold all of the cards. If anyone seeks to take one from me, I will slice open your whore's throat. If she thinks to fight her way free, I will cut her throat, killing her and the unborn brat. It's a win win for me," Loran laughed.

Ryder did not want to negotiate with Loran for it was like he was negotiating with Kaiser directly. His grandfather's will was in play. But he was not sure what to do. One wrong move and Haven would be murdered before his eyes. If only he was at full power. Ryder knew that he could have summoned a killing shot that would have eliminated Loran and saved Haven.

"What is it that you want?" Ryder asked through gritted teeth.

A heavy hand slapped down on his right shoulder. Ryder nearly crumbled under the resulting pain. He managed to right himself before his knees could buckle. "Lord Kaiser wishes to speak with you. Alone."

The crowd hushed and many stumbled to back away. How Rache hid among them without so much as a cold sense touching their hearts was frightening. What was even more scary was the idea that Kaiser was in Twilight. Was he going to attack? If he was in Twilight, why had he not tried to stop the breaking of the Mirror? Everyone's minds were wracked with questions that only increased their anxiety.

"What about?" Ryder asked without turning around. He held himself up as proud as he could. But his energy was flagging.

Rache leaned in to whisper. "Your future." He then looked up and locked eyes with Vorin, Evander, and Aves. Unlike in previous encounters, there was no sense of mirth or joy in his Demon red eyes. "Loran will release the girl and Lord Kaiser will let you through this profane breach if Ryder Coba comes with me. Alone. Should I discover that I am being followed, Lord Kaiser will unleash a sleeping giant that had been contained by the Mirror. With the Mirror broken, it will be free to roam the land and strike whomever and whatever gets in its way."

"I fear no arcane power!" Vorin roared.

Haven cried out, immediately halting the Dragon's fierce response. Loran snickered as he dragged the blade across the skin of his throat. "Be careful. My fingers might slip if you roar again."

"The only thing holding this breach open is the proximity of Kaiser's blood. If you want to save this crowd of wretches, you will do as I say," Rache warned. His eyes scanned the assembly of people and Dragon. He leaned in to whisper to Ryder again. "If you want to save what you love, you will come with me."

It was a choice that Ryder did not want to make. His eyes darted back and forth from Haven to Loran and back to Haven several times. His breath caught in his throat as the inevitable decision made his body shake. "Let them pass. Let her go and I will come with you."

"Then you know the true meaning of sacrifice," Rache whispered.

There was a hint of sadness in the Demon's voice that caught Ryder's attention. He wanted to act upon it but was not sure how. Was it possible that Rache was turning against Kaiser like he thought he would? He managed to glance up to look in Rache's eyes. Sadness was replaced by hard fear. His spirits fell and he hung his head.

THE BREACH CLOSES

No one's eyes left the sight of Rache in complete control of Ryder nor that of Loran with his knife blade pressed against Haven's throat. Vorin's chest rumbled with a low continuous growl. Both Aves and Evander spoke quietly amongst themselves about how to rectify the situation into their favor. They needed Ryder almost as badly as Haven did.

"If only Spirit Wake wasn't in play. We could have used our abilities together to free the Lady Haven," Aves quietly suggested to Evander.

The Lord of the Lightborn shook his head. "It would still leave the problem of freeing Ryder. I doubt that the Demon would release him if we freed Haven. He might even kill Ryder in retaliation."

"Let me burn the Demon bastard," Vorin growled under his breath. "I cannot stand this..." The rest of his statement was lost as he grumbled.

"We cannot sacrifice one for the other. We kill two people if we let the Lady Haven die but we cannot afford to lose Ryder. Kaiser has played us well," Aves said with an exacerbated sigh. He tightened his posture as if he was ready to launch. It was the most unsettled the Lord of the Airborn had been since the Mirror had been broken.

It was a tense situation all around. Loran was in reach for an attack but any strike against him risked the life of Haven. The crowd parted around them with nervous glances in their direction.

Onyx stood further back from the Mirror with an angry expression. He struggled to free himself from Donovan's bear hugging grip. Jarod and Hayden held back Haven's family who were desperate to reach her. What was even more worrisome was that without Vorin's Dragonfire, the breach was starting to shrink and close. A panic started to rise amongst the crowd of Shadowborn and their pace quickened.

After thirty minutes, the last stragglers of the Shadowborn crowd came through the breach and set foot in Branch. Soon, the bridge was cleared and the Alliance soldiers pulled the refugees to safety. Those that refused, stayed behind and armed themselves for a fight. There were at least two thousand men and women at arms and ready. They stood in formation and waited for the command from Vorin, Aves, or Evander. Onyx wrestled himself free from Donovan and took his place at the front of the crowd. He pulled out the royal blade. Donovan soon joined him, standing at his right side with his own sword out.

"We must not be too rash or we risk both of their lives. Your cousin, though powerful in his own right, is weak and exhausted," Donovan said in a low voice.

Onyx bit his bottom lip. He and Ryder had had a very long conversation regarding the steps to take after the breaching of the Shadow Mirror. They had discussed multiple scenarios that ranged from failing to break the Mirror to the darkest one of all. It was one that Onyx refused to let happen: Ryder's death. Going to Kaiser was just as terrible as death, if not worse. No, he was not going to let Kaiser take his cousin away from him or from Haven. But a voice in the back of his mind reminded him that Rache was a more powerful Demon than Iztal. Ryder had told him as much.

"It does not matter," he grumbled.

"What does not matter?" Donovan asked. He looked over at Onyx.

"No matter what happens, we must continue to fight. Even if we are sent to the Spirit World, we must do everything we can to stop Kaiser from destroying this world. I refuse to believe that the Spirits are separated from us now. They will come to our aid and make sure that Terra is saved," Onyx said with absolute conviction. He tightened his grip on the sword hilt. "We must trust in Ryder and we must have faith in the Spirits. In Omu and in the All Spirit."

Donovan nodded. "To Omu and the All Spirit. For truth and peace."

The same feeling passed among the awaiting crowd of soldiers for it seemed that nothing else would be able to save the situation. Each Spiritborn prayed for the Spirits to come. Even the

Gryphons prayed to their ancestors for aid. Vorin only snarled, flashing his sharp teeth. Flames licked his jaws as he eyed the closing breach.

"We must do something before the breach closes otherwise the Shadowborn lands are lost to us," Evander stated, eyeing Vorin's increasing frustration and anger. Aves laid a hand on Evander's sword arm, forcing the Lord of the Lightborn to lower his weapon.

Loran started to laugh out loud. He then turned around towards the crowd of people. "Wow. That is a lot of soldiers wanting to kill me. I am honored that you think I am worth that much."

"We do not give a rat's ass about you. Release Haven now!" Onyx demanded. He brandished his sword and took a step forward.

"Okay," Loran said.

What happened next seemed as if it was happening in slow motion. Loran shoved Haven forward, his blade scratching her neck. Onyx and the soldiers lurched towards the now separated pair. In the blink of an eye, Aves rushed to catch Haven. He took her weight and cushioned her fall. Loran disappeared into Shadow Slide. Everyone slid to a stop as Vorin angrily roared and turned his full fury on the newly reformed Mirror. He blasted it with his hottest fire. The Dragonfire slammed into the Mirror and shot up towards the clouds above. The sky turned bright red as yellow and white lightning jumped between the clouds. Vorin roared even louder and threw himself at the Mirror. Sparks of rainbow energy shot out from between the competing forces of power. The Dragon relented after it was apparent that there was nothing he could do to reopen the breach.

"Damn you, Kaiser! Damn you to the Spiral for all eternity!" Vorin screamed in fury.

While Vorin continued to rage and shout profanities, Aves gingerly held the crying Haven. She laid limp in his arms, blood streaming from the cut on her neck.

"He is gone. Gone forever," she whimpered with quiet desperation. She buried her face against Aves' chest.

Onyx refused to believe that Ryder was lost to them though Haven's cries pulled at his heart. He dropped his head and took a deep breath. He closed his eyes for a moment before snapping back open.

"All of you! Listen to me!" Onyx shouted with a booming voice. He turned to face the assembly of Spiritborn and Gryphons. He puffed out his chest and raised the royal blade into the air. "This is not the end of Peredur Adonis Coba-Silvanus! This is not the end of all that we have fought for! He is the Shadowlord and like the Daylord, he will find us again for a glorious victory!"

Whispers rose amongst the crowd about the possible return of Bane. Vorin even paused in his fury to listen.

"This is not a war against a power crazed madman. This is a war against someone who wants to destroy the very foundations of the world we love and hold dear. Everything Kaiser stands for goes against the Immortal Truth and the Covenant of Spirits. We must protect both with all that we are. Even if it means that we must die. Our ancestors and those that have fallen are watching us, praying for us, and fighting with us. I know this to be true for the Spirits of my father and mother helped me to defeat the Demon Iztal. The Spirits are with us and they always will be.

"We must leave Branch and prepare ourselves to protect the power that holds our world together. We must guard the Immortal Truth and prevent the Covenant of Spirits from being broken and sending Terra back to the Dark Days. The Daylord is coming. I know that he is for I refuse to believe that he has not heard our cries."

"Lord Proto Avis sent a brave Gryphon into the Southlands almost twelve moons ago. The eighth that has flown over the Wall of Crossroads since he first saw the threat of war in the stars above," Vorin offered. He swung his massive body around to stand behind Onyx. "I too refuse to believe that the Daylord has not heard us. I know deep in my heart that he is coming home."

Onyx smiled proudly as he raised his sword up into the air. "This is not Kaiser's victory. Not only will the Daylord come, my cousin will return to us stronger than ever. The Daylord and the Shadowlord will fight together again and cast down Kaiser Adonis once and for all! Nothing can stop the Champions of Truth! Not fear or death! Not even Kaiser! We will win this war united as one heart, body, mind, and soul!"

The defeated mood of the people lifted though it did not leave them. The Shadowborn fell to their knees before Onyx while the other Spiritborn all bowed their heads. Gryphons also bowed their heads. Vorin lifted his head into the air and spit out a jet of red and orange flame. It was a defiant signal.

"He is gone," Haven whispered as she remained in Aves' arms.

"The ones we love never leave us, my Lady," Aves said softly as he lifted her up. He carried her towards her family.

It took a long time but the caravan for Cascade was made ready and began streaming out of Branch. The same two thousand soldiers who had stood strong were joined by another thousand. They had been charged with the defense of Branch and to stand ready if the breach reopened. Vorin stood with them before taking a running start and lifting into the air. He flew over the crowd several times before soaring off towards the south.

"I go to await our champion and King! For truth, beloved kin of Terra! For truth and peace!"

*****

FACE TO FACE

Ryder was not sure how long he had slept. He felt groggy
and like his body had been stretched far beyond his physical limits.
Both of his hands stung with a dull pulsating throb. He reached
back and rubbed the base of his skull. He over extended and his
back locked up. Paralyzed from the pain, Ryder stopped his
attempt to sit up. For an agonizing hour, he shuddered as the pain
rolled through him from the top of his head down to his toes.
When the pain finally faded into the background, Ryder slowly
pushed himself up.

He shook his head and rubbed his eyes. His vision was
slow to clear. Soon, he was able to take a look at his surroundings.
He laughed half-heartedly. The bedroom was in a state of decay
but it was very clearly the room of the Shadowlords of old. He was
sitting in the middle of an ornate four post bed piled high with
pillows and blankets. A mottled gray and black fur was stretched
across the bed that was in desperate need of washing. He ran his
left hand over it, kicking up a cloud of dust. He quickly wiped his
hand on his pant leg and grimaced. He looked up and saw a net of
cobwebs complete with a large family of spiders and several moths
wrapped up in silk. It hurt but Ryder rolled himself off of the bed
and away from the spiders and dusty fur.

He was still wearing his travel worn clothes that were
stained with dirt and blood. A part of him felt stronger in such an
outfit. He pulled at his tunic and the fabric crunched and
crumbled under his touch. When he lifted his arm to further

inspect his clothes, he wrinkled his nose. He was in desperate need of a bath.

The layout of the royal quarters was exactly as he remembered. Ryder had not been here since his father was executed. He had come to take what he wanted of his father's possessions. One thing he had not found that he wanted was the newly created seal for the Coba-Silvanus bloodline. As a result, he had the crest tattooed on his right shoulder. He exited the bedroom and into the sitting room. The fireplace had obviously not been lit in over a year as another next of cobwebs stretched across the opening. Ryder grimaced at the sight. He was briefly reminded of Onyx's father who languished in a state of disconnect for the last ten years of his life. The room reflected Aku's state of mind. Ryder strode over to a second fireplace in the room on the far wall and forced his way through the left hand door.

It took a little effort but Ryder was able to force open the dressing room door. He was surprised to find it clean and dust free. An outfit had been laid out on the mannequin complete with his newly made armor. He stepped up to the armor and ran his fingers over the Shadowlord crest. He tapped the center of it. He wondered how his things came to be here.

"Rache," Ryder said to himself.

He went into the washroom and scrubbed all of the dirt and grime from his hair and body. The bath was refreshing and the warm water soothed his aching muscles. His vigorous scrubbing did however reopen several of his wounds, including the one on his right side that refused to heal completely. The claw marks oozed a black liquid that was tinged with red accents of blood. It was not as severe as before but it still stung unmercifully. It would have been better to use Spirit energy but only Kaiser knew how to heal a Demon inflicted wound in that manner. Only Kaiser could teach him how. He gritted his teeth in burgeoning fury.

At first, Ryder was planning on putting his mangled clothes back on. He picked up his tunic, poking his fingers through the various holes. He looked back up at the armor. If Kaiser wanted to face him, Ryder was going to stand before him as the Shadowlord.

*****

"Look at you all dressed up," Loran snickered as he leaned against the opposite wall with his arms crossed. "Nice armor."

Ryder ignored him and turned towards the left away from the door to the royal quarters. As he walked down the hallway, he started to notice how it was in a poor state of repair and cleanliness. Once bright guild work frames were faded and dull, their paintings covered in a thick layer of dust. Tapestries with intricate designs were frayed and stripped of any embedded jewels or gold and silver thread. Only a sporadic few oil lamps had been lit. Soot coated the wall behind each burning lamp.

"You are about the shiniest thing in this hallway," Loran stated as he followed behind Ryder. "Who made that fancy armor? Was it the endlessly skilled you or..."

Ryder turned around and punched Loran directly in the face. Loran stumbled backwards, holding his nose before falling onto his rear. Blood streamed down his face.

"You broke my nose!" Loran cried as he tried to stop it from bleeding. He constantly wiped his hands over his face, smearing the blood and doing little to help his situation.

"So?" Ryder asked, lifting an eyebrow. He did not care what Loran said or thought. The guy was nearly as useless as his cousin Morin. "I cut your stupid cousin's arm off before I set him on fire. Consider yourself lucky."

Loran flexed his jaw before pushing his broken nose back into place. He spat out a mouthful of blood. "You are just as terrible as Lord Kaiser."

"Ok. So this was just an accident. Just like this is," Ryder snapped before kicking Loran in the face and knocking him out. He snorted towards the unconscious man before turning around and leaving him in the hallway.

Ryder exited the private wing and quickly descended the stairs. At the bottom was Rache, leaning against the railing post. Ryder slowed to a stop a few steps up from where the Demon was waiting. He noticed that Rache was dressed for travel and not in his usual tattered white and tan clothes. He was now wearing a modified Saber uniform with fingerless gloves and the cloak removed. A travel pack rested by his feet, the missing cloak rolled up tightly and strapped onto the top. His flame red hair was pulled back in a loose ponytail. With his hair pulled back, Rache's sharp cheekbones and sullen eyes were on display.

"I do not see Loran with you. Did he not report to his post as his Lord commanded?" Rache asked without looking up.

"He is taking a nap after a well-deserved punch and kick to the face," Ryder commented as he gestured back towards the hallway. "What are you doing?"

Rache let out a deep breath. "I did as my Master commanded. I brought him his grandson alive. Now I am freed from the profane bond as a reward."

"If you are free then why haven't you left already?" Ryder

asked. He had dozens of other questions that he wanted to ask.

The Demon shrugged. "I don't know." He picked up the travel pack and threw it over his shoulder. He turned to face Ryder. "For once in this second life, I do not know what is ahead of me. Perhaps that is the negative of coming back from the dead. Too many paths to follow but only one choice to be made. My homeland is barred from me so I am reduced to wandering this world to find purpose or death again."

Ryder had known Rache his entire life. For the longest time, he hated the Demon. To him, Rache was an attack dog who lived to spill blood and cause destruction. But the individual standing before him looked defeated and lost. The distant expression in Rache's eyes made Ryder pity him. He watched as Rache walked away, his shoulders bent. It was not the same Demon that so famously killed the celebrated hero Begin Anu.

He buried his thoughts about Rache as he headed for the throne room. It wasn't long before he found himself before the tall ebony wood doors. No team of guards flanked the doors. In fact the entryway was utterly abandoned. He pushed open the heavy doors and went inside.

As expected, Kaiser was lounging on the royal chair. This time, he was fully dressed and did not appear drunk on wine. Ryder stopped ten feet away from the raised dais and locked his hands behind his back. Kaiser grinned as he swung his legs around and sat up.

"Welcome back to Cross, my dear grandson. That new armor suits you well. Your other grandfather would have approved," Kaiser said with a pleasant smile.

"Not like I had a choice. Be selfish and let the one I love die or sacrifice my freedom to ensure her and our unborn child's safety? Sometimes sacrifices have to be made," Ryder stated. He shifted his weight. "I am sure that my other more noble grandfather would have made the same decision. Sacrifice himself for the greater good."

Kaiser chuckled as he lowered his head. He clapped his hands once before looking back up. "You know? I got the glorious privilege to watch Madhuri Coba die. I only regret not wielding the assassin's blade myself."

"That is not news to me. I know Rache killed him at your command," Ryder replied. He moved to cross his arms tightly.

"Much like your hush hush news about your unborn spawn with that whore? That is not news to me either. In my day, such blessings were shouted from the rooftops. The royal family is growing! I would say let's celebrate but I am offended that you did not tell me."

"Like you even care considering you used Haven and my child as a bargaining chip for my cooperation," Ryder snapped. He was starting to feel angry.

"At least now you see why I have not subjected myself to the weakness of love. It can make you do funny things. Spend your wealth out of blind foolishness. Take leaps and bounds to the point of self-harm in order to win a fair maiden's heart. Chain you down into a life of monotony. Take away your very freedom. Is that what you want? To live such a dull and fruitless life full of love and sickening emotion?" He put his hands out to the side and shrugged his shoulders.

Ryder gritted his teeth. He hated how Kaiser kept calling Haven a whore and his unborn child a spawn. "She has a name. I desire a life with Haven and our future family above all else. To live in peace and joy instead of constant war."

"Well that's boring." Kaiser sat back in a huff.

"If that is so boring then what do you want in life?"

Kaiser remained silent for a long time. He crossed his legs and looked up at the ceiling. He tapped his fingers on the armrests of the chair. He then smirked. "Oh no. It will not be that easy. My mind is an impenetrable fortress. It will not be so easily breached like you did the Shadow Mirror. Perhaps I was a bit too distracted by other events to keep up my vigilance otherwise the effort would have killed you."

What other events could he be talking about? What was more pressing than an attack on the Shadow Mirror? The Daylord had to be on the move.

"You're afraid."

Kaiser's smile dropped from his face. "What?"

"You're afraid of the Daylord," Ryder offered.

"I am not afraid of Bane Arlis! Just so you know, he is a farmer from the Eastlands. Not a glorious warrior gifted with an amazing power. His appearance in the Northlands was an accident. An accident! Just like you!" Kaiser leaped up from the chair and pointed accusingly at Ryder. "I know that some people say my war would have never happened had you taken the throne. Well guess what! They were wrong!"

"You are trying to distract me from the truth. You are afraid of death and dying. You see? You have already died once so you know how final it is. Those who have never died and are afraid of death are afraid because they believe that they will lose what and who they love. That they will lose what makes them strong. You are afraid of death because you know that to be true. So you started this war in an attempt to order it as you see fit so that you will never feel powerless again. You create chaos out of your own fear. Everyone else does not matter. It's all about you."

"Wow. You think that just because you share my blood that you know me. I hate to break it to you but you don't. You know nothing of death." He turned away from Ryder. "Death is eternal and no one can escape it. It cannot be destroyed. Life after death is even more terrible. You can neither die nor truly live. You are so open to all planes of existence that if you rest for one moment, it will consume you utterly. For over a thousand years, my existence has been a constant war. So yes, it is all about me!"

A silence fell between them and Ryder resisted the urge to speak. He took a few minutes to work up the courage. "Then tell me the story that no one knows but you. Not the one you have boasted about. The real story. The one about your death."

"Why should I tell you? You have done nothing to earn my trust or my respect." Kaiser refused to turn around to face him. He clenched his fists tightly.

"You say that I am your heir. By that right, do I not deserve the tale of your legacy?" Ryder asked.

Kaiser stomped down the dais and came to stand face to face with Ryder. He snarled, curling back his lips.

"Fine. You want to know how I died? My own father murdered me. Cut me right across the throat," he said as he mimicked the action by dragging his thumb over his black scars. "He had the nerve to cry as he watched his own son bleed to death. Then I was buried in the cold ground and left to rot. Nothing more than a terrible memory and an unfortunate embarrassment."

"Why?" came Ryder's quiet question.

"Why?!"

"Yes. Why would a loving father be driven to take his son's life? What did you do to force him to do what he did?"

The expression on Kaiser's face was one of indignation and shock. He stammered to find the words, not out of shock but out of pure anger. A vein pulsated on his forehead over his left eye. "Are you blaming my murder on me?!"

"No. I am saying that you had a good life that was full of love and you threw it away because your ridiculous pride and obsession with power and glory. Your father and mother loved you. Your brother adored you. I just cannot understand why you turned on them. Why you turned your back on the world."

Kaiser stamped away, fuming. His back was stiff and his fists clenched so tightly that blood seeped from between his fingers. His entire body shook. "Shut up."

"You could have been great. Greater than you are now."

"Shut up!" Kaiser yelled as he turned back around.

"You could have brought eternal glory to the name Adonis.

All you have brought it is eternal shame."

"I SAID SHUT UP!" Kaiser roared as he struck Ryder with a powerful right hook.

Ryder was thrown back by the force and collapsed on the ground several feet away. He coughed and spat as he rubbed his jaw. He winced in pain. Once he had gathered himself, he slowly stood back up. He faced Kaiser head on.

"No I won't. You need to know that there are people who will stand up to you and tell you the truth!" Ryder retorted. He wished that he had a sword or knife but all weapons had been taken away from him. He felt that Soja's knife would have at least been sufficient.

Kaiser was beyond angry, steam rising up from his body. "You want to know why my father killed me? You want to know the honest truth? He hated me and I hated him. I hated my mother and my brother. I hated them all. By right of blood, I was an Anu Prince, a direct descendent of the Farlander hero Begin Anu. I deserved the power that was rightfully mine. Of course, the Silvanus family was in the way. I had to do something. I beat Aday to within an inch of his miserable life. I was about to kill him until my father pulled me off.

"He begged Sin Silvanus to let him deal with me. He dragged me back home to Umbra. My stupid brother," Kaiser snarled and looked away. He took several deep breaths but they did little to calm him. "He got in my way and I throttled him until he turned blue and was coughing blood. Apparently that was the last straw for the great Cian Adonis. I was too angry and aggressive to be controlled and that it was only going to get worse. Nothing could be done to save his heir."

It was strange when Kaiser started to cackle like the entire situation amused him. It clearly didn't for his posture was so tight with anger that Ryder thought he would snap his own bones. He took a tentative step back to put some distance between them.

"He took me out to the wilds, telling me that it was going to be a session of tough love and retraining. No, he took me out there to execute me to save his family, reputation, and his legacy the embarrassment. I am sure that he concocted some ridiculous story that a stray Demon tore me to pieces. No! The coward backed down and I realized what was going on.

"I felt betrayed and I attacked him with all of my might. I laughed at him and called him a coward. I shouted that he did not deserve his life of comfort and influence while I languished in the shadows. I came at him blow after blow until an errant strike of his sliced open my throat. I was done."

Kaiser pulled out a small silver knife from his belt and

twisted it around. "Recognize this blade? It is the one dear Soja Rokar gave you before you tried to assassinate me. It is a nice knife. I think that I might keep it. You threw it away and Rache kindly picked it up for me."

Ryder wanted to rip the knife from Kaiser's hand. He unclenched his right hand. In the blink of an eye, Kaiser had appeared before him and shoved the blade through his chest plate and buried it in his heart. He gasped as all strength to stand left him in an instant. Kaiser held him up and shushed his attempts to speak.

"To hear the rest of the story, you will have to ask the Spirit World yourself. I promised you that the next time we meet, I was going to kill you. I always keep my promises. So say goodbye to all that you hold dear and see just how final death really is."

*****

Kaiser let Ryder drop to the floor, the knife still embedded in his chest. Blood bubbled out of the wound and streamed onto the floor. He twirled his left hand and the Living Map appeared. The energy flowed over Ryder's dying form. Whenever the energy touched the blood, it sparked and hummed. The sight made Kaiser laugh softly before it built into a booming sound. It bounced off the walls and ceiling and echoed back to him.

"Let the world know that the Shadowlord is dead. Let them weep tears before they weep blood."

BLOOD IS THE LIFE

Rache entered the throne room with a great deal of caution. He closed the doors behind him and turned to face the center of the room. Thankfully the Living Map was nowhere to be seen and even Kaiser was gone. The feeling in the air was cold. Rache slowly stepped out of the shadows and towards Ryder's pale form. A large puddle of sticky blood surrounded the body. The silver pommel of the knife still sticking out of Ryder's chest glinted in the moonlight. Rache bent down by his side and pressed two fingers to his neck. He felt no pulse. He lowered his head.

"Such is your fate, Peredur. The world has lost another good soul to the evil of Kaiser Adonis. I am sorry that I played my part in your death," Rache started to say. He looked away and wrung his hands. "A year ago, I would have been glad to drink your blood like a parasite. Now I question why I ever did drink blood in the first place."

It was a thought that Rache had battled with for quite some time. Demons by nature drank blood to read the memories of others. There were established rituals and in some cases, celebrations when a particularly desirable victim had been identified. He used to be that Demon who thrilled in the hunt and delighted in the kill. He had bathed in the blood of those he killed. For what? Rache was starting to question why. He was starting to question everything he was.

"In a strange way, I saw myself in you. Someone to be hated and yet you did not let it control you as I did. The bastard of

Akakios made something of himself and now the world will miss everything you became and represented. In my world, the more you killed, the better your reputation. Just as easily as you could rise, someone greater could come along and take you down. Perhaps Demons are too consumed by the darkness." He laughed half-heartedly. "They should come and live amongst the Spiritborn as I did. I guess I should thank Kaiser for that."

Rache gathered up Ryder's body, wrapping it in the blood stained black cloak. He slung the heavy weight over his right shoulder. He did not care that blood got on him. He had never been bothered by blood and normally saw it as a sign of power. Now, it gave him a sense of sorrow. More questions about his existence and everything he was swam in his head as he left the throne room.

At first, Rache did not know why he had decided to go see what had become of Ryder. He was certain that Kaiser was not going to sway him. Ryder had made it very clear that he would never join forces with his grandfather. Thus the only alternative for Kaiser was to kill his only descendent. No one was ever going to see the world as he did. No one was going to follow him with blind love and dedication. Even Loran had toyed with the idea of leaving to return to a life at sea. But Rache had warned him then that Kaiser would know as soon as he left. Even he had deluded himself into thinking that his former Master was not aware of his changing heart. Kaiser had claimed not to have the ability to read minds but Rache was not so sure. He had never met a soul so aware of the world around him.

The castle was empty of all guards, servants, and court officials. It made Rache wonder if they had mixed themselves into the crowd of refugees in Twilight. It did not matter anymore. Those people were probably halfway to Cascade by now. Rache had not rushed back to Cross so they might even be in the Earthborn capital already. He exited the castle out of a side door frequently used by the castle staff. The path twisted around through an avenue of spindly trees before opening up into a stable yard.

There were only four horses left in the stables. Three of them were black and one was white. The white horse stamped its hoof against the stall door and snorted loudly. Rache bypassed the animal and chose a large and spirited horse with a white blaze mark down its snout. He set Ryder's body down on a bale of hay and leaned his travel pack against it. He then set about saddling the horse. After he finished, he looked over again at the white horse. Soon, Rache had both horses equipped with saddles and bridles. On the black horse, he secured his travel pack and Ryder's body. He grabbed both of their reins and led the horses out of the yard and into the city.

The city appeared to be just as empty as the castle. Only a sporadic few houses had smoke rising from their chimneys. Every window was tightly boarded up. Even the usually active taverns and inns were quiet. There were no stray dogs or cats though Rache thought he spotted a thin sewer rat diving out of sight. The feeling was rather cold. Rache found that he missed the energy of the Shadowborn capital. He missed the store owners shouting at passersby to come inside. The children chasing each other and begging street vendors for sweet treats. In his thousand year service to Kaiser, he had grown to admire and admittedly love the joy for life in the Shadowborn.

He mounted the white horse and settled into the saddle. He secured the reins of the second horse to the saddle horn. He glanced back over his shoulder at the black horse that was resigned to its place in line. It was if the horse knew who was on its back and felt sadness for the loss. Instead of going right through the eastern gate of the city, Rache found himself stopping in place. Both horses snorted but otherwise remained still.

Cross had been part of his second life and his identity was connected to it. Though Kaiser had raised him from the dead in Umbra, the capital city was where he had lived for the last thousand years. As he thought about it more, it was where he had been chained into a life of servitude instead of freedom. At first, it did not matter. He was alive again! So what if he was bound to a young and ambitious Shadowborn. Little did he realize back then what Kaiser was and would become. How frightening his ideas would be. He urged his mount forward and the other horse followed.

"I guess I should have had some sort of clue when he raised me from the dead that he was something more. Especially using that ritual. I was too delighted with taking my first breath, feeling the air in my lungs again. My senses were alive. I could hear everything. See everything. It was like it used to be. So what if I was enthralled to a Shadowborn younger than I? Soon enough, I would overpower him and be free to bring terror to the world. No one could control Rache the great killer of Begin Anu!"

Rache laughed quietly to himself as he passed under the gateway. To the left and right were the massive iron studded doors, overgrown with vines and weeds. Sprigs of grass broke through the stone street, growing in thickness until the stone gave way to the natural soil.

"Did you know that Demons do not have cities? Nope, Demons are nomadic. Rarely do we congregate in large numbers unless it is for war and treasure. Demons are very apt to kill each other over the smallest of slights. In our beast forms, we are even more aggressive thus when we do come together, Demons will retain a humanoid form. I doubt there is much truthful literature out there about my race. I remember being surprised at Kaiser's knowledge of my kind. He knew things that only Demons should know."

He was certain that Kaiser did not possess any Demon blood but it was frightening how he knew the innermost secrets and deep history. Granted, Demons did not make a point of teaching history or providing any sort of education for their youth. In the Darklands, it was fend for yourself and hope you don't get killed by someone bigger and stronger. Rache could not remember his childhood nor who his parents were or if he had siblings. Now that he thought about it, he could not remember his early life at all prior to the Dominion War. And he found himself longing to know where he had come from.

"Sometimes I wonder why I was born a Demon if I was born at all. I know precious little about my origins or how my race functions. As a matter of fact, are there any Demons left behind the Daylord's Mirror? I would like to know. I want to know the truth."

Once he had uttered those words, it felt like a door opened from somewhere deep within him. It was an odd sensation that he strangely welcomed. Yes, he wanted to learn more about his origin and about his race. He wanted to travel the world. He glanced back over his shoulder at Ryder's limp body.

"I envy you. You have seen the vast reaches of this world and you are still young," Rache said as he returned his focus forward. "To be wild and free without a care in the world. Burdened by nothing but where to go next. But then, you were always burdened by who you were. Son of an executed Shadowlord. Potential heir to the throne. Descendent of a terrible soul determined to make war. You have never been free. Just like me in this second life. In this way, we are alike. Trapped by Kaiser's influence. He really is terrible and must be stopped. We must stop him before he destroys the Immortal Truth and breaks the Covenant of Spirits. We must before it is too late."

Rache had to face the fact that he helped Kaiser by acting as a shield against assassination. He had also killed hundreds if not thousands under his command. He had wrought death and destruction all in Kaiser's name. Where could he go where he would not be hated or persecuted? Even if he did help to end the war, his dark legacy would follow him wherever he went.

"I need to make amends. Even if it does little to sway the hearts of good people, it will go a long way to ease my Demon consciousness. I cannot erase my past but I can certainly change my future."

*****

Rache had originally planned to take Ryder's body and cast it into the Mirror Sea. Now, he had a different idea that took him towards the northwest. He rode day and night without rest through the woods and hidden trails. At the last minute, he wondered if a being such as himself would be barred from entering the Site of Ascension but he had to risk it. The moon was high in the night sky, nearly full, and surrounded by twinkling stars. He tied the horses' reins to a low hanging branch. Hoisting Ryder's body over his shoulder, Rache brought him to the center of the clearing and laid him on his back. He looked down at Ryder's pale face.

In the few days since leaving Cross, the body had lost all color and warmth. Arms and legs were stiff, both from rigor and from the chill in the air. Rache detected the slight odor of decay as he bent over the chest wound. He slowly wrapped his fingers around the hilt of the knife and pulled it out. It sounded wet and sticky. No blood seeped out of the deep wound.

"I do not know if this will work," Rache mumbled to himself as he sliced open his right hand. He clenched his fists and brought it over the wounds. A thin stream of blood dripped from his hand and disappeared within Ryder's chest cavity.

"Truth be told, let the shadows fall and the day rise. For dawn is here and I can see the light. Let the sun shine down on me as I walk this land until its last goodbye. From day to night, time passes on and all will begin again. Blood is the life and energy for the Spirit..."

Rache continued to chant long into the night, ignoring the chill of the invocation that had once bound him to Kaiser. He repeated it over and over until the moon disappeared and the horizon started to brighten with the light of dawn. With an exhausted sigh, Rache sat up and closed his eyes for a moment of peace. He let out a deep breath before opening his eyes. Soja's knife had fallen into the dirt beside his knee. He pulled his bleeding hand back and examined Ryder, searching for signs of life. Nothing.

*****

SON OF RYDER

Onyx sat leaning forward over his knees with his head in his hands. His hair was a tangled mess and he was in desperate need of a bath. He had barely slept since arriving in Cascade. He was exhausted mentally and physically. He sat up and rested his back against the wall. He let out a deep breath. The bench shifted slightly as another person sat down beside him.

"How are you doing?" Luna asked as she rubbed his left shoulder.

"I've been better," Onyx mumbled. He opened his right eye and looked over at her.

Luna sighed deeply as she pushed back a lock of her brunette hair. "You need to sleep and recover some strength."

"Are you ordering me to bath and bed?" Onyx asked sarcastically.

"No, I am asking as a concerned friend. I know that you want to wait by the Lady Haven's side for the child's arrival but you will do her no service in your current state." Her hand dropped away from his shoulder.

Onyx had truly been glad to reunite with Luna. She was just as kind and friendly as he remembered. They even managed to joke about cliff diving as a way to relax. But Onyx could not shake the burden of what went down in Branch. He ran his fingers through his hair and let out a deep breath. His muscles ached and his old Demon inflicted wound on his right leg was acting up again. He bent down to massage his calf.

"I am Ryder's only family. I promised him before he was taken that I would be there for Haven and for their child," Onyx stated.

Both he and Luna looked up when the bedroom door opened. His grandmother stepped into the hallway. Her dress of forest green and gold swirled as she adjusted her grass green shawl. Her golden hair was pinned back in cascading waves down her back. She wore a circlet of bronze that was studded with emeralds.

"My Lady," Luna said as she leapt up from her seat and curtsied demurely.

Willow nodded and gestured for Luna to stand up straight. She looked at Onyx to do the same. She watched as he slowly got to his feet and attempted to pull at his tunic hem to neaten it.

"Onyx, you have been outside of this door for three days. I think it is high time that you got some rest. There are plenty of good people watching over your cousin's wife," Willow stated with firm gentleness.

"I worry though about leaving her," Onyx replied.

"Childbirth is women's work. You can do little to aid her save by getting some rest. It would be unseemly for you to greet this new boy or girl in your current state. Come now. I know that your quarters are not far. Luna? Can you stay here? Should something happen, I want you to fetch my grandson as quick as your feet will carry you."

Luna curtsied again. "Yes, my Lady."

Onyx reluctantly followed his grandmother. He was not sure why he did it. She had no political power over him as she was Earthborn by blood and title. He was Shadowborn and the heir to the throne. Yet as he thought about it, he did not feel like the heir anymore. Ryder had declared himself the Shadowlord and thus the soon to arrive baby was the heir to the throne. He was not sure what his role was anymore.

"Here we are. Just around the corner. You are not far," Willow smiled softly. She then suddenly embraced him tightly and sniffled. Onyx returned the embrace. "I am glad that you are safe. You have suffered so much on your own."

It felt strange to be hugged for as Onyx quickly realized, the Shadowborn were not so open with their softer emotions. "Thank you."

Willow pulled back, keeping her hands on his shoulders. "You look so much like your mother. She and your father would be very proud of the man you have become."

He knew that everyone meant well when they told him that he needed to rest and wash up. But with the uncertainty of Ryder's fate, Onyx felt obligated to stay close to Haven as a protector. He wanted to believe that his cousin was still alive but every time he thought about him, a shiver went through his body. He wondered if Haven would know first due to her deep connection as a Spirit Anchor. How did that work after all? He could not remember if Ryder had taught him about Spirit Anchors. Haven had been quiet for the last four days but he choked it up to impending child birth. Even he had been quiet. He laughed to himself as he went to find the washroom.

The washroom had a black and white tile floor with dark wood walls. A second door led into the stool closet. A gold hook was attached to the wall next to an enclosed gray stone tub. A hot water bath had already been prepared for him. He peeled off his clothes and slipped into the water. The heat was immediately soothing to his sore body. He dipped beneath the water and quickly came back up. He slicked back his hair and leaned back against the ledge.

Everyone was right. The bath did feel good. His right leg was no longer hurting him. After dressing in clean clothes, Onyx laid back on the four poster bed. The mattress was soft and comfortable. He swung his arms back and forth over the plush surface. It was not long before he closed his eyes and fell asleep.

His dreams were chaotic with no sense of story or direction. Memories flashed in bright bursts before disappearing into the darkness of his mind. Pain shot through him in sporadic waves and then silence.

*****

Onyx woke up to the sound of frantic banging on the bedroom door. The sound paused before beginning anew. He managed to push himself off of the bed and stepped over to the door. He opened it while in the midst of a yawn.

"Come on!" Luna shouted. She reached out and grabbed him by his shirt, pulling him forward.

He stumbled after her and nearly fell to the floor. Luna hopped up and down in nervous excitement as she waited for him to right himself. At first, he could not figure why she was so jittery. She grabbed his hand and began pulling him again. She was desperate to get him to follow her. It then occurred to him what was going on. A broad smile crossed his face and he eagerly took up pace with her. He and Luna slid into the hallway and found a small crowd.

Hayden and Jarod stood guard to either side of the bedroom door while Haven's father, brother in law, and two nephews sat on the bench facing it. The young boys swung their legs back and forth. The older of the two leaped up when he saw Onyx and ran to embrace him. The younger boy was quick to follow. Onyx had to admit that he had no experience with children but something about the gesture felt warm and healing. He returned the embrace. They both began yapping about what was going on until their father hushed them. They returned to their seats.

"My grandmother was right. Childbirth is women's work," Onyx said as he settled down on a second bench.

"She and your aunt are both inside. They have been for several hours," Luna said as she gestured towards the door. "As soon as it started, Commander Abendroth took up guard and hasn't moved an inch."

Even when Onyx looked over to Hayden, the stoic Saber did not move or change his expression. It was strange to see him with his cowl pulled forward and his face mask in place. Only his sharp silver eyes were visible. The Saber Commander had left his head uncovered until now. There was also no risk of danger deep inside of the Earthborn capital. As soon as he had that thought, Onyx dismissed it. He shook his head. They were at war. Their Shadowlord had been taken and was surely dead. Danger could be waiting just around the corner. Hayden was showing that he was on the watch for the soon to arrive child.

"How long was I out?" Onyx asked Luna in a whisper.

"About twelve hours. Labor started eight hours ago. Everyone thought to alert you then but your grandmother and aunt requested that you be allowed to rest. They sent me as soon as they felt that the child would be born," Luna replied. She worked to rebraid her hair after it had fallen loose.

Onyx was sure he could have slept through the night and into the next day. But the birth of Ryder and Haven's child was far too important to miss. He felt obligated as Ryder's only family to be present. But as he thought earlier when the two boys hugged him, he had no experience with children or babies. He could not think of a specific memory of ever interacting with children his own age or younger. He thought that he would be scared but he found himself bouncing with excitement. He tapped his feet on the floor and brushed his hands over his knees repeatedly.

Everyone shared his feelings as none of them could sit completely still. Haven's father appeared the most nervous as he chewed on a thumbnail. He muttered something under his breath that Onyx thought was my youngest girl and grandfather again. He caught Ivan smiling as he wrung his hands. The two boys picked at each other in boredom while their father did his best to keep them quiet. It quickly came to Onyx's attention that Donovan was not present or Kader Erebus who he had joyfully reunited with.

"He is with the Shadowborn camp and I am too old to run these halls," Kader said in a huff when he saw Onyx ask Luna and looking around. "Even a council meeting cannot be so easily interrupted. Mind if I sit down and rest my weary feet?"

Luna slid over and Kader sat down beside her. "It seems that the Lords have been locked away every hour of the day since Onyx and the Shadowborn arrived. What is there still to talk about?"

"Many things. Organizing seven nations with different approaches to war and battles is a logistics nightmare. This is not including the questions regarding Kaiser's abilities and his resources. I had to beg Lord Aves for leave so that I could be present here," Kader explained with an exacerbated sigh.

"Then you have arrived just in time, Master Erebus," Willow said as the bedroom door opened. The sound of a baby crying could be heard in the background. "The Lady Haven would like to see my grandson first as representative of the child's father."

Onyx gulped hard as he stood up. He smoothed down the hem of his tunic and stepped forward. His grandmother smiled and stepped to the side to allow him in. He had fought a Demon and yet, he was more unsettled about seeing a newborn baby. Once inside the room, he saw his aunt, Haven's mother, and two sisters surrounding the bed. Haven, pale and weary, was reclined in the bed with a gray bundle of cloth in her arms. She looked up at him and smiled.

"I want you to bring an announcement to the Lords of the Northern Alliance. A son was born this day and his name is Torin Ombre Coba-Silvanus," Haven said before she pulled back the cloth.

A red wrinkled face was revealed. Onyx could not tell if the baby resembled Ryder or Haven more. Its eyes were closed and he could only see the smallest tuft of dark hair over its brow.

"He's so tiny," Onyx commented.

"But this boy is long. He will be as tall as his father someday," Haven's mother grinned. She brushed back a lock of her daughter's hair. "He is a beautiful boy."

Near instant love swelled up in Onyx's chest as he gazed upon the baby. Here was an example that there was still good in the world. For the first time since Ryder was taken, Onyx felt a sense of joy and happiness. He couldn't wait to spread the news. But he felt rooted to the spot by Haven's bed. It now entered his mind that this child was frail and defenseless. Kaiser could kill the baby just because it had Silvanus blood.

"Torin, you will never want for love for there are already so many that adore you," Onyx declared. He nodded once. "I will gladly bring such joyful tidings to the Lords. Even if I must bust down the council room doors, they will know that the Spirits are with us and have given us a great gift of life."

Onyx moved through the castle like a bolt of lightning, leaving all who had gathered by the bedroom door in the dust. It was almost as if he was flying for no obstacle or bystander could slow him down. He felt powerful and fearless, ready to take on any challenge. Yet, there was a sense of emptiness that he could not shake. The feeling brought him back to the harsh reality that Ryder was not in Cascade. He slowed his pace before stopping completely outside of the throne room. To his right were tan wood doors with intricate carvings of animals and flora. To his left was a floor to ceiling window. There were no shutters or curtains. Beams of sparkling moonlight streamed through the glass and illuminated him and the doors.

*****

"Onyx, what are you doing here?" Palani asked under his breath. He gripped the armrests of his chair.

Onyx ignored his uncle's less than welcoming words and stepped towards the center of the room. He looked about the circle of Lords. His uncle sat upon the throne with Oren on his right side. The two Gryphons, Paladon and Stellaris, glanced at him with narrowed eyes. Aves remained as quiet as ever but this time, Evander was sitting beside him. There was an empty seat on his uncle's left side and Onyx wondered if that was where Kader sat. Argos looked bored and did not lift his eyes in Onyx's direction. For a moment, Onyx forgot why he was there.

"Though matters of war are of great importance, I bring word of a blessing from the Spirits. A son was born this day. He will be named Torin Ombre Coba-Silvanus, son of Peredur and Haven. The blood of Shadow Night shall live on!"

The room erupted into a round of applause and cheers. Onyx could not help but smile as he turned about to see each of the Lords celebrating. Paladon and Stellaris cried out in their native tongue as if they were shouting to the skies above. Oren embraced his son tightly. Argos joined in, wrapping his arms around both of them. Onyx turned and nodded towards Aves who was the most reserved.

"That is certainly news worth interrupting council for. The Spirits have not forgotten us in our trials and loss and given us one of many precious things to fight for even harder," Evander declared. He got up from his seat to join Onyx in the center of the room.

"That is news worth celebrating to those who care about such things," a forbidding voice said darkly. Everyone turned towards the doors. Standing a few feet from them was Kaiser or what appeared to be him. The body was see through and everything from the knees down was surrounded by a gray haze.

Stellaris leapt up with wings flared and a furious expression in his eyes. He charged forward, sliding to an ear splitting stop. Everyone cringed as his talons dragged across the floor.

"You blood traitor and foul Demon!" Stellaris snarled. He spat out a further series of words in the Gryphon tongue.

"Well that is not very nice and so not true. I am not a Demon nor a wingless monster of utter darkness. But go ahead and slash me to pieces with your claws. They will simply pass through me as if I was never here." The astral Kaiser pressed his torso with both hands then looked up and shrugged.

Everyone got up from their seats and surrounded Onyx, Evander, and Stellaris. Even the peaceful Paladon had a look of anger in his eyes as he stood by his Gryphon kin.

"You have much to answer for," Aves stated as he stayed Evander from pulling out a long knife from his belt.

"Like what?" Kaiser innocently asked.

Such a question when the evidence was clear was beyond infuriating. Stellaris roared and surged forward. It took both Argos and Paladon to hold him back. He struggled to break free.

"Enough of these games, Kaiser. You know what you have done even if you do not see it as wrong," Aves continued. He stopped when Kaiser raised a hand to silence him.

"I did not come here in this form to argue or negotiate a surrender. I will not accept surrender anyway. I will only accept your total destruction," Kaiser said flatly.

They watched as Kaiser swept his left hand towards the right and then to the right. The image changed into two people. Ryder stood in profile on the left while Kaiser, also in profile, stood on the right. Kaiser flashed a knife before driving it into Ryder's chest. Once the knife made contact, a spray of red sparks shot out. Ryder slowly fell backwards and disappeared out of sight. The image returned to Kaiser shrugging his shoulders.

Onyx gritted his teeth and clenched his fists. "I refuse to believe..."

"What? That your beloved cousin and Shadowlord is dead by my own hand? Did you honestly think I would not eliminate a threat to my power even if he shared my blood? Peredur is dead and you will never see him in anything but your dreams and memories," Kaiser interrupted. He began to laugh out loud.

"SHUT UP!" Onyx shouted. Kaiser closed his mouth and frowned. "I will have no more of your vicious lies or disgusting love of destroying all that we hold dear! You have taken everything from me. But no more! The Spirits may have abandoned you but they will not abandon us. We fight for truth and we will win."

"Well if you are fighting for truth, you are doing a really bad job. One nation has already fallen under the watch of the Immortal Truth and two Shadowlords dead by my hand." He held up three fingers. "That is how many are left of Shadow Night's kin. Yes, I know of the child who is now taking his first breaths. I listened politely to your announcement before I decided to speak up. Of course, you must be asking. Who is the third? Well that is my little secret for now. However that is who is left to protect the Silvanus bloodline: a boy Prince, a bastard baby, and an unknown vagabond weaker than the two combined."

The astral Kaiser began to dissipate, laughter ringing out. Argos and Paladon let go of Stellaris and the massive Gryphon charged forward. He slashed at the image just as it disappeared. He whipped his head around before turning to look at the others.

"I will fight to save the line of the Shadowlord no matter what that wingless monster says. We are all sons and daughters of the Immortal Truth and Guardians of Terra. Together, we will defeat the plague of Kaiser's evil," Stellaris growled.

"For truth and for Torin," Onyx replied.

*****

JOURNEY NORTH

"Wow. It has been quite some time since I looked upon Garhune," Bane stated.

Gyr and Charon climbed up the small hill and stood to either side of Bane. Both did not share his jovial mood. Charon pulled his travel pack off of his back and dropped it by his feet. He pressed his hands onto the small of his back and pressed down hard. He twisted from left to right before raising his arms into the air and stretching.

"I would be just fine not stopping there," Charon commented.

"I agree," chirped Gyr before he rolled his body vigorously and flapped his wings. He folded them after another good stretch.

Bane chuckled softly. "You are going to let a few foolish men and women keep you at bay just because they hurt your feelings? A couple of unkind words do not compare to a battle against Dark Spirits."

"Charon was born in Garhune and yet the people treat him like an outsider," Gyr quickly stated when Charon was too sheepish to speak up. "As much as I wish, I must keep my dignity and not take revenge for the slight against my friend."

"Why not?" Bane asked. "Charon has proved himself in my eyes and both Meras and Sawn have honored him with gifts."

Charon gulped as he thought about his new travel clothes and chainmail shirt that suddenly felt heavy on his body. He nudged the travel pack at his feet, hearing the soft clink of the steel plate and leather armor. Strapped to the outside was a sleek long bow and quiver with twenty black fletched arrows tucked inside. He absentmindedly fingered the pommel of his new broadsword. He had been grateful for the gifts but now felt unworthy to keep them. He shuddered when Bane put a comforting hand on his left shoulder.

"Don't let them make you feel ashamed of who you are. They should be proud that you are from their city. I think that they need to be reminded of how special you are," Bane said before pulling his hand away. He turned towards Gyr. "I say for dignity's sake, a few harsh words are in order."

"I'd rather not now that I am a bit wiser to the ways of Mortals. They are odd," the Gryphon quickly stated.

"They can be just like any Immortal or Gryphon. I too once thought as you did when I met my first Mortal. I quickly learned that I am just as odd to them," Bane explained.

"Were there Mortals in the Eastlands?" Gyr asked curiously.

Bane shook his head. "Not to my knowledge and if there were, I am sure that they are gone now. This may surprise you but I do not know if the Eastlands was heavily populated or sparsely settled. My home was in a small settlement outside of Norsov, a village deep in the forest. There was a town just over the border between the Southlands and Eastlands but I forget the name. I met my first Mortal there though I did not know it at the time."

"It is odd how similar in appearance Mortals and Spiritborn are when the origins are so different," Gyr commented. He looked towards Garhune and let out a deep sigh.

When Charon started to question the comment, Bane pointed to his eyes and mouthed a response. He had to wonder if his half breed status made the details muddled. He looked at his hands and then at the sword attached to his belt. He was stronger, faster, and more durable but he had met Mortal soldiers of impressive skill to rival his own. Most of those soldiers were based in Arken, the biggest center of trade in the Southlands. Of course, the best of the best needed to guard an area where so much money and goods were exchanged. Sometimes he questioned why he did not settle in Arken.

"The Mortal people are lucky that they do not have to bear the burden of our long lives. To be Immortal is to be a scion of time until the weight of centuries becomes too much. In a way, it is a loss of innocence and real appreciation of life." Bane shook his head. He closed his eyes and took in a deep breath of air. He let it out slowly. "I have lived a very long thousand years with many more ahead of me."

It already made Charon feel strange that he was one

hundred years old with the appearance of a man in his late twenties. That was one of the many reasons his Garhune neighbors wanted nothing to do with him. When he had entered his forties with no signs of aging, people started to take real notice of him and believed his mother's few words regarding the identity of his father.

"Can't we just pass Garhune and head straight to Crossroads?" Charon pleaded.

"Not without teaching them a lesson first about respect and reminding them just who it is that lets them live their lives in peace," Bane deviously grinned.

The town was bustling with activity. A crowd of people had assembled in the market square with several families still streaming in. A large stage had been constructed from wooden crates nailed together. The white haired mayor stood in the center and was addressing the crowd. It was odd to Charon that no one seemed to take notice of Gyr and he could tell that the Gryphon was miffed. A number of children did side eye the Gryphon but their parents pulled them closer to their sides. No one wanted to interrupt the proceeding. Charon thought to ask Bane but he held up a finger to his mouth, indicating silence. Ever since the trio had entered the city, Bane had kept his fur lined hood up to shield his face. They kept to the back of the crowd at Bane's order.

"Who here knows someone in Meras or Sawn? Yes, I see quite a few hands. I know you trade with that jeweler," the mayor said pointed to a tall thin man with red hair. "And I remember your sister and her husband," he said to another person in the front of the crowd. The mayor went on, pointing at four more people before throwing his arms up in the air.

"All of those people he mentioned are still alive due to our intervention," Bane said under his breath.

The mayor cleared his throat. "I do not know what manner of monster attacked our sister cities but I do know that I do not want them here. I want nothing of Demons or Immortal. They have brought nothing but pain and destruction to our town. Here we live in the shadow of the Wall of Crossroads, a cliff face that rises up so high that it touches the clouds. Though they did not raise the cliff themselves, the Immortals promised our ancestors that the Wall of Crossroads would protect them and they too would keep evil at bay. I would have to say that they broke that promise. Meras is in ruins and Sawn is reeling from attack. That is just what happened in the recent months."

Gyr cringed as the man listed numerous attacks and murders that spanned hundreds of years. He glanced at Charon when the mayor talked about his mother's death. Charon appeared to diminish when the mayor spotted him at the back of the crowd and pointed at him.

"Look there and see two souls of Immortal blood. See how they intrude on our proceedings? Go back to where you belong! We want no Immortals bringing harm to our people anymore. Leave the Southlands and never come back!" the mayor declared harshly. "Or would you like to come up and answer for your crimes? Please the stage is open to anyone who wishes to speak."

Gyr furrowed his brow and prepared to go towards the stage. Bane stayed him with a small hand gesture. The Gryphon sat back down and frowned.

"The mayor is sorely misinformed regarding the actions and activities of what I spoke to his ancestors about. I suppose that I deserve the blame," Bane stated quietly before he left Gyr and Charon.

The crowd parted around him, allowing Bane to walk to the stage unmolested. All had fallen silent as he climbed onto the makeshift stage. His hood was still shading his face.

"And who are you? Are you from Arken for your fine attire suggests that you come from there?" the mayor demanded. He leaned away from Bane.

"I came forward so that I could be heard for I have several questions. Who was it that spoke to your ancestors?" Bane asked, keeping his voice low.

"The Daylord. He told them of the Immortal Truth and how it was supposed to protect us and leave us in peace. He is the only Immortal who has protected us when our need was greatest," the mayor replied.

"I have never seen this Daylord. What does he look like?" Bane asked politely.

The mayor went about telling the various stories that described the Daylord's appearance. Occasionally people in the front of the crowd and closest to the stage interjected with their own tales or corrections. When it seemed that the stories stopped, Bane pushed back his hood. Gasps erupted from the crowd with shouts that he was the Daylord.

"A thousand years ago, I came to Garhune with the thought of establishing relations with the Mortal people of the Southlands. Before I gained my title, I had the privilege of living amongst you as a refugee from the fall of the Eastlands. Back then, I and the Immortals with me were treated with great respect as we presented the Immortal Truth. We promised protection not perfection for we are not gods to be worshipped nor are we miracle workers. Strife and trouble will still exist regardless of what we do or do not do. Are Immortals perfect? No and I will freely admit that. But you do not see me insult and treat Mortals with the same amount of vile hate that you do for the Immortals. Your ancestors would be ashamed for all they wanted was peace."

The mayor stammered for an answer to Bane's strong words. He swallowed hard. "But..."

"Immortality does not mean we can heal diseases and stall death for the Mortals. That is something beyond our power. What I promised your ancestors is that through the Immortal Truth, we would fight to keep our wars from spilling over into the Southlands. Those who follow the Truth abide by its laws but there are those that curse it and act as they please. I go north to fight such an individual. If he is not stopped, consider your homes lost and your lives forfeit."

Several people in the crowd clapped with delight at Bane's verbal lashing of the mayor.

"Hate will not stop evil from happening and I think that if that is your way, perhaps someone else should stand in your place and lead Garhune properly." Bane left the stage to raucous cheers and rejoined Charon and Gyr. He leaned in to whisper to them. "I was not about to tell him that his ancestors refused to join the others with establishing relations and how others called them cowards. I think that I have embarrassed him enough."

Charon could not have been more thrilled at the turn of events. He listened as the people called for the mayor's dismissal and cried out for a new election. He looked over at Gyr who was holding his head up high. He had to wonder if the evil Shadowborn that the Gryphon had told him about would be so easily swayed.

WALL OF CROSSROADS

It was not long after Bane, Gyr, and Charon left Garhune before they were looking upon the Wall of Crossroads. Charon had travelled in sight of the wall before. This time, he felt daunted by it. What truly lay on the other side? Was the war that Gyr had warned him about going to be even worse? Question after question rattled through his head and he turned away.

"What is it?" Gyr asked. He slowly stepped over and put his right wing around Charon. He leaned in to listen.

Charon bit his fist to keep himself from crying and shedding tears. He let out a deep breath as he composed himself. "Somehow this feels wrong. Like I should not climb that wall."

"Well of course we are not going to climb it. That would be silly," Bane said. He stepped back a few steps looking into the sky towards the top.

"I am not going to fly you up there. The two of you on my back would be too heavy," Gyr quickly pointed out. He withdrew his wing and folded it on his back. He turned around and sat on his haunches. "You may be my King but I cannot physically do it."

"I appreciate your honesty. However, I said that we will not climb the wall. I did not ask you to fly either one of us up to the top. I will ask if you can on my behalf fly to Crossroads and round up some of your kin," Bane suggested.

Gyr bounced up to his feet and flared his wings. "It will take a few hours to get to Crossroads. The air currents that undulate there can be quite difficult to navigate even for an experienced flyer."

"You are of the line of Mistress Gia, one of the best flyers of her day. I trust that you can handle it. I will keep Charon company until our transport arrives," Bane said with a nod of the head.

Gyr took three bounding leaps forward, flapping his wings the entire time. On the third leap, he rocketed into the air. He beat his wings with deeper motions to gain altitude. He swayed back and forth before disappearing into the mist and clouds.

Bane pulled off his travel pack and dropped it by his feet. He then sat down and lay back on the grass. His cloak acted as a comfortable blanket as he reclined in the sun. "You might as well sit down. It is three hours to Crossroads by flight through the wind shears. Right before autumn is when they are at their worst."

"Has it really been a year since I last wandered here? Those peaks towards the east is where I first met Gyr," Charon pointed before he sat down a few feet away.

"Almost," Bane replied. He closed his eyes and rested his hands behind his head.

Charon picked at the grass by his boots. "What brought you here all those months ago? Gyr said you had not been seen for a thousand years. Why did you appear then?"

He was not sure that was what Charon wanted to say but Bane caught the meaning. It was a question that he had mentally refused to dwell upon for it would open a floodgate of pain and guilt. He had to dig deep into his mind for the memory of that day. When he felt the twinge of guilt, he quickly steeled himself against its overwhelming nature. In truth, he did not know why he had gone to the eastern peaks of the Sol Mountains. Especially during heavy snow. It was unusual that such snow fell when it was not even winter. It was if that the Spirits of the dead Gryphons fought to bring an unnatural chill to the area in retaliation with a few wind blowing wing beats. Or was it the Spirit World's attempt to draw him back to where he belonged?

"Why did you leave the Northlands?" Charon cautiously asked when Bane had not said a word.

Bane let out a deep breath. "You are too young to understand the truth behind my decision."

His voice was forbidding and Charon found himself shivering out of fear. He had not forgotten that Bane was much older than him and yet, he felt like he had. He continued to pick at the grass until he had pulled away the first layer of soil. He leaned back and brushed his fingers across his knees.

"Then help me to understand what I am about to get myself into," Charon challenged in a quiet voice.

No answer was forthcoming and it disappointed him. Charon had thought and believed that Bane had connected with him during their trials. Bane had even expressed that he was more comfortable with him than with Gyr. How would Bane act when Gyr brought more Gryphons to fly them over the wall? He found himself getting excited about meeting more of Gyr's kinsmen. Or was the proper term kinsbirds? He made a mental note to ask Gyr when he came back.

Bane stirred as he sat up and unlatched the gold chain that held his cloak. It slid from his shoulders and fell to the ground. He looked over at Charon.

"The Northlands is a vastly different place to here. Time can seem to be at a standstill. There is no such thing as disease of the body though the mind can be affected. Fecundity is low thus children are view as blessings from the Spirits. Age is a number, not a physical ailment though the oldest Gryphons complain of creaky joints. Rarely will you find individuals over one thousand. Rarer still are those two thousand years old and more. So Immortality does not mean we live forever. Just until something comes along and kills us. Eternity is forever. That is what Spirits are. Eternal but without physical bodies."

Finally! Bane was talking even if he was not answering direct questions about himself. A plan started to form in Charon's head and he knew immediately that it would take clever word play.

"So I won't die unless someone else takes my life?" Charon asked.

"Pretty much. However living for centuries can burden the mind. There is nothing I can say that will prepare you. It will have to be something you deal with on your own," Bane mused. He then opened his eyes and turned to look at Charon.

Charon sheepishly shrugged. "Everyone says how courageous you are. Fearless in battle and a terror to the dark. I wish that I could be the same."

Bane sat up in a swift movement. "If the stories have made you think that I love war, I do not. I abhor it. To me, war means death and loss."

He was not sure how to respond to that statement as he had never fought in a war before. And now, he was heading to a land embroiled by it. Gyr had not held back in his description of the atrocities that Kaiser Adonis had committed. Countless people murdered. Many more intimidated into silence out of fear for their lives. He shook his head in an attempt to break his thoughts. He closed his eyes and took in a deep breath before letting it out slowly. He rested his clenched hands on his knees.

"It is wrong of me to forget how you lost your brother before you could get to know him and your father whose mind was too twisted to be saved. I may hate war but I understand it." Bane lowered his head for a moment as if he was questioning himself about something.

"Who did you lose?" Charon quietly asked.

"A wife and two young children. My son was eight and my daughter was four when they were killed after my beloved Sora was killed. The loss of three people I loved and held dear drove me to near insanity. All I wanted was revenge. I know that you want revenge too. I warn you not to let it consume you as it did me. The choices I have made while in that state." Bane looked down briefly. "I can barely begin to verbalize the reasons why I left the Northlands without being overwhelmed with feelings of uncertainty and guilt."

Charon was starting to wonder if going to the Northlands was going to open a floodgate of more than celebration. It made him even more nervous. He worried about his own identity as a half breed bastard of the once thought dead Aday Silvanus. What would the people of the Northlands say about him?

"The Wall of Crossroads does little to protect us from the most dangerous enemies: ourselves. What we say, do, think, and feel in life will follow us wherever we go. No wall or great expanse of time and space can break that. When we get to the Northlands, you will have some of your questions answered regarding my past. But many more will rise up as you discover your Immortal heritage. Always look towards the light of truth and it will guide you."

*****

Gyr rocketed into the first wind shear at a sharp angle. It pushed against his shoulders and forced him back. He snarled as he pumped his wings to maintain his balance. The wind tore at him again and he twisted towards the left to avoid the brunt of it. He brought his wings up over his head before forcing them down. The motion gave him enough lift to try breaking through the first shear. This time, he zigzagged back and forth, following the troughs whenever they appeared. As soon as he felt the trough move towards an updraft, he folded in his wings until they almost touched his body. He allowed the uprising wind to lift him higher. He followed this pattern for over an hour to moderate success.

He managed to break through the wind shear only to be hit by the second layer. He shouted out a Gryphon cheer and began his fight anew. This time, it required rolling back and forth to the left and right at high speeds to avoid the wing tearing downdrafts. Gyr kept telling himself over and over that failure was not an option. He was going to break free and reach Crossroads.

"Winds of Terra! You cannot stop me! You cannot break me!" Gyr cried out.

The success of this flight meant everything to him. It meant that he had done what no one had been able to do in a thousand years. He had flown into the Southlands, battled against Dark Spirits, and was now bringing word that the Daylord was coming home. He had survived when countless others of his kin had not. He whispered a quick prayer to those Gryphons who had lost their lives on their mission beyond the wall. His success meant that they would not be forgotten. He would make sure to have a memorial place by the top of the cliffs that would look out over the Southlands. No, his fallen kin must not be forgotten.

The third layer of powerful wind was the strongest yet. It twisted and turned so fast that Gyr barely had time to react. He flew on pure instinct without a thought to distract him. He let his wings guide him and his tail direct him. He trusted in his entire body and senses. It was foolish to close his eyes as the wind could drive him into the rock face. But he had to make sure that fear of what he saw was not going to defeat him. He had trained to know the intricacies of air and how it flowed from subtle breezes to raging storms. This would be no different.

An old Gryphon song came to mind as he battled the winds. It was one he had learned in during his power flight lessons.

> *I can fly through anything*
> *I can fly through everything*
> *My wings are strong*
> *My will is calm*
> *The wind will carry me on*
> *On through the storm*
> *On through the night*
> *I will not lose this fight*
> *I am the master of flight*

THE DAYLORD IS COMING HOME!

"THE DAYLORD IS COMING! HE IS COMING HOME!" Gyr shouted as soon as he cleared the edge of the cliff. He overshot the landing and flapped his wings with uncontrolled excitement. He banked towards the left, heading straight towards the white and gold towered citadel.

Gyr continued to shout in both the common tongue and his native tongue with wild abandon. He wanted everyone to hear the good news. He wanted to let them know that he was alive. Most of all, he wanted hidden enemies to know that the Daylord was coming back. He was happy beyond words as he flew over the rooftops. Each time he shouted that Bane was coming, cheers erupted from the people below. He glanced down to see them jumping up and down and waving at him. A shiver ran down his spine. He was going to be remembered forever as the Gryphon herald of the King. It was not something he had considered until just this moment. For a second, he allowed his pride to swell until he felt like he would burst. To release the sensation, he cried out again with a joyous whistle.

*****

Proto Avis and Vorin were both laying down on the flat top of the observation tower. The Dragon had brought the old Gryphon

520

up there in hopes of lifting his Spirits. The news that Ryder had been killed by Kaiser overwhelmed the joy of his son's birth. As a result, Proto's health declined and he no longer seemed to enjoy life as he once did.

"What is that commotion?" Proto Avis halfheartedly asked. He had had little sleep and even less energy.

Vorin arched his neck towards the east and narrowed his eyes. He strained to hear the growing number of voices and what they were saying. His eyes then snapped open and his tail twitched back and forth.

"It is Gyr! Thank the Spirits! Gyr has returned to us!" Vorin cried out with relief. He stamped his feet.

Proto Avis's head shot up as he rose from his reclined position. His bones creaked with every movement. He shook his body and rolled his shoulders. He stumbled slightly but Vorin was quick to catch him from falling by using the tip of his wing to keep him level. Proto thanked him as he sat down by the Dragon's right side. Vorin stretched out his right wing in a gesture of protection.

"Are you certain?" Proto asked, not wanting to get his hopes up. He felt that he did not have the energy to handle anymore disappointment or tragedy.

"I am a Dragon and my sight is as good as the day I entered this world," Vorin momentarily grumbled. "That is a child of Mistress Gia's line no doubt about it."

"I wish my senses were as strong as yours. It seems that the trials of my long years have caught up to me," Proto said as his head dropped.

"He is shouting that the Daylord is coming home!" Vorin roared.

Proto perked up and felt as if all of his burdening thoughts were washed away in an instant. He and Vorin watched as Gyr came closer. It was clear that the young Gryphon was flying at top speed, continuing to shout the news of Bane's return. His flight was excitable and erratic as he swept up high into the air in twisting loops and flips. He soared high above their heads before coming down in a tight spiral. Vorin helped Proto back up as Gyr skidded in for a landing.

"The Daylord is coming! He is coming home!" Gyr said in between breaths. "He waits at the bottom of the Wall of Crossroads for me to bring an escort for him and his companion."

"No need to worry. I will fly him home myself!" Vorin shouted with glee. "Make sure Lord Proto Avis is properly tended to while I am gone. We have a very important guest to welcome."

Vorin gingerly stepped around and away from the Gryphons. Once he was certain that Gyr was by Proto's side, he unfolded his wings and flapped twice to get some lift. The maneuver was just enough to get him into the air. He dropped over the edge of the tower, flapping deeply to regain altitude. He tipped his left wing down to back towards the right, narrowly avoiding a flag pole. The flag whipped violently in his wake. Once he flew past the edge of the cliff, he tucked in his wings and stooped into a fast dive. The Dragon disappeared from sight.

"Is what you say true? Is Bane really..." Proto was too excited to finish his question.

Gyr proudly bowed his head. His chest was still heaving so it took him a while to find the words to speak. "It is true, Lord Proto Avis. I promised that I would not return until I had our King with me. I have a great deal to tell you. Especially about the Daylord's companion."

*****

The wind shears were no problem for a creature as large and powerful as Vorin. He had flown them so many times that he knew the weak spots by memory. He could navigate the shears with his eyes closed. Vorin felt his weight shifting as the winds attempted to slam him against the rock face of the wall. He tightened his wings and legs to his body, causing him to fall faster and out of the shears. As soon as he was free, he whipped his wings back out to slow his descent and control his direction. His head darted back and forth as he searched for sight of Bane. Two small dots appeared on the edge of his sight and he folded his wings in again.

*****

"Is that a Dragon?" Charon fearfully asked as he hid behind Bane. He gripped the hilt of his sword.

"It is indeed. Vorin is a dear friend of mine. It makes me happy to see him again after all these years. You will never find a more loyal soul than a Dragon. Keep in mind, that you will also never find a more fearsome creature if you are their enemy," Bane said with a smile.

"What if he thinks that I am an enemy? He is not going to roast me is he?" Charon blurted out. He was feeling more frantic. Dragons had always been exciting characters in fireside tales. To meet one in the flesh was frightening.

Bane chuckled softly as he set his hands on his hips. He nudged his travel pack with his foot. His folded cloak slid off on to the grass.

"I doubt he will considering you are so scared that you are ready to wet yourself. That he does not think of an enemy. Prey maybe but not an enemy," Bane stated as he looked up into the sky.

That was the last thing that Charon wanted to hear. He prepared himself to run but Bane reached back and stayed him. Instead, Charon dropped his travel pack and cowered behind Bane.

Vorin flared out his wings and beat them to slow his descent until his back feet touched the ground. He landed on his front feet with a heavy thud. "Do my eyes deceive me or is one of my oldest and dearest friends standing before me?"

"My self-proclaimed herald spoke true. I am no illusion. I am truly Bane Arlis in the flesh," Bane replied.

The Dragon brought his head forward and Bane embraced his muzzle. "Words cannot express the joy of seeing you again after all these years. So many memories missed without you close by to share them."

"I have much to answer for but for now, I am glad to see you," Bane said softly. Vorin pulled away, the expression in his eyes warm and happy. "You have not aged. Dragons are truly the greatest of all Immortals."

Vorin studied him and was about to voice a response when he spotted Charon cowering behind Bane. His eyes widened with a hint of recognition. "You look like Aday Silvanus. Are you he?"

Charon was too frightened to answer. He gulped and swallowed hard. Bane reached back and pulled him forward. Charon tried to resist but Bane's grip was surprising strong and unyielding. He knew that his face was as pale as snow and that his teeth were chattering. He at least managed to shake his head no. He thought that he might faint when the Dragon stuck his muzzle within inches of his face. Hot breath blasted on his face as Vorin sniffed him.

"No, you are not him. But you smell like him. You smell young as well. Who are you?" Vorin asked.

Seeing Charon's distress, Bane chose to answer for him. "This is Charon, son of Aday and a Mortal woman. He provided Gyr with a great deal of assistance in navigating the Southlands. He has also proven himself brave against incredible odds. He accompanies me now out of a desire to avenge those lost and to discover his heritage. As such, this is his first time meeting a Dragon."

"If my friend thinks you worthy, then I think you worthy. Do not be afraid. My flame is reserved for only those I consider enemies," Vorin said, doing his best to sound encouraging.

"Hello," Charon squeaked. As scared as he was of Vorin, he was more frightened by flying upon his back.

"Do not worry. Courage will return to you soon enough," Bane chuckled. "You fought against Dark Spirits. Flight on Dragon back will be a pleasant walk compared to that."

Still, Charon was not so sure. He rubbed his hand over the pommel of his sword so hard that he was irritating his palm. He glanced down at his hand when he started to feel pain and saw a large raw spot. It stung when he tried to close his hand. He startled when he saw that Vorin was focused solely on him.

"All will be well for the Daylord is coming home. I am sure that you will see your home again someday and you will show your mother's kin that you are worthy of great praise. Like my friend, I too will help you to navigate the Northlands. Your future is bright as is all of ours." Vorin turned his gaze over to Bane. "Kaiser will now learn the meaning of fear. Come. I will fly you both and bring you to Crossroads."

*****

LET THE SPIRITS TALK

"So, you think that by bringing your hero home that victory is close at hand. I drove him away once. I can do it again. This time, I will make sure that he does not return. I will make him experience a pain so deep and terrible that it will tear him apart from the inside out. I will make him feel betrayal and fear a thousand times stronger than what I felt when my own father murdered me. I have been far too conservative in my efforts. Far too dependent on others to fight my war. Well Terra, you got what you wished for. I will unleash everything that I have and tear your lands apart. I will kill everyone and everything in my path! I will rip open the veil and show you a power too terrible to imagine! I will destroy you!"

Kaiser snarled as he stared hard at the flying image of Vorin with Bane and Charon on his back. The Living Map undulated around him, sparking as a result of his rising fury. He then roared as he swept his hands from front to back, tearing the Map. The broken energy swelled above him before dropping down in a twisting spiral. Kaiser glowed with a reddish orange light as he absorbed the energy into his body.

"Let them have their Spirit powers back. Let the Shadow Mirror fall. With each of their gains, my power will increase a thousand fold! Did you not once think that it took power to maintain the Shadow Mirror I raised? Once it is gone, that power returns to me. I will become stronger than you ever thought possible. I do not need an army of disillusioned followers that I put the fear of death into. I do not need Spirit Wake anymore. You hear that, Omu? You can come to strike me down!"

As if summoned, the great wolf Spirit appeared with hackles raised and lips curled back over his teeth. Omu was now bigger than a draft horse, his eyes glowing white. A deep throated roar rumbled in his chest, waiting to be unleashed.

"Go ahead. Kill me. Strike me down from where I stand," Kaiser invited as he held his arms wide open. He reached in with his left hand and tapped his chest. "I am unarmed."

"Kinslayer. Destroyer. Betrayer. Traitor. Those can only begin to describe you as you truly are. There is no curse dark enough that I can use against you," Omu snarled.

"What's that? I did not hear you," Kaiser said as he cupped his left ear. He started to laugh when Omu did not immediately respond. "The entire world wants me dead and I give you an opportunity to grant them their wish. Yet you, a great Spirit and guide to the dead hesitates. Why?"

Omu still did not rise to the challenge and it made Kaiser laugh even louder. It was if he was frightened deep down and worried about something. Kaiser took full advantage of it. He pointed accusingly at the wolf Spirit. Before Kaiser could speak, Omu unleashed his powerful roar. The roar shook the throne room, breaking stone from the ceiling and cracking the floor. Every window shattered, sending out a spray of broken glass. One piece slashed open a deep gash on the right side of Kaiser's face.

"I do not fear you. I fear what you intend to do. I fear that world coming to fruition and a return to days so dark that even the All Spirit is stirring. Every great Spirit of our World is awakening their power after millennia of slumber. Relish in your victories now for it will not last much longer," Omu warned.

Kaiser scoffed as he wiped the blood from his face. He showed Omu his bloody hand. "Do you see this? This is blood, the essence of a physical life. One that none of the High Spirits will ever see again for there is no force powerful enough to do what you did to me. Even now, you question how I came into being what I am today. I still bear your claw marks across my back and the brand burnt into my skin. I am sure that you still bear the marks of our contest underneath that pelt."

"I bear the burdens of many for I guide the dead to their eternal resting place. I once guided you to the Spiral and handed you over to the guards. How you broke your chains, I may never know. Right now, I do not wish to know for I cannot undo what has already been done."

"Then why are you here if you are not going to strike me down or impede my efforts?" Kaiser curiously asked.

"Because there is someone who wished to speak to you," Omu stated.

The wolf Spirit stepped to the right and looked back. Kaiser watched as a familiar figure appeared out of the mist and took shape. It was his father Cian still wearing his glorious war armor and black cloak floating behind him. A deep slash mark marred the steel plate armor. It ran down from Cian's right shoulder down towards his left hip. A second slash cut across Cian's throat towards his breastbone. The third and final slash mark cut down from Cian's left shoulder and ended over his heart.

"One would have thought to have granted you more dignity in death and covered your wounds," Kaiser growled.

"That was your responsibility as my son upon my death but then you were also my murderer. A terrible conflict of interest," Cian replied. His voice was deep and burly in sound with a slight rasp.

Kaiser pulled down his shirt collar to expose the black scars on his throat. "Where was my dignity when you murdered me and buried me in an unmarked grave? Imagine my fear when I woke up in darkness and covered in cold earth. This is all your making!"

"I will never be able to forgive myself for what I did and the damage my actions have caused. Curse me now to the end of time. I will bear your hate and discord as I once bore your love as my son."

"I loved you as your son? When?" Kaiser demanded.

"I do not know when you turned to hate but there was a time when you looked at me with purity and love for me as your father. You were small and gladly did anything you could to please me. Perhaps in your desperate desire for acceptance, your love turned into obsession and then into the hate you bear now," Cian explained. He looked away briefly before looking deep into Kaiser's eyes. "I failed you as a father and look what it has done."

Another Spirit appeared on Cian's left, materializing by his side. Kaiser immediately knew the Spirit to be that of Shadow Night Silvanus. There was no mistaking his tall and muscled frame and the crest etched into his chest plate.

"Your father speaks to you with honesty. Well I speak to you with warning. I knew you as untrustworthy from the day that you tried to murder my grandson Aday. You have sought to destroy my line, leaving my blood in ruins," Shadow Night started to say.

Kaiser held up his bloodied hand and showed him three fingers. "Three. That is what is left of the mighty Silvanus bloodline. Three children of no worth other than bearing your name. If you were truly as great as the world believed, you would have been able to stop me."

"No, but I will."

Kaiser watched as Cian and Shadow Night took a step to the side. Ryder's Spirit materialized in mid stride as he came to stand in the space between them. His chest wound had turned black and blood stained his front.

"Good. You made it to the Spirit World. Did you know that your whore gave birth to a son? I think your spawn even has a name," Kaiser mocked with a sneer.

Cian and Shadow Night each placed a hand on Ryder's shoulders. Omu stepped in closer, snarling.

"The end is near for you, Kaiser Adonis. To what end only time will tell. But I promise you that the Immortal Truth will never be broken. Whether by victory or defeat, you will be alone. Lost forever to your own selfishness and pride. You are no god, Kaiser. You do not even have a soul," Ryder declared.

"Well that is cruel of you to say. People, both living and dead assume that I care for nothing but myself. That is simply not true." Kaiser gestured towards Cian. "I cared enough to spare you the pain and embarrassment of being my father. To you, Shadow Night, I helped you rejoin your beloved first son in the afterlife. And dear Peredur, I spared you an eternity of suffering under my command. In a way, I set you all free."

The wolf Spirit snarled loudly as he stepped in front of the three Spirits. Each of them slowly dissipated as Omu appeared to grow in size. The mist surrounded him like a thundercloud. It rumbled and shot out sparks of lightning. Kaiser pretended to be scared as he wrapped his arms around himself and shivered. He then broke out into a fit of laughter.

"ENOUGH!" Omu roared. The room shook again and more pieces of stone and guild work fell from the ceiling.

Kaiser stilled himself and squared his shoulders. "Fine. Enough is enough."

Omu barely had time to get out of the way when Kaiser fired a blast of silver and black Spirit energy. It shot towards him like a massive lightning bolt. He rolled to the right, the bolt slamming into the pillar above his head. The air sizzled around him in a way that frightened him. He felt himself being pulled back into the Spirit World against his will. He did not know if it was the All Spirit calling him back or Kaiser's profane energy attack.

Kaiser watched as Omu disappeared in a cloud of smoke. He scoffed once before turning around and walking away.

"The will of the Spirit World is broken and lost. The High Spirits are no longer the mighty beings they once were. They deserve their fate as does Terra. The Covenant of Spirits should never have been written. The Immortal Truth should have never been written. They have put this world into a prison with no regard to its future. This is no way for a world to survive. Terra needs to be free of all bonds. I will set Terra free."

As Kaiser walked out of the throne room and down towards the front gate, black energy leapt out of the surrounding shadows and wrapped around his body. The energy formed and hardened into shining black armor. He reached out both of his hands towards the side as a flowing black cloak formed and floated from his shoulders. The shadowy energy twisted around his arms and settled into each of his hands. The energy transformed into gleaming ebony swords with thin curved blades.

"I am death. I am chaos. I am eternity."

APPENDIX A

NOTE

With Flight of a Hero still to be released, I have included as much information as possible without spoiling story secrets. More information will be revealed with subsequent books.

RACE AND CULTURE

In Flight of the Broken and Flight of the Lost, there are many different types of races and cultures that all originate from the Spirit energy of Terra. Each is unique in their values. Since it may not be easy to see the basic details within the text, I am providing them here for you.

GRYPHONS

LANGUAGE: When they speak their language, it consists of the sounds birds can make. They use sound rather than words. When speaking the common tongue, transitioning from sound to spoken word is difficult. It takes a lot of practice to speak in the common tongue and usually a Gryphon speaks with an accent. It takes many years of repetition to speak without an accent. It is very difficult to learn the Gryphon language though it can be done. Gryphons can also understand the nonspeaking avian species of the world and converse with them.

NAMES: Names come from real world bird scientific names and usually from the corresponding species of bird of prey. Family group names come from the genus but are usually not shared outside of Gryphon society. Most Gryphons are called by their birth names (first name). Parents name their children when they hatch out from the egg. Some Gryphons will acquire nicknames based on deeds or environment and will go by them throughout their lives.

SOCIETY AND BEHAVIOR: Gryphons are essentially animals with a few human traits and characteristics. The lion part influences the desire to live in groups but Gryphons are perfectly happy and capable of living alone. They mate for life and if a mate dies, the survivor usually doesn't live much longer afterwards. Children are highly prized as vectors to carry on the family legacy and for their purity and joy. Both parents participate in raising children (usually 1-3 per nesting period). Children age similar to how normal birds of prey do and then when they hit maturity, they start training in various services. Usually after the Gryphon graduates their training, courtship begins between young Gryphons. Courtship can take a while and a male will present a gift to the female's parents when he has chosen her as his mate and is seeking their blessing. Gift is usually a small wreath of personal feathers and flowers which is later worn by the female during the mate ceremony.

POLITICS: Leadership is held by two Gryphons chosen to be the Lord of War or Lord of Peace. When the world is as war, the Lord of War is the primary decision maker. When the world is at peace, the Lord of Peace is the primary decision maker. They balance each other out to ensure that no rash decisions are made.

HOMELIFE: Gryphons do not wear clothing but may wear pieces of light armor, crowns, and jewelry. They fancy trinkets and nature made gifts. Steps and furniture are not very common in Gryphon homes and very few read and write non-Gryphon books.

VALUES: Gryphons are closest with Dragons and Airborn and hold high regard to those who have proven their worth. They respect other Lords and sages. They dislike those that seek to dominate others and will defend friends and allies fiercely. They can be slow to act when old or quick to act when young. Gryphons do have faults in how they interact with the Spiritborn and they seem haughty and unsociable. Since they depend on instinct, they are seen as good judges of character but they can be fooled if a person is a good enough liar.

DRAGONS

LANGUAGE: Dragons speak with guttural sounds, growls, and vocalizations. Only Vorin, the only named Dragon, is known to be capable of speaking the common tongue of the Spiritborn and understanding the Gryphon tongue.

NAMES: Names are given based on appearance, deeds and bloodlines. It is unknown if surnames are granted, when birth names are given, and if names differentiate between genders.

SOCIETY AND BEHAVIOR: Dragon society operates in a similar manner to the Gryphons in that they are beasts and not of the humanoid race. They are known to be distant from Spiritborn society. Dragons are usually very independent but fiercely loyal to those they consider friends.

POLITICS: The only known fact about Dragon leadership is that when the Immortal Truth was written, Vorin was elected to survive the Dragon race's sacrifice. Successors are chosen by the reigning Lord of the Dragons for unspecified reasons.

HOMELIFE: Unknown

VALUES: A dying Dragon's last words are imparted to a memory keeper who is either a relative or a chosen successor. Last words are considered sacred and are only shared in the greatest of need. Vorin is considered to be the last Dragon alive and has adapted to living with Gryphons and Spiritborn to where his original instincts have been buried deep within his mind.

DEMONS

LANGUAGE: Unknown but it is believed that when Demons speak, the words sound harsh and dark. The timbre of their voices cause non Demons to feel afraid.

NAMES: It is not known how true Demon names are given out but Spiritborn society names them according to the terrible deeds they were known for.

SOCIETY AND BEHAVIOR: It is the goal of all Demons to

destroy the good people of Terra as they believe themselves to be the rightful rulers. Independence and treachery run rampart and leaders last only as long as they can fight off challengers. Demons kill or harm each other in power struggles. They are opportunistic and will participate in any possessions, rituals, or invocations so long as it ultimately benefits them. There is no true organization to their society.

POLITICS: Generals would be chosen to promote and advance the Demon race's idea of conquest and rule. Fear and promises of power are the few things that can motivate a Demon to follow a group and obey orders.

HOMELIFE: Demons are most often nomadic with few permanent settlements. Nothing is known about family dynamics if any exist. All Demons have various levels of power and all can transform into a monstrous beast form. Many Demons will drink blood as a sense of control over the weak. They do get some sustenance from it and can read blood memories. They can eat and drink normal meals. Attire can be anything as they regularly take from their victims. Armor and weapons tend to be sharp and cruel in appearance.

VALUES: Demons value power and dominance. Loyalty is not highly valued and most Demons will fake loyalty until a better opportunity arises. Intellectual learning is a low priority and skills in war are prized. Demons are not particularly book smart but are very street smart.

SPIRITS/GHOSTS

LANGUAGE: Spirits will speak the language of the person they are visiting with fluency. It is unknown if they have a separate language of their own.

NAMES: Names are derived from what the Spirit was in life. There is no true naming system.

SOCIETY AND BEHAVIOR: All Spirits live in the Spirit World, a realm that borders the land of the living. It is difficult to cross over but if the call is great enough, a Spirit can walk in the land of the living. As no one ever comes back from the Spirit World, the structure of their society is unknown. It is believed that Spirits carry on their lives as if they had never died. Older Spirits act as guides to the living.

POLITICS: The All Spirit lords over the Spirit World with the High Spirits who are responsible for various aspects of life. One such example is Omu who guides the dead.

HOMELIFE: Within the Spirit World, there is a prison called the Spiral where the most evil of Spirits reside.

VALUES: Values depend on the nature of the Spirit of the deceased but most Spirits tend to be good hearted. Dark Spirits are a separate group of mindless entities, remnants of the days of Terra's beginning.

SPIRITBORN

LANGUAGE: The common tongue is spoken universally among the six tribes. It is the primary language of politics, negotiations, and the economy.

NAMES: Names can vary among the six tribes. Many are named for future hopes, environment at time of birth, virtues, in honor of ancestors, family, and friends, deeds or whatever the parents like.

HISTORY: The six tribes were at one time one unified race. As spirits were born into flesh, the environment they entered into influenced the separation of the original race. Each tribe can breed with each other and produce mixed children. It is very rare to find a pure family line that have members capable of expertly controlling their respective element. Many of the Spiritborn tend to have at least one different tribe member in their background. All of the tribes are related to each other but have differences based on their home environments. But there are always exceptions within an individual tribe.

SPIRITBORN: SHADOWBORN

NAMES: Though the Spiritborn can have a name of their choosing, most Shadowborn tend to have either their first name or middle name relate to the following words: shadow, night, black, silver, wolf, moon, and dark.

SOCIETY AND BEHAVIOR: The Shadowborn come from the high mountain forests. Many Shadowborn are serious and focused. Men are fiercely protective of what they care about and normally do not admit their inner feelings. Women are very similar if confronted but are more compassionate. Both men and women participate in a warrior based society though men predominate in the militaristic orders. Men tend to have first preference in inheritance however daughters can inherit if no other male family exists. All Shadowborn are capable of tapping into their shadow Spirit energy and using the innate power. The most common technique is Shadow Slide.

POLITICS: The Shadowborn are led by the Silvanus family as Lord of the Shadowborn and Lady of the Shadowborn. The throne is usually inherited by the eldest son though sometimes it falls to the next available son of the Silvanus bloodline. It is believed that should the Silvanus family fail, Shadowborn society would collapse. The royal family is beloved by the people as symbols of strength and stability. Military order commanders hold an equal amount of respect. The Shadow Council that advises the royal family and consists of fourteen members: the Shadowlord, Lord Regent, Lord's Chancellor, Master of Trade, Master of Roads, Master of Homeland, Treasurer, Master of Shadowborn Affairs, Commander of the Sabers, Commander of the Armed Forces, Master of Justice, Master of Education, Master of Spiritual Affairs, and the Ambassador.

HOMELIFE: Black, silver, and armor dominate everyday attire and many Shadowborn carry some form of a blade on their person at all times. Shadowborn tend to wear clothes suited for the cooler mountain weather. All Shadowborn are eligible for military services and to become a Saber, one of the personal guards to the royal family, though nobles are usually picked over lower born people. However, if a Shadowborn has proven him or herself, their efforts are rewarded with favors and positions. All Shadowborn have black hair and most have silver eyes.

VALUES: Loyalty to the throne, the Immortal Truth and family are some of the most important values to an average Shadowborn. Respect and admiration are common for warriors who have proven themselves. When considering the Silvanus bloodline, there are some Shadowborn who believe that only a legitimate born son can inherit the son. Others believe any son of the line, legitimate or not, can inherit so long as he has proven himself strong and worthy.

SPIRITBORN: LIGHTBORN

NAMES: Similar to the Shadowborn naming rules but first or middle names relate to the following words: light, bright, shine, gold, yellow, sun, and star.

SOCIETY AND BEHAVIOR: The Lightborn come from the grasslands and tend to be aloof and distant. Men and women are equals and any child regardless of gender can inherit. They hate the idea of killing and murder and prefer to disarm opponents. Most Lightborn seek intellectual pursuits and try to understand the workings of the world.

POLITICS: The current leader of the Lightborn is Evander. Teachers and scribes make up the advisory council.

HOMELIFE: Attire consists of airy robes of white or lightly colored cloth. Most Lightborn have blonde to stark white hair. Education is a top priority for children and both sexes participate.

VALUES: They value learning and despise war. They are the ones most concerned with what will happen in the future and are believed to have knowledge gifted to them by the ancient Spirits of Terra.

SPIRITBORN: FIREBORN

NAMES: Similar to the Shadowborn naming rules but first or middle names relate to the following words: fire, heat, red, desert, lion, coal, and burn.

SOCIETY AND BEHAVIOR: Fireborn come from the desert and tend to have vivacious and fiery personalities once they get to know others. They are cautious when first met. They are hotheaded but fierce warriors loyal to protecting what they care about. They love celebrations and parties. Men and women are equal and can inherit as the eldest regardless of gender.

POLITICS: The Fireborn are led by Lord Argos and his queen.

HOMELIFE: Attire is light, sun protective and appropriate for desert life. Hair is almost always a shade of red.

VALUES: Fireborn value good cheer and enjoy the company of others. Feats of strength, control, and speed dominate their society and they don't value learning as much as other Spiritborn.

SPIRITBORN: WATERBORN

NAMES: Similar to the Shadowborn naming rules but first or middle names relate to the following words: water, cool, blue, ocean, ice, river, and flowing.

SOCIETY AND BEHAVIOR: Waterborn love to be in or near any source of water, finding comfort and protection. Most are serious and quiet in their dealings with the other nations. Warriors tend to be experts when fighting in and around water. When on land, they tend to be clunky in their movements.

POLITICS: The leadership of the Waterborn belongs to Lord Marinus after the failed war with the Shadowborn.

HOMELIFE: Waterborn commonly wear robes and clothes of blue, gray, and white. They feel at home when around water and become nervous when away. Hair is usually shades of blue, blonde or white.

VALUES: They value learning and the healing arts. However, they have withdrawn from Immortal society after Akakios' failed invasion and currently have a hard time trusting others. The main target of their animosity is Akakios' bastard son.

SPIRITBORN: EARTHBORN

NAMES: Similar to the Shadowborn naming rules but first or middle names relate to the following words: earth, nature, wood, rock, green, and forest.

SOCIETY AND BEHAVIOR: Earthborn come from the forests and tend to be carefree and loving. Men and women are equal in society and can inherit as the eldest child regardless of gender. Scouts and healers predominate but there is a standing army of bowmen and swordsmen. They are very agile and fast but not particularly strong. They use their environment in everyday life. Though different classes exist, discrimination is a rare occurrence and the crowds mix together without trouble. Earthborn also work with the Gryphons in scouting pairs separated into day time patrols and night time patrols.

POLITICS: The Earthborn are led by the Kano family. The royals are well loved and their names are held sacred after death.

HOMELIFE: Festivals and balls are common social events that all Earthborn can attend. Families tend to live close together or in the same house. Children are encouraged to see the world as part of their education.

VALUES: They value family, friends, nature, and protecting the innocent. Earthborn like to believe the best in people and that all bad souls are capable of being saved.

SPIRITBORN: AIRBORN

NAMES: Similar to the Shadowborn naming rules but first or middle names relate to the following words: air, storm, thunder, white, flight, bird, or sky.

SOCIETY AND BEHAVIOR: Airborn come from the high mountains and tend to be quiet and thoughtful. They are effective assassins and spies as they can move in silence. Men and women are equal and can inherit as the eldest regardless of gender. They are the lore masters and guardians of the original Immortal Truth for Terra. They live and share the mountains with migrant Gryphons and are the only Spiritborn competent with speaking the Gryphon tongue.

POLITICS: Aves and his queen rule the Airborn with equal power. Because the Gryphons share and participate in Airborn society, they serve on the advisory council with native Airborn.

HOMELIFE: Attire can vary depending on where Airborn travel. If they are in the high mountains, they tend to wear heavy cloaks and robes. If they are travelling in the lower valleys, they are usually seen wearing tribal style outfits. Hair is always white with streaks of gray and black. Airborn like to wear feather ornaments.

VALUES: Airborn are respectful of others and the world like the Earthborn and distant like the Lightborn. They prefer to make observations and consider all actions, rarely acting without reason.

MORTALS

LANGUAGE: The Mortals speak the same language as the Spiritborn but the tone of their voices is even and unremarkable.

NAMES: Mortals have a similar naming system to the Spiritborn but they do not use the environment or the elements as inspiration. Carrying on the name of ancestors is the most common method for naming. Mortals use surnames as badges of honor to promote their interests.

SOCIETY AND BEHAVIOR: Mortals see Immortals as otherworldly super warriors and they hold the Daylord in the highest regard.

POLITICS: Each Mortal settlement has a mayor or leader that is answerable to the capital city of Arken.

HOMELIFE: Mortals live in family based settlements and their daily lives are directed by their professions. Attire depends on location and profession but is generally less flamboyant than those of the Northlands. They celebrate weddings, birth, and achievements. The dead are burned on funeral pyres.

VALUES: Manners and courtesy are highly prized. Premarital relations are frowned upon. Illegitimate children, especially those of mixed blood, are treated like unwanted outcasts.

APPENDIX B

CHARACTERS MET OR DISCUSSED BY OTHERS

GRYPHONS

- Lord Proto Avis- An ancient Eagle Gryphon known for his great intellect and wisdom. Lives in Crossroads.
- Arik Barr- A young Barn Owl Gryphon in the scout patrol. Partnered with Haro.
- Stria- Day captain of the Western Scout Patrol.
- Whisper- Night captain of the Western Scout Patrol.
- Lana- A desert Falcon Gryphon and messenger between the Fireborn and Crossroads.
- Savanna- A desert Falcon Gryphon and trainer of messengers in Crossroads.
- Grinus- A gray Falcon Gryphon general mentioned by a Gryphon messenger.
- Paladon- An Osprey Gryphon and the current Lord of Peace.
- Stellaris- A large Eagle Gryphon and current Lord of War.
- Pala- Daughter of Paladon. Twin sister of Palas.
- Palas- Son and heir of Paladon and twin brother of Pala.
- Voci- A fish Eagle Gryphon in the company of Palas and Pala.
- Nova- A gray crested Eagle Gryphon and top level commander. Sometimes Regent of the Gryphon homeland.

- Harper- Son of Nova. Friend and traveling partner of Ryder Coba.
- Razila- Harper's mate.
- Togra- A Wood Owl Gryphon in service of the Earthborn during their stay in Crossroads.
- Gyr- A white Falcon Gryphon messenger sent south to alert the Daylord.
- Gia- Ancestress of Gyr and a famous flyer.
- Bellico- Famous Gryphon Lord and world traveler.
- Amke- Favorite messenger of the Gryphon Lords.

DRAGONS

- Vorin- Dragonlord and friend of Proto Avis.
- Ogon- White Dragon and Vorin's predecessor.
- Drako- First Lord of the Dragons.

DEMONS

- Rache- Kaiser's Demon servant.
- Iztal- A low level Demon in the service of Kaiser. Possesses Aku when summoned.
- Axum- An ancient Demon general in the service of Kaiser. Currently terrorizing the Mortal people.

SPIRITS/GHOSTS

- Omu- The Wolf Spirit of shadow and guide to the Silvanus bloodline.
- Halia- The Eagle Spirit of the Airborn.
- The Gray Lady- A ghost of unknown origin that gives Rache advice.
- All Spirit- Lord of the Spirit World.
- Spirit of Creation- Responsible for shaping Terra and creating the Mortal people.
- Spirit of Destruction- Resides in the Spiral with the Dark Spirits. Made the Demon race.

SPIRITBORN: SHADOWBORN

- Shadow Night Silvanus- The ancestor of the Silvanus bloodline and first Shadowlord.
- Lord Shiloh Silvanus- Former Shadowlord and father of Aku.

- Kaiser Adonis- A pure blooded Shadowborn from Umbra with aspirations for power. Antagonist.
- Madhuri Coba- Former Commander of the Armed Forces and husband to Mali Silvanus. Father of Akakios Coba-Silvanus.
- Lord Aku Silvanus- The broken soul and current occupant of the throne of the Shadowborn. Father to Onyx Silvanus.
- Akakios Coba-Silvanus- Son of Mali and Madhuri. Father of Ryder
- Morin Win- The new Commander of the Armed Forces and henchman of Kaiser Adonis.
- Peredur Adonis Coba-Silvanus- Bastard son of Akakios and Aylin. Unnamed heir of Kaiser Adonis. Commonly known as Ryder Coba.
- Kader Erebus- Former Lord's Chancellor and rebel leader against Kaiser.
- Onyx Silvanus- Son of Aku Silvanus and Nuru Kano. Of Shadowborn-Earthborn origin.
- Sai Parahazur- Commander of the Sabers and rebel leader against Kaiser.
- Sin Silvanus- Second son of Shadow Night Silvanus and father to Aday, Mali and Shiloh.
- Zoras Rokar- Former Commander of the Sabers and current Lord's Regent of the Shadow Council. Father of Soja and rebel leader.
- Soja Rokar- Personal Saber guard to Onyx and son of Zoras. Friend to Ryder.
- Mali Silvanus- Mother to Akakios and wife of Madhuri Coba.
- Sage Silvanus- Youngest son of Shadow Night.
- Aday Silvanus- Eldest son of Sin and older brother to Shiloh. Believed to be insane.
- Den- Former student to Kader Erebus and Saber informant.
- Rothe Abendroth- Saber of middling rank and nephew to Saber Captain Hayden. Servant of Kaiser.
- Donovan Shunga- Former Saber guard to Aku and rebel leader under Zoras.
- Haven Ombre- A lowborn girl from Umbra and rebel fighter. Ryder's lover.
- Cian Adonis- Former General of the Northern Border and father of Kaiser.
- Anu Silvanus- Eldest son of Shadow Night Silvanus. His death served as inspiration for the creation of the Sabers.
- Hayden Abendroth- Saber captain and uncle to Rothe. Rebel captain under Zoras.

- Sasha- Sister of Sai Parahazur and wife of Bard.
- Baron- Husband of Sasha and rebel informant.
- Khan Adonis- Younger brother of Kaiser Adonis.
- Adonis Anu- Eldest son of Begin Anu and ancestor to the Adonis Family.
- Loran Win- Cousin of Morin. Called the Mirror Sea Pirate.
- Aylin Adonis- Mother of Ryder.
- Jarod- Former suitor of Haven Ombre.
- Commander Sorin – Former Commander of the Sabers.
- Ivan Ombre- Haven's father and master sword smith.
- Nora Ombre- Haven's mother.
- Sabrae- Eldest sister to Haven.
- Tara- Second elder sister to Haven.
- Garrett- Son of Sabrae and nephew to Haven.
- Riven- Son of Sabrae and nephew to Haven.
- Ira Shunga- Father of Donovan.
- Baya Shunga- Mother of Donovan.

SPIRITBORN: LIGHTBORN

- Evander- Lord of the Lightborn.
- Commander Solar- General of the Lightborn forces.
- Rayn- Chamberlain to Evander's household.

SPIRITBORN: FIREBORN

- Forges- First Lord of the Fireborn.
- Argos- Lord of the Fireborn. Has five daughters.
- Ilana- Eldest daughter and heir to Argos.

SPIRITBORN: WATERBORN

- Nereus- Former Lord of the Waterborn.
- Marinus- Current Lord of the Waterborn.
- Sir Myst- Music master of Lough and former sailor.
- Alton- Crowned Prince of the Waterborn.
- Admiral Marina- Female sailor under Alton's command.
- Admiral Storm- Friend of Sir Myst and sailing legend.
- Admiral Titus- Waterborn sailor.
- Admiral Warren- Waterborn sailor.

SPIRITBORN: EARTHBORN

- Nuru Kano Silvanus- Mother of Onyx and wife to Aku. Daughter of Oren and Willow and sister to Palani.
- Oren Kano- Former Lord of the Earthborn and father to Palani and Nuru.
- Palani Kano- Current Lord of the Earthborn and uncle to Onyx. Father of Flynn and two deceased children (a daughter and son).
- Haro Artemis- Scout of the Earthborn and partnered with Arik. Older brother to Luna.
- Willow- Wife of Oren Kano and mother to Palani and Nuru.
- Avani- Captain of the Western Scout Patrol.
- Luna Artemis- Lady of Flora in service to Gaia. Younger sister to Haro and friend to Onyx.
- Avana Kano- Wife of Palani and mother to Flynn.
- Flynn Kano- Son of Palani and cousin to Onyx. Crowned Prince of the Earthborn.
- Odin Kano- First Lord of the Earthborn and ancestor to the royal family.
- Gaia- Daughter of Odin and former leader of the Earthborn.
- Captain Oaken- Earthborn captain of the palace guards.
- Tessa- Friend of Luna.

SPIRITBORN: AIRBORN

- Aves- Lord of the Airborn.
- Seli- Daughter of Aves and Princess of the Airborn.
- Eru- A champion fighter that Ryder defeats in the Crossroads warrior matches.

MORTALS

- Chane- Mayor of Sawn.
- Captain Howe- Sailor from Sawn.

OTHER

- Bane Arlis- An Eastlander known as the Daylord.
- Begin Anu- An ancient war hero that came from the Farlands. Killed by Rache.
- Sando Ateru- A prophet of mysterious origins.
- Cassiel Cipher- Scribe of the Covenant of Spirits.
- Sora Arlis- Bane's deceased wife.

APPENDIX C

PLACES VISITED, DISCUSSED, OR SEEN ON MAP

REGIONS

- Terra- The name of the world where the story takes place.
- Spiritlands- The name of the landmass where most of the Immortal and Mortal races live.
- Farlands- A mysterious and distant land south of the Spiritlands.
- West Gatelands- A small group of islands to the west of the Spiritlands.
- Stormlands- A group of islands between the Spiritlands and the Farlands.
- Darklands- A desolate land where the Demons live.
- Northlands- Home of the Immortal races.
- Eastlands- A wild and untamed land where Bane Arlis comes from.
- Westlands- A forbidding land that is said to be desolate and dangerous to explorers.
- Southlands- Home of the Mortal races.
- Dragonlands- Home of the Dragons protected by a stormy sea.
- Spirit World- A mysterious realm where the Spirits of the dead roam.

- Spiral- A dark and endless path full of torment for evil Spirits.

CITIES

- Tempest- Capital city of the Airborn. Guards the cavern where the stones of the Immortal Truth are kept.
- Cross- Capital city of the Shadowborn. Home of Onyx Silvanus and many others.
- Crossroads- Capital city of the Northlands. Home of Proto Avis.
- Cascade- Capital city of the Earthborn. Home of the Kano Royals.
- Coal- Capital city of the Fireborn. Home of Argos and his family.
- Lavan- City of the Fireborn. A major trade center.
- Garhune- A Mortal city visible from the Wall of Crossroads.
- Lough- Capital City of the Waterborn. Home of the royal family.
- Dusk- City of the Shadowborn. Twin city of Agin.
- Eclipse- City of the Shadowborn. Notorious for pirate raids.
- Twilight- City of the Shadowborn. Birthplace of Soja's mother.
- Branch- City of the Earthborn.
- Moor- City of the Shadowborn.
- Horizon- City of the Shadowborn.
- Agin- City of the Earthborn. Twin city of Dusk.
- Range- City of the Earthborn.
- Mys- City of the Waterborn.
- Umbra- City of the Earthborn. Birthplace of Kaiser Adonis and Ryder Coba.
- Blaze- City of the Fireborn.
- Isle- City of the Waterborn.
- Forde- City of the Waterborn.
- Coast- City of the Waterborn.
- Fog- City of the Waterborn.
- Roar- City of the Fireborn.
- Ornith- Gryphon capital.
- Prism- Capital city of the Lightborn.
- Arken- Capital city of the Southlands.
- Meras- City of Mortals.
- Sawn- City of Mortals.
- Norsov- City in the Eastlands and hometown of Bane Arlis.

- Koa- A city of Mortals formally located by the border between the Eastlands and the Southlands. Relocated to west of Arken.
- Silver- A mysterious Shadowborn city.

LANDMARKS

- Demon's Eye- Lake in the Darklands.
- Daylord's Shadow Mirror- The magical barrier between the Darklands and the land of the Shadowborn.
- Sea of Truth- The northernmost body of water that borders the Spiritlands.
- The Mirror Sea- A western body of water notorious for pirates and barbarian raiders.
- Shadow Point- A piece of Shadowborn land that juts out into The Mirror Sea west of Eclipse.
- Howling River- A river in the Shadowborn lands.
- North Bend- Outpost to the Western Scout Patrol.
- The River Shadow- A river that serves as the border between the lands of the Shadowborn and the Earthborn.
- The Heights- A high wall of mountains surrounding the city of Cross.
- Kaiser's Shadow Mirror- The invisible barrier that has sealed the Land of the Shadowborn.
- Water's Eye- An island in the Waterborn lands.
- Red Desert- A desert in the Fireborn lands.
- West Shadow- The western branch of The River Shadow near Crossroads.
- East Shadow- The eastern branch of The River Shadow near Crossroads.
- Wall of Crossroads- Rock wall between the Northlands and the Southlands.
- East Road- The main roadway out of the city of Cross towards the border.
- Northern Forest- Forest north of Cross.
- Site of Ascension- Place north of Cross where Shadow Night first was named Lord of his people.
- Crossroads Arena- A place for combat matches and training in the city of Crossroads.
- East Road Bridge- The bridge over The River Shadow that leads towards Agin.
- Sol Mountains- The place in the Southlands where Gyr and Charon meet for the first time.

- Last River- A river in the Southlands that passed close to the Wall of Crossroads.
- Sacred Cavern- Mountain cave where the tablets of the Immortal Truth are kept. Located outside of Tempest.

APPENDIX D

SPIRIT ENERGY AND THE POWERS OF TERRA

THE NATURE OF SPIRIT ENERGY

All abilities come from a Spiritual origin. Spirit energy exists in the world of the living as reserves left over from the Dark Days and within the Spirit World. Some beings have a stronger connection to that innate power than others. The Immortals have the strongest connection while Mortals have the weakest connection. Everyone is capable of using Spiritual power to manipulate their environment except for Demons. The Demons lost the ability to tap into their own Spirit energy and their anger resulted in the First Dominion War. The power and how great it can be is directly related to bloodlines. Blood is a powerful element with which to transfer memories, seals, and magic. When one signs in blood, they are bound to what they signed and promised. The world will otherwise function without a person's manipulation. Very few can affect the world on a big scale. Only the oldest of souls can do so. Sometimes the world and Spirit World act as one to create and destroy. That is when a miracle or a cataclysm can happen.

THE SPIRIT POWERS

- SHADOWBORN

- **Shadow Mirror**- A power exclusive to Begin Anu and the Farlander bloodlines. To raise a Shadow Mirror, a summoner uses their own life force to draw up a shield that can only be breached by those the summoner wishes. Anyone of the summoner's bloodline can cross through with no trouble. Only the summoner's command or death can break a Shadow Mirror.
- **Shadow Shock**- To produce Shadow Shock, a Shadowborn must tap into the electrical energy of their heartbeat and guide it to the dominant hand. Shadow Shock can have a paralyzing effect when one is struck by it.
- **Shadow Wolf**- A Shadowborn projects their Spirit energy in the shape of a black wolf. The ability can be amplified based on level of rage and requires extreme focus.
- **Shadow Slide**- The most basic skill available to a Shadowborn. To go into Shadow Slide, a Shadowborn must center themselves by aligning their heartbeat to the cool pulse of a shadow. The ability becomes easier to use as one practices and gets older. Shadow Slide is an evasive defense move and one cannot attack while in it. Inside, it can dull pain and have a chilling effect but if one stays in too long, they risk being pulled into the Spirit World. It allows a Shadowborn to move quickly across great distances.
- **Shadow Shield**- A technique that can mimic a Shadow Mirror and cut off another's ability to project or send out Spirit energy. It can directly lead to a contest of wills until one person gives up.
- **Shadow Shade**- A Shadowborn can project images of themselves to fool or misdirect others. A fully trained Shadowborn can project any number of Shadow Shades to train for combat matches.
- **Shadow Trail**- A basic power where a Shadowborn leaves behind a trace of Spirit energy as a signal to others or to direct more complex techniques.
- **Shadow Blind**- An outlawed technique where a trained Shadowborn can alter or block part of another's mind and senses. It can be used to create an army of loyal followers. Difficult to break.
- **Shadow Sleep**- Another questionable technique that causes others to fall unconscious. Two fingers of the

caster's dominant hand must be pressed to the center of the receiver's forehead in order to direct the thread of energy.

- o **Shadow Shock Wave-** A more powerful version of Shadow Shock using both arms.
- o **Shadow Guide-** A stabilizing ability used in Shadow Slide to guide others and keep them from being pulled into the Spirit World.
- o **Shadow Break-** A technique meant to force someone out of Shadow Slide. Requires extreme concentration on the natural pulses of one's surroundings.
- o **Shadow Draw-** A power meant to pull shadows closer to the Shadowborn for use in other Spirit energy shadow abilities.
- o **Shadow Call-** By placing a hand over the heart and the forehead, a Shadowborn centers themselves and uses the focus to detect Spirit energy in another person.
- o **Shadow Shot-** A way to transmit messages or objects through any barrier.
- o **Shadow Touch-** A Saber technique said to be a more physical attack than a Spirit energy attack.
- o **Shadow Jump-** The ability to move several Shadowborn people at once. Only for experts due to dangers of being drawn into the veil.
- EARTHBORN
    - o **Earth Touch-** A basic Earthborn skill to touch and sense the invisible magnetic field in the earth.
    - o **Earth Call-** A basic Earthborn power where an Earthborn can use their connection to the natural field to send out a signal with Spirit energy.
    - o **Earth Command-** An intermediate technique where an Earthborn can direct stone or plants to move and act. It can be used for artistic or combat purposes.
    - o **Earth Shift-** An ability that requires great strength to execute. An Earthborn acts as the focal point, using Spirit energy to move large stones. They must remained connected to the ground to maintain power.
    - o **Earth Strike-** A basic skill where an Earthborn charges up Spirit energy in their dominant hand and punches stone hard enough to break it.
    - o **Earth Draw-** A basic technique where an Earthborn taps in the natural pulses and pulls them into their

body to stabilize injuries or provide added strength.

- AIRBORN
  - **Air Push-** An Airborn manipulates the air flow around them to push and pull people and objects.
  - **Wind Blast-** A technique used primarily in combat. An Airborn must begin charging Spirit energy while executing a spinning jump. The air then must be directed with the dominant hand towards the target.
  - **Wind Storm-** An advanced power where an Airborn leaps high into the air in a full spin. The continuous spinning charges up Spirit energy that pulls air into a large funnel cloud. The Airborn then flips around and dives at the opponent at full force. The entire thing looks like a tornado.
  - **Wind Spiral-** A technique where an Airborn directs their Spirit energy to twist around one or both arms. The twisting air can be used to attack or deflect.
  - **Wind Falcon-** An advanced, more stylized version of Wind Storm. Spirit energy is projected out to look like a large falcon.
- FIREBORN
  - **Fire Shot-** A very basic power where a Fireborn charges up Spirit energy to combust the heat in the air. Commonly used alongside staves to direct the shots.
  - **Heat Ward-** A simple charm used to hold heat or turn it away. Can appear in the form of runes.
- WATERBORN
  - **Water Heal-** A basic ability using water to heal surface injuries on contact. The more a Waterborn concentrates, the more thorough the healing is. Uses a cooling effect to dull pain or ice over broken bones.
- GRYPHON
  - **Feather Whisper-** A practice where a Gryphon charms a feather with a single breath to hold voices. The breath activates the latent Spirit energy. The bigger the feather, the more words the energy can hold. Another breath from a Gryphon will charm the feather whisper to release the spoken words only to the intended recipient.
- DRAGON
  - **Dragon Fire-** Dragons produce their fire by combusting the acid in their stomachs to blistering

temperatures. They then suck in air to shoot out a stream of flames from their mouth. They have a very hot core of Spirit energy that can be used at will. Can burn anything except for Spirit Walkers.

- DEMON
  - **Demon Fire**- A remnant of the days when a Demon could use Spirit energy, they transform their rage into a malleable force. A fire must already be present in the environment for a Demon to use their rage to direct it. They cannot produce a flame by themselves.
  - **Demon Ward**- A mysterious charm crafted by Bane Arlis to protect the city of Crossroads from Demons. The strength of the ward is believed to be influenced by the presence of the Shadowlord.
- SPIRIT
  - **Spirit Energy**- The invisible power of Terra that was left over from the days before the Covenant of Spirits separated the world of the living and the world of the dead.
  - **Living Memory**- A phenomenon that can occur to an individual when entering a space that has been charged by latent Spirit energy. A vision of the individual's past is brought to life right before their eyes.
  - **Spirit Ward**- A harmless technique where an individual crosses their heart in a form of protection from coming into contact with too much Spirit energy.
  - **Spirit Call**- The ability to sense an individual's Spirit energy and compel them to move towards the caller.
  - **Living Map**- A map that has been insourced with Spirit energy to depict the world with realistic detail.
  - **Spirit Roar**- A higher form of Spirit Call utilized by Spirits to summon allies or frighten enemies.
  - **Spirit Fire**- A technique where Spirit energy is directly combusted into a silver or golden flame for combat purposes.
  - **Spirit Dragon**- A more advanced, stylized version of Spirit Fire where the caster projects the form of a Dragon.
  - **Spirit Poison**- A darker practice that utilizes various ingredients to create a toxin that can block Spirit energy.
  - **Spirit Anchor**- The sign of a truly deep connection

between two souls where each person is aware of where their partner is and if they are living or dead.

o **Spirit Song-** A phenomenon where the world declares that a wandering Spirit has found its way to the Spirit World. Hearing a Spirit song leaves a listener with a sense of peace and happiness thought they do not remember the words.

o **Spirit Bond-** A phenomenon that occurs between a Spirit of Creation and a living bloodline. The connected Spirit will come to an individual when the need in their heart is great enough.

o **Astral Projection-** Sending one's image across great distances to interact with others.

- BLOOD
  o **Blood Memory-** A natural phenomenon that occurs in both the Immortal and Mortal races. When the blood of an individual is tasted, a taster is privy to the individual's power and strongest memories. The clarity of the blood memory increases when the number of blood relatives decreases in an act of preservation.

  o **Blood Magic-** An outlawed and forbidden dark practice involving torture, poisons, and mental manipulations.

  o **Blood Seal-** A method created by Kaiser Adonis to help his followers bypass the Shadow Mirror. He imbues traces of his blood in metal pendants to mask and suppress the Spirit energy of a carrier.

- COMBINATION
  o **Shadow Shock Spirit Fire-** A technique invented by Ryder Coba combining the paralyzing power of Shadow Shock and the burning Spirit Fire.

  o **Shadow Quake Line-** A power invented by Onyx Silvanus combining the speed of Shadow Slide and the power of Earth Strike.

  o **Demon Shadow Rise-** A dangerous summoning ritual created by Kaiser Adonis using the blood sacrifice of his three Shadowborn family members to bring forth Demons.

  o **Demon Shadow Bond-** Another technique created by Kaiser Adonis to bind his summoned Demon in a powerful bond to protect himself from injury.

  o **Shadow Mirror Mist-** A defensive maneuver invented by Kaiser Adonis in which a small bone shattering shield of air and water is created.

APPENDIX E

THE WRITTEN WORD: LAWS

THE IMMORTAL TRUTH

The Immortal Truth is an ancient code of laws governing the Immortal races and their interaction with Terra. It names the Shadowlord and the Daylord as Champions of Truth. It first addresses how the world of Terra was created and the Spiritual origin of the Immortal races. It gives a history of the world up until the sealing of the Darklands. At this point, the code of laws begins. The role of the Champions is first stated and the role of all Immortals to protect the short-lived and innocent is detailed. All Immortals are to defend against the Demons of the Darklands. These are the high laws of Terra. The lower laws are more targeted to each individual race's day to day lives. Though the Immortal Truth is the law of Terra, each race has their own laws within their border regarding their innate powers, religion, celebrations, and general courtesies. The Immortal Truth was signed in blood by a member of each good Immortal race, imbuing the words with power. This power becomes a ward and barrier against the dark powers. If one of the signer bloodlines fails, the ward is broken and the terror of the Dominion War will return in full force.

THE COVENANT OF SPIRITS

Written by the Farlander, Cassiel Cipher, the Covenant of

Spirits separated the world of the living from the world of the dead. It acts as a barrier against the wild and dangerous flow of energy that exists from the Dark Days. To break it invites destruction and uncontrolled energy fluctuations. Anyone who threatens to undo the binding power of the Covenant will be punished with execution.

THE WRITTEN WORD: SONGS AND INVOCATIONS IN ORDER OF APPEARANCE

GRYPHON SONG OF PARTING

To my brothers and sisters,
Fly free forevermore.
Up into the sky,
And beyond the shore.

Soar to the stars,
And glide to the moon.
Climb with the wind,
Escape the sun at noon.

Remember that you are loved,
So dearly missed.
Remember the Spirits,
Of the ones you once kissed.

DEMON INVOCATION OF BLOOD SACRIFICE

Three hearts for one
A vessel of blood
For the dark soul
A shadow of ancients to guide
And the will to control

SHADOWBORN SONG - THE HUNGRY DOG

Here is the song of the howling dog,
Who wails and sings all night long.
He paces the yard from east to west,
Begging for the meat that he likes best.
The juicy flesh, the nice white bone,
The kind that makes his belly groan.
All he asks for it a bit of meal,
Maybe some chicken, maybe some veal.
Or perhaps a filet of mountain fish,

Something to make a nice hot dish!

THE IMMORTAL TRUTH - INCOMPLETE

Lift up the Immortal Powers
With voices singing of ages long past
Life up the Mortal Spirit
Innocence of the future to come

Shadow, light, air
Earth, water, fire
Feather and scale
Blood and darkness

We once lived in fear at the time of birth
With no guidance before a terrible foe
But a shining light came from afar
To cast down a Demon monster

Shadow against evil
Master of the night
Crowned by the moon
Praises sung by the wolf

The champions are named by all
Shadowlord and Daylord
Guardians of truth and memory
Warriors of power and heart

Light against evil
Master of days
Crowned by the sun
Praises sun by the dove

United the bloodlines come together
To write a bond of truly great power
A promise is made to protect the innocent
And to make a code of laws...

Duty in times of war
We are the sword
We are the shield
We are the guardians against the dark...

Duty in times of peace

We are the word
We are the song
We are the teachers of light

Life is sacred
Life is precious
Death is endless
Death is forever...

By these words shall we live
By these words shall we die
The Spirit reigns
The Immortal Truth reigns

SHADOWBORN SONG OF LONGING

Fear not the night
For all is not lost
Fight with all your might
No matter the cost

Fear not the night
The moon will show you the way
Follow the silver light
And return to me one day

Come back to me
My lost and wandering soul
Come back to me
Come back to me

GRYPHON SONG – FLY HIGH

Fly high, sky high
Soar among the stars
Your loved ones are watching
Love them, honor them
Show all your heart
Your legend is beginning

SPIRIT INVOCATION OF LOYALTY

To the blood loyal,
No hand will slay.
All will obey.

MORTAL SONG OF VICTORY

Victory to our king
He is the best that has ever been
He has pushed back the night
And brought us the dawn
He slayed the Demon monster
And rescued dear Sawn

SHADOW MIRROR INVOCATION

When Shadow meets Light,
Dark becomes bright.
I command with all that I am,
For the power to set the world right
No more will chaos stand,
For Truth is our might.
SPIRIT BREAK!

SONG OF RESURRECTION

Truth be told
Let the shadows fall
And the day rise
For dawn is here
And I can see the light

Let the sun shine down on me
As I walk this land
Until its last goodbye

From day to night
Time passes on
And all will begin again

Blood is the life
And energy for the Spirit...

GRYPHON SONG – MASTER OF FLIGHT

I can fly through anything
I can fly through everything
My wings are strong
My will is calm
The wind will carry me on

On through the storm
On through the night
I will not lose this fight
I am the master of flight

ACKNOWLEDGEMENTS

The dream continues as I have reached another milestone with writing my second book. I thank those who have given me an opportunity to share my books with the world.

FLIGHT OF A HERO

The world is broken and lost. The truth has been laid bare. Kaiser is a destructive force beyond all reckoning. Lands are being turned to ash in his march towards the east. For in the east lies the greatest of all treasures: the stones of the Immortal Truth. Should he win the way to the sacred cavern, chaos will reign for eternity.

Once a nervous young Prince, Onyx is now a fully-fledged leader and icon for the war effort. He fills the void left behind by his famous cousin with steadfast resolve. The world knows his painful story through the words of his heart. The time has finally come to him to discover where his path has led.

After one thousand years, Bane returns to the north and reunites with the likes of Vorin and the Gryphon sage Proto Avis. Despite the joy of his return, Bane must answer for his absence. But there is no time for talk. Only action in the last attempt to stop Kaiser Adonis.

Warriors become heroes. Heroes become legends in the epic conclusion to the Immortal Flight trilogy.

ABOUT THE AUTHOR

Ashley Causey writes and lives in South Carolina. For more news and updates, go to Facebook and visit the Flight of the Broken Official page.